The ROMAN the TWELVE & the KING

WHAT KIDS, TEENS, AND ADULTS ARE SAYING

Kids and Teens

After reading this book, you'll never think of Rome the way you did before. You'll never think of Handel's *Messiah* the way you did before. And most importantly, you'll never think of Jesus the way you did before. This is a marvelous book that I will treasure always. It has truly helped my relationship with God, as I now understand all the pain and suffering He had to go through for a sinner like me. I understand that I'm unworthy of God's grace, but through Jesus' blood I am made worthy. I now understand that I am loved and that I am able. And I can do all things through Christ who strengthens me.

—**Tara Shultz,** 17, Eden Academy, Yucaipa, CA

The best book in the *Epic Order of the Seven* Series so far. Who would have thought it could get any better? Well, it did!

—**Abby Shamblin,** 9, Cornerstone Academy, Dandridge, TN

This is the BEST book ever! Since reading this book, I've been able to answer every question anyone has asked me about Jesus' life. With all the fun characters, even the new ones like cute Clarie and Shandelli, this is the best book yet!

—**Rachel Shamblin,** 9, Cornerstone Academy, Dandridge, TN

The Roman, The Twelve, & The King was such a good book that my Dad asked to read it with me. We enjoyed learning about the composer George F. Handel and *The Messiah*. Jenny L. Cote is an amazing writer who describes the real Messiah's life in an interesting and creative way. And she kept our attention with funny new characters like my favorite, Shandelli, the Italian stick bug.

—**Kyle Martin,** 11, The King's Academy, West Palm Beach, FL

Another awesome book by Jenny! Putting down the book was ever so difficult as the storyline was so absorbing, and I found myself going through the adventures with Max and Liz with every turn of the page. Jenny not only made the story come alive through her mastery of English, she also introduced different perspectives of the Bible through her insightfulness. I will definitely recommend this book to all my friends. Thank you, Jenny, for blessing us with this amazing book, and I can't wait to wait to embark on the next adventure with Max and Liz! Please hurry, Jenny!

—**Clara Tan,** 14, Singapore Chinese Girl's School, Singapore

I simply love this book. For people who do not like reading the Bible because they think it's boring, this is a great way for them to learn about what is in it in a fun way. Jenny L. Cote is an awesome writer with a God-given gift!

—**Cabell W. Jones,** 10, Providence Classical School, Williamsburg, VA

This is Jenny L. Cote's best book yet! It was so interesting how she portrayed the Order of the Seven with Jesus and his disciples. Gillamon remains my favorite character! I recommend *The Roman, The Twelve, & The King* to every kid who loves Jesus Christ and loves to read.

—**Anna E. Boustany,** 12, Atlantic Shores Christian School, Chesapeake, VA

This is my favorite book in the series so far. I love the new characters and their new secret abilities in the IAMISPHERE. I also love Al and his addiction to fish. Also the most musical book so far.

—**Jacob White,** 12, Upwey High School, Melbourne, Victoria Australia

WOW! This book has everything you could ask for . . . suspense, music, animals, action, history, and finally, the truth of the gospel. This brilliant book "takes the biscuit!"

—**Sophia Shedd,** 14, Homeschooled, Chesapeake, VA

I loved everything about this interesting book. I could barely put it down. The story was painted with fascinating details which allowed me to picture the events as they happened. I enjoyed seeing the story of Jesus through different points of view including the Roman Centurion Armandus. In this book, Mrs. Cote created an environment that made Jesus' life more real to me.

—**Alana Dapper,** 11, Sherwood Christian Academy, Albany, GA

This is the best book yet! *The Roman, The Twelve, & The King* has shown me a new perspective of looking at the life of Christ. Jenny L. Cote brought the story alive with her insight into what it might have been like for Jesus to speak with the Epic Order of the Seven!

—**Jordan Sims,** 13, Bellingham Christian School, Bellingham, WA

Anyone who wants to get to know Jesus should read this book! I felt like I got to meet him and know what it was like back in his time. Al is one of my favorite animal characters in the book. He loves to eat all the time like me, and he makes me laugh out loud.

—**Kaitlyn Greer,** 9, Rosa Parks Edison Elementary, Indianapolis, Indiana

Another fantastic book by Jenny L. Cote! *The Roman, The Twelve, & the King* is full of joy, sadness, adventure, suspense, and humor. This book really helps me realize how much Jesus sacrificed for us to be forgiven. I love how the story of Jesus' life is so detailed and it makes me feel like I'm actually there and witnessing all of Jesus' miracles. It showed me all the pain and suffering that Jesus went through before his death, and that he went through all that for us. He didn't have to be whipped and mocked, he didn't have to die, but he did so that our sins could be forgiven and that all the prophecies about his death could be fulfilled. Mrs. Cote described Jesus' life perfectly and showed me just how incredible Jesus was. There is excitement in every part of the book, and I'm always turning the page to find out what happens next!

—**Gillian Hilscher,** 11, Patrick Henry Middle School, Sioux Falls, SD

I love the way Jenny L. Cote combines real stories with funny, fictional characters. The Epic Order of the Seven can clarify events that would otherwise be confusing, add detail to the stories, and provide humor in all the right places. Al cracks me up! More importantly, the wisdom and humor of the animals communicate the true message of the life of Jesus and the composing of Handel's *Messiah*. Jenny describes the stories so vividly that it seems like I am there watching it happen. You can clearly see Jenny's fascination with history in the detail of this book.

—**Faith McColl,** 14, Johnson Ferry Christian Academy, Marietta, GA

I've read each book in the Max and Liz series and was anxiously anticipating to journey through *The Roman, The Twelve, & The King*. I was not disappointed! At times, I experienced humor and fun but then as I continued, I witnessed events where there was sorrow and sadness. It has been an adrenaline rushing, powerful, and full-of-excitement adventure. I loved how I could vividly imagine Jesus as he walked about performing great works: casting out demons, giving hope, stirring the faith of those who watched and listened, and healing those with physical needs. Jesus came to life in a different way for me. Jenny L. Cote has done it again! Long live the Epic Order of the Seven.

—**Analiese L. Delgado,** 10, Vincent Shalvey Academy, Stockton, CA

Jenny L. Cote has always been my favorite author, but this time she has outdone herself! *The Roman, The Twelve, & The King* was truly touching. I was laughing so hard at Al's missions and almost crying during the crucifixion. Sometimes I have a hard time relating to how people must have felt during the Bible time period. However, when I read the way the animals felt during the crucifixion it just touched my soul and it made me realize how deep Jesus' followers must have felt. This book has also taught me so much about Handel's life. I won't be able to listen to Handel's *Messiah* without remembering this fantastic story. Jesus is KING OF KINGS and LORD OF LORDS!

—**Hannah Rotter,** 15, Homeschooled, South Elgin, IL

I have read and reread all of Jenny L. Cote's previous novels, but *The Roman, The Twelve, & The King* "takes the biscuit" thus far. Flowing with detail, intrigue, and suspense, this captivating account of the life of Christ comes alive in a more personal way than I've ever read before. The way that Jenny tangibly reveals Jesus' emotions and the words He speaks is so powerful and thought provoking, that it causes me to examine my own life. The touching scenes of the Passion Week make me appreciate more fully what my Savior did for me, bringing me closer to him. This is a truly inspirational book!!!

—**Joshua Mark Midwood,** 12, Homeschooled, Springfield, MA

This book is really a blessing to anyone who reads it. It had me crying at times, laughing at times and always feeling blessed to be reading about my Savior's life. I would recommend this book to people because it just has all the things we love about our Savior!

—**Madison Abercrombie,** 14, Chestatee Academy, Gainesville GA

The Roman, The Twelve, & The King is simply amazing! Reading it was like getting back to an old friend! In the book I got to see Jesus in a new point of view. I liked seeing through the animals' eyes how they felt about Jesus and what he really went through. Thanks for being such a great author!

—**Megan Marotz,** 11, Summit Christian Academy, Cedar Park, TX

After her last book, I honestly didn't know how Jenny L. Cote could top herself. Yet in this newest installment, the beautiful, wonderful story of the life of Christ is gilded by the ever witty pen of Mrs. Cote. Truly her 'Magnum Opus', this is a book you'll want to read again and again.

—**Stephen Brentlinger,** 14, Homeschooled, Williamson, GA

WOW! What an amazing insight into the life of Christ, not to mention the life of Handel! Having heard Handel's *Messiah* before, and now reading this book on how and who influenced its composition, is just truly inspiring! This is without a doubt one of the best so far in the series and I would strongly encourage anyone to read this God inspired book. It will change your life as it did mine. It's truly AMAZING!

—**Calum Entermann,** 14, Brisbane Adventist College, Ipswich, QLD, Australia

The Roman, The Twelve, & The King really touched me in how it explains the death of Christ in a way that made me feel His pain and agony. The book also showed me that all His teachings and healings truly changed many lives. When I read this book I felt as if I were really standing with Jesus as He did His miracles. It is an EPIC book!

—**Natalie Mears,** 9, Sugar Hill Christian Academy, Sugar Hill, GA

The Roman, The Twelve, & The King is amazing! Jenny L. Cote makes Jesus' story come to life, making you feel like you're right there with him! Thank you, Jenny!

—**Mariahney Stuart,** 13, Metrolina Christian Academy, Mavin, NC

I have thoroughly enjoyed reading this book. I have enjoyed being able to see through the eyes of The Order of the Seven the way that Jesus lived, and how he loved. They say that if you're a child, it will be hard for you to understand Jesus. As we see in the Bible, at the age of twelve Jesus was baffling scholars with spiritual truths. At just fourteen, Mary was pregnant with the Son of God! David was chosen to be king at sixteen! Proof that God doesn't care about your age; he cares about what's in your heart! This book has definitely helped me gain a deeper understanding of what it truly means to be a Christian, and has made me want to live and love more like Jesus.

—**Chance Riley Kester,** 13, Northside High School, Fort Benning, GA

Reading this great book helped me to understand how Jesus' disciples felt when Jesus came. It also helped me to get closer to God. I noticed many of my Sunday school lessons in church involved what I was also reading about in *The Roman, The Twelve, & The King!*

—**McKenna Walters,** 11, Independence Elementary, Monroe, OH

The Roman, The Twelve, & The King is an AMAZING story about the lives of Handel and Jesus. Max, Liz, Kate, and Al take very important roles in this book. In my opinion this is probably Jenny L. Cote's best book yet. It is an amazing book, and anyone who is able to get their hands on it will be amazed, astonished, laugh at times and might even cry at times. It is one of the best books you can read.

—**Connor Chapman,** 12, Warwick River Christian School, Yorktown, VA

This book is AWESOME! It has everything: humor, adventure, and love. Mrs. Cote has a way of painting pictures in your head of what is happening in the story, and writes in such a way that you can relate to the characters. Mrs. Cote has helped me understand the Bible better.

—**Hannah Miller,** 10, Homeschooled, Thirsty for HIM Learning Academy, Bentonville, AR

This book brought Jesus to life in a way I had never experienced before. He seems more accessible, rather than a character from stories in the Bible who did everything perfectly. He seems like someone I want to get to know, someone who loves me and is a friend as well as my Lord and Savior. Mrs. Cote does an amazing job weaving the fictional characters in with the actual Bible. Her research and dedication in bringing the truth of the Bible to life with fun and engaging characters draws me back to these books again and again. This is a true EPIC!

—**Kendyl Born,** 13, Homeschooled, Evergreen, CO

This series contains a mixture of biblical and fictional characters, and is a lot of fun to read. I enjoyed learning about Jesus and all of the other biblical characters that I've grown up reading about. I was also surprised to learn who the seventh member of the Epic Order was! Keep writing, Mrs. Cote! I can't wait until the next book!

—**Savannah Reeves,** 15, Whitehouse High School, Whitehouse, TX

It was neat to see how Mrs. Cote brought the Antonius family back into this book, and my favorite part was when Armandus realized who Jesus really was. My favorite character was the Italian stickbug Shandelli, because he was so unique and different from the other animals. I loved all of the history and symbolism that was explained throughout this book, and I enjoyed Liz's lessons just as much as Kate did!

—**Abby Brewer,** 14, Faith Academy, Semmes, AL

I have been enthralled with Jenny L. Cote's writing since the first paragraph of *The Ark, The Reed, & The Fire Cloud*. All the characters are so real and experience real life situations. They all rely on God for direction and assistance in making wise choices. In *The Roman, The Twelve, & The King*, I love Nigel's dedication to Handel. He tirelessly plays into Handel's ear, so that the next morning the composer is able to write the notes to the most inspiring piece of music ever written. It was comforting to know that when things seemed darkest for Handel, God used his disappointment to remind him of God's mercies and grace to persevere and create this masterpiece. This was particularly important to help me remember that God is always there beside me, guiding me, watching over me, and comforting me when things don't go as I had anticipated. I appreciate Jenny's books, because they have a wide audience and the message of Christ will be shared. I can hardly wait for the next one!!

—**Sophie Jones,** 11, Coronado Heights Elementary School, Oklahoma City, OK

"Brilliant!" as Nigel would say. Mrs. Cote's words and details created images in my mind of Jesus' horrifying crucifixion. I can't imagine the intense pain that He went through for such a wretched sinner like me. I'm so happy to know that He rose from the grave. My God is not dead: He's alive!

—**Laura Hammer,** 10, Homeschooled, Morristown, TN

Jenny L. Cote once again has written a marvelous book! One of the best parts of the book is that the reader can bond with Jesus, not just read about him. You can experience his thoughts, emotions and pain. I would highly recommend this book to everyone.

—Emma Harris, 12, California Montessori Project, Shingle Springs, CA

I've had a blast being part of yet another grrrrrand adventure (as Max would say) by joining Max, Liz, and the whole gang in *The Roman, The Twelve, & The King*! It's amazing the way Jenny has spun together a whirl of history, adventure, and excitement in yet another superb book! I highly recommend all of Jenny L. Cote's books, especially this one.

—**Grace Woods,** 15, Homeschooled, Winston-Salem, NC

I LOVED *The Roman, the Twelve, and the King!* This book shines with the perfect blend of comedy in sharing the story of Christ. I especially loved the part when Max conquered his long-standing fear of water. The adventures of Max and Liz become more exciting with each book. Outstanding literature! All ages will love this book! Miss Jenny, you rock!

—**Warren Raymer,** 13, Mount Paran Christian School, Marietta, GA

Jenny L. Cote's newest book brings history to life like never before! Through her exceptional writing style, you will feel transported through time page after page. Interesting plot, exceptional humor, and accurate facts will make you fall in love with *The Roman, The Twelve, & The King*. As I read about Jesus' life, I felt more connected with him than ever before. I thoroughly enjoyed this wonderful book, and I would highly recommend it to anyone looking for an amusing storyline with a wholesome message!

—**Sarah Wheeler,** 14, Chesterfield Christian Academy, Midlothian, VA

I really liked that the story goes through the time period of Jesus up to modern times. What inspired me the most was how the author brought the Bible stories to life, with Jesus playing and talking with the animals, giving Him a fun-loving, human side. There are many interesting, mysterious spots in this book where you just can't stop reading. Building the violin for Nigel was my favorite part. I would strongly recommend this novel by Jenny L. Cote to anyone who is learning about Jesus and likes to read the Bible.

—**David Straub,** 12, St. Jude the Apostle Catholic School, Sandy Springs, GA

These books are great, and I can't stop reading them! I can't wait until the next book comes out! I like how the animals go back and forth through time, following Jesus around and learning from him. My favorite character is Al because he has a good sense of humor and he loves to eat.

—**Jacob Curry,** 11, Rochester Central Lutheran School, Rochester, MN

A must- read for all ages. *The Roman, The Twelve, & The King* has all of the character-istics I look for in a book. At times funny, exciting, serious, or sad, but always touching and educational, this is my new favorite book that has inspired me so much in many different ways. Thank you, Mrs. Cote!

—**Colleen Magee-Uhlik,** 15, University High School, Tucson, AZ

I could not put this book down! There are no words to describe Jenny L. Cote and her amazing works of art—she always takes my breath away! As Liz would say, *"Ces livres sont vraiment spectaculaires!"*

—**Taylor Weaver,** 12, Manteo Middle School, Manteo, NC

I loved this book that is certainly the best one yet. What I enjoyed the most about this marvelous book was the descriptive wording that opens your eyes to what really hap-pened during the life of Christ. I will always remember this epic experience.

—**Aubrey Greene,** 13, Sherwood Christian Academy, Sylvester, GA

***

Adults, Teachers, and Families

As a home educator and a parent, I see both the hearts and minds of my children, and I have had the blessed privilege to develop both in the Lord through the journeys we have taken with Max, Liz and friends. Through these stories, our family has held our breath in anticipation, cheered, yelled in surprise and cried tears of great sadness, and joy. We have experienced moments of wonder so amazing it has seemed as if we were present with our animal friends on their adventure. I cannot think of any other book series that has touched our lives so deeply. Mrs. Cote, thank you for wrapping deep spiritual truths in a way that is delightfully appealing to both children and the young at heart, and impacting our lives forever. YOU are loved!!

—**The Krueger Family,** Mount Prospect, IL

Incredible!! *The Roman, the Twelve, and the King* is a masterpiece, one you will want to add to your collection of favorites! I honestly felt like I was walking the roads of Israel with Jesus and his furry and beloved companions! I was captivated by the words and life of Jesus. Scriptures that I had read many times before came alive with new and fresh meaning. Readers should be ready for a story so rich and engaging that they will not want to put it down. When they finish, they will be applauding and wanting more. Bravo, job well done!

—**Jenny Keeton**, Lead Teacher, Mount Pisgah Christian School, Johns Creek, GA

The Roman, The Twelve, & The King is by far the best book I have ever read! Reading it took me to Jesus' side as I watched Him teach and perform miracles—what an incredible feeling! My relationship with the Savior has been deepened and strengthened. My children, Anna Grace and Abigail, watched me laugh a lot and cry a lot as I journeyed through this latest adventure with the Epic Order of the Seven. Thank you!

—**Christi Browning,** 41, Teacher, 7–12th graders at Hillcrest Christian School, Jackson, MS

Jenny's true love of history is revealed in the detail that only comes from exhaustive research. Her writing sheds new light and perspectives on how we view and understand these amazing and important turns in history. This book is for those who have ever wondered what it would be like to be a fly on the wall during some of the most influential events of human history! It will challenge your perceptions of these historical characters, give you true, accurate depictions of the events that took place, and challenge how you perceive history and Christianity.

—**Michael Tenkate,** 27, Police Officer, Sydney, Australia

This book makes the life of Christ more real than movies or other books that I have read. Jenny goes into tremendous depth and background study of the probable situations that our Lord encountered and makes them live for us in a way that we can understand. I recommend this book to both young and old who really want to see Jesus in the culture in which he lived, in order to impact *your* life and times.

—**Dr. Paul Mims,** 74, Pastor, Cornerstone Baptist Church, Cherry Log, GA

My eight year-old son Brian and I read this book with a great deal of fascination. He barreled through it in about three days. His favorite part was Clarie becoming whatever character that was needed. I have a Theology degree and felt I knew the story of Jesus' life pretty well until I read this. This book brings the stories alive in a way I have never seen before. I had to put the book down several times because I was blown away by the truths that came through the writing and then snatched it up to see what God was going to make more real next. The whole series is fantastic but this book is incredible!

—**Alice,** 56, and Brian, 8, Herrick, Wisconsin Rapids, WI

Jenny L. Cote's amazing way of interjecting her animals into her writing has opened a whole new vista on how I view God's ability to inspire His authors of the Bible. The biblical lessons are impactful and enlightening. Any pet owner understands the influence that comes from interaction with our animal friends, and Jenny takes that interaction to the next level. A must read for all ages.

—**Jim Redovian,** father of six children, grandfather of eleven grandchildren, and former member of the DeKalb County School Board, Atlanta, GA

We read and hear about Jesus every day. We talk about Him, listen to praise music about Him, but now, I KNOW Him. I already knew most of the words He spoke in this book, but there is a difference between knowing His actions and knowing *Him*. In this venue He was speaking to me, and I heard Him and love Him even more than ever. Thank you so much for writing this book that brought us so much closer to Jesus. We are inspired anew to boldly speak of Jesus, our audience of One.

—**Nancy,** Mike, Kimberly, and Aaron Hopper, Suffolk, VA

In *The Roman, The Twelve, & The King* Jenny L. Cote does a masterful job describing the judgmental perfectionism of the Pharisees, and she challenges us to reject those same attitudes in our own lives. At the same time, we are freshly reminded of the power and love of Christ, and are filled with a growing appreciation of the privilege of calling Him our Savior, Lord, and Friend.

—**The O'Briens,** a Homeschooling Family from Colby, KS

As a music teacher, I thoroughly enjoyed Jenny's imaginings of Handel's work on his great masterpiece, *Messiah*. The highlights for me are Handel's glimpse of heaven as he was writing, and then his receiving Heaven's applause at the first performance. Max, Kate, Al, Liz, Nigel, Clarie, and Gillamon have quickly taken their place alongside four of our family's other heroes — Peter, Susan, Edmund, and Lucy. . . . Hallelujah!

—**Karla LeBlanc,** Mom of Four, Ottawa, Ontario, Canada

I loved EVERY MINUTE of reading this book! I was tingling from my head to my toes! I felt like I was there in London, Jerusalem, and Ireland! I felt the strong emotion of heartache, joy, pain, humor, and truth. Jenny has a wonderful gift, and I hope she will keep on sharing it. Long live the King of Kings!

— **Sara LeBlanc,** 9, St. Jerome Catholic School, Ottawa Ontario, Canada

We have read all of the books in the Max and Liz series so far and couldn't wait to get our hands on *The Roman, The Twelve, & The King*. I am so happy to have books like these to read to my children. They paint a picture of the Bible that they can relate to without taking out the truth. Thank you, Mrs.Cote, for being an amazing writer.

—**The Eskew Family,** Douglasville, GA

"Is something afoot with the mission. . . ?" Liz, the petite French black cat inquired. It is London 1735 and once again the Order of the Seven led by Max: a Scottish Terrier, faithful leader of the team and Liz are about to embark on another exciting adventure to assist George F. Handel. It will be one of great importance that will be timeless in its impact. *"The Maker always has greater plans in mind than men, and it is He who will truly determine greatness."* How is the criminal's sign, nailed to the gnarled cross more than just that—what answer does it hold?

—**Vanessa Caldwell,** Faith Christian School Teacher/ Homeschooling mother of 4, Brisbane, Australia

It was so exciting I couldn't stop reading. There's so much mystery, adventure and comedy. Thanks for writing the books. I'm a big fan.

—**Geoff Caldwell,** 12, Homeschooled, Faith Christian School, Brisbane, Australia

"Words are wanting to express the exquisite delight . . . the most elevated, majestic, and moving words. . . . " As I read this I could not think of any other way to express my gratitude for Mrs. Cote's time, love and passionate endurance that was poured into this divinely inspired creation! Many a time as I sat reading aloud for my children I would literally become speechless, as the children would not want me to stop and my voice would give out! I love how you love Jesus through your words, I love the dedication to each of the people from Scripture, and I feel that I came to know them more intimately. Thank you, Jenny!

—**Sara Scheel,** 35, Homeschooler Mom, Lincoln, NE

I love this book. I think it is fun, and my favorite part was when Al flew into the statue and said, "Hello, me love," to the carving of Liz. I have read all of the books and am rereading the first one . . . AGAIN!

—**Lucia Scheel,** 9, Proverbs 22:6 Homeschool, Lincoln, NE

I thought that leading up to the story of Christ through an interesting frame story really "took the biscuit." I've read your other books and the characters have never been more vibrant than in this one with all of their qualities so clearly shown. And amazingly, these two epic stories were put together at a decent length. Typically, this is too much to take in but all of the necessary information is in there. Excellent! (And I don't say that lightly.)

—**Brian Scheel,** 15, Proverbs 22:6 Homeschool, Lincoln, NE

Jenny L. Cote has skillfully woven two stories into one and made each amazing in its own way. This book is impossible to put down, laden with sudden twists that are unexpected and turns that leave one speechless.

—**Carrie Scheel,** 14, Proverbs 22:6 Homeschool, Lincoln, NE

EPIC ORDER OF THE SEVEN

The ROMAN, the TWELVE & the KING

JENNY L. COTE

LIVING INK BOOKS

Writing Worth Reading™

Epic Order of the Seven®
The Roman, The Twelve & The King
Copyright © 2012 by Jenny L. Cote

Published by Living Ink Books, an imprint of AMG Publishers, Chattanooga, Tennessee
(www.LivingInkBooks.com).

Print Edition	ISBN 13: 978-0-89957-791-3
ePUB Edition	ISBN 13: 978-1-61715-355-6
Mobi Edition	ISBN 13: 978-1-61715-356-3
ePDF Edition	ISBN 13: 978-1-61715-357-0

First AMG Printing—September 2012

EPIC ORDER OF THE SEVEN is a trademark of Jenny L. Cote.

Cover and internal illustrations by Rob Moffitt, Chicago, Illinois.
Photography by Kelly Mihalcoe
Interior design by KLOPublishing.com & theDESKonline.com.
Editing and proofreading by Rich Cairnes and Rick Steele

Printed in Canada
20 21 22 - M - 8 7 6 5 4

There is no human worthy of dedication for this work,
save Messiah himself.
So I dedicate this book to you, Jesus—
King of Kings, Lord of Lords, and my Messiah.

Soli Deo gloria

This book contains fact, fiction, fantasy, allegory, and truth.

For the entire true story, read Matthew, Mark, Luke, John,

and the biography of George Frideric Handel.

. . . he marked out their appointed times in history . . .

—Acts 17:26

CONTENTS

PART THE FIFTH - ENCORE: LONG LIVE THE KING!

Note to Parents: Chapters 60–62 contain scourging and crucifixion scenes. Although written with great care with children in mind, if you have any concerns about such graphic detail, please read these chapters before or with your child.

Acknowledgments

It's too bad there's not enough room on the front cover of this book to list all the names of people who played a role in the book you hold in your hands. Given the tremendous impact they've had, it seems rather selfish of me to list my name alone. At least I can list them here.

Jesus

It's all about you, literally. Thank you for entrusting me with the task of writing your story. You know how unworthy I feel for such a tall order. But thank you for gently handling me as you did Matthew the prodigal turned writer and Peter the loud-mouth, boisterous, denying follower turned speaker. Both of them eventually came around and made you proud. This prodigal girl loves you for letting me knock you over in the road when I came running back into your arms, and hopes she'll make you proud as well.

Family

Casey and Alex, thank you for your love and support as I remained chained to my writing desk all winter, and for letting me go to London on my carpe diem excursion. Dad and Mom, thank you for being there for every phone call and reading. Max and Liz, much love, me wee ones.

Historical Information Heroes

Michael P. Monaco, thank you for inspiring the entire plot line and walking me through the history of Handel, Greene, Jennens and the writing of *Messiah*. Nigel was thrilled about the role he got to play with his tiny violin, and said to extend his most heartfelt thanks. You know you hold a special place in his heart.

Richard Schumann, here you are helping me research Patrick Henry for *The Voice, the Revolution and the Jewel* and voila—you gave me the crucial plotline link of David Henry with *this* book. Wow, I got two books in one with you...so far. Thank you, my brilliant friend.

Mark Schneider, my Roman "patriarch"! Thank you for allowing me to borrow yours and Armand's names again for this book, as well as naming Armandus' horse: Achilles was perfect. Thank you also for sharing your extensive knowledge on the Romans in Britannia. And just wait 'til you see what your Roman grandsons do in *The Way, the Road, and the Fall!* I'm glad "I've got you" as a dear friend.

"Patrick Henry Historian Queen, "Miz. P" Edith Poindexter, and Patrick Henry descendant Karen Lawless, thank you for assisting me with information about David Henry. It was invaluable to bringing his character to life.

(Hmmm…there's a pattern going on here with these Virginians… keep an eye out for them in a future book.)

Rick Larson, you've infected me with your ancient coin collecting bug. Thanks for teaching me about the Roman Star Coin and spurring me on to get my own, even though it's not as nice as yours. I promise I'll buy us the big kahuna gold star coin when I become a millionaire. Thanks also for your insights on the veil in the Temple. Can't wait to see your next film. You're such a STAR.

Handel House Museum, London: Ella Roberts and Sarah Bardwell, I can't begin to thank you enough for allowing me to write in Handel's composing room all day. I know I was the first to make such a request, but I hope I'm not the last. I hope others will long to visit Handel House and learn more about this incredible man. Thank you also for accommodating Lori Marett and me as we filmed there for the CHAIRS documentary. I look forward to seeing all of these exciting things come together.

Foundling Museum, London: Katharine Hogg, never could I have imagined I would get to actually hold the 1759 score of Messiah! I'm still pinching myself, and owe you a debt of gratitude for all you showed us when we visited and filmed there. Nigel especially enjoyed his tour of the museum and his pictures with Handel.

Supporting Sistahs

Claire Roberts Foltz, thank you for suggesting that I go to London before God gave me the definitive word. You know how dangerous it is to suggest something crazy to me. You know I'll do it.

Lori Marett, you've captured it all on film! Thank you for going with me to London and filming my experience at Handel House, Foundling Museum, Westminster Abbey and all over the royal town for the CHAIRS documentary. To consider our time in Oxford following C.S. Lewis around as a 'bonus' feels like a bit of an understatement! I can't wait to see all that comes from our divinely inspired jaunt across the pond. Thank you for being my screenwriter, producer, traveling companion, and above all, my sister in Christ.

Michelle Sauter Cox, you prayed Lori and me all the way to London and back. Thank you for being the "Barnabas" we both needed throughout this project.

Ann McColl, what would I do without you running my calendar? Thank you for helping me tell the world about the Epic Order of the Seven, and especially about Messiah by scheduling all of my events.

Kate Wisenbaker, not only have you given me "Kate" the dog, but now you've inspired an Italian stickbug for my book. Shandelli and I say, "Grazie!"

Theological Book Heroes

Dr. Chuck Swindoll, it seems you wind up in every book I write because of the books you've written. Among my long list of 40+ books as resources for this book, your book *Jesus: the Greatest Life of All* was at the top of the stack, with almost every sentence underlined. You provided such amazing imagery and insights that helped me bring Jesus to life, and for that I am deeply thankful. I had chills when I read your suggestion about Barrabas sitting in his cell and hearing his name shouted among the crowd. I hope you are pleased with how I ran with that idea, and truly your name should be listed with mine on the front cover as your ideas are spread across my pages.

John F. MacArthur, Jr., I marvel at how you write so boldly, accurately and with such authority on tough subjects as you have unapologetically done in your books. Thank you for being such a voice of truth regarding Pharisees—then and now— in *The Jesus You Can't Ignore*. WOW, you truly shaped how I developed those characters and I now understand why Jesus was always the first one to "pick a fight" with them. And your masterpiece book, *Twelve Ordinary Men*, was crucial to my understanding of the twelve disciples. Thank you.

Critique Team

These awesome people keep me going with feedback and encouragement, chapter by chapter. Love and appreciation to Paul and Janice Mims, Claire Roberts Foltz, Lisa Hockman, Lori Marett, Faith McColl, Stephen Brentlinger, Michelle Sauter Cox, and Mike Tenkate.

Publishing Team

An EPIC thank you to the people who take what comes out of my pen and turn it into something so beautiful to hold and read! Illustrator Rob Moffitt, Editor Rich Cairnes, Interior Designer Katherine Lloyd, Literary Agent Paul Shepherd and the AMG Publishing Team: Dale Anderson, Rick Steele, Trevor Overcash, Warren Baker, Mike Oldham, Gin Chasteen, Amanda Donnahoe, Donna Coker and the support staff.

Readers

As Liz would say, "You have no idea," how you keep me going with your encouraging notes, letters, pictures, cards, emails and Facebook posts! Thank you for the privilege of being able to continue to write the books in this series. Let me know how you like this one at jenny@epicorderoftheseven.com. I'll keep writing as long as you keep reading! Much love!

CHARACTER PROFILES

ORDER OF THE SEVEN

Max: a Scottish Terrier from (where else?) Scotland. Full name is Maximillian Braveheart the Bruce. Short, black with a large head, always ready to take on the bad guys. Faithful leader of the team who started with the first mission of Noah's Ark in *The Ark, the Reed, and the Fire Cloud.* Loves to mess with Al, "encouraging" him to work on his bravery. Can't swim. Immortal.

Liz: a petite, French, black cat from Normandy. Full name is Lizette Brilliante Aloysius. Brilliant, refined, and strategic leader of the team, beginning with Noah's Ark. Loves the study of history, science, the written word, culture, and languages. Prides herself on knowing the meanings of names, and simply adores gardens. Immortal.

Al: a well-fed, Irish, orange cat. Full name is Albert Aloysius, also called "Big Al" by his close friends. Hopelessly in love with his mate, Liz, since Noah's Ark. Simple-minded, but often holds the key to gaining access to impossible places, and figuring out things everyone else misses, including deep spiritual truths. Lives to eat and sleep. Scared of everything. Immortal.

Kate: a white West Highland Terrier, also from Scotland. The love of Max's life ever since they 'wed' on the way to the Ark. Has a sweetness that disarms everyone she meets. Is also a fiery lass, unafraid to speak her mind. Always sees the good in others, caring for their needs. Immortal.

Nigel: a jolly, British, white mouse with impeccable manners and speech. Wears spectacles and is on the same intellectual level as Liz, joining her in the thrill of discovery. An expert Egyptologist who joined the team on their mission to Egypt with Joseph in *The Dreamer, the Schemer, and the Robe.* Taught Liz all about Egypt, giving her the endearing term "my pet"—the mouse was the teacher and the cat was his pet. Able to travel quickly and easily via carrier pigeon. Spies to help carry out missions. Immortal.

Gillamon: a wise, kind mountain goat from Switzerland. Moved to Scotland, where he raised orphaned Max and served as his mentor. Died before the Flood, but serves as a spiritual being who delivers mission assignments from the Maker to the team. Can take any shape or form, and shows up when least expected.

Clarie: a sweet little lamb from Judea. Shepherds gave her to Mary and Joseph as a gift for Baby Jesus in *The Prophet, the Shepherd, and the Star.* Enabled the family to escape to Egypt without harm and joined Gillamon as a spiritual being member of the team. Serves as all-knowing guide in the IAMISPHERE when the team goes back in time to events in history. Can take any shape or form.

xxvi

Open your ears to what I am saying,
for I will speak to you in a parable.

I will teach you hidden lessons from our past—
stories we have heard and known,

Stories our ancestors handed down to us.

We will not hide these truths from our children;
we will tell the next generation about the glorious deeds
of the LORD, *about his power and his mighty wonders.*

—PSALM 78:2–4

The ROMAN, the TWELVE & the KING

PROLOGUE

A DARK DAY IN JERUSALEM

Armandus Antonius stood as motionless as a Roman statue while bloody mud splattered his feet. Stinging rain pummeled his face, but he felt nothing. Nothing, that is, except confusion and despair.

Oddly opposing sounds swirled around him. How could both cruel laughter and gut-wrenching wailing be observed in the same day's events? The Roman centurion clenched his jaw as he watched the mother fall to her knees with arms raised, eyes pleading as she cried, "Please, with care, with care!" He instinctively took a step toward her to offer aid, but others rushed to her side, supporting her there on the filthy ground. Armandus remained where he was, but anger consumed him as he turned his gaze upward to see the work of his soldiers.

Two soldiers stood on ladders leaning against the gnarled cross as they carried out with callous precision the task they had performed countless times before. One legionnaire hammered the iron spikes back through blood-drenched wood while the other slipped a rope under the dead body to catch it as it fell forward, slowly lowering it to the ground. The soldiers carried on, laughing about their winnings from casting lots for this dead man's cloak.

"Maybe they'll treat me like a king when I stroll through the city tonight wearing that robe!"

"Hail, great Ulixes!" the other soldier, named Velius, replied with a sarcastic bow as they reached the ground.

The cold-hearted soldiers ignored the group of Jews gathered around the dead man's body, weeping and clinging to one another. The mother refused to be comforted. She held tightly to her son, her head thrown back as she wailed in sorrow, rocking his lifeless form back and forth.

Ulixes picked up the spear belonging to Armandus and together the soldiers walked over and stood face-to-face with their commander. Ulixes wore a look of inappropriate humor and silent indignation as he handed the bloody spear to the centurion.

"Our work is finished here, Sir. Are we relieved?" Velius asked.

Armandus grabbed his spear so tightly his knuckles turned white as his eyes bored into the face of Ulixes. How he wanted to thrust the cold blade into this one who had tortured and mocked the dead man! Yes, these were typical, brutal Roman soldiers who carried out their assignments with undeniable precision and impeccable obedience. But this one—Ulixes—there was something evil about him. He had pushed the limits of Roman brutality today, enjoying every minute of it in a way that could be described as nothing short of inhuman. All Armandus could muster was a nod of agreement as he struggled to maintain self-control. He couldn't allow himself to stoop to the level of mindless brutality as did this soldier, despite the rage he felt.

With that the soldiers picked up their personal effects from their crucifixion post and prepared to depart. Suddenly, something caught Ulixes's eye. He grinned wickedly and walked over to the cross. He looked back at Velius. "We forgot something."

Ulixes climbed back up the ladder with an iron bar and pried loose the wooden sign that had been nailed in place above the head of the dead man. Its purpose was to tell all who gazed upon the criminal the nature of his crime, so no one would dare repeat the crime lest they suffer the same fate.

Ulixes jumped from the ladder and landed on the ground with a thud, splashing mud onto the mourning family. He smiled as he read the sign and carried it over to Armandus.

"The criminal's sign, Sir," he said with false sincerity. "An untimely death but a fitting end to his reign. We have protected our emperor from the threat of this one today. Hail, Caesar!" The depraved soldier saluted his commander and waited for a reply as rain splashed off his outstretched arm.

It was all Armandus could do to return the wicked soldier's salute. Not to do so would signify treason against their sovereign Roman emperor. He quickly saluted and the wicked grin grew on the face of his subordinate. Armandus leaned in and got eye-to-eye with Ulixes, allowing the tip of the spear to rest on the man's chest. "Never usurp my authority again, or it will be you facing an untimely death."

Ulixes gritted his teeth. "Yes . . . Sir." The soldier tossed the wooden sign into the mud.

"Get out of my sight," Armandus scowled as Ulixes turned away.

Velius picked up the dead man's robe and draped it around Ulixes's shoulders. Ulixes and Velius left the scene and walked back down the steep hill. Their laughter and mocking resumed once they were out of earshot of Armandus. Other soldiers joined in the fun of hailing the "royal Ulixes" in his new robe as he gallantly walked back into Jerusalem.

Armandus returned his attention to the grieving mother. Suddenly, two well-dressed men approached her, with servants in tow. They knelt down to place their arms around the mother. *Pharisees? What should they care?* Armandus questioned himself. *They are the ones who condemned this man to death. How dare they pay respects to his mother!*

But as Armandus watched, he noticed that these men cared not that their expensive, prestigious robes were quickly drenched with the blood and mud that ran over the ground in a torrent. Their grief was genuine. One of the men suddenly looked up at Armandus with pain in his eyes. The centurion and the Pharisee shared a moment of strange bewilderment. The man stood and walked over to the centurion.

"I am Joseph of Arimathea," he explained with a hand over his heart. "Pilate has given Nicodemus and me permission to remove the body."

Armandus felt something he couldn't quite identify. Relief? Gratitude? Finally, here was a show of respect for this dead man that Armandus was, due to his position, incapable of giving. Shame. He felt shame.

"Of course," Armandus uttered after clearing his throat and dropping his gaze to the ground.

Joseph stood there, waiting, not daring to touch the Roman. Armandus lifted his head and gazed deeply into the eyes of this Jew. The Pharisee did not speak immediately, but strove to peer into this warrior's soul, somehow understanding the depth of regret buried there. "Know this," Joseph finally said. "You are not responsible for this man's death."

Confusion swept over Armandus. His mind silently screamed, and all he wanted was to escape this scene. He clenched his jaw, brusquely straightened up, and nodded to the strange man. "Be swift with the body."

The Roman centurion looked once more upon the grieving mother. As the servants gently took her son from her arms, she locked her eyes with Armandus's and in them he saw the pain only a mother having lost a child could express. Her eyes. The dead man had her eyes. And in that powerful moment before his death, those eyes looked directly at Armandus with such compassion that the man in charge of the day's proceedings finally realized who the dying man was.

Armandus shook his head and turned away. He could not accept what was happening. He was responsible! How could this Jew say such an outrageous thing? It was his sole responsibility to carry out this despicable deed. *Enough!* his mind silently screamed as he now hurried away from the horror of this dark day in Jerusalem.

At a distance, the animal friends stood in silent grief as they watched the humans carry the body away from the three now-empty crosses. The rain continued to lash down upon the earth, as if nature itself were furious with what had happened here. Already nervous from the earlier earthquake and now this torrential downpour, the humans quickly departed the "place of the Skull" and made their way home. The small creatures walked to the scene, barely able to speak as they gathered around the pool of mud and blood at the foot of the cross.

"No amount of prophecy could have prepared me," Liz said softly, her voice breaking with each word, "for the reality of this day."

"Aye," Max echoed as he put a paw gently on Kate's back. He softly nuzzled his mate, who shook with silent sobs.

"Indeed," Nigel added, wiping his eyes unashamedly.

Al's lip quivered as he sobbed uncontrollably. "I jest don't understand. Why? Why Him? Why?"

Nigel walked over to the sign lying in the mud, rain splattering off it and covering his white fur with drops of diluted blood. "Because of this."

The animals gathered around Nigel and the sign. Liz closed her eyes and nodded in understanding. Max's brow wrinkled with anger. Kate shook her head in grief. Al cocked his head to one side. "Mousie, what does 'INRI' mean?"

Nigel adjusted his spectacles and cleared his throat.

"INRI is an abbreviation for the Latin inscription IESVS•NAZARENVS•REX•IVDÆORVM," Nigel responded, placing his paws respectfully on the crude wood. He looked up at Al and the others and took a deep breath before continuing. The mouse could hardly bear to speak another word. He slowly looked into the grieving faces of these who had walked with Messiah from the joyous moment of his birth and now stood in the sorrowful moment of his death.

Suddenly Liz stepped forward and placed her dainty paw on the sign, her tears falling onto the wood. *"Mon Cher Dieu!"* she exclaimed, looking up at the cross. She turned her gaze to Nigel. "This is more than just a wooden sign. It is an answer."

"I'm afraid I don't follow you, dear girl," Nigel replied as he examined the sign.

"It is the clear answer to the question the Magi asked when they first arrived in Jerusalem," Liz explained with great emotion in her voice.

"Aye, the question aboot Messiah that led ta that dark day in Bethlehem," Max added with a frown, remembering King Herod's response.

Kate smiled sadly as she thought about the happy days before that horrible night. She recited the Magi's question: "Where is he, the newborn King of the Jews?"

The friends stood there for a moment as they remembered the events that followed that night so long ago.

"So ye're sayin' the Wise lads asked the question way back then and the Roman lads answered it today by writin' on this sign?" Al finally asked, not realizing the profound meaning of his question.

Nigel tightly closed his eyes and nodded his head in agreement. He opened his eyes, cleared his throat, and reverently translated the Latin inscription on the sign: "Here is Jesus of Nazareth, the King of the Jews."

PRELUDE TO THE COMPOSITION

Do you see a man skilled in his work?
He will stand before kings.

Proverbs 22:29

THE KING'S MUSICK

D oes he know the king?" Al asked, gazing into the murky water of the meandering river. A soft breeze rippled the lush, green grass on the riverbank, and the warmth of the sun settled on the orange cat's fur. Squinting against the sun, which danced on the water like diamonds, he eagerly swished his fluffy tail back and forth as he spotted a fish.

"But of course, old boy! George Frideric Handel is quite friendly with King George II. That's why we're expecting good news today," Nigel replied, breathing in the fresh country air, basking in the welcome sunshine after the rainy days and dank air of London. Perhaps the clouds were also clearing for his musical mentor this day. The small white mouse preened his whiskers, certain of the outcome of the king's decision. "The King commissioned Handel to write four anthems for his royal coronation when he took the throne. I daresay, after the majestic tune of *Zadok the Priest* whom else would the king choose?"

The big orange cat scratched his head, clearly clueless about what Nigel was talking about. The mouse closed his eyes and smiled warmly. "Let me enlighten you, old boy." Nigel lifted his paw in a fist and boldly sang the coronation piece, punctuating each line with dramatic flair:

"Za-dok the Priest, and Na-than the Pro-phet anoint-ed
Solo-mon King.

And all the people rejoic'd, and said:

God save the King! Long live the King!

May the King live forever,

Amen, Allelujah."

Al, not being musically inclined, was unmoved by Nigel's performance. "Sure, and what does Tim have to do with the George and Zadok laddies?" Al wanted to know, turning his gaze back to the elusive fish. "No, I meant Tim. Does *Tim* know the king?"

"Tim?" Nigel asked, removing his spectacles and holding them up to detect a smudge. "I'm dreadfully sorry, old chap, but whom*ever* are you talking about?" Nigel blew onto the glass before cleaning it with a cloth hanging out of Al's knapsack.

"Ye know—*Tim*," Al replied, drawing a confused look from Nigel, who was replacing his spectacles. "The lad they named this river after. *T-I-M'S River?*" Al gestured to the river in front of them. "I figured any lad with a river named after him must know the king, even if he can't sing a note."

Nigel's whiskers quivered as he chuckled and held his paw to his forehead, shaking good-humoredly. "T-H-A-M-E-S, not Tim's!"

Taking his gaze off the water, Al wore a puzzled look. The simpleminded cat was confused by the same-sounding name of the river and its imagined honoree. "Sure, isn't that what I said?"

"Forgive me, dear boy," Nigel answered, wiping back the tears of laughter. "We British do sometimes have peculiar ways of pronouncing things. But no, there is no 'Tim.'"

"*Oui, cher* Albert," Liz added, sauntering up to the two friends, softly laughing. "The Thames River was not named for a person. The name comes from the Celtic name *Tamesas*, or in Latin *Tamesis*." The petite black cat adored sharing the origin of names, one of her favorite hobbies. She lifted her dainty paw and pointed to the river. "The

Thames is the second longest river in England and is quite important. Even Julius Caesar wrote about the Thames during his expedition here. The Romans established Londinium, or London as we call it today, where the river was narrow enough for a bridge but deep enough for seagoing vessels. This is how London became the capital of the British Empire. Fascinating how water can impact power and kingdoms, no?"

"Yes, yes, yes, my pet, you are indeed correct!" Nigel enthused. "Water indeed can establish kingdoms and announce kings. Our dear Mr. Handel wrote and performed his fabulous *Water Music* for King George I's royal water party one summer night out here on the Thames. Ah, what a splendid occasion! Crowds gathered on the banks of the Thames as the sounds of that glorious music danced off the water." Nigel swirled his paw in the air, imitating the "king's wave." "More than fifty musicians on a barge played Handel's masterpiece three times during that evening cruise. They were terribly exhausted, I'm afraid, but the king was seen in a whole new light by the people, many of whom had never before had the privilege to hear such music or see the dreadfully shy king of England."

5

Playing an imaginary violin in the air, Nigel started joyfully humming part of the *Water Music.* The mouse was a hopeless lover of music, and to him, George Frideric Handel was the greatest composer who ever lived. Nigel made a point to study his music and attend every performance of his operas in London. He longed to play the violin so he could bring Handel's masterpieces to life himself, but a mouse-sized violin just didn't exist.

Al gazed thoughtfully at the Thames. "So ye're tellin' me that Tim's River started a kingdom and announced a king as he jest drifted along? Well, I've seen better water stories aboot kings and such. Sure, and Max could tell ye that better than me."

Liz smiled at her musical mouse friend and gazed at a riverboat docked nearby. "But of course, Albert. We all have. Water seems to be very important to the Maker, *n'est ce pas?* Even our first mission on Noah's Ark involved water, the likes of which the world will never see again."

"Aye, and thanks to Messiah, Max should love water music now," Al said with a grin as he listened to Nigel's serenade. "He would've hated it back on the Ark."

"Make ready!" the voice of the king's courier shouted as he approached the waiting riverboat. "I have the king's letters."

"Quickly! Into the boat," Liz instructed as she and Nigel made their way to the stern, or back, of the small vessel, staying hidden from the humans. Al grudgingly left his fish-staring post and joined them. Now he was hungry.

Nigel's whiskers were quivering with excitement. "This is terribly exciting! I can't wait to see Handel's face when he opens that letter!"

"What exactly is this letter all aboot?" Al asked, digging through his knapsack. The Irish cat long ago learned to have food readily on hand —especially fish—for any excursion. Ignoring the drool running down his chin, he grinned wide and pulled out a lone dried fish. The round cat eagerly gobbled it down and burped loudly. Liz rolled her eyes at his crude manners.

"The King has chosen his next 'Master of the King's Musick,' which is the greatest honor in all the musical world! These letters hold his decision, and I'm certain Handel will be the chosen one," Nigel said with an air of confidence, adjusting his spectacles. "He and King George II are both German, and as I've explained, Handel has remained popular with the Royal Court since King George I sat on the throne. King George II just needs to make it official with this appointment. There just is *no one* more worthy of the post."

The animals hid as the men cast off from the pier where the boat was tied in front of the Royal Palace of Hampton Court. The king resided both here in the countryside and at Kensington Palace in London, but the beauty of the gardens set here on the banks of the Thames made for an exquisite setting that he preferred. He didn't mind traveling the eleven miles or so from London to Hampton Court on the Thames. There was much here to occupy the monarch's time, including the incredible maze sculpted from tall, green shrubberies.

Liz had agreed to come along with Nigel to await the king's courier, as she of course adored gardens, and wanted to see this famous maze. She maneuvered through it with ease, her brilliant mind finding it rather simple. Al, on the other hand, was lost for what felt like hours, panicking and wailing when he couldn't find his way out of the green puzzle. Liz smiled to herself as she remembered the look of relief on Al's face when she went in to rescue him, hearing him exclaim: "Aye! I once were lost, but now I be found! Sure, and it be a grand feelin'—maybe even better than fish and bananas."

Liz's smile faded as she thought about the matter now at hand. While in agreement that Handel was indeed the best musician for the post, she had a bad feeling about this situation. She wanted to get a look at the letters, but they were firmly in the courier's grasp. *A simple distraction is all that is needed, no?* Liz decided to risk being seen by the humans. She came out of hiding, walked along the deck and meowed, *"Bonjour,"* as she jumped up on the bench next to the king's courier. She purred and batted her eyes, slowly nudging the man's ornate red coat. The man smiled and set the letters in his lap as he reached to pet Liz.

"Well, where did you come from, little stowaway?" the courier asked as he stroked Liz's fur.

"If you only knew, Monsieur," Liz meowed, purring and glancing over to see two envelopes adorned with the elegant royal writing and seal. She pushed them aside as she sat on his lap. One letter was addressed to Mr. George Frideric Handel. The other was addressed to Dr. Maurice Greene. Liz frowned as she gazed over at Nigel. He was beaming with pride as he looked at the gentle wake of their boat as they glided along the magnificent Thames River, leaving Hampton Court behind. *The king's decision may not be as certain as Nigel believes, poor dear,* Liz thought. She knew how Nigel longed for good news for his musical mentor who had been passed over time and again for the recognition he deserved. *Handel and Greene competed for a musical post before, and their friendship after that interlude was anything but harmonious,* Liz recalled. *Some of the ugliest chords I've ever heard were struck then—when Handel lost to Greene.*

The riverboat arrived at the London wharf later that afternoon, but storm clouds were swirling over the city. The wharf was encased in a grey haze of mist, and thunder rumbled in the distance. Liz meowed, *"Merci,"* and jumped off the boat onto the dock before the king's courier could try to keep her. There by the dock was an ornate coach with a beautiful carriage horse patiently waiting.

"Farewell, little stowaway," the king's courier said with a smile. Raising a hand to the waiting coachman he stepped off the boat. "Good-day,

Benjamin. Take me to Brook Street near Hyde Park to the home of Mr. George Handel," he ordered.

Benjamin respectfully touched his black tricorne hat and opened the coach door for the courier to step inside. "Of course, Mr. Mims, Sir, right away."

Nigel and Al waited for the proper moment and joined Liz on the wharf where she hid, listening to where they were going. She studied the horse-driven coach that was used for the king's official business. The men from the riverboat were loading a few parcels on a platform into the back of the coach.

"It appears we can be stowaways by coach to get to Handel's house," Liz said with a coy grin. "When I give the word, we'll jump onto that platform and hide behind the parcels."

"Brilliant, my pet!" Nigel agreed. "I rather fancy a ride in the king's coach. Do you think Max and Kate will be waiting when we arrive? I do want everyone there for the big moment."

"This is the plan, no? I took the liberty of locating a butcher shop on Brook Street across from Handel's house where Max and Kate have offered their assistance in rounding up rats. They are to be on the look-out for our return," Liz explained.

Nigel shuddered with a look of distain on his face. "Rats. Utterly dreadful."

"Ye think Max can get me some scraps then?" Al asked with a wide grin.

Liz smiled sweetly in reply to her ever-hungry husband. "We'll see, *cher* Albert. For now, quickly, get to the carriage!"

Nigel climbed onto Al's back and together they jumped up on the platform next to Liz. They heard Benjamin climb into his seat and snap the reins. The horse took off clip-clopping over the cobblestone streets of London.

"Splendid! Hyde Park! We're almost there," Nigel exclaimed as he peeked out from behind a parcel to see they were riding down Tiburn Lane.

Al looked around fearfully. "What exactly is there to hide from in these parts?"

8

Nigel threw back his head with a jolly laugh. "Once again, old boy, our British spelling has dealt you a geographic misnomer!"

Al looked at Nigel with a blank look on his face, as he had no clue what Nigel had just said, supposedly by way of explanation.

Liz placed her dainty paw on Al's shoulder. "H-Y-D-E, Albert. This is one of London's grandest parks. Kensington Gardens are on the opposite end near the Palace. I adore it there! And of course, the beautiful Serpentine snakes through the park."

"Serpentine? Snakes? Aye, that's what I were talkin' aboot, Lass!" Al said with paws up to his eyes. "I'm hidin' already."

Liz shook her head. "No, Serpentine *lake*, Albert, named for its shape."

"Aye, but there be snakes in that lake, am I right?" Al asked.

"I suppose . . ." Liz started to say.

Al held up a paw and closed his eyes with a determined shake of his head. "'Nuff said, Lass. I learned me lesson long ago aboot snakes and gardens. Ye won't find *me* in that park."

Liz and Nigel both shrugged their shoulders and shared a grin over Al's worldview.

"WHOA!" Benjamin said as he pulled on the reins. The clip-clop of the horse suddenly ceased. "25 Brook Street, Mayfair. Mr. Handel's abode, Sir."

Liz, Nigel, and Al jumped off the platform as the coach came to a stop in front of a three-story brick townhouse. They hid behind a nearby shrub as the king's courier stepped out from the coach.

"Wha' kept ye? We were catchin' r-r-rats, but the beasties all be gone now," came a voice from behind with a deep Scottish brogue. "With Maximillian Br-r-raveheart the Br-r-ruce on the lookout, no vermin dares bother the butcher on Br-r-rook Str-r-reet."

9

OVER SOMEVON'S DEAD BODY!

"**B**onjour, Max. I knew you and Kate would provide the best protection for the butcher, no?" Liz said with a smile as she kissed Kate on the cheek. "*Bonjour, mon amie.*"

"Good-day, Liz. The butcher's shop is nice an' clean now," Kate replied as she happily wagged her tail. "He even made us a nice bed ta sleep on."

"Aye, an' he gives us all the scr-r-raps we can eat!" Max added, licking his chops.

Al eagerly gripped Max's shoulders. "Can I work there, PLEASE?!"

"I do hate to break up this splendid greeting but we must attend to the matter at hand," Nigel whispered loudly. "The king's courier is approaching Handel's door!"

The animals huddled behind the shrub as the courier entered the wrought iron gate in front of the brick townhouse. The courier donned his white gloves, straightened his gold-trimmed tricorne hat, and glanced over his red coat, then knocked on the door. The tall man clasped his hands behind his back as he waited outside. Soon the door opened and the courier was greeted by Handel's servant, Peter le Blond.

"Good day, Sir," the courier said with a touch of his hat. "I am Mr. Mims, courier to the king. I bring a letter from His Majesty King George II to Mr. George Frideric Handel. Is Mr. Handel home at present?"

Peter gave a respectful bow. "Good day, Mr. Mims. I'm afraid he is out at the moment, but I shall be glad to give Mr. Handel the letter upon his return. I am his personal servant."

"Very well," the courier said as he handed the letter to Peter. "See to it he opens this posthaste. I am sure Mr. Handel has been waiting for this news."

"Indeed. I shall have it at the ready when he returns," Peter assured him with a nod. He took the letter and held it with a sense of awe. "Thank you, Mr. Mims. Long live the king."

"Long live the king," the courier echoed as he turned and made his way back to the coach. Benjamin tended the door for him, then resumed his seat at the reins. The clip-clop of the horse soon faded away.

"Brilliant! Handel is not yet home!" Nigel exclaimed. "This gives us time to find a way into his dwelling."

"I propose we enter through the back of the building via the basement kitchen," Liz suggested.

"AYE! Through the kitchen," Al agreed with a goofy grin on his face.

"Lad, ye best not touch a thing," Max warned with a frown. "Ye remember wha' a mess ye made in Pharaoh's kitchen, an' the tr-r-rouble it br-r-rought the poor baker an' cup bearer lads. This time stay out of sight."

"*Oui*, Albert, Max is correct," Liz added. "We will need to remain hidden while inside Handel's home, so do not touch *anything* as we quietly make our way upstairs."

Al's ears flattened. "Me and kitchens. Such a beautiful thought, but such a dangerous combination."

"Attaboy, lad," Max said with a burly paw to Al's shoulder. "I'll get ye a nice snack from the butcher when we're done here."

Al's gaze brightened. "Sure, and I'll be a good kitty then!"

"Right!" Nigel agreed. "Let's be on our guard as we make haste to the back of the building. I'll go in first to make sure the coast is clear." The mouse scurried ahead of the animals as they stealthily made their way around the corner.

The aromas of fresh-baked bread and roast beef drifted out of the kitchen as Nigel peered in the open window where sat two pies cooling

11

on the windowsill. Humming a light-hearted tune, the plump cook was busily preparing supper. The kitchen door was propped open to allow fresh air inside.

Al was about to swoon from the delicious smells. Max instinctively put his paw up over Al's nose. "Steady, Big Al."

"I daresay, this will be quite the challenge," Nigel said with a furrowed brow. "We need to get past the cook."

Liz jumped up onto the windowsill and curled her tail slowly up and down, deep in thought as she studied the kitchen. The hearth was laden with several cooking pots the cook was tending. The pantry was full of food with boxes and barrels labeled "ITALIA."

"It appears our Mr. Handel is quite the connoisseur of fine food, most notably from Italy," Liz observed.

"Indeed, my pet," Nigel answered. "He is the rather robust eater, having gained an appreciation for Italian cuisine during his years in Rome and Florence," he explained as he adjusted his spectacles. "This poor cook must be exhausted from the amount of food she prepares daily."

"No doubt Albert and Handel would make fast friends, no?" Liz giggled. "Very well, I believe we can sneak past the cook while she is tending the pots. I shall give the signal for everyone to quietly pass through the kitchen. Nigel, please proceed first so you can ensure that the coast is clear in the stairwell."

"Splendid suggestion, my dear," Nigel said as he and Liz watched the cook remove some spices from the pantry before returning to the cook pots. "Cheerio! I'm off," Nigel whispered as he carefully scurried onto a chop block and down to the floor, hiding behind the table legs as he darted through the kitchen. He gave a salute back to Liz once he was safely across.

Liz returned the salute and called to the others below. "Kate, on my mark, please proceed."

"Will do, Liz," Kate replied, peering inside the kitchen door. After a moment, Liz gave the white Westie the signal, and she passed through easily to the stairwell where Nigel waited.

Liz sighed as she considered Al making it through the kitchen without falling prey to his weakness for food. "Max, I believe it will be most wise to have you accompany Albert so he will not be tempted to sample Mr. Handel's supper."

12

Max nodded and got right in Al's face. "Okay, lad, we're goin' in, an' ye best not cause any tr-r-rouble." The Scottie looked at Al's knapsack and had an idea. "Give me yer knapsack."

Al obediently pulled off the knapsack that was draped across his back. Max plopped it over Al's face. "I can't see anythin'!" Al complained holding his paws out in the air.

"Exactly. See no evil. Smell no evil," Max replied with a grin. "Ye stay right next ta me as we go through."

Max gave Liz a nod. As soon as the cook returned to the pot, Liz gave Max the go-ahead and he proceeded with Al close behind. Liz, Kate, and Nigel all held their breath as the two animals entered the kitchen. Suddenly the cook turned and walked over to the large wooden kitchen table. Max stopped in his tracks and put his paw up to Al's chest. The Scottie pulled Al under the kitchen table to wait for a clear shot to the stairwell. The cook's skirt swished right over them as she hummed along and picked up a knife and a potato. After what seemed an eternity, the cook went back to the hearth, and Max took off toward the stairwell, pulling Al along.

13

Liz sighed when they were safely across, closing her eyes with relief. It wasn't long before she was able to make her move and join the others.

"Brilliant!" Nigel exclaimed. "Now, let's be off to the composing room!"

Nigel scurried up the stairs and Max took Al's knapsack off his head. Liz kissed Al on the cheek. "Well done, *cher* Albert. I'm so proud of you."

Al melted with her kiss. "Yea, though I walk through the valley o' temptation . . ."

Kate softly giggled as they quietly walked up the staircase leading to the first floor. "Al is mixin' up his verses then. I'm glad we made it inside. I know Nigel wanted us all ta be here for Handel's big moment. I've never seen him so excited, the dear mouse."

"*Oui,* I'm glad we're here. Friends must encourage one another, no?" Liz said, keeping her concerns to herself. She knew Nigel might need their encouragement more than Handel when that letter was opened.

Max, Al, Kate, and Liz came up behind Nigel, who stood gaping in awe of the room where Handel did his composing work. The little mouse's mouth hung open as he gazed through the chocolate brown doorway into the room. The lead grey paneled walls were adorned with exquisite paintings and green silk curtains hung in the windows. A large brown chair sat in front of a desk, and sitting next to the desk was the instrument Handel played as he wrote music.

Nigel's whiskers quivered with excitement. "I can't believe I'm actually here! Oh, the majestic music that has been born in this room!" Overwhelmed, he ran over to embrace the legs of the odd-looking instrument.

"Wha' in the name of Pete is that thing?" Max wondered, staring at the instrument.

"Why, it's a *clavichord,* my dear fellow," Nigel answered, running up the legs to reach the keyboard. "It is a keyboard instrument that makes sound by striking these brass strings with small metal blades. Vibrations are transmitted through the bridge here to the soundboard." Nigel pointed out the various pieces of the instrument.

"Why does he not use a harpsichord, Nigel?" Liz asked.

"Well, his harpsichord resides in the front rehearsal room where he practices with other musicians and sometimes gives quaint performances," Nigel explained, running his paw respectfully across the keys. "But this instrument has a soft sound and is compact, which is fine for composing music. I heard tell that as a young lad, our dear Mr. Handel arranged for one of these instruments to be brought up to the top floor of his parent's house. He would play it secretly when his family had gone to bed!"

"Why would he do that?" Kate asked, walking around the room.

"Well, unfortunately, his father wished him to study law and forbade him to have anything to do with music," Nigel said with a chuckle. "Of course, that only spurred Handel on."

"His father must have been daft then!" Max said with a furrowed brow. "Didn't he know his lad had a gift of music?"

"Old Mr. Handel eventually came around when young Handel was about eleven years old. After a church service, the boy took to the organ where the duke of Saxe-Weisenfels observed his remarkable skill, and demanded to know about the extraordinary boy," Nigel relayed, preening his whiskers. "When he learned that Handel's father discouraged the lad, he exclaimed he 'could not but consider it as a sort of crime against the public and posterity, to rob the world of such a rising Genius!' Handel's father humbly explained his wishes for his son to study law, which the duke thought was admirable. But he told the father that Handel would be more likely to succeed 'if suffered to pursue the path that Nature and Providence seemed to have marked out for him.'"

"A very wise duke," Liz interjected. "Children should be allowed to pursue the gifts they have been given. According to his divine purposes the Maker gives gifts to each one, no?"

"So wha' happened then?" Max asked.

"Handel's father didn't abandon the law path but did indeed allow for his son to receive proper music lessons," Nigel replied. "Unfortunately, Handel's father died soon thereafter, which grieved the lad terribly."

"Oh, the poor dear, ta lose his father so young!" Kate said sadly.

"Yes, dear Kate. Five days before his twelfth birthday, young Handel wrote quite a tribute to his father for the funeral," Nigel replied somberly. "He wrote, 'God—who has at present taken from me my dear father's care through his death—still lives. He will, henceforth, care and provide for me and help me through all anxiety and distress.'"

"*C'est magnifique,*" Liz said with eyes brimming with tears, "for such a young boy to have such a faith in the Maker in the face of death."

Nigel clasped his paws behind his back and rolled up and down on the balls of his feet. "Extraordinary indeed. I believe this is why Handel has such charity for children, especially orphans. Anyway, once Handel's musical instruction began in organ, harpsichord, composition, and violin, he surpassed his master, and the rest, as we say, is history."

Suddenly they heard a booming voice coming from the outer hall, followed by the front door slamming shut. "Pater! Did my box come today?"

"It's Handel!" Nigel said with his paws to his face. The mouse stood there frozen.

"Hurry! Everyone hide behind the curtains!" Liz exclaimed. "Nigel, come along before Mr. Handel finds a mouse on his clavichord!"

"Right!" Nigel said, snapping out of his excited stupor. He jumped to the bench and then joined the others behind the curtains.

Soon the animals heard the pronounced footsteps of George Frideric Handel as he entered the composing room. He was rather large and had

15

an awkward gait as he walked over to his desk. He grunted as he took off a large black overcoat, calling, "PATER! PATER! Did you hear vat I said?" Handel wore an enormous white wig that shook when he shouted.

"Yes, sir," Peter said as he hurried into the room, taking the coat from Handel. "Welcome home. I did hear you, but no, your package unfortunately did not arrive. But perhaps something more important came today—a letter from the king." Peter held out the letter to Handel and smiled broadly.

"This is it!" Nigel whispered excitedly.

"Oh! Ya, I've been vondering ven dis vould arrive," Handel replied as he took the letter and sat down. "Let us see vat de king says."

Handel held the envelope, broke the royal seal, and pulled out the letter. He began reading aloud, "From George de Second, by de Grace of God, King of Great Britain, France, and Ireland, Defender of de Faith." Turning to Peter, he chuckled and said, "It's good de King didn't put his seventeen other titles, or it vould all day take me to read dis!"

Handel's eyes scanned the letter. His smile was suddenly replaced by a scowl as he leaned forward, his eyes wide. The animals could see his face turning red and his jaw clenching as he read the letter. Liz put her paw on Nigel's shoulder.

"Vat de dyfil?! GREENE! AGAIN!" Handel shouted as he shook the letter in the air.

"Sir, what happened?" Peter asked in alarm.

"De organist at St. Andrews died, and GREENE vas appointed to take his place! Den de organist at St. Paul's died, and GREENE got de commission! DEN de organist at Chapel Royal died, and GREENE got DAT appointment! NOW, de Master of de King's Musick dies, and GREENE gets de job!!" Handel screamed. "SOMEVON HAS TO DIE BEFORE GREENE GETS A COMMISSION!"

"It can't be!" Nigel said as his heart sank to his stomach. "Not again! Handel deserved that commission, not Greene!"

"Steady, Mousie," Max whispered from behind.

"Yet de KING asked ME to compose his musick for ven he vas made KING! Ven de royals vant a special vork of musick, who do dey ask to write it? ME!" Handel shouted, pulling off his wig and tossing it onto the floor. "But GREENE! He only gets asked to write musick over somevon's dead body!"

16

Peter picked up Handel's wig and clutched it to his chest while trying to offer some word of encouragement. "Oh, Mr. Handel! I'm in
shock! There was clearly no one more qualified to be Master of the
King's Musick than you!"

Handel slammed his fist on the desk and his inkwell bounced, splattering blobs of ink all over the letter. "*Col pugno!* Ya, dis I know!" he
shouted in disgust as he stormed out of the room. Peter quickly followed him. The animals heard the composer's heavy footsteps climb the
stairs as he continued to rant.

Max, Kate, Liz, and Al huddled around Nigel. The little mouse was
devastated. He held his head in his paws, and shook it back and forth.

"*Quel dommage, mon ami.* I am so very sorry about this news," Liz
said sadly. "We all know how much you wanted this commission for
your mentor."

"Aye, 'tis a shame, lad," Max added.

Kate put her paw gently on Nigel's back. "It be so hard when
ye expect somethin' an' get the opposite. Life can be disappointin'
sometimes. I jest wish Handel knew how much he is admired by ye,
Nigel."

Al's lip was quivering. "First he lost his father, now this!" Although
almost forty years had passed between those events, having just learned
what happened to Handel as a boy touched Al's heart.

Nigel rubbed his eyes and stood tall. "Thank you all, my good
friends. I appreciate your support. At least we know the truth of the
matter. Handel is the finest composer in all the land whether he has an
official title from the king or not."

Nigel walked over to jump up on Handel's desk. He wanted to read
the letter for himself. Max, Kate, and Al gathered around on the floor
while Liz joined Nigel on the desk. The mouse quietly read the words
and shook his head. "I just can't believe it." He turned his back on the
letter and sat on the desk, crestfallen.

"*Oui,* it is difficult to understand," Liz said, suddenly wrinkling her
brow as she studied the letter. She was staring at a large ink blob that
had formed when Handel slammed his fist on the desk. "Nigel, I think
you need to see this."

"Oh, my pet, I read it all. It's too disappointing to read again," Nigel
replied.

17

"No, not the letter, Nigel," Liz implored. She looked up at Nigel with excitement in her eyes.

Nigel wore a puzzled look and came back to view the letter with Liz. "Whatever do you mean, my dear?"

Liz pointed to the ink blob right next to the king's crest. It had changed from ink to wax and from black to red.

Startled, Nigel quickly looked at Liz. "By Jove, it's the Seven Seal."

18

HANDEL'S MAGNUM OPUS

Nigel folded his arms over his chest and tapped a finger on his chin as he stared at the Seven Seal. "Extraordinary. Do you suppose the sudden appearance of this seal has anything to do with what just happened here with Handel?"

"Well, there's only one way ta find out, Mousie. Ye best br-r-ring that letter down here," Max instructed eagerly. "When ye br-r-reak the seal we need ta be standin' together."

Kate grinned and wagged her tail excitedly but saw the look of fear on Al's face. "Wha's wrong, Al dear? Aren't ye excited ta see him again?"

Al held his paws up to his mouth. "Aye, I always love to see *him,* but I get nervous seein' pictures o' *me* everywhere at the same time." The nervous cat patted his body. "I always wonder if part o' me will get left behind somewhere in there."

"Not to worry, *cher* Albert," Liz assured her mate with glowing eyes as she and Nigel jumped to the floor. "You will not be separated from yourself as we enter the IAMISPHERE. Is everyone ready?"

"Aye! Chew away, Mousie," Max exclaimed. "Gillamon awaits!"

"Very well," Nigel said with a nod. "Gather around, everyone."

As Nigel nibbled through the seal, the animals were suddenly enveloped in a sphere of light seventy feet high. Swirling around them were countless scenes of themselves across different points in history. The team had been in the IAMISPHERE countless times. It was so named for the great I AM, for whom time is all the same. Being outside of all time, the great I AM sees the past, present, and future as one. It was here inside the IAMISPHERE that the Order of the Seven received their mission assignments and, when necessary, revisited moments in the past.

Max nudged Al in the ribs with a laugh and pointed to a scene. "Look, Big Al! There's Don Pedro r-r-runnin' after ye in that field. I don't think I ever saw yer eyes get so big."

"Sure, and I'm glad ye were there to save me life," Al gulped and said, watching the Spanish bull chasing him on their way to Noah's Ark. Al's face eased as he saw Henriette the French hen enter the scene, ordering the humbled bull around. "And that obnoxious hen saved me every day after that."

"Aye," Max chuckled. "One of me favorite memories."

"Look! It's Daniel readin' his scroll at the magi school in Babylon," Kate pointed out excitedly. "Ah, wha' a sweet lad he were."

"*Oui*, Kate. Nigel and I spent many nights reading on that desk," Liz added with a smile.

The soft sound of rushing wind filled the sphere, and suddenly there before them stood a tall, majestic mountain goat. His white goatee and blue eyes gave his face an image of sublime wisdom and kindness.

"And don't forget *that* desk," the mountain goat said, pointing to a scene of Liz and Nigel sitting on the desk of Isaiah, where the prophet wrote about the promised Messiah. "Greetings, my friends. How wonderful to see you all!"

Max ran to Gillamon and embraced him. "It's gr-r-rand ta see ye! How long has it been?"

Gillamon smiled and looked around the IAMISPHERE. "Just a moment in time, as usual."

"I say, you've come at quite the surprising moment," Nigel said. "I just don't understand why Mr. Handel has once more been passed over for greatness by the king. Is something afoot with a mission involving Mr. Handel?"

"Something is afoot indeed, Nigel. I think you will soon be glad to hear about what is to come for Mr. Handel." Gillamon smiled warmly at the little mouse. "The Maker always has greater plans in mind than man. He is the One who truly determines greatness."

20

Nigel's heart lifted and a smile grew on his face as Liz placed an encouraging paw on the mouse's shoulder. *"Bonjour,* Gillamon. Please do tell us our mission, *s'il vous plaît.* We could use some good news, no?"

"Indeed," Gillamon told her as he circled around the group of animal friends. He pointed to a scene of Handel, drifting down the Thames conducting his *Water Music.* "Your next mission is to assist George Frideric Handel with writing the most important piece of music that not only *he* will ever write—but that will *ever* be written. Timeless in its impact, it will touch more hearts than any other music from the very first performance throughout the ages. This work will be Handel's most important. It will truly be his Magnum Opus."

"What's an opus?" Al asked. "Sure, and what's a magnum, for that matter?"

Liz brightened. "May I, Gillamon?"

"By all means," Gillamon replied with a smile. He knew how the brilliant French cat loved explaining words.

"Opus is the Latin word for 'work' and is used mainly in the fields of music and architecture. The plural of opus is *opera,* which our dear Mr. Handel is fond of writing, no? The Romans used the word *opus* to describe various building methods and styles. Musicians use opuses to number their works composed in order. *Comprenez-vous?"* Liz asked to make sure her audience was still with her.

"Aye, Liz," Kate answered happily. She loved Liz's lectures.

Liz nodded approvingly. *"Bon. Magnum* is Latin for 'great.' So a *Magnum Opus* is a musical piece that crowns a musician's career with respect and admiration as his greatest work."

"Handel's Magnum Opus," Nigel quietly remarked, deep in thought.

"Très bien, Liz," Gillamon affirmed. He then turned to stand in front of Nigel, towering over the little mouse. "And you, Nigel P. Monaco, will assist Handel in creating this musical piece that will not just be recognized by one king for a brief period of time, but by a string of kings and millions of people across time."

Nigel's eyes grew wide. He humbly bowed with his paw draped across his chest. "It will be my honor, Gillamon."

"Very well. Nigel, Liz, and Al, you are to spend the next six years observing the progression of Handel's work before he begins his Magnum

Opus," Gillamon explained. "You will see a decline that must happen for his greatest good. Crucial to your mission will be the introduction of Handel to a chap by the name of Charles Jennens. Everything hinges on this meeting as Jennens will supply Handel with the words for his music. Liz, just as you sat on Isaiah's desk, so, too, will you sit on Jennens's desk as he writes."

"C'est magnifique!" Liz exclaimed.

"Aye, an' wha' should Kate an' me be doin'?" Max asked, feeling left out.

Gillamon turned and smiled at his longtime friend, whom he had raised from a pup. "I have something completely different, but nonetheless very important, for you and Kate to do. You are to assist a fellow by the name of David Henry. I think you'll like this assignment, Max, for he is Scottish."

"AYE! Now that's a gr-r-rand assignment—ta help a fellow Scot!" Max enthused.

"Wonderful! How are we ta help the lad?" Kate added.

"How does matchmaking sound, Kate?" Gillamon asked with a knowing grin. Kate beamed at Max and wagged her tail. "You will help him marry a special lass named Mary Cave. This will in turn help him with his writing career here in London."

"Writing? But this is what Nigel and I specialize in, no?" Liz questioned.

"Indeed," Gillamon nodded. "You can give Max and Kate pointers when they need it, but this fellow David Henry wants to be a reporter for a newspaper. He constantly writes down his thoughts and will serve an important role in the decades to come. And, he will give Handel encouragement he needs at just the right time."

"Nigel, please step forward," Gillamon instructed. "You will have the greatest impact of all on Handel's music."

Nigel smoothed his whiskers and stood attentively in front of Gillamon with his chest raised in proud anticipation of his assignment.

"You must spend the next six years learning to play the violin. When the time is right, divine music will come forth when you play the violin in Handel's ear as he sleeps. Handel will wake up inspired and ready to compose this music," Gillamon instructed.

Nigel's shoulders sank. "But how? How can I possibly play the violin? I'm terribly small and could never hope to hold a bow!"

Gillamon smiled but did not respond right away. "Is anything too hard for the Maker?"

"Nothing is too hard for the Maker, but such a task is formidable for *me*, being such a small animal," Nigel replied honestly. He felt a weight of inadequacy on his shoulders to perform for his musical mentor.

Al stepped up and cleared his throat. "I don't know much aboot opuses and such, but I'm big enough to play a fiddle. I'll volunteer to help Mousie."

Liz happily rubbed her head on Al's cheek. "Oh, Albert, how noble of you!"

Nigel smiled weakly and placed his paw on Al's arm. "It's utterly splendid of you to offer, dear boy, but I'm afraid this assignment is one I'll have to figure out myself."

Gillamon leaned over and got right in Nigel's face. "If the Maker gives you an assignment, he always makes a way for you to accomplish it, no matter how impossible it may seem. Just look up at the scenes around you. How many of these events seemed impossible at the time?"

The animals stood and gazed at the thousands of images from points in history they had been privileged to be part of. From escaping pyramids to parting seas to fiery furnaces to lions' dens, the animals were reminded of the Maker's reliable provision each and every time right when they needed it.

Nigel straightened up and fiddled with his spectacles. "By Jove, you're right. Although I have no idea how I shall accomplish this mission for Mr. Handel, I know the answers shall indeed come."

"And in his perfect time," Gillamon added. "This music will inspire like no other piece for it will be inspired like no other piece."

"Gillamon, what will be the subject of Handel's Magnum Opus?" Liz asked.

"A subject you all know quite well, for you were there when it happened," Gillamon said with reverence. "The Subject is Messiah."

The IAMISPHERE began swirling with scenes from the life of Jesus. The animals saw him with Mary and Joseph as a baby, then in the Temple as a young boy, and as a man healing broken bodies and giving hope to broken hearts.

"There were lots of impossible things in that mission," Max reminded

Nigel as they stood gazing at the scene of Jesus walking on the Sea of Galilee. "Compared ta the Messiah mission, fiddlin' the Messiah music for Handel will be easy, lad."

Nigel smiled. "Indeed. Nothing is impossible after what we saw our Messiah do."

"Gillamon, will we get ta see her during this mission?" Kate asked. She was taken back to a fond memory unfolding before her in Jerusalem.

"Time will tell, dear Kate," Gillamon replied with that familiar twinkle in his eyes. "It always does."

A feeling of reverent awe came over them as the Crucifixion came into view. Liz's eyes filled with tears and she held her paws to her face, overcome with the honor of writing about Messiah. *"Merci, mon Dieu."*

The empty tomb brilliantly swirled into view and the animals tingled from head to toe, reliving the indescribable feeling of that morning.

"Sure, and that were his best impossible move ever," Al whispered.

Next a scene from the Roman Forum appeared in front of them. A younger Handel walked down the Via Sacra, touring the ruins of ancient Rome. Within moments he was sitting in a room there in Rome, sheets of freshly inked music spread across his desk. Handel carefully studied a coin he held in his hand.

Nigel's whiskers quivered with excitement and curiosity. "I say, what was he composing there in Rome, Gillamon?"

Gillamon approached the scene. "That would be the first oratorio Handel ever composed: *The Triumph of Time and Truth*. Quite prophetic for our dear Mr. Handel."

Gillamon placed his hoof in the scene and the animals watched in awe as he faded into the background. He was leaving them, and they knew they must return to Handel's desk in 1735.

"In time, truth always prevails," Gillamon said, his voice trailing off as he disappeared. "Time to go, Nigel. Truth awaits."

PROPER
INTRODUCTIONS

The tantalizing smell of delicious chocolate wafted through the air as Peter slowly carried the bowl of steaming hot cocoa up the stairs from the kitchen. Sitting next to the cocoa on the silver tray was a letter that had arrived the previous night. Handel had returned late from the opera house, so Peter waited until this morning to give him the letter. Peter took great care not to spill the cocoa onto the beautifully penned letter. As he approached the composing room, he heard Handel playing and humming his latest work in progress.

"Good morning, Sir," Peter greeted the composer with a wide smile as he entered the room. "You are up and at it early today, I see."

"Ya, good morning, Pater," Handel replied, marking a correction on the sheet music. He wore a red dressing gown over a crisp white shirt. A matching red cap covered his shaved head, making him look quite different from his public wigged appearance. "Ah, dis is a good day! God has given me favor vit my *Alcina.*"

Peter set the silver tray on the desk. "Congratulations, Mr. Handel. The word about London is that *Alcina* is considered your greatest triumph in opera yet. I understand the king and queen have given their full support to your work."

"Ya, de Royals vonce again *love* my vork." Handel shook his head and threw a hand in the air to dismiss the royal brushoff he had earlier received for the position of Master of the King's Musick. "Vell, I know some people are growing tired of true opera, but I hope my *Alcina* will help tings. Dat dreadful *Beggar's Opera* makes fun of Italian opera! I tink it will kill Italian opera if people vant dat silly comedy instead of real musick, ya? De people's taste is changing," Handel went on, taking a sip of the chocolate. "Ah, but *dis* is de sweetest taste to my tongue, Pater! Tank you. And vat is dis?"

Peter handed the sealed letter to Handel, who set down his cup. "This arrived last evening, from a Mr. Charles Jennens."

"Jennens? Who is dis?" Handel asked as he broke the seal.

"Read and you will find out, *Monsieur*," Liz whispered to herself and Nigel behind the curtains.

Handel raised his eyebrows with a smile. "He says he has subscribed to my music for many years. Ah, dis must be a good man!"

"Indeed," Peter replied with a smile. He stood politely by with his hands folded in front of him as Handel continued to read.

"I knew Handel would like hearing that Jennens is an admirer of his music," Nigel whispered to Liz as he preened his whiskers. "Thank you for adding it in, my dear. I must say your penmanship was exquisite."

"You are most welcome, Nigel," Liz replied with a coy smile. "And *merci*. Handel possesses some new metal-tipped quill pens. I have never used these before, so it was a challenge, no? I had to practice with them to not leave an ink smudge with my paw."

"Mr. Jennens vould like to have coffee vit me dis afternoon," Handel relayed, scratching his scruffy chin. "Dis I vill do, ya."

"Very well," Peter said, taking the letter from Handel, reading the details of the suggested meeting place. "Your schedule is clear, Sir. I see the coffeehouse is nearby."

"Ya, I vill valk on dis beautiful spring day de Lord has made," Handel told him, taking a big gulp of the chocolate and handing it back to Peter. He patted his belly and grinned widely. "I vill too stop by de butcher to see if my box has come. You know how I love to visit de butcher."

"Brilliant!" Nigel exclaimed with his paws clasped together. "Now let's hope Handel's invitation to Jennens meets with the same response!"

"AL! Don't touch the bacon!" Kate scolded as Al reached for the freshly cut meat left on the counter. "If the butcher finds meat missin' he'll come after Max an' me first!"

Al wore a sheepish grin. "Sorry aboot that, Lass. Me mouth is waterin' with all this yummy food. I don't know how ye and Max stand it."

"Ye got ta have patience, lad," Max admonished, tossing a scrap of meat to Al. "The butcher gives plenty of scr-r-raps but ye got ta wait. It's a good thing the butcher is lettin' ye stay. As long as we keep the r-r-rats away, the scr-r-raps will come."

Al gobbled up the scrap and rubbed his belly. "Aye, I'll wait, if it takes forever! Well, at least for as long as I can stand it."

"That's a good lad. Keep an eye out for beasties comin' in the butcher's boxes then. Ye can better jump up ta see them than we can," Kate instructed.

"Aye, Lass," Al replied with a salute. He proceeded to jump up on a group of crates just delivered to the shop, sniffing and peering inside the slats of the wooden crates.

27

Suddenly they heard the door of the butcher shop open, followed by the booming voice of Handel.

"Good day, Mr. Smythe," Handel greeted the butcher with a warm smile. "I vas vanting to check on my box."

"Always wonderful to see you, Mr. Handel!" the butcher replied enthusiastically as he wiped his hands on his apron. "I certainly wish to keep our resident musician happy! Let me go check. I received a large delivery of crates just this morning."

"Vonderful, tank you, Mr. Smythe," Handel replied as he gazed over the shelves stocked with tasty delicacies. His mouth watered.

Al walked around the stack of crates and stopped at a small one marked *ITALIA* and *G.F. HANDEL*. He peeked inside the slats and smelled the wonderful aroma of prosciutto, carefully packaged and sadly out of his reach. He could feel the drool building in his mouth as he gazed at the jar of olives and other Italian delicacies surrounded by the fine straw packaging. Suddenly Al saw something move in the shadows behind a tin of biscotti. He whipped his tail and started to meow.

"Off you go, cat," Mr. Smythe said as he lifted Al off the crate and set him on the floor. "Ah, yes, here it is."

To his terror, Al saw the butcher pick up the crate and carry it to the front of the shop where Handel eagerly waited.

"Max! There's a beastie in Handel's box!" Al cried. "What do we do?"

Max, Kate, and Al gazed to see Handel tuck the box under his arm and tip his tricorne hat to Mr. Smythe in farewell.

"Well, it's too late," Max growled. "Al, ye'll have ta follow that box an' get the beastie when Handel isn't lookin'. The beastie will hide in the straw an' wait for its chance ta sneak out."

"Ye can do it, Al," Kate told Al with a reassuring paw on his back. "Max an' me have ta stay here."

Al gulped. "Aye, I'll follow the beastie. At least it must be small to fit in that crate."

Max grinned. "Aye, Big Al. Ye can handle that Italian beastie. If all else fails, use yer charm."

Puzzled, Al furrowed his brow. "Me charm? I didn't know I had any."

28 The orange cat quickly scooted out of the butcher shop and followed Handel down Brook Street. But Al soon realized Handel wasn't headed home. He was walking right toward Hyde Park.

"Look, he's there!" Nigel exclaimed happily. "By Jove, I believe we've pulled it off!"

Nigel and Liz gazed at the coffeehouse windowfront from behind a bush. They could see Charles Jennens sitting at a small table with two chairs, obviously waiting for Handel.

"*Oui!* Jennens is there!" Liz enthused. "And here comes Handel. Well done, *mon ami!* Your idea for the two of them to meet worked."

Nigel straightened his spectacles and smiled broadly as they watched Handel enter the coffeehouse. "Thank you, my dear. This is terribly exciting, knowing what awaits these two fine gentlemen!"

"I'll tell ye what awaits them if Handel opens his package—terror!" Al nervously exclaimed behind them. "There's a beastie in that box!" Al looked around fearfully at their location by Hyde Park. "There be beasties everywhere."

"Whatever do you mean, Albert?" Liz replied in alarm, stunned to see her big orange mate.

"Handel jest picked up that box at the butcher's and I saw two big eyes starin' at me from inside. But the butcher gave it to Handel before I could do anythin' aboot it," Al exclaimed.

"Oh, dear! How utterly dreadful!" Nigel said, his paws up to his mouth.

Liz's tail swished back and forth as she thought through the situation. "I do not believe that Handel will open his package while in the coffeehouse, as he would not wish to share its contents with a complete stranger. We need to monitor this, of course, but I feel certain Handel will have his coffee and discussion with Mr. Jennens and leave with the crate unopened."

"Max told me to be sure to get the beastie when Handel isn't lookin', sayin' it would hide until the coast is clear," Al explained.

"Let us hope Handel allows the cook to open the box in the kitchen as usual," Liz reasoned. "Otherwise, we could have a paper-chewing rat around our composer's work, and this would be unacceptable, no?"

Nigel closed his eyes and grimaced. "Rats. Utterly dreadful."

"Have ye spotted any beasties around here?" Al whispered, looking over at the park.

"No worries, *cher* Albert," Liz smiled reassuringly, returning her gaze back to the coffeehouse. "Just two expected gentlemen for proper introductions, per our mission assignment. This was rather simple to arrange, no?"

Nigel clasped his paws behind his back and rolled up and down on the balls of his feet. "Elementary, my dear," the mouse agreed with a grin. "The power of the pen is indeed extraordinary."

THE BIG-EYED BEASTIE

n hour passed while Liz, Al, and Nigel watched the two men
in the coffeehouse. Handel's box remained unopened as the
two men enjoyed a lengthy conversation. Jennens wore an
expensive green coat with large cuffs and gold buttons. His white wig
was quite smaller than Handel's, and his beady, hazel eyes appeared
emotionless.

"The other lad looks grumpy," Al noted as he stared at a grim-look-
ing Jennens. "Sure, and he hasn't smiled the whole time."

"I daresay you are right, old boy. He's quite the serious lot, isn't he?"
Nigel agreed. "From what I hear he is a country gentleman—rather
wealthy, opinionated, and dreadfully cruel in his criticism. Like Handel,
he has never married."

"No wonder," Al said with a frown. "Who'd want to live with a
grump like *him*?"

"*Oui*, but our Mr. Jennens is very well educated and has impeccable
taste in music, art, and literature, no? I was quite impressed with his art
collection when we stopped by his house last night with the letter 'from
Handel,'" Liz recalled with a knowing smile. "I have always found it
fascinating how the Maker chooses humans for his purposes. They all
have at least one personal fault, *n'est ce pas?*"

"Brilliant observation, my pet," Nigel replied with a chuckle. "Many
times, humans have more than one issue, but the Maker uses them in
spite of themselves. If only mice, cats, and dogs ruled the world!"

"More often than not, I believe we do, *mon ami,*" Liz added with a wink.

Handel and Jennens stood and shook hands. Handel reached down and picked up his box before heading out the door of the coffeehouse.

"Here they come!" Nigel exclaimed while climbing on Al's back. "Make haste, old boy. Follow that composer!"

"Aye, and that beastie," Al replied.

Once back at 25 Brook Street, Handel entered the front door, and the three animals sneaked in through an open upstairs window after climbing the ivy on a trellis against the back of the brick townhouse. Liz had figured this to be an easier way to enter the house than through the kitchen.

To the animals' surprise, instead of taking the box to the kitchen, Handel headed right for his composing room. He put the box on his desk while he turned to remove his coat. Al's fur rose as he saw two eyes peeking out through the slats.

"That beastie looks ready to jump out!" Al worried.

Nigel scowled. "Al, old boy, you must capture that beast at the first possible moment!"

As Handel lifted the lid, he leaned his head to look inside the box and breathed in deeply. "Ah, now dis is vat I've been vanting!" He took out the biscotti, the olives, and the prosciutto and tossed the box onto the floor. He was soon crunching the mildly sweet Italian biscuit, dropping crumbs everywhere.

"I see your box arrived, Mr. Handel," Peter noted as he entered the room, frowning to see the mess Handel was making all over his desk. "May I take the liberty of having Mrs. Rice prepare you a plate in the dining room? I think you will enjoy it far more in there."

"Ya, dis is a good idea, Pater. I vill go change," Handel replied with his mouth full of biscotti. He held up the prosciutto to Peter. "Just smell dis! A sweet aroma, aged two years! De best prosciutto comes from de nort of Italy." Handel proceeded to wipe off his crumbs and gather up the biscotti while Peter took the meat and olives for the cook.

"How was your meeting with Mr. Jennens?" Peter asked as he and Handel walked toward the door.

31

"Very interesting. He vants to write someting for me," Handel replied. "But he vill have to prove he can make vords to fit my music."

Immediately after the men left the room, Al pounced on top of the box. "All right, beastie, I've got ye covered and there be no escape!"

Nothing. Silence. Al sniffed around the box in a frenzied panic, trying to keep the animal contained. He began throwing the packing straw everywhere, making a greater mess than Handel had.

Liz walked over to join Al in looking around the box, frowning as straw flew all over her shiny black fur. "Careful, Albert."

"Oh dear, do you suppose the beast escaped?" Nigel worried as he joined the cats, peeking around Liz.

As the three animals huddled around the box, a voice came from behind them. *"Mi scusi. Che cosa c'è?"*

Al, Liz, and Nigel looked up at one another and slowly turned to see what or who had spoken to them . . . in Italian.

It was a lanky brown stick bug with huge round eyes that popped off the side of his face. Attached to his skinny body were three pairs of twig-like legs, and protruding from the top of his head were two small antennae. He stood six inches tall and wore a piece of dark string around his neck. Liz couldn't help but smile as she gazed at those large eyes.

"Careful, Lass," Al said as he put his paw in front of Liz, frowning at the stick bug. "He looks like a suspicious beastie. No tellin' what he jest said."

"I believe he said, 'Excuse me, what is the matter?' I do not find him threatening, Albert," Liz said, lifting Al's paw off her chest. She walked over to the stick bug. "Pardon, but you are Italian, no?"

"Si, Signora, grazie," the stick bug replied with a wide grin. *"Mi dispiace*—I am sorry I alarmed you while I was hiding in the box."

Al got right in the stick bug's face and squinted as he stared at the bug's big eyes. "Aye, that be the beastie I saw hidin'. What be yer business here, ye big-eyed bug?"

"Allow me to introduce myself," the stick bug replied with a twiggy arm raised high. "I am Signor Antonio Vivaldi Stradivari Shandelli, at your service."

Nigel's ears perked up. "Astonishing! I say, by the sound of your name you must be a musician like me."

"Ah, *sì, Signor* mouse, but please—call me Shan-*dell*-i," the stick bug replied, emphasizing the second syllable.

"It's a pleasure, Shandelli. I am Nigel P. Monaco, your humble servant," Nigel said as he bowed with a paw draped across his chest. "Do call me Nigel."

"*Bonjour, Signor* Shandelli. I am Liz and this is my husband Albert," Liz told the bug. "It is obvious you have traveled from Italy. What brings you here?"

"The great Handel, of course! All my life I've dreamed of meeting him, and now here I am," Shandelli stated, then paused in awe as he looked around the composing room.

"Antonio Vivaldi Stradivari? These three names I know well. But Shandelli? Is this for Handel that you have named yourself?" Liz asked, curious about his names.

"*Sì!* I named myself for the greatest violinist of all— Antonio Vivaldi, and the greatest violin maker of all, Antonio Stradivari, but of course I had to make the greatest composer of all *sound* Italian," Shandelli replied.

"*Oui!* I see, so Handel became Shandelli," Liz continued.

"And here I thought he were a destructive beastie," Al murmured.

"Brilliant! How *thrilling* to meet an Italian music lover! I'm quite the music aficionado myself," Nigel shared, grooming his whiskers proudly. "We've only recently arrived to meet Mr. Handel ourselves. I say, have you had the privilege of meeting Vivaldi or Stradivari?"

Shandelli leaned over and blinked his big eyes at Nigel with a large grin. "Not only have I met Vivaldi, but I have *lived* in the workshop of Stradivari all my life."

Nigel's eyes got almost as large as Shandelli's. "THE Stradivari? He makes the greatest violins in the entire world! You actually *lived* in his workshop? Utterly staggering!"

"*Sì*, and being a stick bug I could sit among the wood shavings on his desk and watch him without him even knowing I was there," Shandelli said. "But when I heard that the great George Frideric Handel ordered delicacies from my hometown of Cremona, I knew I had to come meet him myself. So I stowed away in that box."

Al shook his head and put his paw on the stick bug's skinny back. "Ye poor laddie. I know it were sheer torture to be with all that food for the long journey."

33

"Actually a few leaves were plenty of food," Shandelli replied, his big eyes at the level of Al's large belly. "It appears you have an appetite like Handel, eh?"

Liz immediately had a thought. "Shandelli, since you watched Stradivari at work, do you know how to construct a violin?"

"Naturalmente! Having watched the master I know everything there is to know about making the finest of violins," Shandelli replied. He fiddled with the string tied around his neck. "I even kept part of the leftover violin string he used to make his most prized violin—'The Messiah.'"

Nigel's whiskers quivered with excitement as he and Liz shared a knowing smile. "This is stupendous! My dear boy, I am thrilled beyond belief for you have *no* idea what this means," Nigel said as he went up to look closely at the violin string around the stick bug's neck. "May I?"

"Naturalmente," Shandelli replied with a puzzled look as Nigel reverently touched the string.

"What Nigel means is that we have a mission from the Maker to inspire Handel to compose the greatest work of all time, but he needs a mouse-sized violin so he can learn to play," Liz explained. "Could you help Nigel make this violin?"

Shandelli's eyes grew even larger with this news. "A mission from the *Maestro*?! *Sì, sì, sì!* Of course I will help you, Nigel. *Ciò che Dio vuole, Io voglio.* What God wills, I will. It will be an honor, *Signor* Monaco."

"You shall have my eternal thanks and, of course, the thanks of the Eternal," Nigel replied as he and Shandelli vigorously shook hands.

"Prego," Shandelli smiled. *"Detto fatto."*

"Ye best not be talkin' aboot me," Al complained with a pout.

Liz giggled. "No, *cher* Albert. He said, 'No sooner said than done.'"

"Aye, okay then," Al grinned sheepishly. "Shandelli, yer eyes are goin' to really pop when ye hear the aboot the music Handel's goin' to write."

"Per favore, do tell me," Shandelli pleaded with his tiny hands out in an exaggerated gesture.

Nigel straightened his spectacles and closed his eyes with an unbelieving nod to himself about this miracle unfolding before him. "The subject for the work we will assist Handel in writing is none other than," he announced as he once again held the violin string in his hand, "Messiah."

"Glorificare Dio!" Shandelli exclaimed as he held his four twiggy arms high in the air. He looked at Nigel, who gazed longingly at the violin string. Shandelli reached down and removed it from around his neck. "And with this string from Stradivari's Messiah violin will we make *your* violin, *amico* Nigel."

"Magnifique!" Liz exclaimed. "Gillamon said a way would come, *mon ami!*"

Nigel threw his head back with a jolly chuckle. "Little did I know the way would come in a box of food from Italy."

"Sure, and that makes perfect sense to me," Al said. "Food is always an answer to *me* prayers."

THE SCOTTISH
CONNECTION

LONDON, 1736

W hat good could ever come out of a tax collector?"
A trio of wealthy London businessmen stood on the corner of the Merchant Exchange and watched Edward Cave
walk away, shaking their heads at his heavy gait. They continued their
dissecting of the questionable man who had been in the bank.

"Word is he's been a troublemaker ever since he was a boy, stealing
roosters, selling completed lessons to his classmates. Evidently he was a
good student and sought to make money from it."

"As I said, his first job was as a *tax collector*, of all things. What
a despicable profession! Seems Mr. Cave chose the perfect first job to
match his character!"

The businessmen enjoyed a moment of laughter before continuing
their assessment of the big man who towered over them in size. They
wouldn't dare speak of him this way in his presence.

"I for one will *never* forget the incident of his opening our mail
when he became postmaster! Served him right that we had him fired
for that offense—even if we never could prove he actually committed
the crime."

The men continued their laughter until they were joined by the Governor of the Bank of England, who overheard their remarks.

"Good day, gentlemen," he greeted them with a touch to his tri-corne hat. "From your conversation, it sounds as if you are disrespecting one of the most successful businessmen in all London." The governor squinted at the men, who exchanged uncomfortable glances. He held a newspaper up in the air. "Surely you aren't jealous of the success of Mr. Edward Cave! Although he has outsmarted every last one of you, and has made more money than your businesses combined." The governor laughed and slapped the newspaper into the chest of one of the men.

The businessmen huddled and gazed at the paper: *The Gentleman's Magazine*. One of them looked up with a question on his face. "You mean to tell us that the Editor—Sylvanus Urban—is . . . ?"

"Mr. Edward Cave himself," laughed the Governor as he started to walk off. "Editor of the most well-known and highly respected publication in the English-speaking world today."

Max grinned from behind the group of now speechless men who had been put in their place. "These pompous lads must not r-r-read their Holy Wr-r-rit, or they'd know that even tax collectors can make somethin' gr-r-rand of themselves."

Kate smiled. "Aye, me love, but let's leave them be. Time ta follow Mr. Cave ta his house an' see where his sister Mary lives."

Max winked at Kate. "Ye're jest lovin' this assignment, ye r-r-romantic lass. Very well, let's be on our way then."

The two dogs started trotting down the street, but Max fell behind Kate. He gazed up at the men huddled there, noses together, reading the latest issue of *The Gentleman's Magazine*. He simply could not resist leaving his mark on the shoes of the man who had made that tax collector remark. Max caught up to Kate and wore a wide grin, showing his white teeth.

"Wha' be so funny, Max?" Kate asked.

"Sometimes I jest enjoy givin' the uppity Brits a bit of Scottish cheekiness," Max laughed.

Twenty-five year-old David Henry sat on a stone bench in Hyde Park, his handsome face buried in this month's hot-off-the-press edition of *The Gentleman's Magazine*. Kate wore her perky grin and wagged her tail as she observed his concentration from her hiding place behind a shrub. He nodded as he agreed with one article; he laughed when he read a funny one. She couldn't wait to officially meet him. She and Max had staked out where David Henry as well as Mary Cave each lived, per their assignment from Gillamon. The pair of dogs had also studied their daily patterns of work and life to know when and where they could arrange a "meeting" of sorts.

David was an avid reader, working in the publishing world as a printer's apprentice in London. How he longed to become a reporter and work for such a fine magazine as the one he read on this bench! His family back in Aberdeen, Scotland, had wanted him to pursue the ministry, but he had to follow HIS passion and came to London at the age of fourteen to find his way. Eleven long years had passed and he had not yet made his mark in the written word. Still, he kept his good humor. And his humor was as grand as his dreams.

38

"Here she comes!" Kate exclaimed, hitting Max in the chest.

"Aye, Mousie, are ye r-r-ready?" Max asked Nigel, who sat there, laying his spectacles aside in the soft grass.

"I suppose so, if it's for the cause," Nigel said, squinting, with his paws reaching out in front of him. "I say, I've become quite blind after wearing my spectacles for so long. I hope I don't run straight into a fountain." The mouse chuckled at the thought.

"No worries, Mousie. I'll tell ye where ta r-r-run," Max replied with a paw on the mouse's small form. "Remember, we'll r-r-run around jest like we did in the market in Egypt."

"This time, please try not to slobber so," Nigel said, straightening his whiskers.

"Shhhhh! She's almost at the bench," Kate reported excitedly. "On me mark."

Mary Cave walked slowly down the path, a basket draped over her arm as she meandered along the edge of Hyde Park. Her one lone auburn curl bounced on her shoulder from under her pretty hat as she took in the beautiful flowers growing there. She smiled at the first signs of spring. She wore a new blue dress and grey satin buckled shoes, gifts from her brother for her recent birthday. She breathed in deeply, happy to be outside on this lovely day. Little did she know what awaited her down the path.

"Ready? GO!" Kate exclaimed, giving Max a push. Max in turn nudged Nigel.

"Right! Cheerio!" Nigel shouted as he took off running straight toward Mary Cave.

"A little bit ta yer r-r-right, Mousie!" Max shouted from behind the mouse as he scurried along the path. Nigel was having a hard time seeing to stay straight.

David Henry looked up from his paper when he heard the barking dog approach. He grinned at the sight of a Scottish Terrier. *Never a finer breed*, he thought to himself. He proceeded to watch the dog chase a small white mouse in and out of bushes, chuckling as he heard the distinctive growl of the Scottie chasing a pest. David looked in the direction where the mouse was running when he saw the beautiful girl walking toward him. Her upward gaze into the blue sky made her oblivious to the commotion heading her way. David's smile faded as the mouse-chasing dog blazed past his feet. He knew what was going to happen.

"AHHHHHHH!" the girl screamed as she grabbed her skirts to herself. The mouse had run under her long skirts to hide and was running around her feet. "HELP! HELP!"

David dropped his paper, jumped off the bench and ran to her side as the dog ran around the outside perimeter of the girl's skirts. "DOWN, BOY!" he exclaimed as he quickly knelt to try to grab Max.

"Don't make it too easy, old boy!" Nigel exclaimed from under Mary's layered skirts.

"AYE! The lad's got ta be a hero then!" Max barked in reply.

Max proceeded to ignore David's attempts at catching him as he quickly ran around and around, barking at Nigel.

"Don't be afraid, dear lady, I shall rescue you!" David shouted above the barking dog, scrambling on the ground to catch the black dog by the fur. Max was too fast for him.

"EEEK! There's a mouse under my feet!" Mary screeched, her eyes wide with fear.

"There's no dog better to catch him than this breed!" David replied, still trying unsuccessfully to grab Max. He finally stood up.

Mary couldn't take it anymore and threw her arms around David, literally jumping into his arms. Surprised but delighted, David lifted the girl above the ground, revealing the mouse. Together they watched as the dog continued to chase the mouse around them. But then their gaze turned to each other. David and Mary shared a smile as he held her there above the chaos at their feet.

"Thank you, Sir, for rescuing me. Do forgive my being so forward," Mary requested shyly. "I cannot stand mice."

"Not at all! I am your humble servant, fair lady," David smiled in reply. He stood there gazing into her beautiful blue eyes, wishing the dog would chase the mouse around their feet for hours.

Kate beamed as she watched the arranged meeting of David Henry and Mary Cave unfold so perfectly before them. How she loved the early moments of love! She trotted over to where David dropped his paper, picked it up in her teeth, and went over to stand below them. She gave Max and Nigel the "signal" and they proceeded to act out their parts as planned. Max grabbed Nigel with his mouth and sat proudly down at their feet with his "catch."

40

"Well, I believe this fine Scottish dog has routed your dreaded foe," David quipped as he gently placed Mary on solid footing. "But we haven't been properly introduced. I am David. David Henry of Aberdeen."

"I cannot thank you enough for protecting me from certain terror, Mr. Henry," Mary said as she extended her hand. David bowed and kissed her hand before looking up. They both shared a laugh at the funny turn of events. "It appears the fierce Scottie has a mate," Mary said as she bent down to take the paper from Kate's mouth. Kate wagged her tail.

"Splendid! This must be a fine dog lass to rescue the best publication in all the world," David said as Mary unfolded *The Gentlemen's Magazine*. He proceeded to pet Kate on the head.

Mary smiled as she held the paper and tilted her head to study David's face. "So you are a subscriber to this publication? What makes it so grand?"

"Indeed, yes, I am! No other publication has such variety as *The Gentlemen's Magazine!* It has news on the latest inventions, explorations, public affairs of the people, business, military news, poetical essays, mathematical theories, maps, stories, and one of my favorite passions— music," David enthused as Mary grinned at him. "I would give *anything* to be part of such a publication. I'm in printing myself, but nothing like this. The Editor Edward Cave was brilliant to come up with this idea. I especially find his use of the pen name Sylvanus Urban to be most clever. I think I would prefer to write anonymously myself, for greater intrigue." David stopped and realized how he was rambling on and on. He smiled sheepishly. "A thousand pardons, dear lady. As you can see, I'm terribly passionate about the world of writing and publishing. I could talk about it all day."

Mary didn't reply but smiled and folded the paper, handing it to David. "I see. Well, perhaps you would like to join me at my brother's house for dinner this evening? I am so grateful for your assistance and would love to repay your kindness."

David bowed and extended his hands in a gesture of gratitude. "I would be honored, Miss . . . I'm afraid I don't know your name."

Mary looked at Kate, who sat there smiling at the interchange of the two humans. She looked up and gave a knowing grin to David. "My name is Mary. Mary Cave."

David's eyes grew wide at hearing her name. He swallowed hard, but didn't reply.

"I'm sure you and my brother, Edward, will have much to discuss," Mary said, taking David's arm as the two walked down the pathway, leaving the dogs behind.

"Bleck!" Max belched as he deposited Nigel on the ground. "Mousie, ye can get out now."

Nigel shook from head to tail, eagerly grooming himself. "Betwixt the blurry vision and the bath of saliva in Max's mouth, it has not been the most splendid of afternoons."

"I wouldn't say that," Kate said dreamily as she watched David and Mary walking away arm in arm. "Things couldn't be more splendid!"

"Aye, looks like the lad an' the fair lass got along for a first meetin'," Max observed.

"Well, well, I do say, that went rather *swimmingly,*" Nigel chuckled as he squinted to see the couple. "Bravo!"

"Mission accomplished," Max said with a definitive nod. "Now all David has ta do is impress Edward Cave with his writin' an' publishin' skills an' he'll be on his way as a reporter."

"There's *more,* ye know! It's not jest aboot a job for the lad," Kate protested, giving Max and Nigel a frown. "It's aboot love!"

41

Nigel cleared his throat and exchanged a good-humored look with Max. With Kate it was always "aboot love."

SIX MONTHS LATER

David gazed deeply into Mary's eyes. "I wish to share something with you, my love." He took her hands into his and kissed them gently. He proceeded to get down on one knee, the crisp autumn leaves crunching under his weight.

Mary put her hand to her throat and took a deep breath, anticipating what he was getting ready to say. "Oh, David!"

David tightened his lips, nodded, and smiled before beginning to dramatically recite a poem:

"May those who love us, love us.
And those who don't love us,
May God turn their hearts;
And if He doesn't turn their hearts,
May He turn their ankles,
So we will know them by their limping."

Mary sat there, puzzled. She had been expecting a proposal of marriage.

"It's one of my favorite Scottish sayings," David quickly said with an impish grin. "Since some of your family hasn't been too keen on the idea of us getting wed, I thought I'd share my sentiments on the matter first."

A deep laugh started building in Mary as she thought about what David had just recited. He continually caught her off guard with his dry wit and humor. He made her laugh all the time, and that was one of the things she loved most about him. Soon she was bent over laughing so hard she couldn't stop. "Mr. Henry, only you could make me act like this when I should be serious."

"But I do have something else to add then," David said, delighting in her laughter.

Mary wiped her eyes. "Yes, dear David?" she chuckled.

David reached in his pocket and took out a simple ring. Mary stopped laughing but her smile remained.

"Will ye be me forever Lass?" he asked in a Scottish brogue as he placed the ring on her finger.

"Yes, my love." Mary looked at the ring and leaned over to kiss David. "And may all those who don't love us limp all the way to the church."

A soft glow came from the flickering fire in the hearth of Handel's kitchen. The dying embers popped now and then, causing sparks to escape up the chimney. The animals gathered here occasionally at night to warm themselves and discuss the events going on with their mission. Al was about as happy as a cat could be. Sleeping soundly on his back, his orange fluffy belly was full of milk and scraps from the butcher, and it gurgled while he purred and snored. Nigel chuckled as he listened to the symphony of sounds in the kitchen, mostly coming from Al.

"'Tis wonderful ta see David an' Mary so happy together then! The weddin' were beautiful," Kate happily reported.

"*C'est bon, mon amie!* I know it was a happy day," Liz smiled and said with a paw under Kate's cheek.

"Aye, an' the lad seems ta be on his way for wr-r-ritin' then. He wr-r-rites a lot, an' gets loads of letters back. We thought ye might like ta see this," Max added, placing a letter with a broken "H" seal at Liz's feet. "Seems our Mr. Henry has family in the colony of Virginia."

Liz smiled as Nigel unfolded the crisp parchment. "*Ah, merci*, Max. Virginia is such a lovely place. But it was rather difficult to get those early settlers through that long winter, *n'est ce pas?*"

"Aye, I never thought *we'd* make it, much less the humans," Max recalled. He shivered, remembering that first cold winter in America.

"I say, had it not been for those splendid natives assisting us, there wouldn't have been a Jamestown settlement in the spring," Nigel added, fiddling with his spectacles. "That Chief Powhatan fellow was such a good chap."

"An' his pretty lass Pocahontas were so sweet," Kate echoed, wagging her tail. "Especially when she an' John Rolfe fell in love."

"*Oui,* I believe our work of getting the natives together with the settlers was one of our proudest moments. It's not every day the Order of the Seven helps to establish a nation," Liz said with a coy smile. "I am

43

very pleased to see the colony doing so well." She proceeded to read the letter out loud:

From   John Henry,
        Hanover CO, VIRGINIA
        31 Jan 1737

To   Mr. David Henry,
        READING, England

Greetings, Cousin:

I received your letter of 15 November. My heart was gladdened with the news of your writing livelihood finally prospering in England. This Edward Cave fellow at *The Gentleman's Magazine* will be a solid help to you, both in your work and now as your brother in marriage. And I am overjoyed about your fair bride, Mary. I send a Scottish blessing for you both:

> *If there is righteousness in the heart,*
> *there will be beauty in the character.*
> *If there is beauty in the character,*
> *there will be harmony in the home.*
> *If there is harmony in the home,*
> *there will be order in the nation.*
> *If there is order in the nation,*
> *there will be peace in the world.*
> *So let it be.*

May the good Lord bless your union, and give you strong children, as he has given me. I, too, have news. Sarah and I have a son, born last May, in the year of our Lord, seventeen hundred and thirty-six, and I named him after my brother. His name is Patrick Henry.

I look forward to your next letter, Cousin, and the latest news from London. Until then, I remain,

Your faithful humble servant,
John Henry

"Aye, now there's a fine Scot!" Max exclaimed. "That John Henry's got a good head on his shoulders ta be quotin' such a gr-r-rand blessin'."

"Many nuggets of wisdom in that blessing." Nigel proceeded to fold the letter and hand it back to Max for return to David Henry's desk. "Sounds like a splendid chap indeed."

"Aye, especially after some of the Cave family didn't take a likin' ta our David at first," Kate said with a frown. "Seems they like their own British kin instead of us Scots. But they be warmin' up ta him now. He's such a charmin' lad."

Al let out a loud snore and rolled over. The cozy fire popped and fizzed. Liz pondered the letter.

"Patrick Henry," Liz said softly.

"Wha' aboot the lad?" Kate asked.

"Noble ruler of the house," Liz replied, still deep in thought. She walked over to the letter as the fire's glow illuminated the "H" seal. "That is what the child's name means, no?"

"Hmmmm, *what* house? I wonder," Nigel posed, tapping his fingers on his chin.

"I cannot put my paw on it, but I have a feeling about this boy," Liz said as she traced the seal on the letter. The petite black cat paused and looked around at her friends. "Like he is destined for greatness."

"As Gillamon always says, 'Time will tell,'" Max added.

Liz gazed into the fire. "*Oui*. It always does."

HANDEL'S REST AND NIGEL'S VIOLIN

LONDON, 1737

"Buon giorno, *Signor* Monaco!" Shandelli exclaimed with his twiggy arms extended in greeting. "Today is our big day, eh? We shall start to make your violin!"

Nigel enthusiastically shook the stick bug's tiny hand. "I'm terribly thrilled, *Signor* Shandelli! I say, I do hope I shall make you proud as a student of the violin when I can actually play upon it."

"*Sì, sì,* I'm sure of it. You already have the *musicale* gift, eh? I have taught you the finger positions, so now we will give you a real wood instrument," Shandelli replied. He put his big bug eyes right in Nigel's face. "Above all you already have the most important thing to play the violin. You have the passion in your heart to play, and to play *well* for the *Maestro.* And when you have this passion, nothing is impossible!"

"*Bonjour, mes amis,*" Liz said as she entered the shed behind Handel's house, followed by Al, Max, and Kate. A soft spring rain was beginning to fall. "Are we late? Al had to get done with his *petit déjeuner.*"

"Aye, and I had to finish off me breakfast," Al added, along with a drawn-out belch. He patted his belly with a goofy grin. "It's the most important meal o' the day."

Max rolled his eyes. "He'll never learn his Fr-r-rench then, even mar-r-ried ta the lass all these millennia." Max gave Al a playful nudge. "Daft kitty!"

"No, *Signora*. I was just about to explain the plan to Nigel," Shandelli replied.

"I must confess before we begin that I am terribly concerned whether Mr. Handel will even need me to play the violin, now that he has suffered a stroke," Nigel lamented. "He's been gone six weeks to soak in the healing baths of Aix-la-Chapelle, but we've received no word of his condition. I simply do not understand why the Maker allows such things to happen to his servants, I'm afraid."

"*Sì, sì,* it is tragic, eh? For the great Handel to lose the ability to use his *right hand* of all things!" Shandelli said, shaking his head. "But when the great ones work as he does, *naturalmente* their bodies suffer. He is only human."

"Jolly right you are. I've never seen a composer work so hard, yet get so little in return," Nigel replied, now pacing with his paws clasped behind his back. "He is passed over by the king for the recognition he deserves, he slaves over his operas day and night, he fights against a competing opera house that is out to destroy him financially, he is barely making ends meet, and sadly he sees his beloved opera dying. The people just do not enjoy it anymore, but still he keeps on composing. And now this!" Nigel shook his head. "April 13 will forever be a *dreadful* date, the date Handel was struck down."

47

"Ah, but we were told by Gillamon that greatness is coming for Handel, no?" Liz reminded him. "His heart is good, and he seeks to serve the Maker in all he does."

"Aye, an' we've seen our fair share of lads an' lassies go through hard times when workin' for the Maker," Max added. "Sometimes they need ta lose everythin' they think is important so they can gain wha' *really* is important."

"Maybe the Maker decided Handel needed ta rest then," Kate suggested. "By still waters."

"Well, ye can't make music without rests," Al said, drawing looks of amazement from the others. He was lying on the floor, his paws behind his head. "If all ye got is lots o' notes and no rests, the music isn't too good. So seems like the lad writin' the notes needs rests, too."

"Why, Albert, that is quite profound!" Liz said delightedly, giving Al a kiss on the cheek. "I did not realize you were paying such close attention to Handel and how he composes his music."

"It's hard not to," Al said, yawning. "I still like what comes out o' his kitchen more than his composin' room though."

Nigel took off his spectacles to clean them, grinning broadly. "Al, old boy, you are indeed correct. Perhaps the Maker decided Handel needs rest, even if it is a forced rest. We were told greatness is coming, so we must not lose faith!"

"Attaboy, Mousie! Aye, we've got a mission still, includin' yer fiddle playin'," encouraged Max with a wink.

"*Certamente!*" Shandelli exclaimed with his twiggy hands clasped in victory. "So, we will continue our part, and trust the *Maestro* with the rest, eh?"

"Right! So what comes first, old boy?" Nigel enthused.

"Beautiful music always begins with a carpenter." Shandelli unrolled a diagram of the parts of a violin, complete with measurements and needed supplies. "The wood used for the violin is the most important part!"

"What kind of wood is best?" Nigel asked, holding a paw to his spectacles as he studied the diagram.

"Spruce and maple are *migliore*—the best. Spruce for the top and maple for the ribs, neck, and bridge," Shandelli explained as he pointed to each part of the violin on his diagram.

"I see," Liz nodded. "We need a carpenter who carries such wood. I propose a furniture maker."

"Aye, there be a Thomas Chippendale lad who makes gr-r-rand furniture not too far from here," Max suggested. "Mousie doesn't need a big violin, so we can get some scr-r-raps from him then."

"Scraps?" Al chimed in excitedly, sitting up. "I love scraps!"

Kate put her paw on Al's back. "*Wood* scraps, Al dear. I don't think ye'd like ta eat them, no matter how hungry ye got."

Max leaned over with a grin and whispered to Nigel, "I'm not so sure aboot that."

"Very well, Max and Kate will see to the wood. What else do we need to get for you, Shandelli?" Liz asked.

"*Grazie!* I already have the catgut string for the violin, so we need glue, and," Shandelli said, closing his eyes and holding his tiny hands up in a dramatic gesture, "the *anima*."

Al's eyes got wide with fear and he gripped his belly. "Catgut! What kind o' a sick beastie are ye?!"

Liz quickly placed her paw on Al's shoulder. "Do not worry, *cher* Albert. Catgut is not from cats."

"That's a relief." Al's face eased, then turned to confusion.

"*Sì*, it is from sheep," Shandelli explained matter of factly.

"Then why call it catgut?!" Al's eyes got wide again. "I don't think Clarie would appreciate this at *all*. Good thing she's not here to be yer *anima!*"

"Albert, sheep gut is not taken until a sheep is deceased," Liz assured him. "But Shandelli, what exactly is *anima?* I am not familiar with this term."

"It is the *soul* of the instruments. We Italians call it *anima*," Shandelli explained, pretending to play a violin. "It is the bow with which to play the violin. The bow makes the violin sing!"

"*Oui*, the bow. And what do you need to make a bow?" Liz asked.

"A stick," Shandelli replied slowly, "and the hair from a grey male horse's tail."

"Well, *ye're* a stick!" Al said, poking Shandelli in the belly. "But I suppose ye won't be volunteerin' to be Nigel's stick, will ye, lad? Humph!" Al was still upset about the catgut issue.

Nigel let loose a jolly laugh. "Al, my dear fellow, even if our Shandelli here offered himself for the bow, I fear he would not be able to fulfill the task. He may look like a stick, but remember he is indeed a BUG!"

Al pouted. "Well, if sheep and horses are givin' up parts, I jest figured the big-eyed beastie could, too."

Shandelli graciously ignored Al's jab. "The great Stradivari uses brazilwood for bows."

Liz immediately nodded. "Ah, from the Fabaceae family, found in South America, no?"

Shandelli's eyes got even bigger. "You *know* this tree, *Signora?*"

"Liz knows everythin' aboot plants, flowers, an' trees," Kate chimed in happily.

"*Oui*, botany is one of my favorite hobbies," Liz agreed. "But this

49

wood is difficult to come by here in England. Max, perhaps you can locate a good, solid stick for Nigel to use, no?"

"Leave it ta me, Lass!" Max replied, wagging his tail.

Shandelli turned to Al and smiled. "There is something you could contribute, Al, *per favore.*"

Al instinctively grabbed his belly and looked at the stick bug suspiciously. "What?"

"Since you are able to jump so well, perhaps you can jump on a grey male horse and pluck just the right tail hair for Nigel's bow," Shandelli explained.

A goofy grin appeared on Al's face. He liked this idea. "I think I can do that. Aye!"

"And I shall locate some glue. Everyone has their assignments then?" Liz confirmed with a nod to the animals. "*Bon!* Let us all meet back here with the items. Albert, I suggest you go with Max and Kate in your quest. It may be best if they are with you when you pull a horse by the tail."

Al suddenly grew worried and swallowed hard. "I didn't think how the horse might feel aboot this."

Suddenly they heard Peter yelling from the open door in the kitchen. "Mrs. Rice! It's a miracle! Mr. Handel is healed! The nuns at Aix la Chapelle prayed for him and soon found him playing the organ in their chapel! He's coming home!"

The animals looked at one another excitedly. Liz smiled broadly. "Look lively, everyone. It appears our Mr. Handel's rest has come to an end."

"Time for the music to begin!" Shandelli exclaimed, pretending to play the violin.

Max, Kate, and Al darted in and out of doorways as best they could. It was a typical rainy day in London, and they were soaked to the bone.

"How much farther?" whined Al as he landed in another puddle. "I can't feel me paws, they be so cold and wet."

Max looked back at Al. He looked pitiful. His ears were flat, his whiskers droopy with rain, and he squinted with one eye open from the drops that splashed onto his face. He brought his knapsack to carry the wood, and it was also soaking wet. "Big Al, ye look more like wha' the cat dr-r-ragged *in* than the cat!" he said, chuckling.

Suddenly Al let loose a big sneeze, spraying Max. "Sorry."

"Bless ye, Al! The poor dear!" Kate said. "Max, I don't want Al catchin' a cold. Let's hurry."

"Aye, Thomas Chippendale str-r-raight ahead," Max said, shaking the spray off. "We best go around back."

The three friends located the side alley that led to the back of the furniture maker's shop. The back door had a lower gate that was closed, but the upper part was open to allow fresh air in. The strong smells of varnish used on the wood escaped the door.

"Al, we need ye ta jump up an' unlock the lower gate then," Max directed. "Can ye do it, lad?"

"Ah-CHOO!" Al sneezed again, wiped his pink triangle nose, and nodded. "Aye."

Al jumped up on the ledge and released the black wrought iron latch below. Max stuck his nose in the door and pushed it open wide enough for him and Kate to get inside. A warm fire blazed in the room, but thankfully no humans were present.

Al immediately made his way to the fire and stuck his behind up to the blaze. "Ah, that feels toasty!"

Max grinned. "Okay, kitty, get yerself warm an' dry while Kate an' me look for the wood."

Al held a paw in the air and looked up at the ceiling, anticipating another sneeze. "Ah-ah-ah-CHOOOOOOOOO!"

"Let's make it quick, Lass," Max instructed Kate as they walked on to the supply room. Stacks of various kinds of wood were piled high in the room, and the aromas made it smell like a forest. "How can ye tell which wood is which?"

"From wha' Shandelli told me, wood is either hard or soft, with grain that's either close or coarse," Kate explained as they walked around the wood. "Spruce and some maples be softer an' lighter, so they make the violin easy ta hold."

The dogs walked around the room, trying to find the right kind of wood. "Aye! There be the spr-r-ruce!" Max exclaimed.

Kate joined him in front of a pile. "That's grand, Max! How did ye find it?"

51

"I can r-r-read, Lass," Max grinned as he pointed to the sign on the wall, indicating what type of wood was stacked where. "Now that we know wha' it looks like, let's get the scr-r-raps we need an' get out of here."

As Max and Kate used their paws to pick through a pile of wood scraps and Al warmed himself, a pair of glowing eyes watched from the shadows.

"AH-CHOO!" Al sneezed, spraying Max again, just as the Scottie dropped the wood at his feet,.

"Thanks . . . a lot," Max said, wiping his face and shaking all over.

Kate untied Al's knapsack to put the scraps of wood inside. "Next we need a stick for the bow."

"And I have to get the horse tail hair," Al added with a paw in the air.

"Well, don't sneeze all over the beastie when ye pull his tail," Max scowled, drawing a crooked grin from Al.

"Let's try the horses near Hyde Park, then we'll go by the butcher shop on our way ta Handel's house," Kate added.

"Can I get a scrap at the butcher's?" Al asked hopefully.

"Yes, Al dear, we'll get ye scraps when we finish our mission," Kate smiled.

The glowing eyes watched the three animals leave, then followed, keeping out of their sight.

The rain lifted, and it wasn't long before Al, Max, and Kate made their way around Hyde Park. They walked down the row of carriages parked along the edge of the park, looking for just the right horse.

"I'm wonderin', do I ask the lad before I take it?" Al stopped and asked.

"I think that would be the most polite thing ta do," Kate answered. "Even though he wouldn't miss it."

"But what if he says no?" Al asked nervously.

"Well, then I'll have a word with him," Max affirmed, starting to walk again. "An' if he still r-r-refuses then we might need ta get r-r-rough with the beastie!"

Al swallowed hard. "Ye know I don't like violence."

Soon, before them stood a massive grey dappled horse harnessed to a fancy red coach. Black blinders covered the horse's eyes, and ornate black leather reins were attached to his halter. The animals looked up and down the street and saw other-colored horses—blacks, browns, and whites. But this was the only grey one in sight.

"Aye, now there's yer beastie, lad. Go on," Max nudged Al from behind.

Al smiled weakly and walked to stand below the horse that towered over him. The orange cat cleared his throat. "Top o' the mornin' to ye!" Al cheerily greeted the horse. The horse stood there ignoring Al.

"Did ye hear me then, horsie?" Al asked. The horse continued to ignore him. "I said . . ."

"What do you want?!" the horse finally replied in a brusque tone, stomping his foot.

Al jumped back. "Oh, aye, well, then, I wanted to ask ye a favor. We need a horse tail hair and wondered if we could have one o' yers."

The horse lowered his head and snorted in Al's face, "What for?"

Al's ears flattened and he leaned back on his hind legs. "Uh, we need it for a violin bow. Ye know, to make music like Handel plays. Actually, for Handel *to* play then. But not the wee violin. Nigel is goin' to play it. See?"

The horse stamped the ground impatiently. "Of COURSE I know about music. Whose carriage do you think I lead around London?"

Al leaned over and saw on the coach was carved a "G." He wrinkled his brow. "Uh, King George?"

"HA!" the horse laughed and snorted. "NO, you simpleton! I lead around none other than Dr. Maurice Green, the Master of the King's Musick. No one makes better music in the kingdom, so Handel should give it a rest. Go away and stop bothering me."

"How *dare* he!" Kate growled. "We even asked politely. He's jest bein' rude!"

Max was incensed, and trotted over to whisper in Al's ear. "Big Al, leave this ta me. Ye go around back an' jump on the carriage from behind. I'll distract this pompous horse while ye get yer tail hair."

Relieved to have Max's help, Al did as he was told and jumped up on the carriage, walking along the rim to the coachman's footrest, which was just above the horse's rump. The rude horse swished his tail back and forth. Al reached his paw out to grab the tail but got whacked in the face, falling back on the footrest.

53

"Now ye listen here, ye mangy beast! I don't care if ye lead the king hisself ar-r-round! We need one of yer tail hairs, an' we don't intend ta go away until we have it!" Max growled.

"Or you'll do what?" the horse said as it lowered its nose to Max's face with a sneer.

Max grinned and quickly jumped up and used his teeth to grab the halter around the horse's face. Startled, the horse pulled its head back, lifting Max two feet off the ground. The Scottie's strong jaws were clamped down on the halter, and he spoke through clenched teeth. "Ye must not have ever tangled with a Scot!" The horse tried to shake Max lose, but Max wasn't going anywhere.

"Now, Al!" Kate yelled. "Grab that horse by the tail!"

Al got up again and reached out for the horse hair. He swiped his paw and got his claws stuck in the horse's bushy tail. The horse began to violently swing Al side-to-side with his tail as he swung Max side-to-side with his head.

"AHHHHHH!" Al cried as he flew around in the air, his claws hanging on.

"Al, ye jest need one!" Kate barked.

"AHHHHHH-CHOO!" Al sneezed with such force that his paw let go of the horse's tail. He went sailing through the air, landing in an ash tree. The big cat struggled to hang on to a branch slippery from the rain. Al swung around hanging on for dear life. His weight was soon too much for the branch and he fell into the bushes below.

Kate ran over to where he disappeared. "Al, are ye okay?"

An orange paw rose up through the green shrubbery and attached were several horse tail hairs waving in the wind. "Got extra!" Al said with a goofy grin as he lifted his head out of the bushes to see Kate shaking her head at him good humoredly. He lifted his other paw and in it was a piece of an ash branch. "And I got a stick!"

"Then ye deserve extra scraps, I'd say," Kate chuckled and said. She turned to Max, who was still hanging on to the horse's halter. "Okay, Max, ye can let go now!"

With that Max let loose his grip on the horse's halter and landed on the ground with a thud. The horse neighed and shook his head. "Now don't ye ever tangle with Maximillian Br-r-raveheart the Br-r-ruce again, ye hear me, lad?" Max scolded.

54

The coachman returned and jumped up in his seat, grabbing the horse's reins so he couldn't reply to Max. Soon the clip-clop of the rude horse's hoofs went down the cobblestone street. Max gave a solid nod and grinned as Al and Kate joined him. "Aye, looks like a fine stick, Al! An' way ta go with the horsie tail hair." He gave Al a pat on the back. "Yer sneezin' came in handy."

"Looks like we got all we need for Mousie's violin," Kate added cheerfully.

"I never knew fiddlin' were so complicated," Al replied as the three friends went happily down the street toward the butcher shop before returning to Handel's house.

The pair of glowing eyes saw what it had been waiting to see—their final destination.

55

NIGEL'S FIRST PERFORMANCE, AND HANDEL'S LAST

Nigel paced back and forth in front of the fire, where the animals were all gathered, eager for Shandelli's arrival. Tonight the Italian stick bug was presenting Nigel with his long-awaited violin. He had asked not to be disturbed as he worked so he could have full concentration to carve, shape, and mold the mouse-sized instrument. After helping Shandelli make the tiny tools needed to carve the violin, Nigel had not been allowed to see it until completion. The mouse was understandably nervous, excited, and eager.

"Ye're goin' ta wear a hole in the floor, Mousie," Max observed with a grin.

Nigel stopped and chuckled his jolly laugh. "Yes, yes, yes, old boy, I know I am quite antsy. But it's terribly exciting, you know."

"You have waited a long time for this moment, *mon ami,*" Liz smiled. "We are happy for you, and cannot wait to hear you play."

"I do hope I am able to play well," Nigel said, adjusting his spectacles. "The Maker is counting on me."

"Well, as Gillamon said, if the Maker asks ye ta do somethin', he'll help ye do it," Kate said. "Ye'll be grand, Nigel."

Al sat on the sill of Handel's kitchen window, his fluffy orange tail curling up and down as he waited for Shandelli. "Aye, and I can't wait to hear the rude horsie's tail hair make music!"

Suddenly the stick bug landed on the windowsill, startling Al as his big eyes caught the reflection of the fire light. *"Buona sera!* I am here!"

Nigel's heart leapt in his chest and he took a step forward as Shandelli proceeded to jump down to the stone floor. Under one of his arms the stick bug carried a package wrapped in thick, red fabric. He walked up to Nigel with his twiggy front arms opened up in greeting, smiling broadly. "Ah, *Signor* Monaco! The night has come, eh?"

Nigel and Shandelli eagerly shook hands in a moment of triumph. "Indeed. I am most eager to see my violin!" Nigel answered.

Shandelli carefully took the package and removed the red fabric to reveal a beautiful, polished, mouse-sized violin and bow. The firelight reflected on the beautiful wood, and all the animals gasped to see how lovely the instrument was.

57

Nigel blinked hard and held out his hands as Shandelli carefully placed the instrument into his paws. "It is an honor for me, Antonio Vivaldi Stradivari Shandelli, to present to you, *Signor* Nigel P. Monaco, this violin. May it honor the *Maestro* as you play it in his service."

The animals all applauded as Shandelli bowed and Nigel humbly took the violin in his hands, studying the intricate details Shandelli had carved into it. The mouse looked up at the stick bug, overcome with emotion. "Thank you, my friend. It is exquisite. I shall ever be in your debt."

"C'est magnifique!" Liz exclaimed. "Well done, *Signor* Shandelli!"

"Aye, looks like a gr-r-rand fiddle!" Max added. "Mousie, play us a tune, then."

"Oh, please do, Nigel," Kate implored, wagging her tail.

"Very well," Nigel agreed, feeling nervous for his first performance. "What should I play?"

"How aboot a good Irish dancin' tune?" Al suggested with a goofy look on his face.

Shandelli wrinkled his brow and lifted his tiny hand. "I suggest you begin with the piece we have worked on to study the notes and finger movements. Something from *La Resurrezione?*"

"*Oui!* The Resurrection! One of Handel's first pieces written in Rome," Liz enthused. "*Oui, mon ami,* this is quite fitting since your violin has strings from the Stradivarius Messiah violin."

Nigel nodded and bowed humbly. "Very well." The mouse cleared his throat and lifted the violin to rest under his chin. He took the bow and gently placed it on the strings. He closed his eyes, took a deep breath, and began to play.

Beautiful music filled the room and Nigel was instantly caught up in the joy of finally being able to play an instrument he desperately loved, but never could hold because of his size. He smiled, swayed, and was soon lost in the music as he played from memory the notes of *La Resurrezione.* The animals clung to each other in awestruck wonder at the sound coming from Nigel's violin. He had thought it impossible that he could ever play and do what the Maker had asked him to do. But together with the help of his friends, here he was, playing music about the resurrection of Christ. And more of that was to come as he would soon play to inspire Handel. The Maker, or as Shandelli liked to call him, the *Maestro,* had made it all possible.

Tears filled the animals' eyes, not only from the splendor of the music but from the joy of watching a dream come into being for their small friend.

LONDON, 1739

"PATER! Have you seen my hat?" Handel yelled while hurriedly picking up pieces of sheet music. "I am late to practice at Covent Gardens, ya! Dey vill not play my musick vitout me and I vill not be dere vitout my hat!"

"I have it here, Sir, right where you left it," Peter said with a grin, holding Handel's fancy tri-corne hat. He was used to Handel's boisterous ways. He knew Handel was especially on edge that night. Things were not going well for the great composer. Had it not been for an anonymous article printed earlier in the week in the *Daily Post,* Handel might not have been going out for a performance at all.

"Tank you, Pater," Handel said with a strong slap on the servant's back. "You I can alvays count on, ya."

"Indeed you can, Mr. Handel." Peter bowed as he replied. "I trust tonight's performance will go well. You certainly have a secret admirer out there who wishes it." He smiled and handed Handel a copy of the April 13 *Daily Post*. Perhaps it will give you a boost to read this article again before tonight's performance."

"Ya, I vonder who dis 'A.Z.' is," Handel replied, taking the paper. He held it up. "But maybe his vords vill help fill de house tonight! If de good Lord vants *Israel in Egypt* to succeed, it vill happen. Good evening, Pater." Peter opened the door and Handel walked out of 25 Brook Street to head to the concert hall of Covent Garden Theatre.

Nigel poked his head out from behind the heavy curtain on the stage of Covent Garden as the crowds gathered into the theatre. He and Liz always came together to the concert hall. The mouse held tightly to his little violin and bow. "I do hope they come in droves tonight. Handel needs a boost."

59

Liz sat reading Handel's copy of the April 13 *Daily Post* offstage. "It appears he already has received one, *mon ami,*" she replied, tapping her paw on the paper. "Thanks to our David Henry, the anonymous writer 'A.Z.'"

"Brilliant! How do you know it was David Henry?" Nigel asked, delighted.

"Max and Kate heard him talking about it with Mary," Liz smiled. "He felt he had to do something to help Handel after the dismal small crowds attending the first two performances of *Israel in Egypt*. Listen to what he said about the performance:

"I was not only pleased but also affected by it, for I never yet met with any musical performance, in which the words and sentiments were so thoroughly studied, and so clearly understood; and as the Words are taken from the Bible, they are perhaps some of the most sublime parts of it. I was indeed concerned, that so excellent a work of so great a Genius was neglected, for though it was a polite and attentive audience, it was not large enough I doubt to encourage him in any future attempt."

"He goes on to beg Mr. Handel to please give another performance," Liz said with a smile. "And *voila!* Here we are."

"By Jove, that's utterly splendid!" Nigel enthused. "I suppose one word of encouragement is all it takes sometimes for the show to go on."

"*Oui*, and did you notice the *date* of this word of encouragement? April 13, *the dreadful date*," Liz said playfully.

Nigel's eyebrows lifted. "Well, I say, perhaps there will be a resurrection for that dreadful date in my calendar after all!"

"*Oui*, and once again the power of the pen has moved the masses," Liz enthused.

They heard the sounds of the orchestra warming up and the applause of the crowd as Handel entered the orchestra pit. He bowed before the crowd, one foot held forward in respect.

"Look! The Prince and Princess of Wales are here!" Nigel exclaimed as he looked out over the audience who filled the theatre. "Bless David Henry! I must warm up now, my dear, if I am to give aid to tonight's performance."

Liz's heart filled with gladness as she watched Nigel lift his violin and tune it for the performance. He brought it to each performance, playing along with Handel's orchestra, hidden offstage. This enabled Nigel to learn the violin by playing for Handel himself! Never had Liz seen Nigel so happy.

Another was not so happy. The pair of glowing eyes squinted in anger from the top of the balcony as the crowds erupted in applause at the end of Handel's concert.

LONDON, 1740

The trio of wealthy London businessmen stood on the corner outside the Merchant Exchange. For months they, along with all of London, were forced inside by the bitter winter that consumed the city. It was too cold to leave firesides, so as spring came the public breathed easier, including Handel, who was able to resume performances. His latest composition of *Alexander's Feast* was enjoyed by many Londoners, including David Henry.

"Here's another anonymous praise for Handel in *The Gentlemen's Magazine*! Some sot has written a *poem* to the man:

"TO MR. HANDEL, on hearing 'Alexander's Feast', 'L'Allegro, ed il Penseroso,' etc.

... Handel's harmony affects the soul, to sooth by sweetness or by force control ..."

The man looked up with disgust at the other two men, who frowned. He scanned to the bottom of the lengthy poem and continued:

"... To form thee, talent, travel, art combine,
And all the powers of music now are thine."

"We'll just see about that," one of the men snapped. A wicked grin grew on his face, and he rephrased the tribute to Handel with his own insidious twist:

'To break thee, money, avarice, and nobility combine,

'Til all the powers of music are no longer thine.'"

The three men erupted in laughter and walked away discussing how they would make their twisted poem come true. The public's musical taste was changing, and in order to stay in business, the theatres and opera houses had to find ways to meet the public's demands. As the primary investors in the competing opera house, the trio of men needed to make sure Handel's music was quieted, and soon.

61

LONDON, MAY 1741

"HE DID WHA'!?" Max roared.

"Che cosa c'è?!" Shandelli asked in alarm. "What is the matter?!

"The nobility have *shunned* him and are turning the public against him! This is utterly despicable!" Nigel lamented, holding a paw to his head as he paced back and forth in front of the fireplace. He was inconsolable with the news.

"Evidently, Handel said or did something that has offended some powerful noblemen," Liz said calmly, trying to settle the group. "They have responded with such a fury that they are pulling down the handbills announcing his concerts as fast as he can put them up. The streets are littered with them."

Shandelli shook his head. "If he's done something like he did that time he held that Italian singer out the window, I can see how people could be mad with him."

Nigel looked at Shandelli in disbelief. "What*ever* are you talking about, old boy?"

A grin appeared on the stick bug's face in spite of the seriousness of the conversation. "This happened long ago, but even the great Stradivari heard of this story back in Italy, eh? Francesca Cuzzoni was one of Handel's Italian opera soprano singers, but she got quite the big head as the public loved her," Shandelli explained. "One day at rehearsal, she refused to sing a new aria, and Handel picked her up by the waist and carried her to the window, with her complaining the whole time. He said if she kept it up, he would throw her out the window!"

Nigel held a paw to his mouth, trying to suppress his laughter. "Oh my, I say, she must have been quite the prima donna!"

"Handel never would have done it, of course, but I admit that Italian singers can be difficult to work with," the stick bug explained, shrugging his shoulders.

"I know of a rather funny story with a difficult *English* singer," Liz chimed in. "A man named Gordon complained of how Handel was accompanying him, and threatened to jump on Handel's harpsichord to smash it to pieces."

"*Per favore*, how did Mr. Handel respond, eh?" Shandelli asked, his eyes even bigger than usual.

Liz giggled. "Pardon my German accent, but I will try to say it like Mr. Handel: 'Oh! Let me know ven you vill do dat, and I vill advertise it. For I am sure more people vill come to see you jump dan to hear you sing!'"

The animals laughed at the funny story. Indeed, that was George F. Handel, all right.

"I know Handel can be a bit boisterous at times, but his heart is so good," Kate said.

"Aye, like when he saw those orphans beggin' outside the coffee-house, he couldn't stand it so he held a concert ta r-r-raise money for the poor lads," Max recounted. "Where were the nobility then?! Sittin' in their fine houses an' stuffin' themselves while poor orphaned children were starvin'!"

"Yes, yes, yes, we know Handel has a temper, a big heart, dedication to the Maker, and a fierce passion for his music," Nigel said, continuing to pace back and forth. "The question is, how do we help him with this dreadful situation now? I overheard him talking to Peter that perhaps this next concert will be his last. He is so depressed about all that has happened he might even return to Germany!"

The animals sat for a moment, thinking about what in the world they could do.

"Jennens," Liz said. "Charles Jennens. Don't you see? Handel is being forced out of the public eye in London. Not only is his beloved opera dead, but the people have turned their backs on him, and his money is dwindling. But because of opera's decline, Handel has created the English oratorio! This is exactly what needed to happen!"

"What's an ora-oreo?" Al asked.

"Ora*torio,* old boy," Nigel corrected. "Opera is a play about history or mythology set to music with an orchestra, choir, and soloists who portray characters in the story. Opera has elaborate sets and costumes and is always performed in the theatre, you see. But *oratorio* is strictly a concert piece about sacred topics from the Bible, so is usually performed in a church."

"Oh, so what happens if an ora-oreo isn't performed in a church?" Al asked, scratching his head.

63

Liz and Nigel looked at one another. This very question plagued Handel, who had already pushed the limits of his oratorios being performed not in the church, but in the theatre. It was one of the reasons he had fallen out of favor with religious types. "Well, the church people do not approve and can get quite upset," Nigel lamented.

Al wrinkled his brow. "Seems like church people would want everybody to hear music about the Bible. Seems like they should be happy that ora-oreos are played other places than church then."

"Indeed, *cher* Albert. This is how it should be, no?" Liz said thoughtfully. "But happily Jennens has already provided Handel with several successful oratorios the past couple of years, so he has already proven his worth to Handel. Handel and Jennens may not have the most perfect relationship, but they have proven to each other that Jennen's words and Handel's music combine to create powerful oratorio. The time has come, *mes amis,* for the most powerful oratorio yet!"

"Aye, and it's been six years, just as Gillamon said!" Max pointed out.

Al stretched out and rolled over. "Sure, and Mousie is good with his fiddle now, too. He can play an ora-oreo better than any beastie."

"By Jove, you're right!" Nigel exclaimed with joy. "Oh, everything is in place for the mission we've waited for. It's time to write *Messiah!*"

"That's grand news!" Kate added happily. "But I think Handel needs some encouragement right away."

"*Oui,* Kate, of course," Liz agreed. "If Handel is to have one final concert, no one is better able to get the theatre packed to bid Handel adieu than David Henry."

"What exactly are you thinking, my pet?" Nigel asked, cleaning his spectacles.

"I think I shall write my own anonymous letter to Mr. Henry," Liz replied with a coy smile.

Max and Kate watched from a distance as David Henry opened the package they left on his doorstep. It was a crumpled handbill for Handel's last performance, and an "anonymous letter" explaining how Handel had unintentionally made a terrible *"faux pas"* and how the nobility and public were against him. David clenched his jaw in anger. He immediately went inside, picked up his pen, and wrote to the *Daily Post:*

> I wish I could persuade the gentlemen who have taken offense at any part of this great man's conduct (for a great man he must be in the musical world, whatever his misfortunes may now too late say to the contrary): to take him back into favor, and relieve him from the cruel persecution of those little vermin, who, taking advantage of their displeasure, pull down even his bills as fast as he has them pasted up; and use a thousand other little arts to injure and distress him. I am sure when they weigh the thing without prejudice they will take him back into favor. But in the meantime, let the public take care that he wants not. That would be an unpardonable ingratitude, and as this Oratorio of Wednesday next is his last for this season, and if reports be true, probably his last forever in this country, let them, with a generous and friendly benevolence, fill this his last house, and show him on his departure, that London, the greatest and richest city in the world, is great and rich in

virtue, as well as in money, and can pardon and forget the failings, or even the faults of a great Genius.

"The house is packed! Well done, my pet!" Nigel said excitedly from backstage. "David Henry's anonymous letter worked! London has been buzzing for days about Handel's last performance. No one wanted to miss it."

Liz smiled and put her dainty paw on Nigel's shoulder, looking out at the massive crowd that left standing room only in the concert hall. "I am so pleased, *mon ami.* With the money Handel receives from this concert, and with the concern of the people who still love him, I believe he will make it until *Messiah* comes."

"But Messiah has already come, my dear," Nigel quipped.

Liz realized what she said and laughed. "You know what I mean, until the *oratorio Messiah* comes!"

"Just a bit of humor to get rid of the pre-concert jitters, dear girl," Nigel laughed, looking out to see who was in attendance at the concert. "I say, none other than David Henry is here!"

Liz smiled as she saw David and Mary make their way to seats near the front of the concert hall. "Well, Max, Kate, Albert, and you have carried most of the load so far in this mission. Charles Jennens and Handel were introduced to begin a working relationship. David Henry and Mary are wed, and David's successful writing career has helped our Mr. Handel in more ways than one. I suspect he is only getting started with the publishing world. And you, *mon ami,* have worked very hard to master the violin."

Nigel groomed his whiskers and bowed with a paw draped humbly across his chest. "Thank you, my dear. It has been my joy and honor."

"*Bon.* Now it is up to me to do *my* part," Liz said.

Just then they saw Charles Jennens enter the concert hall and find a seat. He wore his usual grumpy face despite his elegant attire. Liz's tail curled up and down as she watched him settle into his seat for the concert.

"Tomorrow, Mr. Charles Jennens will be the proud owner of two new cats," Liz said with a knowing grin. "One who will eat him out of house and home, and one who has a way with words, no?"

THE SUBJECT
IS MESSIAH

Summer arrived with days so swelteringly hot some Londoners dreamed of the bitter cold days of the previous winter to make them "feel cooler." Relief came with the setting sun, and windows remained open to let cooler evening breezes inside.

"Sure, and he lives in a fancy house," Al said, his jaw dropping at the size of Jennens's elaborate home, made of brick and stone. Elegant landscaping and an impressive entrance immediately gave onlookers the impression that here lived someone of great wealth and importance.

Liz didn't reply, as she was deep in thought, studying the outside of the house. She searched the open windows, looking for where Jennens's study might be. Suddenly she saw him walk by the window, light a candle, and take a seat at his harpsichord. Jennens began to play and the music flowed out the open window.

"Albert, this is indeed a fancy house, and in order for us to get inside and live in this house, I need your help," Liz implored. "You have always been able to live in palaces of pharaohs and kings, so I am sure you will have no trouble getting into the home of one Charles Jennens of Bloomsbury, London."

"Aye, I have lived in some fancy palaces," Al grinned happily. "What do ye need me to do, love?"

"I need for you to meow on pitch with what Jennens is playing," Liz instructed. "He is quite alone in this house, and I have a feeling he would enjoy our company. But we must be unusual to him to catch his interest."

"I can be unusual!" Al eagerly offered.

"Oui mon cher, this is very true," Liz agreed, rubbing her chin against him. "So, jump up on the windowsill and you can begin to sing along with Jennens. Remember to use your charm."

"Jumpin' and singin' be easy," Al said. "Don't know much aboot charm but I'll try." He took off toward the house and jumped up to the open window in Jennens's study. Liz stayed in the shadows.

Al sat for a moment and listened to the melody. Then he began to meow along with the notes. Liz winked at him and nodded as Al put his full gut into his performance. Soon Jennens stopped, and Al stopped. When Jennens began again, Al resumed singing along. Jennens stopped and Al stopped. Jennens began and Al began. This went on for a few minutes until suddenly Jennens got up from the harpsichord and poked his head out the window. He saw Al sitting there on the windowsill. Al smiled his goofy grin and purred.

Jennens couldn't help but smile, which took Liz aback. She had never seen the man smile. "If I'm not mistaken, you, feline, were singing along with me as I played. Extraordinary."

"Aye!" Al meowed in reply. He went over and headbutted Jennens, purring loudly.

Jennens chuckled softly and picked Al up, bringing him inside. Liz shook her head in amazement as Al once again was able to easily get in wherever he went. He didn't realize how irresistibly charming he was. Liz followed along and let herself in the window. Jennens's study was immaculate, with fine oil paintings lining the walls and expensive furniture filling the room. Hundreds of books lined his shelves and his desk was covered with blank paper, ink wells, and the most expensive pens Liz had ever seen. Everything she loved filled this room, including her husband. Jennens put Al up on his harpsichord and continued playing to see if Al would keep singing along. Liz kept out of sight for a moment and walked around the room while Al entertained Jennens.

"Extraordinary! I've never seen anything like this," Jennens said. "You must be the most brilliant cat I've ever encountered."

That was her cue. Liz jumped up next to Al and rubbed her cheek on him to show she was his mate. *"Bonsoir, Monsieur Jennens,"* Liz meowed as she walked over and blinked her eyes affectionately at the man. *"We are here on a mission for the Maker, and wish to stay with you until you have finished writing the most important libretto that will ever be written."* Liz smiled to herself and thought that if Jennens understood what she had just meowed, he would know *she* was the most brilliant cat alive. She headbutted him affectionately.

"Well, it appears there are two of you," Jennens said, softly petting Liz's silky black fur. "This is highly unusual but I have a great deal of work ahead of me, and I might enjoy your company. Would you like something to eat?"

"I thought ye'd never ask, lad!" Al meowed excitedly, jumping down to encircle Jennens's legs.

68

After a delicious visit to Jennens's extensive kitchen full of every delicacy imaginable, Al and Liz returned with him to his study. Al's belly was full and sleep was coming on. He curled up in a ball on the leather chair next to Jennens's desk. Liz, however, jumped up on his desk and quietly sat down out of his way.

In addition to the paper, on his desk was the Holy Writ—the King James Bible—and the Common Book of Prayer. He proceeded to open the Bible and thumb through it. Liz sat silently, watching what he would do. "I must write something for a composer named Handel. I don't suppose you've heard of him, have you, little midnight cat?" Jennens muttered.

Liz beamed and thought to herself, *If you only knew, Monsieur.*

"He is struggling to survive as a composer, and needs work. I wish to come up with just the right subject for a new oratorio," Jennens said, more talking to himself as he turned the pages of the biblical text. He was of course oblivious to the fact that Liz not only knew all he was saying, but that she was here for the sole purpose of helping him write the new oratorio. Liz sat with him for about an hour as he continued looking through the Bible, yawning as the hour grew late.

He took his pen and dipped it in the inkwell. At the top of the page he wrote, "The Subject is _____," and left it blank. "The subject is, the subject is," Jennens murmured to himself as he yawned. He put down his pen, rubbed his eyes, and stretched long and hard. He looked over at Al, who was sound asleep. "I believe your mate has the right idea. It is time to retire. Make yourself at home. I will see you in the morning and hopefully the idea will come to me."

Jennens left the room and Liz waited until she heard him climb the stairs. She walked over and lifted the pen from the inkwell. On the paper she completed his title, adding the word "MESSIAH."

"The idea has most certainly come, *Monsieur* Jennens," Liz smiled, returning the pen to the inkwell. "And in the morning, we shall begin writing it."

The tweeting of birds outside the open window slowly started to rouse Al from his long sleep. He opened one eye, then the other, and sat up quickly, looking around the room, clearly startled.

"Bonjour, Albert. Did you sleep well?" Liz asked from Jennens's desk. She was flipping through the Old Testament in Jennens's Bible.

"Sure, and I forgot where I were," Al said groggily, rubbing his face rapidly with his front paws. He stood up, stretched long and hard, and gave a groaning yawn. "I dreamed I were singin' on the stage and people were throwin' bananas at me."

Liz chuckled. "So they must have loved your performance to throw you your favorite food, no?"

"Aye, I were a hit," Al agreed, jumping up next to Liz and giving her a good morning kiss. "Ye're up early, Lass."

"Oui, I believe I have found the perfect opening for *Messiah*," Liz said as she pointed to the Scripture. "Isaiah 40:1–3: *'Comfort ye, comfort ye my people, saith your God. Speak ye comfortably to Jerusalem, and cry unto her, that her warfare is accomplished, that her iniquity is pardoned . . . The voice of him that crieth in the wilderness, Prepare the way for the LORD, make straight a desert highway for our God.'"*

Al's face lit up. "I remember him! He were a prophet. I loved the olives from his olive tree."

Liz patted Al on the cheek with her paw. "A prophet, *oui,* and one we spent many years with as he wrote these very words," Liz remembered tenderly. "I'll never forget the day we first met him, when he was out meeting with King Ahaz. It was the day he first prophesied about Messiah by name—*'Behold, a virgin shall conceive, and bear a Son, and shall call his name Immanuel.'"*

"That would be a good one to put in yer ora-oreo," Al said.

Liz giggled at Al's pronunciation of *oratorio.* It was just too cute to correct him. *"Oui, cher* Albert, indeed, I think it belongs in there, too. In fact, many words Isaiah wrote belong in *Messiah."*

"Psssst!" a voice came from the window.

"Mousie!" Al exclaimed happily. "What are ye doin' here?"

"I wanted to come wish you well as you begin the wonderful work on the libretto," Nigel encouraged, scurrying inside to join Liz and Al on the desk.

"Merci, Nigel," Liz said as the mouse took her paw and kissed it. "The Maker has given me some wonderful ideas this morning."

"Aye, and yer prophet laddie Isaiah is goin' to start it," Al noted, thumping the open passage.

"Splendid!" Nigel said, adjusting his spectacles as he read Isaiah 40. "Good show. I remember that passage well. What led you to this one as the opener, my dear?"

"Well, if *Messiah* is going to tell the story of Jesus, it must start at the beginning, with prophecies about him, no?" Liz explained. "And the purpose of Messiah coming was to bring comfort to God's people after heaven had been silent for more than four hundred years. Before you give someone good news, do not you always say, 'I have good news!'?"

"Brilliant, my pet!" Nigel clapped rapidly. "I think it's perfect." He proceeded to scan the Scripture. "I say, I think you could add verses 4 and 5 to follow. What do you think?"

"'Every valley shall be exalted, and every mountain and hill shall be made low; and the crooked shall be made straight, and the rough places plain. And the glory of the LORD shall be revealed, and all flesh shall see it together: for the mouth of the LORD hath spoken it,'" Liz read out loud. *"Oui,* Nigel, I agree," Liz nodded. "Now the challenge will come with getting Jennens to write what we've selected."

70

Nigel walked over to the blank page with the title. *"The Subject is MESSIAH.* Did he write this?"

"He started it," Liz said shyly. "I wrote MESSIAH."

Nigel gave a jolly chuckle. "My dear, I have no doubt you will find a way to get Jennens to do your bidding. You've already given him the subject, now it will just be a matter of leading him to the right Scriptures. If you were able to help Isaiah himself write some of these words, you shall be able to get Jennens to copy them!"

Liz put her paws on both pages of the open Bible. "Genesis to Revelation. Do you realize we have been able to walk through the pages of every book in the Bible? *C'est incredible."*

"Aye, and we were *there,* too," Al said, jumping down from the desk. "Bye, Mousie, I'm goin' to go find some breakfast."

"Cheerio, old boy," Nigel replied with a smile as Al left the room. Turning to Liz, he told her, "My pet, we have been the most blessed creatures in history. Indeed, the only other One who also is on every page from Genesis to Revelation is Messiah himself."

"Oui, in history. *His story.* It is overwhelming, no? How does one tell the story of Messiah in a way that captures everything?" Liz asked. "I have the beginning, but I don't know where to go from here. So many stories, so many writers are here that I could choose from."

"Well, musically speaking, oratorios are traditionally written in three parts," Nigel instructed. "I would suggest dividing up his story that way."

Liz looked up quickly at her old mouse friend and her heart leapt with inspiration. "Of course! *Cher* Nigel, that is the way we must do it! Three parts! *Un, deux, trois! Bon! Un*: The Prophecies and His Birth; *Deux:* His First Coming and Passion; *et Trois:* His Second Coming and Final Victory. Perfect!" But then her face fell. "Still, this is much ground to cover, no?"

Nigel put his paw on her petite frame as she slowly curled her tail up and down on the desk, deep in thought. "My dear, if anyone can do this, you can. Of that I have no doubt."

Liz smiled. *"Merci, mon ami.* Pray for me, *s'il vous plaît,* as I will need it, no?"

"I already have," Nigel said. "And I shall not stop until Jennens writes AMEN at the bottom of *Messiah!"*

They heard footsteps creaking down the stairs. Jennens was up and heading toward them.

Nigel scurried to the window. "I'm off, my dear. May the power of the pen be yours this day!" he said with a fist of victory raised in the air. "I shall return."

"Au revoir, mon ami!" Liz said, blowing a kiss in farewell. She quickly pushed the Bible open to Isaiah 40 right next to Jennens's title page, sat down, and waited, her paws resting on top of the passage.

Jennens walked in the room and a slight grin appeared on his face as he saw Liz sitting there. He looked rather disheveled, his hair askew and still wearing his blue velvet bedclothes. Liz started purring. He walked over and petted her. "And how are we today?" he asked mindlessly as he noticed the title page sitting on his desk. He stopped, picked it up, and wrinkled his brow. He held it to his chest and looked up. "I don't recall writing this. Hmmmm." He took a seat and rubbed his stubbly chin.

"The Subject is MESSIAH," he said, reading out loud. He put the page on the desk and stared out the window. Liz tried to read his reaction as he thought this through. After a moment he sat upright with a start and leaned over to his Bible. Liz sat with her paw pointing to Isaiah 40, purring.

"Comfort ye," he read softly, tapping his finger on his lips. "Comfort ye my people."

Come, Charles Jennens, Liz thought as she willed him to grasp the idea. *Prophecies! It must begin with the prophecies!*

Jennens raised his eyebrows and sat back in his chair, staring at Liz. *"Messiah.* I like it. I must have written this subject down when I was half-asleep last night. What do you think of my subject, little midnight cat?"

Liz blinked her eyes affectionately. *"Oui, you have come up with a grand idea,"* she meowed in approval.

Al came into the room, meowing, *"Top o' the mornin' to ye, lad!"* He was followed by a plump lady dressed in proper servant attire.

Jennens looked down at Al, who obviously had just had his fill of breakfast. "So, my singing cat, I see you've met my kitchen servant, Martha."

"Good morning, Mr. Jennens, sir," Martha said with a thick Cockney accent. "I found this cat in the kitchen, meowing and wrapping himself around my legs. I figured you know about him? He wouldn't let me walk until I put milk down for him."

"Of *course* I know about him. He and this black feline will be staying with me. Make sure they are well fed," Jennens said with an abrupt tone, as was his way of talking with humans.

Al spread out on the floor, grinned broadly, and mouthed to Liz, "*I . . . LOVE . . . HIM!*"

"Will you be eating breakfast in the dining room?" Martha asked.

"No, I must begin my work right now," Jennens replied. "Bring it in here, please."

"Yes, Mr. Jennens, sir," Martha said as she hurried out of the room to prepare his breakfast.

Jennens lifted the Bible, and his finger scanned through Isaiah. He nodded, took a fresh piece of paper, dipped his pen in the inkwell and wrote at the top of the page:

MESSIAH:
AN ORATORIO

He blew on the ink as he read the words he had written. Liz slowly read it upside down. Her heart burst to overflowing with joy to see the words in the fresh ink. MESSIAH! She looked up at him and purred wildly.

Liz's heart was beating hard as Jennens wrote with a fury. Clearly the divine inspiration that flowed through Liz was now pouring out of her and into Jennens's pen. He took a second sheet of paper and quickly scratched out the following:

PART THE FIRST
SINFONY (Overture)

RECITATIVE

Comfort ye, comfort ye my people, saith your God; speak ye comfortably to Jerusalem, and cry unto her, that her warfare is accomplish'd, that her iniquity is pardon'd. The voice of him that crieth in the wilderness, prepare ye the way of the Lord, make straight in the desert a highway for our God. (Isaiah 40:1–3)

SONG

Ev'ry valley shall be exalted, and ev'ry mountain and hill made low, the crooked straight, and the rough places plain. (Isaiah 40:4)

CHORUS

And the Glory of the Lord shall be revealed, and all flesh shall see it together, for the mouth of the Lord hath spoken it. (Isaiah 40:5)

Tears filled Liz's eyes as she watched Jennens write with such fervor. It was as if she were writing it herself. She marveled at seeing Isaiah's name on this page. She had sat on Isaiah's desk long ago as the prophet wrote these very words. Now she sat on Jennens's desk as he put Isaiah's words into a libretto that would be sung for all the world to hear. It was a surreal moment for Liz. She got Jennens started, and the process of Divine Inspiration was now consuming him.

The day flew by. Jennens's breakfast sat there uneaten. He flipped from Scripture to Scripture, poring over the prophecies and writing them into the libretto. Haggai. Malachi. Isaiah. Liz was struck with the segment on Malachi and the prophecies of Jesus' harsh treatment of Israel's priestly line. He was sent to purify the brood of vipers.

RECITATIVE

The Lord whom ye seek will suddenly come to his Temple, ev'n the Messenger of the Covenant, whom ye delight in: Behold He shall come, saith the Lord of Hosts. (Malachi 3:1)

SONG

But who may abide the Day of his coming? And who shall stand when He appeareth? For He is like a Refiner's Fire. (Malachi 3:2)

CHORUS

And He shall purify the Sons of Levi, that they may offer unto the Lord an Offering in Righteousness. (Malachi 3:3)

Liz closed her eyes, recalling that day when Jesus cleared out the Temple with such anger at the sons of Levi, who had turned it from a house of prayer into a den of thieves. No one stood against him when he appeared and blazed like a refining fire through the Temple courts that day.

Jennens then moved to the New Testament and the Christmas story: Matthew— the tax collector turned disciple.

RECITATIVE

Behold, a Virgin shall conceive, and bear a Son, and shall call his name Emmanuel, GOD WITH US. (Isaiah 7:14, Matthew 1:23)

Liz got a lump in her throat when Jennens wrote Isaiah 7:14. She was there not only when Isaiah wrote those words, but earlier in the day when he *spoke* them aloud in a field to King Ahaz! And she was there when Isaiah's prophecies were fulfilled, as she stood over the manger, gazing into the perfect face of that newborn baby, Emmanuel. Messiah. Jesus. This was a surreal moment for her. *Merci, Mon Dieu,* Liz prayed as she was swept away with grateful emotion.

Jennens rubbed his eyes, took out a new sheet of paper, and wrote out one final chorus for the day. Liz couldn't make out what he was writing until he got up from the desk and left the room. She walked over and stood before the paper as the ink dried.

CHORUS

For unto us a child is born, unto us a son is given: and the government shall be upon his shoulder: and his name shall be called Wonderful, Counsellor, The mighty God, The everlasting Father, The Prince of Peace. (Isaiah 9:6)

A feeling of warmth washed over Liz as she recalled the moment she saw these names for Messiah penned for the first time ever—not by Isaiah, but by Gillamon. Their wise leader had written them out in hieroglyphics way back in Egypt after their Joseph mission. He gave Liz and Nigel a code to decipher that foreshadowed the names they were to share with the prophet Isaiah. She would never forget that day later in history when she sat on Isaiah's desk and witnessed the prophet write these names in his scroll. The thread of Messiah through time astounded her.

But suddenly Liz's gaze zeroed in on this verse as if she had never read it before. She was always delighted by the living Word of God, which would give fresh meaning to itself when she least expected it.

The government shall be upon his shoulder.

Liz sat a moment and pondered this. Across time, the kings and the lords of this world claimed control of governments, but ultimately, the government was on HIS shoulder. Messiah's shoulder. He was over all kings and lords. He was the true Sovereign.

She went to Jennens's Bible and flipped through the Scriptures to Revelation. *Ah, dear John,* Liz thought fondly as she remembered the disciple Jesus loved. *Our time on Patmos was hard, but look at the jewel that came from your pen on that island of exile!* Her paw scanned the pages and she soon found the verse she was looking for. *This* would be the verse that would provide the defining chorus for *Messiah.*

Liz yawned, her eyelids heavy with sleep. She couldn't risk not having Jennens latch onto this Scripture when he started work tomorrow. So there she decided to sleep, sprawled across the pages of Revelation.

76

HALLELUJAH

LONDON, JULY 1741

The white horse, with Rider aboard, ran like the wind, followed by an army also riding on white horses. The lead Rider's eyes were ablaze like fire, and the multiple crowns on his head shimmered with brilliance. His blood-dipped robe blew majestically behind him, his title—'the Word of God'—apparent to all. Suddenly a sharp sword came out of his mouth to strike the nations. On his robe was written this title: King of all kings and Lord of all lords.

Liz watched in awe and wonder as the Rider led his faithful army to administer justice over all the earth. *"Mon Dieu!* With just a word from his mouth he has won the battle in a single day!" she exclaimed.

Al stood over Liz, who was obviously dreaming wildly on the desk. Her body was twitching and her eyelids fluttered at what she "saw" in her dream. He hated to wake her from her deep sleep, but he could hear Jennens walking around upstairs, preparing to come down. He decided he would "sing" her awake.

"Good mornin' to ye, good mornin' to ye, good mornin' me beauty, good mornin' to ye," Al softy sang over her. She slowly opened her eyes to see Al with a big, goofy, lovesick grin on his face. He kissed her and said, "Ye're still sleepin', Lass."

Liz sat up quickly, her heart racing. She put a paw up to her head. *"Bonjour, mon cher.* I was dreaming," Liz said, trying to bring herself to the waking reality of where she was. London. 1741. Jennens's study.

"What were ye dreamin' aboot?" Al asked.

Liz stood and looked down at what had been her "bed" for the night. Jennens's Bible was opened to Revelation 19, where she had been reading before she fell asleep. She put her paw reverently on the text. "I have been reading about wonderful things, Albert! About Messiah's second coming, when he will speak and put an end to all evil."

"Sure, and it sounds like a nice dream," Al grinned and said.

"Oui, but this is a dream that will come *true,"* Liz echoed excitedly.

They heard Jennens's heavy footsteps creaking down the stairs. He was headed for the study. "I'm goin' for me breakfast. Want some?" Al asked, jumping off the table.

"Perhaps later. I have work to do first," Liz said, eyeing Jennens with a determined look as he walked into the room.

"Top o' the mornin' to ye!" Al meowed at Jennens, wrapping himself around the man's legs.

Jennens leaned over and petted Al, feeling his wide belly. "It seems you are eating us out of house and home, singing cat."

"Aye, that's what I do best!" Al meowed in reply as he trotted off to the kitchen.

Jennens sat down at the desk. "And you, little midnight cat, what do you have for me today?" he laughed to himself. "As if you can read. You are a peculiar feline, to play with these pages." Liz rolled her eyes at the man.

Jennens reached to turn the pages of his Bible, but Liz slapped her paw on the open text of Revelation 19, preventing him from turning. Jennens frowned, pulling the Bible from Liz's touch to see what her paw marked. "Revelation? I was last in Matthew," he said, removing Liz's paw from the text. "Well, that's not where we need to be. Luke is where we need to be." He proceeded to flip the pages back to the gospel of Luke.

"Monsieur, oui, of course Luke is important, but you must see this passage," Liz meowed in protest.

Jennens ignored her as he put his nose in the text and picked up his pen, dipped it in the inkwell, and started adding to the libretto.

RECITATIVE

There were Shepherds abiding in the field, keeping watch over their flock by night. (Luke 2:8)

Liz twitched her tail forcefully back and forth, showing her displeasure that Jennens was ignoring her. Still, she was pleased with what he was writing, as it was an excellent passage to continue the story of Messiah's birth. *"We will return to Revelation, Monsieur. Of that I will make sure,"* Liz meowed.

The days passed quickly. Jennens worked diligently through the book of Luke, pulling beautiful passages about the Advent of Messiah, and adding some passages of Zechariah, Isaiah, and Matthew that foretold Messiah's ministry on Earth.

RECITATIVE

Then shall the eyes of the blind be opened, and the ears of the deaf unstopped; then shall the lame man leap as a hart, and the tongue of the dumb shall sing.   (Zechariah 35:5-6)

SONG

He shall feed his flock like a Shepherd: and he shall gather the lambs with his arm, and carry them in his bosom, and gently lead those that are with young. Come unto Him, all ye that labor, come unto Him all ye who are heavy laden, and He will give you rest. Take his yoke upon you and learn of him; for He is meek and lowly of heart: and ye shall find rest for your souls. (Isaiah 40:11, Matthew 11:28-29)

Every night Liz would look over Scripture and select a key passage to leave open for Jennens to find the next day. She decided she would wait until Jennens progressed in the story of Messiah before returning him to Revelation. He obviously wasn't ready for it. As they moved into the second part of the *Messiah* libretto, the scenes of Jesus' crucifixion left her spent as she relived the heartbreak of the Passion of Messiah.

PART THE SECOND
CHORUS

Behold the Lamb of God, that taketh away the sin of the world. (John 1:29)

SONG

He was despised and rejected of men, a man of sorrows, and acquainted with grief. He gave his back to the smiters, and his cheeks to them that plucked off the hair; he hid not his face from shame and spitting. (Isaiah 53:3, Isaiah 50:6)

CHORUS

Surely He hath borne our griefs and carried our sorrows: He was wounded for our transgressions, He was bruised for our Iniquities; the chastisement of our peace was upon Him. (Isaiah 53:4–5)

CHORUS

And with His stripes we are healed. (Isaiah 53:5)

CHORUS

All we, like sheep, have gone astray, we have turned ev'ry one to his own way, and the Lord hath laid on Him the iniquity of us all. (Isaiah 53:6)

Liz wept as she remembered the night she saw Isaiah at his desk bent over with grief, weeping as he wrote about the suffering Messiah. That was the night she had done the unthinkable—what she never thought she would ever do—speak out loud to a human. She smiled as she remembered that exchange with Isaiah, knowing how joy-filled he must now be to find himself in the presence of Messiah. Liz then thought that if she couldn't get Jennens to use her passage from Revelation, she might have to do the unthinkable again.

Liz awoke early. Jennens's writing had progressed on to the Resurrection and it was time to end Part Two. She turned his open Bible back to Revelation 19 and sat completely on top of the Scripture. She had no intention of moving until Jennens agreed to write from this passage.

Jennens entered his study and plopped down in his chair as usual. He looked at Liz, who was twitching her tail back and forth and staring back at him with eyes of determination. He leaned over and could barely make out where Liz had the Scripture marked. "I see you have turned the Scripture back to Revelation, little midnight cat," Jennens said. "If you only understood what you were sitting on, you would realize that that book is far too complicated for people to understand in song."

"Monsieur, you are wrong," Liz meowed in protest. *"Do not make me speak to you. I somehow think you will not deal with it well. But if I must, I must."*

Jennens raised his eyebrows at Liz's lengthy reply. "Methinks you doth protest too much." He reached over to take the Bible away from Liz but she would not have it. She dug her claws into the pages. Jennens frowned and forcefully picked her up, setting her down on the floor. When he turned to his Bible, he saw that the cat had torn the page. "Now look what you've done! You've torn my Holy Writ!"

Liz jumped back up onto the desk and hesitated. Her heart pounded, but she knew what she had to do. "If you do not lay out your whole genius and skill on this work to include this passage," Liz blurted out, "you may as well tear up your entire libretto."

Jennens's eyes got wide and he pressed his back deep into his chair in alarm. They sat for a moment in silence, but Liz saw how terrified the man was upon hearing his "little midnight cat" speak. Beads of sweat appeared on his forehead and his pulse was racing. Liz decided he couldn't take anymore. She would not speak again. Liz knew she didn't need to. Her few words were sufficient. She jumped off the table, and sauntered off with her tail in the air, smiling a coy smile as she left the room.

81

Liz decided to leave Jennens alone all day. She would not explain herself as she did with Isaiah. And she was sure the fright she gave him would make Jennens write with even greater haste to finish the project. She wondered if he would put the two cats out of the house, but she realized that would actually work out in their favor. Liz returned to the study that evening when Jennens left the house. Al was asleep in the chair. Jennens had made tremendous progress that day, working well into Part Three of *Messiah*. She grinned when she saw what he finally wrote.

"Good evening, my dear," Nigel whispered as he jumped onto the windowsill and then Jennens's desk. "How is *Messiah* coming?"

"Ah, *bonsoir*, Nigel," Liz said with delight, then added with a giggle, "but he has already come, no?"

"Jolly good humor, my pet!" Nigel chuckled. "How is *Messiah*, the *oratorio*, coming?"

"Jennens has finished Part Two and is well into Part Three," Liz replied. "Nigel, I had to do it. I had to speak aloud to Jennens. He simply would not pay heed to a passage I knew he simply *must* use."

Nigel's eyes grew wide. "Good show, my dear! I say, how did the old boy take it?"

"Not well, I'm afraid. I spoke briefly and left the room," Liz explained. "He was shocked, of course, but I do not plan to speak to him again. I am sure he will come to believe he imagined it."

"I think that is wise, my pet. I'm sure he had a jolly good fright!" Nigel chuckled. "Tell me, did our Mr. Jennens do your bidding?"

Liz smiled and pulled out the page, pointing to the addition. "Indeed, he did."

CHORUS

Hallelujah! For the Lord God Omnipotent reigneth. The Kingdom of this World is become the Kingdom of our Lord and of his Christ; and He shall reign for ever and ever. King of Kings, and Lord of Lords. Hallelujah! (Revelation 19:6; 11:15; 19:16)

Nigel looked at Liz with great seriousness. "My dear, I have chills from reading this chorus. Somehow I feel this will be the most important part of *Messiah* that Handel will set to music," he said, putting his small paw over the words. "If I will first play the music for this Hallelujah Chorus for him, may heaven inspire it like no other piece."

"I thought the same, *mon ami*. This is why I had to take drastic measures and speak to Jennens. I simply felt he could not miss this passage." Liz put her paw on Nigel's back. "I know that all the music for *Messiah* will be divinely inspired, no?"

"Indeed it shall!" Nigel exclaimed with a fist of victory raised in the air. "And I'm sure a little kick in the proverbial pants will do Jennens good. Might make him finish *Messiah* sooner."

"The Maker motivates in mysterious ways, no?" Liz said with a smile. "Especially when you see the men he chose to write Scriptures we shall use in *Messiah*. Of course some are faithful friends, followers, and servants of Jesus, but included in this group are a tax collector, murderer, adulterer, and a notorious Christian killer."

"Splendid! I find it very fitting that no one is kept from talking about Messiah, or being used by him. He did come to save all, did he not?" Nigel remarked in wonder. "Even Saul, that former killer of Christians who 'saw the light' and went on to write most of the New Testament as Paul. He was quite the handful at first, but of course he turned out splendidly."

"*Oui,* indeed, Nigel. And only two writers were actually ever with Jesus: Matthew and John," Liz observed. "These passages we've chosen were written by ten men. If you add the work of Jennens and Handel, twelve men in all will be responsible for *Messiah*. Twelve."

"And a cat and a mouse," Nigel added with a wink. "Of mice, cats, and men, I say!"

"But I'm sure Max and Kate would like to be included, as they helped with your violin," Liz giggled. "Oh, and we cannot forget Shandelli who made your violin and taught you to play."

The pair of glowing eyes peered into the window of Jennen's study, furious as Liz and Nigel carried on in such joyful tones, recounting their efforts to bring *Messiah* into being.

Suddenly they heard Jennens entering through the front door. The glowing eyes disappeared from the windowsill. Nigel scurried to the floor and hid in the shadows. Liz remained on the desk, and greeted Jennens as he sat down, meowing, *"Bonsoir, Monsieur."*

Jennens eyed Liz with nervous suspicion. *Did I imagine that this little cat spoke to me?* he thought to himself. *How could this cat have spoken words? It must be exhaustion setting in from working on this libretto.* He studied Liz and a nagging doubt remained. *But if these felines were miraculously used to inspire me, I will send them on to Handel so they may do the same for him.*

"I must send a letter, little midnight cat," he said, then adding quickly, "please do not reply."

Liz meowed, *"Do not worry. I will not startle you again, Monsieur."*

Jennens was relieved to hear the cat speak in her native tongue. He took out some fresh paper and dipped his pen in the inkwell. Liz smiled as she watched what he wrote to an Edward Holdsworth:

July 10, 1741

Handel says he will do nothing next winter, but I hope I shall persuade him to set another Scripture collection I have made for him, and perform it for his own benefit in Passion Week. I hope he will lay out his whole Genius and Skill upon it, that the composition may excel all his former compositions, as the Subject excels every other subject. The Subject is Messiah.

IN TIME WITH
THE MAESTRO

Handel sat quietly at his desk, fiddling with the ancient Roman coin he picked up when he was a young man studying in Rome. He kept it with him all the time, as it reminded him of the glory of Rome and how that ancient city inspired his writing, most significantly his operas. He sighed. Opera was dead. Would it simply now pass into posterity as did ancient Rome?

The aging composer held the coin close to his face and studied the six-pointed star above the image of Caesar Augustus. He had always wondered about that star. The Roman Emperor Tiberius minted the coin in AD 16 in honor of the events of 2 BC that marked the 750th anniversary of the founding of Rome as well as the twenty-fifth year of the rule of Caesar Augustus. In honor of the occasion the Roman Senate gave Caesar the honored title of Pater Patraie, or "Father of the Country." According to tradition, the brightest star ever seen appeared that year, and the Romans believed it was sent by the gods in honor of this event. It was obviously Caesar's star. *Or was it?* Handel wondered.

Nigel sat high on a shelf, watching his musical mentor, thinking how sad he appeared. Handel rubbed his finger across the unusual indentation on the side of the coin, evidently put there some time in history. Because of the imperfection, the young George F. Handel had been able to buy the coin for a steal at the Forum in Rome. It was a treasured keepsake. He hoped he would not be forced to part with it if times got hard.

A forceful knock sounded at the front door, and Peter quickly answered it. Nigel and Handel listened to the muffled sounds coming from down the hall. Soon Peter quickly walked toward Handel's composing room.

"Mr. Handel, you have a delivery," Peter said, a bit uncertain of the situation. "Mr. Charles Jennens has sent you a package."

Handel's face brightened and he sat up. "Ya? Jennens? Vat did he send, Pater?"

Peter handed over a stack of paper. "It appears he has written a new libretto for you! Isn't that grand news? A project you can begin work on *immediately,*" Peter enthused. In his hand was a basket.

Handel laid the composition aside on his desk, then scanned the cover letter from Jennens. "The subject is Messiah, hmmm . . ." Then suddenly he came to a halt. *"I hope dey vill aid you in your vork?"* He quickly looked up at Peter and the basket in his hand. "Pater, open de basket, vill you?"

Peter placed the basket on the floor and opened the lid, and out popped Liz and Al. "Cats?" Handel said. "Dat Jennens is a strange fellow, ya? He said dese cats helped him write de libretto, and he hoped dey vould help me. BAH! Vat do I need vit two cats?"

Liz and Nigel locked eyes and she gave him a wink. Al followed the instructions Liz had given him earlier and walked over to Handel, rubbing against the composer's legs and meowing. Handel chuckled at seeing Al's robust frame and patted his belly. "Dis von looks like he loves food as much as me!"

"Aye! I do, I do, I do!" Al eagerly meowed. *"Can I have some now?"*

"I think these cats will bring you great company, Mr. Handel. I will make sure they are well taken care of by Mrs. Rice," Peter offered. He was happy about the delivery, as these animals might lift Handel's spirits. Peter had been trying unsuccessfully to help Handel get out of his disinterested and depressed state.

Liz jumped up on Handel's desk and blinked her eyes affectionately at the composer. As the man leaned over to pet her, she headbutted him and meowed a soft, *"Bonjour."*

Nigel gripped his violin expectantly, watching this encounter with Liz and Handel. How he wished he could be face-to-face with his mentor! Little did Handel know that Liz and Al had been secretly sneaking into his kitchen for years. Al would be overjoyed to finally enter the kitchen freely and eat at will, not having to worry about sneaking by Mrs. Rice. Sadly, Nigel still had to remain in the shadows.

Handel stared deeply into Liz's eyes. "You, feline, look very intelligent, ya. Okay, Pater, dey vill stay." He got up, patted his belly, and started walking to the door. "I am hungry. Have Mrs. Rice get my dinner, please. I vill change, ya."

Peter looked at the unread libretto sitting on Handel's desk. "But Mr. Handel, Sir, wouldn't you like to look at the work Mr. Jennens has sent you?"

Handel glanced at his desk and threw his hand in the air to dismiss it. "Later." He walked up the stairs to his bedroom. Peter's shoulders slumped. Handel wasn't enthusiastic about work these days. Al meowed. "Come on, then," Peter instructed as he made his way to the kitchen. He went to inform Mrs. Rice that dinner needed to be ready early, and that they would have two new permanent guests. Al trotted along behind him, triumphantly.

Nigel scurried down from the shelf in an instant, joining Liz on the desk. They shared a brief embrace. "Splendid welcome, my dear! I'm terribly glad Handel has warmly received you two. Now we can enjoy each other's company with freedom."

"Oui, mon ami. It is good to be here at last," Liz said, looking around Handel's desk. Her eyes suddenly saw the coin. She bent down for a closer look and shot her head back up. "Nigel! Do you realize what Handel has here?"

"I'm afraid I don't, dear girl," Nigel said as he closely examined the coin, rubbing his paw over its surface. He quickly felt the unusual indentation. Startled, his gaze met Liz's as smiles grew on both their faces. "It's the coin."

"Oui, the coin," Liz said, touching it softly. "If Handel only realized where this has been, he would never part with it."

"Oh, dear, I overheard Handel talking to Peter about things he might need to sell if his funds run too low," Nigel lamented. "This coin was mentioned."

"No! He must not sell this coin, and that is all there is to it," Liz protested. "Even if we have to hide it from him."

"Agreed, my pet," Nigel affirmed. "I took the liberty of inviting Max and Kate over after the humans have retired. They will sneak away from the butcher and arrive late this evening. Shandelli will also join us from the garden, as he spends most of his time out there, of late."

"*Bon.* It will be wonderful for us to be together again and discuss this next part of our mission," Liz said, softly touching Nigel's precious violin. "But from here, it is really up to you, no?"

Nigel closed his eyes and nodded his head excitedly. "I am a bit nervous, but the time has come."

"Why don't you join us for dinner, hiding cleverly, of course? I shall obtain some cheese for you," Liz suggested.

"I would be delighted, my dear," Nigel said happily. "Let me put my violin away." Nigel stowed his violin behind a stack of books on the bookshelf and he and Liz left Handel's composing room to go to the kitchen.

88

The pair of glowing eyes squinted with glee from the open window. Finally.

The house was quiet early. Handel dismissed his servants and turned in, not even looking at the *Messiah* libretto sent by Jennens. He was disinterested in the project. The animals decided to meet in the garden on this hot summer night.

"Ah, *buona sera!*" Shandelli exclaimed as Liz, Al, Kate, and Max joined them in the mulberry bushes. "What do you think of my garden, eh? Well, I tend it to keep the pests away."

"*Bonsoir, Signor* Shandelli," Liz greeted the stick bug, looking around with delight at the garden. "I am quite partial to gardens. You have done a wonderful job. The flowers are lovely."

"*Grazie, Signora.* I try," the stick bug said with his arms out in a gesture of humility.

"Mousie, seems like a fine night for some fiddlin' then," Max said, looking up at the beautiful night sky. "Why don't ye get yer violin an' play a tune for the lassies?"

"Brilliant suggestion, old boy! I shall return posthaste," Nigel said with a nod. He scurried back into the house.

Al let out a long burp. "I think I be in heaven. I get to live in Mrs. Rice's kitchen. Did a kitty ever need anythin' else?"

"Jest don't cause tr-r-rouble, lad," Max said, poking Al in the belly.

Suddenly they heard Nigel screaming from inside the house. The animals looked up at the open window of Handel's composing room in alarm. "Wha' could be wrong?" Kate asked worriedly.

"I don't know but we'd best get inside," Max said with a growl as he started running for the door.

Nigel sat weeping on the floor of Handel's composing room, his back to the open door. Max and the others ran up behind him and their eyes widened when they saw the terrible tragedy that had caused Nigel's scream. They didn't need to ask *what* had upset him. But they had no idea *how*.

The precious mouse-sized violin so carefully carved and put together lay in a pile of rubble, completely destroyed. The bow was snapped in two.

89

"How did this happen, Mousie?" Max growled.

Shandelli walked slowly toward the rubble, his twiggy arms stretched out in bewilderment and sadness. *"Mi dispiace, Signor* Monaco, but how is it your violin is destroyed?"

Nigel looked up, tears flowing steadily down his face. "I . . . I'm afraid I do not know," he said sadly, gently lifting a broken piece of the tiny mangled violin. "I came in here to get my instrument and found it like this."

"Who could have done this?" Kate asked angrily. "It weren't a human."

"Quel dommage, mon ami. I am so sorry," Liz said tearfully, wrapping her paws around Nigel's shoulders. "Kate, you are correct. And this was no accident. Someone knows what Nigel is supposed to do with this violin. We are evidently not alone."

Al trembled with fear, his paws up to his mouth. He jumped up onto the desk to get away from the carnage on the floor. "Ye mean evil beasties were here?" He backed up on the desk, trying to get away from the unknown menace, and knocked over Handel's inkwell.

"Aye, ye'd have ta be evil ta do such a thing," Max answered seriously.

"It has ta be the doin's of the evil one. Mousie, seems yer fiddlin' is more important than even ye thought, lad."

Al looked behind him and got doubly scared when he saw he had caused a huge mess all over Jennens's letter. He didn't want anyone to know, so he tried to wipe the spilled ink up with his paw, but he only left a huge pawprint on the letter. Terror gripped him at the thought of being banished from the kitchen for his poor behavior. But before Al's eyes, he saw the Seven Seal forming on Jennens's letter, right over the words 'The Subject Is Messiah.' His eyes got wide and he looked down at everyone surrounding Nigel on the floor.

"Um, I think ye should see this," Al said. The animals looked up and he pointed sheepishly at the letter.

Liz jumped up and immediately saw the Seven Seal. She looked at Al and they shared a knowing silence. She then gazed down at Shandelli. He had to leave their presence in order for them to break the seal. Although he knew about their mission, no one was allowed to see the IAMISPHERE but the Order of the Seven. "*Signor* Shandelli, may I ask a favor? Would you please go get Nigel a bit of cheese from the kitchen? I think he looks weak from the shock of losing his violin. It might help him as we discuss what to do."

"*Certamente,*" Shandelli replied as he somberly left the room.

"It's Gillamon," Liz explained, jumping down on the floor with the letter. "The Seal has returned. Quickly, Nigel, before Shandelli returns."

Nigel nodded silently, understanding Liz's sense of urgency. He began nibbling at the seal and immediately the seven animals were encased in light. Swirling panes of moments in time surrounded them, and Gillamon stood there, waiting to greet them in the IAMISPHERE.

"Greetings, dear friends. You have accomplished much," Gillamon said with warmth in his gentle voice. "The Maker is well pleased."

"Aye, Gillamon, but Nigel's violin has been destr-r-royed!" Max reported with a scowl.

"Indeed," Gillamon said calmly. "This was expected."

Nigel looked up quickly at the wise old mountain goat. "Expected? How can this be?"

Gillamon smiled at the small mouse whose emotions were torn apart with the sadness of losing something precious to him. "Nigel, what if I told you that was only your practice violin? What if I told you the one you needed to make and use for *Messiah* would come from items not in this time?"

Nigel took off his spectacles and rubbed his eyes. "I'm afraid I don't follow you, old boy."

Liz stepped forward. "Gillamon, are you saying that we must construct another violin for Nigel? But we must go find the items elsewhere than 1741?"

"That is exactly what I am saying, Liz," Gillamon said with a smile. "Also, music does not just come from words on a page, waiting to be adorned with notes. It must be born of passion. Right now, Mr. Handel has none. And you, Nigel, as enthusiastic as you are, are truly not ready to play the music that will be divinely inspired. You need a fresh touch. From the *Maestro* himself."

The wise mountain goat lowered his head to look right in Nigel's sad, confused eyes. "Just a moment in time will make all the difference."

"Where do ye want us ta go then?" Max asked.

"Back to Messiah, of course," Gillamon replied.

The animals were taken aback. Liz spoke up first. "So we shall revisit our time with Jesus? I think I can speak for everyone that we will be most honored to do so. To which moment in time are we to go?"

"You are to enter time just before Jesus knew he was Messiah. You will then relive life with him up until . . ." Gillamon paused. "Well, you will be told when the time with him is sufficient."

"Aye, an' do ye have instructions of where we're supposed ta get the things for Nigel's violin?" Max asked.

Gillamon didn't answer right away, as was his habit. "Remember that you will not be aware of why you are there shortly after your arrival. But you will not be alone in this quest."

"She'll be there then!" Kate exclaimed in a perky voice, wagging her tail.

"Most certainly, dear Kate, as always," Gillamon chuckled. "Nigel, attend."

Nigel walked to stand before Gillamon, and smoothed his whiskers respectfully. "Deep in your subconscious will be these things to watch. They will give you a fresh passion you will need when you return to 1741. As you go back in time to Jesus, watch him, the *Maestro*, again. Watch as he carefully chooses his twelve *instruments,* tuning them to perfection in order to bring a full *symphony of purpose* into being. Once more feel the *crescendo* of his life symphony to its climactic end in the Passion." Gillamon stopped and lifted his head with eyes closed.

Nigel's heart was beating rapidly, thinking of the life of Messiah in these musical terms. It was already helping his spirit as he pondered what Gillamon said.

After a moment Gillamon opened his eyes and looked intently at Nigel. "Feel the thrill of Messiah's mighty *encore*, which has left believing audiences applauding ever since that day. You see, in order to truly make beautiful music, one must know the Subject well, and feel it deep in the soul."

"And the *Subject* is Messiah." Nigel bowed humbly. "It will be my honor."

"Attaboy, Mousie," Max cheered. "This will be a gr-r-rand adventure back ta Messiah."

"*Oui,* parts of this journey will be difficult, but seeing him again will be worth it!" Liz seconded enthusiastically. "Gillamon, when do we leave?"

The panels swirled in a fury until they blurred into one single, large pane. The small village of Nazareth came to life in front of them. Gillamon walked in front of the pane, and lifted his hoof, his blue eyes twinkling with anticipation for the Order of the Seven.

"There's no time like the present."

ENTER THE MAESTRO

BACK TO NAZARETH

The sound of rushing wind enveloped the animals as they stepped into the IAMISPHERE. For a brief moment they were suspended between AD 1741 and AD 7. The animals could not speak, nor could they move until they entered the other time. They tingled from head to toe with blazing light surrounding them and the powerful voice of God proclaiming, *"I AM, I AM, I AM."* The animals could not survive long in the IAMISPHERE, as the overwhelming presence of God was more than they could handle physically, emotionally, and mentally.

In the blink of an eye they were on a dirt road leading into the city of Nazareth. And there waiting for them was a spotless, white lamb.

"Clarie!" Kate gushed with delight. The Westie ran up to the lamb and they shared an emotional embrace. Kate and Clarie held a special bond, ever since that day the lamb was orphaned and Kate had been the one to wipe her tears. "Oh, how we've missed ye."

"My dear Kate," Clarie replied, a tear of joy slipping from her eye. "I know it feels like forever for you in earthly time, but it's only been a moment since we parted."

Max, Liz, Al, and Nigel happily joined the reunion with Clarie, the other spiritual member of the Order of the Seven. Gillamon was the leader of the Order, having become a spiritual being before the Flood, and now provided assignments, guidance, and protection to the earth-bound team of animals. Clarie was the final member added to the team, joining Gillamon in the spiritual realm.

The lamb was given the honor of joining the Order of the Seven after she sacrificed herself to save Jesus, Mary, and Joseph in their escape to Egypt the horrible night of the slaughter of the innocents. Evil King Herod had sent his soldiers to Bethlehem to kill all the baby boys age two and younger, and Clarie prevented the Roman centurion, Marcus Antonius, from pursuing the fleeing family. They were saved but in his rage over the child's rescue, the evil lion Lucifer killed Clarie. He vowed revenge on the family of Antonius, claiming that the sword of Antonius would reach Messiah yet. Clarie's role was to be the team's guide whenever they entered the IAMISPHERE to visit another earthly time. Like Gillamon, she could take any physical form, and unlike the team, she would always know the time they had traveled from.

"Bonjour, chère Clarie!" Liz said warmly. "I know our time is short. Please review the rules so everyone knows what is to come."

"Very well. Welcome, my friends. It is so good to see you!" Clarie began, her precious face aglow. "Because you have come from the future back to a time you already have lived through, you must not be allowed to know you are from the future. Otherwise, you may act differently than you did when you were here as these events took place, and history could be altered."

"Right. We have seven minutes before we forget, if I'm not mistaken," Nigel added. "My dear, we must find items to make my violin. We need a special piece of wood, a stick, and the tail hair from a grey male horse."

"Yes, Nigel, Gillamon has given me the list. After seven minutes, I will be the only one who will know you are actually from 1741. You will behave just as you did in real time in AD 7," Clarie explained. "I will help you with what you are to find, although you may not understand at the moment why I ask you to do certain things. When it is time for you to return to 1741, I will help you regain your memories of current earthly time and return there."

"This time travelin' always amazes me, little lass," Max said, grinning. "Ye're a gr-r-rand guide as always, an' I know we'll be in good hands then."

"So let us review where we are in time with Jesus, no?" Liz posed. "It is now AD 7. Jesus is nine years old, and he is living with his family.

96

Max, Kate, and Nigel traveled with them to Egypt when Jesus was a baby and returned here when it was safe following King Herod's death. Max is called 'Tovah' and Kate is called 'Chava' by the humans. Albert and I were staying with the Roman family of Marcus Antonius the night the family fled to Egypt, but we rejoined the family here in Nazareth, along with Clarie. They are, of course, unaware that Clarie died that night and has returned. They are especially unaware that she is immortal, as are we all."

"I remember how happy Mary were when she saw us again after so long," Al remembered. "She calls me 'Ari' and Liz 'Zilla.'"

"Very good memory, Albert," Liz remarked with a smile. *"Oui,* she always wondered how we made our way from Jerusalem to Nazareth. That was a happy day."

"And today is a happy day," Clarie chimed in. "Gillamon decided that for this mission you did not need to revisit the moment of Jesus' birth, but should begin with the moment Jesus knows who he really is."

"Mary's journal!" Liz exclaimed. *"Oui,* this is a happy day indeed! I am so glad we will get to see this again."

Clarie started walking. "Follow me, as you will soon forget *when* and *where* you are from. Jesus is out playing with his friends. We will join him there."

"This be so excitin'!" Kate exclaimed happily. "I always love this part!"

As the six friends walked down the road toward Nazareth, something strange and wonderful began to happen. Max, Liz, Kate, Al, and Nigel felt blissful warmth overtake their bodies, starting with their tails and reaching toward their heads. As soon as the sensation reached their heads, their minds felt the gentle touch of the Maker whispering, *"Remember always: I AM."*

Clarie looked at her friends to see if they had made the mental transition. She decided to test them with an idea. "So, I think this could be the day."

"The day for what exactly, *mon amie?"* Liz asked as they walked along.

Clarie smiled. The transition was complete. "I think this is the day Jesus might find out who he is. I heard Mary and Joseph talking about it this morning. Mary was wondering the best way to approach Jesus, as this will come as quite a shock to him."

"He's jest a boy, after all," Kate chimed in. "Even though he is the Maker's lad."

97

"Aye, how do ye go aboot tellin' yer lad that he be GOD?" Max posed.

"Mary's journal," Liz answered. "She has written down all the wonderful events that have happened since before Jesus was born, no? It would be easy for her to simply share this with the child."

"Brilliant, my dear! Utterly brilliant!" Nigel enthused. "It shouldn't be too difficult to bring it to mind. What about the wise man Ahura's letter?"

"Perfect, *mon ami!*" Liz replied. "She keeps it tucked in her journal, and it would be the perfect way for her to begin. I shall bring it to her memory."

They soon heard the sounds of life echoing from the town streets. Two men were arguing over the width of a beam needed to support a walkway leading to a new home. Sounds of hammers on wood added to their loud discussion. A group of ladies laughed as they sat together milling grain for bread. Children shouted and chased each other down the street. Then came an unmistakable voice.

"AMOS! Where have you run away to now, eh?" Rabbi Isaac yelled at his ever-wandering donkey, who had ventured down the street. "I am an old man and here you make me chase you all over Yisrael! *Oi!*"

Al's face lit up and his tummy rumbled. "Sure, and I wonder if Rabbi Isaac made some more dried fish. I ate it all up the other day." Al happily trotted over to follow Rabbi Isaac, who took Amos by the reins to lead him home.

"Come, follow me!" they heard a young voice exclaim as the group of children went running by. "I know the perfect place!"

Max, Liz, Kate, Nigel, and Clarie sat just off the side of the street, watching the happy children run along. Liz smiled at the young boy with the deep brown locks of hair falling into his piercing green eyes. His olive complexion glistened with sweat from running, and his smile was magnetic.

"Jesus doesn't even realize he is practicing for what he has come to Earth to do," Liz said softly. "To lead everyone to the perfect place."

13

EXPECT THE UNEXPECTED

Mary sat alone with her thoughts as she mended a piece of clothing. Her three children were outside playing, so she took advantage of the quietness to ponder what she must do. She couldn't get away from the feeling pressing on her spirit that the time had come to tell Jesus who he was. *So soon?* she asked herself. *I thought I would have more time with Jesus as simply my son. How will I tell him?*

Joseph was busy working on a new piece of furniture in his carpentry shop out back. They had agreed that morning that it was time to tell Jesus he was not just the son of Joseph, but the son of God. Joseph tenderly smiled and gripped her hand. "The Lord has not failed to direct our steps this far. I know he will guide us in this, too. We will pray, and the answer will come."

Max and Kate ran off with the children to play while Liz, Clarie, and Nigel made their way to Mary and Joseph's home. "A word of warning," Clarie said. "The evil one has come before in the form of creatures against you and your mission. This time he will come against Jesus by hiding in men."

Liz looked at Clarie with solemn understanding. "We have been charged with protecting him, but as Jesus begins his mission, I am uncertain as to what we will need to do. Certainly he won't need our help, as he is the all-knowing, all-powerful Messiah. How could we small creatures ever be of help to him?"

"He will tell you what you are to do, for you will certainly be needed," Clarie affirmed.

"These past nine years have been utter joy," Nigel said. "I wonder if he will begin acting like Messiah right away, or if it will take some time."

"The fact that he knows he is Messiah will not change his character and how he treats others," Liz suggested. "Jesus is an obedient, respectful, loving child, and he will always act this way, no?"

"Indeed, Liz. But his time will come," Clarie posed. "For now, enjoy his childhood and watching him grow into a fine young man."

Clarie remained outside while Liz slipped in the front door of the house. Nigel soon followed but stayed in the shadows.

"Ah, Zilla, my little shadow," Mary smiled, patting the rug where she sat. "Join me." Liz purred and rubbed her cheek on Mary's outstretched hand.

"It's time, Zilla. We have to tell Jesus who he is," Mary said as she softly stroked Liz's shiny fur.

"*This is a big day, mon amie,*" Liz meowed. She looked up to the shelf where Mary kept her journal. She walked over to stand under the shelf and looked back at Mary, willing her to follow. "*Your journal, Mary. Use your journal.*"

Mary listened to the meowing cat. "What is it, Zilla? Are you hungry?" Mary got up and walked over to where Liz stood. "I have some dried fish. Do you smell it? Rabbi Isaac brought it this morning, but I put it up here so Ari wouldn't get into it. You know how he loves dried fish." As Mary grinned and reached for the pouch of dried fish, her gaze landed on the scroll. She stopped suddenly and picked it up, along with the fish, turning to sit back down on the floor. She mindlessly gave Liz a piece of dried fish while she read through the journal.

Liz played along and ate some fish although her attention was on Mary as she read the words she had penned for nine years to her precious little one, Jesus. Nigel had arranged this leather scroll for Mary while she was staying with Zechariah and Elizabeth for three months until Jesus' cousin John was born. Zechariah had taught Mary how to read and write, and this journal gave Mary a wonderful outlet to write down her thoughts. Liz's heart warmed as she saw Mary's face glow with joy when she read about the miracle of Jesus' birth. Mary unrolled the scroll and out fell the letter from the old wise man, Ahura.

When the Magi from the East visited Mary, Joseph, and the toddler Jesus in Bethlehem, they brought with them gifts of gold, frankincense, and myrrh. But there remained back in Babylon a wise man who had not been able to make the journey. Ahura Yazda was his name, and he was the Chief Magus at the school founded by Daniel more than five hundred years earlier during the Babylonian Captivity. Ahura had instructed the three magi, Faraz, Naveed, and Caspar, as they studied the heavens and searched the scrolls of prophecy about the newborn king of the Jews. It was his wisdom that led the Wise Men to find Jesus, but he himself was too old to travel so far. As the Magi were departing on their quest, he handed them a letter to be given to the parents of the child.

Mary unfolded the letter and tears brimmed up in her eyes as she read his words of wisdom and kindness, as she had read countless times before. Suddenly she looked up and saw Liz staring at her quietly. "This is it, Zilla! Ahura's letter! We will share it with Jesus!"

"Oui, mon amie," Liz meowed, delighted that Mary came to the same conclusion that this was the best way to tell Jesus that he was the long-awaited Messiah.

Mary got up and ran out to Joseph, Ahura's letter in hand.

The group of ten children were enjoying a game of hide and seek in the grove of olive trees. Max and Kate were running around, enjoying the sheer delight of the children's laughter and innocence while at play. Jesus was responsible for his little five-year-old brother James and four-year-old sister Sarah, and took great care to make sure they had a fair turn. Sometimes the older children would pass them by, but Jesus stood up for them. The other children respected Jesus for his kindness.

Jesus was in a good hiding place up in one of the olive trees. Suddenly Sarah tripped and fell, scraping her knee. "Ahhhh! Jesus, help me!" she cried. Max and Kate immediately ran to her side.

Jesus didn't think twice about leaving his hiding place above where the children were searching for him. He jumped down from the tree, ran to Sarah, and scooped her up in his arms. "It's okay, Sarah. Shhhh," he said gently as he examined her knee, which was beginning to bleed. "It's just a little scrape. Do you want me to take you home?"

Sarah held her fingers in her mouth and nodded silently with her lower lip out. She sniffed as Jesus wiped away her tears. Max and Kate were eye level with Jesus. He smiled at them. "See, Tovah and Chava are here, too. Look how cute they are." Little Sarah looked at the two dogs, whose tongues were hanging out from running around with the children. A smile slowly appeared on her face and she reached her small hand to touch the friendly dogs. Max licked her hand and Kate wagged her tail excitedly.

"Let's go," Jesus said as he stood, holding Sarah. "James, better come on home with us." James told the other children good-bye and the three children of Joseph and Mary walked home with their two dogs by their side.

ידיד

102   Joseph and Mary were sitting inside enjoying some pistachios and dates when the children arrived. Al had returned, stuffed with dried fish, from Rabbi Isaac's house, and was sleeping in the corner. "Mother, Sarah fell," Jesus said as he gently placed her on the floor by Mary. "She has a little scrape."

"Oh, Sarah, I'm sorry," Mary said as she kissed the girl on the head. She took a cloth to dab in a bowl of water and tenderly cleaned her knee. "It's not too bad, my sweet girl. Would you like a date?"

Sarah brightened as Mary gave her the sweet treat. Little James held his hand out for one and giggled as he bit into the fruit. "Thank you, Jesus, for watching over your brother and sister," Joseph said with his hand on young Jesus' shoulder. "We can always depend on you."

"I think you two need to lie down and rest for a while," Mary told Sarah and James as she led them to their mats on the floor in the next room.

Jesus sat on the floor next to Joseph and cracked a pistachio, popping it into his mouth. Joseph studied his son's face, and marvelled at the miracle of how he had come to be their son. His heart was heavy but grateful that Jesus would soon know he, Joseph the carpenter, was his father not by blood but by adoption. Mary came back and sat with Joseph and Jesus, locking eyes with Joseph as she removed Ahura's letter from the folds of her skirt and handed it to her husband. Mary's journal rested on the floor next to her.

Max, Kate, Clarie, and Liz sat together in the corner. Max nudged Al awake. "Ye don't want ta miss this, lad." Their hearts were pounding with what was getting ready to happen in the humble home of this family not rich in wealth but wealthy in the riches of God. Nigel scurried over to huddle with the animals, eager to witness Jesus' reaction.

Joseph cleared his throat and nodded to Mary, then began, "Jesus, there is something your mother and I need to share with you. This might be hard for you to understand, as you are still young, but we know that Jehovah will speak to your heart and make it clear with time."

Jesus looked at Joseph and then at Mary with a question on his face. "What is it, Father?"

"You are no ordinary boy," Joseph began. He looked at Mary, still uncertain of how to say the right words. "You have heard us teach you about God, our people, and the prophecies since you could speak. Even though you didn't understand at first, you now understand the Law of Moses and the history of our people." Joseph took a deep breath. "So you know about the prophecies of Messiah."

"Yes, Father. Messiah has been promised to the people. When he comes he will comfort them. He will save them," Jesus said simply.

Joseph nodded and placed his strong hand on Jesus' shoulder. "Indeed he will. And according to the prophecies of Daniel, the time for Messiah's arrival is at hand. Daniel wrote in Babylon about Messiah's arrival." He hesitated and handed Jesus the letter from Ahura. "Another wise man from Babylon also wrote to confirm that Messiah, the King of the Jews, has now come."

Mary's eyes brimmed with tears as Jesus looked at her and Joseph with curiosity. Jesus carefully unfolded the letter, written in Hebrew, and began to read:

Greetings, Blessed Ones:

I send this letter to you, the parents of Messiah, as my gift for the child. My heart longed to be there to see the promised child with my eyes, but my age kept me from the journey. I write to you with this affirmation. Your Son is the Chosen One of God, as foretold by the prophet Isaiah. I

103

have studied the prophecies as well as the heavens for the signs of his arrival. As Magi, it is our duty to approve the validity of kings for our nation. It appears from what was revealed to us that we also have the privilege of approving the validity of your Son as King of the Jews. I shall recount for you the events that were recorded in the heavens that led us to Him.

On the night of Rosh Hashanah, the King Planet Jupiter passed the King Star Sharu, in the constellation of the lion, the symbol of the tribe of Judah. But there was more. The crescent moon followed Virgo as the sun passed through, symbolizing a virgin and new birth. According to Isaiah, "The virgin will conceive a child. She will give birth to a son and will call him Immanuel."

We studied the ancient scrolls of the Hebrews, and in the book of Numbers we read that "a star will rise from Jacob; a scepter will emerge from Israel." That star did rise, announcing the birth of the One who will hold a scepter: a King. Nine months after the first wondrous events in the heavens on Rosh Hashana, the brightest star the world has ever seen shone in the sky, right over Judea. We had been waiting for this moment, and our hearts rejoiced on that day. Isaiah even foretold our rejoicing, writing, "In the west people will respect the name of the Lord; in the east they will glorify him." We knew we must come to Him when we further read this passage: "Vast caravans of camels will converge on you, the camels of Midian and Ephah. The people of Sheba will bring gold and frankincense and will come worshipping the Lord." We knew then that this King was not just a man, for worship alone belongs to God.

We also read that "Jerusalem gives birth to a son," verifying the location of the star and the place we must begin our search. If you are reading this letter, my fellow Magi indeed found you, and have brought gifts for your Son. The gold is for His royalty, and the frankincense is for his deity. The myrrh is for his humanity. I was overcome with

104

emotion as I read from Isaiah that he would be a man of sorrows, acquainted with grief, and would be struck down with the sins of all laid upon him.

I knew as I read about this King of the Jews that he would be and do the unexpected. Only God could become man from a virgin. Only God could be sinless to pay for sin. And only a man could die as Isaiah foretold. The King of the Jews is coming, not to rule as a man, but to die as a man—to save the people as God.

I must confess I do not understand the great mystery about your son. Expect the unexpected with him. But know that what has happened to you with his birth was prophesied by Isaiah and revealed to us Gentiles in word and with a star. All nations will come to his light.

May the God of Abraham, Isaac, and Jacob bless you as you raise this special child. And when the time is right, may the words I have written be shared with him, the Messiah, the King of the Jews.

Ahura Yazda

Nigel, overcome with emotion, squeezed Liz's paw when Jesus finished reading. The mouse had been there when Ahura wrote the letter. Now to hear it read by Messiah himself was surreal.

Jesus slowly put the letter in his lap and looked up at his parents in reverent awe. He didn't speak but tried to absorb what he had just read. Mary handed him her journal.

"Jesus, there is more. I have written to you since before you were born, about the miracle of my pregnancy with you, about the day of your birth, and about events ever since," Mary explained softly. "The Magi did come to see you with those gifts. We saw the star the night you were born. It was the most incredible thing I had ever seen, except of course for you. Shepherds also saw the star and came," she said, looking over at the animals. "They are the ones who gave us Clarie, Tovah, and Chava. It's all there in my journal."

Jesus looked back at the animals and smiled. Their hearts leapt within them. His gaze was somehow different. He saw Nigel hiding under Max's legs and locked eyes with the small mouse. Nigel started to hide, but something told him it was okay. He beamed back at the boy, showing himself for the first time to a human without fear of being chased away.

"Do you understand what we are sharing with you, Jesus?" Joseph asked.

"I am . . . Messiah?" Jesus asked in wonder.

"Yes, Jesus. You are Messiah, the King of the Jews," Joseph answered warmly. He looked around their humble home. "I know this doesn't look much like a palace."

"Expect the unexpected," Jesus softly murmured, echoing Ahura's words. He looked deeply into the eyes of Mary and held her journal to his chest. He was overcome with emotion. "Mother, Father, may it be for me as you have said."

Joseph and Mary enveloped Jesus with their arms and the blessed family shared a quiet moment together.

106

Early that evening Jesus took Mary's journal and told his parents he needed some time alone. Mary and Joseph hugged him and told him to take all the time he needed.

"He's leavin'," Max said to Kate. "I think I need ta be with the lad."

"Go, me love," Kate said with a nudge of her head.

"*Oui,* I feel the need to go as well," Liz said, standing.

Max barked and together he and Liz trotted outside after Jesus. He looked and saw the two black animals running behind him. "Want to come along?"

Jesus led them on a ten-minute hike up the hill and looked out at the incredible view of Galilee. He took a deep breath as he gazed out at the land where so many events had taken place in the history of God's people. Looking north he gazed across the beautiful hills and valleys to the snow-capped Mt. Hermon out in the distance. Just three miles away was Jonah's ancient hometown. Jesus smiled as he thought about Jonah trying to run from God and landing in the belly of a big fish for three days before he obeyed and went to Nineveh.

Jesus turned and looked south to see the beautiful Plain of Esdraelon that ran from the Jordan River to the Mediterranean Sea. Nearby was the spring of Harod, where Gideon and his three hundred men defeated the Midianites. He could see Jezreel, where wicked Jezebel met a bad end after killing many of God's servants. Jesus also saw Mt. Gilboa, where the Philistines killed King Saul.

Ten miles to the west was Mt. Carmel, where Elijah had a contest with the priests of Baal and called down fire from heaven. Just eight miles south was Shunem, where Elisha had raised a boy to life. *I wonder what that would feel like?* Jesus thought. He felt an overwhelming sense of destiny as his gaze then took him ten miles to the southwest to view the pass of Armageddon.

So much history to take in, all within view of this hill. Jesus loved to come here, but after what he learned today, the realization that this history all pointed to Messiah's coming became even more important to him. He sat down in the cool grass. The setting sun was giving the sky a beautiful pink hue, and big puffy clouds slowly drifted across the sky. Max lay down next to Jesus, putting his head on his front paws. Liz sat quietly by, her gaze on Mary's journal. Jesus slowly rubbed Max's head as he read Mary's entries about his birth in Bethlehem. The Star. The Shepherds. Clarie. So much to take in. After a while Jesus closed his eyes.

107

"Father, thank you for showing me your purpose for me. Help me do what you ask me to do. Show me how," Jesus prayed.

He sat in silence for a long time, communing with his heavenly Father. Max and Liz prayed, too. It was a holy moment.

After a while, Jesus opened his eyes and put a hand out to softly pet Liz. "So you were there the night I was born."

Liz blinked her eyes warmly at Jesus and meowed, *"Oui, mon Roi."*

Max lifted his head. "And so were you," Jesus said, grinning at Max.

"Aye, lad," Max barked happily at Jesus' touch.

Jesus nodded slowly and gave them both a knowing look. He then turned his gaze to the setting sun and there in the sky appeared the Fire Cloud. Max and Liz gasped in awe as the cloud that had led them to the Ark so long ago now blazed in fiery glory before them. Their fur stood on end at the power of the cloud. But the emotions they felt were far surpassed with Jesus' next words.

"Ah oui, le nuage de feu. Est-ce ainsi que vous vous en souvenez, Liz?" Jesus asked. Liz's jaw dropped, for he had just said, "Ah yes, the Fire Cloud. Is this how you remember it, Liz?"

"Wha' aboot ye, Max?" Jesus asked with a Scottish brogue, turning to the speechless Scottie. "Ye followed this Fire Cloud a long way, lad."

Max and Liz looked at each other, tingling from head to toe to hear Jesus speak to them in their native tongues. But besides that, he knew who they were!

"Jesus, you . . . you know who we are?" Liz finally asked.

"Of course. My Father just told me," Jesus answered with joy. "He told me about all of you. Kate, Al, Nigel, and Clarie, too. But don't worry. It will be our secret. I am glad to finally meet you in person."

"Enchanté, mon Roi," Liz said, bowing her head in respect and awe. "It is an honor to serve you."

"Aye," Max echoed, "but I am a wee bit surprised then. We've never talked ta a human before."

"Speak for yourself," Liz corrected Max.

"Yes, Liz, Isaiah told me you talked to him," Jesus said, then shook his head in wonder. "How did I know that?"

Liz put her dainty paw on Jesus' hand. "But you have come from heaven, no? I believe you will remember things as they come back to you, when the Maker thinks you should recall them."

"This is hard for me to understand," Jesus said. "I'm just a human kid. But I'm the Son of God. I guess that makes me the Son of Man."

"I'm glad we can be here for ye, Jesus," Max said. "Jest tell us wha' ta do, an' we'll do it."

Jesus gathered Max and Liz into his arms. "Just be my friends. That's what I need. This is going to be hard. Besides my parents, you animals will be the only ones who really know who I am."

"Aye, jest like ye're the only One who knows who *we* be," Max affirmed.

"Of course, Jesus. We will be with you every step of the way," Liz promised. "But there is another human who knows who you are. Rabbi Isaac knows and believes in you."

"Rabbi Isaac?" Jesus replied with surprised delight. "He is my teacher! I can actually talk to him about this?"

"Oui, but of course," Liz replied. "He is the one who stood up for your parents with blessing when the village discovered your mother was pregnant. You can trust him."

A wide grin grew on Max's face. "I jest thought how Al is goin' ta react when Jesus talks ta him with an Ir-r-rish br-r-rogue! He's bound ta jump r-r-right out of his fur."

Jesus and Liz laughed at the thought. The three of them sat together and watched the sun finally fade away, leaving the Fire Cloud illuminating the night sky as God's gift of affirmation. The Great I AM hovered over them, delighting in their bond of friendship that would last for all time.

109

14

JESUS AND RABBI ISAAC

The next morning Jesus was up early working with Joseph. Max and Liz told Nigel and Clarie about their incredible encounter with Jesus. Nigel couldn't wait to speak with him, but of course, Al slept through the discussion. They decided they would let the sleepy cat get the shock from Jesus himself.

"I finished my chores, Mother. Father has gone to work on Samuel's home. Can I do anything for you here?" Jesus asked, wiping the sweat from his brow. Mary sat on the floor grinding the grain for bread. He plopped down next to her and took a piece of grain in his fingers, studying it closely.

"Thank you, Jesus, but you've worked enough for today." Mary smiled at her Son. "How are you feeling about things? Is there anything you would like to talk about?"

Jesus wrapped his arms around his knees and thought a moment. "Tell me about that Roman family you mentioned in your journal."

Mary nodded fondly. "Yes. Marcus and Julia Antonius. We met them the day we dedicated you at the Temple in Jerusalem. We stayed in Bethlehem after you were born, and your father was blessed with solid work in Jerusalem. These Romans had moved from Rome to Jerusalem for Marcus to assume his role as centurion there. His wife Julia and their son Armandus were riding by when a wheel came off their carriage.

Your father assisted them, and I could tell that Julia was quite lonely. We showed them kindness and followed them back to their home." Mary paused and looked up at Jesus. "We did the unthinkable for Jews. We entered their home."

"Rabbi Isaac teaches that to enter a Gentile's home defiles a Jew," Jesus said. "What made you do it?"

"I felt in my heart that Jehovah wanted us to reach out to this pagan family," Mary said, putting her hand over her heart. "It seemed more proper to see them as individual people lost in darkness than as a race that would taint us. You were in my arms, Jesus, and I felt that Roman home needed your light brought inside."

"So what happened?" Jesus asked, now leaning back with his hands on the floor behind him.

"Well, your father did some work on their home and we became friends with this family. Julia and I talked about matters of the heart frequently. They were so spiritually hungry, Jesus!" Mary exclaimed, remembering that unusual encounter. "Their little boy Armandus was a couple of years older than you, and was such a bundle of energy. He loved it when we came over to visit. Once he said he liked your eyes." Mary leaned over and squeezed Jesus' foot affectionately. "Even as a baby you were touching lives with joy."

Jesus smiled and placed his hand over hers. "Well, I have a mother who shows me how to treat people with love. So, you never saw them again? Marcus and Julia?"

"No, one horrible night we had to flee to Egypt, and we have never returned to Bethlehem. Your father was told in a dream when Herod died it was safe to return to Israel, but he was warned in another dream not to return to Judea where Herod's wicked son Archelaus ruled. So we decided to come back home, here to Nazareth," Mary explained. "Of course we go to Jerusalem every year for the Passover feast but we travel with such a large group that we go unnoticed by those who sought to harm you. I've often wondered about the Antonius family."

Jesus hung his head and shook it sadly. "I can't believe all those babies were killed because . . . Herod sent those soldiers looking for *me.*"

Mary reached out and cupped Jesus' face in her hand. "I have wept for those mothers since that night. Such is the evil that will stop at nothing to extinguish the Light of the world. You should know that Rabbi

111

Isaac lost his only grandson on that terrible night in Bethlehem."

Jesus' eyes widened in grief and alarm. "Oh, Mother! That breaks my heart for Rebbe. He is such a good, wise, big-hearted man." Jesus' face grew angry at the thought. "I hate death."

Mary pondered silently for a moment what Jesus had said. She knew a sword would pierce her heart someday but she couldn't think about it now. She shook her head in an attempt to clear her mind. "Jesus, you can trust Rabbi Isaac. Besides your grandparents and us, he is the only other one who knows that you are Messiah."

"I think I will go see him," Jesus said, giving Mary a kiss on the cheek. "Thank you, Mother."

"*Shalom*, dear one," Mary replied as she watched Jesus leave their humble home. "Go give Rebbe your light."

Nigel was waiting for Jesus outside. "Pssst!" he called as Jesus walked by the stone wall where the mouse sat, giddy with excitement. Jesus stopped and looked up to see Nigel there. The boy grinned and looked both ways to make sure no one else was around.

"Good morning, Nigel," Jesus said with a wink. "May I?" Jesus gently picked Nigel up and placed him in the palm of his hand.

"Utterly thrilling to officially meet you, Jesus! Well, I've known you since you were a wee chap, but never having had the pleasure to actually *chat* with you, this makes for a splendid occasion for me," Nigel enthused as Jesus held the small mouse up to his face. The mouse bowed humbly with his small paw draped over his chest, one foot forward. "Nigel P. Monaco, your humble servant."

"Nice to meet you officially, too, Nigel," Jesus said. "Thank you for helping me all along the way." Jesus touched his finger to his eyes. "I like your . . . what do you call them?"

"Spectacles, dear boy," Nigel said, straightening them and looking around Jesus' hand. "I'd be blind as a bat without them, I'm afraid. I say, I've never experienced this sensation of being held by a human. Quite smashing!"

"Well, I can carry you around with me whenever and wherever you like," Jesus said with a broad smile. "Would you like to go with me to see Rabbi Isaac?"

"That would take the biscuit!" Nigel said. "Al is already there, eating the poor Rabbi out of house and fish."

"I haven't met Al officially yet, but I hear he's *quite* funny to talk to," Jesus said with a playful British accent as he started walking down the street with Nigel in his hand. "Of course he's funny just as a simple house cat."

Nigel chuckled. "I look forward with great eagerness to watching his response to you."

"I tell you this, cat, you have more *chutzpah* than any cat I've ever seen to come here day after day, eating all my dried fish. True? Of course, true!" Rabbi Isaac said with a wave of his hand at the plump orange cat. The old man playfully complained, but in truth, he loved Al's company and made sure there was always dried fish on hand for the hungry feline.

Al stretched out long and hard and rolled on the floor with his belly exposed. *"Aye, lad. Thanks for the fish."* Al's eyelids grew heavy. He felt a nap coming on.

113

Jesus and Nigel arrived but Jesus stopped at the door. "I guess you'd better stay out of sight, Nigel. I'll set you down when we get inside, okay?"

"Of course," Nigel agreed. "Never fear, I've been hiding from humans for centuries!"

Jesus knocked on the door and was greeted by a delighted rabbi. "Ah, *shalom*, Jesus! What brings you to my house? Come in, come in, eh?" Rabbi Isaac eagerly ushered Jesus in.

"Shalom, Rebbe," Jesus replied, following the old man inside. He knelt down and quickly released Nigel to go find a hiding spot. "I wanted to talk with you if you have a moment."

"For you, *yeled*, of course. Have a seat, eh?" Rabbi Isaac motioned to the mat on the floor and the two of them sat down.

Jesus saw Al sound asleep on the floor and smiled. "I see Ari has made himself at home and helped himself to your fish as usual."

Isaac chuckled and leaned forward to whisper. "Yes, that cat is *meshuga*—crazy— but don't tell him I like his visits every day," he said with a wink. "Now, tell me what do you wish to discuss?"

"Rebbe," Jesus started, hesitating. "My father and mother told me the truth about my birth. They told me who I am."

Rabbi Isaac's eyes widened and he nodded slowly. "So the time is here. Yes, you are Messiah. I have looked forward to this day when we could talk freely about it. I know it came as a shock. It isn't every day you find out you are God, *nu?*" He patted Jesus on the back with affirmation. The wise old man always had a way of making people feel at ease. "I am humbled that my Lord would allow me to know you like this."

"I'm grateful that you're in our lives, Rebbe. You were the one who helped my parents when the village discovered my mother was obviously pregnant before they wed," Jesus said. "I know it was risky to do that."

"I had *ein brerah*—no choice, eh? These people didn't know whose child they were dealing with. You are Messiah, so I must do what Jehovah would have me do," Isaac replied. "It was a privilege then and it will continue to be a privilege to stand up for you."

"My mother also told me you lost a grandson in Bethlehem, when they were after me," Jesus said somberly. "I'm so sorry, Rebbe. Your grandson died in my place."

114

Rabbi Isaac's eyes filled with tears and he clenched his jaw to hold back his emotions. "And you, Jesus, would do the same if you could. True? Of *course,* true." He wiped his eyes and got a determined look on his face. "The years ahead will be hard for you, Jesus. You are not what the people expect Messiah to be. And when people's expectations are not met, they rise up in protest. But know this," he said with a finger raised in the front of them. "I will stand by you no matter what comes. I give you my word."

"Thank you, Rebbe. I don't understand everything about what I am to do. But for now I will learn from you as you teach me the Torah—the Law—and the Prophets, and my Father will show me what to do," Jesus replied. "It's good to know I'm not alone."

"*Yihyeh beseder*—it will all work out," Rabbi Isaac said with hands raised. "With the help of Jehovah, you will do what he has brought you here to do. But for now, you are a boy, eh? We will talk of this from time to time, but focus on just being *Jesus.* Don't worry about the rest."

Jesus smiled. "*Toda*, Rebbe. Thank you. That helps. I'm glad I don't have to have all the answers now."

"Good, good," Isaac replied with a pat on Jesus' back.

Al yawned with a loud groan and stood to stretch and arch his back.

He saw Jesus sitting there and walked over to headbutt the boy.

"I guess Ari and I will be going now," Jesus said, picking Al up in his arms. "Thank you for your time, Rebbe. *Shalom.*"

"*Shalom,* Jesus," the old man replied. "Come by anytime. I am always here." Amos hee-hawed at that moment from the stall in the other room, where the old man kept his animals. Rabbi Isaac rolled his eyes. "Except for when I'm out looking for Amos. I was glad your parents gave him back to me when they returned to Nazareth, but he has the itch to get out and travel even more now. True? Of course, true!"

Jesus laughed and looked on the floor for Nigel. When he saw the mouse scurry out the door he waved good-bye and carried Al outside. Al loved to be carried by humans so he didn't have to walk. Nigel jumped up on Jesus' tunic and climbed up to his shoulder.

Al suddenly saw Nigel sitting there on Jesus' shoulder and a look of fear and panic spread across his face. He tried to make eye signals to Nigel to get off before he was caught. *"GET . . . DOWN!"* he mouthed to Nigel. The mouse grinned back at Al and tipped his hand in the air as if to say, "Hello, old boy!"

Al looked from Nigel to Jesus and back to Nigel nervously. Jesus looked down at Al and smiled. "What is it, Ari? Something bothering you?"

Al smiled weakly and continued to try to signal to Nigel that he'd better get off Jesus' shoulder or he would be caught.

Jesus stopped and turned his head, seeing Nigel there. Al's paws went up to his mouth in panic. Jesus and Nigel shared a smile before the boy looked at Al and spoke in a thick Irish accent. "Sure, and there's nothin' to be worried aboot, Big Al. It's jest Nigel."

Al's eyes got as wide as saucers before they rolled up in his head and he fainted right there in Jesus' arms.

"Jolly good show!" Nigel said, holding his stomach with laughter. "I say, you've given Al quite the shock of his life!"

Jesus stroked Al tenderly and laughed. "Don't worry, I'll wake him up gently soon. Something tells me I'm going to have that effect on people a lot when I grow up."

"Indeed, Jesus, I'm quite sure you will," Nigel agreed, sitting on Jesus' shoulder. "But that's just what the world needs from Messiah—a stunning shock followed by a gentle awakening."

15

The Passover Lamb

THREE YEARS LATER

I think we have everything, Joseph," Mary told her husband as she handed him the last remaining satchel for their trip. Joseph carried it outside to pack it onto Amos. She turned to her mother, Sarah, who was holding their young toddler Joses by the hand, and smiled at her daughter Sarah, who was making Joses giggle. "Mother, thank you for watching the children and the animals while we're gone. We'll be in Jerusalem eight days for the Passover feast. Four days travel there and four days back, so we'll be back in a little over two weeks. Do you think you can manage?"

"Of course, Mary," her mother replied. "Little Sarah can help me take care of Simon and Joses. James is excited about feeding the animals while you're gone. Don't worry about us."

Mary embraced her mother and leaned down to kiss little Joses. "Thank you, Mother. This is a big trip for Jesus, and it will be easier without the little ones in tow. Jesus? Are you ready?"

"Almost, Mother. Be right there," Jesus called back.

Liz and Nigel sat on the floor with Jesus while he packed his knapsack. "How I wish I could go with you two," Liz lamented. "I know it will be a special trip."

"I wish you could go, too, Liz," Jesus answered, giving Liz a petting on the head. "But since there are so many people traveling in the

116

caravan, we have to pack light. My younger siblings are even staying home, so please make sure they are safe. Nigel, you can hide in my headscarf on my shoulder, okay?"

"I understand, of course," Liz said. "We will make sure all is well here."

"Right! I shall stay hidden and try not to tickle your neck," Nigel said, climbing into the folds of Jesus' headscarf. He snuggled down and poked his tiny face out. "Cheerio, Liz."

"Farewell, *mes amis. Bon voyage,*" Liz said as Jesus walked outside to join the growing caravan lining up in the street.

Max, Kate, and Clarie stood outside, watching Joseph pack. "Looks like a gr-r-rand adventure awaits," Max said as Jesus leaned over to pet them farewell.

Jesus whispered, "Aye," and winked at Max and Kate. "You take care of things, okay?" He came to Clarie and stared intently into her eyes. "I'm glad you are staying here, little one."

Clarie nodded. *"Shalom,* Jesus."

117

"Amos, are you ready? Why would you not be ready with Joseph packing you up so well, eh?" Rabbi Isaac said, patting the donkey on the rump. "You get your annual trip to Jerusalem but you may not be happy with an old man like me riding you, *nu*"? He proceeded to climb onto Amos as Joseph gave him a hand, grunting as he hefted himself up. *"Oi!* This gets higher every time I get up here!"

"Hee-haw!" Amos groaned as the old man wiggled his backside around to get comfortable. Isaac saw Jesus' brother James holding the orange cat, Ari. "James, I almost forgot," he said, tossing a pouch to the boy. "There should be enough dried fish to hold him." James caught the bag and Al immediately started pawing at it.

"A partin' gift!" Al meowed gleefully. *"I'll try to make it last."*

"Let's be off," Joseph said, leading Amos by the reins. Mary and Jesus waved good-bye and blended into the caravan of people, carts, and donkeys making the eighty-mile trip to Jerusalem.

The sights and sounds of several hundred thousand people descending on Jerusalem was staggering. Dust kicked up from the countless donkeys, camels, and horses riding by with Roman soldiers eyeing the crowds for troublemakers. Travel-weary yet grateful, Mary looked behind at the long line of sojourners in their group of about a hundred people from Galilee to get a glimpse of Joseph and Rabbi Isaac. "Do you see them, Jesus?"

Jesus' eyes were gaping at the walls surrounding the magnificent city, and the throngs of people making their way up the ancient ramps to enter the gates of Jerusalem. "Look, Nigel," he said quietly. "Jerusalem! We made it!"

Nigel peeked out and smiled as he recalled the delicious moment of arrival in this city after the long, hard journey from Babylon with the Wise Men long ago. That trip was several hundred miles compared with the eighty they had made from Nazareth, but the wonderful feeling of arrival was just as sweet. "Ah, the splendor of Jerusalem!"

"Jesus, did you hear me?" Mary asked again.

"Oh, sorry, Mother," Jesus said, looking back along the line of children to the women and finally to the men, who traveled in the back of the caravan. "I don't see them yet."

118

"Well, let's wait off to the side until they catch up with us," Mary said, pulling Jesus aside. "Then we can find our way to cousin Micah's house. But, we're here!" She wrapped her arm around Jesus and together they looked up at the magnificent city. Memories flooded back into her mind, both happy and sad. But she thought of the wonderful experience ahead for Jesus. "I can't wait for you to experience your first Passover in Jerusalem."

Jesus nodded. "I've looked forward to this, too, Mother. Now that I'm twelve years old, I'm just about ready to join the men in the back of the caravan. Maybe next year I can walk back there with Father and Rabbi Isaac."

"You are growing into such a fine young man, Jesus. Yes, and maybe you can even join them back there on the way home," Mary replied with an affirming smile. The children and women always walked in the front of the caravan to set the pace so they would not be left behind. The men walked at the back to protect the caravan.

A group of shepherds approached with a flock of bleating sheep, merging into the mass of people entering the city. The sheep were being taken to the Temple for sacrifice. Mary and Jesus stepped back to let them pass. Mary looked at Jesus. "The sacrifical lambs. Father will get one for us when we get in the city."

Jesus nodded silently as he watched the lambs joining the ranks of a quarter million sheep that would be slaughtered for the Passover. So much blood. So much sin to atone for. So much death. Never-ending death.

"Here we are," Joseph said, smiling as he guided Amos over to where Mary and Jesus stood. "Let's get in the city, and then, Jesus, you can go with me and Rabbi Isaac to sacrifice a lamb while your mother prepares the meal."

Jesus nodded. "I'm ready to see how this is done, Father."

Joseph put his hand on Jesus' back and together the family walked into Jerusalem.

The chaos around the Temple grew with each passing hour. Beggars packed every corner, playing on the sympathies of pilgrims whose minds were focused on God and doing what pleased him. Merchants sold sacrificial animals and special items needed for the Passover meal. The sounds of haggling and moneychanging mixed in with the bleating of lambs and the shouting of men. Priests continually sang the Hallel, Psalms 115–118, after the sacrifice of each animal whose blood was splattered on the altar. The blood of thousands of animals ran like a river off the altar out the back of the Temple grounds. It flowed down the hill into the Kidron Brook until it was blood red, following a southward course into the Valley of Hinnom.

Joseph, Rabbi Isaac, and Jesus entered this scene unfolding on the grounds of the magnificent Temple of Herod. Jesus gaped in awe at the height of the Temple walls and the size of the massive menorah candelabras. Fires burned with the aroma of incense rising into the air. The throngs of Jews assembled for this occasion came to Jerusalem for the Passover as one of the three annual festivals to remember God's provision for his people. Passover lasted only one day but was followed by the Feast of Unleavened Bread, which lasted seven days. While many Jews only came for two or three days, Joseph and Mary showed their deep commitment to the Lord by staying for the duration.

"What do you think, eh? A fine lamb!" Rabbi Isaac said as he and Joseph paid the merchant and gave the lamb to Jesus. "You will take him to the priest yourself, Jesus."

119

The lamb bleated and Jesus looked into its face, touching it tenderly. He looked up at his father with pain in his eyes but knew what needed to happen.

"A male lamb without blemish, Jesus," Joseph said, touching Jesus on the shoulder. "An acceptable sacrifice to the Lord to pay for sin."

Jesus picked up the lamb and carried it as he walked with the men to the sacrificial altar. The priests slaying the sacrificial animals were covered with blood from the endless stream of lambs. Jesus looked at the severity of the process and felt the weight of God's anger at sin. It must be paid for. Man could never pay for it himself, so the bloodshed would never end. That is, until the time came. Jesus knew he would be the Lamb of God who would take away the sins of the world. The reality of his mission came rushing into his spirit, but so did the grace of God. While Jesus' heart broke, it was enveloped by the peace that passes understanding.

As they stepped up to the priest, Jesus held the lamb close to his heart and whispered in its ear, "Thank you, little one. *Shalom."* A tear slipped from his eye as he handed the spotless lamb to the priest. He watched as the lamb was slain, its blood sprinkled on the altar.

This process took a while, and the lamb was prepared with its fat burned on the altar while one of the priests held his hands up and sang,

"The LORD is my strength and my song; he has become my salvation. Glad songs of salvation are in the tents of the righteous: 'The right hand of the LORD does valiantly; the right hand of the LORD exalts, the right hand of the LORD does valiantly!' I shall not die, but I shall live, and recount the deeds of the LORD."

"Amen," Nigel whispered softly in the ear of Jesus, who was wiping the tears from his eyes.

Finally it was time to take the lamb back for the Seder meal. *"Mazal tov,* Jesus!" Rabbi Isaac said with a slap on Jesus' back. "You have completed your first sacrifice according to the Law."

Joseph smiled and said, "Well done, Son. Now we take the lamb for the Passover feast. We must eat it tonight, leaving none of it until morning. We must also take care not to break any of its bones. The women will prepare the lamb's body with spices and bitter herbs."

Jesus nodded and obediently followed Joseph as they departed for the home where they were staying in Jerusalem. He looked at the lifeless form of the lamb. "Your blood was shed, and now your body is broken for us."

Nigel took in from his hiding place every word Jesus said, moved to the depths of his soul by what he knew this ritual meant today, and what it would mean at a future Passover in Jerusalem.

The candlelight flickered on the wall of the *kataluma,* or guest room, where the family and friends reclined around the outside of the U-shaped table. They supported their upper bodies by leaning on their left elbows as they reclined on the colorful cushions. Traditionally, only freemen ate while reclining. While the first Passover meal in Egypt was eaten in haste while standing, tradition changed as rabbis taught that Jews should eat the Passover meal reclining as a free people to show that God had redeemed them from Egypt.

The family and friends sang psalms to worship God and celebrate the redemption he gave them through the lamb. At the end of the meal, it was time for the tradition of the oldest son asking his father an important question. Mary nodded to Jesus and smiled.

Jesus sat up and asked Joseph, "Why is this night different from all the others?"

Joseph lifted his hands and replied:

"With a mighty hand the Lord brought us out of Egypt, out of the land of slavery. When Pharaoh stubbornly refused to let us go, the Lord killed every firstborn in Egypt, both man and animal. But those who had slaughtered a lamb and put the blood on the doorpost of the home were saved. The tenth plague—the Angel of Death—passed over the home that was protected by the blood of the lamb. Salvation came only through the sacrificial lamb."

He was oppressed and afflicted, yet he did not open his mouth. Like a lamb led to the slaughter, Jesus suddenly remembered from Isaiah 53, swallowing hard as he thought about the prophecies about Messiah. About himself. *My righteous Servant will justify many.*

"*L'chaim!* To life!" Rabbi Isaac said as he raised a glass. "Praise Jehovah for his goodness!"

"L'chaim!" the family and friends there echoed as they broke into songs of praise to the Lord.

To life, Jesus thought to himself. *No . . . More . . . Death.* He remembered the words of Hosea and in that moment claimed them as his own: *I will ransom them from the power of the grave; I will redeem them from death: O death, I will be thy plagues; O grave, I will be thy destruction!*

Nigel sat high on a shelf enjoying the celebration. He tilted his head, squinting with one eye closed as Rabbi Isaac started singing off key. Nigel pointed his finger up in the air, willing the old man to hit the right pitch. No matter. It was a joyful noise. *What a splendid idea, to set Scripture to music,* Nigel thought to himself. *How I would love to do that someday.*

A very full Rabbi Isaac slowly got up from the table and patted his belly. "I don't care if you think I'm *meshuga* with my big feet, I must dance, eh?!" The old man started to dance, lifting his hands in the air and singing at the top of his lungs as the people clapped, slowly at first but gaining volume and speed. Joy and laughter filled the room at the celebration of life. *"Oi, HaRosh mistovev!* My head is spinning!" Rabbi Isaac said with a hand to his head as he turned around and around. The circle of dancers grew with hands held together and hearts lifted in song.

Joseph gave his hand to Jesus who joined him in the circle to dance in praise to God. Jesus gazed into the faces of Rabbi Isaac, Joseph, and Mary and smiled, knowing that someday the celebration would never end. When death was no more.

"How do you like the matzah, eh?" Rabbi Isaac asked, nibbling a piece of the flat bread. "It looks like it has been pierced, *nu?* And see here the stripes where it is grilled," Rabbi Isaac pointed out. "Do you remember why we must eat this bread of life for seven days after Passover, Jesus?"

Jesus held the flat bread up to the light and saw the holes. He then studied the grill marks. *He was pierced for our transgressions,* Jesus recalled from Isaiah 53. *By his stripes we are healed.*

"We eat this bread made without leaven, or yeast, to remember how the Israelites didn't have time to let their bread rise when they fled Egypt. They had to leave in haste, taking it with them to eat for their journey," Jesus replied, taking a bite of the matzah. *Bread of life.*

"And what does the leaven symbolize in Scripture?" Rabbi Isaac continued, crumbs falling into his salt-and-pepper beard.

"Leaven represents sin, so this is why we had to clean the house of any leaven before Passover," Jesus replied. "It's like a search to remove any hypocrisy or wickedness in the house. Matzah means 'without sin.'"

Rabbi Isaac held his hands out with emphatic delight. "What a smart boy! True? Of course, true!"

Joseph and Mary shared glances of pride at their son. "Well done, Jesus," Joseph told his boy. "I think this has been a great week of celebration and learning in Jerusalem!" He patted Jesus on the knee. "We're proud of you, Son."

"Thank you, Father," Jesus replied humbly. "Thank you, too, Rabbi Isaac, for teaching me so much. I could sit and talk like this all day!"

"Well, it is time to go home. Mary, we need to pack this last bit of food and get Amos ready," Joseph instructed. "I want to take Jesus around part of the city before we leave. We'll meet up with the caravan at the Golden Gate. Jesus, grab your knapsack."

"Very well, Joseph," Mary said, wrapping up the food and gathering their few remaining items as Jesus went to get his things. "You take Jesus, and Rabbi Isaac and I will meet you there soon with Amos. Oh, and I told Jesus that maybe he could walk in the back of the caravan with the men."

Joseph raised his eyebrows. "Ah, well, we'll see. Jesus is certainly mature enough, isn't he?" He gave Mary a kiss and whispered in her ear, "I'm a blessed man. Thank you, my love, for giving me such a wonderful son. A father couldn't be more proud."

Mary cupped Joseph's face in her hands. "Thank you for believing me about him so long ago. You are such a wonderful father, Joseph."

"Okay, I'm ready," Jesus said, fiddling with his headscarf, trying to get Nigel situated.

"We'll see you there, Mary, Rebbe," Joseph told them as he and Jesus left the house.

Although most of the crowds had departed the city, it was still extremely crowded in the narrow streets of Jerusalem. Joseph took Jesus around and showed him the Pool of Siloam and explained about Hezekiah's Tunnel, which brought water into the city.

"King Hezekiah was preparing the city for a siege by the Assyrian King Sennacherib and had this tunnel built so the people would have water," Joseph explained.

"Remind me to tell you about that cheeky Sennacherib fellow and how I routed his general and his troops with my pigeons," Nigel whispered in Jesus' ear with a chuckle.

Jesus smiled. "Hezekiah's Tunnel is amazing, Father. There is so much history here, it's hard to take it all in."

"Yes, Jehovah has always protected his people within these walls when they submitted to his authority," Joseph said. "But when they turn their backs on Him, certain destruction comes, as it did when King Nebuchadnezzar of Babylon took the people captive and sacked the city."

"Oh, I have so many stories about Daniel when he was taken to Babylon, too!" Nigel whispered. "Quite the splendid fellow. Had it not been for Daniel, the Wise Men would not have found you as a baby. Brilliant!"

"But Jehovah always has his remnant of people who keep believing and trusting him," Joseph said, wrapping his arms around his son. "Even though many turn away, Jehovah only needs a few faithful followers to accomplish his purposes. Remember that." Joseph looked at the rising sun. "We'd best go meet the caravan. Time to go home."

As Joseph and Jesus made their way to the Golden Gate they walked by the Temple and Jesus saw a group of men seated in the courtyard, having an intense discussion. Curious, he stopped to listen. They were discussing Daniel's prophecies. "Father, can we stop a moment and listen?"

Joseph hesitated but knew how eager Jesus was to hear such discussions. The greatest Jewish teachers in all the Roman world had gathered here in Jerusalem for the Passover feast, constantly discussing the Law, the Prophets, poetry, history, and, of course, Messiah. These were expert minds, and Jesus absorbed like a sponge the things they talked about. Joseph knew it would take a little while to finish packing up the caravan.

"Okay, look, you see the Beautiful Gate right there?" Joseph said, pointing to the entrance of the Temple area. "Just past that is the Golden Gate. We'll be waiting for you with the caravan."

"Golden Gate. Caravan. Okay, Father," Jesus answered, already pulled into the discussion of Daniel's Seventy Weeks Prophecy. He leaned his head forward, listening intently to what the teachers were saying.

Joseph left Jesus there and walked on to the caravan.

Hundreds of people were gathered around the Golden Gate with their donkeys and carts packed with provisions for their various journeys. Traveling in large groups was always beneficial to protect the families from thieves. At every stop for the night, some families would peel off to go to their villages. Mary stood with Rabbi Isaac and Amos with their caravan waiting to head for Galilee, watching for Joseph and Jesus to join them. Children were running around, laughing with glee. It was a chaotic scene of people, animals, and noise.

"Simon, wait for me!" the little boy yelled, trying to keep up with his older brother.

"Come on, Andrew! Last one to the cart is a rotten fish!" Simon said.

"Spoken like a true fisherman's son," a woman laughed as she and her husband passed Mary. "Zebedee, tell Jona that I'll watch Simon and Andrew at the front with the children. They can walk with James and John."

"Very well, Salome," Zebedee said, squeezing her arm. "May Jehovah give you patience with those four boys on the journey back to Capernaum. You're going to need it." Zebedee winked and laughed as he carried a large satchel to join the men in the back of the caravan.

Joseph saw Mary and waved a hand. He came over and took Amos's reins to guide him, with Rabbi Isaac on his back, to the rear of the caravan to join the others. "Jesus will be joining us shortly," Joseph explained. "He was listening to some of the teachers at the Temple."

"What did I tell you about this boy, eh? Smarter than any student I've ever had!" Rabbi Isaac exclaimed, petting Amos. "Even Amos knows this! *Oi!*"

Mary smiled. "He just can't get enough teaching, can he? Very well, I'll see you men when we stop tonight."

Mary assumed Jesus would be joining Joseph in the back of the caravan when he arrived from the Temple. Joseph assumed Jesus would be joining Mary at the front of the caravan. So neither of them was watching for Jesus, who never showed up at the caravan at all.

16

MY FATHER'S HOUSE

N igel, I can't explain what this week in Jerusalem has done to me," Jesus whispered to Nigel while looking for a place to sit close to the teachers. "My mind is just on fire with thoughts. God's thoughts! I'm so excited about God's truth, it's all I want to talk about."

"That's completely understandable, dear boy," Nigel replied. "You *are* Messiah. You've been coming to grips with that reality these past three years, and as your mind and spirit are growing, it's only natural that your passion is, too. You've witnessed the Passover in a new way, and the truths pointing to you I'm sure are *powerful.*"

Jesus looked around at the sea of experts gathered here, discussing divine truth. "I want to know what *they* think about Messiah. Do they think the time has come for me to be here? What do some of the prophecies mean? I'm still trying to understand all this."

"Then, ask," Nigel said, eager to be witness to an audience completely unaware Messiah himself was in their midst as they discussed him.

"I will, Nigel," Jesus said, finding a good spot. "For now, though, I'm just going to listen."

Time flew by and neither Jesus nor Nigel gave a thought to the fact that the caravan had left without them. They were completely engrossed in the discussion, and didn't bother to get up from where they sat. This opportunity simply could not be missed.

Word came forward from the back of the caravan that it was time to stop for the night. The caravan had traveled twenty miles, and everyone was exhausted. Cheers erupted from the children and the women. Mary had enjoyed a lengthy discussion with Salome about her family and their fishing business on the Sea of Galilee. But she was glad now to rejoin her family and settle in for a night of rest. She couldn't wait to hear how Jesus enjoyed his first day in the back of the caravan with the men.

Mary started making her way to the back, passing the throngs of dust-covered travelers who started making camp. She soon saw Joseph unloading the pack holding their mats and food. Rabbi Isaac was stretching his back, yawning.

"Joseph, what a long distance we made today! How is everyone?" Mary asked, looking around for Jesus.

128

"Yes, I'm glad we were able to get so far," Joseph agreed, handing the satchel of food to Mary, who was looking behind her. "If we can go five miles farther tomorrow that would be great. Is Jesus still playing with the children?"

Mary's face froze. "No, he . . . isn't he with you? I thought he was going to walk with the men!"

"No, didn't he walk with you? I figured when he didn't show up in the back of the caravan he had decided to keep you company up front," Joseph said, dropping the mats on the ground. "JESUS!" he yelled, starting to get worried.

Mary's heart started beating out of her chest. "Joseph! Jesus *HAS* to be here! Maybe he walked along with some of his friends," she hoped as she and Joseph started running along the caravan looking for their son.

"JESUS! JESUS!" they called frantically, stopping at every family fire and gathering, searching for him. "Have you seen Jesus?!"

Mary and Joseph ran down the complete stretch of people, donkeys, and carts, but there was no sign of their son. No one had seen him all day. The blood drained from their faces when they realized where he was.

"We've got to go back!" Mary said, trying to pack up everything when they reached Rabbi Isaac.

"Where is our boy, eh?" Rabbi Isaac asked, growing concerned.

"He's evidently in Jerusalem," Joseph answered. "No one has seen him all day. Last place I saw him was at the Temple."

"Oh, my boy! He must be terrified being alone in that big city!" Mary said, her voice shaking. "We have to get back to him!"

The sun was almost down for the day. "Mary, we will, but we have to wait until morning. We've lost daylight and we're too exhausted to turn right around and go now. We have to rest."

"He's right, Mary," Isaac said, putting his hand on her arm as she, now starting to cry with worry, frantically tried to pack Amos's satchel. "Shhhh! Jehovah will take care of him. True? Of course, true."

"BESIDES, HE'S NOT ALONE!" Amos hee-hawed. *"NIGEL'S WITH HIM!"*

"He knows he can go to cousin Micah's house," Joseph offered, feeling relief at the thought. "Yes, I'm *sure* he'll go back there and wait for us."

Mary lifted her gaze at the ray of hope that Jesus had a place to go. The tears streaked her dust-covered face. "Yes, yes, that has to be where he will go," she said, still shaking with the sickening feeling of having left her child alone. "Cousin Micah's house."

Joseph wiped her face and pulled her close to his chest. "We will leave early and find him tomorrow night," he assured Mary. "He's a smart boy. Our Jesus will be okay."

"Oh, Father, please, keep him safe," Mary whispered in prayer as she melted into Joseph's arms, weak with a panicked heart only a parent could understand. A child lost was unbearable. Thinking of Psalm 31, which she and all good Jewish mothers taught their children to pray before bedtime, she prayed it for her son. "Into your hands I commit his spirit."

Jesus was about to burst. If he didn't speak soon, he knew he would explode. The discussion of Daniel's Seventy Week Prophecy had led the group of teachers right into the topic of Messiah's arrival. Jesus waited for his opportunity and when a pause came, he took it.

"Teachers, may I ask a question?" Jesus respectfully requested.

All eyes turned to the young boy sitting in their midst. One of the discussion leaders, named Gamaliel, smiled and lifted his hand in approval. "I've noticed how you have been listening to all that has been discussed here. What is your question, young man?"

"According to the Seventy Weeks Prophecy, isn't the time for Messiah's arrival upon us?" Jesus asked. "Isn't it possible he is already here?"

"Brilliant!" Nigel whispered with a tap on Jesus' shoulder.

Gamaliel looked around at the faces of the teachers. No one was answering. "Yes, according to the timeline given by Daniel, Messiah could be here anytime."

"But if Messiah is already here, I believe we would already know about his birth," another teacher offered.

"Yes, for such a mighty warrior as Messiah will come with prominence and power," another teacher added.

"His birth will be one that the world would certainly take note of," still another chimed in.

The teachers murmured among themselves, some stating they would not know if Messiah had been born.

"Where do the Scriptures say Messiah will be born?" Jesus asked, knowing full well the prophecy, but wanting to make a point.

"According to Micah, in Bethlehem: *But you, Bethlehem Ephratah, though you are small among the clans of Judah, out of you will come for me one who will be ruler over Israel,*" one of the teachers readily offered.

"And is Bethlehem a place where powerful people of influence live?" Jesus asked.

"No, of course not," they replied in unison.

"So if Messiah is born there, to unimportant people, how would the world know of his birth?" Jesus asked, looking at their faces as he saw them thinking this through. "Would a sign be given?"

"Of course a sign would be given," a teacher readily answered.

"What kind of sign?" Jesus simply asked. "Would angels from heaven announce the birth?"

Two of the men in the crowd, Joseph from Arimathea and Nicodemus looked at one another. They each had an immediate flashback to a group of rowdy shepherds the teachers had dismissed years ago.

"Wasn't our great and powerful King David also born in Bethlehem in a humble home of shepherds? Did the world know of David's birth at the time?" Jesus asked. "But then he was not Messiah."

130

The teachers looked around at each other, but no one offered a reply.

"And how could God be born in Bethlehem?" Jesus continued. "Isaiah wrote about a sign foretelling his birth: *'The Lord himself will give you a sign. Behold, the virgin shall conceive and bear a son, and shall call his name Immanuel.'"* Jesus paused and looked around at the faces staring at him in wonder. "God with us. Isn't that a sign? A virgin birth?"

"We are amazed at your questions, young man," Gamaliel said after a lengthy silence.

"What about the words Isaiah used to describe Messiah? He said, *'For to us a child is born, to us a son is given; and the government shall be upon his shoulder,'"* Jesus stopped there. "What does that mean: 'The government will be upon his shoulder'?"

Gamaliel spoke up, ignoring the fact they couldn't answer the boy's previous questions. This one, however, was clear. "Look at the Roman soldiers stationed here and throughout Israel. We are ruled by Caesar the Roman Emperor. Our people Israel are ruled by a government of oppressors and Gentiles. When Messiah comes, he will take over the government that rules Israel, just as did King David of old."

131

"So Messiah must be a military warrior to do this?" Jesus asked.

"Of course! How else could Messiah overthrow such a powerful government as Rome without mighty military force?!" another teacher echoed.

Jesus nodded his head to show respect to their comments. But he continued, "Isaiah then adds to the names of Messiah: *'His name shall be called Wonderful Counselor, Mighty God, Everlasting Father, Prince of Peace.'"*

"*'Of the increase of his government and of peace there will be no end, on the throne of David and over his kingdom, to establish it and uphold it with justice and righteousness from this time forth and forevermore,'"* spoke another teacher, emphatically finishing Isaiah's passage.

"How could a Prince of Peace be a mighty military warrior?" Jesus posed.

"Peace is often won through military strength, to overcome evil," Gamaliel observed.

"Indeed, this is true, as we saw with David's military victories in establishing the security of Israel," Jesus agreed. "What about Wonderful Counselor?"

"He will have the wisdom of Solomon, of course," a teacher answered. "Never has a man had wisdom such as Solomon's to rule."

"But is Messiah a man like Solomon and David, or is he God?" Jesus asked. "Isaiah calls him Mighty God."

Again, the teachers were struck silent.

Jesus continued, "He will be called, 'Everlasting Father.'" He looked around at the Temple, the earthly house of his Father. "When Malachi says, *'Have we not all one father?'* is he not referring to our Creator and the Father of Israel, his covenant people? So how is Messiah, born of man, here on earth, to be 'Everlasting Father'?"

Silence. No one could answer him. Jesus knew he had given them much to ponder, but he was also pondering these things himself. *Father.* Suddenly Jesus thought of Joseph and realized he and Nigel had never joined them in the caravan. The sun was about to set.

"I must go. Thank you for allowing me to speak. Thank you for hearing me," Jesus said, standing to bow respectfully to his elders. "May I join you again?"

132

Gamaliel spoke up quickly, "Of course you may. The hour is late for all of us. We will be here again in the morning." He stood and looked at Jesus. "Israel has a strong future ahead if its sons are half as passionate as you are in learning the truths of Jehovah!"

The other teachers there murmured their approval of this amazing young boy. Jesus smiled and continued to express his thanks as he left the teachers there, dumbfounded by what they had heard.

"Nigel, I didn't meet my parents at the caravan," Jesus whispered as he quickly made his way out of the Temple area and on toward the Golden Gate.

"Oh, dear," Nigel said, now worried. The mouse had also been caught up in the rapture of the incredible time in the Temple and had forgotten all about the caravan. "But I must say, you were utterly brilliant in your line of questions. I'm sure the greatest minds of Israel will lose sleep tonight as they search for answers."

Jesus soon stood outside the Golden Gate, looking around, but there was no caravan to be seen. They were gone.

"Evidently they thought you were with them," Nigel assumed, looking out from under Jesus' headscarf. "I know they would not have left you here on purpose."

"I'm sure you're right, Nigel. No doubt they will return," Jesus said without a word of panic in his voice. He was secure in who he was, and was immersed in the sovereignty of God and his purposes. Why was being alone in the city something to worry about? "Well, I know where to go and what to do while we wait. We'll go to my Father's house."

Jesus and Nigel were walking back to the Temple grounds when Jesus realized he was hungry. The merchants were closing up their tents for the night, but Jesus didn't have any money. He stopped and knelt down to search his knapsack. "Ah, Nigel, I have some almonds. Here," Jesus offered, handing one to Nigel. He sat down and popped a few almonds in his mouth. Just then they heard people coming down the street, obviously looking for someone. One of them was a Roman soldier.

"Armandus! Where are you?" the woman called out. She was dressed in the expensive finery only nobles wore. Her beautiful green robe was made of silk, and her lovely headdress was adorned with gold trim.

"Julia, I'm sure he's down here," the soldier said. "He wanted to get some items to take back to Rome."

As they got close, they didn't notice Jesus sitting on the ground with his back to the wall. But Nigel noticed *them*. His eyes got wide and he poked Jesus on the shoulder. "It's them! Jesus, it's Marcus and Julia Antonius! After all this time."

Jesus sat up, eager to see the Roman family his mother had written about. He looked at the handsome Roman soldier with the strong jawline and distinctive Roman nose. He was a centurion, in his forties, and wore the impressive sculpted body armor and red plumed helmet of his position. Suddenly Jesus saw a young man walking slowly toward Marcus and Julia, not paying attention to his surroundings, but studying a piece of pottery in his hand. His light brown hair fell into his eyes, and he reached up with his other hand to brush it back, revealing beautiful blue eyes. He was a few years older than Jesus, about fifteen years of age. His arms were toned and he also wore the clothes of one who obviously had means. He stopped right in front of Jesus and for a brief moment, all time seemed to stand still.

The young Roman looked directly at Jesus and noticed his worn clothes. He figured him to be an orphan or just a poor, underprivileged Jewish boy.

"There you are," his mother exclaimed with relief. "Your father and I have been looking for you."

"Look what I bought. It's an oil lamp," Armandus said. "I like the way it's carved."

"It's lovely, Armandus," Julia said. "It will be a nice memento from your time here."

"It's *functional*, and I expect you to use it on your desk for studies," Marcus said. "Come, the hour is late and we get an early start tomorrow. Julia, take Armandus home in the carriage. I'll meet you there tonight. I have some remaining business to handle at the Praetorium before we depart."

Armandus looked up and gave Jesus a parting glance. Jesus smiled and the young Roman returned the smile, noticing the Jewish boy's captivating green eyes. He hesitated for a split second, a distant feeling of familiarity coming over him. Armandus then turned and walked with his parents down the street to their waiting carriage that would carry them to their stately home in the wealthy section of Jerusalem.

The next day Joseph and Mary left the campsite just before sunup after a restless night of sleep. Mary was anxious to get on the road. Rabbi Isaac decided he had better continue on with the caravan, and Joseph made arrangements for him to ride in a cart so they could use Amos. The anxious parents arrived in Jerusalem just at nightfall and went immediately to cousin Micah's house.

"He never came here?" Mary asked their cousin. "You haven't seen him?"

"No, Mary, I'm sorry. Had we known Jesus was lost we would have been out looking for him ourselves. Perhaps he didn't remember how to find his way back here," Micah reasoned. "Jerusalem is a maze of tiny alleys and streets, and many of the buildings look alike."

"We'll find him, Mary," Joseph reassured her. "We'll make a full search of the city, and we'll find him."

"I plan to start right now," Mary said, dropping her satchel and heading out the door. She wasn't about to sit down, knowing her son was out in the streets of Jerusalem. Joseph followed her and they spent most of the night looking for their son, frantically looking in every place they could think of. Still, with no success they reluctantly returned to their cousin's home, heartsick and exhausted. They would begin their search again when the light of day came.

Jesus slept in the Temple area two nights, and Nigel kept him company, curling up next to the boy. A kind woman had given Jesus some bread and cheese, so their hunger was satisfied. Nigel was especially happy about the cheese. Jesus was unconcerned about their situation, having no doubt his heavenly Father would provide all their needs. And just before he drifted off, he quoted Psalm 31 as his mother had taught him to do before he went to sleep: *Into your hands I commit my spirit.*

In the daytime they stayed in the Temple courts, continuing to listen to the discussion of the teachers who gathered each morning. Jesus' fervor and questions grew even more intense, and the men assembled there marveled at his knowledge and wisdom, well beyond his twelve years.

135

Early on the third day, Mary and Joseph began their search once again for their son. They checked the Golden Gate, the market area, and finally thought they would check the Temple. When they arrived, Mary's knees almost buckled with relief when she saw Jesus there, sitting among the teachers. She grabbed Joseph's arm. "He's there! Praise Jehovah, Jesus is all right!"

Joseph let go a deep breath, as he too was flooded with relief. "I knew he would be fine. Let's go to him."

Mary and Joseph quickly made their way through the courtyard and Nigel saw them coming. "Jesus, your parents are here! Look!" he whispered joyfully.

Jesus turned and smiled as they approached. Mary's joy suddenly turned to frustration as she came up to the men sitting there.

"Young man, why have you done this to us?" Mary exclaimed, her voice trembling from her emotions, which had been churning the last three days. "Your father and I have been going out of our minds looking for you!"

Jesus stood and calmly answered her. "Why were you looking for me? Don't you know that I had to be here, in my Father's house?"

Joseph and Mary shared a look of confusion and dismay. *What does he mean?* their eyes asked each other.

At that moment, Mary felt for the first time pain in her heart from her son. Never had she seen Jesus act this way. He wasn't disrespectful. He hadn't been hiding from them, disobeying or defying them. But she felt in that moment a relational break from Jesus. He was still their son, and would continue to be raised in their home, but something had changed. Jesus had come to Earth to do the will of his *heavenly* Father, not his earthly father, and his bold declaration made this abundantly clear. He would someday be the Savior doing what his Father demanded and would cease to be simply her son, doing only as *she* wanted.

Mary looked up at the Temple. The words of Simeon came rushing back to her mind from that day she and Joseph dedicated Jesus on this very spot. The old priest knew who Jesus was when they placed the baby in his arms, having been told by the Holy Spirit that this child was Messiah. *A sword will pierce your very soul.* Simeon's words echoed in Mary's mind and she clutched the front of her tunic over her heart. And this was only the beginning.

136

"Come along, Son. Time to go," Joseph said, clearing his throat. Jesus' words were hard for him to hear as well. Joseph knew he wasn't Jesus' real father, but the Lord had asked him to raise the child as his own. Mary at least had a physical connection to him. Joseph felt even further removed relationally than Mary, to hear Jesus talk about 'his Father' only to realize he wasn't referring to Joseph. "Thank you, kind sirs. I hope our son has not been a distraction to you."

Gamaliel stood. "Not at all. We have enjoyed having him with us. You have a remarkable boy, unlike any of the students I have taught in Israel."

"Thank you. *Shalom,*" Joseph responded as he, Mary, and Jesus left the area to go home.

A young boy entered the courtyard from the other side as Jesus' family walked toward the Beautiful Gate. He gazed at them for a moment before Gamaliel caught his attention.

"Ah, Saul, I'm glad you're here," Gamaliel said. "Take a seat. Teachers, this is one of my new students visiting from Tarsus. Some day he will study with me full time here in Jerusalem."

"*Shalom,*" the teachers greeted the young boy.

"I'm sorry you missed our discussion today," Gamaliel said, handing Saul a scroll. "We've had quite the debate about several of the messianic prophecies. The young boy I told you about was with us again today and was quite eager to discuss the prophecies in Isaiah. We were just discussing Isaiah 8."

Saul unrolled the scroll of Isaiah and read, *"He will be a sanctuary; but for the two houses of Israel, He will be a stone to stumble over and a rock to trip over, and a trap and a snare to the inhabitants of Jerusalem. Many will stumble over these; they will fall and be broken; they will be snared and captured."*

Saul wrinkled his brow and watched as Jesus and his family left through the Beautiful Gate. "Who was that boy, Master?"

"I don't know," answered Gamaliel, holding his hands out and shaking his head. "We never got his name."

17

THE GLORY OF ROME

ROME, AD 18

Marcus and Armandus Antonius heard the roar of the growing masses as they walked through the crowded, dark entrance corridor to the Circus Maximus. The walls vibrated from the throngs of spectators eager for the races to begin. Numerous shops were packed with people buying food, souvenirs, or even cushions for the hard stone benches. Gamblers milled about, making bets on the four teams: Red, Green, White, and Blue. A merchant was shouting and holding up a terra cotta oil lamp that caught Armandus's attention. He walked over to look at the lamp that was intricately carved with a victorious chariot and horse in the Circus.

"I'll give you a good price on this fine lamp!" the merchant enthused as he put the lamp in Armandus's hands. "No better carving of a victory scene from the races than on this lamp!"

"See something, Armandus?" Marcus asked, walking up behind his son. He smiled, "Another oil lamp?"

"I enjoy light, Father," Armandus quipped. "And I appreciate fine craftsmanship on things large and small." He held the lamp close to his face and studied the carving, running his finger along the outer edge.

"Indeed. Your commander says you have an eye for excellence in architecture and a skill for building. He said you were invaluable to their expedition in Gaul," Marcus observed proudly. "Your mother says you would go through gallons of olive oil when you were at home, lighting lamps around the house," Marcus remarked, pointing at the lamp. "She misses you, and can't wait for your short time with us before your next assignment. We'll go to the villa after the races and some business I have at the Forum."

"Achilles," Armandus read from the placard above the horse on the lamp.

"What? Where?" Marcus asked, pulling the lamp over for a closer inspection. He smiled. "He's a celebrity for our Red Team. You'll see him today."

"Yes!" the merchant exclaimed. "Achilles is the most powerful horse in Rome!"

"Then I must buy this lamp, for luck!" Armandus said with a wide grin.

"Here," Marcus said, wanting to dote on his son, pulling some coins from his pouch to hand the merchant. Even though Armandus was a grown man of twenty-two, it gave Marcus joy to give him gifts like this. He motioned to the merchant that they would buy the lamp and a basket of food to enjoy for the races.

"Certainly, sir," the merchant said enthusiastically. His booth was filled to the brim with goods and food, crates and baskets piled high behind him. A pair of cats sat on top of the crates, and one of them stared intently at Marcus. The merchant eagerly packed the basket and counted out the change, handing it to Marcus one coin at a time.

"Thank you, Father," Armandus said. "You know how I like to be reminded of important places and events. This lamp will remind me of this day."

Marcus smiled as he fiddled with the change the merchant gave him. A coin caught his attention. He frowned and clenched his jaw as he stared at the six-pointed star above the image of Caesar Augustus.

"What is it, Father?" Armandus asked, noticing the change on Marcus's pensive face.

"It's a coin, recently minted by Tiberius," Marcus replied, holding the coin in the palm of his hand. "It's to commemorate the events twenty years ago when Caesar Augustus was given the honored title *Pater Patraie,* or 'Father of the Country.' Do you see the star, just there?"

Armandus studied the coin and the star and nodded. "What does it mean?"

"The night before I was given my assignment to go to Judea, there appeared in the sky the brightest star ever seen. All of Rome saw it, and assumed it was a sign from the gods declaring their favor on Caesar," Marcus explained. "I first learned about this star when getting my orders at the Forum, but I later learned that it was seen by others, far from Rome."

"How far away?" Armandus asked, taking the coin in hand for a closer inspection.

"Persia. A group of Magi from the East claimed to have seen this star and thought it was the sign that a new King of the Jews had been born. They studied the Jewish prophecies and came to Jerusalem to Herod's Palace, asking where they could find this new King," Marcus remembered. He ran a hand through his hair, which was beginning to grey at the temples. "I was a centurion at the time, and Herod called for me in a rage, threatened by this potential Jewish king. It fell to me to carry out his despicable orders." Marcus shook his head with regret.

Armandus put his hand on his father's shoulder. "What were you required to do?"

"Herod ordered the death of all baby boys two years old and younger in the Bethlehem area. I led the charge of soldiers into that town and we went from house to house, slaying those children," Marcus explained sadly. "It was horrific."

Armandus' eyes widened as he imagined the carnage of that night. "I know it was, Father. Did you find the newborn King?"

"If we did, we'll never know because he's dead," Marcus explained, turning to look his son in the eye. "Soldiers must sometimes do difficult things in the service of the Emperor. You must shut down your emotions and see it through. Always remember that." He looked around to make sure no one heard what he said next. "But even I betrayed this directive, Armandus. There was one family that got away. I entered their home and saw them in the distance. They had escaped out the back door."

"Why did you spare them?" Armandus whispered so he wouldn't be overheard.

"Your mother and I knew this Jewish family. They befriended us

140

when we arrived in Jerusalem. The father did some carpentry work on our home, and the mother would bring their baby boy and visit with you and your mother," Marcus recalled with a sad smile on his face. "These Jews were different and went against the dogma of their religion that a Jew would be defiled if he entered a Roman's home. These people were more concerned about us as people than if we were one of them. They called us . . ." He paused, memories flooding his mind. "They called us friends. When I saw their pet lamb in the house, I realized who they were and couldn't go through with it."

The merchant called out, "Will there be anything else, sir?"

Marcus shook his head and turned his back on the merchant. The black cat kept her gaze on the Roman father and son.

"That is the only time in my military career I have ever defied orders. If you someday find yourself in such a situation, you must be sure that the high risk of what you do is worthy of such a decision," Marcus whispered. "But that act led your mother and me to sympathize with the Jews. The Jewish family frequently talked about this one God they serve, and I feel there is something to this God. Armandus, be kind to the Jews. For the sake of my memory, be kind to them, as I carry a heavy burden for what I did."

141

"I will, Father. May I keep this coin?" Armandus asked. "It will remind me of what you've told me."

"A good reminder, Son, of course," Marcus said. "Now, enough of this. Time to enjoy our day together at the Circus." He smiled and motioned for Armandus to follow him down the corridor leading to the block of seats they had been assigned.

The black cat watched the two men trail off. She turned to the merchant. "They're gone, *mon amie*."

"Did you hear what they said? Marcus gave Armandus the full story!" the merchant replied. His eyes were smiling.

Liz smiled. "And he even mentioned *you*. I am glad Armandus knows the truth. Your oil lamp was the perfect bait." She studied the dirty merchant. "But I am having a difficult time getting used to you as a human, much less a *man*, no?"

"I'm a sheep in man's clothing!" Clarie laughed. As a spiritual member of the Order of the Seven, she had the ability to take any shape or form, including human. "I am glad we made this trip. It was important for you to be here for this moment. More will come from this conversation than you now know. From here we will follow Armandus to Britannia, or England, as we animals know it. Of course you realize it will be a long journey, but there is a purpose in the Maker's plan."

"Can ye give me some o' yer dried fish then, little lamb, sir?" Al said eagerly, his mouth drooling at the baskets of fish in the booth. "I'm hungry."

"If you promise to behave when the races start," Clarie replied, handing a few fish to Al.

Al stuffed his mouth and mumbled, "Ye have me word, Lass!"

Armandus put his hand up to shield his eyes when they emerged onto the platform next to their seating section, the sun blinding him for a brief moment.

"Ah, the glory of Rome!" Marcus said, looking around at the massive arena. He pointed to their rows below. "It's a spectacular day for racing. Our seats are just down there, behind the senators."

Armandus looked at the expanse of the incredible Circus Maximus that stretched almost 700 yards long and just shy of 160 yards wide. It was situated in a valley between two of Rome's seven hills, the Palatine and the Aventine. Both of the long sides of the oblong arena were filled with stands holding one-hundred-fifty thousand spectators, divided according to social class. Sections of the first tier were reserved for priests and the six Vestal Virgins, Senators, and for wealthy Equestrians. Marcus fell into this latter class, as he was a Knight in the Equestrian Order, serving as a Commander of the Imperial Army.

At one end of the oblong were twelve starting gates, arches with iron gates that kept the chariots and horses at bay until the races began. From the third tier of seats on the Palatine Hill side of the track rose a marble building resembling a temple, which housed the emperor's special box. From here, the emperor could be seen by the people when he attended the races, with his hand raised to drop the white cloth, or *mappa,* to signal the start of a race.

In the middle of the race track was the *spina,* or central island barrier, surrounded by high stone walls. Each end was rounded off with turning posts, and statues of gods, marble altars, and shrines were placed along the middle of the island barrier. At either end were lap counters, with seven dolphins on one end and seven eggs on the other. As the charioteers finished each lap, a dolphin or an egg would drop so the screaming fans as well as the racers would know how many laps remained. In the center of the spina was a huge obelisk, towering over the other structures and close to the white finish line.

Armandus stared at the obelisk. "Father, where did that come from?" he said as he pointed to the imposing monument.

"Augustus had it brought here from Egypt," Marcus explained as they took their seats behind the senators. "As Egyptians worship the sun god, who for us is Apollo, Augustus wanted to honor him here at the Circus. Apollo is the divine patron of the Circus and the games." He motioned to the race course. "This circuit mirrors the heavenly course of Apollo in his four-horse chariot, or *quadriga*, pulling the sun across the sky from its rising to its setting. As the emperor is Apollo's earthly equivalent, he oversees the games. Of course, Augustus was far more excited about the races than Tiberius, who rarely comes. But perhaps we'll see him today."

Suddenly they heard the unmistakable sound of the *cornu*, or G-shaped trumpet, announcing the parade of entrants into the Circus. The crowd erupted as a grand procession of dignitaries, team flag bearers, musicians, and dancers filed into the arena. Priests carried statues of the gods and goddesses who would "watch" the games alongside the Emperor Tiberius, who appeared in his viewing box. Then the thundering of hooves filled the air as twelve charioteers with four horses each came racing down the track. The crowds began cheering for their preferred team. Lots were cast among the charioteers to determine their starting position, and they made their way to the starting gate stalls.

"Which Red Team has Achilles?" Armandus asked as he anxiously watched the teams race by. There were three teams for each of the four colors.

"That one," Marcus said, pointing to the first Red Team to race by, with Achilles on the far left position of the four-horse team. He was a magnificent grey Arabian stallion, with a wide forehead, large eyes, and large nostrils that flared as he ran with blazing speed and power down the track. His muzzle had streaks of black and his hind quarters were dappled with darker grey spots. His deep grey mane and tail had streaks of light at the tip. Achilles stood five feet tall at the shoulder and his sculpted muscles projected his unmatched strength.

"Run, Achilles!" Armandus shouted excitedly.

The charioteers lined up and soon a hush fell over the crowd as Emperor Tiberius stood with the white cloth, the *mappa,* in his hand. The suspense captured the crowd, who were hungry for the race to begin.

"Citizens! I welcome you to these games provided for your entertainment by the divine empire of Rome. I dedicate these games to you, its citizens," Tiberius bellowed with his loudest voice. "You have come to these games to witness the glory of Rome manifest in the running of the chariots. Let us honor those who race today!"

The crowds erupted in cheers of praise as Tiberius held his hands toward the chariots at the starting block. The forty-eight horses stomped their hooves and snorted at the deafening sound, eager to bust out of the gates. The cheers slowly grew into a unified chant of "Hail, Caesar; hail, Caesar; hail, Caesar!"

Tiberius motioned for the crowds to settle. "To the winner of the race, a crown of victory!" He slowly raised his arm and released the *mappa.* As it floated to the ground, the iron gates were sprung, releasing the twelve chariot teams that thundered onto the track. The crowd roared to life and rose to their feet.

Marcus leaned over and had to shout so Armandus could hear him. "The strategy is to pace the horses for seven laps while trying to hold a position close to the barrier and rounding the turning posts as closely as possible without hitting them."

Armandus nodded but kept his eyes on Achilles and the Red Team. The forty-eight black, chestnut, white, and grey horses kicked up a massive cloud of dust behind them. The charioteers stood in their chariots with the reins tied around their waists, which was extremely dangerous should something go wrong. And that is exactly what the crowd hoped for.

Ravenous fans screamed curses against their opposing teams, hoping to bring down the competition. The charioteers deliberately slammed into one another, hoping to cause harm to the other chariots. On the second lap, a White Team chariot suddenly slammed into the *spina,* flipping over while the horses fell into a chaotic heap, struggling to get up. A team of slaves carrying a stretcher ran out onto the race course to recover the charioteer, bloodied from the crash, unable to get up on his broken legs. He screamed in agony as the men quickly lifted him onto the stretcher. Another team of men got the horses upright to lead them off the course. They barely got out of the way before the remaining chariots closed in on their position.

Achilles thundered down the track, responding with perfection at the slightest touch of the reins from the charioteer. His nostrils flared with every breath as he ran the four miles with blazing speed. Sweat poured off his dappled coat and his mane blew majestically behind him. The other three horses followed Achilles's lead, kicking up a cloud of dust that rose into the air as they took the lead position in the race.

Liz, Al, and Clarie sat watching the spectacle from high above the Circus. "Sure, and that Achilles would outrun even Giorgio," Al said, remembering their Italian stallion friend from Noah's Ark.

Liz's tail twitched back and forth and she found herself holding her breath in the suspense of the race. *"Oui,* I have never seen a faster horse. He is *superb!"*

A Blue Team chariot collided with one from the Green Team, and the charioteers were caught up in a physical struggle. The Green Team's driver used his whip to hit the Blue Team's driver. The crowds yelled and screamed with delight, hoping for another wipeout. Suddenly one of the wheels fell off the Blue chariot, yanking the charioteer out of the chariot and onto the course. The charioteer was powerless as he struggled to reach his knife to cut himself free of the reins tied around his waist. It was no use. He couldn't do anything but hang on as he was violently dragged along the course, almost crushed by another team racing by. Another group of slaves rushed onto the track to grab the horses and lead them out of the way. The wounded charioteer lay bloodied and passed out while they removed him from the track.

One Red Team entry hit the curb of the *spina* and turned over its chariot, leading to a domino effect that eliminated three other chariots. Now the race was down to six teams, with four teams slowly trailing behind the lead Red and Green Teams. Suddenly the Green Team began closing in on Achilles and the Red Team. The sixth dolphin lap marker dropped. This was the final lap.

"What's that thing stickin' out o' the green chariot then?" Al asked with a full mouth, pointing with a fish.

Liz stared intently at the wheels of the Green Team chariot and her eyes widened. "Blades! This is how they took out the Blue Team chariot!" she screamed in alarm over the din of the crowds. "It could take out a horse as well!"

The Green Team entry edged its way up along the left side of the Red Team chariot, but Achilles pushed to stay clear of them. The white finish line was barely fifty yards ahead. The Red charioteer saw the blades and at just the right moment dropped back and pushed the Green Team with the full force of his horses into the *spina*. The blade on the opposing chariot caught a gap in the curb, flipping the chariot over and sending its charioteer under the pounding hooves of its horses, killing him instantly. Al quickly put his paws up to his eyes and Liz's face wore a look of horror. Still, they were relieved that the Red Team prevailed.

The crowds immediately started chanting the name of Achilles as the Red Team ran toward the finish line in victory. Armandus grabbed Marcus by the shoulder, exclaiming, "He won! He won! Achilles must be the finest horse in all of Rome!"

"Indeed, he is!" Marcus shouted in agreement, giving Armandus a knowing smile. "And he is far too fast and powerful to be wasted here at the games."

The Red Team chariot stopped in front of the Emperor's box and the charioteer climbed to the podium, where Tiberius placed a laurel wreath on the winning man's head. He raised his hands and the crowds clamored to celebrate the victory of the Red Team and Achilles.

"What do you mean, Father?" Armandus asked, keeping his eyes on Achilles as another driver led the team off the race course. The driver looked up at Marcus and gave a wave of recognition.

Marcus waved back, drawing a look of question from Armandus. "A horse as fine as Achilles should be in the service of the Empire for more important purposes than entertaining the citizens of Rome."

"I agree, Father," Armandus enthused. "How I would love to have a horse like that!"

Marcus smiled. "Come then," he told his son as he started exiting their row.

"Where are we going?" Armandus asked, disappointed and picking up his lamp. "Aren't we going to stay for the rest of the races?"

Marcus didn't answer but led Armandus down the stairs. Liz was just as curious as Armandus. "We need to see where they are going," she said as she sauntered off in their direction. Al burped and followed along behind. "Whatever ye say, love." Clarie followed, a knowing grin on her face.

Marcus led them through the winding corridor to the holding area where the horses were being unharnessed and cooled down from the exhausting race. Armandus saw Achilles eagerly drinking water and ran over to stand next to this amazing horse. Marcus grinned and followed his son to stand with Achilles.

"You have been given a rare opportunity for a legionnaire to visit Britannia because of the skills you possess," Marcus told Armandus while stroking Achilles on his shoulder. "Ever since Julius Caesar's expedition there, Rome has wanted to add that mysterious land to the empire, but has been unable to amass forces and resources because of the empire's other pursuits. But the empire will have a presence there one day, mark my words."

147

"Yes, Father, I look forward to seeing Britannia," Armandus replied, reaching up to also touch Achilles. "Word is that the taxes on trade of luxury goods from that land into Rome bring in more money than conquest, but I, too, see that land as part of Rome's future empire." Armandus was well educated and well trained in the operations of the Roman army, having served as a legionnaire these past five years. His family's tremendous wealth and prestige enabled his favorable attention from his commanders, but his remarkable insight and intelligence earned him their respect.

"Although you are not yet in the Equestrian Order of the Imperial Army, for this expedition you will need a fine horse to carry you on the important business of the Emperor," Marcus instructed.

Armandus blinked and quickly looked into his father's eyes. A slow grin appeared on Marcus's face. Armandus returned the smile with building anticipation. "Father, you don't mean . . ."

"I own Achilles. He is mine to do with as I wish," Marcus said, turning to look at the magnificent animal. "And I wish to give him to you."

Armandus put his hands excitedly on Marcus's shoulders. "Father! You're giving Achilles to me?!"

Marcus laughed. "Only if you want him."

"*WANT* him?!" Armandus exclaimed, pushing past his father. He got eye-to-eye with the horse and placed his hand under Achilles's muzzle. Achilles snorted and sniffed at the young man's hand, picking up his scent, and meeting Armandus's gaze. The two exchanged a silent bond of understanding. Respect. Courage. Loyalty. Armandus slowly stroked the horse's long nose and spoke softly into the horse's ear. "Achilles. You and I will see the world. And conquer it for the Emperor."

Armandus smiled broadly and turned to Marcus, who stood there erect, hands clasped behind his back. "I don't know what to say, Father. Thank you!"

"It is done then," Marcus said, walking up to Achilles and patting his muscular shoulder. "You two were meant to know the bond of horse and rider. Achilles will serve you well."

Liz, Al, and "Clarie" the merchant stood in the shadows. "*C'est bon!* I am so happy for Armandus!" Liz exclaimed.

"Aye, the lad's got a grand horse," Al echoed. "But doesn't Achilles have a bad foot?"

"Only in Greek mythology, Al," Clarie explained. "This Achilles is perfect in every way." She looked from the horse to Liz and Al and grinned to herself. "He is a *grey* stallion. And he is destined for *great* things."

"Father, why was Achilles's name not changed from the Greek to Roman?" Armandus asked, continuing to examine the horse up and down.

"Achilles was a Greek hero, not a god, so we didn't adapt his name as we would with the gods we worship," Marcus explained. "As you know, when Rome conquers a nation, we invite their gods to come inhabit Rome. We believe it adds to our power."

Armandus patted Achilles and looked at Marcus. "What about this Jewish god you mentioned? Has he been invited to inhabit Rome?"

"No," Marcus replied cautiously. "I shudder to think what would happen to Rome if the Jewish God came to inhabit this city."

"He'd take over, *that's* what would happen," Al remarked, drawing looks of amazement from Liz and Clarie.

Marcus wrinkled his brow as he remembered what the Jewish family had told him about their God and his unmatched power. This God also exhibited unmatched love for his people, which, for Marcus, held a far

148

greater weight. Never had he heard of such a god. He had never gotten away from the longing in his heart to know more. And he carried the burden deep inside that he had defied the Jewish God by killing their newborn king, so long ago. He clung to the hope that the one child he had saved would count for something to clean the blood from his hands.

The roar of the crowds announced the beginning of another race for the glory of Rome. *The glory of Rome*, Marcus thought to himself. They were supreme rulers of the world, yet the thought left him with a hollow feeling. Rome's conquests resulted in the deaths of countless thousands. Endless, bloody death. Death of enemies, death for sport in the arenas with gladiators and games. Even death today at the races, thrilling the bloodthirsty masses.

But there was no comfort, no end of death, Marcus knew. Not even from their gods, which held the route to the spiritual realm. The countless stream of gods in Rome demanded tribute or else certain punishment. The wealth he and Julia had amassed meant nothing. Marcus moved up through the ranks and was a knight with special privilege in the empire. He loved his family with a fierce love, but something was missing.

There has to be more than the glory of Rome, Marcus thought. *There has to be more to life than this.*

"If only he knew," Clarie lamented, staring at Marcus, seeing the heaviness in his eyes and knowing the void in his spirit. "If only Marcus knew the Life he preserved long ago, he would know he had captured the favor . . . of the God of the Jews."

149

The Assignment of Armandus Antonius

"Mousie would love to be here again," Al said, his tail swishing back and forth as he stared into the flowing river, watching a school of fish. One day in the distant future, this water would be known as the Thames River, but that fact was known only to Clarie. "Sure, and I miss the greenery o' these lands meself."

Liz sat studying the wide expanse of the river that flowed through the countryside. *"Oui, cher* Albert. There is nothing like these northern lands. I am grateful we were able to travel through my beloved France on the way to Britannia."

"I never imagined it could be so pretty and green here," Clarie added, nibbling some grass in her original sheep form. "And delicious!"

"Well, ye ain't seen green until ye visit ME land o' Ireland!" Al protested. "It's jest across the water, but these Roman laddies haven't found it yet."

"It is rather comical that the Romans believe there to be only three continents, no?" Liz said with a paw to her mouth, stifling a giggle. "Europe, Africa, and Asia are all there is in their world, along with the Sea. Little do they know there are *seven* continents."

"So you met animals from all over the world when they came to

Noah's Ark?" Clarie asked, fascinated by the great expanse of the earth. "That must have been wonderful!"

"It was, *mon amie*. And the Maker allowed us to see bits and pieces of the world on the Ark, since the natural habitats of the animals formed around them," Liz remembered with wonder.

Al suddenly had a craving for bananas, remembering how he had ventured to the monkey stalls daily for his favorite food. "Best trip o' me life."

"But the Romans believe this land of Britannia to be a suspicious place, full of monsters beyond the limits of the known world," shared Liz. "They have conquered much of the world but haven't been able to seize power here. Yet."

"It will come," Clarie said, watching Armandus leading Achilles by the reins to get a drink of water from the river. "For now the Romans are content to keep Britannia as a client kingdom with King or 'Rex' Verica in charge of this Atrebates region. Armandus has gathered some important information to take back to Rome about these lands and the potential here."

151

Liz, Al, and Clarie hid behind the river shrubs and watched as Armandus was joined by the Roman-appointed King Verica and a group of his tribesmen. The animal friends had remained in the shadows as Armandus travelled with a small squad of legionnaires on this temporary post as an "Immune," meaning he was exempt from hard labor and tedious tasks of the regular legionnaire soldiers. He was sent here to scope out the land, collecting engineering, trade, and military intelligence, and strengthen the bonds of the Rome-Britannia alliance. His superiors noted his diplomatic as well as engineering skills early on, realizing he would be perfect for this assignment. He had the ability to build bridges not only physically as he had in Gaul, but also in terms of relating to cultures different from Rome.

"This is the part of the river I wanted to discuss with you," Armandus said, pointing out a place where the water narrowed. Verica studied the stretch Armandus referred to. "My men and I have studied the water here and found it to be narrow enough to build a bridge, but deep enough for Roman ships to enter and make port."

This comment drew suspicious looks from the tribesmen, who were wary of the Roman conquerors coming to Britannia for more than just an alliance through trade. They feared a military invasion. Verica held his hand up. "Surely you mean for purposes of trade."

Armandus had to tread lightly as he knew that Rome wanted to conquer this land with military force, but the day had not yet come for that to happen. For now, they had to shore up the balance of power in the south of this strange island land, investigate how it could benefit Rome, and bide their time.

"Well, indeed for trade," Armandus answered. "But if you could see the cities Rome offers its provinces, you would welcome what Rome has to offer Britannia. And to *you*, Rex Verica. Rome seeks to give local, existing rulers the business of the Imperial administration."

"You mean collecting taxes," Verica confirmed. "This fuels Rome and the empire. What do I get in return?"

"You get the glory of Rome here in Britannia!" Armandus enthused. "You get the status and prestige of being a Roman citizen once a province is officially founded here."

152

"The Romans are brilliant with this plan," Liz explained to Al and Clarie. "If a man in a local province sees that the best way he can advance himself is through the Roman system, he won't try to overthrow Rome. He'll *adopt* the Roman way of life. What better way than to take over a people who are willing to submit to all things Roman? You make people *want* Rome by offering them its wealth, luxury, and way of life."

Armandus pulled out some coins from his pouch, showing them to Verica. "You see on these coins the wealth of Rome—how we dress, eat, act, spend. Rome offers to build coliseums, baths, markets, and roads throughout its provinces. Given the land in this area and the expanse of this river, I see this as the perfect place for a major city in Britannia."

Liz envisioned a "mini-Rome" built on the site of this river. Mini-Roman cities that reflected the glory of Rome were spread across the empire, especially in the south of France, or Gaul, as the Romans called it. "As long as you do Roman things and adopt the Roman way of life, you can be a citizen of Rome," Liz continued. "It doesn't matter what culture, country, or bloodline you have."

"Yes, but some cultures will not adopt the Roman way of life, such as the Jews in Israel," Clarie added.

"Well, I can't see the Maker bein' too happy with the idea o' his people runnin' after all the god and goddess lads and lassies these Romans have," Al added with a frown. "Ye got to give the Jewish people credit for that."

"*Oui*, even while the Romans oppress them, they hold fast to Jehovah and stubbornly refuse to be Romanized," replied Liz, shaking her head as she considered the plight of the Jews in bondage to the Roman state. "Someone like Armandus could be a wonderful relational bridge builder for the Jews."

"That's what Armandus's superiors think as well," Clarie said with a knowing grin. She turned to look at Liz and Al. "We'll be leaving Britannia soon. Armandus is getting ready to receive a new assignment."

Liz perked up. "Where is he—or are *we*—going?"

"After returning to Rome to give his report on Britannia, he'll be promoted to centurion in the province of Galilee," Clarie reported, smiling. "He'll be stationed in the city of Capernaum."

"Galilee!" Liz exclaimed joyfully. "Then we'll be rejoining Jesus and the others soon, no? Capernaum is on the Sea of Galilee."

"Aye, and there be lots o' fish there!" Al added, purring wildly at the thought of returning to the source of Rabbi Isaac's dried fish.

"Oh, but I cannot wait to see Jesus again," Liz said fondly. "How I've missed him."

"Yes, but it was important for you to follow Armandus's journey," Clarie affirmed. "Someday you will put all these things together. Watch!"

Achilles started to nervously snort and raise up, neighing, knocking the coins out of Armandus's hand onto the riverbank. Liz's fur stood on end when she saw what had startled Achilles.

"Whoa, what is it, Achilles?" Armandus exclaimed, alarmed by the horse's movements, and tightening his grip on the reins.

Suddenly a grass snake appeared on the riverbank and raised itself up at the feet of the powerful horse with a threatening hiss. Achilles snorted loudly and proceeded to stomp his hooves repeatedly to hit the snake, killing it. The men saw what the problem was and stood back as the horse took care of the unwelcome reptile.

One of the tribesmen grabbed a stick and lifted the dead snake. "You have a horse that knows how to protect you, Armandus," he said, tossing the snake in the river. "Or at least take care of itself."

Armandus patted Achilles on the side of his face, calming him down. "Well done, Achilles!"

"Magnifique!" Liz exclaimed. "Achilles is very brave, no?"

"Aye, the lad killed the attackin' snake," Al observed, relief covering his round, orange face. "He'd be good to keep in a garden then."

The tribesman bent down to gather the scattered coins, handing them to Armandus. "Your coins, sir."

"Thank you," Armandus said, caring only about one coin that had been knocked out of his hand. It was the coin his father had given him in Rome, with Caesar Augustus on the face. He called it his Star Coin. As he placed the coins in his pouch, he saw a Roman courier approaching on horseback.

"Armandus Antonius?" the courier asked. "Your men said I would find you here."

"Yes," Armandus said, taking a small scroll from the man.

"Here it comes," Clarie said.

Armandus unrolled the scroll and nodded to himself before rolling it up and putting it in his pouch. "Gentlemen, if you'll excuse me, I have to depart. I've been called back to Rome for another assignment, and need to make arrangements to leave immediately. I will come bid you farewell before I leave Britannia." He shook hands with Verica and the tribesmen, mounted Achilles, and headed back to camp.

Armandus lit his oil lamp on his rough wooden desk to write out the reports he needed to take with him to Rome. He paused and watched the flame dance in the lamp, illuminating the form of Achilles etched in the terra cotta carving. He thought of the day he spent with his father at the Circus Maximus when he bought this lamp, smiling as he remembered that it was also the day he got Achilles. And what a tremendous horse he was! His speed was unmatched, and his power was just as evident, as seen today when he killed the snake. Armandus had not had to take Achilles into battle, but knew he would be just as fearless then.

Armandus reached for his pouch, taking out the special Star Coin. He wiped off the mud and noticed a slight indentation now on the coin. Evidently Achilles had stomped on it when trying to kill the snake. Armandus frowned, but no matter. Achilles was safe and he still had the coin, imperfect though it now was. Its value was not the coin itself, but what it represented.

As his fingers ran along the new indentation of the coin, he glanced at his new orders from Rome. He was to receive not only a promotion but a new assignment, seemingly following in his father's footsteps. He was to be a centurion stationed in Capernaum, in the land of the Jews. His orders indicated that since he had been raised in the province of Judea and was familiar with its strange culture of people, then his myriad of skills and previous military experience would serve the Empire well. He would soon be in charge of one hundred men plus servants, in a coastal town on the Sea of Galilee. He would soon be administering Roman law to a people who did not welcome Roman rule, and did not want any of the things Rome had to offer, such as he had told the king of Britannia about just that day. They despised the Romans. And why shouldn't they? The Romans oppressed them in every way, and had even killed their promised newborn King.

"Be kind to them", Marcus's voice echoed in Armandus's mind. *"I carry a heavy burden for what I did."*

"I will, Father," Armandus said softly to himself, gripping the coin tightly in his hand.

155

While Armandus readied himself to depart Britannia, Clarie wanted to take Liz and Al somewhere with future significance. Although she knew they wouldn't realize it now, Clarie felt it would be meaningful to them after this mission when they regained their memories.

"Armandus is right. Someday this area will be an important city," Clarie told her friends as she led them through the grassy countryside away from the river.

"You sound like Gillamon, teasing us with tidbits of information about the future," Liz said, looking around at this land that seemed to hold no more future than for sheep to graze.

Sometimes it was difficult for Clarie to bite her tongue and not say anything more than she should about future events. But she was fascinated with the layering of time, especially over geographical places. She wanted them to see what had happened today with Achilles and the coin, for someday it would mean something.

Suddenly Al stopped in his tracks and looked around. "Why does this feel familiar? Sure, and I think I'm havin' one o' those *déjà vu* things."

"Oh, Albert, it must be from when we visited this area with Nigel so long ago, when he wanted to show us his beloved homeland after our mission in Egypt," Liz explained.

Clarie smiled to herself. She knew what London looked like now, layered over time in this very place where they stood. And she knew that in reality, her animal friends were on mission *from* London, visiting this previous point in time. Liz and Al didn't realize the ground they walked on would someday be known as 25 Brook Street, London. The home of George F. Handel.

LEAVING MARY

Jesus grinned as he read an early entry from Mary's journal:

My Little One,

Your cousin was born today! It was such a blessed event to be here to help with the delivery. To see the miracle of this child foretold by Gabriel has strengthened my faith about you. As I hold baby John and look into his sweet face, my heart is so full, knowing he will one day tell everyone about you.

John came out loud and crying! Perhaps he is practicing for the day when Isaiah said he will be "a voice crying in the wilderness to prepare the way for the Lord." The Lord. Messiah. Jesus. My baby. You.

I felt you flutter in my belly for the first time today. Were you celebrating John's birthday?

Jesus rolled up the scroll containing Mary's journal with the words she wrote to him so long ago. Mary had been with Elizabeth when Jesus' cousin John was born. John had leapt in Elizabeth's womb when Mary greeted her. The two mothers shared their wonderful stories, beyond the belief of anyone outside their family. Their boys were chosen for greatness by God. John was the prophet foretold by Isaiah who would prepare the way for Messiah. And Jesus, of course, *was* Messiah.

These cousins knew one another as children, and were only six months apart in age, but it had been years since they had seen each other. Once Zechariah and Elizabeth passed away in their old age, young John went to live with distant relatives. The cousins had simply lost contact with time and distance. Jesus wondered if Elizabeth had told John before she died that he was a prophet of God, as Mary had done in sharing with Jesus who he was. John was filled with the Holy Spirit even before his birth, so had an unusual capacity to understand such things with solid belief. And God was faithful. Just as he had allowed Simeon to recognize the infant Jesus as Messiah in the Temple, so, too, would he make sure John knew Messiah when he saw him.

Mary came up behind Jesus, wiping her eyes. "When will I see you again?"

Jesus turned and enveloped his mother with a strong, loving embrace. "Soon, Mother, I promise. I'll see you at the wedding at least. You can plan on me being there." A lump grew in his throat to think of her alone without him. When Joseph died years ago, Mary leaned on Jesus to lead the household as he grew into a strong man. He carried on Joseph's carpentry business and they had such a happy life together. Of course there were plenty of other family members here in Nazareth to watch out for her, but Jesus was her firstborn son, and the one who was responsible for her care. Given the miracle of their relationship and their thirty years together, their bond was unbreakable. Mary knew this day would come. Jesus didn't come to Earth to be a carpenter. He came to be the Savior of the world. She couldn't have him all to herself any longer. Jesus had been hers for a time. Now the world needed him.

Jesus kissed Mary on the head and then gazed deeply into her eyes, holding her by the shoulders. "I've talked with my brothers and sisters, as well as Rabbi Isaac, and they will make sure you are all right. And I'll see you before too long, I promise," he said, his eyes now welling up with tears as he thought of her sadness, and how the nature of their relationship would be changed forever. "Thank you, Mother, for the wonderful home you've always provided for me. No son could have known more love growing up."

Mary sniffed and blinked back the tears, nodding in agreement. She cupped his face in her hands. "How I love you, Jesus! A mother could never be as proud of a son as I am of you. But I know your heavenly Father has called you to begin your ministry. I'll always be here for you. Always."

Jesus pointed his finger gently at Mary's heart. "And I will always be here for you. Always."

The mother and son shared another long embrace, and shed a few more tears. Finally they let go and Mary watched as her son, Jesus of Nazareth, walked out the door and down the dusty road leading out of town. She felt the sword pierce her soul again, but breathed a prayer of thanksgiving for the privilege of having raised this remarkable son: *Into your hands I commit his spirit.*

A VOICE CRYING IN THE WILDERNESS

JUDEA, AD 28

Travelers lined the roads from Jerusalem and from all over the region around the Jordan River. They walked briskly, and with visible excitement. There was a buzz among the people, and a sense of urgency to get to the river that fed this desert area. Crowds had been on the move like this for six months. For the first time in four hundred years, Israel had a voice who spoke the truth with bold authority. This voice was dynamic, forceful, and flew in the face of the religious establishment that offered nothing but the same old judgmental murmurs, reminding the people to bring their sacrifices—and their offerings—and follow the burdensome laws—or else.

This voice shouted salvation, forgiveness, the mercy of God, and the promise of a bright new day about to dawn after these dark days in the life of Israel. The message was so powerful that people were turning back to the Lord. Peace entered homes as fathers' hearts were turned back to their children, and those who lived rebellious lifestyles gravitated to the wisdom of living a just, honorable life. Rough lives felt the smoothing effects of grace and forgiveness, and experienced deep joy as a result. As a king's highway is cleared and prepared before he arrives, something wonderful was happening in the lives of these people who were expectant about the arrival of the promised King.

Could it be that the time for Messiah was almost here? The people longed for a king who would come save them from Roman oppression. They longed for freedom to live and worship and enjoy life as they once had in the days of their greatness under David and Solomon. Regret for their rebellion against God still hung in the hills of this land. They had paid a steep price for worshipping idols and going their own way, ignoring the commands of the Lord. Ever since the Babylonian captivity they had struggled to rebuild and remake themselves, but they could never achieve as a nation what they had before. So when *this* voice shouted hope, the spirit of the nation of Israel responded with eagerness. This voice belonged to the first prophet of God they had heard from since heaven had fallen silent four hundred years before, leaving them to themselves. The last words from the prophet Malachi said that for those who feared the Lord's name, the sun of righteousness would rise with healing in its wings. But before that awesome day, God would send another Elijah to prepare the way.

161

It was as if this prophet had stepped out of the pages of ancient time and into their current day. He even looked like the prophets of old. He dressed like the prophet Elijah had when he shouted to their ancestors. This prophet wore scratchy clothes made of camel's hair, with a leather belt tied around his waist. He identified with the poor because he lived as they did. He chose to abandon social norms and lived in isolation out in the wilderness. He ate wild honey and locusts. His hair was long, he didn't shave, and he didn't care about appearances. That alone was refreshing, for appearances seemed to be all the religious leaders cared about.

"Repent! For the kingdom of heaven is at hand!" John shouted loudly to the crowd gathered on the banks of the Jordan River. He walked into the water until he was waist deep and lifted his hands, beckoning people to come. "It's not enough to just say you're sorry for what you've done! Confess your sins before God and change the direction you've been going in life!"

Tears streamed down the faces of those who felt the stinging, wonderful prodding of truth to make a change. Men, women, and young people came into the water to be baptized by John. As they rose up out of the water, they hugged one another from the joy they felt. They were forgiven! They were willing to submit their hearts to Jehovah and stop living in sin.

"This water doesn't save you," John said as he baptized individuals, "but it symbolizes the cleansing that is taking place in your heart."

"Thank you, John," a young man said, clasping the prophet's fore-arms and smiling broadly. "May Jehovah have his way with me from now on."

"That's the way!" John said, smiling as well and patting the young man on the back as they walked together out of the water. John's smile faded as he saw a group of Pharisees and Sadducees from the Temple in Jerusalem gathered there on the riverbank. They frowned and looked down their noses at the unkempt prophet whose camel hair clothes dripped with water as he stood on the bank. Anger filled John at the display of these holier-than-thou types who were here because John's baptism had become so popular with the people. They knew *they* didn't need it, of course. They were the sons of Abraham. They were safe in the security of their bloodline—or so they thought.

162

John lifted his hand and pointed a finger accusingly at the religious leaders. "You brood of vipers! What do you think you're doing slithering down here to the river? Do you think a little water on your snakeskins is going to make any difference? It's your *life* that must change, not your skin! And don't think you can pull rank by claiming Abraham as father." John stopped and picked up a stone in each hand. "I tell you, God is able from these stones to raise up children for Abraham." He threw the stones down to the ground in disgust and moved closer to them.

"What counts is your life. Is it green and blossoming? Because if it's deadwood, it goes on the fire," John warned them as he continued to boldly drill holes in their pious reputations.

"Then what are we supposed to do?" a man from the crowd shouted.

John picked up a coat that belonged to the young man he had just baptized, and handed it to him. "If you have two coats, give one away. Do the same with your food."

Two tax collectors nervously approached John, convicted by the way they had treated the people. "Teacher, what should we do?"

John lifted a finger and wagged it back and forth to emphasize his point. "Don't collect any more than what you've been authorized."

There were some soldiers from the Temple guard who approached

John, much to the anger of the religious officials. "And what should *we* do?"

"Don't take money from anyone by force or false accusation; be satisfied with your wages," John replied. He saw the looks on the faces of the people who gazed at him in awe. He knew what they were thinking, for he had heard the discussions going on around him, wondering if he could be the Messiah. The thought made him cringe.

"Who are you?" asked the leader of the Pharisees, named Zeeb.

"I am not Messiah," John answered honestly.

"Who then? Elijah?" another Pharisee named Jarib pressed.

"I am not," John replied.

"The Prophet?" Nahshon the Sadducee asked.

"No," John calmly answered.

The religious leaders were becoming exasperated with this "prophet." Another Pharisee by the name of Saar spoke up. "Who, then? We need an answer for those who sent us. Tell us something—anything!—about yourself."

163

John paused and breathed deeply. "I am a *voice of one crying out in the wilderness: Make straight the way of the Lord*, just as Isaiah the prophet said."

"Why then do you baptize if you aren't the Messiah, or Elijah, or the Prophet?" they asked.

"I baptize you with water, for repentance, but he who is coming after me is mightier than I," John said, with a hand draped over his heart and his head hung in humility, "whose sandals I'm not worthy to carry. He will baptize you with the Holy Spirit and fire." He looked up and thought about the implications for the religious elite.

John stared directly at the apparent leader of the religious men still standing there. "He's going to clean house—make a clean sweep of your lives. He'll place everything true in its proper place before God." John turned his back on them to walk away. He stopped and had one more piercing remark to make. "Everything false he'll put out with the trash to be burned." He eyed each of them before turning again and walking along the banks of the river, changing his tone to share the joy of the good news with the people. The eager crowds followed along behind him, hungry for more teaching.

When John was out of earshot, the group of Pharisees and Sadducees huddled together, murmuring among themselves about this outrageous John the Baptizer, who was threatening the status quo of their religious world. Finally the ringleader silenced them with his hands and stared out in the distance at the prophet with the booming voice to whom the people were clearly listening, and responding in droves.

"We have a problem," Zeeb said. "This man is not only opposing *us,* but he has even condemned Herod Antipas for immorality over his questionable marriage to his brother's wife, causing political trouble in this region."

"How can this *nobody* have such an effect on the people? He has no formal education, he is not associated with the priesthood," Saar posed angrily. "Look at how he lives, like a wild animal out here in the wilderness, but the people are willing to travel a day's journey from Jerusalem to hear him!"

"We cannot allow him to continue to interfere with our handling of the people," Jarib pointed out. "But John is so popular, I don't know how we can stop him."

164

"We have to protect the people from false prophets and messiahs," Zeeb explained as he crossed his arms over his chest with a scowl on his face. "Even if that means eliminating them."

The next day broke with abundant sunshine across the countryside, and the Jordan River glimmered as the sun danced off its waters. Jesus sat on a hillside, gazing at the gathering crowds where John was baptizing, but he wasn't alone. Max, Liz, Kate, Al, Nigel, and Clarie sat there with him. The animals also had left Nazareth, but were careful to stay out of sight of other humans as Jesus traveled along. Jesus had a solution to how they could better travel together, but that would come with time. For now, they needed to lie low.

"Well, this is the big day," Jesus said.

"We are so honored to be with you as you begin your mission," Liz said. "Is it permissible for us to go down to the river as long as we stay out of sight?"

Jesus smiled and softly petted Liz. "Of course—I want you there."

"Aye, we can hide in the r-r-reeds then," Max suggested. "I'll find us a perfect spot."

"Splendid suggestion, old boy!" Nigel agreed.

Clarie grinned at Jesus. "The *reeds* will be perfect. We will be in earshot of everything you say, but out of sight."

"Very good. Pray for me, and pray for John," Jesus told them as he stood to leave. "This is a big day for him as well."

"We will all be praying for both of you, *mon ami,*" Liz said warmly, wrapping her tail around his legs. The other animals also gathered around Jesus for an affectionate embrace.

Suddenly they heard John bellowing to the crowds. His voice was so loud it carried up the hillside to where they sat.

"My, wha' a grand voice he has," Kate said happily, wagging her tail as she looked at John. "He's such a grown lad now. I remember he were such a sweet boy."

Al stared at John's clothing and wrinkled his brow. "What is he wearin'?"

"His clothes are made of camel hair," Liz explained.

"Well, that explains it," Al said with a nod of realization.

"Explains wha'?" Max asked.

"Sure, and he's as loud as Osahar the shoutin' camel were," Al explained matter-of-factly. "Must be the camel hair."

Everyone paused a moment before breaking out in laughter, especially Jesus.

"Oh, Al, the things you say," Jesus said, shaking his head. "Thanks for the jubilant sendoff."

With that Jesus made his way down the hill to the riverbank.

Max led the animals to a spot along the river where a large cluster of reeds grew. The wind was softly blowing the reeds and he smiled as he thought of home. His entire adventure with the Maker had begun with humming reeds along the loch in Scotland when Max heard the Voice calling him to the Ark. He half expected the reeds to speak now. No one uttered a word as the group hid. A holy moment was about to unfold.

John lifted an older woman from the water, and gently led her to the riverbank after her baptism, where she was joined in a loving embrace by her son. Jesus smiled tenderly at them, thinking of Mary. His gaze

165

then turned to John, and he walked straight toward him.

When John saw Jesus, his heart immediately jumped in his chest. His pulse started to race and he was flooded with the realization of who Jesus was. Scenes of their childhood encounters flashed through John's mind as he now saw the mature face of this one he had called "cousin." Now, he knew he must call him *Messiah*.

Jesus stepped into the water and the two men locked arms in greeting, but John shook his head in protest. This couldn't be right. This man was sinless!

"I need to be baptized by *you*, and yet you come to *me*?" John objected.

Jesus put his hand on John's shoulder and smiled at him with love. "Do this, John. God's work of putting things right all these centuries is coming together right now in this baptism."

"Why does John not want ta baptize Jesus?" Kate whispered.

"John's baptism follows people's repenting of their sins," Clarie explained quietly. "Jesus doesn't need to repent."

"So he is identifying with the sinners he came to save," Liz realized in awe.

"Exactly," Clarie affirmed. "And he is giving us a picture of what is to come."

John let go a deep breath and agreed to baptize Jesus. Together the remarkable cousins walked out to deeper water and John baptized Jesus.

For a moment Jesus was hidden under the water. All of a sudden the wind picked up and Jesus rose up out of the water, his head held back with eyes closed and his arms out. The reeds hummed and Jesus opened his eyes to see the heavens opening above him. John started tingling from head to toe, as did the animals.

Suddenly what appeared to be a dove landed on Jesus and from heaven came a commanding Voice. "THIS IS MY BELOVED SON! I TAKE DELIGHT IN HIM!"

Jesus basked in the love and affirmation of his heavenly Father. Oh, it had been so long since he had heard his Voice! Not since he left heaven to come to Earth had the three members of the Trinity been together, but now here at the Jordan River, Father, Son, and Holy Spirit were reunited. It was a glorious, holy moment!

John was filled with such joy to see this sign that had been promised to him now unfolding before his eyes. John was told the dove would light and remain on the promised Messiah, and this One would baptize with the Holy Spirit. John was witness to the affirmation of God!

"The Voice!" Max shouted excitedly, not caring if he was heard or not.

"That be the Maker!" Kate added.

"*Oui!* I shall never forget the first time I heard that Voice," Liz said with emotion.

"Aye, I'd know that Voice anywhere," Al said happily.

Nigel gaped at Jesus and John embracing in the water. "I say, I'm speechless."

Clarie smiled at her friends. "Max, why don't you chew off one of these Jordan River reeds to keep as a reminder of this special day?"

"That's a gr-r-rand idea, Lass, but I don't have anythin' ta carry a stick with besides me mouth," Max said, nosing his way through a clump of reeds.

Clarie considered Nigel's size. "A small one will do. In fact, if you get a really tiny one I can keep it tucked in my wool. Nigel, would you help Max?" "Of course, dear girl," Nigel exclaimed happily as Max easily pulled out a tiny reed no longer than Nigel's arm. The mouse scurried up to Clarie's back and tucked the tiny stick behind her ear. "How is that, my dear?"

"It's perfect," Clarie said, grinning to herself.

"Look, Jesus is leaving," Liz exclaimed. "We best go meet up with him."

The animals watched as Jesus walked up onto the riverbank and toward the far hillside.

"Aye, he'll be expectin' us," Max said, trotting off in Jesus' direction, the others following behind.

A serious expression grew on Clarie's face as she brought up the rear of the group. She knew that Jesus wouldn't just expect them. He would *need* them for the hard days ahead.

167

21

FORTY HUNGRY DAYS WITH THE TEMPTER

The animals ran through the countryside to catch up with Jesus. He was walking away from the river toward the Judean desert. Jesus heard them coming and turned to greet them with his warm smile. He squatted to get eye level with them, giving each of them a gentle petting.

"It was wonderful to see your baptism, Jesus!" Liz exclaimed with delight. "You must be feeling like you are on the top of the world, no?"

"I'm glad you were all there. Yes, it was wonderful to experience the approval of my Father like that," Jesus replied. "I'm excited to begin fulfilling my purpose of coming to Earth. But no one can stay on top of the world for long. Not here." Jesus opened his hand for Nigel so he could put the mouse on his shoulder. Nigel grinned and happily joined Jesus as he stood to start walking again.

"Where are we going, Jesus?" Nigel asked, sitting down comfortably on Jesus' shoulder.

"Into the wilderness," Jesus replied. "For a time of testing."

"Why do ye need ta be tested? Don't ye know *everythin'*?" Al asked with a confused look on his face.

Jesus smiled at Al's wonderful simplicity. "Not that kind of testing, Al. This is the kind of testing to prove I am worthy of the title 'Messiah.'"

"Who will be there to see this test?" Liz asked.

"My Father will be the main one watching, of course, along with all the heavenly beings," Jesus explained. "But the Tempter will be there."

"Satan?" Kate asked in alarm, moving next to Max. "He'll be there?"

"Yes, he will be the one giving the test," Jesus answered. "But he is coming only for me, so have no fear of him."

Max's fur stood on end at the thought of the snake who had tricked him so long ago on the Ark. Not only tricked him, but killed him and Liz. "If that snake lays so much as a *scale* on ye, I'll bite him in half!"

"You are indeed brave, Max," Jesus affirmed. "But understand that nothing will happen at the hand of this devil that hasn't already been approved for God's purposes—and will be used without his realizing it to fulfill the prophecies."

"So wha' are we supposed ta do in this mission ta help ye?" Max asked, feeling helpless. If there was anyone he wanted to protect, it was Jesus.

"Your mission for now is to give me comfort and support, and to watch and learn from me. Soon you'll meet a group of men I will call my disciples. Get to know them well, for they will need your help when I'm gone," Jesus explained. He stooped down again to look Max right in the eye. "When my time comes, you must let it come." Jesus continued again to walk forward, the animals walking on either side of him.

Max wrinkled his brow and breathed a heavy sigh. "Aye."

"But why do ye need ta prove anythin'?" Kate asked, still concerned.

"People across time will hear and someday even read about what happens out here in this wilderness," Jesus started. "This test is for them. They will know that I am exactly who I say I am by how I handle the test."

"Might I inquire as to how long we'll be out here in the wilderness?" Nigel asked.

"Forty days," Jesus said.

"That's how long it rained when we were on the Ark!" Al exclaimed, proud to remember something important.

"*Oui,* and this is also how long Moses was up on Mt. Sinai to get the Ten Commandments," Liz added.

"Brilliant observation! I might add that the prophet Elijah spent forty days on Mt. Horeb if I'm not mistaken," Nigel pointed out.

"An' Israel spent forty *years* in the wilderness," Max added. "Aye, that were a long spell. I thought it would never end."

"Yes, it was, Max. But where Israel failed in their testing, I will not," Jesus said determinedly.

"I do love a touch of *déjà vu*, no?" Liz remarked. "There is nothing like being reminded of things."

"Indeed, my pet," Nigel said. "And as we've seen across time, the humans need quite a bit of reminding!"

Jesus and the animals came to a place where the greenery of the Jordan Valley started to be sparse. They were leaving a place of beauty and provision, and heading into a desolate, rocky place lacking every comfort. Jesus stopped and gazed up into the wilderness area, anticipating what awaited him there.

"If you really want to know where we're going," Jesus said with solid resolve, "we're going into battle."

Jesus walked ahead while the animals looked at each other nervously. Clarie looked them all in the eye. "Don't worry. This battle is one we'll watch, not fight." Their gaze followed the strong, good, secure person of Jesus walking confidently into the wilderness. "Besides, I think we all know who will win."

170

By late afternoon they came to a flat area protected by a cluster of boulders and one lone tree. Behind them was a rock cliff that rose in gradual, ragged ledges to a high peak. Sand blew around their feet and dry scrub brush peppered the ground around them. The tree gave little shade, and looked parched. Broken rocks and stones lay everywhere. Jesus sat down in the shade and stretched out his legs, leaning his head on the trunk of the tree. He inhaled deeply through his nose and slowly breathed out through his mouth. He was tired.

"I'm starved. When can we eat?" Al asked pitifully as the animals gathered in a circle around Jesus.

"Aye, I could do with some vittles then," Max echoed, looking around. There appeared to be nothing to eat in sight.

Liz gave a thorough look around at their setting and frowned. "I do not see any food here. Perhaps we need to follow this dry creek bed to find some."

Jesus opened his eyes and pointed in the distance. "If you go about half a mile down that way you'll find some date palm trees and a small spring of water. Also a jujube tree."

"A jujube tree! *C'est bon!* I've always wanted to see one!" Liz enthused, ever excited about plant life.

"Jujube? Wha' kind of tree is that?" Kate asked.

"It's a beautiful little tree in the Ziziphus genus of the Rhamnaceae family," Liz rattled off easily. "It has thorns but small, delicious green fruit that tastes like an apple."

"I love apples!" Al exclaimed. "Sure, I like bananas better but apples will do. Can we get some now?"

"I'll lead the way then," Max ordered as he began trotting off.

"Jesus, can we bring you some fruit?" Clarie asked, putting her sweet face near his.

Jesus turned and placed his hand on her blemish-free face and smiled. "No, but thank you, Clarie. I won't be eating for a while. I need to fast so I am ready."

"I say, a fast helps one to focus on matters of the mind and spirit," Nigel said, wiping off his dusty spectacles. "Splendid practice, fasting. How long do you plan to fast, Jesus?"

"Forty days," Jesus replied.

Al's eyes got as big as apples and he gripped Jesus' leg with wild concern. "Ye're not eatin' for FORTY DAYS?!"

"No," Jesus said simply.

Al put his paws up to his mouth in concern. "But there'll be nothin' *left* o' ye!"

"Trust me," Jesus said, giving Al a comforting pat on the head. "This will make me strong. You'll see."

Al shook his head in confusion and worry. "I jest don't see how. I can hardly make it forty *minutes* without food, much less forty days."

Clarie studied Jesus. "Everyone, let's go down to the spring. Jesus needs some time alone."

Jesus met her gaze and nodded.

Kate put her paw on Al, who was beside himself over Jesus going without food. "Our Jesus knows best," she reminded him.

"*Oui, cher* Albert," Liz agreed as they moved on. "Jesus has more important things to occupy his mind and spirit right now."

The animals walked to the spring and refreshed themselves with water and food while Jesus sat alone. They were soon to find that this solitude and discipline would be vital for what was to come.

Late one afternoon Max came back from the spring and didn't see Jesus under the tree. His alarm went up and he began to race around the scrubby brushes, looking for Jesus. "Jesus! Jesus! Where ye be?" Max called.

Max's shouting caught the attention of the others, who came running back to the tree.

"Where is he?" Liz asked.

"I can't find him!" Max yelled.

"Oh, dear," Kate lamented, looking around anxiously. Nigel rode on her back and put his paw to his eye to give a good look around. Suddenly they heard Clarie.

172

"Over here," Clarie called from up on a jagged ledge, her fluffy little tail waving.

Nigel pointed to where the lamb called from. "That way, dear girl!" he directed Kate.

Max, Liz, Kate, Al, and Nigel joined Clarie up on the ledge, and couldn't believe what they saw. Jesus was sitting on another ledge in the distance next to a lion, its front paws dangling off the edge.

"Is it . . . Lucifer?" Nigel asked Clarie, jumping off Kate to stand by the lamb. The evil one had taken the form of a wicked lion the night Herod slaughtered the newborn boys in Bethlehem. Nigel had been too late to get to Clarie, who had encountered Lucifer alone.

"No, Nigel," Clarie smiled and said. "It's just a lion. Jesus has been with the wild beasts all morning. There were a pack of hyenas and a few wild boars here earlier. He blessed them all."

Liz studied the scene of Jesus and the lion and could tell he was talking to the king of the beasts. Jesus was examining the big cat's paw while the lion winced. He gently pulled what looked like a large thorn from its paw. Liz smiled. "It appears Jesus is helping my larger cousin."

"Aye, that beastie is lickin' him then," Max added, shaking his head in wonder as Jesus laughed while the lion licked his face.

"Jesus made these beasties after all," Al remarked casually, chewing on a jujube fruit. "I'm sure he's missed playin' with them in heaven."

Everyone looked at Al in amazement. It was astounding to consider that Jesus, the Word who was God and was with God as all of creation was brought into being would delight in simply *being* with his creation.

Jesus leaned over and hugged the lion. It was a tender moment. The animals gazed in awe of Jesus with this ferocious beast that was now as docile as Al. Jesus patted the lion's back and leaned against the wild beast, closing his eyes in complete peace.

"If we observed nothing else with Jesus, seeing the wildest of animals come to him is enough to show he is indeed Messiah," Nigel said with his paws clasped behind his back. "Isaiah said, 'The Spirit of the Lord will rest on him,' as we saw at his baptism, and one day all creatures of creation will lie down together in harmony."

"Oui," Liz whispered softly, thinking of Isaiah's prophecies of Jesus as a lamb. "The lion will lie down with the Lamb."

173

Over the course of the next few days there were so many wild animals coming and going it became routine to see Jesus with a hedgehog or a porcupine, a gazelle or a jackal, a wolf or a fox. The animals marveled at his control over creation, and his delight in it.

Everyone was gathered quietly around Jesus, who sat under the tree, praying. Max' head snapped up and a growl entered his throat when he saw a black snake slithering toward Jesus.

"It's probably jest another wild animal comin' ta see him," Kate said quietly, putting a paw on Max. "Isn't it?"

Suddenly their fur stood on end. This was no ordinary snake.

Jesus opened his eyes and placed a hand on Max, who now stood with ears and tail up, growling. As the snake got close, it suddenly rose up and kept rising until it morphed into the human form of a man, wearing the same black as its scales had been. He cricked his head back and forth with his hands to work the kinks out of his neck. Then he turned his gaze on the animals and gave a sinister chuckle.

"I see your little friends are with you. How sweet," Satan said with a sneer.

Jesus stood and walked in between Satan and the animals, who huddled in close together behind him. "What do you want?"

Satan cocked his head and studied Jesus. A wicked grin grew on his face. He knew Jesus had been fasting and was terribly hungry. "Let's talk about what *you* want."

Satan picked up two stones and rolled them over in his hands. "If God can use these stones to raise up sons of Abraham, surely they can be used to satisfy your hunger." Satan held them out to Jesus. "If you are the Son of God, tell these stones to become bread."

Jesus looked Satan in the eye with such fierceness that the sneer left the devil's face. "It is written: Man does not live on bread alone, but on every word that comes from the mouth of God."

Satan gripped the stones so tightly his knuckles whitened and his eyes turned red. He stood there fuming under Jesus' powerful gaze. His angry grip suddenly crushed the stones into dust, and his body also turned into dust, disappearing before their eyes.

"He's gone!" Max said, stepping forward.

Jesus calmly turned and sat down again under the tree. "He'll be back."

174

A week passed after that terrible experience of seeing Satan confront Jesus with his first test. Everyone was on edge, waiting for the snake to reappear at any moment, except for Jesus. He continued to fast, commune with the wild beasts, and spend hours alone in prayer. Jesus was anything but weak. Although he hadn't eaten in weeks, his spirit was as solid as the rock he sat on.

One morning while Jesus was off praying, Clarie told the animals to follow her to a special spot behind a cluster of rocks.

"It's time for the second test for Jesus, but we cannot be with him. Still, we will be able to witness what happens," Clarie promised, pointing to a Seven Seal that was affixed to a rock.

"We're going into the IAMISPHERE?" Liz asked. "Nigel, can you break the seal?"

Nigel stepped up to the rock and adjusted his spectacles as he studied the seal. "Right. I believe I can nibble it on a rock, although I am used to paper. Let's give it a go, shall we?"

"Steady, lad," Max said to calm a very nervous Al, who never liked doing this. Al put his paws up over his eyes and nodded.

Nigel nibbled the seal and instantly they were in the IAMISPHERE. And of course, so was Gillamon.

"What do you think of our Messiah?" Gillamon said with his warm eyes and gentle voice.

"Ah, Gillamon, there's no one like Jesus," Max said, running up to embrace his old friend. "It's gr-r-rand ta see ye."

"He's the most loving person we've ever known," Kate said happily, watching scenes of Jesus' life swirling around them.

"*Oui*, what a joy he is!" Liz added, smiling at a scene of Jesus playing hide and seek with the children in Nazareth.

"The wild beasties like him, too," Al said, removing his paws from his eyes. "But he hasn't eaten in *weeks!* I'm worried aboot the lad."

"No need to worry about him," Gillamon said, smiling. "Watch."

Gillamon put his hoof up on the wall of the IAMISPHERE and all the panels swirled into one large pane that proceeded to completely encircle them. Each of the animals turned around and gazed at this incredible 360-degree view of Jerusalem. It felt as if they were *actually* in the scene, but they remained in the IAMISPHERE.

175

They saw Jesus and Satan standing at the highest point in the Temple complex in Jerusalem, up on the flat-topped corner of Solomon's porch. Below them was the Kidron Valley. The second test was starting.

"If you are the Son of God, throw yourself down, for it is written: 'He will command his angels concerning you, and they will lift you up in their hands, so that you will not strike your foot against a stone.'"

Jesus shook his head at Satan's attempt to use Scripture as a weapon. "It is also written: 'Do not put the Lord your God to the test.'"

"That devil is sadly mistaken," Nigel said, wrinkling his brow in anger. "He's twisting what the psalmist wrote about stumbling with Jesus deliberately jumping off this high point!"

"*Oui*, we cannot test God's faithfulness to his Word by forcing him to act in certain ways," Liz added, swishing her tail back and forth in contempt.

Gillamon put his hoof into the pane and it swirled around them so fast they had to close their eyes lest they get dizzy. The scene slowed down and they soon saw that Jesus and Satan were no longer in Jerusalem. "Observe," Gillamon said. "The third test."

They were on the top of a mountain so high they could see all the kingdoms of the world spread out below them. It was surreal. Israel, Persia, Egypt, Rome, and other lesser kingdoms glistened like gold in the sun. It was as if the wealth amassed in these kingdoms was on display, but it was more than treasure. There was a feeling of power that radiated over the kingdoms.

Satan placed his fists on his hips and took in a deep breath as he smiled and nodded, reveling in the fact he had been given temporary authority over the earth. He turned around and smiled at Jesus as a gracious host would greet a welcome guest, with his arms spread out to communicate that what was his could belong to Jesus.

"All this will I give you," Satan said, arrogantly raising his chin in the air, "if you will bow down and worship me."

Anger welled up in Jesus at the brazen offer of this wicked devil. He lifted his arm and pointed his finger to the distant horizon. "Get out of here, Satan! For it is written: 'Worship the Lord your God, and serve him only.'"

Satan shrank back at Jesus' rebuke. He dropped his hands to his sides and the arrogant smile melted off his twisted face. He lowered his head and immediately vanished. Jesus stood there looking out at the kingdoms of the earth. A tear fell from his eye as he looked with love upon these cultures of peoples who chased many gods. But not the one true God. Suddenly, Jesus vanished as well.

Gillamon once more put his hoof in the pane and it swirled until they were again viewing the one lone tree in the wilderness where they had been with Jesus for forty days. All of a sudden they all broke through the pane and were standing there together. This time Gillamon remained with them. They had just witnessed two more tests from Satan that Jesus had passed with perfection. Their emotions swirled like the panes of the IAMISPHERE, and their minds reeled with questions.

"Will he be back?" Al asked timidly, wondering if they should expect the evil one again.

"Yes," Gillamon said, clenching his jaw as he looked down through time in his mind. "When the time is right. He'll be back."

Jesus was suddenly there under the tree, but he was not alone. He was surrounded by scores of angels ministering to him.

"Would ye look at that?" Max emphasized triumphantly. "The very same help that Jesus turned down when it would have put the Maker ta the test is now r-r-right here at his side. If that's not a gr-r-rand turn of events, I don't know wha' is!"

"Satan used all he has, but failed," Gillamon noted. "He only has three weapons of temptation to throw at anyone. He used the same ones on Adam and Eve."

"Only thr-r-ree?" Max asked, wide-eyed.

"All temptation comes from the Devil and can only be one of three things: the desire of the flesh, the yearning of the eyes, and the pride of life," Gillamon explained. "In other words, he'll try to get you to want something physically because it looks like something you would enjoy."

"Like in the Garden, no? Satan tempted Eve with a piece of the most delicious-looking fruit she had ever seen, and she wanted to taste it," Liz observed.

Gillamon nodded in affirmation. "That's right, Liz. He'll also make you want things and possessions to such a point you'll do anything to get them, even hurt others. Worldly possessions aren't wrong *per se*. But *how* you get them and use them can be."

"Ye mean like when thieves steal ta get tr-r-reasure?" Max asked with a scowl.

"Or, I daresay, when students cheat to get good grades in school?" Nigel added. "I saw this sometimes in the Egyptian school where I lived for years. Simply dastardly practice!"

"Precisely," Gillamon replied. "Finally that snake will try to get you to want things because of what they can give you, like power, fame, wealth, or glory."

"But isn't it correct that temptation is not sin?" Liz posed.

"Right again, Liz. To be faced with a situation and *think* about what to do is not sin. Sin happens when you *desire* the opportunity, and take it," Gillamon explained. "And know this. You can only be tempted with something *you* would want. What tempts one creature may not tempt another. So what does that tell you about the enemy?"

"The enemy must get to know you well enough to know what would tempt you," Nigel observed with a frown.

"Jesus used God's Word ta beat that snake," Kate said with force.

"Dear Kate, you have discovered the secret weapon that will beat the Devil every time it's used. If humans and creatures throw God's Word at him, he has to run away," Gillamon instructed them with a reassuring smile.

Clarie's eyes filled with tears as she realized Jesus had passed all three tests. "Satan tried to keep Jesus from being a suffering Messiah by giving him an easier route than the cross."

"Indeed," Nigel affirmed. "He offered Jesus the option of being a *prideful* Messiah to use his powers for his personal use of making bread, and not for the glory of the Maker."

"Or to be a *spectacular* Messiah by gaining followers with a miraculous stunt of jumping off the Temple," Liz added.

"Or of bein' a *compromisin'* Messiah an' bowin' a knee ta that snake so he'd give him all the earthly kingdoms," Max scowled.

"Sufferin' were the route he chose, above all others," Kate said reverently.

Nigel cleared his throat with emotion. "What he will someday do to save the world, he will do willingly. It will be by his choice."

"And that is why he alone can hold the title of Messiah," Gillamon said softly.

The Order of the Seven sat for a long while, watching the angels ministering to Jesus. They brought him food and water, cleaned him up, and surrounded him with adoration. Jesus eventually fell asleep, exhausted from those forty long days of hunger and testing in the wilderness. Angels hovered over him as he slept, not leaving his side for a moment as the blanket of bright stars lit up the dark wilderness sky.

The animals were also exhausted from all they had seen and experienced that day. They each began to yawn and lie down quietly. No one spoke another word.

Gillamon looked at them fondly, and whispered softly as the animals began drifting off to sleep. "Rest well. Tomorrow we leave this wilderness." He turned his gaze to Jesus, who was sound asleep. "And the ministry of Messiah begins."

22

Come and See

A l's nose twitched. *Sniff, sniff.* He stirred, half-asleep and not wanting to come awake. But the aroma that tickled his nose was stronger than his need for sleep. Drool ran down his chin. *Sniff, sniff, sniff. Bread? BREAD?* Al's eyes flashed open and he sat up straight. There before him was an old man cooking bread over a fire.

"Good morning," the man winked and said. "Hungry?"

"Am I *hungry*?" Al asked, then thought to himself, *What a silly question!* "AYE!" Al jumped up and excitedly took the bread offered to him by the old man. Joyful tears filled his eyes as he devoured the delicious bread. It had been so long since he had had anything hot to eat, having been out here in the wilderness with Jesus. "Yummm-mmmmmmmmm!" Al moaned as he chewed with eyes closed in utter delight. Suddenly it dawned on him he had taken bread from a complete stranger. Swallowing hard, Al opened his eyes and squinted at the man. "Who are ye?"

The old man wore a dusty brown shepherd's robe, and had a long, white beard that matched his bushy white eyebrows. His skin was weathered with deep laugh lines around his warm, blue eyes. Next to the old man stood a donkey with saddle bags draped over her back. The old man patted the donkey, laughed softly, leaned over, and offered Al another piece of bread. "Al, don't you recognize us?"

Al looked him over suspiciously and slowly took the bread. He turned around and saw the others gathered by Jesus: Max, Liz, Kate, and Nigel. Soon realization spread across his face and he broke out in a wide grin. "Gillamon? Clarie?"

The donkey suddenly blurted out, "HEE-HAW!"

Gillamon leaned back and slapped his knee lightheartedly. "I have to admit, this never gets old." He held out his hands to look at them front and back, and wiggled his fingers. "It's nice to have fingers. Humans don't realize how easy they have it with these ten little tools."

"Aye, like for makin' breakfast!" Al enthused. "So why are ye a man and not a goat then? And why is Clarie a donkey and not a lamb?"

"I'm going with you all as Jesus heads back to the Jordan River," Gillamon explained. "Clarie and I will be your 'cover' so people will think I'm just an old man traveling with my beloved animals. Clarie will help us carry supplies, and if you like, carry *you* for the journey. It wouldn't do for Jesus to have all of you around as he starts to call his disciples."

"What's a disciple?" Al asked.

180

"*Bonjour,* Albert," Liz said, giving him a good morning kiss. "A disciple is a student, one who learns."

"So Jesus is goin' to be a teacher?" Al asked with his mouth full, crumbs falling into his fluffy, orange fur.

"He already is," Nigel said with a hearty chuckle. "I say, are we about done here? Jesus is ready to depart."

"Just let me put out this fire," Gillamon said, removing his baking stone, but quickly dropping it. "Ouch!" He shook his hand and the donkey reached over to lick his fingers.

"Guess ye forgot those ten little tools feel heat then," Al said, stretching long and hard.

"Indeed," Gillamon said, shaking his head at himself. "Thank you, Clarie."

"We have an exciting day ahead," Jesus greeted them, stretching his back.

"Jesus, how many disciples will you have?" Liz asked.

"Thousands will follow me as I teach, just as they have followed John the Baptist," Jesus replied. "But I will eventually name twelve of them to be my official disciples. This won't happen for many months. When the time for training comes, I will call them by name."

"I say, this is terribly exciting!" Nigel shared, fiddling with his spectacles. "I expect you'll be calling the brightest scholars, who can grasp your level of teaching. Will you call rabbis? Or scribes perhaps?"

"Come and see," Jesus replied, smiling without an answer. He stooped to offer Nigel his hand. Nigel happily scurried into Jesus' open palm and Jesus placed the mouse gently on his shoulder.

"Aye! Let's be on our way then," Max answered. "Gillamon, I'm glad ta be yer dog."

"Good boy," Gillamon said, patting Max on the head.

"Me, too!" Kate chimed in, wagging her tail and waiting in line for a petting from Gillamon, who gave her a good scratch behind the ears.

"I understand we will part company as we approach the river area," Liz posed.

"Yes, we will peel off with Gillamon, and go ahead of Jesus to prepare a place for him to bring his disciples," Clarie confirmed. "Liz and Al, do you wish to ride with me?"

"Aye, let's get out o' this wilderness and back to real food," Al exclaimed.

Gillamon lifted Al and Liz to place them in Clarie's saddlebags.

"Al, I couldn't agree more," Jesus said, smiling and scratching Al under the chin. "And just wait until you see the kind of food we'll be eating with my disciples."

Al purred and thought about what it could be. "Bananas?" he asked wishfully.

Jesus threw his head back and laughed. "Fish!"

A big, goofy grin appeared on Al's face. "Well, what are we waitin' for then?"

Jesus began walking away from the one lone tree, the Order of the Seven following along behind. He was finished with his time here in the wilderness. He had passed the test and now had a divine appointment with a group of unlikely men who would someday turn the world upside down.

"There he is," Liz observed as they came to the bank of the Jordan River. They saw John the Baptist in the distance.

Gillamon walked up to stand next to Jesus. "I will have everything ready, Master."

Jesus stopped and smiled. His heart raced with the thrill of what was getting ready to begin. "Very well. I will see you shortly."

As Jesus walked toward the riverbank, Gillamon and the animals proceeded along the road. "Let's go set up camp. Company is coming."

John the Baptist stood with two of his followers on the riverbank. They were in a deep discussion.

"So when Isaiah wrote, 'The government will be upon his shoulder,' he showed that Messiah will be a ruler," John the follower said. "That much is clear."

"Indeed, Isaiah says just a few verses later that, 'Of the increase of his government and of peace there will be no end, on the throne of David and over his Kingdom, to establish it and to uphold it,'" Andrew added. "Messiah will definitely be a *King*."

John the Baptizer saw Jesus coming in the distance and was in awe of the presence of the Holy Spirit clearly on his cousin. He kept his eyes on Jesus but answered his two followers, Andrew and John. "Yes, he will be a king. But he will also be the final lamb needed to take away the sin of the world . . ." John trailed off, taking a few steps forward and meeting Jesus' gaze. They locked eyes and Jesus smiled, but kept on walking.

John pointed his finger at Jesus and said in a loud voice, "Behold, the Lamb of God!"

Andrew and John quickly turned to see who John the Baptist was talking about. They had heard him speak of the One who had come to him for baptism—the true One they should follow as Messiah. It was this kind of teaching that had attracted these men and their friends. This man John the Baptist wasn't trying to build a religious empire for himself, but was simply preparing the way for the One men should truly follow. So Andrew and John were prepared, ready at a moment's notice to follow John the Baptist's lead. Immediately they ran after Jesus. John the Baptist crossed his arms and nodded his head in approval as his two followers left him. *This is how it should be,* he said to himself. *They are yours now, Jesus.*

Jesus heard the two men running up behind him. He turned and stopped. "What are you seeking?" he asked simply.

Andrew and John looked at one another, seeing who would speak first. "Teacher," Andrew finally blurted out awkwardly, rubbing his hand on his brown tunic. "Where are you staying?"

John nodded enthusiastically in agreement. Jesus smiled, fully aware these men wanted to know far more than simply where Jesus was staying. "Come and see."

Together the three men walked across the countryside toward the place where people coming to see John the Baptist stayed. A tiny village of huts and makeshift camel-hair tents was off the main road, a short walk north of where they were. They got to know each other as they walked along.

"I'm Andrew, son of John, originally from Bethsaida," Andrew started.

"Ah, so you don't live there now?" Jesus asked.

"No, my brother Simon and I now live in Capernaum," the young man replied, feeling a little more comfortable. "We're fishermen."

"So are we," John interjected. "I mean, my brother James and I. We're fishermen, too."

"Fishing is an important job. It feeds many," Jesus affirmed. "Do you enjoy it?"

Andrew shrugged his shoulders. "It's hard work, but good work. Simon is the one who handles all the business. I just do what he asks."

Jesus looked at John. "What about you, John?"

"We're sons of a fisherman, so it's a family business," John explained. "I do sometimes wish for more in life."

"When you're doing what you were truly made to do, then work takes on a new meaning," Jesus noted. "It becomes your passion."

"And what is your passion?" John asked Jesus.

Jesus stopped and put his hand on John's shoulder. "To seek and save those who are lost."

John glanced at Andrew and the two men shared a look full of anticipation.

"John the Baptist told us you were the promised One for whom Israel has waited," Andrew related with growing excitement.

"He said we should follow you now," John quickly added.

"John speaks truth," Jesus said. He locked eyes with Andrew and John and they shared a brief moment of understanding. The fishermen didn't even know how to respond. They were walking down the road with a man who was possibly the promised Messiah, foretold by prophets and expected for hundreds of years by the people of Israel. How could they respond?

183

Suddenly they heard Max barking. Jesus smiled, turned, and pointed to a tent up ahead. "Ah, here we are."

Jesus led them to the tent where Gillamon sat just outside with a small fire, baking more bread. He stood when Jesus, Andrew, and John came up to him.

"This is where I'm staying. Please, meet my friend," Jesus stopped and said, giving a knowing look at the old man, "Gillamon."

"Shalom. Please, sit and I will serve you," Gillamon said as they gathered around the fire.

"Thank you," Andrew and John answered in unison, sitting down with Jesus.

"I see you have many animals," John said as Liz came up to him, purring and rubbing her cheek on his blue tunic.

"Bonjour," Liz meowed. John smiled and petted her head.

"Yes, they are my friends," Gillamon said warmly, handing the men some bread. Al came into the midst of them, batting at the bread. "But watch out for this orange one. He'll eat anything in sight."

Max and Kate came up wagging their tails and sat next to Andrew. Nigel peeked out from Clarie's saddlebag. The animals were excited to witness the beginning of Jesus' ministry with these young men.

"I say, they don't look like rabbis," Nigel whispered in Clarie's ear as he scurried up onto her head.

"Remember what Ahura said about Jesus," Clarie whispered. "Expect the unexpected."

The hour grew late. Andrew and John had spent the day with Jesus. They were amazed and filled with excitement at all they had heard.

"Teacher, may I please go get my brother?" Andrew asked. "I want him to meet you."

"Of course," Jesus replied. "I'll be here until tomorrow."

Andrew got up quickly. "It can't wait until tomorrow. I'll be right back!" He ran off down the road, leaving Jesus there with John and Gillamon.

Andrew ran to the tent where he and his brother were staying. There he found Simon lying on his mat, with his eyes closed. Simon was a big man, with wild, curly black hair and dirt all over his deep red tunic.

"Simon, get up!" Andrew said, kicking his brother's foot.

Simon opened his eyes and kicked Andrew back forcefully in the shin. "What is it?!" he scowled, scratching his thick black beard.

"Ow!" Andrew rubbed his shin, and squatted down next to Simon. "We've found Messiah!"

Simon's scowl turned into a look of surprise. Andrew grabbed his hand and pulled Simon to his feet. "Come on, get up! Come and see!"

Together they hurried back to Jesus as Andrew rattled on and on about this man they had met. When they came to Jesus' tent, Simon stopped short. Andrew pushed him forward. "Teacher, this is my brother, Simon."

Max and Liz sat by one another. Liz immediately looked the rough, burly man over and nudged Max in the side. "This one reminds me of you, *mon ami.*"

Max cocked his head to the side. "Why, Lass?"

Liz shrugged her shoulders. "Just a feeling, no?"

Jesus studied the big fisherman for a moment. "So, you are Simon the son of John," he said as he stood to walk over to the man. He placed his hand on Simon's shoulder. "You shall be called 'Peter'!" Jesus laughed and slapped Peter on the back. "Come, sit with us."

185

Simon looked at Andrew with a "What have you gotten me into?" look. Andrew grinned and shrugged his shoulders.

"So the first thing Jesus says ta the man is that he's goin' ta give him a nickname?" Max whispered to Liz.

Liz's tail swished back and forth as she considered Jesus' unusual greeting. *"Oui.* Do you know what 'Peter' means?"

"No, Lass, but I'm sure ye do," Max replied.

"Peter means 'rock,'" Liz explained. "But I don't know why Jesus has done this."

Max studied Peter. "Maybe he sees somethin' in him we don't?"

"Undoubtedly," Liz replied, marveling at Jesus' approach. She looked up at the night sky to the stars that were by now lighting up the darkness. The words of the psalmist came to mind: *"He determines the number of the stars and calls them each by name."* Twelve disciples. Hmmm."

"Wha' does that have ta do with Peter?" Max asked. "Jesus called him a rock, not a star then."

"Perhaps he will be both," Liz pondered. "We can't see the stars when the sun is shining. But when the sun disappears, that's when the stars shine."

The next morning they got up early. Jesus decided they would be going to Galilee, and had invited Andrew, John, and Peter to join them for the journey, as they had to make their way home as well. It was time to get back to their fishing business. As they were nearing the turnoff to Capernaum, Jesus found a young man along the way who was also traveling in their direction.

"Follow me," Jesus commanded the young man.

His name was Philip. The young man joined in the conversation with Andrew, John, Peter, and Jesus and immediately was caught up in the excitement of who he "just so happened to meet" on the way home. After a while they stopped to rest and to eat.

"Teacher, there's someone I need to go find," Philip said, lifting his hands and motioning in the distance. "I'll be right back."

Jesus nodded. "We'll be here."

Philip went running down the road and soon came to a house with a fig tree growing out back. He ran around to the back of the house and there he found his best friend Nathaniel sitting under the fig tree with his eyes closed, meditating. Several scrolls sat on the ground around him.

"Nathaniel!" Philip shouted and fell down next to him, breathing hard from running all the way.

Nathaniel quickly opened his eyes. "What?! You startled me!"

Philip saw the scrolls he knew very well, as he and Nathaniel had studied them together. They constantly pored over the prophecies, eager to discover Messiah, for they knew from Daniel that his time was near. He lifted the scroll of Moses and held it up triumphantly. "We have found the One about whom Moses wrote in the Law. The Prophets wrote about him, too. His name is Jesus, the son of Joseph, from Nazareth!"

A sarcastic grin appeared on Nathaniel's face. "Nazareth? There's no talk of Nazareth in the prophecies. *Bethlehem* is where Messiah is supposed to be from," he argued. "Besides, can anything good come out of Nazareth?"

186

Philip put down the scroll and smiled at his sarcastic friend. Nathaniel was from Cana, and Cana and Nazareth were rival towns. Nazareth was known for its roughness and low-class citizens. But it was a larger city than Cana, so boasted more importance from trade. Cana was such a puny, out-of-the-way place that no one went there unless they had a good reason. It was always a side trip destination. Philip ignored Nathaniel's expression of doubt, which he understood was well-founded. Nathaniel had a good heart and was genuine in his quest for Messiah.

"Come and see," Philip said, standing up and holding his hand out to Nathaniel.

Soon they neared the place where Jesus and the others were resting. Jesus stood with his hands on his hips and grinned broadly as Nathaniel approached. Jesus pointed to him and said, "Here is a true Israelite; no deceit is in him."

Nathaniel stopped and looked at him, clearly uncomfortable with this greeting. "How do you . . . know me?"

Jesus walked up to Nathaniel and looked him in the eye. "Before Philip called you, when you were under the fig tree—I saw you," he said with a smile and a look that peered deep into Nathaniel's soul.

Nathaniel's eyes widened and a wave of truth washed over him with such force he knew in an instant Jesus was genuine. Even though he didn't understand, he knew. "Rabbi, you are the son of God! You are the King of Israel!"

Jesus leaned his head back and looked at Nathaniel. "Because I said, 'I saw you under the fig tree,' you believe?" He chuckled warmly and leaned in close to Nathaniel's face again. "You will see greater things than these. You will see heaven opened and the angels of God ascending and descending on the Son of Man." He winked at Nathaniel.

Philip came up and gripped his best friend by the shoulders, shaking him good humoredly. "What did I tell you?"

Together the men shared a laugh as Andrew, John, and Peter introduced themselves to Nathaniel. Gillamon leaned against the tree with his arms folded.

"Gillamon, what exactly did Jesus mean by all that?" Nigel asked from between the branches next to his head.

"Jacob the deceiver wrestled with God one night at Bethel," Gillamon started. "That night he had a dream about a ladder reaching

187

to heaven. Unlike Jacob, Jesus knows Nathaniel's heart is genuine. He wanted to show him that just as Jacob received a supernatural revelation, so will Nathaniel and these disciples experience such supernatural things, affirming that Jesus is the Christ, Messiah."

"Brilliant! And am I correct to assume that Jesus' analogy makes him the new Ladder now to reach heaven?" Nigel asked excitedly.

"Indeed he is, Nigel. It's a new dream followed by a new day dawning." Gillamon looked at Jesus and these five disciples with a look of deep satisfaction. "Jesus is now the way to God. And it will be up to these men to do exactly as they've already done so far."

Nigel nodded. "The disciples will tell people to 'come and see.'"

HASTE TO THE WEDDING

"A weddin'?! I LOVE weddin's!" Al enthused.

Liz smiled and shook her head at her big, lovable mate. She knew that the part Al loved about weddings had nothing to do with the joining of two lives in holy matrimony before God. It was the food.

"Can we go now?" Al said, pulling on Gillamon's cloak. "These things only last seven days, ye know. We'd best be on our way so we don't miss *any* o' it! I'd hate for them to run out o' anythin' before we get there."

"Jesus and his disciples have been invited to the wedding in Cana, but I don't recall seeing your name on the guest list," Gillamon teased.

"How do I get me name on the list?" Al implored, now grabbing Gillamon's cloak with both front paws. "I've *got* to get to that weddin'!"

Jesus stood behind Al, listening to the ever-hungry cat's pleadings. He and Gillamon shared a look and it was all Gillamon could do to keep from bursting out laughing. Jesus put a hand on his stomach and laughed silently. Finally he regained his composure and decided to put Al out of his misery.

"What's this about the wedding?" Jesus asked.

Al turned abruptly and ran to Jesus. "Jesus, pleeeeeeeeease let me go to the weddin' with ye! I promise to be a good kitty and not be in the way." He gave Jesus his best big-eyed, lovable smile.

"Why, Al, I didn't realize you were so passionate about weddings," Jesus replied. "But since we are guests of this family in Cana, we shouldn't impose with any more guests on their list. These people do not have much wealth, so it will be a modest wedding."

Al frowned. "But will it last seven days?"

"Yes, that is the Jewish custom," Jesus answered.

"Well, it's their job to feed their guests while they're there so if they have seven days o' food, they must have enough then," Al insisted, wiping the drool accidentally spilling from his mouth at the thought of so much food. "I don't eat much."

Jesus frowned and gave Al a convicting look. Al's ears went back. The plump cat swallowed and held up his paws to make a show of how much he'd eat. "Sure, I do eat a lot but compared with what the humans eat it's not much. PLEASE, Jesus! Let me go with you!"

Jesus crossed his arms and tilted his head as he observed Al. A slow grin appeared on his face. "Al, I do admire your persistence. That is an admirable trait. Other kitties would give up, but not you," he said. "You have promised to not be in the way and to be a good kitty. You can come, Al. I will have Gillamon bring you some scraps from the feast. But you must stay out of the main guest area, agreed?"

"Aye! I promise! Oh, thank ye, Jesus!" cried Al, embracing Jesus' legs with his paws and closing his eyes in gratitude. "I'll be a good kitty."

Jesus leaned down and scratched Al on the head. "Very well. We're leaving now, so go over to Clarie."

"Aye! Right away!" Al exclaimed as he ran over to Clarie to stand obediently until Gillamon lifted him up for the ride. He started humming a merry tune, bouncing his head side-to-side with joy.

Clarie looked down at Al as she listened to his little song. She knew he was humming an Irish dancing tune called *Haste to the Wedding*. Even though the animals had temporarily forgotten they were from the year 1741, Clarie grinned when they would do things with insight from the future. "That's a sweet little tune, Al. What's it called?" she teased.

"Hmmm . . . I don't remember where I learned it, Lass," Al replied as he kept bobbing his head and then began dancing an Irish jig around Clarie. "Did ye know we're goin' to a weddin'?!"

"Yes, I did," Clarie said, smiling.

Jesus leaned and whispered into Gillamon's ear. "Al doesn't need to know he was coming to the wedding all along. Persistent asking for things is a good quality, especially when my creation comes to me. If the request is for something good that will bless them, it gives me delight to grant it." "And I might say, you give with generous extravagance," Gillamon replied. "But I'll keep this between us."

"Good man," Jesus said with a wink to Gillamon. "Let's go."

"Master, I am glad we are able to attend this wedding with you," Nathaniel told Jesus with excitement. "It is an honor to have you in my hometown of Cana."

"I'm glad as well, Nathaniel. Cana isn't out of the way for me. It's an important destination," Jesus affirmed.

"That's the house, just up there," Nathaniel pointed, running a little ahead. "I can hear the music!"

"AYE! Here we be!" Al said happily, rubbing his paws together. "Do ye think we missed anythin'?"

"Now, Albert, you promised Jesus you would stay out of the main guest area, so be patient until Gillamon can bring you some food," Liz reminded him.

"Aye, an' if ye get any ideas, I'll be here ta stop ye," Max added.

"I promise," Al said humbly. Gillamon was unloading Clarie's saddlebags and setting up an area outside the main house in a grove of trees. The animals settled in with Gillamon while Jesus and the five disciples went inside to the wedding feast.

"Jesus!" Mary exclaimed, running up to him with a tight embrace. "How I've missed you!"

"It's good to see you, Mother," Jesus said. "Ah, and there are my sweet sisters!" He proceeded to embrace his sisters and brothers, who also got up from their tables to greet Jesus. "Here, meet my friends." Jesus proceeded to introduce Andrew, Peter, Philip, Nathaniel, and John to Mary and his siblings.

"Good, now come, say hello to the bride and the groom," Mary instructed. Jesus agreed and gave his greetings to the happy couple, who sat under a wedding canopy. The bride was beautifully adorned with a colorful gown and head dressing, with plenty of borrowed jewels sewn into her garments. The couple came from families who didn't have much money. This wedding was a strain but the parents did the best they could to provide for this happy day. Jesus blessed the young couple and gave his congratulations to their parents.

"I have seats for you," Mary said, leading them to a sitting area of pillows around a low, flat table. Jesus and his disciples followed her and got comfortable while servants began filling their cups with wine. Mary instructed the servants to bring plenty of food for them.

Mary was a typical Jewish mother who ruled the affairs of the family inside the home, wanting things to be just so. The bridegroom's family were dear friends of hers, and she had spent weeks helping to get everything ready for the happy occasion. Mary remembered her wedding day and how happy the celebration had been. But soon afterward the village of Nazareth learned she had been pregnant before she married Joseph. It put a damper on Mary's joy as the well-wishers from her wedding day slowly turned away in judgment of her assumed bad behavior. Little did they know that Mary was pregnant with Jesus by the Holy Spirit. Although Mary knew the truth, she still was a typical young girl who wanted her wedding to be one that people would remember with joy. So weddings became something she was very passionate about, especially after losing Joseph. When Mary was satisfied everyone was taken care of, she sat down next to Jesus and enjoyed the feast. She wanted to hear all about Jesus' experiences since he left home.

"I know how that felt, to have the Holy Spirit come upon you," Mary said after Jesus shared about being baptized by his cousin John. She held her hand to her belly. "I'll never forget that moment. It was glorious." She turned and smiled at her son, placing her hand on Jesus' arm. "But I know it is far greater for you, still. You will be able to do things never before seen."

Jesus smiled at his remarkable mother, thinking of all she had sacrificed personally for him. She was obedient when Gabriel came to tell her she was chosen above all others to bring the promised Messiah into the world. It cost her so much. It cost her Joseph's trust at first, until Gabriel told Joseph the truth. It cost her her reputation with the people. And Jesus knew that when his time soon came, it would cost her terrible pain. She had already known losing the love of her life in

192

Joseph. Jesus hated the pain of death and loss. He looked around at the joy of this day and gazed through time to a future wedding feast that he would enjoy with his followers in heaven. When there would be no more pain, and no more death—just joy, forever! Days like today were glimpses of that joy. And Jesus knew, for Mary, this day was special. He wrapped his arm around her and kissed her on the cheek. All he wanted for her was joy.

"John was such a good son to Elizabeth, just like you are to me," Mary said, returning his embrace. "He has accomplished what he was born to do," she said with eyes brimming. "His parents would be so proud."

Jesus leaned over and whispered in her ear. "They are, Mother. They are."

Mary gave him a quizzical look, followed by a smile of understanding that her son knew the hearts of people regardless of where they were. That reality never ceased to fill her with awe.

"Mother, you'll be happy to know that Zilla, Ari, Tovah, and Chava are outside," Jesus said, giving the names Mary had used to call her beloved animals Liz, Al, Max, and Kate.

"They're here? They're with you?" she replied happily. She tilted her head and tapped her fingers on her chin. "They are special, aren't they? No animals live as long as they have."

Jesus winked. "Yes, they are. They serve my Father, and were there to minister to you and Father so long ago. They travel with me and my friend Gillamon, who helps provide food for my disciples and me." Jesus paused. It would be too difficult to explain about Clarie, so he didn't bring her into the conversation.

"I know Ari must be hungry!" Mary exclaimed, getting up. "I will get some food for him, and of course the others. Enjoy the feast. I'll be back shortly."

Al sat outside eagerly awaiting some food. He could hear all the laughter and music, and his stomach growled at the thought. "When, when, when?" he moaned lying with his paw draped over his eyes. Mary approached with a basket of food and Al jumped up and ran to her. *Mary! Ye brought food! Thanks, Lass!* Al meowed. *"Oh, and it's grand to see ye, too!"*

Liz's heart was full of joy to see Mary again. She also ran up to Mary, purring and meowing her greeting: *"Bonjour, mon amie."*

Mary placed the basket on the ground, squatted down, and enveloped the cats with her arms. "I've missed you, my little ones," she said. "But Jesus told me about you. Thank you for taking care of him, as you took care of me."

Liz and Al looked at one another, unsure of what to do. Liz simply blinked her eyes affectionately. Mary unpacked the food. She looked at Al with a big grin. "For you, Ari, plenty of food, including Rabbi Isaac's dried fish!"

Tears filled Al's eyes as he gobbled up the goodies. Mary chuckled and then turned to greet Gillamon. "I am Mary, Jesus' mother. Please, join us inside," she implored. "We have plenty of food for one or two unexpected guests. These animals will be fine here."

"Thank you, I am grateful," Gillamon said. "Everyone stay here." He winked at Clarie.

"Aye, I'll keep them all in line," Max barked.

"Good to see you, Tovah and Chava," Mary said, petting the two dogs on the head. "You take care of things."

The friends watched Mary guide Gillamon inside. "I say, I'm small enough to go unnoticed. I shall go take in the sights of the feast and give you a full report," Nigel promised, scurrying off to run up Gillamon's cloak and hide in the folds of his head covering.

"Mary, we have a problem," the groom's mother said, wringing her hands.

"What's wrong?" Mary asked, concerned.

"We've run out of wine," the mother replied, her voice trembling. "We didn't have much to begin with, and were hoping it would last. This will cause so much embarrassment for our family. I haven't told our host who is overseeing the feast. I don't think I can bear it!"

Mary wrinkled her brow and wrapped her arm around her worried friend. "We'll think of something. Go sit back down and let me see what I can do."

The mother nodded gratefully and returned to her seat. Mary looked at Jesus and all those gathered around him, enjoying the feast.

194

She knew he could do something about this. She made her way back to their table and sat down next to Jesus.

"They've run out of wine," Mary said quietly, but it caught the attention of Nathaniel. He in turn whispered it to the other disciples. This was a terrible situation. All eyes turned to Jesus.

Jesus looked at Mary with a wrinkled brow. "Is that any of our business, Mother—yours or mine? This isn't my time. Don't push me."

Mary sat there with a look of such despair for her friend. Her eyes implored Jesus to please help. She didn't want to overstep her bounds as Jesus' mother. She understood who he was and what he was capable of. Jesus' reply reminded her that he must operate on the timetable of his heavenly Father, not her timetable. He was not planning to unveil his miraculous powers yet.

As Jesus gazed into her eyes, his look softened. He looked around the room and saw all the guests enjoying themselves. He observed the young couple starting out on this life journey, and Jesus wanted to bless them with a joyous beginning. He thought of his mother's joy as well, and about the image of the future wedding feast that would flow with wine. Jesus observed his disciples looking up at him to see what he would do. He glanced at Gillamon and words from this morning's conversation came to mind. *"Persistent asking for things is a good quality, especially when my creation comes to me. If the request is for something good that will bless them, it gives me delight to grant it." "And I might say, you give with generous extravagance."* Jesus closed his eyes and nodded. "Very well."

195

Mary clasped her hands up to her face with a smile. Together they stood and walked over to a group of servants. "Do whatever he tells you to do," Mary instructed. Then she respectfully backed away, not wanting to interfere with Jesus any further.

Six huge stoneware water pots were sitting over in an alcove off the main area where the guests sat. Jesus directed the servants to follow him there. He looked into these pots that were used for ritual washings and saw they were empty.

"Fill these pots with water, to the brim," Jesus instructed.

The servants quickly ran to gather the smaller pitchers filled with water and did as Jesus directed. While the servants ran back and forth, Jesus silently prayed. Soon the pots were filled to the brim with thirty gallons of water each.

Jesus held his hand over the pots for a moment. Then he turned to the servants. "Now fill your pitchers and take them to the host," Jesus directed.

The servants did as they were told while Jesus made his way back to the table. He sat down next to Mary and gave her a warm smile. She turned her gaze and watched the servant pour from his pitcher into the host's cup. Instead of water, out poured wine! The servants looked at one another in shock, not understanding how this was possible. The host was oblivious as to what had happened with the water and the wine.

The host took a sip of this new wine and his eyes grew wide with delight. He stood and lifted his cup, calling out to the bridegroom. The entire wedding party stopped and listened to what the host had to say. "Everyone serves the good wine first, and when people have drunk freely, then the poor wine is served. But you have kept the good wine until now!"

196

Cheers erupted as the servants began pouring the new wine for all the guests. The bridegroom's mother looked over at Mary and held her hands up to her face, showing wonder and gratitude. Mary's eyes filled with joyful tears. She leaned over and placed her head lovingly on Jesus' shoulder. "Thank you, Jesus," she said softly.

Jesus kissed his mother's head. "You're welcome," he whispered back. He turned to see his disciples, whose jaws hung open in wonder. They had witnessed the very first miracle of Jesus, and were overcome with his glory.

When it came time for them to depart for Capernaum, the animals gathered around Nigel to hear about all that had gone on inside at the wedding.

"Utterly thrilling! Spectacular! Nothing short of brilliant!" Nigel raved, pacing around the animals excitedly with his hands raised in the air. "I've never seen anything like it! Jesus turned the water into wine, and not just any wine, but the *best* wine! He saved the day for this family, I assure you."

"*C'est magnifique!* There were six pots, you say?" Liz asked. "That adds up to 180 gallons of wine! Not only did Jesus provide the wine, he provided an *extravagant amount* of wine! That's more than this wedding party could ever even consume."

"Oh, our Jesus be so good." Kate wagged her tail and wore a wide grin. "I be happy for the bride an' the groom. Their day wasn't ruined, but made better than they could have even dreamed!"

"Aye, so Jesus performed his first mir-r-racle then. Wha' a gr-r-r-and day!" Max echoed.

"After seeing this miracle, those disciples believe Jesus is indeed Messiah," Gillamon said, walking up to the group to get Clarie ready to go. "The beginning of their faith from these first few days with Jesus was strengthened to new levels today."

"And he's just getting started," Clarie said with a knowing grin.

Al was asleep on his back with a full, fluffy belly from the abundance of food he had eaten from the wedding feast. He was drooling in his sleep and wore a goofy grin of contentment.

Jesus walked up to the group before the disciples, who were helping Mary and others get their things. They would all travel on to Capernaum together for a couple of days before heading to Jerusalem for the Passover feast.

Jesus looked at Al and leaned down to rub his fluffy belly. Al roused and cracked his eyes open and smiled. "I love weddin's."

"I do, too, Al," Jesus said with a smile. "I do, too."

197

24

But Who May Abide the Day of His Coming?

A s usual, Jerusalem was packed for the Passover. Jesus and his disciples were herded into the city with the pressing crowds trying to get to the Temple to make their approved sacrifices. The Temple courts were bustling with the activity of merchants selling sacrificial animals to the travel-weary pilgrims. At least the long journey was made easier without having to travel with bleating sheep, bawling oxen, and cooing doves. The merchants in the Temple courts provided the convenience of buying preapproved animals right there on site—for a premium price—and pocketed large amounts of money in the process.

Because people traveled from all over the Roman world, they carried Roman coins with images of Caesar and other idolatrous beings. These coins were of course not acceptable for Temple offerings. According to the Temple rulers, only an approved kind of half-shekel coin could be used. So the money changers sat there in the Temple courts, changing out the pagan coins with the approved half-shekel coins. They, too, charged a premium fee to exchange the coins for the weary travelers— and pocketed large amounts of money in the process.

The weary travelers coming to worship God through the burdensome laws of sacrifice were unknowing victims of greed by the Temple authorities and swindling merchants. The sons of Levi, charged with taking care of God's chosen people, were cheating the very ones they were supposed to minister to.

Jesus stood back, watching all this unfold. He clenched his jaw as his gaze followed the smoke drifting up in the sky toward heaven, supposedly as a pleasing sacrifice to the Lord. But the source of the sacrifice was anything but pleasing. It was revolting, for it was accomplished by hearts full of greed and wickedness. People argued and bickered over prices for the animals and birds. Animal sounds and smells filled the air with such a stench it was difficult to breathe. The shoving and pushing of crowds of angry merchants and irritated travelers made this entire setting one of misery. This Temple, supposed to be a holy place of peaceful refuge, was anything but. This was not the atmosphere for reverent worship of God. This was the atmosphere of evil chaos, administered by the sons of Levi.

Jesus frowned as he looked around at the filthy stone platform of the Temple court. It was littered with dirt, straw, animal droppings, and pieces of leather straps used to bind up the sacrificial animals. Jesus bent down and started picking up the scraps of leather as he walked silently around the Temple court.

"What is he doing?" James asked his brother John. James was a new follower of Jesus, having met him when Jesus and his disciples arrived in Capernaum.

John observed Jesus and wrinkled his brow. "It looks like he's . . . making a whip." John and James shared a confused look.

Jesus calmly walked along the row of merchants and money changers, bending down now and then to add another piece of leather strap to the whip he was slowly braiding together. The disciples huddled together and just watched their Rabbi, uncertain of what he was doing.

Gillamon, Liz, and Nigel sat off to the side, also watching Jesus. Max had agreed to stay with the others and keep watch outside the city walls while these three came inside. Liz frowned as she studied Jesus.

"He is not happy," Liz observed, her tail switching back and forth.

"No, he is not," Gillamon affirmed, wrapping his arms around his knees. "The Sanhedrin have allowed the Temple to become nothing more than a cheapened marketplace that deceives and burdens the people."

"I say, can you please refresh me on the Sanhedrin, old boy?" Nigel

199

said, adjusting his spectacles. "It does get a bit confusing on how this all works."

"The Sanhedrin is the religious ruling body of Israel, and is made up of seventy-one members— chief priests, elders, and scribes," Gillamon began. "Chief priests are the ranking leaders of the priestly line of Jews. Elders are key leaders and influential members of important families but they are outside the priestly line."

"And the scribes are the scholars, no?" Liz interjected. "They are not of noble birth as are the chief priests and elders, but they are the experts in the Jewish law and traditions."

Gillamon nodded. "Indeed, Liz. So these are the three types of members of the Sanhedrin. There are two parties of belief in the Sanhedrin: Sadducees and Pharisees. The chief priests and elders are predominantly Sadducees and the scribes are dominated by Pharisees."

Nigel twirled his whiskers in thought. "And as I understand it, the Sadducees do not believe in life after death, or in angels. They only follow the five books of Moses and pay no attention to the Prophets."

"That is why they are sad, you see?" Gillamon quipped. "Indeed, Nigel, the Sadducees are outnumbered by the Pharisees when it comes to the people of Israel, but they hold the majority power in the Sanhedrin. They are more interested in keeping the power granted them by Rome than in the practice of Judaism."

"Dreadful! And on the opposite extreme, the Pharisees are so obsessed with Judaism and the Law that they keep the people in bondage with their rules," Nigel protested, pacing with his paws behind his back.

"*Oui,* the word *Pharisee* means 'separate.' That is exactly how they act with the people, no?" Liz added. "They love to show how pious they are, wearing long tassels on their garments and continually washing, observing strict diet rules, and keeping the Sabbath. The people can't possibly live up to their standards."

"Their religion has become more important than God himself!" Nigel fumed. "Nothing is more evil than false religion."

Gillamon pointed to Jesus, who continued to braid his whip. "And that is why Jesus is angry at these sons of Levi who are supposed to be the shepherds for God's people. They give the *appearance* of being devoted to God, but are more devoted to their traditions that aren't even scriptural. They are self-righteous, thinking they are better than the people. And here in the Temple courts, they are even making money from the system they have created. The shepherds have become wolves in sheep's clothing."

"And the closer the wolves can get to the flock, the easier it is to devour them," Liz added.

"Jesus is the Good Shepherd, and shepherds don't negotiate with wolves," Gillamon added, looking Liz and Nigel in the eye. "They *attack* them and chase them away."

Just then they heard the snap of a whip and turned to see Jesus driving the animals from the marketplace. Chaos erupted as animals broke free from their stalls and began stampeding out of the courtyard, merchants chasing after them. Jesus snapped the whip on the stone pavement, not hitting a single animal or human. But it was enough to send man and beast scrambling.

Jesus moved over to the money-changing tables and began turning them over. His sculpted arms were strong from the hard work of carving and sawing wood, so he lifted the heavy tables with ease. Coins went flying across the stone pavement, clinking and echoing loudly as they landed. Without their tables the money changers were exposed to the people, who saw the excess of money piled up around them. Men scrambled to the ground to scrape up their coins, but Jesus' snapping whip and his ferocious presence made the money changers leave it all and run for cover.

Jesus then lifted a crate holding doves and shoved it into the arms of a wide-eyed bird merchant. He looked down the line of bird merchants and commanded, "Get these out of here! How dare you turn my Father's house into a market!" The frightened merchants quickly stacked the crates to carry them out of the courtyard, stumbling over one another as they fled.

"He's cleaning out the Temple!" Nigel enthused with a fist of victory raised in the air. "Brilliant! Jolly good show!"

"He is fierce yet gentle enough not to harm even a dove," Liz observed. Jesus had not knocked over the crates of doves, as he had the tables. He knew precious life was within them.

A group of Roman soldiers standing guard on top of the Antonia fortress watched as this scene unfolded. From their vantage point they

201

could observe everything happening in the Temple and streets of Jerusalem, and were ready to send soldiers out at a moment's notice.

Armandus leaned over the wall, watching a lone man with a whip driving the animals out of the area. He saw merchants vacating the filthy corral areas and the crooked money changers leaving the area. He was mesmerized by what he saw. Somehow it felt like something positive was happening.

"Sir, should we send soldiers down there?" a sentry asked.

Armandus was one of six centurions assigned to the charge of Herod Antipas's protection in his district of Galilee and when he traveled. Herod always came to Jerusalem for Passover, so Armandus and his men accompanied Herod every year to this city full of cultural oddities and crowds. As the Roman centurion watched Jesus from a distance, all he saw was controlled authority. No riots were breaking out. The people themselves were calm. Once the animals, merchants, and money changers left the area, an amazing peace spread over the Temple courtyard. Armandus saw a group from the Temple guard approaching the lone man with the whip. It appeared they could handle this themselves.

202

"No, we aren't needed now," Armandus replied. "All is in order." He continued to watch from a distance, wondering what was being said.

Peter stood with fists clenching, wondering if he should run over and help Jesus. *"Zeal for your house will consume me,"* he recalled from the psalms. "Look at Jesus' passion for his Father's house!"

John put a calming hand on Peter's shoulder. "Steady, Peter. Here comes that same group of Pharisees who opposed John at the Jordan River."

Liz's gaze followed a group of Jewish leaders who walked close together, dressed in their elaborate robes with long tassels swaying as they walked. They remained calm but wore looks of anger as they stood in front of Jesus. A group of Temple guards stood behind them. Liz's tail flicked back and forth. "Pharisees."

"Indeed. Jarib, Saar, and Zeeb are Pharisees," Gillamon replied, pointing out each one. "Nahshon is a Sadducee. These men are among the most power-hungry of the Sanhedrin, and always the first to pose judgment on the behavior of the people."

"Pfft!" Liz spat in disgust, shaking her head. "They are indeed living up to their names, no?"

"What do you mean, my dear?" Nigel posed.

"*Jarib* means 'adversary, or opponent.' *Saar* means 'storm,' and *Nahshon* means 'snake-bird,'" Liz explained, her tail flicking wildly back and forth. Her gaze zeroed in on the ring leader of the group. "And *Zeeb* means 'wolf.'"

"What miraculous sign can you show us to prove your authority to do all this?" Zeeb said, spreading his arms out over the messy aftermath of Jesus clearing the Temple.

Jesus stared deeply into Zeeb's squinty eyes for a moment before lifting his head to look at the magnificent Temple. His gaze and his thoughts rose above these conniving men. "Destroy this temple, and I will raise it again in three days."

Saar spoke up immediately with a fist pointed to the Temple. "It has taken forty-six years to build this temple, and you are going to raise it in three days?"

The Jewish leaders murmured and nodded in agreement with Saar's question. This radical Jewish upstart named Jesus not only had invaded "their" territory with demands of the merchants on a prophetic scale, but now was making outrageous claims.

Jesus returned his gaze to the fuming Jewish leaders and shook his head slightly at their complete lack of understanding of the sign he had indeed given them. Their small-mindedness didn't warrant a response. Jesus knew they were trying to intimidate him and stake their claim to authority here in the Temple. He wasn't referring to the pristine, gold-trimmed marble structure of the Temple built by Herod. Workmen had labored forty-six years, cutting stones for the walls and beating gold plates to cover the massive doors. Jesus' statement referred not to a mere brick-and-mortar building, but to his own body. No one would understand what he said now until his resurrection.

Jesus dropped his whip at their feet and turned his back on them, giving them no further reply. He walked through the crowd of spectators gathered there and rejoined his disciples, who followed him out of the Temple area. Folding their arms in defiance, the people turned to watch the Jewish leaders to see what they would do. The people sided with Jesus' exposure of the swindling merchants, who were backed by these Jewish leaders of the Sanhedrin.

The religious leaders huddled together as they had done on the bank of the river, ignoring the people. They were flooded with embarrassment, having been exposed and defied by some no-name upstart who instantly gained the approval of the masses for what he had done. In broad daylight Jesus had loudly declared these leaders guilty of defiling the Temple. He didn't cower or back down when they challenged him, but stood his ground with confidence, saying things they didn't comprehend.

"What do we do? Should we have him arrested for disturbing the peace?" Jarib asked.

Nahshon shook his head. "We're too exposed. Arrest would warrant a trial, and there are too many witnesses here to give testimony about the merchants and money changers."

"It's just like the people following John the Baptist," Saar posed. "We can't touch him without the people coming against us."

"We have to let him go for now," Zeeb said as he watched Jesus and a small group of men leaving the now quieted courtyard. "But remember his words."

Gillamon, Liz, and Nigel watched the Jewish leaders huddled together, talking with hatred about this new problem of a Jewish nobody Rabbi who dared oppose them, and on *their* turf. He didn't just *oppose* them, he *exposed* them. And this would not be tolerated by the Sanhedrin. The group of men turned and walked back to their inner sanctum, where they could escape the gaze of the people.

Suddenly Scripture from Malachi popped into Liz's mind, and she recited it out loud: "The Lord whom you seek will suddenly come to his Temple . . . But who may abide the day of His coming? And who can stand when He appears? For He is like a refiner's fire . . ."

Gillamon tilted his head and studied the cat as she snapped her tail back and forth. Liz wore a confused look. "What troubles you, Liz?"

Liz slowly shook her head in puzzlement. "This prophecy, Gillamon. I know we are watching it unfold here before our eyes," she explained, then turned to look into the wise one's eyes. "But why do these words feel so *familiar*? I feel like I've just penned them myself recently. I can't explain it."

Gillamon's eyes twinkled with a knowing, mysterious look. He knew exactly why Liz's emotions were so stirred. She had been sitting on Jennen's desk when he used these words for *Messiah*. This would be a powerful part of the greatest music ever written, as it echoed the power and sovereignty of Messiah, who suddenly came to his Temple to purify the sons of Levi. He would change everything in the worship of God, and this event was the beginning of that purification.

"Your emotions should be stirred, Liz," Gillamon encouraged. "Jesus has just made his public debut in the heart of Israel, and has thrown down the gauntlet of opposition to the ruling religious authorities."

"Nothing will be the same after this," Nigel said with cautious concern.

"Indeed," Gillamon replied as he watched a lone figure come out from the shadows of the Temple columns. He wore the same ornate robes of the Pharisees, but his face wore a different look from that of his hate-filled colleagues. There was a genuine longing in his kind eyes for Jehovah. This man had heard Jesus' words and something stirred deep within his heart. Gillamon smiled at the man known as Nicodemus, who followed along at a distance after Jesus and his disciples.

"So it begins."

205

25

NICODEMUS AT NIGHT

The fire crackled with comforting warmth on this chilly spring-time night. John sat opposite Jesus and studied the remarkable Rabbi who briskly rubbed his cold hands together next to the fire. Those hands. John and the other disciples had witnessed Jesus use those hands to touch many sick and broken bodies this week in Jerusalem. John studied Jesus' strong hands. They were cold now but through them earlier today had come miraculous power to mend a broken arm for a little boy crying out in pain after he fell in the street.

Jesus was the first to hear the boy's cries, and ran to where the child lay in a darkened alley as he rocked and held his mangled arm to his chest. The boy's dark curls were stuck to his sweaty forehead as he writhed in pain. Jesus squatted down next to the boy and winced as he gazed at the unnatural angle of the boy's broken arm. His strong hands gently touched the boy's arm and instantly the boy stopped crying. The boy held out his arm that was now straight and perfect, studying it with awe. The boy looked up at Jesus, first with a confused look on his face, followed by a smile of relief. Jesus smiled back and suddenly the boy's two perfect arms wrapped tightly around Jesus' neck. Jesus closed his eyes and held on to the boy with those strong, loving hands. Jesus finally released the boy and told him, "Go on now. Go and play." The boy grinned broadly and skipped off to join his friends while John and the disciples stood in utter amazement at what they had just witnessed. And they weren't the only ones.

Many spectators saw Jesus work healing miracles with those strong hands. Cheers erupted as those with demons were freed from the stronghold of evil, those with broken bodies were healed, and those who felt hopeless heard they were worth saving as Jesus spoke words about the love and grace of Almighty God. John and the others were excited as they returned to their campsite, telling Jesus his welcome reception by the people who believed on his name must mean his mission was already a success! But Jesus confused them all as he shook his head and said, "Just because the people give a positive response to what I do doesn't mean their hearts have truly believed in me."

Jesus didn't trust the hearts of the people, for he knew what was really inside. Some, of course, did believe, but most were reacting to the thrill of the miraculous. John sat pondering Jesus' words and his ability to see inside human hearts. Jesus knew what men thought and what they felt. Nothing escaped his understanding.

Liz sat in the shadows watching John and the men gathered around the fire. "The disciples are clearly puzzled. What they thought was a fabulous beginning for Jesus isn't at all what this Messiah is about."

"Aye, Jesus is popular for wha' he's done, but wha's popular with humans doesn't matter ta him," Max agreed.

"He cares aboot their hearts," Kate added.

"The people say they believe in Jesus, but he knows better," Clarie said with a sigh.

"So Jesus doesn't have faith in their faith then?" Al asked with a wrinkled brow.

Gillamon smiled. "That's right, Al. People can say the right words that seem genuine, but down deep in their hearts is where the real story lies hidden."

"It must be dark down there," Al said with a gulp. "I'm afraid of the dark."

Nigel folded his arms over his chest in amazement at Al's comment and shook his head in wonder of the simple cat with the deep insights. "Old boy, you've hit the nail on the head, I believe. Darkness is a comfortable place for most creatures. Rats always scurry for a dark corner when light enters the room."

Liz's gaze drifted to Jesus. "But in the midst of the darkness, there is light."

The fire snapped and popped. Al's gaze followed the sparks that flew up into the night sky. "It's dark out here, too."

Max thought about Al and his many fears, including the dark. Max wasn't afraid of anything, except stormy nights and water—ever since that dark night when he lost his mother. Max frowned. He was ashamed he still couldn't swim and held on to these fears, after so long.

Suddenly they heard someone clearing his throat. "Excuse me, may I join you?"

Peter immediately stood to see who it was and was shocked to see a Pharisee timidly standing there in the shadows. Peter looked down at Jesus, who nodded that all was well. "Come," Peter said, motioning for the Pharisee to join them by the fire.

The disciples whispered among themselves, "It's Nicodemus." The distinguished old man gathered up his robes and slowly sat down next to Jesus. John's gaze was fixed on the unlikely sight of one of the most respected elders in the Sanhedrin out here under the cover of night with Jesus, the very man who had invaded their turf earlier in the week. Nicodemus didn't come with an offensive posture of accusation as had the others who approached Jesus in the Temple. John cocked his head as he studied the wise old man who looked around at those staring at him. Nicodemus appeared almost fearful to be seen here.

"Rabbi, we know you are a teacher who has come from God. For no one could perform the miraculous signs you are doing if God were not with him," Nicodemus started, leaning in and holding his hands out in a gesture of graciousness. By calling him 'Rabbi,' Nicodemus suggested that Jesus was an equal with the scholars of Israel.

Jesus brushed off Nicodemus's gracious introduction and immediately confronted the respected scholar with a shocking statement. "You're absolutely right. Unless a person is born again from above, it's not possible to see what I'm pointing to—to God's kingdom."

Nicodemus leaned back and wrinkled his brow, placing his hands on his knees for a moment as he considered Jesus' words. "How can anyone be born again who has already been born and grown up?" Nicodemus finally asked with a hand raised in the air. "You can't re-enter your mother's womb and be born again. What are you saying with this 'born-from-above' talk?"

"You're not listening, Nicodemus," Jesus said with a hand on the old man's arm. "Let me say it again. Unless one is born of water and the Spirit he cannot enter into the kingdom of God. That which is born of the flesh is flesh, and that which is born of the Spirit is spirit. When you look at a baby, it's just that: a body you can look at and touch. But the person who takes shape within is formed by something you can't see and touch—the Spirit—and becomes a living spirit."

"Wha's Jesus doin'?" Max asked Gillamon.

"He's using language Nicodemus can understand. What Jesus just said is nothing new to Nicodemus," Gillamon explained. "As a scribe he is well familiar with the promise in Ezekiel given to Israel during the Babylonian captivity:

> "I will sprinkle clean water on you, and you shall be clean; I will cleanse you from all your filthiness and from all your idols. I will give you a new heart and put a new spirit within you; I will take the heart of stone out of your flesh and give you a heart of flesh. I will put My Spirit within you and cause you to walk in My statutes, and you will keep My judgments and do them."

"*Oui,* this promise speaks about a new life for a dead soul," Liz added. "Jesus is telling Nicodemus that he needs a new heart, not another ritual added to the already heavy burden of dos and don'ts."

"I might add, when a Gentile decides to become Jewish, they are called 'newborn children.' It's a lovely way to affirm them as new sons and daughters of the God of Abraham," Nigel interjected, adjusting his spectacles. "These 'newborn Jewish children' are then baptized into the Jewish faith to symbolize a new life and a new spiritual beginning."

"Correct, Nigel and Liz. So Nicodemus thinks Jesus is telling him he needs to have a similar Gentile conversion experience, but that is not what Jesus is telling the experienced old Jew," Gillamon affirmed.

"*Oui,* when Jesus talked about a baby, he is giving a picture of a creature moving from one way of life to another. A baby is born with all the potential for the new life," Liz explained.

"Sure, but a baby doesn't have to do anythin' to be born," Al added. "The baby's mum does all the work."

"Brilliant observation, old boy!" Nigel exclaimed. "A baby can't do anything to form himself or herself. That is the Creator's job. A baby must simply enter new life."

209

"Shhhh," Clarie whispered. "Jesus has more to say."

"So don't be so surprised when I tell you that you have to be 'born from above'—out of this world, so to speak," Jesus continued. A breeze came through the trees behind them and stirred the embers of the fire, causing the flames to rise. Jesus pointed to the fire. "You know well enough how the wind blows this way and that. You hear it rustling through the trees, but you have no idea where it comes from or where it's headed next. That's the way it is with everyone 'born from above' by the wind of God, the Spirit of God."

Nicodemus put a hand to his head, and leaned forward, now not afraid to be seen as vulnerable and ignorant. His eyes pleaded with Jesus for an answer. "What do you mean by this? How does this happen?"

Jesus looked at Nicodemus with a look of astonishment. "You're a respected teacher of Israel and you don't know these basics?" Jesus clasped his hands together and leaned in close to Nicodemus. "Listen carefully. I'm speaking sober truth to you. I speak only of what I know by experience; I give witness only to what I have seen with my own eyes. There is nothing secondhand here, no hearsay. Yet instead of facing the evidence and accepting it, you procrastinate with questions." Jesus held his hand up in front of Nicodemus. "If I tell you things that are plain as the hand before your face and you don't believe me, what use is there in telling you of things you can't see, the things of God?"

The disciples looked at each other in shock as Jesus suddenly stood, growing animated with his discussion. They could not believe how harsh Jesus was being with Nicodemus. He essentially was telling the learned Pharisee that all the old man's wisdom and knowledge didn't even begin to cover the basics of understanding.

"No one has ever gone up into the presence of God except the One who came down from that Presence, the Son of Man," Jesus said, putting his hands on his chest, referring to himself. He then stretched his hands out wide. "In the same way that Moses lifted the serpent in the desert so people could have something to see and then believe, it is necessary for the Son of Man to be lifted up—and everyone who looks up to him, trusting and expectant, will gain a real life, eternal life."

Kate spoke up. "I remember when that happened. Venomous snakes came inta the camp of the Israelites an' were killin' people. God told Moses ta hold up a bronze snake high for all ta see. When the people looked up an' saw it, an' *believed,* they were saved."

Liz's heart sank and her eyes brimmed with tears. "Now Jesus is talking about the cross. *His* cross."

"Indeed," Gillamon said seriously. "Jesus knows that Nicodemus sees himself in the role of Moses, who saved the people. He's telling this Jewish leader that he needs to see himself as just like every other sinner in Israel in order to be saved."

"Aye, but humans like ta think they be mostly good enough," Max added. "They don't like the idea that the human race be fallen an' helpless on their own. Especially religious leaders like Nicodemus."

"Right you are, old chap," Nigel quickly agreed, clasping his paws behind his back. "Sadly, humans think they can look good enough on the outside to earn their way to being saved. But that's not the way it works, I'm afraid. What the world thinks is 'good' falls terribly short of what God thinks is good."

"Sure, and they all need to act like babies," Al said.

"Shhhh," Clarie shushed them. "There's still more. Listen."

Jesus sat down again next to Nicodemus and peered deeply into the old man's eyes. "This is how much God loved the world: He gave his Son, his *one and only* Son. And this is why: so that *no one* need be destroyed; by believing in him, anyone can have a whole and lasting life." Jesus' voice was filled with power and authority. John took note of how animated Jesus was, gesturing with those amazing hands as he spoke. "God didn't go to all the trouble of sending his Son merely to point an accusing finger, telling the world how bad it was. He came to *help,* to put the world right again. Anyone who trusts in him is acquitted," Jesus said with a hopeful tone of good news. Then his face grew serious and he leaned back. "Anyone who refuses to trust him has long since been under the death sentence without knowing it. And why? Because of that person's failure to believe in the Son of God when introduced to him."

"Jesus is being incredibly bold with what he is telling Nicodemus, no?" Liz observed. "But he knows that the truth must be said."

"Jesus cares more aboot the truth than how Nicodemus feels aboot it," Max added.

"What Jesus is doing shows the highest form of love for Nicodemus," Gillamon stressed. "Nicodemus's eternity is at stake here. Jesus doesn't want him to miss that it is *faith* that will save him, not keeping every detail of the Law and acting like a good model Pharisee in God's eyes."

Jesus put one strong hand on Nicodemus's shoulder. "This is the verdict: Light has come into the world, but people loved darkness instead of light because their deeds were evil. Everyone who does evil hates the light, and will not come into the light for fear their deeds will be exposed," Jesus shared with them, stopping to point to the fire. "But whoever lives by the truth comes into the light, so it may be seen plainly that what they have done has been done in the sight of God."

Nicodemus frowned and nodded, his mind swirling with all that Jesus had shared. The old Pharisee was overwhelmed with how Jesus had just turned over his entire understanding of faith and way of life as easily as he had turned over the merchant tables at the Temple. Nicodemus had nothing else to say. He slowly got up and Jesus met his gaze with pleading love. They shared a brief smile before Nicodemus turned and walked back into the dark of the night.

212

The animals watched as Jesus sat back down and warmed his hands once again by the fire. Nicodemus wasn't the only one whose mind was swirling. All the disciples examined themselves, quietly pondering what Jesus had said to one of the most learned men in all Israel. John was especially moved, and kept his gaze on Jesus. Today this Rabbi's strong hands had perfected that which was shattered in a young boy's arm. Tonight this Rabbi's strong words had shattered that which was perfect in an old man's mind and heart. In both cases he acted with the skill and urgency of a physician. He gave healing care to one, and as a doctor gives a patient a serious report about their life-threatening condition, he gave an honest diagnosis to the other. A good physician will tell a patient the truth so that real healing can take place. No matter how much it hurts.

What kind of Messiah was Jesus? He called himself the Son of Man. He called himself the Light of the world. John's heart was full of wonder and awe. He knew that what he had heard tonight had to be some of the most important words Jesus had ever uttered. Those words were seared into John's heart.

"Nicodemus came to Jesus under the cover of darkness," Liz said, marveling at how Jesus spoke with bold, unashamed truth. "And he met the Light, who exposed everything in Nicodemus's heart."

"Now Nicodemus must decide if he will live in the light," Kate posed.

"This could be dreadful for him with the rest of the Pharisees," Nigel suggested.

"Aye, they alr-r-ready hate Jesus for clear-r-ring the Temple earlier this week," Max growled.

"Things will get ugly with the Sanhedrin from here on out," Gillamon agreed. He saw the shadowy form of Nicodemus in the distance. "But God always has his remnant of believers—even in the midst of the Pharisees."

26

I AM MESSIAH

"John told me himself," Andrew said emphatically. "A group of John the Baptizer's disciples were jealous over how we've been baptizing so many more people with Jesus' ministry, and just down the way from them on the Jordan in Judea. The Baptist had to calm them down, saying it was time that Jesus' ministry take the lead. He told them, 'He must increase, but I must decrease.'"

"Well, it sounds like John the Baptist is okay with what is happening, with his ministry being turned over to Jesus," John remarked as the men walked along the dusty road.

"Of course, *he's* fine with it!" Peter exclaimed, pulling his cloak around his shoulders against the cold December wind. "The ones *not* fine with it are John's disciples who haven't met Jesus. Or the Pharisees in Jerusalem. I hear that bunch of vipers is keeping track of how many disciples Jesus is making now."

"Yes, they know that Jesus has surpassed John," James chimed in. "Jesus said that's why we should head back to Galilee. But I don't understand. If Jesus is getting more disciples than John, wouldn't he want to stay and show the Pharisees that he's the new One the people are following?"

"And why come through Samaria to get to Galilee?" Peter spat. "Why don't we just go around this place like all good Jews. Sometimes I just don't understand the way Jesus does things."

Liz rolled her eyes as she listened to the disciples discuss recent events among themselves. She, Nigel, and Al rode comfortably in Cla-rie's saddlebags while Jesus and Gillamon walked along together in front of them. Max and Kate brought up the rear with the disciples.

"They do not understand that Jesus has a plan and a time for things, no? He knows when to pull back and avoid unnecessary tangling with those Pharisee snakes," Liz said.

"I say, he follows God's direction and purpose," Nigel added, look-ing around. "Even coming through dreadful Samaria."

"Why be it so dreadful?" Al asked nervously. "Be there beasties here?"

"No, Albert, we are traveling through Samaria to reach Galilee. The Jews and the Samaritans despise one another," Liz explained. "Do you remember long ago when that wicked Assyrian King Sennacherib came and attacked Israel, back when we were with Isaiah?"

"Is he the king who sent those soldiers we had to keep from shootin' arrows at Jerusalem?" Al asked, trying to remember the events of seven hundred years ago. A goofy grin appeared on his face. "Nigel's pigeon pooped on that general's face!"

"Jolly good show that was, if I do say so myself," Nigel quipped, preening his whiskers with great satisfaction.

"*Oui*, Albert, that's the one," Liz replied. "But if you recall, King Sennacherib's troops never sacked Jerusalem because an angel wiped them out in one night."

"Dreadful sight the next morning," Nigel shuddered. "Still, Jerusa-lem was spared, unlike the northern kingdom of Israel."

"Precisely, *mon ami*. Which brings us to where the Samaritans came from," Liz continued. "The Assyrians took most of Israel captive, and eventually some of those Jews married with their cruel Assyrian con-querors. Their children became a mixed race of half-Jew, half-Assyrian: the Samaritans. Does this make sense?"

Al scratched his head. "I think so."

"You see, old boy, Jews were told to keep themselves pure as a race before God, but those who married the Assyrians entered into homes that worshipped idols. Still today, the Samaritans hold to the God of Jacob, but they are rejected by Jewish society," Nigel explained, straight-ening his spectacles. "They dwell in this land that once belonged to Jacob and his sons, but Jews won't be caught dead coming through here."

"Except for Jesus," Liz said as Jesus walked toward them. He looked very tired from their long journey.

"We'll get you taken care of soon, little ones," Jesus said, patting Clarie's back. "There's a well up ahead. I'll send the disciples into town for food."

Jesus walked back to his disciples with instructions. They looked at one another with obvious discomfort at the thought of entering a Samaritan village for supplies. Still, they did as Jesus asked. Jesus walked on up toward the well while Gillamon took Clarie by the reins and led her to a cluster of shady trees.

"We'll wait over here," Gillamon said.

"Wait for wha'?" Max asked as he and Kate trotted over to join them.

"That's Jacob's Well," Gillamon nodded in Jesus' direction. "Divine encounters happen at wells. Watch. And listen."

The animals turned to see Jesus sit down at the well. He rubbed his forehead with the back of his arm and let his hand drop into his lap. He leaned over and gazed down into the deep well. He could feel the cool air rising from the water deep in the earth. Jesus suddenly remembered what his mother had written in her journal about going to the well in Nazareth when she was pregnant with him. He ran his hand along the side of the well, recalling her words:

I suppose one of the hardest times for me has been when I go to the well to get water, for that is where the women gang up against me . . . I just prefer not to go to the well when the women are present. I go at midday when no one is there, just to avoid their stares and their cruel remarks. Oh, my Jesus, if you ever meet a woman who is outcast by others, perhaps at a well at midday, please be kind to her. Certainly be honest with her if she does not act properly, but above all, be kind to her and show her grace. I cannot tell you how lonely it feels to be treated like a woman of ill repute.

Jesus looked up at the midday sun and had to shield his eyes from its winter glare. When he lowered his gaze, he saw a Samaritan woman with a jar balanced on her side, walking toward the well. Unlike respectable Jewish women, this Samaritan didn't cover her head, and wore brightly colored clothes. Bangles clinked together on her arm as she walked, and the dark makeup around her eyes left no doubt as to her reputation. She walked alone, coming to get her daily supply of water. Women always came to the well in groups in the morning. No one came to the well at noon. This woman obviously didn't want to meet anyone here. *Just like you, Mother,* Jesus thought to himself. *But this one is not like you.*

Ignoring Jesus, the woman set her clay jar on the edge of the well and unwound the rope that was wrapped around it. As she got ready to lower the jar into the well, Jesus startled her with a question.

"Would you give me a drink of water?" Jesus asked her.

The woman set her jar back down on the well and cocked her head to the side as she studied Jesus. "How come you, a Jew, are asking me, a Samaritan woman, for a drink?"

"Jesus is quite the bold one," Nigel stated emphatically with raised eyebrows. "Jews never speak to Samaritans, and men *never* speak to women in public. This is quite the scandalous encounter, I must say!"

"*Pfft!* Rabbis made up that rule to 'keep women in their place,'" Liz said with disgust at the thought of how women were treated in Jesus' day and age. She studied the woman and curled her tail up and down. "I like her. A submissive Jewish woman would have just drawn the water and not said a word. She has spunk, no?"

Jesus answered, "If you knew the generosity of God and who I am, you would be asking me for a drink, and I would give you fresh, living water."

The woman looked around and noticed Jesus had nothing with him. She put a hand on her hip, grinned, and lifted her chin in defiance. Her voice was full of sarcasm. "Sir, you don't even have a bucket to draw with, and this well is deep. So how are you going to get this 'living water'? Are you a better man than our ancestor Jacob, who dug this well and drank from it, he and his sons and livestock, and passed it down to us?"

"*Oooh-la-la,* she's picking a fight with Jesus!" Liz said excitedly, sitting up tall with a coy grin on her face. "Now she's bringing race into this, asking Jesus if he's better than she is!"

"Aye, those be fightin' words," Kate added, wagging her tail. She was just as fascinated to see a woman act like this. She and Liz were used to watching women being cast aside in society, never permitted to speak their mind. "Let's see how Jesus handles this fiery lass."

"Everyone who drinks this water will get thirsty again and again. Anyone who drinks the water I give will never thirst—not ever. The water I give will be an artesian spring within, gushing fountains of endless life."

The woman's defiant smirk left her face. Her sarcastic tone turned respectful as she considered what this man was offering her. No more trips to the well at midday. "Sir, give me this water so I won't ever get thirsty, won't ever have to come back to this well again!"

Jesus paused a moment, then gave her a directive. "Go call your husband and then come back."

"I have no husband," she said as she dropped her gaze to the ground and bit her lip.

"That's nicely put: 'I have no husband,'" Jesus said with forthright acknowledgement of the facts. "You've had five husbands, and the man you're living with now isn't even your husband. You spoke the truth there, sure enough."

"Brilliant!" Nigel enthused. "Jesus didn't take the bait, but has set a trap for her instead!"

"Aye, he's got her r-r-right where he wants her," Max added with a grin. "Look at the lass squirmin'."

"*Oui*, but look at how gentle Jesus is with her," Liz marveled. "He didn't throw the seventh commandment at her like the Pharisees would have done. He simply told her he knows what she is hiding."

"Amazin' grace!" Kate exclaimed.

The woman's eyes grew wide at Jesus seeing right through her, but she wasn't about to let him dig deeper into her heart. *How does he know that?* she thought as she tried to think of something to deflect attention away from herself. Her defiant attitude returned and she tossed her hair back and said, "Oh, so you're a prophet! Well, tell me this: Our ancestors worshipped God at this mountain, but you Jews insist that Jerusalem is the only place for worship, right?"

"She's trying one more religious race jab, but Jesus is holding his ground," Nigel observed.

Gillamon and Clarie smiled as they watched the animal friends so engrossed in this dialogue between Jesus and the Samaritan woman. Little did those friends know what was coming.

"Believe me, woman, the time is coming when you Samaritans will worship the Father neither here at this mountain nor there in Jerusalem. You worship guessing in the dark; we Jews worship in the clear light of day," Jesus said, lifting his hand to the sun. "God's way of salvation is made available through the Jews. But the time is coming—it has, in fact, come—when what you're called will not matter and where you go to worship will not matter."

"What do he mean by that?" Al asked.

"He's talking about himself," Liz answered softly.

Jesus leaned in and gazed deeply into this lonely woman's eyes. "It's who you are and the way you live that count before God. Your worship must engage your spirit in the pursuit of truth. That's the kind of people the Father is out looking for: those who are simply and honestly themselves before him in their worship. God is sheer being itself—Spirit. Those who worship him must do it out of their very being, their spirits, their true selves, in adoration."

"I don't know about that," the woman said, wrinkling her brow and staring at the ground. Softening, she said, "I do know that the Messiah is coming. When he arrives, we'll get the whole story."

Jesus smiled at her with compassion. "I AM the Messiah. You don't have to wait any longer or look any further."

The woman's head snapped up. Her pulse began to race with a heart full of longing for such acceptance, truth, and hope. Suddenly they heard the disciples walking toward them. The men gave frowning glances at the woman and to each other. Clearly they were shocked at Jesus. They couldn't believe he was talking with that kind of a woman. No one said what they were all thinking, but their faces showed it. The woman took the hint and quickly left, leaving her water jar behind.

"Do you realize this Samaritan woman is the first person Jesus has told he is Messiah?" Nigel asked in wonder. "Astounding. Of all people."

"A woman. He told a sinful woman *first*," Kate added.

"He's beginning to set the Garden right," Liz posed.

"Wha' do ye mean, Lass?" Max asked. "There's no garden here."

"Not *a* garden, *the* Garden—of Eden," Liz replied. "Don't you see, *mes amis?* When Satan appeared to Eve, he appeared to a perfect woman and offered the food of death. Jesus has now appeared to the most *im*perfect of women, and offered her the water of life!"

"Sure, Jesus offered this 'Eve' the way back then," Al noted.

219

Everyone eyeballed Al in amazement.

"Aye, an' look how differently Jesus treated this lass from Nicodemus," Max pointed out. "He were harsh an' br-r-rutal with that r-r-religious lad, but gentle as a lamb with this sinner."

"You're beginning to see how Jesus deals with those inside the religious class who *should* know better about real faith, and with those outside who just *don't* know better," Gillamon chimed in. "He can work with a heart willing to seek forgiveness, like this Samaritan woman's. She longs for Messiah, so he met her right where she was. The religious elite don't long for Messiah, so Jesus can do nothing to reach their cold hearts."

"And look how Jesus is willing to take such risks with his reputation," Clarie added. "He is totally free from all the religious and social prejudice that keeps the Jews and the Samaritans at such angry odds."

"Aye, he doesn't care a shoutin' camel's spit aboot wha' people think!" Max cheered. "His disciples need ta learn a thing or two from him."

"Indeed," Gillamon agreed as he turned his gaze to Jesus and his disciples.

The Samaritan woman ran back into the village, blazing past a group of gossiping women who sat grinding grain. "She's so unpopular with the women of this town because she's too popular with the *men!*" one of them commented snidely. They watched the loose woman run to find a group of men. "Look how she runs after them!"

Something felt different to this lonely, rejected Samaritan woman. She heard the jabs but they didn't faze her. She felt strangely elated, and somehow free in her spirit. *Is this what real hope feels like?* she wondered.

When the woman reached the group of men sitting around eating in a tent, she boldly interrupted them and exclaimed, "Come see a man who knew all about the things I did, who knows me inside and out!" She was smiling and out of breath. She put a hand over her heart. "Do you think this could be Messiah?"

The men looked at one another, several with guilt written on their faces. Some stranger knew about what this woman of ill repute had done. That would mean he would also know about what *they* had done.

They got up from the table and followed her out of the tent. They had to investigate this stranger, Messiah or not.

The group of gossiping, grinding women now watched as the woman of ill repute raced back by them, now with a bunch of men trailing along behind her. They looked at one another in disgust. "What is this all about?" One by one they got up, left their grain, and followed the people out to Jacob's Well.

Jesus continued to sit at the well with his hands folded in his lap while his disciples hungrily ate the lunch they had bought in town. Jesus didn't appear interested in food.

Peter and the others pressed him, "Rabbi, eat. Aren't you going to eat?"

Jesus looked at them with a pensive gaze. "I have food to eat you know nothing about."

The disciples were puzzled, and whispered among themselves. "Who could have brought him food?"

Liz rolled her eyes. "There they go, thinking Jesus is speaking about real food, just like the Samaritan woman thought Jesus was talking about real water."

Jesus said, "The food that keeps me going is that I do the will of the One who sent me, finishing the work he started. As you look around right now, wouldn't you say that in about four months it will be time to harvest? Well, I'm telling you to open your eyes and take a good look at what's right in front of you. These Samaritan fields are ripe. It's harvest time!"

"Aye, he's doin' one o' those metaphorical thingies," Al posed, much to Liz's delight. She kissed him on the cheek and the big cat melted under her affection.

The animals watched as the group of Samaritans from the village came up to Jesus and began to ask him questions. Jesus expressed astounding wisdom, love, and grace to all of them, much to their surprise. The people begged him to come into town and stay with them. Jesus got up and followed them, leaving his disciples sitting there dumbfounded. After a moment they got up and followed Jesus. They had much to learn indeed about this strange Messiah.

"Do you know what this reminds me of?" Clarie asked, her eyes full of joyful tears. "The night Jesus was born."

221

"How so, dear Clarie?" Kate said, nudging her affectionately.

"These half-breed Samaritan rejects of Jewish society are the first ones Jesus told he was Messiah. The shepherds of Bethlehem were also rejects of Jewish society, and *they* were the first ones to hear the good news that Messiah had been born," Clarie explained. "*I* was a reject until Jesus touched me, so I know how joyful they are right now."

Kate's eyes welled up with tears as she recalled the tiny fingers of Jesus touching the lamb's blemished face, making it as white as snow. "Ye know how these people feel more than any of us, Lass."

"*C'est magnifique!*" Liz exclaimed, clapping her paws in sheer delight.

"What a splendid occasion this has been! Our Jesus is continuing to turn tables, I believe. Now he's turning the tables on rejection itself," Nigel said excitedly.

"Aye, well, I think we'll be stayin' here a bit longer than a water stop then," Max guessed. "I don't think these Samaritans are goin' ta let Jesus go anytime soon."

"Well, in that case, I'm goin' into town," Al said, jumping up. "I'm starved. Sure, and the happy Samaritans might give this kitty some happy morsels then."

Two days later Jesus and his disciples bid the villagers farewell as they got an early morning start resuming their journey. Jesus planned to part company with the disciples, who had to make their way back to Capernaum and their fishing businesses while Jesus visited Nazareth. The people watched as Messiah left to walk north. Many people believed in Jesus and their hearts were changed toward God and one another.

The Samaritan woman stood off by herself, now respectfully dressed and already changed in her lifestyle. The crowd turned and noticed her standing there alone.

One man smiled and said to the woman, "We no longer believe because of what you said about him telling you everything you did."

"We've heard it for ourselves, and know it for sure," another spoke up.

Another man raised his hands in gratitude for having met Messiah. "He's the Savior of the world!"

The Samaritan woman smiled, nodded, and rubbed her arms

against the chill of the December wind. But her heart was full of warmth, even for the people who had rejected her here. As the men walked off, the women of the village stood with their water jars and looked at one another. After a moment one of the women stepped forward and placed her hand gently on the Samaritan woman's arm. She smiled, determined to change just as much as this woman of ill repute had already changed.

"Why don't you grab your heavy cloak, and while you're at it, your water jar," the woman suggested. "It's time to go to the well for water."

Tears filled the Samaritan woman's eyes as she ran off to get her jar. "Thank you, Messiah," she whispered prayerfully, "I'll never be thirsty again."

SEVENTH-HOUR
MIRACLE

H e's still here in Cana?!" Tatius exclaimed, wide-eyed and jumping up from the table. He folded the letter he had just received from his wife, sticking it in his travel bag. "May I?" he asked as he reached for some raisin cakes on the table.

"I saw him today in the market," Verus replied, gesturing for Tatius to help himself to the food that he quickly packed in his travel bag. "He's been staying with the family from that miracle wedding feast."

"A miracle worker like that could help my son," Tatius said with cautious hope. He slung his travel bag over his shoulder. "I have to try. Thank you for your hospitality."

"But it's almost the seventh hour. Are you sure you won't spend the night and leave in the morning?" Verus asked with concern.

"I must get back to Capernaum, even if I have to walk all night," Tatius insisted.

"Very well, my friend. I hope your son gets well. Please send me word," Verus requested as he stood to bid his friend farewell.

The two Romans shared an unspoken look of agreement and grave concern as they gripped forearms. "I will," Tatius promised.

With that the nobleman Tatius headed out into the deepening darkness. He needed to find Jesus, the miracle worker.

Max and Gillamon sat by the fire, listening to the murmuring of the people in the courtyard. Gillamon slowly stroked Max on the head while they watched Jesus interacting with the crowd.

"These humans jest want Jesus ta do more gr-r-rand mir-r-racles then," Max said with a frown. "They don't really listen ta wha' he be tellin' them aboot tr-r-ruth."

"Yes, my friend, it appears to go in one ear and out the other," Gillamon agreed sadly. "Jesus has caused quite a stir here, beginning with the water-into-wine wedding miracle. Many of the people from here in Cana then saw Jesus perform miracles at the feast in Jerusalem. Word is spreading about him."

"Aye, but they jest want Jesus for wha' he can do for them," Max growled.

"Jesus knows their hearts," Gillamon offered. "And he loves them. But he also knows how to handle them."

"JESUS! JESUS OF NAZARETH? ARE YOU HERE?" the booming voice of Tatius echoed off the stone walls in the courtyard.

225

Jesus remained seated by the fire, chewing on some figs, seemingly unmoved by the abrupt entrance of the nobleman.

"He's over here," the host directed Tatius. "What do you want?"

Tatius brushed the host aside and rushed over to Jesus, kneeling down next to him.

"Good sir, I am from Capernaum, in the service of Herod Antipas," Tatius began. "I've just received word that my little boy . . ." He became choked up and fought back the tears. "He is sick with a high fever and is on the brink of death. Please! Please come with me back to Capernaum. I've heard that you perform miracles and have healed people all over Judea and Galilee. Please!"

Jesus very calmly turned his gaze to meet that of Tatius, and his eyes were filled with sad compassion. The people all leaned in close to see what Jesus would do. Jesus looked around at the crowd and then back to Tatius. "Unless you people see signs and wonders, you will not believe."

"Please, sir, come down before my little boy dies!" Tatius pleaded, gripping Jesus' arm.

Jesus stared deeply at this nobleman who had the prestige of Herod but the powerlessness of humanity. At this moment he wasn't an influential court official. He was a frantic father, about to lose his son. "Go," Jesus said in an affirming tone. "Your son will live."

Tatius blinked hard and slowly released his grip on Jesus. Somehow, he felt sure of Jesus' words. He nodded in understanding and belief, and hurried out of the courtyard. The people looked at one another and started to murmur about this latest Jesus encounter.

"Did the lad believe Jesus then?" Max asked Gillamon hopefully.

The pronounced smile lines around Gillamon's kind eyes curved upward. "If he didn't, I doubt he would be leaving without Jesus tonight."

Only two more miles, Tatius thought to himself as he neared Capernaum the next morning. He was exhausted, having walked the twenty miles overnight rather than wait for a Roman escort to transport him. This father was driven by the thought of getting to his dying son. All night as he walked he hoped beyond hope that what the miracle worker had told him would be true.

Suddenly Tatius heard the galloping approach of a soldier on horseback. It was his friend, Armandus.

"Tatius!" Armandus called out. "I was coming to get you. When I heard about your son, I asked Herod if I could depart and come get you immediately on my fastest horse. Have you walked all night?"

Tatius stopped and looked up at Armandus mounted on Achilles, shielding his eyes from the sun. The horse snorted and shook his head as Armandus pulled back on the reins. "Yes, my friend. I had to get home to my son. I couldn't wait."

"Here, let me take you the rest of the way," Armandus offered, giving Tatius his arm to pull him up onto Achilles. Once Tatius was situated, Armandus snapped the reins and Achilles was running to clip off the last two miles to Capernaum. The sun glistened across the Sea of Galilee as they approached the beautiful seaside town.

The men had not ridden far when they were met in the street by a group of Tatius's servants. They smiled and waved to Tatius when they saw that it was he. "Good news!"

Tatius jumped off Achilles. "What is it?!"

"Your son is alive and well!" the servants replied excitedly.

"What time did he begin to recover?" Tatius implored, his heart pounding with joy.

"Yesterday at the seventh hour, his fever suddenly disappeared!" the servants answered. "Come and see!"

Tatius wore a look of shock and mindlessly handed over his travel bag to his servant. He looked up at Armandus and shook his head in awestruck wonder.

"That's great news, my friend!" Armandus enthused. "What's the matter?"

"The seventh hour. That's when the miracle worker in Cana told me my son would live," Tatius said, holding his head in growing excitement. He began to run down the road toward home, his servants following along behind.

"Who? What miracle worker?" Armandus called, trotting along behind him.

"Jesus! Jesus of Nazareth!" Tatius trailed off, running as fast as his legs would take him home.

227

Armandus stopped in the road and watched his friend running toward his seventh-hour miracle. His mind raced with questions. *Miracle worker? But the man wasn't even here. This man just spoke and it happened? The boy was healed? Jesus of Nazareth.* Armandus suddenly recalled a buzz of talk around the court of Herod Antipas following the feast in Jerusalem. The man he had seen clearing the Temple with a whip was called Jesus of Nazareth. Herod was relieved to hear that a new prophet was emerging, as he had sought to arrest John the Baptist for preaching out against him and his wife Herodias. Before now Herod had been afraid of the reaction of the people, but word from the Sanhedrin was that this Jesus of Nazareth was gathering more followers than John. Herod seized the opportunity of a new prophet in the public eye, and ordered Armandus to have John the Baptist arrested. *So now John the Baptist sits in prison. But this whip-cracking miracle worker speaks, and what he says comes to pass— twenty miles away? I wonder which prophet is the real danger to Herod—and those power-hungry Jews?*

The Roman centurion felt mixed emotions. He was bound by his duty as a Roman to protect the Emperor and the Roman Empire from all known threats. But he was drawn to this Jesus of Nazareth, admiring him for standing up to the Jews and now for healing a little boy with just a word. *Who IS he?*

Armandus turned Achilles toward Cana, tempted to ride up there and see this miracle worker himself. But his disciplined sense of duty told him he must return to his post, now that Tatius was home and all was well. Armandus squeezed his heels into Achilles's side and rode back into Capernaum, kicking up dust behind him.

Little did Armandus know that soon Jesus of Nazareth would come to *him*.

CHUTZPAH IN NAZARETH

"Oh, how wonderful to be back in Nazareth!" Liz exclaimed happily. The animals walked along the road with Jesus, Gillamon, and Clarie. The cluster of mudbrick homes dotted the hillside, beckoning them back home. Soon they were in the midst of busy streets, children running along laughing, women grinding their grain, and men bargaining, selling, building, and shouting.

Al lifted his nose in the air, sniffing. He broke out in a grin. "Aye, Rabbi Isaac's fish be callin' me!" With that, Al jumped out of Clarie's saddlebag and trotted down the well-worn street to raid Rabbi Isaac's pantry.

Gillamon shook his head as he and Jesus shared a chuckle. "It is good to be back, Liz," Jesus said. His face turned somber as they passed the synagogue. "How I loved it here. I love the people. Such a happy place to grow up. But nothing ever stays the same."

"Wha's wrong, Jesus?" Kate asked, detecting a hint of sadness in Jesus' voice.

Jesus knelt to give Kate a gentle pat on the head. "Nothing that isn't expected, little Kate. Don't worry."

"Jesus!" Mary exclaimed as they neared Jesus' childhood home. "Oh, you're back!" Mary ran up to him and embraced her son with a tight hug.

"Mother," Jesus said, enveloping her in his strong arms. "I'm so happy to see you."

"And how is my little Zilla?" Mary leaned over to lift Liz out of the saddlebag, and held her close. Liz immediately began to purr and rubbed Mary affectionately on the chin.

"You remember my friend Gillamon, and of course your favorite animal friends," Jesus said, his hand on Gillamon's shoulder. Gillamon nodded humbly to Mary. "Can you spare some bread for dinner?"

"Why, of course! There is plenty for everyone," Mary said, stroking Liz. She gave Max and Kate a welcoming petting, and received licks and wags in return. She noticed that Al was missing and grinned. "You don't have to tell me where Ari is. I'm sure he's already enjoying his fish. Come, I've just made fresh bread."

Jesus and the others followed Mary inside. Jesus' brother Simon was there and gave Jesus a big bearhug.

"Jesus! Mother and I were just talking about you! Well, so is the entire town, actually. Word has spread about what my big brother has been doing in Judea and here in Galilee," Simon said, motioning for Jesus to have a seat next to him on the mat. "We had a merchant from Capernaum say you even healed a nobleman's son while you were still in *Cana!* Needless to say, the people here in Nazareth are proud of their native son. They are singing your praises everywhere!"

Max perked up, happy to hear the news of the nobleman's son. He was proud of the reputation Jesus had earned from his miracles and teachings. "If that doesn't convince the people ta believe in Jesus, I don't know wha' will then," Max whispered with a nod to Liz and Kate.

"*Oui,* it is good to hear that word of Jesus is spreading around the region," Liz said, her tail curling up and down. "But humans are quite fickle, no?"

"Aye, but it's grand ta see Jesus welcomed like this in his hometown," Kate added happily. "I know Rabbi Isaac will be happy to see everyone finally believing in Jesus—as he has all along."

"I must warn you, my dear Kate. Believing Jesus' miracles is one thing," Nigel cautioned, coming out from hiding. "Believing he is Messiah is a different matter entirely."

While Jesus enjoyed catching up with his family, Gillamon led Clarie to the back of the humble home to get her fresh hay and water.

230

"I hate to go through this again," Clarie said sadly. "I can hardly bear it for Rabbi Isaac."

Gillamon softly rubbed her donkey nose. "Yes, tomorrow will be a hard day, but as Jesus said, it is expected."

"Max had a hard time dealing with this," Clarie said with eyes full of compassion for her brave, protective little friend.

"Yes, but he made it through before," Gillamon reassured, "and he'll make it through again."

ה וד

"So, are you *meshuga* enough to go with me to synagogue, eh?" Rabbi Isaac asked Al, grunting as he leaned over to tie his sandals. "The people will think I'm *meshuga* to take you with me, but do you think I care if they think an old man like me is crazy?" He waved his hands as if to shake off the thought. "I'll only take you to the steps, hungry kitty, as you are not allowed inside. Mary can take you home after that, *nu?*"

Al sat purring with a full belly, watching the old man get dressed. He didn't care where he was allowed, as long as he wasn't hungry.

"Now if they knew I thought Jesus was Messiah as a boy, they would think such a thing, but not now. True? Of course, true!" Isaac slowly rose up and stretched his back with a groan. *"Oi!* I'm not the young man I used to be, *nu?"* He grunted and groaned as he shuffled his feet across the floor to the room where his donkey Amos stayed. "I'll be back after synagogue, Amos. Maybe Jesus will come see you, too, since he's in town."

"HEE-HAW!" Amos replied excitedly.

Rabbi Isaac wagged his finger with an impish grin at his lifelong donkey friend. "You see, I can tell that you know what I'm saying. No one can tell me Balaam had the only smart donkey in all Israel, eh?"

"HEE-HAW!" Amos snorted again, jerking his head up and down in happy agreement.

Rabbi Isaac cupped a handful of grain to Amos's mouth, and chuckled when Amos's lips tickled him as the animal scooped up every last morsel. He leaned in close to the donkey's ears. "Today should be a great day for Israel, my friend. Maybe at last Jesus will tell them, *nu?"*

The aging man rubbed Amos on the nose and walked back into

231

the other room to clean his hands. He then reverently picked up his white *tallit*, or prayer shawl, adorned with deep blue stripes. Its knotted, twined fringes called *tzitzit* dangled from the four corners of the shawl as Isaac stretched it out before him. Al lifted his paw, tempted to reach out and play with the fringe.

Rabbi Isaac took a deep breath and recited the blessing as he had done countless times before: *"Barukh atah Adonai, Eloheinu, melekh ha'olam* (Blessed are you, Lord, our God, sovereign of the universe), *asher kidishanu b'mitz'votav v'tzivanu l'hit'ateif ba-tzitzit* (Who has sanctified us with His commandments and commanded us to wrap ourselves in the tzitzit.)" He then threw the tallit over his shoulders and brought his hands together in front of his face briefly, covering his head. After a moment he adjusted the tallit around his shoulders and looked down at Al. "I think I am ready, Ari. To the synagogue, *nu?"*

Together Rabbi Isaac and Al walked slowly down the dusty streets of Nazareth toward the synagogue. The beloved old man beamed as he heard the people walking by, mentioning that Jesus was in town. He nodded and lifted his hand now and then. He had waited so long for the people of his town to see Jesus for who he really was. He wasn't just a carpenter, the son of Mary and Joseph. He was Messiah, foretold by prophets, and he was a *Nazarene!* For years, Rabbi Isaac read from Isaiah and the prophets about the promised Messiah who would soon come. Oh, how glorious it would be for the people to embrace Jesus and usher in his Kingdom! Isaac picked up his pace as best he could. He couldn't wait to see Jesus at the synagogue. He already knew he would ask Jesus to read today.

When they reached the synagogue, Rabbi Isaac went inside to get things ready for the morning service. Al joined Gillamon and the others, who were already waiting outside the synagogue in the courtyard.

"Top o' the mornin'!" Al said in greeting as he kissed Liz on the cheek. "I had a grand night. I hope ye did, too, me love."

"Bonjour, cher Albert," Liz replied, petting his belly. "I'm sure you did."

"We figured we'd see ye here, lad," Max greeted him. "Jesus said we'd be leavin' after synagogue, so it's a good thing ye're here then."

Al wrinkled his forehead. "But we jest got here. Sure, and why would we be leavin' so soon then?"

"Jesus has his reasons," Nigel piped up, holding his spectacles up to the light and noticing a smudge. He frowned, breathed on the glasses and used Gillamon's tunic to wipe them off. Placing them back on his head, he smiled. "Ah, that's better. Always good to have a clear view of things, you know."

"*Oui*, and I have a feeling this is what Jesus will be giving here today," Liz said as they watched the people eagerly filing into the synagogue. "But will the people *want* their view clear?"

While the men proceeded to fill up the front rows, the women filed inside last and stayed in the back of the synagogue behind a screen. The men and women were separated according to the Law, so as to keep the focus on prayer and worship alone. Soon Jesus and Mary came to enter the synagogue, along with Jesus' brothers, sisters, aunts, uncles, and cousins. Everyone was murmuring happily to be here with Jesus. Just before he entered, Jesus and Gillamon locked eyes and Jesus nodded with a confident gaze.

233

"Hear, O Israel: the Lord is our God, the Lord is one," Rabbi Isaac began with his aging voice, but still loud enough for all to hear.

"I have to watch this!" Nigel whispered to Liz, looking for a window. "Ah! Up there!"

"I wouldn't miss this, *mon ami*," Liz replied, following the little mouse to jump up on a tiny window ledge.

They peered in and could see everything inside the synagogue. Jesus sat humbly, his head bowed, deep in prayer. He was situated in the front of the room, right next to the wall that faced in the direction of Jerusalem. On the wall was hung the Ark, a cabinet holding the Torah scrolls. Jesus looked up as Rabbi Isaac motioned for one of the men to open the door of the Ark, which was a tremendous honor. The man bowed respectfully and as he walked to the Ark, the people in the synagogue stood. Liz squinted to read the carved inscription on the door of the Ark. She read it out loud for Nigel: *"Know before whom you stand, before the King of Kings, the Holy One Blessed be He."*

Liz and Nigel shared a look of awe as they considered Jesus, the King of Kings, standing in the midst of the congregation. Only Rabbi Isaac and Mary fully grasped who Jesus was at this moment. The man appointed by Rabbi Isaac opened the *parokhet,* or inner curtain of the Ark, which imitated the curtain in the Sanctuary in the Temple. There behind the curtain were the scrolls of the Torah: Genesis, Exodus, Leviticus, Numbers, and Deuteronomy. These books were sacred to the people of Israel, for they contained their history and God's laws. The synagogue also held the other scrolls of sacred Scripture, but the Torah was the foundation for the rest. All the people gathered here in the synagogue knew they were God's people, set apart from the rest of the world, and expectedly waiting for the promised Messiah, who would come save them from their oppressors.

After Isaac prayed, the man once again closed the curtain, shut the doors of the Ark and retook his seat. As the people took their seats once the Ark doors were closed, Rabbi Isaac and Jesus locked eyes and shared a knowing look of sacred friendship and mutual respect and love. Their friendship had lasted more than thirty years. Rabbi Isaac had been the only advocate Mary and Joseph had when her pregnancy was discovered. He alone fought for the struggling young couple, daring anyone to come against them. He alone knew that the baby Mary carried was Messiah, and he was determined to protect that child from harm. Isaac looked out and saw Mary, who stood at the very back of the room.

Rabbi Isaac's heart had been full of joy the day Mary and Joseph returned to Nazareth with the toddler Jesus. After Jesus' birth in Bethlehem and their brief stay in Egypt when they fled the wrath of Herod the Great, Joseph brought the family back to Nazareth to raise Jesus. Never in his wildest dreams did Isaac think he could be Messiah's rabbi! What an honor to teach this special boy the Torah, the Law, and the prophecies about himself! Rabbi Isaac comforted Mary and Jesus when Joseph died, and supported Mary again as Jesus left to begin his ministry. Now here, today, Rabbi Isaac felt destiny rolling out before them. His gaze left Mary and he picked up the Isaiah scroll. He took a deep breath and invited Jesus to stand with him in the center of the room at the *bimah,* or pedestal where the scrolls are placed when they are read. Jesus stood and walked over to stand before the *bimah.* The eyes of the people were lit up with anticipation of hearing from their hometown prophet, now famous throughout the land. Rabbi Isaac picked up a scroll and handed it to Jesus.

"Which scroll is it, my dear?" Nigel asked Liz, who had a better view.

A lump caught in Liz's throat. "Isaiah."

Nigel put a paw on Liz's arm and squeezed, knowing they shared a long history with that scroll. Not only had they sat on Isaiah's desk as he wrote it, they also sat on Daniel's desk in Babylon as he read it. Before the animals left Babylon they hid the Isaiah scroll away for the Wise Men to someday find, to aid them in their quest to find the newborn King of the Jews. Jesus and Rabbi Isaac had pored over the scroll of Isaiah as Jesus grew, learning the prophecies and piecing together the miraculous events of Jesus' life. Liz's eyes welled up with tears as Jesus unrolled the scroll and began to read:

> "The Spirit of the Lord is upon me, for he has anointed me to bring Good News to the poor. He has sent me to proclaim that captives will be released, that the blind will see, that the oppressed will be set free, and that the time of the Lord's favor has come."

Jesus rolled up the scroll, handed it back to Rabbi Isaac, and sat down. All eyes in the synagogue looked at him intently. He returned their gaze, longing for them to clearly see the truth. "The Scripture you've just heard has been fulfilled this very day."

The people began murmuring among themselves. Rabbi Isaac clutched his hand to his chest, beaming with the revealed truth of Jesus as Messiah. He scanned the crowd and saw the people who had once praised his words begin to question him.

"How can this be?" one man whispered.

"Isn't this Joseph's son?" another echoed.

Jesus knew what they were thinking. "You will undoubtedly quote me this proverb: 'Physician, heal yourself'—meaning, 'Do miracles here in your hometown like those you did in Capernaum.' But I tell you the truth, no prophet is accepted in his own hometown."

Mary's hand went to her mouth as the pain of what she saw unfolding gripped her heart.

Jesus stood and continued. "Certainly there were many needy widows in Israel in Elijah's time, when the heavens were closed for three and a half years, and a severe famine devastated the land. Yet Elijah was not sent to any of them. He was sent instead to a foreigner—a widow of Zarephath in the land of Sidon. And there were many lepers in Israel in the time of the prophet Elisha, but the only one healed was Naaman, a Syrian."

"Do you realize what he's saying to these people?!" Nigel exclaimed with a paw to his forehead. "These people don't like to be reminded of these stories in Israel's history when God used his rejected prophets of Israel to provide for pagan, sinful Gentiles over his own people. Elijah provided miraculous replenishment of food for the widow, and later even raised her son from the dead. Then Elisha healed Naaman, the commander of the Syrian Army, who had raided Israel and taken people as prisoners back to Syria, when he humbled himself and dipped in the Jordan River seven times. It's as if Jesus is rubbing their noses in these stories of God's bypassing them for Gentiles. He is being quite bold in warning them about faithlessness in God's servants."

"*Oui*, Nigel, but Jesus is also trying to make them understand that salvation is for those who truly have faith in the living God," Liz explained. "These two stories relay how these sinful, unclean Gentiles admitted their condition and received the grace of God. They humbled themselves and believed *before* they had the miracle they desperately needed. They were obedient and willingly saw themselves as those the Messiah was foretold to save: the poor, the prisoners, the blind, and the oppressed!"

"Indeed, my dear, you are right," Nigel agreed as he rubbed his chin. "Jesus is bringing good news to the poor in spirit, to release the captives of false spirituality, to let those spiritually blind see, and to set free those who are spiritually oppressed by the likes of the scribes and Pharisees! He's trying to make the prophecy clear, but the people don't see it."

"They don't *want* to see it, Nigel." Liz frowned as she saw the people's anger rise up in the synagogue. "Spiritual pride is blinding them to the truth."

Rabbi Isaac felt his hopes begin to dash against the rock of pride that these people carried around with both hands. It kept them from embracing Messiah, for whom they had longed. They refused to be talked to this way, especially by a lowly hometown carpenter, miracles or no miracles. They didn't want to admit they needed spiritual saving. They wanted Messiah to change their circumstances, not their hearts. Suddenly loud shouting erupted as the people jumped up and mobbed Jesus.

"Quickly! They've got Jesus!" Nigel exclaimed as he and Liz jumped off the window ledge and ran back to the courtyard to rejoin the others.

"Tr-r-rouble's br-r-rewin'!" Max growled as the throng of people gushed out of the synagogue. The men had their hands on Jesus and were forcing him up the hill to throw him off the cliff. "We've got ta get in there an' stop this!"

Immediately Max and Kate took off running into the crowd, barking and pulling at the legs of the men who sought to harm Jesus. The two dogs darted in and out of the men's legs, tripping them right and left so they fell onto the rocky ground, adding to the chaos of this terrible turn of events.

"Gillamon! What should we do?" Liz cried as they watched the mob of people taking Jesus up the very same hill where Jesus had first spoken to Max and Liz the day he found out who he really was. The scene on the hill that day was majestic, powerful, and holy. Today this hill was filled with hatred, violence, and evil intent.

Gillamon calmly picked up Liz, Al, and Nigel and placed them in Clarie's saddlebags. "Come." He began to steadily lead them down the road and out of Nazareth.

"But Gillamon, we certainly can't leave Jesus at a time like this!" Nigel protested. "I say, please turn back so we can go fight for him!"

"Trust me," Gillamon told them as he continued walking calmly ahead. "The people's praise for Jesus has turned into venomous accusations. They now consider him to be a false prophet for claiming to be Messiah. The Law has conditioned them to kill false prophets, so that is what they seek to do."

Even Al couldn't stand it any longer. "But Gillamon!" the usually cowardly cat argued. "How can we let them get away with this?"

"His time has not yet come," Clarie said.

As the group got farther away from the hillside, the bloodthirsty cries of the people began to diminish. Reeling with confusion, Liz, Al, and Nigel rode along, gazing back at the hill for any sign of Jesus, Max, or Kate.

"There you are!" came a strong voice from up ahead of them.

"Jesus!" Nigel exclaimed in shock to see him standing there on the road with them. "How did you . . .?" the tiny mouse started to ask, jaw dropping and paws raised in question.

237

Liz placed her dainty paw on her chest, flooded with relief. Clarie sighed deeply in gratitude. Al fainted.

Max and Kate came trotting up behind Jesus. "We showed those people a thing or two then! They best not mess with me Messiah!" the proud Scottie exclaimed. Suddenly he noticed they were down on the road and he snapped his head back up to the hill where they had been just seconds before. "How did we . . .?"

". . . get here?" Kate finished Max's question. Her eyes were wide with confusion.

Jesus smiled at the two dogs. "Thank you, Max and Kate, for your bravery. You were very courageous to go up against that angry crowd for my sake." He knelt down to look them in the eye. "But you see, my time has not yet come. No one has any power over me here on Earth. When my time comes, I will lay down my life freely."

"So ye didn't need us, then?" Max asked, deflated and embarrassed.

"I didn't need your protection, dear Max, but I certainly always need your friendship," Jesus said, mussing Max's head.

"Jesus, we are all greatly saddened by the way the people of your hometown treated you," Liz pined.

"The very ones who should have accepted and celebrated you as Messiah were the first to reject you," Clarie added with a frown.

Jesus looked back at Nazareth, getting smaller in the distance behind them. "I am sad as well, Liz and Clarie. But not for me. I am sad for those people, whom I love with all my heart. They don't realize they've rejected the very thing they've been longing for."

"Indeed, the prophecy of Isaiah promised God's gift of freedom to those who clearly see the need to change their hearts," Gillamon posed. "But God cannot offer anything to people who are content with the condition of their hearts."

"Except judgment," Liz added somberly.

"I am especially saddened for Rabbi Isaac, and my mother," Jesus said mournfully. "I know they had such high hopes for today."

Liz thought of Mary, and all she must be pondering at this moment. "It must feel like those early days in Nazareth all over again, when the people wanted to get rid of *her,* an unwed, pregnant mother."

Jesus tightened his lips as he considered his mother's pain. Once again the dagger of burden as the mother of Messiah had pierced her heart. The group walked along in silence for a moment as they reflected on the events of the day.

"I say, will we ever return to Nazareth, Jesus?" Nigel asked.

"Someday," Jesus answered. "But for now, let's be on our way. Capernaum awaits."

Rabbi Isaac sat on a boulder at the top of the hill. The crowds had dispersed and gone home. He sat alone with his thoughts, and wrestled with the reaction of the people as he gazed out over this vast country rich with the blood of its prophets. Gratefully, he knew Jesus had miraculously escaped the clutches of the people, but he was left with a grieving spirit.

"Why?" the old man said softly as he wept, rocking back and forth. "Why couldn't they see him as Messiah? It wasn't supposed to be like this. Why?"

After decades of anticipation for this day, the old rabbi was now devastated. Still, he knew he had believed in Jesus as Messiah since the moment he learned from Mary of his coming birth, and he wasn't about to stop now. He recounted the passage of Isaiah that Jesus had read in the synagogue:

> "The Spirit of the Lord is upon me, for he has anointed me to bring Good News to the poor. He has sent me to proclaim that captives will be released, that the blind will see, that the oppressed will be set free, and that the time of the Lord's favor has come."

"The oppressed will be set free," Isaac mouthed again and again. "The time of the Lord's favor has come."

A sense of peace slowly enveloped Isaac. He lifted his gaze, straightened up, and embraced those words of Isaiah, spoken today by Messiah, for himself. The old rabbi stood and straightened his *tallit*. There in the sky appeared the fire cloud, but he didn't know the full significance of what he saw as he marveled at its beauty. As his heart reaffirmed his steadfast belief in Messiah, the sadness began to dissolve into a deeper level of understanding.

This Messiah's coming was not at all the way Israel had expected it to be. No wonder they couldn't see it! This Messiah wasn't coming to set up a worldly kingdom, but a heavenly one in the hearts of the people. All the Torah and the prophecies of Daniel, Isaiah, and the others suddenly took on new meaning for Isaac. He saw it all so clearly now.

"So the people couldn't see him? They *choose* not to see him," Isaac said sternly out loud to no one. "But as for me and my house, we will serve the Lord! Jesus had the *chutzpah* to confront the people of Nazareth with the truth, so *I* will have the *chutzpah* to keep shouting the truth! And if the people of Nazareth have the *chutzpah* to throw me off this cliff for saying the truth, then let them! *Oi!*"

Rabbi Isaac suddenly was infused with strength and a power from his belief that freed him from the bonds of oppression he had felt moments before. He felt the favor of the Lord washing over him as the warmth of the fire cloud reached out to touch him. He smiled to himself as he walked down the hill, shouting, "I know before whom I stand, before the King of Kings!" He didn't care if the people thought him *meshuga*. "Jesus *is* MESSIAH! True? Of course, true!"

240

FISHERS OF MEN

"N o fish? What do ye mean, there's NO FISH!?" Al pleaded with Max, grabbing the dog's big square head with his fluffy orange paws. "There *has* to be fish!"

"I'm jest r-r-reportin' wha' I saw, lad," Max told him with a wrinkled brow. "Ye can let go of me head now."

Al took his paws off Max's head and put them up to his mouth in distress. Max shook vigorously from head to tail, his fur fluffing up to make Liz giggle. "Ye can go down an' see for yerself. Kate an' me went with Jesus ta the water an' a bunch of fishermen jest got back after fishin' all night."

"They didn't catch anythin'," Kate reported. "They be cleanin' their nets now. Jesus be teachin' a big crowd this mornin'. There's hardly any room ta stand an' hear him then."

"Is this so?" Liz asked, jumping down from a boulder where she was giving herself a bath in the sunshine. "I wish to go hear his lesson."

Gillamon sat whittling a new walking stick. "I think you're all going to want to hear this lesson today—especially the lesson that *follows* the lesson." He laid the stick aside, stood up, and brushed off his tunic. "I suggest we all go down to the lake this morning."

"*Bon,*" Liz replied, turning to walk down the path.

Nigel looked around and didn't see Clarie anywhere. "I say, where is Clarie? She was here earlier."

With that ever-present twinkle in his eye, Gillamon smiled and said, "Oh, she's around."

"Did she go fishin'?" Al asked. "I think I'd like to give it a fair go then."

"Well, today just might be a perfect day for you to start, Al," Gillamon said with a chuckle.

The crowds lined the shoreline to listen to Jesus. The animals darted in and out of the people's legs as they followed Gillamon to a good spot. Jesus was standing at the water's edge, but people were straining to hear what he had to say. Gillamon led the animals to where Peter, Andrew, James, and John were cleaning their fishing nets. Peter was barking orders where to put the nets and complaining about almost everything. Al began to feverishly run around the boats, checking for himself that there were no fish. Max and Kate sat by, looking at each other and then rolling their eyes at their disbelieving, hungry feline friend.

"I hear you had a bad night of fishing," Gillamon noted, pointing to their empty nets.

"Bad doesn't begin to describe it!" Peter snapped back. He picked up one of the heavy, empty nets and let it drop with a thud, catching Al by the tail. "ARRW!" the big cat yelled. Peter lifted the net so Al could get free. "I've never seen such bad luck. We were out there all night long and not one measly little sardine swam into our nets!" He rubbed the back of his neck and yawned hard. "Wasted night."

"Well, maybe your luck will change today," Gillamon suggested.

Peter looked at Gillamon with a sneer and replied in a sarcastic tone, "Well, it *might* if we actually *fished* during the *day*, but there's a reason we *don't!*"

Gillamon folded his hands over his upper arms and just grinned at Peter, not responding to his rude manner. He just chuckled at the brawny fisherman's rough demeanor.

Liz and Nigel were more interested in Jesus' lesson and sat on the bow of one of the empty boats belonging to Peter and Andrew.

"Listen!" Jesus said with an excited tone. A group of children were standing in the front, so Jesus animated the story with his hands, acting out the scene as he spoke. "A farmer went out to plant some seeds. As he scattered them across his field, some seeds fell on a footpath, and the birds came and ate them." Jesus pretended to scatter the seeds all around, then swooped his hand like a bird and plopped the imaginary seeds into his mouth. The children giggled.

"Other seeds fell on shallow soil with underlying rock. The seeds sprouted quickly because the soil was shallow. But the plants soon wilted under the hot sun, and since they didn't have deep roots, they died." Jesus held his hands up to his eyes, shielding them from the sweltering sun. He acted like he was withering in the sun, and the children imitated Jesus, falling to the ground. Jesus smiled as the children helped him act out the parable.

"Other seeds fell among thorns that grew up and choked out the tender plants." One little boy put his hands up to his neck as if he were choking and Jesus pointed to the boy as an illustration. "Still other seeds fell on fertile soil, and they produced a crop that was thirty, sixty, and even a hundred times as much as had been planted! Anyone with ears to hear should listen and understand." The children clapped with joy and acted as if they were eating a big feast with Jesus.

"I daresay, Jesus is certainly in his element," Nigel observed with a jolly tone. "He obviously loves teaching the eager crowds, especially the children."

243

"Oui, that he does," Liz smiled warmly. "How he loves the children! And how clever of him to speak in parables, no? On the way to Capernaum, Jesus told us this story and that it is about God's Word, and what happens when people receive it in various ways."

"Right you are, my dear," Nigel enthused. "The seed on the path represents people who hear the message, only to have the devil come and snatch it away from their hearts, keeping them from believing and being saved. The seed on the rocky soil represents people who hear the message and receive it with joy, but because they have no roots, they may believe for a while but fall away when they face temptation."

"Oui, and the seeds that fell among the thorns represent those who hear the message but all too quickly the message is crowded out by the cares and riches and pleasures of this life. And so they never grow into maturity, no?" Liz added.

Nigel held up a finger and grinned broadly. "Ah, but the seeds that fell on good soil represent honest, good-hearted people who hear God's Word, cling to it, and patiently produce a huge harvest."

"C'est bon! I adore Jesus' stories!" Liz replied. "Shhhh, he has more."

Jesus posed a question to the crowd. "Would anyone light a lamp and then put it under a basket or under a bed? Of course not! A lamp is placed on a stand, where its light will be seen. For everything hidden will eventually be brought into the open, and every secret will be brought to light." He leaned in close to the crowd for emphasis. "Pay close attention to what you hear. The closer you listen, the more understanding you will be given—and you will receive even more. To those who listen to my teaching, more understanding will be given. But for those who are not listening, even what little understanding they have will be taken away from them."

A man shouted from the back of the crowd, "Jesus, we want to hear you, but we can't back here! Please speak louder!"

Jesus stood up on his toes and cupped his ear, trying to make out what the man was saying. He nodded and then looked around. He saw Liz and Nigel sitting on the bow of the empty fishing boat and smiled. He walked over and stepped into Peter's boat, winking at Liz and Nigel.

244

"Simon!" Jesus called over to Peter, who still sat grumbling as he mended his nets. The fisherman looked up and immediately got to his feet.

"What's he doing in my boat?" Peter grumbled.

Gillamon sat silently by, grinning. Al looked up and saw Liz and Nigel in the boat. "If Jesus is goin' fishin,' I'm goin' too!" Al ran over and jumped into the back of the boat, getting tangled up in some nets that were still there.

"Simon, please push your boat out into the water," Jesus asked. "The people are having a hard time hearing me, so if I can get out just a little farther I can better speak to the crowds."

Andrew pushed Simon from where his stubborn feet were planted. "Do it, Simon! This is *Jesus* asking you to do this!"

Simon looked at Andrew and dropped his head, nodding. "Yes, all right, all right." He dropped the net he was working on and walked to the boat. "Looks I won't be making it home to sleep anytime soon anyway."

James and John followed Andrew over to the boats to listen to Jesus. Andrew helped Simon Peter shove the twenty-six-foot heavy wooden boat off the sandy bottom out into slightly deeper water as Jesus requested. The two fishermen then climbed aboard and sat in the back.

Jesus' kind eyes bored into Simon Peter for a moment, making Peter feel uncomfortable. "Thank you, Simon," Jesus finally said. Peter nodded, grumbled a half-hearted 'You're welcome,' and picked up an oar to keep the boat in place.

The people were able to form a semicircle on the shore as Peter positioned the fishing boat just offshore in the center of where they stood. Jesus looked down, then lifted one of Peter's fishing nets to show the crowd.

"Again, the Kingdom of Heaven is like a fishing net that was thrown into the water and caught fish of every kind. When the net was full, they dragged it up onto the shore, sat down, and sorted the good fish into crates, but threw the bad ones away. That is the way it will be at the end of the world. The angels will come and separate the wicked people from the righteous, throwing the wicked into the fiery furnace, where there will be weeping and gnashing of teeth. Do you understand all these things?" Jesus asked the crowd.

"Yes," they said, "we do."

245

Peter and Andrew shared a sobering glance. They could especially relate to this parable, for it was what they did every day. Well, every day that they actually caught fish.

Jesus continued. "What is the Kingdom of God like? How can I illustrate it? It is like a tiny mustard seed that a man planted in a garden; it grows and becomes a tree, and the birds make nests in its branches."

As Jesus kept sharing other parables about the Kingdom of God, Peter and Andrew sat listening with rapt attention. Liz, Al, and Nigel stayed out of the way, but watched every nuance of interchange between these rough fishermen and Messiah. When Jesus was finished speaking, he dismissed the crowds and turned around to face Peter, who sat with his elbows resting on his knees.

"Now, go out where it is deeper, and let down your nets to catch some fish," Jesus directed in a matter-of-fact tone, pointing to the middle of the lake.

Peter immediately reacted with a sarcastic laugh, thinking of how ludicrous Jesus' request was. "Master," Peter started with a patronizing tone, sitting up to meet Jesus' gaze. "We worked hard all last night and didn't catch a *thing.*"

"I noticed," Jesus replied with a smile.

"Come on, Simon," Andrew urged, a hand on Peter's arm.

"AYE!" Al meowed happily. "Let's go fishin'!"

Peter frowned and looked from Andrew to Jesus, shaking his head. "If you say so, I'll let the nets down *again.*" He snickered. "I'll let down the nets . . . in the middle of the day . . . when the fish don't come near the surface . . . because of the *LIGHT.*"

Jesus just smiled at Peter with a knowing grin. "It appears they didn't come near the surface in the dark," Jesus observed, his hands spread out to emphasize Peter's empty boat. "You were fishing at the best time to catch fish, but came up empty."

Peter frowned as he lifted the sail to catch the wind. Soon they were heading out into deeper waters. Andrew stood next to him as they worked on the rigging. Peter whispered to Andrew, "So a preaching carpenter knows all about fishing now? Well, he can preach to the *fish* for all I care!"

"SIMON!" Andrew shushed his obstinate older brother. "Your *chutzpah* astounds even me! For once in your life can you stop that hotheaded, brash talk, especially in front of the Master?"

"Bah!" Simon snapped as he leaned against the mast and folded his hands over his chest. He gazed out at the sun hitting the lake. He looked across the lake that was thirteen miles north to south and eight miles east to west. This lake was his life, and he depended on it for his livelihood. But last night it had betrayed him. Simon Peter rarely felt afraid, but he did so now. He was lashing out at everyone, including Jesus of Nazareth, the supposed Messiah of all people. Peter thought about what he had seen Jesus do in Cana, Jerusalem, and Samaria, but none of those wonderful miracles meant a thing to his empty nets. He started feeling guilty of how disrespectful his tone was toward Jesus, but he didn't know how to set it right. So he just stood there, back to Jesus, ignoring him. He closed his eyes and breathed in the air as the sunlight warmed his face.

"Here. Put your nets down here," Jesus instructed calmly.

Peter opened his eyes, dropped his hands, and made his way to the nets. "Andrew, get the other side." He simply did as Jesus suggested—he and Andrew lowered the nets into the water.

Al stood eagerly on the bow of the boat, waiting for fish. He watched as the nine-foot nets splashed into the water and slowly drifted into the depths. Suddenly he saw one lone fish come up to the surface and flip its fin, splashing Al in the face. Al shut one eye and turned to Liz. "Aye, there be at least one fish splashin' aboot!"

"And how long . . ." Peter started to say when Jesus held up his hand to stop him.

"Wait," is all Jesus said. He closed his eyes.

Suddenly Peter and Andrew were jerked forward and the boat leaned to the side. Peter and Andrew looked at one another in alarm and then down to the depths where the nets dangled in the deep water. They began to pull but the resistance was tremendous. "PULL!" Peter shouted. Peter and Andrew strained with all their might and slowly they saw a massive pool of fish swarming within their nets. "Look! Look at all the fish!"

Peter looked up at Jesus in shock and awe, and felt sudden shame at his disbelief. Jesus simply smiled and then burst out laughing. "Here, let me help you." Jesus got on his knees and helped the two fishermen pull on the nets, but even with three of them it wouldn't be enough. The nets were so full they began to tear.

247

"We're going to need more help," Peter said as he cupped his hands around his mouth, shouting to James and John still on the shore, "HURRY! BRING YOUR BOAT!" He looked down at Jesus and Andrew. "AND MORE NETS!"

"Brilliant! It looks like the catch of a lifetime!" Nigel cheered as he, Liz, and Al gazed into the water teeming with fish.

"*Magnifique!* Jesus has done the unexpected once more!" Liz exclaimed.

"I knew Jesus were a good fisherman!" Al praised, his mouth drooling at the thought of having one of those tasty fish in his mouth.

James and John pulled their boat up next to Peter's and dropped their nets. Soon both boats were so heavily laden with fish that they were on the verge of sinking.

"I think that's enough fish," Peter laughed and said. "Let's get these back to shore."

Al leaned over the edge of the boat, grasping at the fish when that same lone fish came up to him and slapped him in the face. Al fell back into the boat and shook his whiskers. "That must have been a barbel fishy!"

Liz and Nigel gazed at the fish, who came by for a second pass and surfaced. It winked at them and then disappeared into the depths of the lake. Liz and Nigel looked at one another questioningly. "I say, do we know that fish?" Nigel asked, taking off his water-spotted spectacles to wipe them off.

A coy grin grew on Liz's face. *"Mon ami,* I believe we do."

Suddenly Peter fell onto his knees in the middle of the boat before Jesus, weeping. He hung his head low and shook it mournfully. He was awestruck by the miracle Jesus had performed, and realized he was in the presence of holiness. He immediately felt convicted of his sinfulness. "Oh, Lord, please leave me—I'm too much of a sinner to be around you."

Jesus put his strong hand on Peter's shoulder. "Peter, look at me," Jesus ordered him, for the first time calling him by the new name he had given Simon the day they first met. Peter turned his gaze up at Jesus, who looked upon him with grace and love. "Don't be afraid! From now on you'll be fishing for people!"

Peter gripped his hand on Jesus' and felt at that moment the peace of God he had never known before. He knew what he must do. He would follow Jesus to the ends of the earth. He nodded and broke out into a grin, this time shaking his head in delight and wonder over the miracle of forgiveness and acceptance by this amazing Messiah.

"Without you, my nets came up empty, but with you, they were full," Peter said softly. "That's how my life's purpose has felt lately. Just empty."

"Peter, from here on, you will be filling my Father's nets with people who choose to trust his name," Jesus reassured. He gave Peter a good-humored look. "But you have to learn to fish with my instructions, agreed?"

Peter threw his head back and laughed. "Agreed! I never thought I'd be taught how to fish by a carpenter!"

Andrew, James, and John were also caught up in the miracle of what Jesus had done, and the call on Peter's life. Jesus turned to them and shouted, "Come, follow me!" and the men eagerly embraced one another, agreeing on what they had to do.

"By Jove, Jesus has officially called his first disciples! Utterly thrilling!" Nigel cheered.

"*Oui,* and utterly unexpected choices for disciples, no?" Liz replied in wonder. "Jesus has called the most unworthy and unqualified men he could find to do his work. The religious elite would call these fishermen worthless nobodies."

"Well, maybe worthless nobodies be the only kind of people he's got to work with," Al suggested.

Liz and Nigel once again were amazed at Al's insight. "Indeed, old boy, God's favorite instruments are nobodies. Instruments. Hmmmm, I say, why did I think of that analogy?" Nigel puzzled a moment, rubbing his chin, deep in thought. "Instruments."

"*Oui,* God chooses the broken, humble, and weak so there is never any question about the source of power in their lives, no?" Liz offered. "Think of all the humans we have helped across time. They either failed before they were called, during their calling, or after their calling."

"Or all three!" Nigel pointed out.

Al decided to wax philosophical. "Aye, if nobodies think they're somebodies, their pride won't let God be the only body who can really make them somebodies from nobodies, so they'll stay nobodies. But if nobodies *think* they're nobodies then God can turn them into somebodies because he *really is* the only somebody there be."

249

Liz and Nigel sat silently for a moment, trying to process what Al had just said.

"Well, Peter and these others have the raw materials Jesus needs to make them into the kind of men he can use," Liz noted. "The skills they have as fishermen are things Jesus can work with to make them into great men, no? Like patience, perseverance, courage, an eye for the right moment, knowledge of how to bait the fish, and skill to keep themselves out of sight."

"Indeed my pet, but these raw materials are rough at best," Nigel suggested. "Jesus will have to fine-tune these instruments to make those skills work for his purposes." Nigel stopped and threw his paws up in the air and let out a chuckle. "There I go with another musical analogy. Hmmmm. Perhaps I'm in need of hearing some good music."

"Want me to sing a tune then?" Al offered. As he got ready to lift his meowing voice, the boats hit the shore, sending him flying into the pile of fish.

Zebedee, the father of James and John, along with his servants, met the two boats as they landed. They immediately started to yell and cheer over the tremendous catch of fish, helping to pull in the torn, heavy nets. Gillamon stood on the shore with Clarie, Max, and Kate, grinning as he watched Jesus, Peter, Andrew, James, and John get out of the boats and walk away.

"Wait! Where are you going?!" Zebedee pleaded.

"It's all yours," Peter said, motioning to the fish.

"You're walking away from the biggest catch of your life?" a servant asked in disbelief.

Peter didn't reply. He and the others immediately walked away from the fish, the nets, the boats, and the only way of life they had known. From now on they would follow Jesus of Nazareth.

Al was busy running around the fish, not knowing where to begin. He was in heaven. "SO . . . MUCH . . . FISH!"

"Come, Al, time to go," Gillamon said as he lifted Al into Clarie's saddlebag, sharing a grin with the donkey, who winked at him.

250

"But, but, Jesus jest caught all these fish, and we're jest goin' to LEAVE them here?" Al whined.

Gillamon lifted Liz and Nigel into the other saddlebag. He leaned over and picked up a big fish to give to Al. "Here, Al. One for the road," he said with a wink and a laugh. "But don't worry, there's more where this came from."

Al happily wrapped his paws around the fish as Gillamon led the group to follow along behind Jesus and his four new disciples. Suddenly Clarie hee-hawed and shook herself all over. Droplets of water went flying everywhere.

Al stopped in mid-bite of his fish. "Clarie, Lass, how'd ye get so wet?"

30

COMFORT YE MY PEOPLE

It's the finest synagogue in all of Galilee! We never could have been able to build such a fine house of worship without your help," the local Jewish officials gushed. "We are very grateful to you, Armandus. How will we ever be able to repay your kindness?" They were giddy with excitement.

Armandus stood with his hands on his hips as he admired the newly constructed synagogue in Capernaum. "Please, no repayment is necessary. I'm glad it will meet your needs. Just use it in good health as you worship your God, and say a prayer for me now and then."

"You can be assured we will! May Jehovah bless you beyond measure for caring for his people!" the synagogue officials replied. "We have a special speaker today, if you'd like to . . ."

Armandus mounted Achilles and nodded to the Jewish officials. "No, I must be on my way. Until we meet again." He waved and left to report to the headquarters of Herod Antipas.

The Jewish men stood in the street and watched this unusual Roman soldier riding off to fulfill his duties for Rome. They marveled at how a Roman centurion would love the Jewish people enough to build them a synagogue. Why would he do such a thing? they wondered. Little did they know that Armandus Antonius had promised his father Marcus that he would be kind to the Jewish people, however and whenever he could. When he learned that the people in Capernaum needed a new synagogue, he quietly used his own personal funds to pay for it. He wanted no recognition, and in fact, preferred to keep this transaction quiet and out of earshot of his superiors.

"So who is speaking today?" one of the men asked.

"The new resident teacher, Jesus of Nazareth, will be speaking today," one man answered. "He has moved to Capernaum and has already gathered quite a following. I'm sure he will be the perfect one to give the first talk at our new synagogue today. If only Armandus could have stayed."

"If a man has a hundred sheep and one of them gets lost, what will he do? Won't he leave the ninety-nine others in the wilderness and go to search for the one that is lost until he finds it? And when he has found it, he will joyfully carry it home on his shoulders. When he arrives, he will call together his friends and neighbors, saying, 'Rejoice with me because I have found my lost sheep.' In the same way, there is more joy in heaven over one lost sinner who repents and returns to God than over ninety-nine others who are righteous and haven't strayed away!

"Or suppose a woman has ten silver coins and loses one. Won't she light a lamp and sweep the entire house and search carefully until she finds it? And when she finds it, she will call in her friends and neighbors and say, 'Rejoice with me because I have found my lost coin.' In the same way, there is joy in the presence of God's angels when even one sinner repents."

The people were astonished at Jesus' teachings. They knew he spoke with authority, for he wasn't quoting other rabbis as the scribes would do. His stories and words were from a perspective of grace they had never heard. *Angels rejoiced over them?* All was quiet in the synagogue as Jesus taught. That is, until all hell broke loose.

Suddenly a man with wild eyes in the back of the synagogue got up and started spitting as he screamed at Jesus. He was possessed by a demon—an evil spirit—and people cleared out of the area where he stood.

Pointing a finger at Jesus, he screamed, "Go away! Why are you interfering with us, Jesus of Nazareth? Have you come to destroy us? I know who you are—the Holy One sent from God!"

Jesus abruptly stood and walked over to the man, holding his hand up over him. Jesus' eyes blazed with anger and divine authority. "Be quiet! Come out of the man," he ordered.

At that, the demon threw the man to the floor as the crowd watched. The man writhed and foamed at the mouth, but suddenly a rush of calm came over him. He sat up and blinked hard, as if disoriented and not knowing what had just happened. He wiped off his mouth with the sleeve of his tunic and looked up at Jesus, who offered him a hand to lift him to his feet. As Jesus helped the tormented man stand, the man broke into sobs of relief. Jesus smiled and gripped his shoulders. How long had this man sat in the synagogue week after week, tormented by the evil spirit that lived inside him? Oh, but now he was free!

The people started murmuring among themselves, shocked and amazed at what had just taken place. "What authority and power this man's words possess! Even evil spirits obey him, and they flee at his command!"

253

Peter, Andrew, James, and John surrounded Jesus and the man, praising God for what he had done. Together they left the synagogue, and the people quickly filed outside. Word of what Jesus had done spread like wildfire through the streets of Capernaum.

"Why do the wicked beasties want ta be inside humans anyway?" Max inquired, frowning at the thought. The animals were discussing the extraordinary events that had happened that morning at synagogue. They sat in the outer courtyard of Simon Peter's home, where Jesus and his disciples were staying.

"Well, the evil one seeks to destroy all life, including individuals," Gillamon explained with a serious tone. "So he sends his demons to take control of people who do not have the Maker's authority in their lives, to destroy them with sickness or even to make them hurt themselves."

"But the Maker is in complete control of the spirit realm, including those wicked demons!" Nigel interjected, pounding one of his fists into his open palm. "So Jesus has complete authority and power over them, and those spirits know exactly who he is."

"Why did Jesus tell the spirit ta be quiet? It was callin' Jesus by name, tellin' everyone who he were," Kate asked. "Seems ta me he'd want people ta hear the truth."

Gillamon leaned forward and scratched Kate behind the ears. "Yes, dear Kate, Jesus does want the people to know who he is, but not from the witness of demons. That's why Jesus seeks to teach the people, so those who embrace him as the Son of God will tell the world. The truth is important, but the *source* of truth is sometimes just as important."

Suddenly they heard Peter's wife, Naomi, come rushing out of the house to meet Jesus and the others as they approached the courtyard. "Jesus! Oh, please, my mother has become very sick. She has such a high fever she is delirious. Please heal her!"

Jesus placed his hand on Naomi's shoulder. "Show me to her room."

Naomi quickly ran inside and led Jesus to where her mother lay covered in sweat, her breathing very shallow. Jesus stood by her bedside and placed his hand on her forehead. He frowned as he felt the rage of her fever under his palm.

Peter and Naomi stood in the doorway, holding one another. Liz and Nigel peeked around the couple's legs to watch.

"Leave her," Jesus said, rebuking the fever.

In an instant, the woman opened her eyes, her color returned, and she began to breathe normally. Jesus smiled at her and simply asked, "How do you feel?"

She sat up and put her feet on the floor. "I feel well! Thank you, Jesus." She immediately stood and picked up her bed mat, shaking it out. "Well, after I hang this outside and change my clothes, I will get the meal going. Naomi, come, we have work to do and hungry men to feed!"

Jesus and Peter stood there and chuckled as the now healthy, bossy Jewish mother took charge of things. Peter threw his hands in the air and let them drop to his sides. "Jesus, I don't know what to say. First, you give a resounding sermon at synagogue that stirs hearts, then you heal a demon-possessed man, now you heal my mother-in-law. How . . .? I just . . ." Peter stammered, overwhelmed with this day so far with Jesus.

Jesus patted Peter on the back. "With God, all things are possible, Peter." As Peter walked ahead of them to join the others, Jesus looked down at Liz and Nigel and leaned over to whisper, "Are you enjoying this wonderful Sabbath?"

Liz headbutted Jesus with great affection. *"Cher* Jesus, you are a miracle worker!"

"Indeed! Brilliant! I'm simply speechless," Nigel cheered as Jesus nudged the little mouse.

"Wait until the sun goes down," Jesus said with a knowing grin.

The knock came on the door just after sunset. Peter went to open the door and there stood a man holding a little boy with a cancerous knot on his leg. The little boy's eyes were weak and sunken in, and he was extremely thin. "Please, my little boy has been suffering ever since this thing appeared on his leg. He used to love to run, but now he's in constant pain, and he is too weak even to walk." The man choked up as a single tear fell down his cheek. He swallowed hard. "We know he's dying. But I know the Master can heal him. *Please."*

Jesus came up from behind Peter and stepped outside with the distraught father. Filled with compassion, Jesus placed his hand on the boy's leg. Immediately, the boy's eyes lit up with energy as warmth coursed through his frail body. When Jesus removed his hand, the knot was gone.

"Father, I feel like I can stand!" the little boy exclaimed.

The father looked at Jesus who smiled and nodded. He gently placed his son on the ground and the boy began skipping around the courtyard. "I'm well! I'm well! Look, I can even run!"

The father's hands went up to his face as he broke out in tears of joy. "Oh, thank you, Jesus! Thank you for healing my boy!"

Everyone inside the house came out to witness the miracle of the little boy. Jesus gripped the man by the arm. "You are most welcome."

"Mon Dieu!" Liz shouted, with her paw up to her mouth. "He's done it again!"

"Aye, an' it looks like he'll be doin' it again, an' again, an' again," Max added. "Look."

Coming up the road were scores of people heading to Simon Peter's house. The people had waited until sunset on the Sabbath to bring their sick loved ones to the miracle worker who had healed the demon-possessed man in the synagogue. It wasn't long before the entire town had assembled at Peter's door. The animals sat on a rock

255

wall in the courtyard of Peter's house, watching this amazing event unfold.

"Why're they comin' now?" Al asked. "Why'd they wait 'til it were dark? Are they afraid like Nicodemus?"

"No, Al. Under the Sabbath law the people can't labor or carry anyone until the end of the Sabbath, so they had to wait until the long day was over," Clarie explained. "Don't you know they were wishing the hours would fly so they could get here tonight?!"

"*Oui,* and by law, Jesus wasn't supposed to heal on the Sabbath, but that didn't stop him in the synagogue or in Peter's house, did it?" Liz added with a grin.

"Aye! I've said it befor-r-re an' I'll say it again, Jesus doesn't care a shoutin' camel's spit aboot wha' people think," Max asserted with a wide grin.

"When it comes ta Jesus, the only law that really matters is love," Kate added, beaming with joyful tears at the little boy running around. "Love is more important than rules and laws. People be more important ta Jesus than anythin'."

"'Comfort ye my people,'" Liz said softly, quoting Isaiah's prophecy of Messiah. "'He Himself took on our weaknesses and carried our diseases.' Everything is coming true about Jesus, just as Isaiah foretold."

The animals sat and watched as Jesus went from one person to another, speaking just a word. Immediately, no matter what their diseases were, the touch of his hand healed every one. Many were possessed by demons; and the demons came out at his command, shouting, "You are the Son of God!" But because they knew he was Messiah, he rebuked them and refused to let them speak, just as he had done in the synagogue.

While the disciples got tired and sat down, Jesus stayed up until every last person who had come to him for healing was touched. Only then did he call it a night. The city of Capernaum would never be the same for them again.

Before daybreak the next morning, Jesus got up and went out to an isolated place to pray. He was drained from the incredible Sabbath day of healing and casting out demons.

"Look how he goes to his Father," Liz noted softly.

256

"His task is so great," Gillamon added. "He knows he needs divine strength to accomplish all he must do. Today will be a big day as well."

"No r-r-rest for the wear-r-ry," Max said, stretching out long and hard.

"I'm glad we get ta be here, prayin' with him," Kate added. "But we're far enough away ta not be a bother then."

"Did anyone bring breakfast?" Al asked.

"Up here," Clarie nodded to her saddlebag. "You're completely hopeless, Al."

"Aye, but not if I got fish!" Al said happily, jumping up on Clarie's back.

It wasn't long before Simon Peter and the others went out to find Jesus. When they found him, they said, "Everyone is looking for you."

Jesus nodded and put his hands on his knees, pushing himself up to face his disciples. "We must go on to other towns as well, and I will preach to them, too. That is why I came."

"Looks like his disciples need some educatin' then," Max noted.

"*Oui,*" Liz agreed. They think he should take advantage of his growing popularity by doing more miracles in Capernaum, but Jesus' mission is not to be a miracle worker," she added.

"Right you are, my pet," Nigel confirmed. "While he does miracles, he's out to redeem hearts and minds. He's jolly well not out to be a healing spectacle for the masses."

"The disciple laddies jest don't get why Jesus came out here at all," Max huffed. "Jesus wants ta get *away* because of the popularity in Capernaum. It's like I've been sayin' all along. The people only want Jesus ta do mir-r-racles. They don't r-r-really want ta be r-r-ruled by the Maker!"

Gillamon listened to the Order of the Seven analyze the situation with Jesus, his disciples, and the miracles. "Jesus knows when, where, and why to perform miracles, so trust his judgment. If a miracle leads to a heart change, he knows it. If it leads to a word of hope that Messiah has come, he knows it. If it simply leads to people wanting to see a spectacle, desiring only to see something like the magicians pull, he knows it, too. He knows the motivation of the people, but he above all knows *his* motivation."

"Love!" Kate said happily, wagging her tail.

Gillamon closed his eyes and nodded. "Indeed, Kate. Love it is."

257

Jesus and his disciples walked on to the next village and were suddenly met by a shocking scene. A leper approached them in the middle of the road. People covered their mouths and pushed their loved ones inside and away from the unclean man. His leprosy was advanced and the stench from his body was evident to all. The disciples retreated but Jesus stood in place in the middle of the street as the leper boldly approached him.

"Wha's happenin'?" Max asked in alarm.

"A leper is doing the unthinkable!" Liz replied with shock. "A leper is never supposed to mingle with crowds of people. They have such a horrific, contagious disease that by law they must remain separated from society."

"I knew they were dangerous, but I never knew leopards were so contagious!" Al said, putting his paws into his mouth.

"Leper, not leopard, Al old boy," Nigel corrected, his spectacles down on his nose as he studied the man approaching Jesus. "Dreadful disease, leprosy. It's known as the 'living death.' No other disease reduces a human being to so hideous a wreck for so many years."

"How so?" Kate asked, hiding behind Max.

Nigel shook his head. "Well, it sometimes begins with little nodules on the skin that become ulcers. The eyebrows fall out, the eyes sink in, the voice becomes raspy with vocal chords attacked by ulcers, and the breath gets wheezy. The hands and feet of course are covered in sores that eventually cover every square inch of the leper's body. The nerves lose all sensation, so injury occurs without feeling, and wounds are not attended. Muscles waste away. Then comes the loss of fingers, toes, until at the end," Nigel gulped, "a whole hand or foot may fall off. And it's not just the body that decays, but the mind goes as well. Utterly dreadful!"

"So lepers are considered 'walking dead men,'" Liz added with a wince. "*Quel dommage!* Once a leper is diagnosed, he or she is banished from human society. They are separated from their family and friends, never to touch them or anyone again. They have to cover their mouths and shout, 'Unclean!' as they pass people."

"Think of having to refer to yourself that way forever," Clarie said with great sadness. "I know how it feels to know you are unclean and blemished. But imagine having to watch your children grow up from a distance, never being able to hug them again. Oh, I can't imagine!"

258

"We got ta stop him then!" Al said in horror as the leper came right up to Jesus.

"Steady, Al." Gillamon put his hand on Al's shaking frame. "Watch."

Evidently this man had heard of the miracles Jesus had performed in Capernaum and the area. He came and knelt in front of Jesus, begging to be healed. "If you are willing, you can heal me and make me clean," he said.

Jesus was moved with intense compassion for this suffering man. He reached out and touched him. "I am willing," he said with an affirming smile. "Be healed!"

All eyes were glued to the scene when instantly the leprosy disappeared. The man was healed! He looked at the backs of his hands in awe, and opened his ragged shirt to gaze at his chest, now clean and whole.

The disciples held their heads in disbelief, grabbing one another in exultation of watching their Master at work.

"He didn't *have* to touch him," Liz said, her lip trembling and her eyes full of joyful tears. "He didn't *have* to touch him in order for him to be healed. *Ooh-la-la,* how wonderful Jesus is! His touch meant more to that man than words will ever be able to express."

259

Clarie, also weeping as she remembered the touch of Jesus on her blemish, added, "Jesus just welcomed this man back into the family of mankind with his touch."

"And according to Jewish law, *Jesus* is now unclean for touching him," Nigel informed them.

"A shoutin' camel's spit!" Max said, suddenly running up to Jesus and barking with joy around him.

The healed man leaned down and petted Max, marveling at being able to even touch an animal without fear of harming it.

Jesus smiled at Max but then his face grew serious as he approached the man. "Don't tell anyone about this. Instead, go to the priest and let him examine you. Take along the offering required in the Law of Moses for those who have been healed of leprosy. This will be a public testimony that you have been cleansed."

The man looked at Jesus with such ecstatic joy that he bowed and kissed Jesus' hands, exclaiming, "Yes, Lord, yes! I will! Thank you, Jesus! Oh, thank you!"

With that the man went running on two strong, healed legs with ten toes on his feet. But as Jesus watched him go, he knew the man wouldn't be able to contain himself. He would tell everyone. He took in a deep breath and sighed heavily.

"I won't be able to go anywhere without being mobbed now," Jesus muttered to Max. "Well, so be it. Come, my friend, we have more work to do."

Jesus walked on to the next town, his disciples grilling him with questions and acting like giddy young boys at Jesus' miracle with the leper. Jesus had his eyes set on speaking at another synagogue come the Sabbath. He set his sights on the nearby village of Jotapata, and there they went.

People packed the synagogue when they heard that Jesus was going to teach. Jesus scanned the crowd and saw him, hiding in the back row. He smiled and began to speak.

260

"A man had two sons. The younger son told his father, 'I want my share of your estate now before you die.' So his father agreed to divide his wealth between his sons. A few days later this younger son packed all his belongings and moved to a distant land, and there he wasted all his money in wild living. About the time his money ran out, a great famine swept over the land, and he began to starve. He persuaded a local farmer to hire him, and the man sent him into his fields to feed the pigs. The young man became so hungry that even the pods he was feeding the pigs looked good to him. But no one gave him anything.

"When he finally came to his senses, he said to himself, 'At home even the hired servants have food enough to spare, and here I am dying of hunger! I will go home to my father and say, "Father, I have sinned against both heaven and you, and I am no longer worthy of being called your son. Please take me on as a hired servant."'

"So he returned home to his father. And while he was still a long way off, his father saw him coming. Filled with love and compassion, he ran to his son, embraced him, and kissed him. His son said to him, 'Father, I have sinned against both heaven and you, and I am no longer worthy of being called your son. But his father said to the servants, 'Quick! Bring the finest robe in the house and put it on him. Get a ring for his finger and sandals for his feet. And kill the calf we have been fattening. We must celebrate with a feast, for this son of mine was dead and has now returned to life. He was lost, but now he is found.' So the party began.

"Meanwhile, the older son was in the fields working. When he returned home, he heard music and dancing in the house, and he asked one of the servants what was going on. 'Your brother is back,' he was told, 'and your father has killed the fattened calf. We are celebrating because of your brother's safe return.'

"The older brother was angry and wouldn't go in. His father came out and begged him, but he replied, 'All these years I've slaved for you and never once refused to do a single thing you told me to. And in all that time you never gave me even one young goat for a feast with my friends. Yet when this son of yours comes back after squandering your money on prostitutes, you celebrate by killing the fattened calf!'"

Jesus looked intently at the tax collector from Capernaum whom he had seen regularly at his customs table, burdening his fellow Jews by collecting extra tax money to line his pockets. Jesus knew full well this man was spiritually hungry enough to attend a synagogue outside of his own town, where no one would recognize him. He was sitting in the back with slumped shoulders and in complete humility, praying to God this morning, begging forgiveness. Jesus had compassion on this lost son of Israel who had betrayed his fellow Jews to serve Rome. He was indeed a prodigal in need of redemption. The man looked up and Jesus locked eyes with him as he finished the story.

"His father said to him, 'Look, dear son, you have always stayed by me, and everything I have is yours. We had to celebrate this happy day. For your brother was dead and has come back to life! He was lost, but now he is found!'"

Only Jesus saw the tax collector quickly make his way out the back of the synagogue as the people stood to leave. Jesus locked eyes with him one last time.

Matthew's eyes brimmed with tears. He couldn't bare the conviction engulfing him about his life's path. He was the prodigal son, having spiritually left his heavenly Father's home for the glory of Rome. He had to get out of there. He had been seen in the synagogue, where he had been banned because of his profession. But even more urgently, he needed to escape the loving gaze of the One beckoning him home.

261

THROUGH THE ROOF

W e've tr-r-raveled so many miles in Galilee I think we've seen ever-r-ry squar-r-re inch of it then," Max groaned as he plopped down and spread out his hind legs behind him on the cool stone in Peter's courtyard. "I'm one pooped laddie."

"I liked Jotapata, Jotapata, Jotapata," Al repeated, humming and eating some dates.

"I say, why do you pronounce that town thrice?" Nigel inquired.

"It's jest fun to say," Al mumbled with a full mouth, moving his arms back and forth. "Jotapata, Jotapata, Jotapata."

Nigel chuckled. "It certainly has rhythm when you say it like that, dear boy."

"Well, I for one am glad to be back in Capernaum at Peter's house," Liz spoke up. "Perhaps we can rest here a while, no?" she wanted to know, stretching out and licking a front paw.

"A brief rest, yes, but Jesus' time here on Earth is short," Gillamon reminded her. "And he has much to accomplish. Besides, when word gets out Jesus is back in Capernaum, things will get busy soon enough."

"I think it's already happened then," Kate said, looking down the street. Just as before, people came flocking to Peter's house.

Jesus was inside talking with his disciples when people asked if they could simply sit and listen to the Master. Jesus, of course, welcomed them, so every available space in the house was taken with people. They even poured out the door and windows and into the courtyard.

Clarie noticed four men walking up the road carrying a stretcher. "Look at this."

Gillamon and the animals turned to see the men carrying a friend, obviously hoping to bring him to Jesus. The man was unable to move his arms or his legs—a quadriplegic. The men wore looks of determination. When they saw that the house was packed with no way in, they set their friend down while they surveyed the house.

"Wha' do ye suppose they're doin'?" Max asked.

Liz gazed at the men, her tail slowly curling up and down. She watched one of them climb the outside staircase and walk around the roof. He then came running back down to his friends. They lifted the stretcher and began climbing the outside staircase. "They're going to go through the roof!" Liz guessed.

"Oh, how much they must love their friend to do this for him!" Kate offered.

"Utterly splendid of the chaps," Nigel cheered, but then put a paw to his chin in worry. "Oh, dear, Peter will not be too happy about this. Let's hope his patience gets honed a bit by this invasion."

"I wish to see this from the inside," Liz said, walking toward the house.

She easily walked through the people, meowing, *"Pardon, mon ami,"* here and there. The people smiled and let her through, petting her as she climbed over them. Jesus was talking about loving one another when suddenly they heard the sound of the men on the roof, making a great deal of noise. The roof of the house was fitted with wooden beams covered with clay tiles and covered over with a layer of plaster and straw. The men were digging through the plaster to get to the tiles.

Peter looked up, as did the rest of the crowd gathered there. "What is going on up there?" Peter demanded with a scowl.

Jesus sat with his arms clasped around his knees, watching the ceiling. Some sand and dust fell from the ceiling onto his tunic and he calmly brushed it off. Suddenly daylight poured in as the men removed the tiles above. Jesus smiled broadly at what was happening.

"Hey! You're taking my roof apart!" Peter yelled. "You can't just . . ."

"Simon," Jesus said, getting the attention of his hotheaded disciple.

263

He didn't need to speak another word. Peter crossed his arms, clearly irritated, and backed down.

"Make way!" one of the men shouted as enough tiles were removed to leave a big hole. Slowly the men began to lower the stretcher though the roof down to the floor below.

"Clear a space for him," Jesus asked those gathered there.

Some people stood and helped take hold of the stretcher to gently place the helpless man on the floor. His eyes were full of worry, as he didn't know what to expect from Jesus.

Jesus looked up at the four friends who now peered over the edge and smiled at their friend. And when he saw their faith, he turned to the paralytic, took his hand, and said, "Son, your sins are forgiven."

The man closed his eyes and smiled, tears slowly running down his temples as he lay there. His friends up above clung to each other as they gazed at their friend who had suffered for so many years.

Sitting in the room were some of the scribes from the synagogue. Immediately they began thinking to themselves, *Why does this man speak like that? He is blaspheming! Who can forgive sins but God alone?*

Liz's gaze was on Jesus. Suddenly he looked right at the scribes and she could feel his rebuke coming. Her fur stood on end.

"Why do you question these things in your hearts? Which is easier, to say to the paralytic, 'Your sins are forgiven,' or to say, 'Rise, take up your bed and walk'?" Jesus stood up. "But that you may know that the Son of Man has authority on earth to forgive sins"—he turned his gaze to the paralyzed man—"I say to you, rise, pick up your bed, and go home."

All eyes were on the man, and the people gasped as he sat up on his own, using his hands to raise himself up. The man looked up at his friends and started breathing quickly, anticipating what he was about to do. He felt strength fill his emaciated muscles and weak bones. He was tingling from head to toe as he slowly rose to stand before the people. "Look at me! Look at me! Look at me!" he cried in joyous ecstasy. Jesus smiled as the man gripped Jesus' forearms. The man looked up at his friends, who were shouting joyfully and holding their heads in disbelief. "We're coming down!" they shouted and the people could hear their footsteps running off the roof and down the stairs.

The people cleared a path to the door as the man picked up the stretcher that had been his bed, and clutched it to his chest. "Thank you, Master," the man said simply. He was at a loss for what else to say. Jesus nodded silently and smiled in affirmation.

The man walked out the door with his mat and the people erupted in cheers and shouts of amazement. "We've never seen anything like this! Praise be to God!"

The four friends encircled the man as he turned around and around, lifting his legs to show how they were not just well, but strong. The friends enveloped him in a massive embrace and they all began to sing and cheer. Two friends each came alongside the man and the five friends walked arm-in-arm, back down the road they had traveled to get to Peter's house.

Peter stood looking at the hole in his roof, hands on his hips, surveying the damage. Jesus came up to him and Peter smiled. "What's a little clay for a man's new life?"

Jesus nodded his approval of Peter's change of heart, knowing that Peter was gaining an understanding of what was really important in life. Things meant nothing. Lives meant everything.

Nigel came up to Liz as she wiped from her eyes the tears of joy of yet another miraculous event. "Oh my dear, what a blessing for you to have witnessed this miracle! But I noticed the scribes as they left, seeming none too pleased, despite the splendid outcome. Did something bad also happen in here?"

Liz frowned. "*Oui,* Nigel. When Jesus told the man his sins were forgiven before he was healed, the scribes of course thought he was speaking blasphemy. The Jews believe that all sickness is because of sin, and no healing can come until sin is forgiven."

"And no one can forgive sin but God," Nigel finished her thought. "Oh dear, I see. For Jesus to dare to extend forgiveness to the man meant to the scribes that Jesus had insulted God. Pity they don't understand that Jesus *is* God and has the authority to do so!"

"I'm afraid this might start a rift between Jesus and the Jewish leaders here in Capernaum," Liz said, twitching her tail back and forth in concern. "If they don't like Jesus, they will naturally misinterpret his motives and misrepresent all he does from here on."

"Gillamon told us trouble would come as Jesus begins to threaten the religious establishment," Nigel sighed. "I just didn't expect it to come so soon, and on such a happy day."

Liz looked up at the roof that was opened for the good of a suffering man, an act completely discounted as bad by the religious leaders. They cared more about their pious laws than one transformed life. She knew this event would not be forgotten.

"When word of this reaches Jerusalem," Liz said, furrowing her brow, "the Sanhedrin will most certainly go through the roof."

266

Partying
with Sinners

Once again Jesus was by the sea, preaching to the crowds, but today he purposely positioned himself near the tax office where sat Levi, son of Alphaeus, better known as Matthew. He had frequently passed Matthew's desk, usually pulling Peter away as he stood there cursing the despised man. This was before Jesus called Peter to leave his life of fishing to become a disciple. Peter no longer had to pay taxes on his daily catch of fish, but the resentment against Matthew was still there, and it was as deep as the Sea of Galilee.

Today among the crowds were gathered some Pharisees sent by the Sanhedrin in Jerusalem to hear what the blasphemous Jesus had to say. Word had reached them about the audacity of Jesus forgiving the paralytic's sins. So this delegation was sent to observe Jesus. Saar, Jarib, Nahshon, and Zeeb stood smugly in the back, listening. Peter, Andrew, James, and John also stood in the back, observing these same Pharisees Jesus had encountered at the Temple in Jerusalem.

Jesus looked up to see the Pharisees and then his gaze drifted to Matthew, who also sat listening intently. He then looked over the eager crowd and shared a story. "Two men went up into the temple to pray, one a Pharisee and the other a tax collector. The Pharisee, standing by himself, prayed thus: 'God, I thank you that I am not like other men, extortioners, unjust, adulterers, or even like this tax collector. I fast twice a week; I give tithes of all that I get.' But the tax collector, standing far off, would not even lift up his eyes to heaven, but beat his breast, saying, 'God, be merciful to me, a sinner!'" Jesus looked over at Matthew. "I tell you, this man went down to his house justified, rather than the other. For everyone who exalts himself will be humbled, but the one who humbles himself will be exalted."

"Ooooooh, the Phar-r-risees didn't like that a bit," Max whispered to Liz.

"C'est vraiment, mon ami," Liz replied softly, frowning and whipping her tail back and forth as she watched the silent outrage of the Pharisees. "Quite true. This will cause further trouble for Jesus, I'm afraid."

Max grinned wide. "Aye, but I do love it when Jesus shows up those self-r-r-righteous r-r-religious r-r-rogues."

The corners of Liz's mouth curved up. "Those religious men can handle Jesus' miracles, and in fact believe that he has done them, no? What they can't handle is Jesus calling them sinners, and claiming he can forgive sin," she pointed out.

Peter and the other disciples were also grinning. They, too, enjoyed watching Jesus boldly at work. It was incredible to watch Jesus call out the truth no matter how it upset the religious elite. Jesus indeed didn't care what men thought when the truth was at stake.

Matthew hung his head, looking down at his tax table laden with coins. He reached into a bag and lifted up a handful of coins, letting them drop slowly through his fingers. He shook his head in shame. *I've swindled my own people out of this money. No wonder they banned me from their midst.* He looked up at Jesus, who was dismissing the crowds. *But this man says I am justified before God because I repented that day in the synagogue? It's that easy? That's too good for a sinner like me to believe.*

Matthew picked up his pen and rolled open his ledger to make more notes of today's collections. Tatius would be by to take his latest report to Herod Antipas, who had awarded him this tax collection post. He had sold his soul to Rome, and now had to pay his dues. Matthew buried his face in his work, trying to shake off the spiritual torment he felt. Then a shadow fell over his desk. Matthew didn't look up.

"You've come to pay your taxes?" Matthew said gruffly. "Let's see how much you . . ." he stopped in mid-sentence. There before him stood Jesus, quietly staring at him.

268

"Oh, it's you. Jesus of Nazareth," Matthew cleared his throat and muttered, rolling up his scroll as if to hide his shame. He looked both ways before he whispered, "I heard your teaching today. I know you saw me at the synagogue in Jotapata."

Jesus still said nothing, but cocked his head and smiled.

Matthew broke out in a sweat under the gaze of this One who made his heart burn with longing at the words he spoke. The prodigal son. The forgiven tax collector. *He was talking about me,* Matthew realized. "I've studied the Scriptures extensively," he said as he let go a sad laugh. "I've had to study them on my own since I was banned from entering the house of the Lord due to my profession. I'm cut off from God and his people, banned from sacrifice in the Temple and worship in the synagogue. I'm considered worse than a Gentile in the eyes of the religious elite!"

Matthew waited for a response, but still Jesus said nothing.

"So I broke the Law to get inside the house of the Lord!" he pled as he tapped his pen on the rough wooden table. Then he pointed his pen up at Jesus and said, "But according to the Law, it is *righteous* to lie and deceive a tax collector because that's what a professional extorter like me deserves. So why didn't you report me? And how can you tell me I'm forgiven before God because I simply asked for it that day in the synagogue? How can you . . ."

"Follow me," Jesus cut him off.

Matthew took in a quick breath, shocked by Jesus' command. His heart was immediately gripped with the power of grace. He suddenly had the vision of the prodigal son running into the welcoming, forgiving embrace of his father. Tears quickened in his eyes and he stood behind his table, looking down at the life he thought would bring him fulfillment. It had only brought him rejection, dishonor, and isolation. He gripped his pen tightly and turned his gaze to Jesus. "I've also extensively studied what the Scriptures say about Messiah. According to Daniel's Seventy Weeks Prophecy, his time should be at hand."

Jesus simply smiled. "Indeed. Follow me."

Matthew nodded and walked out from behind his desk, leaving everything behind, except his pen, which he unknowingly still gripped in his hand. A rush of excitement coursed through his veins. He shouted out in joy, "Master! Please come to my house! I want all my friends to meet you! I'll throw a big banquet in your honor tonight!"

"Of course, let's go," Jesus answered, leaving his other disciples behind.

As the two men walked away to Matthew's house, Peter was clenching his fists in anger. "How could Jesus possibly call *Matthew?!* MATTHEW!" He stomped off, grumbling, "I'm going home!"

Andrew, James, and John stood there, wondering what to do. They, too, were in shock that Jesus would call such a sinner to be part of their group, but they were at a loss as to how to handle it. They fell in line and followed Peter home, not knowing what else to do.

The animals stayed by the shoreline with Gillamon as they watched Jesus and Matthew head in one direction, and Peter and the others in another.

"What's so bad aboot bein' one o' those tax collectors?" Al asked, casually munching on some fish. "I thought collectin' stuff were a good hobby. I don't know aboot taxes. Is it anythin' like collectin' coins?"

270

"It *is* collecting coins, old boy, but not for the purpose of enjoying them," Nigel began to explain.

"Why would he collect coins if he didn't enjoy it?" Al asked, clearly confused.

"Well, he *does* enjoy collecting coins, but not for the purpose of keeping them," Nigel continued.

"Now ye really got me confused, Mousie." Al scratched his head. "If he collects coins, and enjoys it, but ends up not keepin' 'em, what's the point o' bein' a tax collector?"

Nigel was getting flustered himself, trying to explain this to Al. "Let me try again," the mouse said, straightening his spectacles, then using his paws to gesture as he talked. "Tax collectors work for the Roman government, and Matthew specifically works for Herod Antipas here in Capernaum. Matthew actually bought the rights to have a tax business here. His job is to collect taxes or fees to be paid to Rome for various things like what they make, what they trade, what they travel with . . ."

"And what they catch, like Peter and the others catching fish," Liz interjected.

"Right you are, my dear," Nigel concurred. "So the people have to come to the tax collectors and pay the money they owe Rome, but the tax collectors overcharge in order to line their own pockets, cheating the people out of their hard-earned, and much-needed, income. Sometimes they even hire thugs to force the people to pay. Simply dastardly practice, tax collecting!"

Al held up his fish. "Did this fish have a tax?" he asked fretfully. "I hope some poor fisherman laddie didn't have to pay extra for it."

"*Oui, cher* Albert, that fish was taxed, as was every single one that Peter, James, Andrew, and John caught," Liz explained. "This is why they were always so angry at Matthew, and why they are angry now, that Jesus would call such a despicable man to become a disciple."

Al tapped the fish thoughtfully on his chin. "But Jesus jest talked aboot the story o' the Pharisee and the tax collector, and he said that the bad laddie asked God to forgive him, so he did. Shouldn't Peter and the others be glad that Matthew wants to turn good, like God?"

Gillamon clapped his hands slowly in affirmation of Al's point. "Very good, Albert. And this is the very thing Jesus is trying to teach his disciples today. They must learn to give grace to the most despicable sinners around, just as he does."

271

"Looks like Jesus' parable was as much for the disciples as it was for the Pharisees," Clarie added. "Peter and the others are acting like the Pharisee in the story now."

"Excellent observation, Clarie," Gillamon leaned in and affirmed. "Jesus needs all people to learn they are sinners, from the despicable tax collectors to the self-righteous Pharisees."

"Well, I'm happy that Jesus called Matthew!" Kate added with her enthusiastic grin. "I love it when a lost lad or lassie finds their way ta goodness."

"Aye, an' Peter an' the others best learn this lesson fast, or Jesus will make it clear ta the lot of 'em," Max added. "Should we go ta where Jesus is now, at Matthew's house then, Gillamon?"

"Of course, let's go to the fun party," Gillamon said, leading them up the road.

"Aye! Forget Peter's pity party then," Max added, trotting behind Gillamon.

As they passed by Matthew's deserted table, Gillamon stopped and looked it over. "Matthew took nothing with him, save one thing. Do you know what it is?"

Liz and Nigel jumped up onto the desk to scope it out. The money was there, along with his ledger scrolls and all his business records.

"It appears he didn't take anything, old boy," Nigel said. "I say, what are we missing?"

Gillamon leaned in close enough to make such a point that Liz and Nigel leaned their heads back. "His pen."

"But what does he need his pen for?" Liz questioned.

Gillamon started walking again, chuckling, and answered, "You'll see."

The laughter spilling out of Matthew's house was second only to the wine spilling out of the jars into the glasses of the guests around his table. Every lowlife imaginable had been invited to Matthew's celebration dinner for Jesus, including prostitutes, tax collectors, and even the hired thugs Matthew sometimes used to collect money from unwilling taxpayers. Matthew's friends were all despicable, vile scoundrels.

272

"How *revolting*," Nigel said as they gazed into the crowd of poorly dressed women who shamelessly hung all over the sleazy men as they lounged around the dinner table. Everyone was eating and drinking too much, and the raucous laughter got louder as the evening progressed.

"Why did Matthew invite these people ta his celebration party with Jesus?" Kate asked.

"No one else will associate with Matthew," Liz answered with a sad tone. "They are the only friends he has."

Jesus sat at the head of the table with Matthew, enjoying a conversation with his newest disciple, but not indulging to excess like the rest of Matthew's guests. Jesus offered no judgmental stares or words, but looked around the crowd to assess who was there. Matthew started to feel self-conscious about the heavy partying that was going on. He looked at the crowd and then to Jesus. When he looked back at the door, there he saw Jesus' other disciples, sitting in the doorway.

Matthew could see the lamplight dancing off the faces of Peter, Andrew, James, and John, who dared not enter, as they hadn't been invited. There remained a serious rift between Matthew and Peter, which Matthew was just beginning to realize they would have to overcome. Although he always was at odds with Peter, he admired what a good man, husband, and citizen the fisherman was. He had faith, honor, integrity, and the respect of his fellow villagers. Matthew looked at the only friends he had—the lowlifes of Capernaum—and knew he wanted things to be different from now on.

"Everyone, thank you for coming to my home tonight," Matthew addressed the crowd as he sought to hush his rowdy guests. "This is a big day for me, and I'm going to change the direction I'm going. I wanted you to hear Jesus for yourselves and see what a great man of God he is. His words touch my mind and my heart," he told the crowd, then stopped, locking eyes with Peter. "So I wanted you to hear what he has to say, too. He tells great stories."

"Ooooh! Stories! I love stories! Please tell us a story!" one of the prostitutes shouted, slurring her words. Matthew grimaced at her.

Jesus pulled his knees up and wrapped his arms around them, smiling at the sad, loose young woman. "Once there were two spies sent to spy out the Promised Land that God was to give to his people, who had escaped slavery in Egypt. Joshua son of Nun secretly sent them, saying: 'Go. Look over the land. Check out Jericho.' They left and arrived at the house of a harlot named Rahab and decided this would be a good place to hide. But the king of Jericho was told, 'We've just learned that men arrived tonight to spy out the land. They're from the people of Israel.' The king of Jericho sent word to Rahab: 'Bring out the men who came to you to stay the night in your house. They're spies; they've come to spy out the whole country.'"

Everyone sat in rapt attention, including the animals. Al's paws were up to his mouth in worry, wondering if the spies would be caught. Matthew knew this story well, having studied the Scriptures and the stories about Joshua.

Jesus continued. "The woman had taken the two men and hidden them. She said, 'Yes, two men did come to me, but I didn't know where they'd come from. At dark, when the gate was about to be shut, the men left. But I have no idea where they went. Hurry up! Chase them—you can still catch them!' (She had actually taken them up on the roof and hidden them under the stalks of flax that were spread out for her.) So the men of Jericho began the chase down the Jordan road toward the fords. As soon as they were gone, the gate was shut."

Al's paws dropped in relief.

"Before the spies were down for the night, the woman came up to

273

them on the roof and said, 'I know that God has given you the land. We're all afraid. Everyone in the country feels hopeless. We heard how God dried up the waters of the Red Sea before you when you left Egypt, and what he did to the two Amorite kings east of the Jordan, Sihon and Og, whom you put under a holy curse and destroyed. We heard it and our hearts sank. We all had the wind knocked out of us. And all because of you, you and God, your God, God of the heavens above and God of the earth below.

"'Now promise me by God. I showed you mercy; now show my family mercy. And give me some tangible proof, a guarantee of life for my father and mother, my brothers and sisters—everyone connected with my family. Save our souls from death!'

"'Our lives for yours!' said the men. 'But don't tell anyone our business. When God turns this land over to us, we'll do right by you in loyal mercy.'

"She lowered them down from a window with a rope because her house was on the outside of the city wall. She told them, 'Run for the hills so your pursuers won't find you. Hide out for three days and give your pursuers time to return. Then get on your way.' The men told her, 'In order to keep this oath you made us swear, here is what you must do: Hang this red rope out the window through which you let us down and gather your entire family with you in your house—father, mother, brothers, and sisters. Anyone who goes out the doors of your house into the street and is killed, it's his own fault—we aren't responsible. But for everyone within the house we take full responsibility. If anyone lays a hand on one of them, it's our fault. But if you tell anyone of our business here, the oath you made us swear is canceled—we're no longer responsible.'

"She said, 'If that's what you say, that's the way it is,' and sent them off. They left and she hung the red rope out the window. They headed for the hills and stayed there for three days until the pursuers had returned. The pursuers had looked high and low. The men of Israel headed back. They came down out of the hills, crossed the river, and returned to Joshua son of Nun and reported all their experiences. They told Joshua, 'Yes! God has given the whole country to us. Everybody there is in a state of panic because of us.'

"The time came for the people to invade Jericho. Joshua ordered

274

the two men who had spied out the land, 'Enter the house of the harlot and rescue the woman and everyone connected with her, just as you promised her.' So the young spies went in and brought out Rahab, her father, mother, and brothers—everyone connected with her. They got the whole family out and gave them a place outside the camp of Israel. But they burned down the city and everything in it, except for the gold and silver and the bronze and iron vessels—all those things they put in the treasury of God's house. But Joshua let Rahab the harlot live— Rahab and her father's household and everyone connected to her."

Jesus leaned back on his hands after relating this story. He stared directly at Peter. "This woman with a past now had a new future." He turned his gaze and looked down the row of prostitutes, making eye contact with each one. "Having strange men appear at her door was nothing new for Rahab. But when these two men of God came to her door, she saw her chance to join the cause of the God she had heard of and now feared. She must have wondered if these men would betray her, or if this new God might fail her. But once she made the decision there was no turning back. She risked death to be obedient to the conviction now stirring in her heart. And her good heart immediately went to thoughts of protecting her family and herself."

The row of prostitutes self-consciously started pulling their shawls around their shoulders, trying to make themselves appear more modest in the presence of this man of God, who was filling their ears with words of hope about a woman just like them.

"But the men did not betray her, and God certainly did not fail her," Jesus said with a warm smile. "Rahab went on to have a new life. She had to learn new, healthy ways to relate to men, but God helped her every step of the way. For you see, God knew Rahab. He saw in her not only what she was, but what she *could* be. Because of the change in her choices and in her life, Rahab not only saved those two men and helped the nation of Israel, she became an important woman in the line of King David."

And Messiah is in the lineage of King David, Matthew thought to himself. *Jesus is Messiah! Rahab is his distant grandmother! A prostitute! There is no one that God can't use for his purposes!*

Hope filled the room. Grace drifted in the air as did the billowy smoke from the oil lamps. Matthew knew what he needed to do. He

275

stood and walked over to where Peter and the others sat just outside the door. He smiled and held out his hand, "Please. Won't you come into my home and join us?"

Peter slowly got to his feet as Jesus watched the two men. Peter looked at Jesus sitting around all these sinners who were now quiet and pondering Jesus' words. He then looked at Matthew and from a new source of grace that he couldn't explain, Peter smiled and said, "Yes, we would like to join you."

The two men clasped their forearms as the people watched this miraculous transformation as a bitter relationship turned into a firm friendship. Polite murmurings and soft welcomes ushered Peter, Andrew, James, and John into the room, and the guests eagerly made spaces for the disciples to sit at the table.

"*C'est magnifique!*" Liz exclaimed, her eyes brimming with tears. "Look at the power of grace!"

"And look how Jesus once again has raised the value of lassies!" Kate added. "He's shown these young lassies that even now they can have a new life if they give it ta the Maker."

The once vacant doorway was now filled with the scowling faces of the four Pharisees from Jerusalem. They peered inside with obvious looks of disgust at the good Jewish fishermen who had now joined the company of this blasphemer and these sinners! Their hatred grew quickly until Zeeb shouted, "Why do you eat and drink with tax collectors and sinners?!"

Peter immediately got riled up, and Jesus had to place a calming hand on the disciple's arm. "Those who are well have no need of a physician, but those who are sick. I have not come to call the righteous but sinners to repentance."

The Pharisees gave Jesus a hate-filled gaze and immediately left Matthew's house.

"Jesus told off those four fer-r-rocious Phar-r-risees!" Max growled.

"And what Jesus *really* means by 'righteous' is 'self-righteous,'" Nigel said with a chuckle.

"And what Jesus *really* means by *that* is that all are sinners!" Liz added.

"Sure, and it looks like Peter and the others have come around then," Al cheered.

"By Jove, I think they've got it!" agreed Nigel.

"The disciples have received from the Master their first major lesson in grace," Gillamon observed, his arms folded over his chest as they all sat in the back of the room. "They have all learned something about what this Messiah is really like."

"Aye! He parties with sinners ta br-r-ring them home then," Max offered.

Gillamon looked at Matthew's face, now completely radiating joy and peace for the first time in years. "Yes, and today one prodigal came home to stay."

33

LORD OF THE SABBATH

s they approached the gates of Jerusalem to attend one of the required feasts, Liz couldn't help but wonder what awaited them inside those formidable walls. She had been deep in thought about recent events, especially the clashes with the Pharisees. Now they were once again entering the home turf of the Sanhedrin. Liz wrinkled her brow as she considered that the Pharisees were obviously watching Jesus' every move, and Jesus was deliberately flaunting his contempt for their system. Both sides were getting bolder. Every time Jesus embarrassed the Pharisees, they would fall back, regroup, and rethink their strategy for a way to discredit him. But Jesus was ready for them every time.

Liz looked over at Jesus, who threw his head back laughing at something Al had said as they walked along. Liz breathed deeply and smiled. *Oh, how I love Jesus! Why can't the Pharisees see who Jesus is? Oh, if only they knew, really knew, who he was.*

"Master, Nathaniel and Philip are here, and they've brought a friend with them," Andrew said running up to Jesus. "He asked to meet you."

Jesus stopped and turned to see the men walking toward him and smiled. "I'm glad to see you again, Nathaniel and Philip. And who is this?"

"It's good to see you again, too, Jesus!" Nathaniel said excitedly. "We've told everyone about you, and knew you'd be coming to Jerusalem, so our friend was eager to meet you. This is Didymus, or Thomas, as we call him."

Thomas bowed respectfully as he greeted Jesus, but wore a tight-lipped serious look. "Rabbi."

Jesus looked Thomas in the eye, and couldn't quite contain his humor at Thomas's 'eagerness.' "Thomas, so you are a twin? I'm sure your mother was blessed to have two fine children together."

Thomas maintained his dreary demeanor. "I doubt that."

"Well, I am glad to know you, and happy you will be able to spend some time with us in Jerusalem," Jesus replied with a hand to Thomas's back.

"I wouldn't plan on any quality time with all the crowds," Thomas said with a straight face. "Still, it's nice to finally meet you, Rabbi."

"He's quite the pessimistic lad, ain't he then?" Max whispered to Gillamon.

Gillamon and Jesus shared a knowing grin as they started walking again to enter Jerusalem. "Well, some people just tend to see the negative side of things."

"Jesus should be able ta help him with that then," Kate offered, wagging her tail.

Jesus told his disciples he would meet them in the Temple court, and peeled off toward the Sheep Gate. Gillamon remained with the animals but Nigel scurried into Jesus' robe and hid up in his hood as they walked to the pool at Bethesda. "I say, it's just like old times with you here like this in Jerusalem," Nigel whispered in Jesus' ear. "Thank you for letting me come along."

Jesus smiled as they entered the pool area where there were five roofed colonnades. "I always love to have my little British mouse in tow."

Jesus stopped and surveyed the multitude of invalids—blind, lame, and paralyzed—all desperately hoping the spring-fed pool would heal them. It was the only source of healing these poor people had. Jesus' gaze landed on one man, an invalid very much alone by the pool. He was the picture of helplessness.

"There he is," Jesus muttered.

"Who?" Nigel popped his head out to see.

"He's been lame for thirty-eight years," Jesus replied. "He thinks angels come and stir the waters, and unless he's the first one in, the healing won't come."

"How sad," Nigel noted. "I say, he doesn't take his eyes off the water, does he? So close, yet so far away."

"Indeed," Jesus said, walking straight toward him. "So he'll need quite a distraction to get his eyes elsewhere."

The man lay there, scowl on his face as he stared into the water. His rough skin was etched with deep wrinkles, and he wore bitterness and regret as easily as his filthy clothes.

Jesus stopped right next to the man, casting a shadow on him. The man didn't look up, but kept his icy gaze on the water. Jesus waited for the tension to build, then asked, "Do you want to get well?"

Ha! What kind of man is this to ask such a ridiculous question?! the man thought to himself. He turned his gaze away from the water to look up at Jesus. With a pitiful, whining voice he replied, "Sir, I have no one to help me into the pool when the water is stirred. While I am trying to get in, someone else goes down ahead of me."

Jesus wasn't going to entertain him with sympathy, nor was he going to help him get into the pool. "Get up! Pick up your mat and walk."

At once the man was cured. Heat radiated through his legs and he felt a jolt of strength hit him as if he had been thrown into the water. Jesus stepped back as the man got up, blending into the mass of people there. When the man reached down to pick up his mat, he clutched it to himself and looked for the man who healed him, but he was nowhere to be found. He was in shock with what was happening to him and mindlessly walked to the Temple.

Several members of the Sanhedrin were strolling through the Temple court, observing the people to make sure they were all adhering to the Sabbath rules. Suddenly one of them saw the man Jesus had healed walking with his mat. Immediately their ire rose and they stomped over to intercept the man. They knew this lame man well, for he had been seen at the pool for years.

"It is the Sabbath; the Law forbids you to carry your mat," one of the Jewish leaders sneered, giving no acknowledgment to the miraculous fact that the man was standing straight and tall in front of them.

The man was startled and dropped his mat, not having really thought that he was breaking the Law. He was too focused on the fact that he was walking for the first time in thirty-eight years. "The man who made me well told me, 'Pick up your mat and walk.'"

"Who is this fellow who told you to pick it up and walk?" another Pharisee snapped.

The man looked around in a full circle and shrugged his shoulders. "I have no idea who he was."

The Pharisees all lifted their chins and looked down their noses at the man. They immediately turned and went to their chambers to discuss this with other members of the Sanhedrin. The man stood there and looked at his mat, not knowing what to do with it now that he was told it was unlawful to carry it on the Sabbath. But he couldn't leave it there, either. He looked both ways and picked it up, running to the shadows to hide out.

"I bet you anything it's Jesus of Nazareth," Zeeb said as he slapped his hand on the table at hearing the report of the others. "Sounds exactly like something he would do."

"Heal a man who has been lame for thirty-eight years?" Nicodemus spoke up. "Yes, it certainly does."

"No! Heal on the *Sabbath!*" Zeeb shouted. "I want to go see for myself." With that he stormed to the door, grabbing his other colleagues to go with him.

Nicodemus and Joseph of Arimathea stayed put, sharing a concerned look as their colleagues huffed out of the room.

"Those pompous Pharisees were no better than childhood bullies for how they treated that poor man!" Nigel raged in Jesus' ear. He and Jesus had been privy to the entire scene, staying just out of sight. "Anyone with a *shred* of decency or an *ounce* of feeling would have been rejoicing over the man's healing, but *noooooooooo!* Those callous, cold, self-righteous . . ."

"Calm down, Nigel," Jesus said, putting his hand up on the little mouse. "Consider the source."

"Forgive me, Jesus," Nigel said with a paw to his head. "I just get so angry at these Pharisees and the way they treat the people."

"I do, too," Jesus affirmed, seeing the man hiding in the shadows. He walked over to him and lifted his hand as he looked him over up and down. He let his hand drop to his side, clearly pleased.

"See, you are well again," Jesus said with a smile. Then leaning in close, he gave a stern warning. "Stop sinning or something worse may happen to you."

The man just stood there and nodded. "Might I know your name?"

Jesus told him and then walked off to find his disciples. The man went away and told the Jewish leaders it was Jesus who had made him well.

"What did I tell you?" Zeeb scowled as he and the others left the man to go looking for Jesus. It didn't take long. Jesus was standing in the courtyard with his disciples.

"Jesus of Nazareth," Zeeb bellowed. "What do you think you're doing, working on the Sabbath and violating our laws?"

Jesus slowly turned and took a deep breath, keeping calm as he answered. "My Father is always at his work to this very day, and I too am working."

Zeeb, Saar, Jarib, and Nahshon immediately put their heads together and whispered. "Blasphemy! He's equating himself with God!"

"How dare he?! This has gone beyond breaking the Sabbath law."

"He must be stopped!"

The disciples stood behind Jesus, anxious about this showdown in process.

"This isn't good," Thomas muttered under his breath.

Jesus knew what the Pharisees were saying, and spoke to them. "Very truly I tell you, the Son can do nothing by himself; he can do only what he sees his Father doing, because whatever the Father does the Son also does. For the Father loves the Son and shows him all he does. Yes, and he will show him even greater works than these, so that you will be amazed. For just as the Father raises the dead and gives them life, even so the Son gives life to whom he is pleased to give it. Moreover, the Father judges no one, but has entrusted all judgment to the Son, that all may honor the Son just as they honor the Father. Whoever does not honor the Son does not honor the Father, who sent him."

Jesus was only getting started. He walked closer to the Pharisees, who stood there with hate radiating from their eyes. He continued,

282

"Very truly I tell you, whoever hears my word and believes him who sent me has eternal life and will not be judged but has crossed over from death to life. Very truly I tell you, a time is coming and has now come when the dead will hear the voice of the Son of God and those who hear will live. For as the Father has life in himself, so he has granted the Son also to have life in himself. And he has given him authority to judge because he is the Son of Man.

"Do not be amazed at this, for a time is coming when all who are in their graves will hear his voice and come out—those who have done what is good will rise to live, and those who have done what is evil will rise to be condemned. By myself I can do nothing; I judge only as I hear, and my judgment is just, for I seek not to please myself but him who sent me.

"If I testify about myself, my testimony is not true. There is another who testifies in my favor, and I know that his testimony about me is true. You have sent to John and he has testified to the truth. Not that I accept human testimony; but I mention it that you may be saved. John was a lamp that burned and gave light, and you chose for a time to enjoy his light.

283

"I have testimony weightier than that of John. For the works that the Father has given me to finish—the very works that I am doing—testify that the Father has sent me. And the Father who sent me has himself testified concerning me. You have never heard his voice nor seen his form, nor does his word dwell in you, for you do not believe the one he sent. You study the Scriptures diligently because you think that in them you have eternal life. These are the very Scriptures that testify about me, yet you refuse to come to me to have life.

"I do not accept glory from human beings, but I know you. I know that you do not have the love of God in your hearts. I have come in my Father's name, and you do not accept me; but if someone else comes in his own name, you will accept him. How can you believe since you accept glory from one another but do not seek the glory that comes from the only God?

"But do not think I will accuse you before the Father. Your accuser is Moses, on whom your hopes are set. If you believed Moses, you would believe me, for he wrote about me. But since you do not believe what he wrote, how are you going to believe what I say?"

The Pharisees stood there, clenching their fists, the rage inside of them building. Had they had stones in their hands, they would have hurled them at Jesus.

A group of men stood off next to Jesus' disciples, marveling at what they heard. Their names were Thaddeus, James, and Simon. As Jesus left the speechless Pharisees standing there, these new men filed out along behind him.

"He was brilliant! Magnificent, I tell you!" Nigel cheered, getting the animals caught up on what had transpired at the latest showdown between Jesus and the Pharisees. "A huge crowd was gathered in the Temple courts to hear Jesus tear down the Pharisees and the one source they trust in to justify their power. He told them that Moses himself is against them for not believing in Jesus as the Son of God."

"So Jesus has publicly and definitively claimed that he is not just a prophet or a rabbi, but the Son of God," Liz assessed, wrinkling her brow. "We can expect the Sanhedrin to increase their watch of Jesus. But they are fearful of Jesus' power and presence, and also of the people."

"Typical bullies. They always be the biggest cowar-r-rds," Max grumbled. "Aye, but they cr-r-rawled back under the r-r-rock they came from then, didn't they, Nigel?"

"Indeed, they scurried out of the courtyard, whispering amongst themselves," Nigel told them.

Liz could only imagine what they discussed.

"We need to build a credible case against him," Jarib offered.

Nahshon nodded and quickly added, "Jesus needs to be shown to be a constant and wicked blasphemer."

Zeeb's elbows rested on the table, his hands clasped with his fingers pointed to his mouth, thinking. He slowly put his hands down on the table. "It's not enough just to try to discredit him any longer." The arrogant ringleader of the group stood and walked to the window, clasping his hands behind his back. "Our case needs to be strong enough that we can kill him." Zeeb paused, turning to ensure the others were with him. "Without a challenge from Rome."

"So why're the Pharisees so picky aboot what ye do on the Sabbath then?" Al asked. They were traveling back to Capernaum, but wouldn't make it before sundown when the Sabbath began. The group of disciples following Jesus had grown in number on this trip, which slowed their travel speed.

"The Pharisees have turned the Sabbath into something God never intended it to be," Gillamon answered. "After the Babylonian exile, when the people of Israel were stripped of everything that made them Hebrew, they clung to the books of Moses that spelled out the laws of God. The rise of the Pharisees came out of this obsession with the Law, and legalism became the core of Jewish identity."

Liz saw that Al was confused. "God had simply said to 'rest' on the Sabbath, meaning to cease from working and to rest in the worship of Him. But the Pharisees added a long list of things to rest from."

"Like what?" Al asked.

"Ooh-la-la, but there are thirty-nine categories of forbidden activity," Liz said with a paw to her face. "Carrying, burning, writing, cooking, washing, sewing, tearing, knotting, untying, plowing, planting, reaping, harvesting, threshing, winnowing, sifting, grinding, kneading, building, demolishing, shearing . . ." She paused. "The list goes on, no?" Al's eyes were wide. "That's the most stressful restin' I ever heard."

"Exactly, old boy, so you can see why Jesus openly defies what the Pharisees have made it," Nigel jumped in. "To show you how dreadfully absurd they are, it's considered lawful to do good on the Sabbath, like giving your animals a drink of water so they do not thirst, but unlawful for Jesus to heal a lame man! And mind you, unlawful enough to where the Pharisees could have stoned Jesus to death!"

"Ye got ta be KIDDIN' me!" Max growled. "Ye mean it's okay ta give Clarie here a dr-r-rink but ta fr-r-ree a lad fr-r-rom thirty-eight years of bondage is punishable by death?" The black dog's fur was on end.

"Oui, the people are exhausted with a sense of failure over trying to keep all the Sabbath demands. This is why Jesus is out to take back the Sabbath by never backing off from healing or comforting those who need it," Liz answered. "But rest assured, the Pharisees aren't about to let Jesus have it without a fight."

285

As they neared Capernaum early that evening, the Sabbath had begun. Everyone was hungry. Jesus and his followers were going through the grainfields, and as the disciples walked along, they began to pick some heads of grain.

"Look, there they are *again!*" Nigel exclaimed, pointing to a group of Pharisees from Jerusalem. "Do they ever stop?"

"Not on the Sabbath," Al said, making quite the incriminating statement about the hypocritical Pharisees.

"Look, why are they doing what is unlawful on the Sabbath?" One of the men pointed at Peter and the others who were eating the grain.

"Is pickin' grain on their 'rest list'?" Al asked.

"Evidently they consider picking the grain 'reaping,' rubbing it between your fingers 'threshing,' and blowing away the chaff 'winnowing'! Pffft!" Liz spat in disgust.

286

Jesus looked at the religious leaders and shook his head. "Have you never read what David did when he and his soldiers were hungry and in need? In the days of Abiathar the high priest, he entered the house of God and ate the consecrated bread, which is lawful only for priests to eat. And he also gave some to his men."

The Pharisees looked at one another, but couldn't give a reply. They knew that what Jesus had pointed out was true.

Jesus kept walking and then stopped and turned. "The Sabbath was made for man, not man for the Sabbath. So the Son of Man is Lord even of the Sabbath."

"*Tell 'em, Jesus!*" Max barked. "*In yer faces, ye self-r-r-righteous r-r-rabble!*"

The Pharisees fumed and walked in the opposite direction, making notes and plotting their next move as they walked into darkness.

Everyone woke to a beautiful Sabbath morning. They were happy to be back by the sea in Capernaum. As Jesus and the disciples got ready to go to synagogue, Liz had a hunch that she needed to discuss with Nigel.

"If those Pharisees were sent from Jerusalem to spy on Jesus, we can expect them to be at the synagogue today, no?" Liz posed. "I think they are deliberately trying to catch Jesus in the act of violating their Sabbath rules.""Agreed," Nigel said, cleaning his spectacles. "So what are you thinking, my dear?"

"I think we need to be at synagogue today to watch what happens. Tensions are high enough already, but something tells me to expect another clash today," Liz answered, her tail slowly curling up and down as she thought this through.

"There's a window in the synagogue," Nigel answered with a grin. Then, lifting his paw toward the door, he asked, "Shall we?"

Liz smiled as she and Nigel scurried behind Jesus and his disciples. When they arrived at the synagogue, Liz and Nigel jumped up to the window ledge while the men filed inside.

"What did I tell you!" Liz said, pointing to the Pharisees sitting in the back.

"Your intuition never fails, my pet!" Nigel agreed.

"Now we shall wait for the clash *du jour*," Liz predicted, eyeing the crowd. She spotted a man with a withered hand sitting near the front. He turned and looked back at the Pharisees, who gave him a slight nod.

"It's a plant!" Liz exclaimed. "The Pharisees have actually planted a wounded man right in the middle of the synagogue to see if Jesus will heal him on the Sabbath!" Liz turned her gaze to the heavens. *"Mon Dieu!* How do you put up with them?!"

"A simply dastardly ruse, using that poor fellow for their evil purposes!" Nigel said with a frown. "But this does tell us what they think about Jesus."

"What is that, *mon ami?"* Liz wanted to know, whipping her tail in anger now.

"They know Jesus *can* and *will* heal him," Nigel replied. "They don't doubt his powers or his compassionate heart for people. How utterly absurd that they doubt his Lordship, for who else could do such things but Messiah, for whom they've waited?!"

"Oui, look how far man's pride and lust for power will go," Liz replied sadly.

"To the point of utter blindness," Nigel agreed. "They don't even realize it."

As Jesus got up to speak he saw the man with the shriveled hand. He knew exactly what the Pharisees were thinking and doing.

287

Jesus pointed to the man whose deformed hand was bent inward in an unnatural way. "Stand up in front of everyone."

Then Jesus looked right at the Pharisees and asked them, "Which is lawful on the Sabbath: to do good or to do evil, to save life or to kill?"

But they remained silent.

Jesus looked around at them in anger and, deeply distressed at their stubborn hearts, said to the man, "Stretch out your hand."

He stretched it out, and his hand was completely restored.

Gasps arose from the people as the man held his hand to his face in amazement and joy.

The Pharisees immediately stood up and stomped out of the synagogue.

Liz and Nigel sat on the windowsill as the men walked down the street, gesturing wildly in anger. Liz wrinkled her brow and turned to her mouse friend. "There is something else we know about what the Pharisees think of Jesus' claim to be Lord of the Sabbath."

288

"What is that, my dear?" Nigel asked, folding his arms as they watched the spiritually blind, conniving men.

Liz furrowed her brow. "The Pharisees won't rest until Jesus is dead."

TWELVE INSTRUMENTS

THE TWELVE

The crowds following Jesus were becoming so great he could hardly move about. The people came from all over Galilee, Judea, Jerusalem, Idumea, from east of the Jordan River, and even from as far north as Tyre and Sidon. The news about Jesus' miracles had spread far and wide, and vast numbers of people came to see him. His compassion poured over the people, and he healed all of them wherever he went. And whenever those possessed by evil spirits caught sight of him, the spirits would throw them to the ground in front of him shrieking, "You are the Son of God!" But Jesus sternly commanded the spirits not to reveal who he was.

Jesus finally asked a group of people to accompany him up a mountainside to escape the crowds. When the small group was settled for the night, Max watched as Jesus went off by himself to pray.

"Gillamon, Jesus seems preoccupied with somethin'," Max observed.

Gillamon stoked the fire and glanced over at Jesus as he walked away from the group. He turned his gaze back to the fire and then to the Order of the Seven team gathered around him. "He's going to pray. He has to make some big decisions in the morning, and needs his Father's direction."

"How many decisions then?" Max asked.

"Twelve," Gillamon replied with a knowing grin. "Everyone get some good rest tonight. Tomorrow is a big day."

Gillamon woke everyone early, before the sun was even up. "Jesus wishes to speak with us before the others. Come."

Max, Liz, Kate, Al, Nigel, and Clarie quietly rose and followed Gillamon up the path they had seen Jesus take the night before. They were yawning and sleepy still, but when they saw Jesus there, praying with his head in his hands, they immediately came alert.

Jesus heard them coming and smiled, waving them over. "Good morning, little ones. Come, I have some things to tell you."

The animals looked at each other and walked over to surround Jesus. Gillamon sat down on a rock behind them.

"I've been praying all night, for today I will call twelve men to be my disciples. My Father guided me to the right choices, and I have been praying for them," Jesus began. "This calling is one that will change their lives forever. They've needed their hearts and minds prepared for what I will ask them to do."

292

"Haven't ye already called some disciples, Jesus?" Al asked.

"Yes, Al, but just on a level as students who listen to and learn from my teaching," Jesus answered. "This call will be greater than just discipleship. These disciples will also be apostles."

"Ah, *oui*, disciples are students who learn, but apostles are messengers who are sent, no?" Liz clarified.

"Exactly, Liz," Jesus replied. "These men will be my ambassadors to spread the gospel message of my teachings, and they will eventually hold positions of authority for teaching, and be given supernatural power to work signs and wonders."

"Aye, so they must need ta be r-r-really important laddies then," Max jumped in. "Who are they then? R-r-rabbis?"

Jesus shook his head. "No."

"Scribes? Priests?" Kate asked.

Again, Jesus shook his head. "No."

"I say, you couldn't possibly mean Pharisees or Sadducees?" Nigel asked warily.

Jesus gave Nigel a look as if to say, "Are you completely mental?" Nigel closed his eyes in relief, gripping his chest with dramatic emphasis.

"Not a single one from the religious establishment," Jesus said. "But ordinary, flawed, low-class, rural, unworthy, unqualified men."

"Rabble, not rabbis," Al noted.

Jesus chuckled at Al's play on words. "Right. These twelve represent judgment on organized Judaism, which is now corrupt. Instead of being based on the faith of Abraham, it is now based simply on being physical descendants of Abraham."

"Aye, with a lot of r-r-rules an' r-r-regulations heaped on the people then," Max said gruffly.

"Twelve, just like the twelve tribes of Israel," Liz posed. "Is there a connection, Jesus?"

Jesus nodded. "These twelve will represent a new leadership for a coming new covenant my Father will make not only with his chosen people, but with all mankind. And with these twelve weak men, God alone will get the glory. My strength is made perfect in weakness."

"Brilliant! What better way to confound the mighty than with the weak things of this world?" Nigel enthused.

293

"The time has come to change the focus of my ministry, and to train these twelve men. They will leave everything to follow me, and will be with me everywhere I go. I will not ask them to give up anything that I will not more than make up for," Jesus told them. "They have much to learn, and time is short."

Jesus and Gillamon exchanged a somber look. Liz's heart caught in her chest as she read into what Jesus was saying. His death was looming in the not-too-distant future.

"Jesus, how will you teach them in so short a time?" Clarie asked, knowing what Jesus and Gillamon knew, that only eighteen months remained. "And how can you turn over such authority to the likes of . . ." she started to say, feeling the burden Jesus had before him.

"Aye, wha' if they fail?" Max interjected. "Is there a backup plan then?"

"I will instruct them with patience, encourage them with grace, and correct them with love. They lack spiritual understanding, humility, complete commitment, and power, but I am choosing *them*, so I am responsible for them," Jesus explained. "I know their many faults, but these twelve will turn the world upside down. They will not fail." Then turning to Max, he told them, "There is no backup plan."

"You told us in the wilderness that this time would come," Liz remembered. "You said we would need to get to know them well for they would need our help when you are . . ." She stopped, a lump in her throat. "When you are gone."

Jesus looked into Liz's eyes with tender compassion, for he knew her heart was breaking at the thought of losing him. *"Cher* Liz, indeed. Get to know these twelve well. Learn their strengths, their weaknesses, their fears, and their hidden talents. Someday you will help them as they pick up where I left off."

Max sat there brooding, not liking the thought. Jesus leaned over to Max. "And remember, my small, brave friend. When my time comes, you must let it come."

Max gazed up at Jesus, and nodded with a resolved understanding. "Aye," he sighed.

Jesus gave Max a good rub on the ears. "That's the boy." He stood up. "Now, let's go back to the others. It's time to call the twelve."

Jesus walked ahead of everyone down the path. Gillamon stayed in place, watching each of the animals as they fell in line behind Jesus. "Trust him, now," he admonished them. "He knows what he's doing."

"I'm sure the twelve Jesus has selected will be fine instruments," Nigel said with a jolly tone, then stopped and wrinkled his brow. "Hmmm . . . instruments."

A pink hue filled the early morning sky as Jesus and Gillamon woke the large group of followers gathered there. Birds were announcing the start of the new day and it gladdened Jesus' heart to hear their song of joy.

"Blessed morning to you all," Jesus began as the group stood in obedience to his request. "Today is an important day, and my heart is grateful for the devotion you have given me in my ministry. But the time has come for me to select twelve disciples to be with me in every place and at all times. Although I will continue to speak and teach to the multitudes for a time, I will increasingly need to spend even more time alone with my disciples. So, let me call them by name now."

The group of people looked around at one another in anticipation, wondering if they would be chosen. Some were worried, not knowing if they could follow. Others hoped they wouldn't be chosen. Others still prayed they would be. But the choice belonged to Jesus alone.

Jesus began walking through the group that surrounded him, standing before each of his chosen ones.

"Simon," Jesus said as he placed his hand upon the fisherman's broad shoulder. "I have named you Peter to remind you of what you are to become."

Peter bowed his head in humility and nodded. He lifted his gaze to Jesus, not comprehending why Jesus would choose him. "I will remember, Master."

Jesus nodded to Peter and moved on. "James and John, the sons of Zebedee," he said as the two brothers fidgeted at the honor of being chosen. "You are my Sons of Thunder."

James and John looked at one another and smiled, knowing that Jesus had nicknamed them appropriately.

"Andrew, you appreciate the value of a single soul," Jesus smiled and said with his hand on Andrew's shoulder. "You pay attention to people and details, and were the first to introduce me to your brother Peter."

Jesus moved on to Philip. "Just as you, Philip, did with Nathaniel." He placed his hand on Nathaniel. "I hope you've seen that indeed, good things can come from Nazareth." Nathaniel was surprised and chagrined as Jesus revealed he knew what Nathaniel first thought when Philip told him Messiah was from Nazareth. "There indeed is no deceit in you." Nathaniel smiled and bowed his head in respect and humility.

Matthew's eyes welled up with tears as Jesus approached him and smiled. "Matthew, my prodigal friend." Matthew couldn't resist the urge and eagerly reached out to envelop Jesus in a tight bearhug. "Welcome home," Jesus whispered in his ear as Matthew wept softly. After a moment, Matthew released him and Jesus patted him on the back before moving on to the next man.

Jesus grinned as he stood before Thomas, who proceeded to look behind himself, then pointed to his chest with a questioning expression on his face, not believing that Jesus would choose him. "Yes, Thomas, you, too." The corners of Thomas's mouth curved up and Jesus chuckled warmly.

"Ah, little James," Jesus said as he placed his hands on both shoulders of the small man. "You will do things far greater than your frame, making your father Alphaeus proud."

"And tender-hearted, gentle Thaddaeus," Jesus affirmed the soft-spoken man next to James the Less. "The world needs more men like you."

Jesus raised his eyebrows as he next stood before Simon. "And you, Simon, our Zealot, your passion for God's rule is fierce. He can use you for great things, but you must gain control of your fire."

Simon nodded humbly. "I will, Master. I will."

Jesus finally went to stand before a man who just recently had begun to follow him. He was an outsider, the only one of the twelve not from Galilee, but from a humble town in the south of Judea, Kerioth, so he was referred to as "Iscariot." Jesus took a deep breath and gave the same warm smile he had given the others, placing his hand on the man's shoulder. "Judas, you will be used as an important instrument of God."

Judas locked eyes with Jesus. "Master, I am honored to be included as your disciple, and will do my part." He reached over and kissed Jesus on the cheek, a common custom in the day to show respect and peace. Jesus closed his eyes tightly at Judas's kiss. When his new disciple leaned back smiling, Jesus slowly opened his eyes. He gazed at Judas for a moment, nodded, and then stepped back.

Jesus lifted his arms as the twelve encircled him. "I have prayed for each of you by name. A new chapter for Israel—for the world— is dawning. By God's power alone, you twelve men will change the world," Jesus said, smiling. The sun started rising above the tree line and Jesus squinted as the rays warmed his face. "Let's get started, shall we?"

Jesus began walking down the mountain. The twelve new disciples erupted in cheers and hugged each other as an instant bond formed among them. Grasping each other's shoulders as they followed Jesus, this band of brothers walked into their destiny.

And the destiny of the world walked into them.

MOUNTAIN MANIFESTO
OF THE KING

As Jesus and his disciples descended the mountain, they could see the masses of people gathered at the bottom. Instead of going down all the way, Jesus found a level place on the hillside where he could begin instructing the disciples. He invited the men to sit while he also found a place to get comfortable. Gillamon and the animals stayed back from the group, but close enough to hear what was being said.

"What I'm going to share with you are things you need to learn for yourselves that you will then share with others," Jesus told them, motioning to the crowds at the base of the mountain. "I am going to set before you the laws of the kingdom of Heaven. As my disciples, you all are blessed subjects of the kingdom, and need to understand a new way, a better way to relate to yourself, to the law, to God, and to others."

The men nodded in agreement, eager to learn from their Master. Liz, Al, Max, Kate, Nigel, Gillamon, and Clarie were just as eager to hear what Jesus had to say.

"You're blessed when you're at the end of your rope. With less of you, there is more of God and his rule," Jesus began excitedly.

"You're blessed when you feel you've lost what is most dear to you. Only then can you be embraced by the One most dear to you.

"You're blessed when you're content with just who you are—no more, no less. That's the moment you find yourselves proud owners of everything that can't be bought.

"You're blessed when you've worked up a good appetite for God. He's food and drink in the best meal you'll ever eat.

"You're blessed when you care. At the moment of being 'care-full,' you find yourselves cared for.

"You're blessed when you get your inside world—your mind and heart—put right. Then you can see God in the outside world.

"You're blessed when you can show people how to cooperate instead of compete or fight. That's when you discover who you really are, and your place in God's family.

"You're blessed when your commitment to God provokes persecution. The persecution drives you even deeper into God's kingdom. Not only that—count yourselves blessed every time people put you down or throw you out or speak lies about you to discredit me. What it means is that the truth is too close for comfort and they are uncomfortable. You can be glad when that happens—give a cheer, even!—for though *they* don't like it, *I* do! And all heaven applauds. And know that you are in good company. My prophets and witnesses have always gotten into this kind of trouble."

"*C'est magnifique!*" Liz exclaimed in wonder. "Jesus is telling the disciples how blessed they will be if they simply live these things out."

"Aye, it's not like the Phar-r-risees' long list of wha' ta do or not do," Max added. "It's more like how they're supposed ta *be.*"

"Splendid! I say, this is how *everyone's* attitudes should be," Nigel remarked.

"So they're like 'be attitudes'?" Al asked.

Liz's eyes lit up with delight and she kissed Al on the cheek. "What a wonderful way to put it, *cher* Albert! The Latin word for 'blessings' is 'beatitudes,' so *oui*, they are attitudes followers of Jesus must have."

"Well, I know I'm best at bein' the fourth one Jesus said," Al noted confidently. "Havin' an appetite."

Clarie leaned in close to Al's face. "He meant for *God*, Al. Hungering and thirsting for *God.*"

Al gave a weak grin. "Oh . . . well, I can be that, too."

"Beatitudes," Gillamon said, nodding. "I like it. I like it a lot.

Perhaps one of the disciples will write these beatitudes down for everyone to someday learn."

"Brilliant idea, old boy!" Nigel enthused as he began looking over each of the twelve. "I wonder which of these fine fellows could do that."

"Better not be Thomas," Al said.

"Aye, then they'd be the 'bad-attitudes,'" Max chuckled with Al.

"Sure, he and Henriette would have been best friends!" Al joked.

Kate frowned at the two for teasing Thomas behind his back. "Thomas may have a negative attitude, but he's tryin' ta learn, so ye best stop teasin' him," she scolded. "An' after all these centuries ye jest can't stop jokin' aboot Henriette!"

Clarie rolled her eyes at the big orange cat and the Scottie dog. "And sweet Kate here has just demonstrated the fifth beatitude—*caring.*"

Kate smiled shyly. "Thank ye, Clarie."

Max and Al simmered down and looked at one another, holding in their laughter before it overtook them and they burst out laughing again.

Liz ignored the two, as she was trying to identify who the writer would be among the disciples. "Ah, Matthew's pen!" Liz exclaimed, drawing a smile and a slow nod from Gillamon. "He took his pen with him because he always had it with him to keep notes and reports, no?"

"Exactly, Liz," Gillamon affirmed. "And God will take the skill Matthew once used for bad purposes and use it for his good purposes."

"Jolly good show!" Nigel cheered, a fist in the air.

"Of course, why didn't *we* think of that?" Al cheered, a fish in the air. "Someone will need to record the events of Jesus' life and ministry!"

"*Oui,* Mary has been the only one to do so in her journal," Liz remembered fondly. "So, will Matthew be writing down everything Jesus says, Gillamon?"

"No one could write down everything, but Matthew will have help," Gillamon said. "There's one more of the twelve who will also write about Jesus so everyone will know history."

"This is terribly exciting to know there are two budding writers in the group," Nigel said, smoothing his whiskers in delight. "Who is he?"

"I think I'll let you figure it out as we go," Gillamon said with a wink. Then he pointed to Jesus and lifted a finger to his lips. "Shhh, there's more to hear. Listen."

"Let me tell you why you are here," Jesus said. "You're here to be salt-seasoning that brings out the God-flavors of this earth. If you lose your saltiness, how will people taste godliness? You've lost your usefulness and will end up in the garbage.

"Here's another way to put it: You're here to be light, bringing out the God-colors in the world. God is not a secret to be kept. We're going public with this, as public as a city on a hill. If I make you light-bearers, you don't think I'm going to hide you under a bucket, do you? I'm putting you on a light stand. Now that I've put you there on a hilltop, on a light stand—shine! Keep open house; be generous with your lives. By opening up to others, you'll prompt people to open up with God, this generous Father in heaven."

"Aye, he's right. Salt and light make everythin' better," Al remarked.

"Here's another old saying that deserves a second look: 'Eye for eye, tooth for tooth.' Is that going to get us anywhere? Here's what I propose: 'Don't hit back at all.' If someone strikes you, stand there and take it. If someone drags you into court and sues for the shirt off your back, giftwrap your best coat and make a present of it. And if someone takes unfair advantage of you, use the occasion to practice the servant life. No more tit-for-tat stuff. Live generously."

"Aye, this must be hard for the disciples ta hear," Max offered. "Especially the hotheaded laddies like Peter, the Sons of Thunder—James an' John—and Simon.

"And perhaps another hotheaded laddie we all know and love?" Clarie added, looking Max right in the eye.

Max frowned guiltily. "Shhhh, Jesus be talkin' still."

"You're familiar with the old written law, 'Love your friend,' and its unwritten companion, 'Hate your enemy.' I'm challenging that. I'm telling you to love your enemies," Jesus commanded. "Let them bring out the best in you, not the worst. When someone gives you a hard time, respond with the energies of prayer, for then you are working out of your true selves, your God-created selves. This is what God does. He gives his best—the sun to warm and the rain to nourish—to everyone, regardless: the good and bad, the nice and nasty. If all you do is love the lovable, do you expect a bonus? Anybody can do that. If you simply say hello to those who greet you, do you expect a medal? Any run-of-the-mill sinner does that. In a word, what I'm saying is, Grow up. You're kingdom subjects. Now live like it. Live out your God-created identity. Live generously and graciously toward others, the way God lives toward you."

Nigel shook his head in wonder. "I'm in awe of what Jesus is telling his disciples. It's a whole new way to live and relate to others."

"Oui, it's a manifesto," Liz agreed.

"Wha's a manifesto?" Kate asked.

"It is an Italian word, meaning 'public declaration of principles and intentions,'" Liz explained. "'Manifesto' comes from the Latin word *manifestum,* meaning 'clear.'"

"Jesus is certainly declaring principles quite clear for the Kingdom," Nigel added.

"Oui, it's a manifesto of the King," Liz said, deep in thought.

Jesus continued his lesson. "Don't pick on people, jump on their failures, criticize their faults—unless, of course, you want the same treatment. That critical spirit has a way of boomeranging. It's easy to see a smudge on your neighbor's face and be oblivious to the ugly sneer on your own. Do you have the nerve to say, 'Let me wash your face for you,' when your own face is distorted by contempt? It's this whole traveling-road-show mentality all over again, playing a holier-than-thou part instead of just living your part. Wipe that ugly sneer off your own face, and you might be fit to offer a washcloth to your neighbor."

301

Kate looked at Max and Al, raising her eyebrows as a reminder of what they were just talking about with Thomas. "Is that clear then?"

Max and Al looked at one another, and nodded at Kate, convicted by Jesus' words. "Aye."

"Don't bargain with God. Be direct. Ask for what you need," Jesus said. He saw Liz and Nigel sitting there, listening intently, and smiled. "This isn't a cat-and-mouse, hide-and-seek game we're in. If your child asks for bread, do you trick him with sawdust? If he asks for fish, do you scare him with a live snake on his plate? As bad as you are, you wouldn't think of such a thing. You're at least decent to your own children. So don't you think the God who conceived you in love will be even better?

"Here is a simple, rule-of-thumb guide for behavior: Ask yourself what you want people to do for you, then grab the initiative and do it for them. Add up God's Law and Prophets and this is what you get."

"Brilliant! And so simple!" Nigel exclaimed.

"So simple, it's golden," Al said.

"Be on your guard against false religious teachers, who come to you dressed up as sheep but are really greedy wolves. You can tell them by their fruit. Do you pick a bunch of grapes from a thorn-bush or figs from a clump of thistles? Every good tree produces good fruit, but a bad tree produces bad fruit. A good tree is incapable of producing bad fruit, and a bad tree cannot produce good fruit. The tree that fails to produce good fruit is cut down and burnt. So you may know men by their fruit."

"I know exactly who he's talkin' aboot now!" Max growled. "Them scr-r-ribes an' Phar-r-risees that have been after Jesus, like Zeeb, Jarib, Nahshon, an' Saar. They make the people think they're all r-r-righteous an' holy."

"Sure, and they be rotten to the core like yesterday's apple," Al said, adding his own food analogy.

"*Oui,* and Zeeb's name means 'wolf,'" Liz mentioned thoughtfully. "I wonder if Jesus was thinking of him as he said that."

"It is not everyone who keeps saying to me 'Lord, Lord' who will enter the kingdom of heaven, but the man who actually does my Heavenly Father's will. In 'that day' many will say to me, 'Lord, Lord, didn't we preach in your name, didn't we cast out devils in your name, and do many great things in your name?' Then I shall tell them plainly, 'I have never known you. Go away from me. You have worked on the side of evil!'"

Gillamon spoke up. "Well, the Pharisees and the Sadducees are the obvious ones, but remember, *anyone* can act like they are religious yet not really believe in their hearts."

"Or have other motives," Clarie said, eyeing Judas. She looked up at Gillamon sadly, then turned her gaze to the ground.

"Everyone then who hears these words of mine and puts them into practice is like a sensible man who builds his house on the rock. Down came the rain and up came the floods, while the winds blew and roared upon that house—and it did not fall because its foundations were on the rock.

"And everyone who hears these words of mine and does not follow them can be compared with a foolish man who built his house on sand. Down came the rain and up came the floods, while the winds blew and battered that house till it collapsed, and fell with a great crash."

Jesus leaned back to discuss all these things with his disciples. The disciples looked at one another, dumbfounded by the words of Jesus, for his words had the ring of authority, quite unlike those of the scribes. They hardly knew where to begin, but soon started eagerly asking Jesus endless questions so they would clearly understand. Their hearts and minds were on fire.

"Smart lad, that one who built his house on the r-r-rock," Max said with a definitive nod.

"Aye, who would build their house on the sand?" Kate asked, shaking her head. "Seems obvious ta me that's a foolish thing ta do."

"Jesus' point is well taken, and is something people can understand when thinking about how to build their lives," Gillamon added. "Either on God's solid truths or the world's shifting lies."

"Some people choose rocks, others choose sand," Nigel observed.

"So people choose their future before they even start buildin'," Al said, drawing looks of amazement from the others for his insight. "What?"

"Al, if the disciples are half as smart as you, they're going to succeed indeed," Gillamon said with a playful scratch on the orange kitty's head.

303

Al closed his eyes, grinning as he enjoyed the scratch and the compliment. "Well, whenever a king gives a manifesto, it best be clear, I always say."

36

THE ROMAN, THE TWELVE, AND THE KING

"How did it happen?" Armandus exclaimed in alarm. "How is he?"

"I don't know, he must have lost his footing," Bella explained sadly. "He was working on our new roof and fell. He landed on his back and is in terrible pain. I've tried to make him as comfortable as possible, but I don't know if he'll make it, Armandus."

Armandus's new wife was grief stricken over the accident. She wiped her beautiful, deep green eyes and held her hand to her mouth, shaking her head. She knew how much this slave meant to her husband. Caius was a special servant, having been with Armandus's family in Rome. Although he would never want his superiors to know it, Caius was more of a friend than a servant. When it became clear he would be in this Roman province for an indefinite period, Armandus sent for Bella to come be his wife, and requested that Caius escort her here. And, faithful to his master, Caius delivered Bella to Capernaum safe and sound.

Caius was now working on their new seaside home, another benefit of the wealth that Armandus carried from his family's status, along with the privilege to keep a home while in the service of Herod Antipas.

Caius slipped on some loose tiles and broke his back when he fell.

Armandus held his wife by the shoulders and the pain in his eyes revealed his heart for his servant, his friend. His voice cracked as he calmly said, "Take me to him."

Bella took Armandus's hand and led him to the room where the other servants had carried Caius. Armandus grimaced as he heard the weak moans of Caius crying out in agony. The Roman centurion rushed to his side and knelt by his bed.

"Caius, oh Caius, I'm so sorry!" Armandus said, not touching the man but looking him over to try to assess his pain.

Caius's eyes were full of pain and he couldn't keep the tears from falling. He was afraid he was going to die. "I'm . . . sorry . . . Master . . . I was . . . careless." Every physical effort caused him pain.

"Don't speak," Armandus said. "And I will not have you apologizing for what has happened. If anything, I am the one who is sorry."

Armandus looked up at Bella, feeling helpless. "Is there nothing we can do?"

Bella quietly shook her head, looking up at the ceiling as she wiped her eyes.

Grief and anger welled up in Armandus. He wasn't used to not being able to control a situation. He was responsible for a hundred men who depended on his wisdom to solve problems and overcome obstacles. Herod Antipas himself depended on Armandus to keep his district running smoothly. Armandus could figure out how to fix anything. But as he looked at his suffering friend, he was at a loss. Then suddenly a thought came to him. *The Miracle Worker.*

Armandus quickly looked up at Bella. "Tatius! Remember me telling you about Tatius and how a man by the name of Jesus of Nazareth healed his son?" Armandus leaned over and whispered in Caius's ear, "Hang on, my friend. I'm going for help."

Armandus stood and hurried out of the room, Bella following him down the hall. He continued to remind her of the story. "Tatius's son was very ill here in Capernaum, and his wife sent word to where he was in Cana. Tatius went to Jesus, who was also in Cana. The man just spoke and the boy was healed. When the servants told him the next day his son had been healed, he discovered that the boy got well at the exact hour Jesus gave the word."

305

"Do you think this Jesus will heal Caius?" Bella asked hopefully. "Where is he now?"

Armandus hurried outside where Achilles was tied. "He's been in and out of Capernaum, from what the Jewish community officials have told me." He pulled himself up onto Achilles and got ready to ride off. "I'm going to find him. Keep Caius comfortable. I'll be back."

With that Armandus took off down the road on Achilles, asking his beloved horse to run like the wind.

Jesus was sitting in the shade of some fig trees with his disciples in Peter's courtyard, as it was a hot day. Word was out that Jesus had returned once again to Capernaum. Several of the townspeople were also gathered around Jesus, eager to hear the latest news about his healings and teachings.

The sound of an approaching horse caused Max to stand up and look down the road to inspect things. "Looks like a R-r-roman then, an' he's in a hurry."

Liz sat up and joined Max and Nigel, also wanting to see. "That's not just any Roman. It's Armandus!"

"Right you are, and he is headed straight for Jesus," Nigel confirmed. "Do you realize these two haven't seen each other in person since they were boys in Jerusalem? What could possibly be bringing him to Jesus now?"

A cloud of dust kicked up behind Achilles as Armandus brought him to a sudden halt. He immediately jumped off the horse and strode over to Jesus.

Jesus looked up but remained seated while Peter, Matthew, and Simon stood in alarm at the approach of this Roman. Matthew wondered if the soldier was coming for him for having abandoned his post. But Armandus looked around at the men until his eyes settled on Jesus.

"Armandus, Sir, is there something you need of us?" a Jewish community leader said as he and a colleague also rose. They were on good terms with Armandus and thought highly of him after he showed such kindness in the manner he treated the Jews, especially building them a synagogue.

Armandus was out of breath, but raised his hand and shook his head 'no' to the Jewish leader. He walked up to Jesus and finally could see what he looked like up close, only having seen him from afar on several occasions. "Jesus of Nazareth?"

"Yes?" Jesus answered calmly. "How can I help you?"

"Please, Lord, my young servant lies in bed, paralyzed and in terrible pain."

Jesus put his hand on the ground to raise himself up without a moment's hesitation. "I will come and heal him."

Armandus walked two steps forward and put his hand up to Jesus to stop him. "Lord, I am not worthy to have you come into my home. Just say the word from where you are, and my servant will be healed. I know this because I am under the authority of my superior officers, and I have authority over my soldiers. I only need to say, 'Go,' and they go, or 'Come,' and they come. And if I say to my slaves, 'Do this,' they do it."

Jesus raised his eyebrows in utter amazement as he listened to Armandus. He turned to his twelve disciples and pointed at Armandus. "Believe me, I have never found faith like this, even in Israel! I tell you that many people will come from east and west and sit at my table with Abraham, Isaac and Jacob in the kingdom of Heaven. But those who should have belonged to the kingdom will be banished to the darkness outside, where there will be tears and bitter regret."

The disciples marveled at what Jesus was telling them, and looked to gauge the reaction of the Jewish community leaders. They were shocked at Jesus' words. As much as they loved Armandus, and knew that Armandus loved them as a people, the thought of a Gentile being invited to the great feast in heaven was unthinkable. But they were equally shocked to hear a Roman master so worried about a slave. The Romans viewed slaves as Aristotle had classified them: 'For master and slave have nothing in common; a slave is a living tool, just as a tool is an inanimate slave.' Armandus indeed was unusual.

Jesus placed his hand on Armandus's shoulder and gazed deeply into his eyes. "Go back home. Because you believed, it has happened."

Armandus was immediately caught off guard by a vague sense of familiarity with Jesus. Those eyes. He felt he had seen them before, but he knew he had only watched Jesus from a distance. Still, he wrinkled his brow as the thought haunted him. But the mystery was quickly replaced by the realization of what Jesus had told him. His servant was healed! Armandus's eyes filled with relief and a grateful smile appeared on his face as their gazes lingered a moment longer. Jesus smiled in return.

"Thank you, Lord," Armandus said as he humbly bowed in respect and awe. He looked at the others and nodded as he backed up toward Achilles. "Thank you!" He suddenly pulled himself up onto Achilles and squeezed his heels into the horse's sides, taking off in a flash.

Liz's eyes were brimming with tears and Nigel placed his paw on her shoulder. "What a wonderful reunion, I must say."

Liz smiled and nodded. "Armandus understands the Jewish law, that a Jew is defiled if they enter a Gentile's home. But I was there when they met as toddlers, in his parents' home in Jerusalem. Little does he know that Jesus has been in his home."

"Ah yes, when Mary and Joseph did the unthinkable, and entered the Gentile home of Marcus and Julia Antonius," Nigel remembered.

"I'll never forget the day Armandus made Jesus laugh so hard his little cheeks turned red." Liz watched the now grown Armandus race off to find his servant healed as Jesus had told him. She sighed and a lump grew in her throat as she recalled that day. "As Armandus skipped away from the laughing baby Jesus, he told his mother, 'I like his eyes.'"

37

QUESTIONS AND ANSWER

The grief was more than she could bear. Her son—her only son—was dead. She had lost her husband several years ago, but her son had provided for her since then. He was such a fine young man, and he loved his mother. But sickness came, and though he fought to get well, in the end he lost his battle and died. The woman sat in her humble home and gazed at the lifeless form of her boy. Her chin quivered and tears fell down her face. She was alone now. She was alone in her grief, and would soon be destitute with no one to take care of her. *What is to become of me?* she wondered.

A quiet knock came at her door. The men were there to carry her son's body away to be buried. Her head dropped to her chest as she sobbed in helpless grief. "Oh, my son! My son, my son, my son," she whispered softly. "I wish the sickness had taken me instead of you. You deserved life."

The door opened, and the Rabbi of Nain quietly walked up to the woman. "We are ready."

The woman wiped her eyes and nodded, standing as the men brought in the bier to carry the body. She stood with hands folded as the men gently lifted her son with sheets, placed him on the wooden platform, and covered him with a shroud. She closed her eyes tightly and let out a groan of sadness as his face disappeared from view. The men picked up the bier and took him outside.

The rabbi led the woman by the elbow, following the men out the door of her home and into the street, where a procession of people waited. A large crowd from the town was there to escort her outside the city walls to bury her son.

Jesus and the disciples met the procession in the street. Jesus' gaze landed on the boy's mother and his heart broke at seeing her unfathomable grief. He walked in front of her and stopped the procession. He gazed deeply into her eyes and softly told her, "Don't cry."

She looked up at Jesus, not understanding why he would say such a thing. She watched this strange man as he went up and touched the bier that carried her son. The men holding the bier stood still, looking at one another in confusion.

Jesus looked at the lifeless body. He wrinkled his brow and with a strong voice commanded, "Young man, I say to you, get up!"

The mother's hand went to her face as suddenly her son sat up.

"Mother?" the young man said. "I'm . . . I'm here."

Jesus smiled, pulled the shroud off the man, and helped him to the ground. He led the man over to the woman and gave him back to her. The woman embraced her son immediately, weeping with joy.

The people were all filled with awe and praised God. "A great prophet has appeared among us!" they cried out. "God has come to help his people." The people watched as Jesus and his disciples continued on down the road, in shock at what they had witnessed. The muttering about Jesus and this miracle started with these people, but would soon spread throughout Judea and the surrounding countryside.

The disciples followed along behind Jesus in amazement, filled with a newfound sense of awe and reverent fear. Healing miracles were one thing, but bringing a dead man back to life? That was an entirely new realm.

Jesus walked up beside Gillamon. The animals also marveled at what they had just witnessed. Jesus looked over at them and with great seriousness said, "I hate death."

A slow drip, drip, drip of water echoed in the cave. John lay there listening to it. Sometimes he counted the drips until his mind drifted to something else. He was isolated, cut off from all life. Although at times irritating, the dripping water coming off the wall was at least a constant companion. Suddenly a piece of bread landed on the rock next to him. Then a few dates, followed by several olives that rolled across the stone floor. John looked up to the tiny barred window high above him. He shifted to have a better view and the chains around his ankles dragged along the cold stone.

"John? We have come to bring you news," the man whispered through the outside bars of the prison window. The sound of the man's voice drifted down the twenty feet into the dank dungeon below. "Are you there?"

John looked up, unable to see the source of the voice. "I'm here," John replied, closing his eyes gratefully and taking a bite of the bread. "Tell me."

Several disciples of John the Baptist gathered around the prison window, straining to get a glimpse of the prophet they had faithfully followed for months. His words burned in their hearts and they found new freedom in his teaching. John baptized them and they vowed to stick by him, come what may. Even after he was imprisoned here in this horrific dungeon by Herod Antipas, they sought to care for him as best they could, sneaking up to the fortress to bring him food and information. He always only wanted to know about Jesus.

"He continues to draw crowds with his healing miracles, but he has encountered intense hostility from the Sanhedrin," one disciple said.

"And he was even driven out of his own hometown of Nazareth for his bold teaching," another disciple added. "They tried to kill him for claiming to be the Son of God, but he somehow escaped."

"The Pharisees and Sadducees are so up in arms about him for healing on the Sabbath and what they call blasphemy that sources tell us they seek to silence him," another man said. "They have grounds for putting him to death for blasphemy, John."

John frowned and leaned his head on the slimy wall, filled with concern. "I preached he would come and establish his Kingdom with power, yet he was thrown out of his own synagogue? And they seek to kill him?" He crossed his arms and thought this news through. *This isn't unfolding as I expected it to. I'm in prison, people cheer Jesus' healing powers, but his own people and the Sanhedrin want him dead. Did I*

311

misunderstand Messiah's agenda? I know Jesus is Messiah, but have I gone wrong somewhere in understanding the prophecies?

A rat ran by, trying to nab some of the food the men had thrown down to John. He picked up a rock and threw it at the rodent.

"John?"

"I need you to do something for me," John replied. "Go find Jesus. Ask him, 'Are you the one who was to come or are we to look for somebody else?' Then come back and tell me what he says."

At that moment John's disciples heard the approach of horses and fear fell upon them as a trio of Roman soldiers rode up to Herod's fortress.

"We will. We must go," one of the men said quickly as the group hurried away from the window, hoping they weren't seen by the soldiers.

Armandus was the first to spot them, bringing Achilles to a halt in their path. "You there! What are you doing?"

The men looked at one another in fear. "We just wish to bring word to John the Baptist."

"Word of what?" another Roman soldier snapped.

"Of Jesus of Nazareth," one of the men answered immediately.

Armandus immediately felt a jolt of anxiety run through him.

"So, the *prisoner* prophet wants to hear how the *new, popular* prophet who stole his audience is doing?" laughed one of the soldiers, jumping off his horse, drawing his sword to intimidate the man. "And what did you tell John the Baptizer?"

The man swallowed hard as sweat broke out on his brow. "We . . . we told him about the miracles Jesus has been doing."

"Oh, *miracles,*" laughed the soldier, named Ulixes. "You should see the 'miracles' done in Rome. Why, our people wanted and demanded such wonders that architects made our temples do the impossible."

"Yes, engineered holy water to magically run, doors to open, and even engraved images to dance and spin," the other soldier, named Velius, boasted.

"We heard about Jesus and his water-to-wine miracle," Ulixes chided with a sarcastic grin. "Our temples were rigged to do the same with cleverly designed pitchers and hidden chambers with tubes to create the illusion of water turning into wine," he laughed.

"But our temples did even more," Velius added. "Snake images would hiss from secret steam tubes. Worshippers could hear a mighty storm of rain, wind, and thunder with even flashes of lightning. It's all explainable magic. Only fools believe it."

"So don't tell me some *miracle worker* can do things greater than Rome," Ulixes scowled as he got right in the face of the frightened disciple.

"That's enough," Armandus called out to his men. "These men are harmless. Let them go."

Ulixes smiled at the man, and for a brief moment the man saw a flash of red in the soldier's eyes.

"I SAID, 'ENOUGH!'" Armandus shouted, pulling Achilles up next to the soldier.

Ulixes immediately backed off and he and Velius got up on their horses. Armandus motioned for John's disciples to be gone as he led his men to the fortress. He didn't want his men to know his heart was racing, wanting to fight them for daring to say anything against Jesus of Nazareth. His servant Caius was healed the same hour Jesus told Armandus he would be well. No great magic of Rome could do that. But Armandus kept his experience with the miracle worker to himself. He wrestled with his thoughts. *How can I continue to keep quiet about Jesus, after what he did for me?*

313

John's disciples wasted no time finding Jesus. They didn't know how long John had before Herod Antipas would take measures to silence him for good. Jesus was teaching to a great crowd of people when they came running up to him. "John the Baptist has sent us to you, saying, 'Are you the one who was to come or are we to look for somebody else?'"

Jesus nodded but didn't reply. Instead, he went over to the middle of the crowd where sat a blind man. Jesus touched him and immediately the man could see. He went to another, a little girl who couldn't hear, gently placing his hands over her ears. Suddenly she smiled, hearing Jesus' voice telling her she was precious in his sight.

John's disciples looked at each other and then back to Jesus as he continued walking through the crowd, healing the lame, who instantly stood to walk, then proceeded to dance around with joy. A leper stood off in the distance. Jesus looked at John's disciples and pointed to the man. Jesus then walked straight toward him, even as the man called out, 'Unclean!' Jesus placed his hands on the man and instantly his skin was clean and healed.

"JESUS OF NAZARETH!" came an evil voice screeching in the crowd.

Everyone looked over to see a well-known woman who frequently ran through the streets, spilling over bowls in the marketplace and screaming. Her clothes were torn and her face filled with terror. Her unkempt black hair trailed down her back and her eyes quickly shifted back and forth. She started running right at Jesus.

Jesus stood in the road and held up his hand. "WHAT DO YOU WANT WITH US?!" the possessed woman screamed as she reached him and fell to the ground.

"LEAVE HER!" Jesus said in a deep, commanding voice.

As the woman lay there writhing on the ground, only Jesus, Gillamon, and Clarie could see the demons who came out of her. Jesus' gaze alone sent them fleeing down the road and into the desert. Jesus knelt down and called some of his disciples over to help her. Thaddeus and Nathaniel immediately came and helped lift her to her feet. She kept her gaze on Jesus and began to weep softly, but slowly smiled. Her eyes no longer were filled with rage and chaos. They were serene.

Jesus smiled at her. "Mary, you are free."

"Master," Mary replied softly. "Thank you."

"That's Mary from Magdala," one of the men in the crowd whispered to his friends. "She's been kicked out of every town from here to Tyre."

"But Jesus has healed her!" a woman exclaimed. "She doesn't have to run anymore."

"Every time I think I've seen it all, I find out I haven't," Nigel said in awe of what Jesus was doing. "First raising the dead lad from Nain, now all these healings, and releasing a woman from demons."

"There were seven of them," Gillamon shared. "Seven demons tormented that poor woman."

"Seven!" Kate exclaimed. "No wonder the poor lass were so crazed! Oh, Jesus has freed her now!"

"Look at all the things Jesus heals," Liz added in amazement.

314

"*Oooh-la-la*, but there is so much that needs healing in this world!"

"In the beginning the world wasn't like this," Clarie said sadly. "It wasn't broken. Man was never meant to live with all these diseases and tormenting demons. The Fall in the Garden changed everything."

"Aye, but look how gr-r-rand Jesus is ta set things r-r-right!" Max added. "He's healed thousands of humans by now."

"I say, miracles don't usually happen every day," Nigel agreed.

"Sure, otherwise they'd be called 'regulars,'" Al said simply.

Nigel chuckled and put a paw on Al's back. "Al, old boy, with Jesus they are turning into 'regulars.'"

Jesus finally walked over to where John's disciples stood. "Go and tell John what you see and hear—that blind men are recovering their sight, cripples are walking, lepers being healed, the deaf hearing, the dead being brought to life and the good news is being given to those in need. And happy is the man who never loses faith in me."

The men were speechless, but nodded as they went on their way to report to John.

315

"Jesus has sent John a message that he will clearly understand, no?" Liz said, overjoyed by how Jesus replied to John's question. "He's told him he is doing what only Messiah could do, as foretold by Isaiah: 'Then will the eyes of the blind be opened and the ears of the deaf unstopped. Then will the lame leap like a deer, and the mute tongue shout for joy.'"

Jesus began talking to the crowd about John: "What did you go out into the wilderness to see? A reed swayed by the wind? If not, what did you go out to see? A man dressed in fine clothes? No, those who wear expensive clothes and indulge in luxury are in palaces. But what did you go out to see? A prophet? Yes, I tell you, and more than a prophet. This is the one about whom it is written: 'I will send my messenger ahead of you, who will prepare your way before you.'

"I tell you, among those born of women there is no one greater than John; yet the one who is least in the kingdom of God is greater than he."

All the people, even the tax collectors, when they heard Jesus' words, acknowledged that God's way was right, because they had been baptized by John. But the Pharisees and the experts in the Law rejected God's purpose for themselves, because they had not been baptized by John.

Jesus looked at the crowd, knowing they were caught up in the miracles he performed, yet the religious elite still had unbelieving hearts in the message of repentance preached by both him and John. "How can I show what the people of this generation are like? They are like children sitting in the marketplace calling out to their friends, 'We played at weddings for you but you wouldn't dance, and we played at funerals and you wouldn't cry!' For John the Baptist came neither eating bread nor drinking wine, and you say, 'He has a demon.' The Son of Man came eating and drinking, and you say, 'Here is a glutton and a drunkard, a friend of tax collectors and sinners.' But wisdom is proved right by all her children."

"I wish John were here to see how Jesus is praising him in front of the people," Clarie lamented. "John must wonder if he failed in his mission. But he did exactly as Scripture foretold he would do."

Jesus continued, "From the days of John the Baptist until now the kingdom of Heaven has been taken by storm and eager men are forcing their way into it. For the Law and all the Prophets foretold it till the time of John and—if you can believe it—John himself is the 'Elijah' who must come before the kingdom. The man who has ears to hear must use them."

Jesus stopped speaking and looked at the crowd. He thought about all the people John had touched in his six months of ministry, and then all those he himself had seen as he went from town to town, teaching and healing in the name of God. Many of the towns where he had performed most of his miracles still rallied with great crowds seeking healing, but by and large, the people still did not repent and change their evil ways. Jesus grew angry at the thought of the cities where he had worked the hardest but whose people had responded the least, shrugging their shoulders and going their own way.

"Doom to you, Chorazin! Doom, Bethsaida! If Tyre and Sidon had seen half of the powerful miracles you have seen, they would have been on their knees in a minute. At Judgment Day they'll get off easy compared to you. And Capernaum! With all your peacock strutting, you are going to end up in the abyss. If the people of Sodom had had your chances, the city would still be around. At Judgment Day they'll get off easy compared to you."

Abruptly Jesus broke into prayer: "O Father, Lord of Heaven and earth, I thank you for hiding these things from the clever and intelligent and for showing them to mere children. Yes, I thank you, Father, that this was your will."

Jesus took a deep breath and looked over the crowd. He saw those who truly were grasping his teachings and were hungry for the truth. They weren't the elite or the learned. They were the ones who had been forgiven the most, and who had lost the most in this life. The words of Jesus now sprung into their lives as streams in the desert. Jesus smiled as he looked at the little girl, once deaf, who could now hear. Then at Mary Magdalene, once demon-possessed, now in her right mind. His voice turned tender. "Everything has been put in my hands by my Father, and nobody knows the Son except the Father. Nor does anyone know the Father except the Son—and the man to whom the Son chooses to reveal him."

Jesus stopped. He was emotionally and physically spent from the long day of teaching and healing. And his heart grieved for John. But he had one final word to give the people before he left them for the day: "Come to me, all you who are weary and burdened, and I will give you rest. Take my yoke upon you and learn from me, for I am gentle and humble in heart, and you will find rest for your souls. For my yoke is easy and my burden is light."

317

"'Come to me,'" Liz said thoughtfully. "That's what the Maker told us when he called us to the Ark."

"Aye, 'Come ta me,'" Max agreed. "Except this time Jesus be the Ark for safety an' r-r-rest."

"I say, Jesus has given such a brilliant picture of what life is like with him," Nigel shared. "Walk with him and work with him, and he won't lay anything heavy or ill-fitting on you. With him you'll learn to live freely and lightly. Utterly splendid."

As Jesus and the disciples dismissed the crowds, Mary Magdalene followed along but kept her distance. Gillamon stopped next to her. "Can I help you, Mary?"

She raised her eyes, marveling at the new experience of someone speaking civilly to her, and calling her by name. "Jesus said he is the One. And now he said to come to him and I'll find rest," she said, eyeing Jesus as he walked off up the hillside. "I'm so very weary and I have nowhere to go. So how can I learn from him unless I remain with him?"

Gillamon nodded and smiled with a twinkle in his eye. "I'm

Gillamon. Come, you can help me minister to Jesus and his disciples. I'm sure they're tired of my cooking by now."

Mary clasped her hands and held them up to her mouth, tears quickening in her eyes. "Thank you, Gillamon," she replied, now walking along with him and eyeing Jesus in the distance. "And who are all your little friends here?" She reached out to pet Liz, who sat in Clarie's saddlebag.

"Oh, you'll get to know them soon enough," Gillamon said, winking at the animals. Then he thought to himself, *We're seven new friends to give you joy, replacing the seven demons that caused you pain.*

Mary leaned over and saw Al's robust frame. "This one looks like he'll be my hardiest eater."

"Aye, how's yer fish?" Al meowed happily, making her laugh for the first time in years.

MUCH FORGIVENESS, MUCH LOVE

A re you sure you want this much?" the street vendor asked, looking the woman up and down with a wicked grin. "This is about a year's wages, you know. Or maybe for you, less time than that, eh?"

The woman pulled her crimson tunic tightly around her shoulder, wishing she was like the respectable girls who owned head coverings. "Please give me the amount I requested. Here is the money."

The vendor held out his hand as the woman placed a bag of coins there. He grabbed her by the wrist. "We could always work out a deal if you'd rather hang on to some of this money," he said, looking both ways. His breath smelled as bad as his intentions.

Anger flared in her and she pulled her wrist out of his grasp. "Just count the money and give me the jar."

The man frowned and gave a sarcastic laugh. He opened her bag of coins and once he had counted it out, handed over her purchase. "One alabaster jar, full of sweet perfume."

The woman eagerly took the jar and ran away from the sleazy vendor who called after her, "I'm sure you'll smell real nice for your customer tonight!"

No longer, she thought as she fought back the tears. She made her way down the crowded market street and through the bad section of town over to where the more well-to-do people lived. It wasn't that she wasn't familiar with this side of town. Oh, she had been here. Frequently. But all these residents would deny it. They wanted her services, but they didn't want *her*.

No longer will I put myself in that situation. I'm going home, if they'll have me. I've been gone so long. But I have to try. I have to get out of here. She continued to think through her new future as she searched out her immediate destination. *He showed me a new way to live, so I have to change, no matter what it costs me.*

She could hear the sounds of merriment coming from one of the larger homes and noticed a crowd of people outside. She took a deep breath, looked down at her jar, and boldly walked up to some of the men standing there. "Is this the home of Simon the Pharisee?" she asked.

The men looked at her and then each other, breaking out into slow smiles. "Why, yes it is, but this isn't a good time for you to be here. You should come back later."

Her eyes flashed at what they were insinuating. She pushed past them to enter the house. A large group of people packed the house, lining the walls of the large room where a banquet was being served. Whenever dignitaries were highlighted at events such as this, spectators were allowed to attend, but not participate in the meal or the discussion. Their silent presence was welcome, for it only made the host look more important.

Mary Magdalene was the first one to notice the woman enter the room and stand on tiptoe to look around at the guests. The woman's eyes landed on Jesus and she rushed over to sit directly behind him. Mary and the disciples were sitting with the spectators, as Jesus was the only one whom Simon had officially invited to partake of the meal. She leaned over to Peter and Matthew and whispered, "The town harlot."

Peter and Matthew looked at the woman. Jesus didn't even acknowledge her presence. He was reclining around the table like the rest of the guests, leaning on one elbow with his feet behind him. Peter looked at the host, who immediately froze mid-bite when he saw the woman behind Jesus. A judgmental scowl grew on the Pharisee's face. "This should be interesting," Peter whispered back to Mary and Matthew.

The woman held her alabaster jar and sat there behind Jesus, weeping, her head bent down in shame. Her tears began to fall softly on

320

Jesus' feet. She noticed that his feet had not been washed, which was always an essential formality for guests coming to a home like this. Simon either didn't care about offending his dinner guest, or it was a gross oversight on his part. Either way, it was considered an insult. *I'll clean them,* she thought to herself. But she realized she didn't have a cloth to clean them with.

Slowly she let down her hair, much to the disapproval of the guests who were already murmuring about her. For a woman to let down her hair in public was shameful, and for married women, even grounds for divorce. *Let them think what they will,* she thought. *I don't care.* The only thing that concerned her was caring for this man whose words had changed her life. She had stood in the back of the crowd and listened to him teach about repentance, grace, and salvation. Her heart was changed forevermore. She had to do something. She just had to let him know what he had done for her. Slowly she used her hair to wipe Jesus' feet as her tears were now so profuse they blinded her.

"Jesus isn't even acknowledging her presence," Matthew said.

"But look at Simon and his friends. They can't keep their eyes off her," Mary added.

Peter wrinkled his brow, not understanding what Jesus was doing by saying nothing to this woman of the night. He knew Jesus didn't care about what people thought. "Religious circles like this one revolve around the fear of what men think," Peter shared. "Simon is certainly worried about what his friends will think of this woman being in his home."

"Yes, but Jesus is free from that kind of mindset," Matthew replied quietly. "And I have my doubts about Simon's intentions for bringing Jesus here tonight. Just like the other Pharisees from Jerusalem, I think he was hoping something like this would happen to catch Jesus in yet another act of breaking their laws."

"For Jesus to even allow this woman to touch him makes him unclean in their eyes," Peter said, shaking his head.

After the woman had dried Jesus' feet, she tenderly kissed them. Then she took her alabaster jar and anointed Jesus' feet with the sweet perfume. Jesus still did not turn around to her, but kept his gaze on Simon. The oil lamps burned, illuminating the questioning faces of everyone around the table. The guests, including Jesus, continued to eat, but all conversation had ceased.

Simon snorted and thought to himself, *If this man were a prophet, he would know what kind of woman is touching him. She's a sinner!*

Jesus took a sip of wine to swallow his food and set his goblet down. He had read Simon's thoughts. "Simon, I have something to say to you."

"Go ahead, Teacher," Simon replied, looking around at his guests to gauge their reaction.

"Here it comes," Matthew whispered to Peter and Mary, who nodded in agreement.

"A man loaned money to two people—five hundred pieces of silver to one and fifty pieces to the other. But neither of them could repay him, so he kindly forgave them both, canceling their debts. Who do you suppose loved him more after that?" Jesus asked.

Simon scratched his chin. "I suppose the one for whom he canceled the larger debt."

"That's right," Jesus said. He finally turned to the woman and said to Simon, "Look at this woman kneeling here. When I entered your home, you didn't offer me water to wash the dust from my feet, but she has washed them with her tears and wiped them with her hair. You didn't greet me with a kiss, but from the time I first came in, she has not stopped kissing my feet. You neglected the courtesy of olive oil to anoint my head, but she has anointed my feet with rare perfume."

Simon squirmed as he was embarrassed by his glaringly obvious failure in being a good host to such a renowned man.

Jesus looked at her as she continued to lovingly rub his feet with the perfume. "I tell you, her sins have been forgiven, so she has shown me much love." He looked up at Simon. "But a person who is forgiven little shows only little love."

Then Jesus turned back to the woman and smiled tenderly. She looked up at him with sincere, deep repentance and longing for grace. "Your sins—and I know that they are many— are forgiven."

The woman inhaled quickly and shut her eyes tightly. She welled up all over again, but this time with a rush of relief. As the people stared at her with scorn, Jesus covered her with a cloak of grace and kindness. Her hand went to her mouth as she wept with joy.

The men at the table murmured among themselves, "Who is this man, that he goes around forgiving sins?"

Mary Magdalene leaned over to Peter and Matthew and whispered.

"Simon knows nothing of the love and forgiveness Jesus brings, because he doesn't realize he even needs it." The two men shared a knowing look. It was like the feast at Matthew's house. Jesus would once more be accused, this time of welcoming a sinner and forgiving sins.

Jesus lifted the woman's chin and peered deeply into her soul. "Your faith has saved you; go in peace."

The woman smiled and nodded quickly, wiping her tears with her hands. She then carefully picked up her alabaster jar and stood, looking down at Jesus a moment longer. Jesus nodded and she smiled. She turned and made her way to the door.

Gillamon and the animals were outside and suddenly saw a young woman run out of the house of Simon the Pharisee. She was giddy and laughing through tears. As she ran past them, they heard her saying, "Thank you, thank you, thank you!" They watched as she disappeared down the street and into the night.

Mary Magdalene came outside and smiled as she watched the forgiven woman running toward her new life. "I guess she won't be joining us," she said as she walked up to Gillamon and the women gathered there. Joanna, the wife of Chuza (Herod's household manager), and Susanna had joined Mary to help support Jesus and his disciples. They gave their money, which was common for followers of rabbis to do. They also served the men by helping with food and any needs they had with clothing.

Liz, Kate, and Clarie, of course, were thrilled to have some female companionship. Once again, Jesus elevated the status of these women by giving them importance. It was unheard of for a rabbi to have women followers, but true to himself, Jesus didn't care about the norm. He cared about the people. Kate wagged her tail and looked at Liz and Clarie, cheering, "Lassie power!"

"What happened in there?" Joanna asked. "The girl looked quite happy."

Mary folded her arms over her shoulders and smiled, knowing another life was forever changed by her Lord. "Much forgiveness and much love."

STORMS WITHOUT AND STORMS WITHIN

Jesus sat on the beach, tired after a long day of teaching. His disciples were dismissing the crowds who had flocked to hear him preach again in Capernaum. His days were always full and he gave of himself so completely he was simply exhausted. He yawned as Max dropped a stick at his feet.

"You have more energy than me at the moment, Max," Jesus said.

Max was panting with his tongue hanging out, waiting for another throw. "Please? I love it when ye thr-r-r-ow the stick then."

Jesus chuckled warmly. "Okay, one more time." He picked up the stick and threw it way down the sandy shore. Jesus smiled as Max took off running down the beach, kicking up sand behind him. He overshot the target and had to circle back, growling as he picked up the stick. Max came running back and dropped the stick again for Jesus, giving him another *Please?* look.

Peter walked up to Jesus. "This dog loves to play with you. I know he belongs to Gillamon, but sometimes I think he belongs to you more than his master."

Max and Jesus looked up at Peter and then at one another, enjoying the silent joke between them. Max had belonged to Jesus for longer than Peter could even comprehend. Jesus picked up the stick, stood, and stretched his back.

"I'm tired and would like to get away from the crowds for a while. Let's go for a sail," Jesus said, pointing to the other side of the lake. "Over there, to the other side."

Peter looked to where Jesus pointed and surveyed the skies, nodding. "Looks like a nice evening for a sail. I'll ready the boats, Master." Peter called the other disciples, who made ready two of the boats to take out to sea.

Jesus stood there tapping Max's stick in his hand as he stared at the other coastline of the Sea of Galilee. It was the region known as the country of the Gerasenes, and was also Gentile territory. Max panted and kept his eye on the stick, waiting. Finally, he gave a low whine to remind Jesus he was still there. Jesus looked down, "Oh, Max, sorry. One more time, and then you need to come get into the boat."

"Aye!" Max exclaimed happily.

Jesus threw the stick and then muttered to himself. "You're not going to want to miss this, laddie."

Al and Nigel were already in one of the boats, where they had enjoyed a nice afternoon nap curled up in the bow. Gillamon and the other animals were back at Peter's house, having stayed with the women, who were mending clothes and cooking for the group.

Max came running back with the stick and Jesus squatted down to greet him. "Looks like maybe you're ready for a rest."

"Aye, that I be then," Max agreed, panting heavily. Jesus mussed his head and lifted him into Peter's boat.

"Shove off," Peter instructed James, who manned the other boat. The twelve disciples were evenly divided between the two boats, and each did his part to get out to sea.

Al popped his head up out of James's boat and noticed they were leaving the shore. *"Are we goin' fishin' then?"* he meowed excitedly.

John leaned over and scratched Al behind the ears. "We're just going for a sail," John said, knowing that this orange cat always begged for fish. He reached in his knapsack and took out some dried fish, handing Al a piece. "Here, this will keep you happy for now."

"Aye! Thanks, lad!" Al meowed eagerly, gobbling up a piece of fish. He saw Max over in the other boat and waved at him.

Nigel climbed up behind some of the rigging, but stayed out of sight of the men. "What a splendid evening for a sail, I must say."

Soon the light breeze filled their sails and the boats were gliding along peacefully, slicing through the tranquil water that glistened with the late afternoon sun.

Jesus closed his eyes and allowed the sun to warm his face. He breathed in deeply, yawned again, and shook his head, now realizing fully how incredibly tired he was. He was sitting in the back of the boat, and noticed there were a couple of old pillows there. He patted them and said, "Come on, boy." Max came over and nestled down next to Jesus as the tired Teacher scrunched down to lay his head back on the pillow. Jesus took a deep breath and let go a sigh of relief. "Ah, this feels nice." He closed his eyes and he and Max drifted off to sleep.

BOOM! The clap of thunder was so loud it made Max jump awake. He instantly sat up and was hit in the face with blinding sea spray. Terror filled Max immediately as he heard the howling of the wind that came from every direction to hit the water at an angle. Suddenly lightning cracked and lit up the now darkened sky. The men were screaming and trying to get hold of the sails flapping wildly from the mast, threatening to tear loose from their fittings. Chaos abounded as the boat leaned to the left and a wave crashed over the side. Water pooled in the boat and quickly covered Max's paws. Max's heart started pounding with fear as he looked over to see the other boat also struggling to stay afloat. Even in the midst of the roar of the storm, he could still make out the sound of Al wailing.

"WE'RE ALL GOIN' TO DIE!" Al screamed. "HELLLLP! HELLLLP! HELLLLP!" He grabbed Nigel and clung to the little mouse for dear life. "WE'RE ALL GOIN' TO DIE!"

Nigel was soaked to the bone, as they all were. His spectacles were covered in sea spray but he lifted his gaze to his soggy cat friend and tried to yell above the noise. "WE ARE MOST CERTAINLY *NOT* GOING TO DIE! WE *CAN'T* DIE! PULL YOURSELF TOGETHER, OLD BOY!"

Al was too engrossed in his fear to pay heed to Nigel's reason. But he wasn't the only one.

"We've weathered storms out here on the sea, but I've never seen it like this!" Peter yelled. "Never this fierce!"

326

"The waves are swamping the boat!" Philip screamed as he grabbed the railing. "This wind is kicking up waves higher than our vessel can handle!"

The angry sea churned up foam that now blew into the boats. Another wave came crashing over the disciples, who now could do little more than hold on for dear life. "I can't even see the shoreline!" Andrew shouted.

"If the boat sinks, we'll drown out here!" Thomas cried in despair.

Peter tried to spot James's boat in between the swelling waves that lifted the two boats up and down, bringing them crashing headlong into the angry sea. He saw they were in the same predicament. Another wave hit the boat and all the disciples fell backward onto one another. More water poured in around their feet and they screamed in terror.

"Where's Jesus?!" Judas cried. "We're going to die!"

They all looked to the stern of the boat and there they saw Jesus, still sound asleep. Max cowered next to him, shivering more from fear than the cold water that soaked his fur. Peter struggled to crawl back to wake Jesus, shouting over the raging storm. He tugged on Jesus' leg.

327

"Master! Don't you care that we're going to die!?" Peter pleaded.

Jesus' eyes slowly opened and he sat up. He looked at Peter and the others, but there was no alarm in his eyes, only vague disappointment. Jesus rose to his feet, spread his arms out wide, and with a commanding voice said to the raging wind and the angry waves, "Silence! Be still!"

Instantly the furious wind ceased, and the sea turned to glass. All was calm, and the only sounds were the gentle lapping of the water on the boat's hull and the familiar creaking of the rigging as the sail lazily hung on its mast. James's boat drifted up next to them.

Jesus looked at each of the disciples. "Why are you fearful? Do you still have no faith?" His gaze was penetrating. "Why can't you trust me?"

The disciples were stunned and terrified, first from the storm, and now from Jesus' power to knock the breath out of the wind with a word. They started asking one another in hushed tones, "Who is this? Even the wind and the waves obey him!"

Nigel removed his spectacles and squinted over at Jesus. "Just as with healing people, the effect of his word to nature is *immediate*. He is indeed Lord of all. Brilliant!"

No one could reply to Jesus at the moment. There was too much for them to grasp, and they shied away from Jesus' rebuke. They didn't realize Jesus had been modeling perfect confidence in God as he slept during the storm. They should have done the same, knowing that God Incarnate was in the boat with them. They should have known they would be okay, regardless of the ferocious nature of the storm. The men started to clean up the boat and take care of the ropes and rigging, quietly discussing this miraculous event among themselves.

Jesus sat back down and Max looked up at him with his ears back and eyes filled with shame for being such a coward. Jesus rubbed him on the head.

"I feel like I be more of a Faintheart than a Braveheart," Max lamented. "I've been afraid of storms since I were a pup. And this storm were the worst I ever seen."

Jesus gave Max a reassuring pat on the back. "Maybe it's time you overcome this fear of storms, so you can live up to your name with confidence."

"I've tried an' I jest can't get past it then," Max frowned. "It all goes back ta the night I lost me mum."

"I know," Jesus said gently. "That was a hard night. But Max, you have to realize that whatever happened in your past doesn't have to define who you are today. You aren't the scared, lost puppy whose heart was broken that stormy night. You are Maximillian Braveheart the Bruce, and you serve the Maker in mighty ways. Yes, your pain happened, but it's time to let it go."

Max looked up at Jesus. "How?"

"Give it all to me. Just as I calmed this storm outside," Jesus replied, pointing to the sea. He then pointed to Max's chest. "I'll calm your storm *inside.*"

"Aye, I think I see wha' ye're sayin'. I jest got ta tr-r-rust ye with it, then, an' not be afr-r-raid anymore," Max replied.

"Storms will always come, Max, but I'll keep you safe until they pass . . ." Jesus started.

". . . or until ye give the word," Max jumped in, smiling.

"That's it, Max. No storm lasts forever," Jesus said, smiling. He looked over at the other boat and chuckled at Al peering up now over the railing. "Although Al looks like he's *still* in the storm. Look."

Max peeked around Jesus and broke out in a wide grin. Together he and Jesus laughed at Al, whose face was completely covered in foam.

Daylight came as they neared the far shore, landing in the country of the Gerasenes. The disciples had pulled the boats up onto the beach when they heard a horrible sound. Looking around they saw a crazed man running and screaming from the tombs that dotted the hillside above. As soon as Jesus got out of the boat, the man ran up to him and knelt down before him, his face twisted in terror and agony. Everyone was taken aback by the ferocity of his nature.

The man was clearly demon-possessed and lived in the tombs. No one was able to restrain him—even with chains. He often had been bound with shackles and chains, but had snapped off the chains and smashed the shackles. No one was strong enough to subdue him. And always, night and day, he was crying out among the tombs and in the mountains and cutting himself with stones. His skin was marred with bloody cuts, some fresh and some dried. His wild eyes darted back and forth and he was covered in sweat. His breath was rapid and every part of his body twitched incessantly.

He cried out with a loud, gravelly, almost unnatural voice, "What do you have to do with me, Jesus, Son of the Most High God? I beg you before God, don't torment me!"

Those standing on the shore did not realize Jesus had already told the demons to come out of the man.

Jesus calmly stood and looked down at him. "What is your name?"

"My name is Legion," he answered him, "for we are many."

Nigel, Max, and Al remained in the boats, which were pulled up right next to each other.

"Legion!" Nigel exclaimed in horror. "Do you realize there are six thousand soldiers in a Roman legion? This poor fellow has six thousand demons inside him!" Al trembled and hid behind Nigel. "M-m-m-mary had seven and we thought that were bad."

"Aye, we've seen lots of people with demons, but never one like this. Never this fierce," Max said with a frown. "Wha' does he mean by Jesus torturin' him then?"

"When Satan fell from heaven, he took scores of fallen angels with

329

him who became his minions—his demons. Although they still wreak havoc around the world, the Maker confined many of them to the Abyss, where they must wait until Judgment Day," Nigel explained, adjusting his spectacles. He shuddered. "It's a horrible place of confined evil. These demons know they'll be placed there one day, but they're begging Jesus to postpone that time for now. Demons must have a host, and they'd rather be in pigs than go to the Abyss."

Jesus saw a massive herd of two thousand pigs, then looked back down to the tormented man. He preferred that the demons enter the pigs than remain in this poor soul's body a moment longer. "Go," he told Legion, giving the demons permission.

Suddenly the demons came out of the man and went up the hillside to enter the pigs, who squealed with fear. Everyone watched in shock as the herd rushed down the steep bank into the sea and drowned there.

"The pigs preferred ta drown in the sea than have them demons inside," Max said. "Can't say I blame them then."

330

The group of men who tended the pigs ran off and reported what had happened in the town. Word spread quickly around the countryside, and people soon came out to see what had happened.

Matthew searched in the boats and retrieved a cloak to drape around the freed man's body, for he was naked. The demons had kept him not only in a state of terror, but in a state of shame. The man sat on the ground and Jesus sat down next to him.

The disciples saw people running down the beach toward the boats. They rushed up and gasped when they came to Jesus and saw the man who had been demon-possessed by Legion, sitting there, dressed and in his right mind. Fear gripped the people, for they knew that Jesus must possess a power even greater than that which had possessed the man.

The people gathered around the eyewitness pig herders, who told the people what had happened to the demon-possessed man and the pigs. They began to murmur among themselves and came to agreement about what needed to happen now.

One of the local leaders spoke up for the rest of the group. "Please, leave our region at once. We don't want you here!"

The disciples were shocked at their response. Jesus had saved their region from a terror that kept the people from even burying their dead in the tombs any longer. They lived in fear of what the possessed man might do if he entered their villages. Yet they wanted Jesus now to leave?

"They cared more about the money the two thousand pigs would have brought them than the value of this suffering man," Matthew said, with his arms folded, sickened by their greed. He remembered his own greed. Looking at them was like looking at his former self. How grateful he was Jesus had saved him!

"Well, they lost a considerable amount of money because of what Jesus just did," Judas pointed out.

Matthew looked at Judas in disbelief. "So these people would prefer their *pigs* to Jesus' power in their lives?!"

Judas shrugged his shoulders and Matthew stomped off to the boats, helping Peter, James, and the others. "People will cling to pigs when they don't understand something as wonderful as Jesus," Matthew muttered, shaking his head at what he knew the people were missing in their spiritual blindness.

As Jesus was getting into the boat, the man who had been demon-possessed caught him by the sleeve. "Please, Lord! Please let me come with you!"

331

Jesus placed his hand on the man's shoulder, smiling tenderly at this one who was now free from the consuming rage of evil. "Go back home to your own people, and report to them how much the Lord has done for you and how He has had mercy on you."

The man locked eyes with this One who had saved him from the torment of hell on Earth. In those eyes he saw a love for him that was as fierce in goodness as the demons had been in their wickedness. The man nodded and agreed. "I will, Master. I will tell them all."

Jesus gave him a final nod and squeezed his arm before climbing into the boat. Peter and James shoved off from the shore and the man stood there, waving and bidding them farewell.

As the breeze caught the sails and the boats sliced through the water, Al looked at the man on the shore. "Looks like Jesus calmed the lad's storm within."

Max grinned and jumped up on the bow of the boat, the sun shining bright and the beautiful sea blue and clear. He took a deep breath and grinned. "Aye, wherever Jesus be, the storms have ta hush."

40

TWELVE YEARS NOTED

W e've tried everything," Jairus said in a defeated voice. "No doctor has been able to heal her. She's . . . ," his voice cracked and a lump locked in his throat. A single tear fell down his cheek. "She's slipping away. Twelve years. Twelve short years is all she's had."

Armandus clenched his jaw as he looked into the bloodshot eyes of this man who was such an important pillar of society here in Capernaum. He was the elected ruler of the synagogue and oversaw the concerns of worship, the building, and the conduct of the people. Armandus had worked closely with Jairus when they were building the new synagogue, and had come to respect this man. He was always in charge and calm about all things, but today he was reduced to a helpless father who had exhausted all human resources. His twelve-year-old little girl was the joy and light of his life. Armandus knew that Jairus would gladly take the place of his dying daughter if he could.

"I'm sorry, Jairus," Armandus sympathized. "Had I known you were in the midst of this today I wouldn't have bothered you with business matters. This can wait. Is there nothing else you can do?"

Jairus didn't even acknowledge the business at hand, fiddling with the scroll Armandus had brought him to discuss. "There is one last hope," he said, giving a sad, single laugh. "But I fear I've destroyed any chance of that with the way I've treated him."

"Treated whom?" Armandus asked, although he already supposed the answer.

Jairus shook his head in regret. "Jesus of Nazareth. The blasphemous heretic that I joined my fellow council members in rebuking for *healing* in our synagogue! How could I possibly approach him now?"

Armandus knew that Jesus could heal Jairus's daughter. But he was still hesitant to share his story about Caius with anyone outside of Bella and his household. He thought how strange it was that he and Jairus stood here, concerned about what men would think about their affiliation with not just the last hope but the *only* hope they had.

"From what I've heard about Jesus, he isn't the type of man who bears a grudge or clings to injured pride. His character is above that kind of small thinking. He's a different kind of man," Armandus encouraged. He suddenly thought of something that would give Jairus the encouragement he might need. "Jesus healed my friend Tatius's young son who lay dying like your daughter! And he did so from a distance—just with a word—and for a *Roman,* not one of his followers. I heard he's back in Capernaum today, by the market."

333

Jairus looked up and tears quickened in his eyes. He knew that Jesus could heal his daughter, maybe not for Jairus's sake, but his daughter's. He nodded. "I will go to him. I need to also not cling to injured pride. My daughter needs him."

Armandus smiled. "Go, my friend. I hope your last hope doesn't fail you."

Jairus left the Roman centurion there in the street outside his house, which was located next to the synagogue. Armandus watched as the desperate father picked up his pace and raced down the street. He was stripping himself of everything he had instructed his body of Jewish synagogue goers to cling to. This was life or death. It surprised Jairus to think how irrelevant the law condemning this healing blasphemer had quickly become.

The woman gazed out her tiny window at the crowds following Jesus, longing to be with them. But that wasn't possible. Because of her continual bleeding, she was considered unclean by the Jewish community.

Everything she touched, sat on, laid on, or wore was unclean in their eyes. So she was shut off from attending worship, from fellowshipping with people, and from life. As if having the physical burden of her terrible condition wasn't enough, she also bore the emotional burden of being shunned, isolated, and alone.

Twelve years. Twelve long years I've had this, she thought to herself. *But no one has been able to help me.*

The woman had lost count of how many physicians she had seen. The *Talmud,* or collection of rabbinical law, customs, ethics, philosophy and history, set forth eleven cures for her condition, from tonics and astringents to superstitious remedies. Not only did they not work, some of them made her worse, and were just ridiculous. One of the supposed remedies was to carry the ashes of an ostrich egg in a linen bag in summer, and a cotton bag in winter. The woman shook her head and laughed sadly as she recalled actually trying that remedy, which of course didn't work. *Nothing* worked.

334

She caught a glimpse of Jesus of Nazareth right outside her window and her heart skipped a beat. Word had spread about this miracle worker and the countless people he had healed of every sort of ailment. *If he can heal leprosy, make blind men see and lame men walk, surely he can heal me,* she thought. Suddenly a sense of urgency coursed through her. This might be her only chance to get to Jesus. What did she have to lose? As long as no one recognized her, she could just blend into the crowd and touch Jesus. She knew her condition wasn't contagious, and that she wouldn't put anyone in harm's way by touching them. *Oh, but if I touch Jesus, I could be well!*

The woman quickly put on her head covering, pulling it way down over her eyes to try to hide her face. She suddenly felt a bit lightheaded from the loss of blood, so paused to steady herself. When she felt ready to walk, she took a deep breath, went out the door, and blended into the crowd, slowly inching her way up to Jesus.

Jesus and his disciples were going through the market, purchasing food and supplies. While Gillamon filled Clarie's saddlebags Al practically swooned from the smells within his reach.

"No sampling of the food, Albert," Liz scolded, gently slapping his paw as he tried to get inside the basket containing olives and dried fruit.

Al's ears went back. He knew he had been caught snooping. "Aye, Lass. Sorry."

Liz couldn't resist her husband's pitiful look. He was just too cute. Her mouth curved in a smile and she reached over to kiss him on the cheek. His frown turned upward as a goofy grin appeared on his face.

"Here, Al," Gillamon said, cracking open a pistachio to give the hungry orange cat. "You can have some of mine."

Al gobbled up the tasty nut and held his paw out for another. Gillamon and Liz rolled their eyes and shared a smile.

"I like 'em too, ye know," Max said from below.

Gillamon cracked a few more pistachios and gave some to Max and Kate. Tails were wagging as the two dogs crunched the yummy nuts.

"Don't forget your favorite donkey," Clarie hee-hawed.

"And her tiniest passenger!" Nigel appeared with a paw raised in the air.

Gillamon put his hand out for Clarie to nibble them out of his palm and slipped one to Nigel, who hid back where Liz sat. Gillamon offered one to Liz but she politely refused.

335

"Well, I'm glad everyone is enjoying the pistachio treat," Gillamon said, wiping off his hands and holding them up. "Because I'm all out."

"BANANAS!" Al screamed, spotting them in one of the vendor stalls.

Liz looked sweetly up at Gillamon. "Could we impose on you to get a banana for Albert?"

Gillamon chuckled and gave the vendor a few coins. "How about a whole bunch?" he said as he set the bananas in Al's lap. He quickly counted them. "You have twelve there. That should keep you for a while."

"Come to me, me beauties!" Al said, enveloping the bananas in an affectionate embrace. Ever since Noah's Ark, bananas had been Al's favorite food. Fish were a close second. "Thank ye, lad. Ye done give me more than I expected then."

"You're welcome, Al," Gillamon replied. "I wish everyone were as easy to please as you."

The people were crushing in on Jesus as they slowly walked through the market. Everyone wanted to get to him, hoping to hear him speak or to receive a healing touch. They couldn't get enough of Jesus, and it was becoming increasingly difficult to move about the cities. But Jesus' compassion wore long, and he never turned anyone away who sought him out.

"Make way, make way!" a voice sounded. The crowds began to part as Jairus walked into the market. "Let Jairus through!" The people immediately obliged and made a path for this respected man of Capernaum.

Jesus stopped and a path opened up in front of him. When Jairus saw Jesus he rushed over and knelt before him, pleading desperately for his help.

"My little girl is dying," Jairus muttered, his head held down. He couldn't look Jesus in the eye as he begged for his help. "Will you come and put your hands on her—then she will get better and live."

"Of course, Jairus," Jesus replied immediately.

Jairus quickly looked up and saw Jesus' gaze of compassion and willingness. There was no resentment for past offenses. Indeed this man was unlike any he had ever met. Jesus helped Jairus slowly to his feet. The hopeless father suddenly had hope for his little girl.

The woman was crawling on her hands and knees through the legs of the people who had stopped to listen to the exchange between Jairus and Jesus. *If I can just . . . touch . . . the hem,* she thought as she desperately strained to reach Jesus' robe, *I'll be all right.*

"Take me to her," Jesus said calmly to Jairus. He motioned for his disciples to fall in line behind him.

Jairus smiled and just as they were turning to walk out of the market, the woman made a desperate lunge. *This is my only chance!* The tips of her fingers barely grazed Jesus' robe. Immediately she felt the bleeding stop as warmth filled her womb. She sat back on her heels there in the street, placing her hands over her belly and closing her eyes as she felt the healing take place. She began to sob softly with joy. Twelve years of suffering were ended.

At once Jesus knew intuitively that power had gone out of him. He turned round in the middle of the crowd and asked, "Who touched me?"

Peter furrowed his brow. "You can see this crowd jostling you. How can you ask, 'Who touched me?' Who *hasn't* touched you, Master?"

But he looked all round at their faces to see who had done so. Max and Kate saw exactly who had done it, being on the same level in the street as the woman. They saw the woman begin to shake and look around nervously.

"The poor lass be frightened. She knows she be the one Jesus be lookin' for," Kate said sadly. "But she needn't be afraid with Jesus."

Jesus' gaze finally settled on the woman and she locked eyes with him. One by one, people moved out of his way until he stood a few feet away. She flung herself before him and told him the whole story of her twelve years of agony.

"No one has been able to help me, Master, but I knew you could heal me," she gushed. "You were my last hope. My only hope."

Jesus reached down and lifted her to her feet, smiling warmly at her. "Daughter, it is your faith that has healed you. Go home in peace, and be free from your trouble."

"One touch can change everything," Liz said with eyes full of joyous tears.

While Jesus was speaking with the woman, messengers arrived from Jairus's house. They searched him out and with great sadness told Jairus the bad news. "Your daughter is dead—there is no need to bother the Master any further."

But when Jesus heard this, he turned to Jairus, lifted his hand, and assured him, "Don't be afraid. Keep believing." He then turned to his disciples. "Peter, James, and John, you three come with me. The rest of you, please stay here."

Jairus's emotions were a swirling mass of confusion. His heart was torn asunder with grief at hearing the news his daughter had died but with the hope that this miracle worker told him to keep believing. He simply walked silently forward with the messengers, and Jesus and his three disciples. Liz and Kate were already on their way, too, sneaking through the people to follow Jesus to Jairus's house. They weren't about to miss this.

They arrived at Jairus's house to be greeted with the chaotic weeping and wailing that was expected.

"There sure be a lot of racket," Kate said as she and Liz hid in a bush.

"*Oui,* the Jewish people even have rules for how to mourn appropriately," Liz replied. They watched one of the mourners rend his garment, tearing it at the collar. "Did you know there are thirty-nine rules just governing how to rend garments when mourning?"

Kate looked at Liz in disbelief. "This be gettin' a wee bit out of hand, Lass! There be rules ta tell grievin' people how ta rip their clothes?"

"*Oui,* but there is more. Professional wailers are hired to weep and build up the emotions of visitors as they come to pay last respects to the family," Liz continued. "And no less than two flute players are required for any death. Flutes are associated with grief and death, even in Rome, no?"

Jesus looked around at the wailing people in the house and shook his head. "Why are you making such a noise with your crying? The child is not dead," he told them, looking up at Jairus and his grieving wife, "only sleeping."

The people gathered there greeted Jesus with a scornful laugh.

"They be so caught up in their mournin' they seem ta resent hope," Kate growled. "How crazy can they be then?"

338

"Well, understand they've seen the girl, felt her pulse, and know she's dead," Liz said. "Logically, Jesus' comment would be absurd, no?"

"Aye, but not when Jesus says it," Kate said.

Jesus had Peter, James, and John politely usher all the mourners and wailers out of the house until only Jairus, his wife, and the three disciples remained.

"Take me to her," Jesus said softly once it was quiet.

Jairus held his wife's hand as they went into the room where the child was. The girl lay on a bed, still and lifeless. Her beautiful brown hair fell across her pillow. Her face was ashen and her body completely void of any signs of life. Above her in the room was one small window where light poured in and onto the floor.

Jesus walked over and squatted down by the girl. He took the little girl's cold, ashen hand and softly whispered, "Little lamb, wake up."

At once the girls' eyes fluttered open. She looked up at Jesus and saw the face of the One who had brought her back to life. They shared a tender smile. Twelve years of life instantly restored to continue on.

The little girl sat up and her parents rushed to her side, falling all over her with hugs and kisses. "Oh, our girl is back! She's alive!" Jairus exclaimed.

Jesus respectfully stood and backed out of their way so the family could rejoice in this moment. Peter, James, and John held their heads in disbelief and hugged one another over the miraculous power of their Lord. Jesus grinned as he saw Liz's shadow jump down from the windowsill. She had witnessed the miracle as well.

Jairus stood and was so overcome with emotion he could hardly speak. His lip trembled and he held out his hands. "Thank you, Jesus. Thank you, *Rabbi.*"

Jesus nodded and smiled. "Now give her something to eat. And Jairus, don't tell anyone about what happened here today."

Jairus wrinkled his forehead in confusion. He didn't understand why Jesus would say such a thing, as he had publicly healed so many others. It had nothing to do with the fact that Jesus had touched a dead body, making him "unclean" according to Jewish law. Jesus clearly didn't care about that, and Jairus thought how ironic that he, now, didn't either. He would do whatever Jesus asked of him. "Understood," he agreed.

Jesus then left with his disciples, not giving an explanation to the mourners who were still assembled in the courtyard. They murmured among themselves as Jesus walked by, but rushed up to the door of Jairus's house to see what had happened inside. As soon as they saw the little girl was up and eating a bowl of stew, their mournful weeping turned to joyous singing!

"Aye, now that's more like it!" Kate cheered. "The funeral dirge now be a happy tune."

"*Oui! C'est magnifique!* Jesus has done it again!" Liz exclaimed as she and Kate fell in line behind Jesus and the disciples. "Have you noticed that Jesus breaks up every funeral he attends?"

"Aye," Kate replied happily. "He hates death."

Jesus overheard Kate and Liz chatting behind him and smiled. He turned, glanced down at them, and gave them a wink. He then continued on with Peter, James, and John, who were grilling him with questions.

Kate and Liz were soon back at the market with Gillamon, Max, Al, and Nigel, who greeted them with excitement over the little girl being brought back to life. Liz looked over and saw the woman whom Jesus had healed. She was happily talking with her neighbors about her miracle.

339

"Twelve," Liz pondered. "Twelve seems to be the number *du jour.*"

"Aye, twelve bananas," Al said with a mouthful of the sweet fruit.

Max reached over and bonked Al on the head. "Daft kitty!"

Liz continued, ignoring Al's silly remark. "That woman suffered for twelve years—just as many years as Jairus's daughter had been alive."

Nigel watched as Jesus' twelve disciples surrounded him, rejoicing over the day's events. "And twelve instruments are receiving more fine tuning with each passing day." Nigel put his paw up to his mouth. "I jolly well don't know *why* I keep referring to the disciples as instruments."

Clarie and Gillamon shared a knowing smile. Gillamon pulled out the tiny reed Clarie still carried behind her ear, having taken the reed from the bank of the Jordan River the day John baptized Jesus. "Nigel, tell me, how many notes are there on the musical scale?"

"I say, *twelve,*" Nigel remarked, growing even more curious about his analogy.

Gillamon nodded, rubbing the tiny Nigel-sized reed in his fingers. "Well, just as beautiful music needs twelve notes, Jesus has selected twelve disciples, or 'instruments.'"

"Ergo, Jesus is out to make beautiful music in the world!" Nigel cheered. "Utterly splendid insight, old boy!"

"Well, he's certainly done that for two lives today, no?" Liz posed. "Twelve years of agony ended, and twelve years of joy restored."

"Aye, we even heard the mourners change their tune, from sad to glad."

"That's certainly the kind of music fitting for Messiah," Nigel told them, preening his whiskers.

Gillamon winked at Clarie. Little did Nigel know the full meaning of what he had just uttered.

SILENCING THREATS

Herod's eyes shifted back and forth and he rapidly tapped his fingers on the arms of his ornate chair as he listened to the reports of his informants. Word had spread about Jesus' miracles, from the common people all the way up to the top rulers of the region. Even his twelve disciples were now on mission for their Master, traveling around Galilee, teaching and healing. A movement was growing, and Jesus of Nazareth was its leader.

"Some are saying Jesus is John the Baptist, risen from the dead. That's why he is showing such miraculous powers," one man reported.

"Others say he's Elijah the prophet," another chimed in. "Or another of the prophets of the old days come back again."

Herod Antipas stood and clasped his hands behind his neck. He proceeded to pace about the room, distressed and allowing the full force of his insane, superstitious mindset to sweep over him. His hands went to hold his head and he shook it slowly. With wide eyes he shouted, "It must be John whom I beheaded, risen from the dead!"

Armandus stood in the back of the room, gripping his fists in anger. He had seen the full wrath of this madman unleashed on the prophet, and he knew where this could lead. Herod Antipas was truly his father's son—a drunken, depraved, weak madman, and above all, a killer. Armandus's thoughts drifted back to the horror of the night Herod had John killed, several weeks earlier.

"Music! Music!" Herod said with a slur as he clumsily clapped his hands. "Play me more music!"

The musicians had already been playing for hours and sought a brief respite. They had just ceased playing, but at Herod's command they immediately picked up their instruments and resumed filling the banquet hall with music. No one took a chance by defying Herod, especially today.

Herodias spared no expense for her husband's birthday party, serving an abundance of exotic food and wine. All of Herod's courtiers and top military commanders had been invited to this extravagant event, and she made sure the food was plentiful and the wine flowed. She made especially sure Herod's cup stayed full. When the time was right, she gave her daughter Salome the nod.

All heads turned to see the beautiful young girl who entered the banquet hall. She was dressed in a silky red tunic of airy, sheer layers that trailed behind her as she moved. Gold bangles adorned her arms and ankles, and sewn into her headdress were gold droplets that cascaded onto her forehead. Her deep brown eyes were painted with thick black kohl and her lips with red stain. Salome was young, beautiful, and headstrong, just like her mother.

Herod's jaw fell and his eyes widened as Salome sauntered up to him wearing a coy grin. Her mother clapped instructions to the musicians, who began playing a slow dancing tune. Salome began to dance in front of Herod, much to his delight and the delight of his guests. Herodias smiled smugly as she saw Herod enthralled with her daughter's dancing, which gradually got faster and faster with the music until she fell to the floor with a dramatic finale. Applause and cheers erupted from the guests, and Herod was visibly spellbound by her performance.

In his drunken excitement Herod gushed out, "Ask me anything you like and I will give it to you! I will give you whatever you ask me, up to half of my kingdom!"

Again, the guests applauded the gesture of reward to this beautiful girl who had entertained them. Salome smiled and went over to her mother, who was reclining on the satin pillows around the table.

"What shall I ask for?" Salome whispered.

Herodias lifted her chin with satisfaction, congratulating herself on the success of her scheme. She knew exactly what Salome should ask for.

Herodias had waited for this opportunity for months, ever since Herod arrested John the Baptist and had him bound in prison. The arrest was all on account of Herodias, his brother Philip's wife, whom Herod had married. When John learned of this unlawful, disgraceful marriage, he rebuked Herod publicly. Herodias herself was furious with him for this and wanted to have him executed, but she couldn't do it. Herod had a deep respect for John, knowing he was a just and holy man, and protected him. Herod used to listen to John and be profoundly disturbed, and yet he enjoyed hearing him. So Herodias patiently waited and plotted how she could bring about John's death.

Herodias smiled wickedly. At last the opportune time had come. She instructed her daughter to answer Herod's question, "The head of John the Baptist!"

Salome rushed back to the king's presence, and made her request. "I want you to give me, this minute, the head of John the Baptist on a platter!"

343

Herod was aghast. Even in his drunken state, the shock of Salome's request brought reality crashing into his mind. He looked around at his guests, who waited for him to make good on the oath he had just sworn to the young girl. Then he looked back at the brazen beauty before him. He did not like to refuse his stepdaughter. The pressure of all eyes on him caused him to cave within minutes. Finally he closed his eyes and nodded, giving the partygoers more reason to applaud and cheer.

Herod called over one of the palace guardsmen, who came and leaned down close to the madman. "Bring me . . ." he paused, sickened by what he was doing, "John's head."

"Yes, my King," the guardsman said. The man went off to the dungeon below Herod's fortress.

Herodias studied her husband and could see the turmoil he was in. She gave a sarcastic laugh at his weakness. She knew he didn't want to kill the prophet. But Herod cared more about what the people thought of him. He remained forever imprisoned by the opinions of others, and was more of a captive than John in that respect. Well, now they would no longer have to worry about the opinion of John the Baptist.

The guests audibly gasped when the guardsman re-entered the banquet hall. He carried a large silver tray in both hands. And there on the tray was the head of John the Baptist. He walked over and gave it to Salome, who in turn handed it to her mother.

Herodias took the tray and looked at the once forceful mouth of John the Baptist. "Your opinion is permanently silenced," she mocked, and ordered an attendant to take it away as she laughed. "Music, music!" she demanded, as the banquet hall was quiet from the dramatic scene that had just unfolded. "And bring more wine! We have much to celebrate!"

Armandus was outside the fortress with his men when John's disciples arrived. Once the party guests returned to their homes throughout Galilee, word spread quickly about what had taken place at Herod's party. When John's faithful disciples heard what had happened, they immediately came to the fortress.

"Please, sir, we've come to take away John's body, so that we might bury it respectfully in a tomb," one of the disciples explained. They had cloth and ointments to prepare the body for burial, and carried an empty bier.

344

Velius and Ulixes and some of the other soldiers mocked them. "Looks like your prophet won't have much more to say about Herod now, will he?" they laughed.

"You see what happens when you defy those in Roman authority?" Ulixes said, getting in the faces of the men standing before him in a state of quiet humility. "Yes, that's exactly how you are to respond. Keep your mouths shut!"

Armandus pushed his way through to John's disciples, calling off the soldiers, who continually enjoyed intimidating the Jews. The centurion grew weary of these two in particular, who seemed to have a particularly strange hostility toward the people.

"You may take the body," Armandus told the disciples. "Follow me."

He ushered them in and they hurriedly wrapped John's body with great care, anointing it with love and respect. They quietly whispered among themselves as they went about their task. Finally the four men placed John's body on the bier and carried it off.

"Let me know as soon as you hear anything else," Herod raged at his informants, stomping out of the room. Armandus snapped back from his daydream and stood at attention as the madman passed by. Herod called back as he walked down the hall, "about Jesus of Nazareth."

Armandus frowned. He knew that Herod was plagued with paranoid guilt over the death of John the Baptist. Now he thought Jesus was the prophet brought back to life. Herod would not hesitate to go after this new apparition of the prophet to relieve his warped mind.

How strange, Armandus thought as he considered the acts committed by their fathers. The father of Herod Antipas, Herod the Great, slaughtered all the male children two years of age and under in and around Bethlehem in an attempt to silence the threat of a new King of the Jews. Armandus's father, Marcus Antonius, was the centurion charged with carrying out that despicable act, and it still haunted him to this day. Armandus and Herod Antipas were the next generation in this unfolding historical conflict among the people of Israel.

Jesus of Nazareth was now not only a target in the sights of the Sanhedrin, but of Herod Antipas as well. Newborn babies and John the Baptist had been silenced by these wicked Herods. Armandus couldn't help but wonder which voice would be silenced next.

Jesus sat with the animals up on a mountainside. He had sent the twelve out on mission, giving them power and authority over all demons and to cure diseases, and to spread the good news about the Kingdom of God. Jesus knew they were returning today, and that they would enthusiastically share their experiences of teaching and healing through villages across the region. Jesus explained that this mission was part of the training for work they someday would need to do completely on their own. Jesus also was well aware that Herod Antipas had heard of all that was happening with Jesus' ministry, and that he had murdered John the Baptist. Jesus' heart was grieving over the loss of his cousin.

"John spoke the truth, but truth is a sharp sword of conflict," Jesus explained. "Those who hold it will be hunted by evil, as he was."

"Truth is rarely popular with those who seek to control others," Nigel posed.

"*Oui*, if they can't control those who speak the truth, they'll seek to silence them, no?" Liz added. "Herod and his wicked wife couldn't control John, so they had to silence him."

"John's sword of truth pierced the heart of those hypocrites," Kate said angrily. "An' their wicked hearts bled out resentment an' hatred."

"Aye, do ye think Herod will be tr-r-ryin' ta hunt *ye* down now, too?" Max growled, concerned about Jesus' welfare.

"Nothing will happen outside the appointed time, and the appointed place, and by the appointed men my Father will use to fulfill his purposes for me. So Herod has no power to touch me unless it is given to him from above," Jesus reassured the brave little dog. He looked down the hillside and saw his disciples beginning to return. When Jesus was gone, these men would be responsible to spread Jesus' truth to the ends of the earth. "But when I am silenced for a time, the truth will roar back with these twelve until the whole world hears the truth."

HE SHALL FEED
HIS FLOCK LIKE
A SHEPHERD

T hey can't stop grinning," Liz observed, smiling as she watched the disciples share stories about all they had experienced while on mission for Jesus. "Their faces are animated with joy, no?"

"Utterly splendid to see that the old boys had such a rousing success!" Nigel exclaimed with a fist of victory in the air. "You would never know how tired they really are."

"Aye, Jesus were right ta bring them across the sea for a rest then," Kate said happily. Her front paws were up on the bow of the boat. She wagged her tail as the breeze blew in her face. They were clipping along on the shiny sea, abundant sunshine and blue skies making it a perfect day.

Nigel preened his whiskers, then clasped his paws behind his back. "Indeed, my dear, rests are as much a part of the music as the notes. Without rests, the music would become dreadfully hard to listen to."

"What a wonderful musical analogy, *mon ami!*" Liz praised her little mouse friend. "And look how it relates perfectly to life, no? We think we must be busy, busy, busy all the time, but without rest we all will become dreadfully hard to listen to. I do not understand why humans have such a difficult time with simply resting."

"Rest is a gift from the Maker then," Kate added. "Ye get more done in the long run, too."

"I could rest all day," Al interjected.

"All that may be, but it don't look like they're goin' ta get much of a r-r-rest today then," Max observed, pointing to the shore where they were headed. "Look."

The crowds were already gathering on the other side. Evidently word got out about where Jesus and his disciples were headed, and the people had raced ahead to meet them there. Gillamon and Clarie were among the crowd standing on the beach.

"How'd they'd get here so fast?" Al asked, scratching his head and waving at Gillamon, whose long, white beard blew in the breeze. Everyone looked at Al with knowing grins. "Oh! They can travel at the speed o' time if they wanna then. Sure—I knew that."

Jesus gazed out at the longing faces of the people and took a deep breath. "They are like sheep without a shepherd," he said softly as the boats landed.

348

Jesus stepped out onto shore and immediately began to walk among the people, healing those who so desperately needed his touch. The disciples secured the boats and rallied around their Master, helping to lead the crowds to a grassy hillside where Jesus could more easily teach and be heard. Hours passed and the sun was starting its late afternoon descent.

"There must be five thousand men here," Philip guessed, scanning the crowd.

"Not to mention the women and the children," Matthew added. His hands went to his head in awe. "There could be twenty thousand people on this hillside!"

"Indeed, I think it's the largest crowd that has ever come to Jesus," Philip said. "I hope the Master lets them go earlier than usual today."

"Why?" Matthew asked.

"Well, look at them. They didn't come prepared to camp here," Philip observed. "They don't have provisions with them. They just ran here to find Jesus without thinking about that. It will take time for them to travel home to get food."

Matthew chuckled and slapped Philip on the back. "Always the pragmatist!"

Andrew stood with his hands on his hips, grinning at something.

"What are you looking at?" Peter asked him, looking in the direction of his gaze.

"The orange cat is bugging that little boy over there," Andrew said, pointing.

Al was sniffing all around the little boy, who had a small knapsack. The little boy threw his head back, giggling as Al kept nudging him, meowing.

"Must have fish in there," Peter said, arms folded and shaking his head with a grin at the hungry cat.

"Of course he does! I don't know why the Master allows these animals to stay around us all the time, but they seem to bring joy to others now and then," Andrew replied. "He always has his reasons for doing things, even when they don't make sense to us."

Jesus looked up and motioned for Philip. The disciple went over to Jesus and squatted down next to him. Andrew and Peter went along as well.

"Where shall we buy bread for these people to eat?" Jesus asked him in a matter-of-fact tone.

Philip's eyes widened and he threw his hand out at the sizable crowd. "It would take more than half a year's wages to buy enough bread for each one to just have a bite!"

"How could Jesus ask Philip such a cr-r-razy thing?" Max whispered. The animals were sitting together on the grass near Jesus.

Liz's tail curled up and down slowly and she wore a coy grin. "He's not asking, he's testing."

"Wha' do ye mean, Liz?" Kate asked.

"Jesus already knows what he's going to do," Liz explained. "He's giving Philip an opportunity to learn something, but I am not yet sure what."

Gillamon's smiling eyes watched as Andrew ran over to where the little boy was sitting. "Look."

Al was now climbing all over the little boy, pawing at his knapsack. The boy's face was red from laughing so hard. Andrew squatted down next to them.

"Hi," Andrew said, pulling Al off the boy. "I see you have a lunch there. With our cat crawling all over you like this, I'll guess you have fish."

The little boy sat up and happily opened his pouch. "Yes, two fish, and I have some barley loaves, too." He reached in and eagerly grabbed a loaf. "Want some?"

Al meowed, reaching his paw up to the boy. *"O' COURSE I DO!"*

Andrew laughed, placing his hand on the boy's shoulder. "No, but I know someone who does. Can you come with me to see Jesus?"

"Sure!" the little boy said, standing up. He took Andrew by the hand and together they walked over to Jesus. Al was trailing along behind, staying close to the boy.

Andrew stood behind the little boy and placed his hands on the lad's shoulders. He wore a chagrined look on his face but offered, "Here is a boy with five small barley loaves and two small fish, but how far will they go among so many?"

Jesus smiled broadly and patted the ground, inviting the boy to sit down next to him. "Did your mother pack this for you?"

"Yes, Master, she did," the little boy replied. "But I can share it. Are you hungry?"

Jesus closed his eyes in delight over this precious boy offering all he had. He smiled and gave the boy an approving hug. "May I share some of your lunch with the other people here?"

The little boy looked around and nodded eagerly. "Sure! However far it will go."

Jesus looked up at his disciples, especially at Philip. "Have the people sit down," he instructed.

The disciples immediately went through the crowd and Philip suggested they group people by fifties and hundreds. Soon word spread across the abundantly grassy hillside and the people sat down as asked. The disciples returned to Jesus for further instructions.

"He makes me lie down in green pastures," Clarie said, quoting a psalm as she sat down next to Nigel.

"He shall feed his flock like a shepherd: he shall gather the lambs with his arm," Nigel said. "I say, Isaiah wrote that passage with such prophetic beauty! It has rather a nice rhythm to it." He began to hum a little tune. "It would flow rather well in song, I believe."

Gillamon and Clarie shared a wink.

"Look at the daft kitty sittin' in front of Jesus, waitin' on a piece of fish then," Max said.

Liz shook her head, grinning. "Oh, my predictable Albert."

"If it weren't for Al, Andrew wouldn't have noticed the little boy," Gillamon offered with a twinkle in his eye. "Watch."

Jesus asked the boy, "May I have a loaf?"

The boy smiled and handed over his entire pouch. "You can have it all."

Jesus nodded and smiled. "Thank you, my young friend." He then took a loaf of bread and raised it above his head, closing his eyes. "Father, we give thanks to you for this bread. You are the Giver of all things, the Maker of heaven and Earth, and the provider for all life. I thank you for the small offering of this child who has given all he has. Bless this one whom you will use to bless many. Amen."

Jesus began to tear the loaf apart, and handed the first small piece to Philip. "Don't measure the size of the challenge by what you have to offer, but by what God can do with what you give him, no matter how small."

Philip took the bread and looked at Jesus with questioning obedi- 351 ence. He nodded silently and went over to a group of fifty people sitting in the grass. He tore off a piece of bread and handed it to an elderly woman. She took it gladly. When Philip looked down to tear off some more, his piece was the same size as before! He looked back quickly at Jesus in shock and amazement. Jesus simply smiled at his disciple.

Philip eagerly began tearing off piece after piece after piece, and yet his piece of the loaf remained the same size. "Here! There's plenty for everyone!"

The same happened with each of the twelve disciples, and the miracle astounded the people as the food multiplied. Cries of joy erupted on the grassy hillside. A warm, gentle breeze blew across the thousands upon thousands of people gathered there.

After Jesus had broken the five loaves, he took the two fish and held them in his hand. He leaned forward and whispered to Al. "You found him, so you get the first piece." Al's eyes widened with excitement as Jesus broke off a piece and handed it to the hungry cat, giving him a wink.

Al closed his eyes in delight and rubbed his belly. *"Thank ye, Jesus,"* he meowed. *"I jest can't wait to see if there's more where that came from, like the bread!"*

Jesus threw his head back, laughing. "Of course there is! Eat your fill!"

Jesus proceeded to multiply the fish as he handed it to the disciples, amazing the crowds even further. Some of the people lived on the edge of starvation, so were weeping over having so much to eat. Over the course of the next few hours, the scene on the hillside was one of feasting, celebration, and joy. But a slow murmur also began to sweep through the crowd. "This is the prophet for sure, God's prophet right here in Galilee!"

Jesus knew what they all were thinking—and he would have to do something about it.

"I ate too much," Al said, lying on his back, patting his big fluffy belly.

"Ye think?!" Max replied with a sarcastic flash of his eyes.

"*C'est incredible!* Jesus keeps amazing us all!" Liz said, now giving herself a dainty bath after the delicious meal.

"Jesus took the *biscuit* with this miracle!" Nigel said with an impish grin. "And multiplied it!" He broke out in a jolly laugh, holding his paws over his belly as he chuckled.

"Looks like the disciples each have a basket full of leftovers," Kate said, glancing at the twelve men. Jesus had instructed them to gather up all the pieces so nothing was wasted, and dismissed the crowds.

"Twelve baskets of leftovers," Liz pondered. "Jesus began with seven pieces and ended with twelve baskets."

"Seven and twelve," Gillamon said, winking. "Good numbers for any project."

Al rolled over and moaned. "Aye, but the lad were jest one. He did the addition," Al said, yawning broadly. "And Jesus did the multiplication then."

Everyone looked at Al's surprising math analogy. "Albert! I'm so proud of you!" Liz affectionately nudged her mate with the uncomfortably full stomach.

"Aye, the lad jest gave all he had, knowin' it weren't enough," Max said. "But whatever ye give the Maker with all yer heart, jest watch wha' he'll do. The impossible even!"

"Provision is the Maker's responsibility, not ours," Gillamon added. "He only asks us to offer what we have. I think Philip learned that lesson indeed today. They all did."

Jesus came walking up to them, smiling. "I hope everyone ate his or her fill."

Al raised his paw silently and let it fall to his side with a thump. Jesus chuckled.

"I'm sending the disciples back to the boats, so you best go along with them," Jesus said. "I need to withdraw from the people. They have the wrong idea about me, and wish to force me to assume the role of earthly king."

"But isn't that wha' ye be?" Kate asked.

"Yes, dear Kate, but not the way the people envision it," Jesus explained. "They see my miracles and want me to storm the gates of Jerusalem to overthrow the Roman authority with earthly force. So it's time to withdraw so their emotions will settle on the matter. There will be a time to enter Jerusalem, but not like that."

353

Gillamon stood and grabbed Clarie by the reins. "Come, everyone." He reached down and lifted Al into Clarie's saddlebag. "I know you can't walk a step, Big Al."

"Aye, much obliged, lad," Al yawned.

Jesus whispered in Gillamon's ear and he nodded in response. As the animals began to follow Gillamon, Jesus said, "See you all soon. Max, you come with me."

"Me? Why then?" wondered Max.

"You can be with me while I spend some time praying," Jesus answered. "And you never know what else."

Max trotted over to Jesus, bouncing on his Scottish feet. "Aye, I'll be with ye, Jesus. I like those 'wha' else' moments then."

Jesus waved at the others and he and Max turned to walk up the mountainside together.

Night was upon them, so as the disciples shoved the boats off the beach, they couldn't see that massive storm clouds were building over the Sea of Galilee.

MASTER OF THE IMPOSSIBLE

The wind slowly began to pick up on top of the mountain. Max was lying there with his feet behind him, head resting on his front paws. He lifted his gaze to see the trees begin to blow and bend at the will of the wind. He looked over and saw Jesus still in prayer. As the wind began to howl, Jesus slowly raised his gaze. Max knew he was finished praying, so quietly walked over to where Jesus sat.

"They're in trouble," Jesus said, his gaze fixed on the sea out in the darkness.

Max sat down next to Jesus. "Aye, storm's a br-r-rewin'."

"Yes, it is," Jesus said, wrapping his arm around Max. "How do you feel about storms now?"

"I still don't like 'em, but since I gave ye me fear, I don't feel afr-r-raid then," Max replied. "Ye be the one contr-r-rollin' 'em, so me fr-r-rettin' aboot 'em doesn't do any good."

"I'm glad to hear that, because we're going to go help my disciples," Jesus said as he stood up and began to walk down the mountain.

Max trotted along behind him. "They must be in the middle of the lake by now! How do ye r-r-reckon' ye can get ta them?" Max asked.

"Max, you've held onto two fears all your life—fear of storms and fear of water, since you can't swim well," Jesus said. "We've handled one together, now it's time to put your other fear to rest once and for all."

"An' jest how're we goin' ta do that?" Max asked, uncertain and a bit fearful.

Jesus stopped and looked down at the small Scottie dog. "By walking all over it."

"The wind is just too strong!" Andrew shouted, exhausted and out of breath. He and the others had been rowing against the wind after taking down the uncontrollable sails.

"We're still more than a mile from land, and we're being battered by these waves," James echoed. "We'll never make it!"

"AHHHHH! WE'RE ALL GOIN' TO DIE! WE'LL BE LOST TO THE SEA AND THE SHARK BEASTIES WILL COME GET US!" Al wailed. "IT'S DÉJÀ VU ALL OVER AGAIN!"

"Pull yourself together old boy!! The only way it is *déjà vu* all over again is that we most certainly will NOT die! And there are NO sharks in this sea!" Nigel shouted in the fearful cat's ear.

355

Liz and Kate huddled together under one of the wooden overhangs, giving each other comfort. "I wish Max were here," Kate said fearfully. "But then again, I'm sure he's glad he's not."

"*Mon ami,* I know Max would want to be here to protect you," Liz said. "But we will trust that the Maker will protect us all."

Peter assessed the condition of the boat. Water was pooling in the bottom despite their continual bailing, and their attempts to row against the wind were getting them nowhere except exhausted. But if they didn't row, they could be smashed against unseen rocks at the shoreline. They couldn't sail, as the wind was too strong. He estimated it was around three o'clock in the morning, so daylight was still hours away. *If only Jesus were here,* he thought. He picked up the oar, giving John a much needed rest. "We keep rowing! Pray!"

Jesus and Max stood on the beach, where the water was kicking up foam as it rolled into shore. The wind was stronger than Max had ever seen it, and his fur and ears were blowing back. He looked up at Jesus.

"You need to overcome your fear not only for your own good, but for my purposes," Jesus encouraged.

"Wha' do ye mean?" Max asked, not understanding Jesus.

"One day you will be in a far worse storm than this, and you will need to encourage one of my greatest servants to be brave," Jesus explained. "You've worked on your swimming, so give me your bravery."

Max looked at the raging sea and thought about the little boy who gave all he had to Jesus. Jesus had done the impossible with it. Max had worked on his fear, and had tried to learn to swim, but barely kept his head above water. He didn't know how he was going to do this. He was afraid. But he was tired of being afraid. And this was *Jesus* asking him to do this! Max took a deep breath.

"All r-r-right then! I give it all ta ye, Jesus! Me fears an' me doubts!" Max shouted over the din of the roaring wind. "Jest tell me wha' ta do!"

Jesus smiled and nodded in approval, reaching down to pet Max on the back. "Just follow me. I'll be with you every step of the way. But you must keep your eyes on me, not the storm."

Jesus stood and set foot off the shore, but instead of sinking into the water, he remained on top of it! Max's jaw dropped. Jesus was actually walking on the water! Max hesitated and shook his head in disbelief at what he was seeing. It was impossible that Jesus was doing this! Yet, he walked along on top of the waves.

Max gave a brisk shake all over, set his face with determination, and nodded. He lifted his front paw and held it up for a brief moment. His heart was pounding and the roar of the wind filled his ears, fueling his natural instinct to run and take cover. He closed his eyes, took a deep breath, and placed his paw on the water. It landed on a firm surface. He put his other front paw down and, again, landed on a firm surface. He brought his back paws up and they did, too. He opened his eyes and there he found himself, standing on top of the water! He was doing the impossible, just like Jesus! He was doing the impossible *because of* Jesus.

"Come on, Max!" Jesus shouted.

"Aye, time ta dr-r-own me fears," Max shouted back, keeping his eyes on Jesus, "one step at a time." He took slow, steady steps and marveled at the water kicking up all around him while he stayed firmly in place next to Jesus.

Jesus walked securely ahead, calm, cool, and collected as he traversed the waves. Max kept his eyes on Jesus and didn't allow himself to think about the roaring wind or the wild waves licking his paws.

Suddenly a fish came up next to Max and popped out of the water. "Go, Max, go!" the fish cheered and then disappeared beneath the waves.

"Were that . . .?" Max started, surprised and questioning.

"Yes, it was. Clarie loves being a fish," Jesus laughed. "When we get near the boat, you'll need to go on with her to shore. It's best the disciples don't see a dog walking on water. They'll be alarmed enough when they see me. By now they'll assume you went back to Capernaum with Gillamon and Clarie—Clarie as a donkey, that is."

"Aye, I'll do jest as ye say!" Max responded. "Ye've helped me ta do even more than the possible. Ye've helped me ta do the *im*possible!"

"Just as with the little boy's lunch, when you give me all you have, I'll give it back to you in even greater abundance," Jesus answered. "More than you could ever imagine."

"Thanks for helpin' me, Jesus," Max said. "I be a new dog then!"

"Always remember, Max. If anyone is in me, they are a new creation," Jesus said.

357

The disciples were straining against the oars, about ready to give up. Their hands were blistered, their backs were breaking, and they saw no way out of this storm. They were yelling and screaming and practically drowning in fear. Suddenly the lightning cracked and lit up the angry sky. Nigel was peering out to see if he could spot land when he saw them at that moment. He rubbed the front of his spectacles and squinted against the rain.

"By Jove, it's a miracle!" Nigel exclaimed. "Look!"

Liz and Kate timidly peered out from under the railing when another flash of lightning appeared, briefly lighting up the sky.

"*Mon Dieu!* It's Jesus!" Liz exclaimed.

"An' me Max," Kate added, then questioning, "walkin' on water?"

She and Liz shared a look of sheer amazement, shock, and awe. Al remained hidden under the bow overhang, hiding his eyes. He was too afraid to look.

"Indeed they are!" Nigel cheered, waving at Jesus and Max. Suddenly Nigel saw Max depart from Jesus and begin walking away. "But now he's walking to shore!"

"If Max is with Jesus, then Jesus has told him to do exactly that,"

Liz suggested. Then she remembered Clarie as the fish a while ago and grinned. "And I have a feeling Max isn't alone."

Suddenly the thunder boomed and another crash of lighting hit so close it rattled the boat. At that moment Peter looked up and saw Jesus walking on the water toward them. James and John also saw him and fear hit them all like another violent wave. The three men ran up to the front of the boat where the animals were but only saw Jesus.

"It's a ghost!" they said, and cried out in fear.

Immediately Jesus spoke to them with a loud, commanding voice. "Have courage! It is I! Don't be afraid."

"Lord, if it's you," Peter shouted, "command me to come to you on the water."

"Come!" Jesus said.

Peter kept his gaze on Jesus as he sat on the rim of the bow, putting his feet over the side.

"What are you doing?" John cried, gripping Peter's arm. "You'll be lost to the sea!"

358

"I'm going to the Master!" Peter argued, pulling his arm away determinedly. He put his foot down on top of the water and felt a solid surface. His heart began pounding as he set the other foot out onto the water. He stood there for a brief moment, shocked at what he was doing.

James, John, and the other disciples were all huddled together in fear and wonder of what they were witnessing. Liz, Kate, and Nigel watched from their positions, rejoicing as they saw Max trotting away on the top of the waves in the distance.

Peter started walking on the water and came toward Jesus, who stood there waiting for him. Adrenaline was coursing through Peter's veins with every step. A gust of wind came and a massive wave crashed against his legs. Peter took his gaze off Jesus and looked at the waves and the power of the wind. A wave of fear washed over him and he immediately began to sink.

"Lord, save me!" Peter cried out, holding his hand out to Jesus. He was now bobbing up and down in the waves, at times completely submerged.

Immediately Jesus reached out his hand and caught hold of Peter. "You of little faith, why did you doubt?"

Pulling Peter to his feet, Jesus wrapped his arm around the fearful man and together they walked over to the boat. As soon as Peter and Jesus climbed into the boat, the wind ceased.

The sea was immediately calm and the storm clouds receded, revealing the stars and a crescent moon. No one spoke a word for a moment as Jesus stood in the bow before them, the gentle breeze blowing his hair. Peter abruptly fell on his face, as did the others. One by one, they started saying, "Truly you are the Son of God!"

"This is the first time anyone other than demons have addressed Jesus this way," Liz noted. "The disciples have seen his power over the forces of nature twice now."

"Brilliant observation, my dear!" Nigel said. "I say, I can't wait to hear about Max's experience out on the sea."

Kate looked down to see Al still hiding with his paws over his eyes. "Al, ye can come out now. The storm be over."

Al slowly lifted one paw from his eyes, then the other. He looked around and saw that all was calm. "Sure, so Jesus showed up then?"

359

A soft pink hue gradually began to chase away the dark night sky as the boat approached the shore. Gillamon was sitting by a fire on the beach, cooking breakfast. Kate looked over the railing and there waiting on the shore for her was Max, grinning wide. Her heart leapt to see him safe and sound.

"I smell fish!" Al exclaimed as the aroma of Gillamon's breakfast drifted by on the breeze. He sat up and suddenly jumped over the side of the boat, even though they were still several yards from shore.

"Albert!" Liz said as Al landed in the water.

Al didn't walk on the water, but swam up to the beach. He shook off the water and ran right over to Gillamon, who was prepared for Al's stomach, which was evidently recovered from yesterday's fish and loaves feast.

Max closed one eye as Al's spray hit him in the face. "Thanks, a lot, lad. Did ye think ye'd walk on water when ye jumped out then?"

"Nope, I jest wanted to get to the fish," Al explained. "I can swim jest fine."

As Jesus and the disciples stepped out of the boat, they went to join Gillamon, thankful to be back on dry land.

Kate went running up to Max and they nudged heads. "Oh me love, I were worried when I first saw ye walkin' on the water! But I knew if ye were with Jesus, all would be well."

"Aye, Lass, Jesus helped me take the first steps out onto the sea. But when he told me ta get ta shore, he sent a helper so I wouldn't be alone then," Max explained.

"*C'est bon!*" Liz exclaimed. "Jesus never leaves us alone without a comforter, no? Where is Clarie?"

"Jolly good show, old boy, walking on water and all that!" Nigel congratulated Max as he scurried up to Jesus. "Tell us, how did it feel?"

"It weren't like anythin' I ever felt before," Max started. "But I guess the closest it felt like were walkin' over the soft sod of Scotland. Jesus jest took away me fear of water an' of storms. I'll never str-r-ruggle with that again!"

"Wha' a wonderful blessin'!" Kate gushed. "I'm so proud of ye for trustin' Jesus. He be the Master of the sea!"

360

"Aye, of the sea, of the storms, of the fish, of the loaves," Max continued, looking at Jesus with newfound awe. "And of me fears. He be the Master of the impossible."

"'Nothing is impossible with God.' Those are the words Gabriel spoke to Mary so long ago, and her son has proven that once again today. *Magnifique!*" Liz enthused.

Suddenly they saw Clarie the donkey come walking down the beach toward them.

"*Bonjour, mon amie!*" Liz greeted her. "You've had a busy night, no?"

Clarie winked at Max. "Hee-haw, you could say that!" She shook her head, trying to get out some water that was stuck in her ear, hitting Al.

"Clarie, Lass, why ye be so wet again?" Al asked in mid-bite of fish. "Did ye go swimmin' then?"

"Well, it appears the disciples are quietly thinking about their busy night," Nigel observed. "I say, it's terribly sad that Peter's faith failed him when he was walking to Jesus."

"Aye, but look where he were *when* he sank," Kate countered. "At least he had faith enough ta get out of the boat. I wish I could count the times I been eager ta do somethin' but me fears kept me from it."

"*Oui,* as long as Peter kept his eyes on Jesus, he didn't sink," Liz added. "But as soon as he looked at the storm instead of Jesus, he sank. This is a good lesson for us all to learn, no?"

"Aye, I'm keepin' me eyes on Jesus with ever-r-rythin' from now on," Max affirmed. "I don't plan ta ever sink again."

"Unsinkable Maximillian Braveheart the Bruce!" Nigel cheered. "Has a nice ring to it, old boy."

Max grinned, locking eyes with Jesus, who winked at him from the fire. "Aye. I think I can finally live up ta me name now."

MESSIAH

W ell, things don't seem ta be goin' well," Max growled as they travelled along with Jesus and his disciples. They were on their way to Caesarea Philippi, twenty-five miles north of the Sea of Galilee. "Between the unbelievin' people an' the hypocr-r-ritical Phar-r-risees, Jesus jest has his small band of disciples willin' ta follow him then."

Gillamon could see the frustration building in Max as well as all the animals. They needed to talk this through. "I want you to understand what Jesus is doing. After he fed the five thousand, the people followed him back to Capernaum the next day and still wanted to make him king for what he could do for them. So he gave them some tough teachings that were not only the truth of what his Kingdom is really all about, but also served their purpose by making the people fall away and stop following him. As Jesus told them, they only wanted him for the bread he could feed them. When he explained he was the Bread of Life, they couldn't understand what he meant."

"*Oui,* just like the Samaritan woman at the well, no?" Liz added. "Jesus said she would never be thirsty again as he could give her the living water. He is speaking in ways that are difficult for the people to grasp. And they most certainly did not want to hear Jesus talk about himself having come down from heaven as the Bread of Life that they must eat. He was telling them that he is going to give them life—*his* life."

"Righto, so at that point many of the people turned away and deserted Jesus," Nigel recounted. "That's when Jesus asked his twelve disciples, 'Are you also going to leave?'"

"Aye, then Peter said, 'Master, ta whom would we go then? Ye have the words of r-r-real life, eternal life. We've already committed ourselves, confident that ye be the Holy One of God,'" Max finished. "But wha' has me worried is how Jesus responded: 'I chose the twelve of ye, but one be a devil.' Who could he be talkin' aboot?"

Kate jumped in. "Jesus also had some more run-ins with those bad Pharisees from Jerusalem. They grilled him aboot his disciples not washin' up before supper an' keepin' all their other rules. Jesus let 'em have it!"

"*Oui,* and after Jesus went on to feed another crowd of four thousand with seven loaves and a few fish, the Pharisees had the gall to ask for a sign that Jesus is Messiah!" Liz interjected. "Pfft!"

"But Jesus even had to scold his disciples for not understanding him,'" Clarie reminded them. "Jesus knew his disciples were arguing about not having brought bread on the journey. They thought that's why Jesus warned them about the yeast of those men! So he said, 'Don't you understand even yet? Don't you remember the five thousand I fed with five loaves, and the baskets of leftovers you picked up? Or the four thousand I fed with seven loaves, and the large baskets of leftovers you picked up? Why can't you understand I'm not talking about bread? So again I say, 'Beware of the yeast of the Pharisees and Sadducees.'"

363

"Yes, and at last they understood he wasn't speaking about the yeast in bread, but about the deceptive teaching of the Pharisees and Sadducees," Nigel added. "But it does seem to me there is a lot of activity and discussion about bread."

"Indeed, Nigel," Gillamon said. "When Jesus broke bread for the five thousand, that was the end of his ministry in Galilee. When he broke bread for the four thousand, that was the end of his ministry in the Gentile region."

"I like it when Jesus makes bread, but it seems like when Jesus ends a ministry he breaks bread then," Al suggested. "It's the 'ends' I don't like."

The animals walked along quietly after that, thinking about what all of this could mean.

"Looks like we're here. Caesarea Philippi," Gillamon said. The animals stood and gazed up at the town and the rocky hillside rising above it.

"There is a fascinating history about this place, no?" Liz offered. "Centuries ago it was the place of Baal worship. Later the Greeks called this place 'Paneas' because it became the center of worship of the false god Pan. But Herod Antipas's brother Philip renamed it Caesarea Philippi, to honor Caesar and himself."

"Would ye look at that r-r-rock wall? Must be a hundred feet high an' five hundred feet long," Max said. "There be holes cut out everywhere."

"An' wha' be that big cave? It looks like a big, open mouth with teeth then," Kate added.

"Those are niches carved out of the rock, and in each one would be placed a wooden carving of Pan," Liz explained. "The Greeks called Pan the god of shepherds and flocks, and he was responsible for their fertility. The cave is called the 'Jaws of Death' and inside is water so deep no one has been able to even measure it. It's an abyss."

364

"Utterly dastardly deeds have taken place here," Nigel shuddered and said. "The people gathered at the cave for their chaotic worship, sacrificing animals that they threw into the mouth of the cave, hence the 'Jaws of Death.'"

"I don't think we should be here then," Al said fearfully, putting his paws to his mouth. "Why would Jesus want to come here? It's a place of death!"

Gillamon put his hand on Al's nervous back. "Don't worry, Al. Jesus has his reasons. He's come to this rock where worship of false gods was founded and has taken place for centuries. He likes to use illustrations to make his points, and what better contrast could he have than this place?"

"*Oui*, we must trust Jesus when we don't understand him," Liz consoled Al. She stared at the eerie cave and couldn't help but think that behind the entrance of those Jaws of Death was an abyss of despair. Here the people worshipped Pan, whose very name led to the word 'panic.' It was a place that was alluring but frightening to people who felt they had to sacrifice to have the favor of Pan. *All the powers of hell are at home here in this place of panic*, she thought.

Nightfall was coming and Jesus and his disciples were gathered around a fire on top of the rock wall. Every one of them knew the pagan history of this place. This was a place of evil that worshipped false gods, not the Living God. They knew that evil reigned supreme here, but Jesus chose to invade this place with his presence. Sometimes Jesus taught simply by where he brought them.

Jesus stood and asked his disciples, "Who do people say that I am?"

"Well," Andrew replied, "some say John the Baptist."

"Some say Elijah," Matthew added.

"Others say Jeremiah or one of the other prophets," Nathaniel noted.

Jesus slowly scanned the faces of these twelve men who had chosen to stay with him when others had turned away. "But who do *you* say I am?"

The men looked at one another to see who would answer first. Peter was the first to jump to his feet. "You are the Messiah, the Son of the living God."

365

Jesus smiled and walked over to Peter, placing his hand on his disciple's shoulder. "You are blessed, Simon son of John, because my Father in heaven has revealed this to you. You did not learn this from any human being. Now I say to you that you are Peter (which means 'rock'), and upon this rock I will build my church, and all the powers of hell will not conquer it. And I will give you the keys of the Kingdom of Heaven. Whatever you forbid on earth will be forbidden in heaven, and whatever you permit on earth will be permitted in heaven."

Jesus looked at his disciples. "But listen to me. You are not to tell anyone I am Messiah."

The animals were huddled together with Gillamon behind Jesus and his disciples and immediately began discussing what Peter and Jesus had just said.

"Brilliant!" Nigel enthused. "I see why Jesus brought us here. It's just rife with meaning."

"Peter be the first one ta boldly say Jesus be Messiah!" Max said with a grin.

"Aye, an' he called him the Son of the *Livin'* God," Kate remarked. "Not a false god like Pan that's worshipped here."

"Yes, and Jesus essentially told Peter, 'Since you can tell me who I am, I'll tell you who *you* are,'" Gillamon explained. "Do you understand what he said to Peter?"

"Well, he reminded Peter he is the son of a human, while Jesus is the Son of God, and that he is blessed because only God could have revealed the truth of Jesus as Messiah to him," Clarie replied.

"Oui, and he reminded him of the name he gave Simon the day they met: *Peter,* or 'rock,'" Liz added.

"You see? And look where we are—on top of this massive rock where worship of false gods was founded!" Nigel observed excitedly. "Jesus is founding the true, right worship of the *Living* God right here on top of this pagan place, taking it over. And he intends to use Peter and his belief in Messiah to build a new community of believers—his church. And nothing will be able to stop it—not the Jaws of Death or the very gates of hell! Brilliant!"

Liz's eyes lit up with revelation. "But Jesus is the cornerstone of his church, no? Do you remember what Isaiah prophesied about Messiah? 'See, I lay a stone in Zion, a tested stone, a precious cornerstone for a sure foundation; the one who relies on it will never be stricken with panic.' Do you see? With *PANIC!* Look at this place of panic! But Jesus is the cornerstone and Peter and those who build on top of him will not be stricken with panic like those who chase after Pan and other false gods! *C'est magnifique!"*

Gillamon's eyebrows were raised with delight at the animals' observations. "Well done, Liz and Nigel!"

"Aye, ye're one smart mouse an' kitty," Max said with a smile. "But wha' aboot the keys then? Is Peter the only one who gets them?"

"The keys, I believe, are the words of Scripture that God originally gave the authority of interpreting to the scribes, who were to unlock their meaning for the people," Liz replied. "Since Jesus has called these twelve to replace the old system and is founding his church based on the Good News, he is giving Peter that authority to interpret Jesus' teachings as Messiah. He is giving Peter these keys because of what he just confessed."

"Aye, but if others confess Jesus as Messiah, wouldn't he want them ta spr-r-read the word aboot him, too?" Kate asked.

"For followers of Jesus, their lives and message of good news will unlock the Kingdom of God for the salvation of many," Gillamon assured her.

366

Jesus' face grew serious. He was about to tell his disciples something he had not yet shared, and he knew it would be difficult for them to hear.

"From here we will begin to head toward Jerusalem," Jesus started. He paused a moment and looked at their faces. "I will suffer many terrible things at the hands of the elders, the leading priests, and the teachers of religious law. They will kill me, but on the third day I will be raised from the dead."

Peter's eyes widened and anger overtook him. He put his hand on Jesus' arm and reprimanded him. "Heaven forbid, Lord," he said. "This will never happen to you!"

Jesus turned his gaze to Peter and peered deeply into his eyes. "Get behind me, Satan! You are a stumbling block to me; for you are not setting your mind on God's interests, but man's."

Then Jesus turned and looked around at all his disciples. "If any of you wants to be my follower, you must turn from your selfish ways, take up your cross, and follow me. If you try to hang on to your life, you will lose it. But if you give up your life for my sake, you will save it. And what do you benefit if you gain the whole world but lose your own soul? Is anything worth more than your soul? For the Son of Man will come with his angels in the glory of his Father and will judge all people according to their deeds. And I tell you the truth, some standing here right now will not die before they see the Son of Man coming in his Kingdom."

Shock swept through the disciples, but none moreso than Peter. Only moments before, Jesus had praised him as the rock on which Jesus would build his church. Now he was calling him Satan! Peter shrank back in shame for how he had answered Jesus' disturbing announcement.

"Is Peter the Devil Jesus has talked about being one of the twelve then?" Al asked, clearly confused.

"No, Al, but Peter has just learned an important thing about Satan," Gillamon responded. "He's learned that Satan can fill his mouth just as easily as God can fill it. It's a harsh rebuke, but Peter needs to learn this hard lesson with the responsibility Jesus has given him."

"Indeed, if Peter thinks on the things of men rather than the things of God, or doesn't do the will of God, as Jesus must certainly do, he could be used as an instrument of the enemy," Nigel said with deep seriousness.

"So the rock be a stumblin' block now?" Al questioned, still unclear.

"What Jesus means is that Peter is playing the part of the tempter, trying to sway Jesus away from being obedient to what he must do in Jerusalem," Gillamon explained.

"Aye, but Jesus didn't mention his death without mentionin' his r-r-resurr-r-rection then," Max observed.

"That's right, Max. Jesus is getting the disciples ready as they head to Jerusalem. So he told them who he is and what he is going to do," Gillamon told his friend.

"But why did Jesus tell his disciples not ta tell anyone he be Messiah?" Kate asked.

"People do not understand the real nature and mission of Messiah," Liz replied. "The Jews have expected Messiah to be victorious and powerful, not a suffering, slain Messiah."

"Aye, even Peter don't get why Jesus must do wha' he must do. That's why he told Jesus he mustn't die," Max added.

"If Jesus' own disciples don't fully understand his role as Messiah, you can see how the people at large certainly don't," Nigel said with his paws clasped behind his back. "That's why Jesus told them not to tell the people. They aren't able to fully understand."

"So, when will everyone finally be able to understand who Jesus really be as Messiah?" Al asked.

Liz looked lovingly at Jesus, her heart catching in her throat as she realized the time for Jesus' death was fast approaching. The heartache she felt at what was coming made her eyes brim with tears. Jesus would have to endure the burden he faced without anyone understanding him. He would have to bear it all alone.

"Not until the third day," Liz whispered softly. "No one will really understand Messiah until the third day."

368

CRESCENDO TO THE FINALE

45

ᴀND THE ᴳLORY OF THE ᴸORD

"I s there something we should see, Gillamon?" Liz asked.
"I think you will be enlightened by what you see," Gillamon replied
with a twinkle in his eye. "You two need to follow them. We'll
remain here with the others."

"If you insist, old boy, of course," Nigel replied. Then turning to
Liz, "Shall we, my dear?"

"Bien sûr, mon ami," Liz replied.

They began the ascent up the mountain where Jesus walked ahead.
Peter, James, and John were with him and he led them high up on a
hillside where they were entirely alone. Liz and Nigel stayed out of sight,
but watched as Jesus found a place to pray. The three disciples sat nearby
but soon drifted off to sleep.

"Have you noticed that Jesus has brought just these three along
with him on other occasions?" Nigel posed. "I believe they are his inner
circle."

"Oui, they are the ones who will lead the disciples, but also perhaps
the ones who need the most attention," Liz replied. "Jesus certainly has
modeled for them how important it is to get away and pray."

Nigel nodded and smoothed his whiskers. "Indeed, even the Son of
God is dependent on prayer so he is prepared for his daily challenges."

"But the disciples are *sleeping,* not praying!" Liz noticed. "I am sure

Jesus did not bring them up here to sleep. I wonder what it is that Gillamon . . ." Liz stopped mid-sentence.

Nigel looked at Liz and saw that definite look of her studying something with intensity. "What is it, my pet?" He turned to look in the direction of her gaze. "Do you see something . . . ?" Nigel also stopped mid-sentence.

The two sat for a silent moment as they stared at Jesus. While he was praying, the whole appearance of his face changed and his clothes became white and dazzling. The brightness surrounded Jesus and suddenly two men were standing in the middle of the light, talking with him.

"Jesus is radiating his full glory, from the inside out! Brilliant!" Nigel exclaimed. "And I daresay, that is Moses there with him!" he added, adjusting his spectacles to make sure he was getting a clear picture.

"And Elijah!" Liz added. "Both men are in their heavenly splendor, no? *Magnifique!*"

372

Liz and Nigel listened to Jesus' conversation with Moses and Elijah, and looked at one another in awe.

"They are talking about the path Jesus must take and the end he must accomplish in Jerusalem," Nigel said somberly.

"*Oui,* just as Moses's exodus led the people from the bondage of slavery, Jesus' exodus will lead people from the bondage of sin and death," shared Liz. "How incredible that Moses and Elijah would come to bring Jesus encouragement."

Suddenly Peter awoke, then rubbed his eyes when he saw Jesus ablaze in his heavenly glory, with Moses and Elijah standing there. He hit James and John, who awoke with a start. The three men were awestruck with the transfiguration taking place before them, not knowing what to do or say.

When it looked as if Moses and Elijah were getting ready to depart from Jesus, Peter jumped up and exclaimed, "Master, it is wonderful for us to be here! Let us put up three shelters—one for you, one for Moses, and one for Elijah."

"What in the world could he *possibly* mean by that?" Nigel asked incredulously. "How utterly ridiculous to suggest building three shelters, especially for heavenly beings! What is he thinking?"

"*Oui,* but Peter did not know what he was saying," Liz replied. "He cannot resist an opportunity for a speech, no? Still, I wonder how he knew it was Moses and Elijah. We know them, of course, because we've met them. But Peter? Hmmmm."

Suddenly the fire cloud appeared and awe swept over them all as it enveloped them. A Voice came out of the cloud, saying, "THIS IS MY DEARLY-LOVED SON. LISTEN TO HIM!"

"The Maker!" Nigel whispered hoarsely. "Now the Father has rebuked poor Peter!"

"*Oui,* and he said the same thing he said at Jesus' baptism," Liz softly noted. "The Maker is telling the disciples they still must follow Jesus and obey him, even as he heads to Jerusalem . . . to die."

And while the Voice was speaking, suddenly no one was there in the brilliant glory but Jesus. He stood before them, and the disciples were reduced to silence, shaking with having heard the voice of God and with the glory of the Lord shining over them.

Suddenly the words from Isaiah came to Liz: "And the glory of the Lord shall be revealed, and all flesh shall see it together: for the mouth of the Lord hath spoken it," she quoted softly.

373

"And the glo-ry, the glory of the Lord," Nigel echoed in a melodic voice, "shall be re-vealed." He stopped and wrinkled his brow, putting a paw up to his forehead. "I say, why did I sing that verse of Scripture?"

"I think seeing the glory of the Lord has that effect, no?" Liz said, placing her paw on Nigel's back. "But it was lovely, *mon ami.*"

"Thank you, my dear," Nigel said, draping his paw humbly over his chest.

As Jesus' appearance began to return to its normal, human state, the disciples' fear lessened.

"You must not tell anyone what you have just seen until I have risen from the dead," Jesus instructed them. He began walking down the hillside, the men following him.

Peter, James, and John looked at one another and silently agreed they would not breathe a word. John mouthed, *"What does rising from the dead mean?"* But neither Peter nor James had an answer.

Together they walked along silently until finally they asked Jesus, "Why do the teachers of religious law insist that Elijah must return before the Messiah comes?"

Jesus responded, "Elijah is indeed coming first to get everything ready. Yet why do the Scriptures say the Son of Man must suffer greatly and be treated with utter contempt? But I tell you, Elijah has already come, and they chose to abuse him, just as the Scriptures predicted."

The disciples silently pondered this, but all finally understood that indeed John the Baptist was 'Elijah' returned as foretold in Scripture. Jesus was telling them he would be treated just as John was, and this also was foretold in Scripture.

Suddenly a deep revelation hit Liz as she pondered the Scriptures about John the Baptist. "John was the forerunner of Messiah in more ways than we realized. He told people Messiah was coming. But John didn't come to prevent Messiah's suffering and death," Liz said with deep emotion, "he foreshadowed it with his own."

The next morning they rejoined the other disciples at the base of the mountain. They were surrounded by a large crowd, and some of the scribes were arguing with them.

"Looks like more trouble from the Sanhedrin," Nigel scoffed. Liz and Nigel ran over to where Gillamon sat with the other animals.

"Was your time on the mountain illuminating?" Gillamon asked with a wink.

"Oui, très brilliante!" Liz replied.

"Jesus is indeed the Light of the world!" Nigel reported. "I daresay Peter wanted to stay on the mountain."

"I'm sure he did," Gillamon replied, turning his eyes to the unruly crowd. "But you can't make those mountaintop experiences last forever. The valleys always await."

As soon as the people saw Jesus, they ran forward excitedly to welcome him. The nine disciples who had remained behind stood around, looking defeated by the shouting crowd.

"What is all this arguing about?" Jesus demanded, looking from his disciples to the people.

One of the men in the crowd stepped forward. He spoke up and, pointing to the disciples, explained, "Teacher, I brought my son so you could heal him. He is possessed by an evil spirit that won't let him talk. And whenever this spirit seizes him, it throws him violently to the ground. Then he foams at the mouth and grinds his teeth and

374

becomes rigid. So I asked your disciples to cast out the evil spirit, but they couldn't do it."

The disciples looked at the ground in defeat. Jesus shook his head in frustration. He had given them full authority over all demons, so they had his power at their disposal. When he sent them out to the surrounding region they had succeeded in casting out demons. This time, however, they failed.

"You faithless people! How long must I be with you? How long must I put up with you?" Jesus chastised. "Bring the boy to me."

The disciples brought the man's son, who was sitting alone on a rock. But when the evil spirit saw Jesus, it threw the child into a violent convulsion, and he fell to the ground, writhing and foaming at the mouth.

Jesus wrinkled his brow as he studied the boy. He turned to the boy's father. "How long has this been happening?"

"Since he was a little boy," the father replied, his voice breaking in despair. "The spirit often throws him into the fire or into water, trying to kill him. Have mercy on us and help us, if you can."

"What do you mean, *'If I can'?*" Jesus asked incredulously. "Anything is possible if a person believes."

The father instantly cried out and fell to his knees, clasping his hands up to his chin, "I do believe, but help me overcome my unbelief!"

Jesus saw that the crowd of onlookers was growing. He needed to free this boy and be on his way. "Listen, you spirit that makes this boy unable to hear and speak," he ordered the demon. "I command you to come out of this child and never enter him again!"

The spirit screamed and threw the boy into another violent convulsion and left him. The boy appeared to be dead. His brown, curly hair was wet with sweat, and foam covered his chin. He lay there, motionless.

A murmur ran through the crowd. "He's dead," they said. But he was far from dead.

Jesus walked over to the boy, knelt down, and took him by the hand to help him to his feet. The boy stood up and the crowd gasped in awe. The father ran over and embraced his son with unspeakable joy and relief. He picked him up and clutched him to his chest, carrying him away from the crowd, kissing him repeatedly on the cheek. The scribes folded their arms and wore frowns just as somber as when

375

the boy *wasn't* healed. They soon began walking away as the crowd dispersed.

"Finally those scr-r-ribes be as quiet as the lad," Max said with a growl. "I'm aboot sick an' tired of them."

"I'm sure they would be speechless, too, if they had seen what we saw on the mountain," Nigel chuckled.

"Wha' happened up there?" Kate asked happily. "Seems like ye had a grand experience."

"Kate, my dear, we saw a glimpse of Jesus' glory that is masked by his human form," Nigel tried to explain, his paws raised in wonder.

"*Oui*, and Moses and Elijah were there on the mountain talking with Jesus," Liz added, drawing looks of astonishment from the others.

"Were they in the IAMISPHERE?" Al asked. "Did they show up in one piece?"

Nigel chuckled warmly. "Not the IAMISPHERE this time, old boy. They just appeared in radiant glory. But then the fire cloud appeared!"

"Ye don't say! The Maker were there, too?" Max asked with a wide-eyed grin.

"*Oui*, and he once again said Jesus is his beloved son, and that the disciples should listen to him."

"How grand that ye got ta see them all!" Kate enthused. "But why did all that happen? Why Moses an' Elijah?"

"From what we can deduce, Moses represents the Law, and Elijah the Prophets," Liz explained. "Jesus has come to fulfill both, and gave these three disciples in his inner circle a glimpse of who he really is. But he warned them once again not to tell the others what happened until his resurrection."

"I don't think Peter, James, and John could even *begin* to explain what they saw," Gillamon suggested. "But this glimpse will give them hope when all hope is gone, whether they realize it or not. It's burned on their hearts."

Later the nine disciples surrounded Jesus, begging to know what had happened. "Why couldn't we cast out that evil spirit?"

"This kind can be cast out only by prayer," Jesus replied. "You don't have enough faith. I tell you the truth, if you had faith even as small as a mustard seed, you could say to this mountain, 'Move from here to there,' and it would move. Nothing would be impossible."

"And this is why he keeps showing you how important prayer is, no?" Liz directed at the disciples, her paw up in the air. "Next time try *praying* rather than *sleeping.*"

"Aye, I think the laddies need a lesson or two in pr-r-rayin' then," Max said. "With all that's comin' they're goin' ta need it. A lot of it."

Nigel was sitting by himself, bobbing his head, humming and softly singing, "And the glory, the glory of the Lord shall be revealed . . . for the mouth of the Lord hath spo-ken it." Al came over and plopped down next to him.

"What ye hummin', Mousie?" Al asked.

"Sounds like a nice tune," Clarie added, smiling as she walked up.

"Huh?" Nigel replied mindlessly. "Oh, Liz and I witnessed another of Isaiah's prophecies fulfilled up on the mountain, and for some reason I just keep singing it. You must think me daft!"

"Not at all," Clarie said with a knowing grin. "Why do you think the angels sing all the time?"

377

"Jolly good point, my dear!" Nigel said. "They see the glory of the Lord all the time. If anyone is worthy to be sung about, it certainly is Messiah!"

Gillamon and Clarie shared a wink. "Nigel, you have no idea."

FISHY MONEY AND INFINITE FORGIVENESS

I t was time to start making their way toward Jerusalem, traveling back through Galilee. Jesus didn't want anyone to know he was there, for he wanted to spend more time teaching his disciples. Since many people had fallen away after Jesus' hard teaching, the crowds seeking to follow him everywhere he went had diminished. But there still were those who sought Jesus out for healing. And he never refused them.

As they made the turn toward Capernaum, Jesus told his disciples for the third time what was to come when they reached Jerusalem. "The Son of Man is going to be betrayed into the hands of his enemies. He will be killed, but three days later he will rise from the dead."

No one said a word.

"Did they not hear him then?" Max grumbled.

"*Oui,* they heard him. But they didn't truly understand what he was saying," Liz replied.

"Right, but I believe they were afraid to ask him what he meant," Nigel offered. "After all, Jesus gave Peter quite an unsettling rebuke when he spoke against Jesus' first announcement."

"But this time did you notice what he added?" Liz asked. "He said he would be *betrayed.* This should be further cause for alarm and questioning."

"I want ta know who it be," Max growled, looking down the row of disciples as they walked along. "It's got ta be one of these then."

"Max, remember what Jesus told you," Gillamon cautioned.

Max hung his head and looked away. "Aye, when his time comes, I've got ta let it come. Aye."

After a while the disciples did start talking among themselves. Max wanted to know what they were saying so he snuck up underfoot. What he heard, especially after Jesus' announcement, made his fur stand on end in anger. He stomped back to Gillamon and the animals.

"Ye will NOT believe wha' those laddies be talkin' aboot!" Max growled.

"What is it, Max?" Clarie asked.

Max shook his head. "They be ar-r-rguin' aboot who will be the gr-r-reatest in the Kingdom of heaven! As if they didn't alr-r-ready know, an' this after Jesus jest told 'em he's goin' ta be betr-r-rayed an' DIE?!"

"Steady, Max," Kate encouraged.

"Utterly dastardly discussion!" Nigel railed. "Do these chaps not understand what is going on about *anything*? How dare they get so cheeky when Jesus is facing his end!"

"Calm down, *mes amis,*" Liz urged. "If I know Jesus, he won't let this conversation slide by without adding his own comments, no?"

Everyone at Peter's house was happy to welcome Jesus and the disciples back. Mary Magdalene was especially happy to see everyone in Capernaum, safe and sound.

"We're preparing a wonderful feast tonight!" Mary Magdalene exclaimed. "But we'll be sure to only have our small group and not the entire town."

"Thank you, Mary," Jesus said. "We'll look forward to it after our long journey. And thank you for keeping the dinner party small." He gave her a big smile and squeezed her arm.

"Don't expect twelve baskets of leftovers, unless you're doing the cooking," Mary Magdalene said as she went to help the other ladies with the food.

Jesus threw his head back laughing with the others as they washed the dust off their feet.

Peter was outside with Gillamon and the animals when the collectors of the Temple tax came up to him. "Your master doesn't pay Temple tax, we presume?" they asked with a condescending tone.

Peter's head snapped up and he felt the anger rising in him at this question by these sniveling spies. "Oh, yes, he does!" Peter replied and stormed off inside, leaving the men there. He was trying to work on his temper and felt he'd best just leave before he said too much.

The men put their heads together and whispered as they walked away. Max stood with his tail out and a low growl in his throat.

"Wha's a Temple tax?" Kate asked.

"Jewish men between the ages of twenty and fifty are expected to pay the two-drachma tax for the upkeep of the Temple as prescribed by the Law of Moses," Liz explained. "It is also known as an atonement tax for the soul. It is about two days' wages, but since there isn't a coin in this amount, two men will often pay their tax with a single shekel."

"Ye mean the laddies think they can pay for salvation with a *coin?*" Max grumbled.

380

"The religious leaders from Jerusalem have been following Jesus' tracks over the past year, and I suspect they are looking for yet another way to find him at fault," Nigel interjected. "Officially ordained rabbis are exempt from the tax, but Jesus is certainly not officially ordained."

"Not by humans!" Kate snapped. "Jesus be ordained by the Maker!"

"Aye, an' Jesus be the last person needin' an atonement then!" Max added. "He *be* the atonement!"

"I wish to see how Peter will handle this," Liz said, walking away from the rest of the group. Nigel scurried along beside her.

Gillamon took Clarie by the reins and started walking toward the sea, leaving Max, Kate, and Al sitting there. "We'll be back."

"Where're they goin'?" Al wondered.

"Ye never know with those two," Kate told him.

Peter was inside, trying to think how he should discuss this tax matter with Jesus. But before he had a chance to speak, Jesus looked up at him and immediately asked, "What do you think, Peter? Do kings tax their own people or the people they have conquered?"

Jesus' question caught Peter off guard. *How did he know I was going to ask him about this?* Peter wondered silently, then uttered a reply: "They tax the people they have conquered."

"Well, then," Jesus said, "the citizens are free! However, we don't want to offend them, so go down to the lake and throw in a line. Open the mouth of the first fish you catch, and you will find a large silver coin. Take it and pay the tax for both of us."

Peter's mouth was open like the fish he was supposed to catch. This was by far the strangest request Jesus had ever made of him. He shook his head in confusion, but knew he must do as Jesus asked. "Very well," he answered and went out the door, grabbing a fishing line and a hook. Al took off behind him, as he knew he and Peter were going fishing.

Liz and Nigel rejoined the others outside and didn't notice that Gillamon, Clarie, and Al were gone.

"Brilliant! Jesus knows how to handle each and every situation, even before we ask!" Nigel cheered.

"So wha' happened in there?" Kate asked.

"Jesus explained to Peter that although he is not obligated to pay the tax because he and his followers are children of the King, he would pay it so the collectors would not be offended," Liz reported. "He is paying the tax not for his sake but for theirs, to keep them from stumbling in believing in him should they allow their hearts and minds to be open to him. He will not give them a reason to doubt based on his not upholding the laws of Moses. *Oui,* he is brilliant!"

"So Peter's goin' ta pay the tax?" Max asked.

Nigel chuckled. "Yes, and he will pay it with fishy money! Jesus told Peter to go throw a line into the sea and the first fish he catches will have the needed coin to pay the tax in its mouth."

Max broke out in a big grin. "I love the way Jesus be handlin' this, by givin' the tax laddies their stinkin' money!"

"Jesus doesn't mean it like that, Max!" Kate scolded.

"Aye, I know but it makes me laugh ta think of that coin in their hands an' they won't know where it's been then," Max snickered.

"Where did Al, Clarie, and Gillamon go?" Liz asked, looking around.

"Gillamon and Clarie left a while ago, sayin' they'd be back," Kate explained. "They didn't say where they be goin'."

"An' that daft kitty went tr-r-r-ottin' off with Peter, pr-r-robably wantin' ta eat the fish he catches then," Max added.

Liz and Nigel looked at one another and said at the same time, "Clarie!"

Peter was at the water's edge before Liz, Nigel, Max, and Kate saw him and Al standing on the shore. As they were running to intercept Al from trying to eat Peter's catch, Gillamon stopped them. He was sitting on some rocks up from the shoreline.

"Gillamon, is Clarie doing what we think she's doing?" Nigel asked nervously.

"If you mean delivering a coin to Peter, then yes," Gillamon replied calmly, gazing out to sea.

"But Al is there with Peter!" Liz said with alarm.

"Don't ye think we should stop the kitty then?" Max asked. "He's bound ta want ta eat anythin' Peter pulls out of the sea."

"I think Clarie can handle herself with Al," Gillamon said with a wink. "Stay and watch."

Against their better judgment they agreed to sit with Gillamon and watch the scene unfold.

"Who would ever have thought to fish for money?" Peter asked as he threw the line into the water. "But you don't care about the coin, you only care about the fish, don't you, cat?"

"*Aye!*" Al meowed enthusiastically.

"I'm glad I decided to follow Jesus and leave my fishing business when I did," Peter teased. "You would have eaten all my profits up anyway."

Suddenly Peter's hand lurched forward as a fish took the hook. He immediately pulled quickly to set the hook. "Got one!" He pulled it in, the fish thrashing about on the surface of the water. Al started purring.

"Let's hope it's *the* one," Peter said as he lifted the beautiful white fish out of the water. He held it by the back and noticed its unusual eyes. "Blue eyes? I've never seen a fish with eyes this color before! Fish always have black eyes. Strange."

Peter gently pried the hook out of the corner of the fish's mouth. "Now let's see if it's got the coin." As Peter slowly opened the fish's mouth, sitting there just as Jesus told him it would be was the silver shekel! "Only the Son of God could arrange this!" Peter exclaimed as he reached in and took the coin. "I'm actually going to enjoy paying this tax, cat!"

Al sat eagerly waiting for the fish, drool coming out of his mouth. "Okay, here you go, cat," Peter said as he placed the fish on the sandy beach for Al and stood to go pay the tax with the fishy coin.

"Thanks, lad!" Al meowed. As he walked over to the fish, who by now was flopping in the surf, he reached out his paws to lift it to his hungry mouth. "Come to me, me precious!"

Al opened wide but the fish slapped him in the face, sending him falling backward into the sand. "IF YOU SO MUCH AS LICK MY SCALES I'LL TURN INTO A SHARK AND EAT YOU UP RIGHT HERE ON THE BEACH!" Clarie shouted.

Al's eyes grew wide with fear as he watched the fish flopping around until it got into the current to swim away. "But Mousie told me there weren't shark beasties in this sea!"

Clarie gave a final splash with her fin to send water flying in Al's face. He sat there in the soggy sand, water dripping down his whiskers and left with the humiliation of being defeated by a talking fish. He looked around when he heard laughter behind him from up the beach. Al frowned. Max had seen it all.

383

Max was rolling on the sand, laughing his head off as Al walked forlornly up to them. "I guess she showed ye, lad!"

"She? Who?" Al asked.

"My dear boy, have you no idea that the fish you just attempted to eat was none other than Clarie?" Nigel said with a chuckle.

Al put his paws to his mouth and his eyes grew wide with shock. "I thought I were eatin' a fish, not a little lamb then!"

Nigel placed his paw on Al's disturbed form. "No harm done, old chap. That makes two of us who have escaped your jaws of death!"

Al grinned weakly as Nigel made him remember the day they first met in the market in Egypt. Nigel nearly became his breakfast until Liz put a stop to it, liberating Nigel from Al's mouth. "Sorry again aboot that, Mousie," Al muttered.

"Well, I for one am relieved to know that Clarie can handle any beast she meets in the Sea of Galilee," Liz said, petting Al on the cheek. "Even you, my love."

Later back at Peter's house, the disciples were refreshed and reclining around the table after enjoying the wonderful meal prepared by the women. Gillamon and the animals were sitting quietly in the back of the room with some children.

Jesus asked his disciples, "What were you discussing out on the road?" No one responded because they were embarrassed that they had been discussing who would be greatest in the Kingdom.

"I knew it, no?" Liz exclaimed. "Jesus wasn't about to let them off so easy."

"Whoever wants to be first must take last place and be the servant of everyone else," Jesus began, answering the question.

"Who is greatest in the Kingdom of Heaven?" John asked.

Some children were giggling as they played together on the floor. Jesus smiled and called one of them over to him, placing him where all the disciples could see him. "I tell you the truth, unless you turn from your sins and become like little children, you will never get into the Kingdom of Heaven. So anyone who becomes as humble as this little child is the greatest in the Kingdom of Heaven."

"Oh, how he loves the wee lads an' lassies!" Kate said happily. "They be the most important ones ta him, even though adults don't think anythin' aboot them in this culture, jest like lassies."

"Oui, mon amie," Liz agreed and smiled. "Lassie power and wee one power, no?"

"And anyone who welcomes a little child like this on my behalf is welcoming me," Jesus continued. "But if you cause one of these little ones who trusts in me to fall into sin, it would be better for you to have a large millstone tied around your neck and be drowned in the depths of the sea."

"That's some fierce love then!" Max said.

Jesus continued, "What sorrow awaits the world, because it tempts people to sin. Temptations are inevitable, but what sorrow awaits the person who does the tempting. So if your hand or foot causes you to sin, cut it off and throw it away. It's better to enter eternal life with only one hand or one foot than to be thrown into eternal fire with both of your hands and feet. And if your eye causes you to sin, gouge it out and throw it away. It's better to enter eternal life with only one eye than to have two eyes and be thrown into the fire of hell."

"Aye, and that be some fierce teachin'!" Al added nervously.

"Jesus doesn't mean to literally do those things, old boy," Nigel explained. "He's simply making a point of how very seriously we need to take temptation."

"Beware that you don't look down on any of these little ones. For I tell you that in heaven their angels are always in the presence of my heavenly Father," Jesus added. "If a man has a hundred sheep and one of them wanders away, what will he do? Won't he leave the ninety-nine others on the hills and go out to search for the one that is lost? And if he finds it, I tell you the truth, he will rejoice over it more than over the ninety-nine that didn't wander away! In the same way, it is not my heavenly Father's will that even one of these little ones should perish."

"Children are important enough to have the attention of angels, Jesus, and the Maker," Gillamon observed with a smile as Jesus gave the little boy a big hug. "He's given these humans much to consider, as children are overlooked in this culture. But his warning is severe if anyone causes them to stumble."

385

Peter's mind was thinking about what Jesus said about not causing even the tax collectors to stumble in their possible belief in him. He struggled with his anger over the tax collectors and those who were out to hurt Jesus. "Lord, how often should I forgive someone who sins against me? Seven times?"

"No, not seven times," Jesus replied, "but seventy times seven!"

Peter's eyes widened, as did those of all the other disciples. This was a radical new way of thinking.

"*Oooh-la-la!* Jesus has shocked them with this truth," Liz said. "Rabbis ruled that no one should forgive more than three times, so Peter thought he was being a rather large person to offer more than twice that much forgiveness."

"Four hundred ninety times be a lot of forgivin'," Kate said, doing the math.

"I believe Jesus' equation really means unlimited forgiveness," Nigel suggested.

Jesus went on, "The Kingdom of Heaven can be compared to a king who decided to bring his accounts up to date with servants who had borrowed money from him. In the process, one of his debtors was brought in who owed him millions of dollars. He couldn't pay, so his master ordered that he be sold—along with his wife, his children, and everything he owned—to pay the debt.

"But the man fell down before his master and begged him, 'Please, be patient with me, and I will pay it all.' Then his master was filled with pity for him, and he released him and forgave his debt. But when the man left the king, he went to a fellow servant who owed him a few thousand dollars. He grabbed him by the throat and demanded instant payment.

"His fellow servant fell down before him and begged for a little more time. 'Be patient with me, and I will pay it,' he pleaded. But his creditor wouldn't wait. He had the man arrested and put in prison until the debt could be paid in full. When some of the other servants saw this, they were very upset. They went to the king and told him everything that had happened. Then the king called in the man he had forgiven and said, 'You evil servant! I forgave you that tremendous debt because you pleaded with me. Shouldn't you have mercy on your fellow servant, just as I had mercy on you?' Then the angry king sent the man to prison to be tortured until he had paid his entire debt. That's what my heavenly Father will do to you if you refuse to forgive your brothers and sisters from your heart."

386

"Jesus is teaching a difficult truth," Liz said. "We will never be able to pay our debt of sin, so we are forgiven by grace. Because of that, we must forgive others in turn. If not, we will be just like the unforgiving servant."

"Gillamon, is Clarie back yet, as a donkey?" Al asked. He was thinking about the lost sheep parable and now the forgiveness lesson.

"She should be out in the courtyard," Gillamon replied. "Why?"

"I got to tell the lass I be sorry for almost eatin' her then," Al said.

"That's a good kitty," Max said with a burly paw on Al's shoulder. "Always make it r-r-right when ye aboot eat someone." Kate gave Max a disapproving frown as Al walked off to find Clarie.

"I mean when ye hurt them then," Max called after him, correcting himself. He smiled at Kate and gave her a wink. She shook her head at her teasing mate.

"Well, Al has apologized for nearly eating me, and now for nearly eating Clarie," Nigel chuckled. "Two down out of our seven. Let's hope for your sakes that Al doesn't have to ask for seven times the forgiveness!"

THE PEOPLE WHO
WALKED IN DARKNESS

I t's the seventh day of this Festival of Tabernacles," Nigel noted. "Jesus has certainly stirred the waters with the Sanhedrin this week in Jerusalem, but I suspect more is coming."

"Speakin' o' water, why do the priest laddies keep spillin' water all over the Temple floor?" Al asked, shaking his soggy back paws off. Gillamon had the animals tucked away in an alcove but there they could still see everything going on.

"The Festival of Tabernacles is one of three festivals that Jewish men are required to attend each year," Nigel explained, straightening his spectacles. "First is the Passover, which celebrates the night the Angel of Death passed over the nation of Israel, at that time called the Hebrews, sparing their firstborn sons, and allowing Israel to leave Egypt. Second is Pentecost, which celebrates Moses getting the law on Mount Sinai, fifty days after the Exodus. Third is this festival, which celebrates Israel's deliverance from Egypt, when they lived in tents while they traveled the wilderness, and depended on the Maker for food and water. *Ergo*, the pouring of the water symbolizes the Maker's provision for them in the wilderness."

"*Oui,* and on the seventh day, today, they pour out seven times as

387

much water," Liz added. "This is why there is 'water, water everywhere,' as William Frog once said on the Ark."

"Aye, Jesus be standin' ankle deep in it," Max observed.

Jesus looked down at the water rushing past his feet. He lifted his gaze and saw the multitude of people roaming the streets of Jerusalem, and his heart was full of love for them. He felt a surge of emotion and suddenly cried out, "If anyone thirsts, let him come to me and drink. Rivers of living water will brim and spill out of the depths of anyone who believes in me this way, just as the Scripture says."

Those in the crowd stopped and murmured among themselves, but they were split over who Jesus was.

"This has to be the Prophet," some said.

"He is Messiah!" others claimed.

But others were saying, "Messiah doesn't come from Galilee, does he? Don't the Scriptures tell us that the Messiah comes from David's line and from Bethlehem, David's village?"

388

"Would ye listen ta these people?" Kate scoffed. "Don't they know Jesus were born in Bethlehem?"

"I'm afraid not, *mon ami*," Liz said. "All they know is that he is from Galilee, so that is why they are confused."

"Why don't they ask him?" Kate lamented.

"If only they would," Liz replied sadly as she watched the Temple guards who had been standing by suddenly leave.

"Why didn't you bring him with you?" Zeeb demanded to know when the Temple guards came to give their daily report of Jesus' activity.

"Have you heard the way he talks?" the Temple guard replied, looking at the others for backup. "We've never heard anyone speak like this man."

Saar slapped his fist on the table. "Are you carried away like the rest of the rabble? You don't see any of the leaders believing in him, do you? Or any from the Pharisees? It's only this crowd, ignorant of God's Law, taken in by him—and damned."

Nicodemus couldn't remain quiet any longer. He had been listening and watching all week. He knew the Sanhedrin wanted to arrest Jesus, and he feared they wanted him dead. "Does our Law decide about a man's guilt without first listening to him and finding out what he is doing?"

"Are you also campaigning for the Galilean?" Jarib snapped at the wiser, older Nicodemus. "Examine the evidence. See if any prophet ever comes from Galilee."

Nahshon stood. "The day is coming to a close. Let us go home for the night and think on what we should do."

As Nicodemus and the others filed out of the room, Nahshon called Zeeb aside and whispered in his ear. "I have a plan for tomorrow. It's a trap I think we can use to catch him red-handed."

Zeeb's eyebrows went up and he smiled wickedly. "I'm listening."

After a night spent with his disciples on the Mount of Olives, Jesus went back to the Temple again. He went to the Women's Court, where swarms of people came to him, and he was in the middle of teaching them when a scuffle was heard in the back of the crowd.

"Let go of me!" the woman screamed.

389

Peter, John, and Matthew stood immediately to see what was happening. Coming toward them was the same group of scribes and Pharisees, dragging a half-dressed woman across the cobblestones. Her hair was a mess and she struggled to fix her clothes as the men callously threw her down in front of Jesus. The crowds craned their necks to see the woman, and murmuring rippled throughout the crowd. People began to pick up rocks, ready for what was coming. The woman scurried to the wall and hid her face in her hands, beginning to weep. Jesus kept his gaze on the Pharisees.

"Teacher, this woman was caught red-handed in the act of adultery. Moses, in the Law, gives orders to stone such persons. What do you say?" Zeeb demanded to know. He and the others wore smug looks of superiority.

Jesus bent down and slowly wrote with his finger in the dirt, quietly ignoring the men.

"What is he writing?" Liz whispered to Nigel.

"I intend to find out," Nigel said as he scurried up the wall to a vantage point where he could read what Jesus had written.

Saar stepped forward, gripping a stone so tightly in his hand that his knuckles turned white. "Well?! What do you have to say?"

"Where's the man she were caught with is wha' *I* want ta know," Kate whispered to Liz.

"This is a setup," Liz said with a frown, her tail whipping back and forth. "They don't care about enforcing the law or stoning the woman. They want to stone Jesus." Liz looked up and Nigel gave her a nod. He was coming down.

"Look at how Jesus won't even look at her, to add to her shame," Liz observed. "He is dismissing the case."

Nigel scurried up to Liz and Kate. "Names. He's writing names. Men's names and women's names. I could make out 'Zeeb' and 'Saar' among them, so he's trying to make a point with this poor woman's accusers."

Suddenly a verse came to Liz. "Jesus is fulfilling the words of Jeremiah! 'Lord, you are the hope of Israel; all who forsake you will be put to shame. Those who turn away from you will be written in the dust because they have forsaken the Lord, the spring of living water.'"

390

"Brilliant connection, my dear!" Nigel enthused. "These men have turned away from the Lord, and Jesus just yesterday proclaimed himself the source of living water."

"Aye, an' he's puttin' *them* ta shame," Kate added.

"Answer us!" Saar demanded, taking a step forward and then looking down to see what Jesus had written. He snapped his head up when he saw his name and the one next to it. His eyes narrowed in anger, then panic.

Jesus stood up and calmly looked them right in the eye. "The sinless one among you, go first: Throw the stone." Bending down again, he wrote some more in the dirt.

The woman covered her head, bracing for the stones. Her heart was pounding and she wept tears of regret.

The men looked at one another in alarm. Their trap had backfired. Now they were caught in Jesus' trap. They knew they couldn't claim to be sinless. Jesus had even written their names alongside other names they longed to erase from the dirt. Slowly, each man dropped his rock. The older Pharisees stomped off, and following their lead, so did the younger people in the crowd. One by one, they all left the scene, leaving only Jesus and the woman. The disciples stood off to the side, awed by Jesus' handling of this delicate situation.

Jesus stood up behind the woman cowering at the wall. "Woman, where are they? Does no one condemn you?"

The woman slowly turned her head and saw only Jesus standing there behind her. She exhaled in relief and shock. "N-n-n-no one, Master," she said, trembling.

"Neither do I," spoke Jesus gently. "Go on your way. From now on, don't sin."

She shut her eyes tight with relief as the waters of grace washed over her. She slowly shook her head in disbelief and wiped her eyes. Looking at Jesus, she pulled her tunic up around her shoulders and smiled, nodding silently. The woman hurried off and Jesus' gaze followed her as she blended into the crowd.

"Jesus showed 'em!" Max cheered. "Made all those r-r-rats r-r-run away!"

"And we can be sure this humiliation of the Pharisees will only fan the flames of their evil intentions," Liz said.

As evening came, the parade of torches proceeded through the Temple courts, illuminating the inner court.

"Now this part of the festival is to remember that the Israelites were led by the pillar of fire," Nigel observed as the animals huddled together around Gillamon.

"The fire cloud!" Al said excitedly. "I followed it, too. But to the Ark then."

"*Oui,* as we all did, *cher* Albert," Liz said. Suddenly she saw a group of Pharisees walking toward Jesus, but none of them had been involved in the earlier incident with the woman. "Oh, no, here we go again."

People had once again gathered around Jesus. He pointed to the torch bearers and said, "I am the Light of the world. The man who follows me will never walk in the dark but will live his life in the light."

"You are testifying to yourself—your evidence is not valid," one of the Pharisees protested.

Jesus turned to the self-righteous, robed men standing there. "Even if I am testifying to myself, my evidence is valid, for I know where I have come from and I know where I am going. But as for you, you have no idea where I come from or where I am going. You are judging by human standards, but I am not judging anyone. Yet if I should judge, my decision would be just, for I am not alone—the Father who sent me is with me. In your Law, it is stated that the witness of two persons is valid. I am one testifying to myself and the second witness to me is the Father who sent me."

"And where is this father of yours?" one of them replied.

"You do not know my Father," returned Jesus, "any more than you know me: if you had known me, you would have known him."

The men looked at one another and didn't have a reply.

"Jesus is laying it on rather hard, I daresay," stated Nigel, wrinkling his brow in serious observation.

"Aye, he's shootin' the tr-r-ruth at these r-r-rabble," Max growled.

Jesus spoke to them again. "I am going away and you will try to find me, but you will die in your sins. You cannot come where I am going."

The Pharisees whispered among themselves. "Is he going to kill himself, then? Is that why he says, 'You cannot come where I am going'?"

"The difference between us," Jesus said to them, "is that you come from below and I am from above. You belong to this world but I do not. That is why I told you will die in your sins. For unless you believe that I am who I am, you will die in your sins."

"Who are you?" one of the Pharisees demanded to know.

"I am what I have told you I was from the beginning," replied Jesus. "There is much in you that I could speak about and condemn. But he who sent me is true and I am only speaking to this world what I myself have heard from him."

"They clearly do not know what he is talking about," Liz whispered.

"When you have lifted up the Son of Man, then you will realize that I am who I say I am, and that I do nothing on my own authority but speak simply as my Father has taught me. The one who sent me is with me now: the Father has never left me alone for I always do what pleases him."

Nicodemus stood in the shadows and Jesus' words gripped his heart. *I believe,* he thought to himself.

Others gathered there were also so moved by Jesus' teachings that they believed. Jesus turned away from the Pharisees and spoke to these others. But mixed in the crowd were those who didn't believe and wanted Jesus dead.

"If you are faithful to what I have said, you are truly my disciples. And you will know the truth and the truth will set you free!"

"But we are descendants of Abraham," a man replied, "and we have never in our lives been any man's slaves. How can you say to us, 'You will be set free'?"

"Excusez-moi?!" Liz exclaimed. "Never been slaves? Do you not recall Egypt? Babylon? And now you are under Roman occupation? Pfft!"

Jesus returned, "Believe me when I tell you that every man who commits sin is a slave. For a slave is no permanent part of a household, but a son is. If the Son, then, sets you free, you are really free! I know that you are descended from Abraham, but some of you are looking for a way to kill me because you can't bear my words. I am telling you what I have seen in the presence of my Father, and you are doing what you have seen in the presence of your father."

"Our father is Abraham!" several of the men argued, stepping forward.

"If you were the children of Abraham, you would do the sort of things Abraham did. But in fact, at this moment, you are looking for a way to kill me, simply because I am a man who has told you the truth that I have heard from God. Abraham would never have done that. No, you are doing your father's work."

393

"We are not illegitimate!" the people protested. "We have one Father—God."

"If God were really your Father," replied Jesus, "you would have loved me. For I came from God, and I am here. I did not come of my own accord—he sent me, and I am here. Why do you not understand my words? It is because you cannot hear what I am really saying. Your father is the devil, and what you are wanting to do is what your father longs to do. He always was a murderer, and has never dealt with the truth, since the truth will have nothing to do with him. Whenever he tells a lie, he speaks in character, for he is a liar and the father of lies. And it is because I speak the truth that you will not believe me. Which of you can prove me guilty of sin? If I am speaking the truth, why is it that you do not believe me? The man who is born of God can hear these words of God and the reason why you cannot hear the words of God is simply this, that you are not the sons of God."

"This is heating up," Gillamon said to the animals. "Come along. We're leaving."

At this they all quietly followed Gillamon out of the courtyard. The people didn't have an answer for Jesus, so they began to hurl insults at him.

"How right we are," one of the men shouted, "in calling you a Samaritan, and mad at that!"

"No," replied Jesus, "I am not mad. I am honoring my Father and you are trying to dishonor me. But I am not concerned with my own glory: there is one whose concern it is, and he is the true judge. Believe me when I tell you that if anybody accepts my words, he will never see death at all."

"Now we know that you're mad," replied some of the men listening. "Why, Abraham died and the prophets, too, and yet you say, 'If a man accepts my words, he will never experience death!' Are you greater than our father, Abraham? He died, and so did the prophets—who are you making yourself out to be?"

"If I were trying to glorify myself," returned Jesus, "such glory would be worthless. But it is my Father who glorifies me, the very one whom you say is your God—though you have never known him. But I know him, and if I said I did not know him, I should be as much a liar as you are! But I do know him and I am faithful to what he says. As for your father, Abraham, his great joy was that he would see my coming. Now he has seen it and he is overjoyed."

"Look," said one of the religious leaders to him, "you are not fifty yet, and has Abraham seen you?"

"I tell you in solemn truth," returned Jesus with a bold, resounding voice that echoed off the walls of the Temple, "before there was an Abraham, I AM!"

The people's anger immediately roared to life and they bent down to pick up stones to hurl at him. When they looked up Jesus had disappeared and made his way out of the Temple.

Nicodemus remained in the shadows as one by one the people dropped their stones and walked into the darkness of the night. His mind and heart were swirling with all that Jesus had said. He was the living Water and the Light of the world. He was Messiah. Nicodemus no longer had any doubt. Suddenly the prophecies started becoming clear to him, and filled his mind. *"The people that walked in darkness*

394

have seen a great light: they that dwell in the land of the shadow of death, upon them hath the light shined."

Nicodemus turned to walk home, and planned to pore over this prophecy from Isaiah and to find others to see anew how Messiah was foretold. Alarm coursed through him as he suddenly remembered what Jesus said, *"When you have lifted up the Son of Man, then you will realize that I am who I say I am . . ."* *Lifted up.* Nicodemus picked up his pace. Everything was becoming too clear to him. He remembered the conversation he had the night he went to Jesus, now more than two years ago, when Jesus said, "In the same way that Moses lifted the serpent in the desert so people could have something to see and then believe, it is necessary for the Son of Man to be lifted up—and everyone who looks up to him, trusting and expectant, will gain a real life, eternal life."

"Oh my," Nicodemus muttered out loud to himself and he remembered more of Jesus' words that night: *"Light has come into the world, but people loved darkness instead of light because their deeds were evil. Everyone who does evil hates the light, and will not come into the light for fear that their deeds will be exposed."*

Jesus is in grave danger, Nicodemus thought to himself, thinking of the Sanhedrin. *He exposed their evil deeds today. And they won't stop coming after him until his light has been extinguished.*

395

THEN SHALL THE EYES OF THE BLIND

I like it," Caiaphas the high priest said, nodding and raising his eyebrows in affirmation. "Anyone professing Jesus as Messiah will be thrown out of the synagogue. Well done."

Zeeb, Nahshon, Saar, and Jarib all stood in a row before Caiaphas, the leader of the Sanhedrin. They were seeking power and using this ongoing issue with the Galilean to further their interests.

"Thank you, Caiaphas," Zeeb offered eagerly, bowing in false humility before the most powerful man in the ruling council of Israel. "If we can't stop Jesus from teaching, we'll shut down his followers by threatening them with expulsion from our midst. We feel this will squelch his movement."

"If no one will follow him, then Jesus will fade into obscurity with the other false prophets," Caiaphas replied. "Let me know how effective this threat is. The people look to us for leadership in these matters, so it should be successful."

"We will keep you informed," Zeeb said. He and the others filed out of the room.

They couldn't wait to further control the people by spreading the word about this threat of expulsion from the synagogue. They knew it would work. It had to work. They were going head-to-head with Jesus of Nazareth over the loyalties of the people. If they failed, they would be in a worse position than before.

Jesus and his disciples were making their way out of Jerusalem, as the Feast of Tabernacles had come to a close. Jesus planned to travel on to Bethany. Gillamon and the animals had gone ahead of the disciples, all except for Nigel. He was tucked away in Jesus' tunic.

"Please, alms, alms! Have mercy on me, a blind man!" the man cried as he pounded his stick on the stone pavement with one hand and held out his other hand, hoping for people to place a coin there. His eyes were open, but his surroundings were dark. His head moved with the sounds around him, trying to detect movement of passersby. He could feel the sun on his face, so a cool shadow meant someone was there. His clothes were worn and ragged, and he had begged in this place day in and day out for years.

Peter grabbed Jesus' arm as they approached the man. "Rabbi, who sinned: this man or his parents, causing him to be born blind?"

Jesus gazed at the blind man with compassion. "You're asking the wrong question. You're looking for someone to blame. There is no such cause-and-effect here. Look instead for what God can do. We need to be energetically at work for the One who sent me here, working while the sun shines. When night falls, the workday is over. For as long as I am in the world, there is plenty of light. I am the world's Light."

"Who's there?" the blind man asked, turning his head in the direction of their voices.

"Jesus is with us," Peter told him, placing his hand on the man's shoulder.

Peter gave a questioning look as he watched Jesus then spit in the dust and make a clay paste with the saliva. Jesus nodded to Peter to hold the man while he rubbed the paste on the blind man's eyes.

The blind man struggled against them, so Peter held him fast. "What are you doing to me!? Stop it!" the blind man cried, dropping his stick.

Jesus ignored the man's pleas as he determinedly rubbed the clay on his eyes and held it in place with his thumbs for a moment. Finally, he looked up at Peter and the other disciples and removed his hands from the man's face. "Go, wash at the Pool of Siloam," he instructed the man.

"My eyes are burning! What have you done to me?!" the man cried.

Peter helped the man to his feet as John and some of the others surrounded the man to escort him to the pool. Jesus walked into the Temple courtyard.

"This should be something to see—no pun intended!" Nigel cheered in Jesus' ear. "I say, for you to heal a man born blind will certainly be something that has never happened before."

"This man has suffered long enough," Jesus said. "It's time for his life to begin and for God to be glorified."

"Utterly dreadful that the Pharisees think this man's blindness was caused by someone's sin, either his parents' or his," Nigel replied. "Since Esau fought with Jacob in the womb, they actually believe one can sin before birth!"

398

"The blind leading the blind," Jesus muttered. "I told the people I am the Light of the world. Now they will see it in this man's eyes."

The man continued to wail as the disciples helped him over to the pool. They led him down the steps and put his hands in the water. The man splashed the water repeatedly on his eyes, the cool water bringing immediate relief to the sting he felt. John handed him a cloth and he pressed it to his eyes for a moment. The burning sensation ceased. He removed the cloth, opened his eyes, and immediately saw light dancing on the water in the pool. His eyes widened in shock, as these were the first things he had ever seen. Water and light.

"I can see! I can see!" the man said with a voice shaking from raw emotion. He put his hands on John's face. "I can see you!" He turned and looked at Peter, James, Andrew, and a growing crowd of people who rushed over to see what was happening.

The murmuring blazed through the crowd of his relatives and those who year after year had seen him as a blind man begging. One man pointed to him and said, "Isn't this the man we knew, who sat here and begged?"

"It's him all right!" a woman replied.

Some people in the crowd objected, "It's not the same man at all. It just looks like him."

The man looked at them as they carried on this discussion and he shook his head. He placed his hands on his chest and exclaimed, "It is I, the very one!"

"How did your eyes get opened?" a man shouted, echoed by the others. They all wanted to know.

"A man named Jesus made a paste and rubbed it on my eyes and told me, 'Go to Siloam and wash.' I did what he said. When I washed, I saw."

"So where is he?" one of the men asked, looking around.

"I don't know," the man replied.

Some of the men grabbed the man by the arm to march him to the Pharisees.

Saar saw them first. "Something is happening in the crowd."

Zeeb, Nahshon, and Jarib turned to face the mob who brought the man to stand right in front of them. "He claims Jesus healed him," one of the men said, pushing the man forward. Nicodemus and Joseph of Arimathea walked up to join them.

399

They couldn't believe their eyes. They knew this blind beggar well. But here he was, no longer blind. And it was the Sabbath. *Jesus of Nazareth,* Zeeb muttered under his breath, sneering.

"Well, what do you have to say for yourself?" Jarib asked. "How is it that you are seeing when we saw you just this morning begging in the street?"

The man was taken aback by how cold these Pharisees were acting. Shouldn't they be rejoicing over his miraculous healing? He held out his hands and shrugged his shoulders. "He put a clay paste on my eyes, and I washed, and now I see."

"Obviously, this man can't be from God," Saar scowled. "He doesn't keep the Sabbath."

Joseph of Arimathea spoke up. "How can a bad man do miraculous, God-revealing things like this?"

"You're the expert," Zeeb said as he looked the man up and down with a condescending stare. "He opened your eyes. What do you say about him?"

"He is a prophet," the man replied, looking at this group of Pharisees who were blind to the fact a miracle had occurred.

The crowds were debating among themselves and the Pharisees saw they were split over not only Jesus but if the man was even blind to begin with. "Bring his parents to us," Zeeb demanded. Two of the men who knew the beggar ran immediately to get them. He turned to whisper to the others, "Now we'll see if our threats are effective."

Soon the parents of the man stood before the Pharisees. Nahshon asked them, "Is this your son, the one you say was born blind? So how is it that he now sees?"

His parents looked at one another, clearly in shock. The joy they felt over seeing their son healed was overshadowed by the intimidation of the Pharisees.

The man's father spoke up. "We know he is our son, and we know he was born blind. But we don't know how he came to see—haven't a clue about who opened his eyes. Why don't you ask him? He's a grown man and can speak for himself."

Zeeb smiled. The intimidation was working with the parents; now to move in on their son. He motioned for the man a second time. "Give glory to God by telling the truth," he said. "We know this man is a sinner."

The man shook his head. "Whether he is a sinner or not, I don't know. One thing I do know. I was blind but now I see!"

The faces of the Pharisees turned angry. Saar stepped forward and demanded, "What did he do to you? How did he open your eyes?"

"I've told you over and over and you haven't listened. Why do you want to hear it again?" the man asked, looking them each in the eye. "Are you so eager to become his disciples?"

With that they jumped all over him. "You might be a disciple of that man, but we're disciples of Moses. We know for sure that God spoke to Moses, but we have no idea where this man even comes from."

The man replied, "This is amazing! You claim to know nothing about him, but the fact is, he opened my eyes! It's well known that God isn't at the beck and call of sinners, but listens carefully to anyone who lives in reverence and does his will. That someone opened the eyes of a man born blind has never been heard of—ever. If this man didn't come from God, he wouldn't be able to do anything."

Fury burned in their eyes and they spat at the man. "You're nothing but dirt! How dare you take that tone with us!"

400

Zeeb called the Temple guards, who came running over, and instructed them to throw the man out in the street. The crowds were stunned and looked at one another in fear. The Pharisees had made good on their threat about anyone endorsing Jesus as Messiah. Evidently saying Jesus was sent by God was enough for them to enforce their mandate. While the four Pharisees with the threat plan stormed back into their chambers, some of the other Pharisees milled about the crowds to gauge the response of the people.

The man sat in the street and he studied his hands, marveling at how they were made. But he realized that now his hands would have to find work. He could no longer sit here in the street and beg.

Jesus came walking up to the man after searching for him. The disciples reported everything that happened between the man and the Pharisees. "Do you believe in the Son of Man?" he asked him.

The man got to his feet. "Point him out to me, sir, so that I can believe in him."

Jesus smiled. "You're looking right at him. Don't you recognize my voice?"

401

"Master, I believe," the man said. He fell to his face and bowed at Jesus' feet in gratitude.

"I entered this world to render judgment—to give sight to the blind and to show those who think they see that they are blind," Jesus told him, tenderly placing his hand on the man's head.

Some Pharisees standing nearby heard him and asked, "Are you saying we're blind?"

"If you were blind, you wouldn't be guilty," Jesus replied. "But you remain guilty because you claim you can see."

With that, the Pharisees stormed off to report to Zeeb and the others.

Jesus squatted down and lifted the man to his feet. He smiled and gazed deeply into the man's eyes that now saw everything, and most importantly, that saw Messiah.

"The lack of sight doesn't mean that the light isn't there," Jesus told him. "Light reveals the condition of the eye, and the Light of the world reveals the condition of the soul. These Pharisees think they can see clearly but are steeped in darkness. But you have been given sight with both today."

"Yes, Master, thank you." The man smiled back and eagerly embraced Jesus' forearms with his hands.

"Go now and be light for those who will listen," Jesus instructed him.

"I will, Lord! I will!" the man responded, "beginning with my parents!" He ran off toward home to tell his family Jesus was the true Light of the world.

As Jesus watched the man run away, happy to begin his new life, he folded his arms and smiled as he stood there in the street.

"Brilliant!" Nigel exclaimed. "I say, I believe this might be your most intimidating miracle showdown with the Pharisees yet."

Jesus wrinkled his brow as he looked off in the direction of Bethany. "Not quite. There remains one more event that will seal my fate with the Sanhedrin."

"Oh dear, I know it's coming but I must tell you I dread the darkness," Nigel lamented. "The Pharisees will think they've won."

402

"Don't fear the darkness, Nigel, as hard as it will be," Jesus comforted him. "Remember, when the light returns, the rats run for cover."

"Then shall the eyes of the blind be opened!" Nigel cheered, quoting Isaiah and thinking of the people who now were following the darkness of the Pharisees.

"Exactly," Jesus said, petting Nigel affectionately.

"Rats," Nigel remarked. "Utterly dreadful."

THE GOOD SAMARITAN, THE GOOD PRAYER, AND THE GOOD-BYE

FIVE MONTHS LATER, ONE MONTH BEFORE PASSOVER

T he crowds are growing again," Liz observed, looking down the long line of people gathered around Jesus and his disciples. "Between Jesus' travels and sending out the seventy to spread the good news throughout the region, word about Jesus has spread to a new level."

"Aye, but there be some who don't like that the cr-r-rowds be gr-r-rowin'," Max growled. "Them Phar-r-risees be there at every turn!"

"Teacher!" a man said, standing up in the crowd. "Teacher, what should I do to inherit eternal life?"

"Wha' were I jest sayin'?" Max said with a frown.

"I believe this chap is not a Pharisee but a Levite, who is an expert in the law," Nigel corrected.

"Aye, but they be in cahoots together anyway, seein' how the Levite laddies assist the Phar-r-risees in the Temple," Max replied. "I bet ye he's out ta tr-r-rap Jesus like the r-r-rest of 'em."

"Rest assured Jesus will not be trapped, old boy!" Nigel exclaimed.

"Shhhhh, I wish to hear Jesus' response, no?" Liz whispered.

403

Jesus looked at the man, a Levite who knew the Law well. "What does the Law of Moses say? How do you read it?"

The man had a ready reply. "'You must love the Lord your God with all your heart, all your soul, all your strength, and all your mind.' And, 'Love your neighbor as yourself.'"

"You have answered correctly," Jesus replied. "Do this and you will live."

The Levite quickly added, "And who is my neighbor?"

"This is where Jesus will catch the Levite in his own trap," Liz said with a coy grin.

Jesus sat up and wrapped his arms around his knees as he began to tell a story.

"A man was going down from Jerusalem to Jericho, when he was attacked by robbers. They stripped him of his clothes, beat him and went away, leaving him half dead. A priest happened to be going down the same road, and when he saw the man, he passed by on the other side. So too, a Levite, when he came to the place and saw him, passed by on the other side . . ." Jesus paused for effect, leaning back on his hand.

404

"Look at the laddie squir-r-rmin'," Max grinned as the Levite looked around uncomfortably.

"I told you Jesus would catch him," Liz replied.

Jesus continued the story. "But a Samaritan, as he traveled, came where the man was; and when he saw him, he took pity on him. He went to him and bandaged his wounds, pouring on oil and wine. Then he put the man on his own donkey, brought him to an inn and took care of him. The next day he took out two denarii and gave them to the innkeeper. 'Look after him,' he said, 'and when I return, I will reimburse you for any extra expense you may have.' Which of these three do you think was a neighbor to the man who fell into the hands of robbers?"

The Levite quietly replied, "The one who had mercy on him."

Jesus told him, "Go and do likewise."

The man stared at Jesus, defeated by the obvious points Jesus made in the story. This was a grace and a type of attitude that the man could hardly understand. It was completely foreign to the way Jews and Samaritans related in their world. They hated each other with blinding hatred. Yet, Jesus was telling them to actually *love* one another? This was hard teaching to swallow.

"Jesus has turned the usual order of things upside down once again," Nigel commented. "Love of one's neighbor must go beyond the boundaries of race, nationality, religion, or status in this life. Simply brilliant!"

The animals watched the Levite get up and depart from the crowd.

"Guess he had enough of bein' showed up by a good Samaritan," Max observed.

"He's doin' it again," Kate observed. The animals sat, watching Jesus, who was off by himself deep in prayer.

"*Oui,* he is consistently praying, no?" Liz agreed. She looked over at his disciples and saw Andrew staring at Jesus. "But the disciples still seem to not understand how to pray."

"Perhaps they need a lesson," Nigel added. "If Jesus could give them some sort of model to go by, that would help a great deal."

"Aye, the laddies need it, especially with wha's comin' soon," Max noted.

The moment Jesus raised his head and opened his eyes, Andrew went over to him. "Lord, teach us to pray, just as John taught his disciples."

The other disciples gathered around Jesus and he nodded in affirmation. "Jolly good!" Nigel cheered. "It's as if Andrew read my mind!"

Jesus looked around at his disciples, who were eager to follow his example. "When you pray, you are not to be like the hypocrites; for they love to stand and pray in the synagogues and on the street corners so that they may be seen by men. Truly I say to you, they have their reward in full. But you, when you pray, go into your inner room, close your door and pray to your Father who is in secret, and your Father who sees what is done in secret will reward you.

"And when you are praying, do not use meaningless repetition as the Gentiles do, for they suppose that they will be heard for their many words. So do not be like them; for your Father knows what you need before you ask Him." Jesus held up his hands and closed his eyes. "When you pray, say:

"Our Father in heaven: May your holy name be honored; may your kingdom come; may your will be done on earth as it is in heaven. Give us today the food we need. Forgive us the wrongs we have done, as we

405

forgive the wrongs that others have done to us. Do not bring us to hard testing, but keep us safe from the Evil One. For yours is the kingdom and the power and the glory forever. Amen."

"Jesus is teaching them priorities in prayer," Gillamon observed. "You must always recognize the Maker and his agenda before your own."

"*Oui,* then you may ask for your daily bread," Liz added. "I've heard Jesus say that if you forgive others the wrongs they have done to you, your Father in heaven will also forgive you. But if you do not forgive others, then your Father will not forgive the wrongs *you* have done."

"Right, so one best not come to ask forgiveness until one is willing to do the hard task of forgiving those who hurt him or her," Nigel said, adjusting his spectacles. "Forgiveness is a difficult business, but the Maker takes it quite seriously."

"I like how Jesus mentions guarding ourselves against tests that could tempt us into sin," Clarie added. "The Maker can keep us safe from ourselves."

406

"Aye, and keep us safe from the Evil One," Al added. "I like that part best."

Liz smiled at Al, and even though he was the most visibly fearful of them all, she knew that every one of the team had fearfully encountered the Evil One. She also knew that the Maker alone could keep them safe. But even when he allowed the Evil One to seemingly triumph, as with Charlatan at the Ark or Lucifer with Clarie, ultimately the Evil One could not touch the most important part of their being—their soul. "But everything in the end belongs to the all-powerful Maker, and he deserves the glory, no?"

"I say, I believe we've all learned how to pray better today," Nigel cheered. "Utterly splendid way to have a conversation with the Maker."

"Aye, now that be a good prayer," Kate agreed.

Nicodemus and Joseph of Arimathea were out of breath when they reached Jesus and his disciples. Jesus had pulled back again across the Jordan to an unpopulated area where John had baptized. They were in the middle of Herod's territory. John and Peter saw them approaching and went to greet them.

"Nicodemus?" Peter said. "What brings you out here?"

"Please, we must speak to the Master," Nicodemus responded. "It is a most urgent matter."

"Certainly, we'll take you to him," Peter said, escorting these Pharisees over to where Jesus sat by the banks of the Jordan River, teaching a group of people.

Jesus smiled at their approach, and stood in respect for these men who believed on him as Messiah. God had his remnant of believers in Israel's ruling authority with these Pharisees. Before he could speak they gushed out warnings.

"Run for your life!" Joseph cried, lifting his hands in alarm.

"Herod's on the hunt. He's out to kill you!" Nicodemus warned, his face full of anguish and concern.

Jesus' smile turned to a look of challenge against this powerless threat. "Tell that fox that I've no time for him right now. Today and tomorrow I'm busy clearing out the demons and healing the sick; the third day I'm wrapping things up. Besides, it's not proper for a prophet to come to a bad end outside Jerusalem."

407

Nicodemus and Joseph looked at one another in astonishment at Jesus' boldness.

"Wha' do Jesus mean by that?" Kate whispered. "Will things happen in three days?"

"No, Jesus simply means he is working on his own timetable, and that Herod is powerless to stop him," Liz explained. "Herod's threats are meaningless, for no one can kill Jesus before his time."

"Indeed, but that time is fast approaching," Nigel pointed out with a furrowed brow. "In Jerusalem."

Jesus swallowed hard and his eyes filled with tears. His heart broke over Jerusalem, the city he loved. "Jerusalem, killer of prophets, abuser of the messengers of God! How often I've longed to gather your children, gather your children like a hen, her brood safe under her wings—but you refused and turned away! And now it's too late: You won't see me again until the day you say, 'Blessed is he who comes in the name of the Lord.'"

"It sounds as if Jesus is telling Jerusalem good-bye," Liz posed. "Gillamon, what does Jesus mean by quoting this psalm?"

"It's too late now for Israel," Gillamon said. "They've had their day of opportunity to believe in the true Messiah, but they've rejected him.

In a way, Jesus is telling Jerusalem good-bye, in terms of hoping for their belief. Someday they will acknowledge him as Messiah. But not today."

Jesus walked away from Nicodemus, Joseph, and the others gathered there. His heart was heavy.

Gillamon heaved a heavy sigh. "As with the prophets of old, Jesus will die in and at the hands of Jerusalem."

IF ONLY

The countryside was exploding with flowers of every color and type imaginable. Springtime in Israel was a welcome relief with warm days and less frigid nights as well as incredible beauty everywhere. The lush green hillside was interspersed with pockets of red, yellow, blue, orange, white, lilac, and pink. Liz was in heaven as she walked in the midst of the beauty, pointing out various flower species to the others.

"Now here we have the exquisite *Romulea,* named after Romulus, the founder of Rome," Liz lectured. "Notice the dramatic pointed lilac petals with the dark center."

"Wha' be this kind?" Kate asked, putting her nose into a bunch of low-lying red flowers bursting with color.

"Truly a beautiful specimen, *mon amie!* This is none other than *Glaucium Corniculatum,* or Blackspot Hornpoppy," answered Liz.

"That's fun to say," Al said, goofily repeating Liz as he jumped across the meadow. "Blackspot Hornpoppy, Blackspot Hornpoppy, Blackspot Hornpoppy."

"Ah, now this is one *you* should like, Gillamon," Liz said. She lifted up a beautiful flower with purple large outer petals surrounding a tight ring of darker purple petals dotted with yellow. "This is *Geropogon Hybridus,* better known as Goat's Beard."

"Liz, your knowledge of flowers is truly amazing," Gillamon chuckled, pulling his beard through his fingers. "Sometimes I miss being a mountain goat. That looks like one tasty flower."

"I simply adore flora," Liz said, breathing in the fresh air.

"I say, a day like today just takes the biscuit!" Nigel exclaimed. "I'm enjoying our time out in the countryside away from the crowded villages. This is refreshing to the spirit."

"Aye, an' after that last heated encounter in Judea, it's gr-r-rand ta be out here," Max said. He sniffed a bush of dainty pink flower clusters.

Liz walked up to Max and examined the flowers. "*Ricotia Lunaria,* an annual with four pink petals arranged in the form of a cross."

"Even out here, there's a r-r-reminder of wha's comin'," Max frowned. "An' soon."

"Liz, tell us about these tall green trees," Clarie asked. "We see them everywhere."

"*Oui,* these are *Cupressus Sempervirens,* or cypress trees," Liz began. The animals gathered around her and looked up at the tall, pointed trees, now lush with new growth.

410

"There is a fascinating Greek myth about this tree. Supposedly a youth named Cyparissus killed his playmate stag, and begged the gods to let him mourn forever. Therefore he was turned into a cypress tree by Apollo," related Liz.

Al's eyes grew wide as he stared up at the tall tree towering over him. "Ye mean, this tree could be a laddie?"

"Daft kitty," Max said, bonking Al on the head. "Myths aren't r-r-real. They jest be made up by humans ta explain why things happen."

"Jest checkin'," Al replied with a weak grin.

"Because the tree resembles a candle, it is extensively planted in and around cemeteries," Liz continued. "This tradition stems from the sacred association of these trees with the Roman god Pluto, whom the Romans believe is the ruler of the underworld. The Egyptians also associate the cypress with death, and connect it to their beliefs of the afterlife. They use its fragrant wood for preservative properties, and in mummifications."

"Well done, my pet! Oh, how I did enjoy a good mummification back in Egypt," Nigel remembered, preening his whiskers. "Utterly fascinating how they prepare the mummies."

"I think I've heard enough aboot death for one day," Al whined. "Let's talk aboot the Blackspot Hornpoppy instead!"

Just then they saw a man riding a horse toward Jesus and his disciples.

"Ain't that the servant we saw at Mary an' Martha's house?" Kate asked. "He were a friendly man when we stayed there."

"Yes, Kate. He works in the home of Mary, Martha, and Lazarus, Jesus' dear friends in Bethany," Gillamon replied. "Let's go see why he's come."

As the man reached the disciples he quickly jumped off the horse and ran up to Jesus. "Lord, Mary and Martha sent me to find you. Your dear friend Lazarus is very sick."

"This servant had to have travelled an entire day to reach Jesus. For Mary and Martha to send him, it must be serious," Nigel suggested.

Jesus wore a concerned look and placed his hand on the man's shoulder. "Lazarus's sickness will not end in death. No, it happened for the glory of God so that the Son of God will receive glory from this." He looked in the man's eyes. "Go, I'll be there."

"Thank goodness," Al said. "I don't want any more death talk today."

"*Bon!* Surely Jesus will heal Lazarus, no?" Liz suggested. "He has assured the servant that Lazarus will not die."

Gillamon and Clarie shared a knowing frown.

"Jesus loves Martha, Mary, and Lazarus, but sometimes love is expressed in strange ways," Clarie said.

411

Jesus sent the servant back to Mary, Martha, and Lazarus, but gave no specific word of healing. The servant left, mystified by Jesus' response. He expected Jesus to follow him back immediately, but Jesus remained where he was. At least he could tell Mary and Martha what Jesus had said. But by the time he reached Bethany, Lazarus was dead. Nothing made sense, so he didn't know if he should share what Jesus had said about Lazarus not dying. *How could the Master be wrong?* he wondered.

Two days later, Jesus stood and said to his disciples, "Let's go back to Judea."

But his disciples immediately objected. "Rabbi," Peter said, "only a few days ago the people in Judea were trying to stone you. Are you going there again?"

Jesus replied, "There are twelve hours of daylight every day. During the day people can walk safely. They can see because they have the light of this world. But at night there is danger of stumbling because they have no light." He gazed in the direction of Bethany. "Our friend Lazarus has fallen asleep, but now I will go and wake him up."

Matthew spoke up, "Lord, if he is sleeping, he will soon get better!"

Jesus knew that his disciples thought he meant that Lazarus was literally just sleeping. They needed to fully understand the situation.

"Lazarus is dead," Jesus said plainly. "And for your sakes, I'm glad I wasn't there, for now you will really believe. Come, let's go see him."

Thomas stood and boldly proclaimed to the other disciples, "Let's go, too—and die with Jesus."

"Well, will ye look at that?" Max said. "Thomas has gr-r-r-own some cour-r-rage then."

"Oui, although he still looks at the situation from a negative point of view, thinking they will die if they return to dangerous Judea," Liz added.

"At least Thomas realizes he'd rather die with Jesus than be left behind," Nigel observed.

"Sure, that's what I call heroic pessimism," Al said.

Jesus and the disciples began the journey to Bethany. Gillamon and the animals brought up the rear.

Liz wrinkled her brow, deep in thought. Like the servant, she too was perplexed by Jesus' statement Lazarus would not die.

"What's troubling you, Liz?" Gillamon asked.

"I am puzzled by Jesus' handling of this situation, no?" Liz replied. "He has always broken up every funeral he has ever attended, and he said Lazarus's illness would not result in death. Yet he died. And why was Jesus glad he wasn't there? *Je ne comprends pas.*"

"This is one of those times you must trust him, even though you don't understand," Gillamon assured her. "You can imagine how Mary and Martha must feel by now. Lazarus will have been dead four days by the time we get there."

"Aye, but Jesus said Lazarus jest be sleepin', an' that he were goin' ta wake him," Kate remembered. "How can he be asleep an' dead at the same time?"

"May I take a stab at this?" Nigel asked. "According to Jewish burial customs, the general belief when someone dies is that the spirit hovers around the body for three days, waiting for the possibility of reentry. But on the third day the body loses its color and the spirit is locked out, therefore having to go to *Sheol*, or 'the place of the dead.'"

"Sure, if only ye'd stop all this death talk." Al put his paws up over his ears.

"So, for those who believe in the Maker, death is no more sinister than sleep, for the spirit never dies," Nigel explained. "Only the body."

"But the mourners will have lost all hope, since the third day will have been passed," Liz said, now sitting up in anticipation. "Jesus said he was glad he wasn't there because now God would be glorified, as would Jesus. This can only mean one thing!"

When Jesus arrived at Bethany, he was told Lazarus had already been in the grave for four days.

413

"Lazarus was a well-respected man of influence," Nigel observed by the crowds who had gathered to console Martha and Mary in their loss. "Many of these people have come from Jerusalem."

"*Oui*, Jerusalem is only two miles away," Liz noted.

When Martha got word Jesus was coming, she went to meet him. But Mary stayed in the house.

Martha was dressed in black and her eyes were swollen from crying. Her nose was red and she was drained from sorrow. As she went up to Jesus, she fell into his chest and he lovingly embraced her with compassion.

"Lord, if only you had been here," Martha said, her chin trembling, "my brother would not have died. But even now I know that God will give you whatever you ask."

Jesus placed his hands on her arms and stared into Martha's eyes. "Your brother will rise again."

"Yes," Martha said, "he will rise when everyone else rises, at the last day."

Jesus looked out over the crowd of mourners. "I am the resurrection and the life. Anyone who believes in me will live, even after dying. Everyone who lives in me and believes in me will never ever die." He turned to lock eyes with her. "Do you believe this, Martha?"

"Yes, Lord," she told him. "I have always believed you are the Messiah, the Son of God, the one who has come into the world from God."

"Go, get Mary," Jesus said gently.

Martha nodded, and was escorted by several women as she returned to get her sister. The house was full of mourners, wailing and crying out in sorrow. Martha called Mary aside from the mourners and told her softly, "The Teacher is here and wants to see you."

Mary's eyes filled with tears, and she immediately got up and went to him. When the people who were at the house consoling Mary saw her leave so hastily, they assumed she was going to Lazarus's grave to weep. So they followed her there. The crowds immediately recognized Jesus.

When Mary arrived and saw Jesus, she fell at his feet and cried out, "Lord, if only you had been here, my brother would not have died."

When Jesus saw her weeping and saw the other people wailing with her, a deep anger welled up within him, and he was deeply troubled. "Where have you put him?" he asked Mary, helping her to her feet.

"Lord, come and see." Together Mary and Martha held onto one another as they slowly walked to the cave where Lazarus's tomb had been carved out of the rock. A large stone was rolled over the entrance to seal the tomb. The sound of grief echoed off the cold stone as mourners joined Mary and Martha. The tall cypress trees planted in this place of death held their silent vigil of reverence.

Jesus looked at the brokenness of these he loved so deeply. Tears filled his eyes and he wept.

"See how much he loved him!" one of the people standing by exclaimed.

But someone else added, "This man healed a blind man. Couldn't he have kept Lazarus from dying?"

Jesus was still angry as he arrived at the tomb. He clenched his jaw tight as a solitary tear rolled down his cheek. "Roll the stone aside."

"Lord, he has been dead for four days," Martha protested. "The smell will be terrible."

Jesus responded, "Didn't I tell you that you would see God's glory if you believe?"

Martha bowed her head in submission and nodded. She looked at some of the men standing there. "Do as he says."

414

The men struggled to roll the heavy stone aside, and they immediately fell back. A hush fell over the crowd as Jesus walked to stand in front of the tomb. Then Jesus looked up to heaven and said, "Father, thank you for hearing me. You always hear me, but I said it out loud for the sake of all these people standing here, so that they will believe you sent me."

Jesus stared at the open tomb and slowly stretched out his arms. In a bold, commanding voice, he shouted, "Lazarus, come out!"

The crowd leaned forward in anticipation as the seconds passed with no movement. Suddenly a collective gasp rippled through the crowd as Lazarus appeared at the entrance to the tomb. His hands and feet were bound in graveclothes, his face wrapped in a head cloth.

Mary and Martha clutched one another tightly and their hearts pounded in joyous awe.

Jesus slowly lowered his arms and breathed in deeply. "Unwrap him and let him go!"

The sisters ran over and surrounded Lazarus in a tight embrace, pulling the cloth from his face. He looked at Jesus and their eyes locked. Jesus was the only one whom Lazarus could look to at this moment. Jesus was the only one who fully understood the spirit realm where Lazarus had been these four days. Jesus gradually smiled as did Lazarus and the two men stepped toward one another and embraced.

"Welcome back, my friend," Jesus whispered in Lazarus's ear.

"My Savior and my Lord!" Lazarus wept with joy. "You are the resurrection and the life!"

People were cheering and holding their heads in disbelief of what they saw. The disciples hugged one another, giving Thomas a rough and tumble embrace. Men began running through the streets, spreading the word about this staggering miracle. Immediately the wailing of the mourners ceased and the women began to sing and dance in joyous celebration.

Al brightened. "Hooray! Jesus hates death again!"

Liz's eyes brimmed with tears as she quoted Jeremiah: "Then young women will dance and be glad, young men and old as well. I will turn their mourning into gladness; I will give them comfort and joy instead of sorrow."

Nigel watched a group of frowning men huddled together, talking.

"I'm afraid there are some here who are none too pleased with Jesus' miracle."

"Phar-r-risee spies," Max growled, his fur bristling. He watched as the group of grumbling men immediately made their way down the street.

"Oh dear, this must be what Jesus was referring to," Nigel said, looking up at the cypress trees surrounding them.

"Wha' do ye mean, Mousie?" Max asked in alarm.

"He told me there was one final miracle that would seal his fate with the Sanhedrin!" Nigel exclaimed as he began running up one of the trees.

Liz walked up to Max as they watched their mouse friend disappear into the branches. "Where is Nigel going?" Liz asked.

"Beats me, Lass," Max said. He and Liz stared up into the cypress tree, waiting to spot Nigel.

Suddenly they heard the flapping of wings and the cooing of a pigeon. Nigel emerged from the cypress branches riding on the bird's back. He directed the pigeon to swoop down by Max and Liz.

"I'm off to Jerusalem!" Nigel shouted and waved as they flew by, then shouted in the pigeon's ear, "Follow those spies!"

416

51

Death and Ambition

T ell us everything!" Zeeb instructed as the spies were ushered into the chambers of the high council of leading priests and Pharisees. The men nervously looked around as they entered the hallowed room filled with the most respected and revered leaders in all Israel. The pious leaders were dressed in their robes of finery and head-dresses of prominence, and their intimidating faces were lit up by oil lamps that cast a glow around the room. The high priest Caiaphas himself was here, seated in his chair of authority. The spies swallowed hard and sweat broke out on their foreheads as the eyes of the Sanhedrin bored into them.

Nigel saw the perfect window ledge outside the Sanhedrin chambers. "If you would be so kind as to land there, my dear."

The pigeon softly landed and the fluttering of her wings on the ledge caused Caiaphas to briefly turn his gaze to look up at the noise. He slowly returned his attention to the men standing before him. He sat in his chair, chin resting on his thumb with his fingers covering his mouth. He quietly listened to the report of the spies.

"We saw him ourselves! Lazarus was dead and placed in the tomb four days ago," one spy reported. "Mourners have been there ever since. They weren't faking this."

"Yes, then Jesus of Nazareth arrived today and commanded that the stone be rolled away," the second spy said, "despite the pleading of Lazarus's sister. After the stone was moved he called to Lazarus to come out of the tomb. And he did, still wrapped in his graveclothes."

The chamber erupted with the priests and Pharisees murmuring and shaking their heads.

"I even went for a closer look and it was Lazarus all right," a third spy spoke up and claimed over the din of voices. "I waited 'til they removed his headcloth so I could see it for myself. It was Lazarus, risen from the dead."

"What are we going to do?" Saar asked with a desperate tone.

"This man certainly performs many miraculous signs," one of the more reserved priests noted.

"If we allow him to go on like this, soon everyone will believe in him," Nahshon warned.

"Then the Roman army will come and destroy both our Temple and our nation," Jarib predicted.

"Yes, if there is an uprising of these people with Jesus as their leader, Rome will see it as a breach of their conditional peace," another priest surmised. "We'll lose our positions of authority that Rome has allowed us over Israel."

418

The room once again broke out with the men debating the potential outcome of these events.

"You plainly don't understand what is involved here," Caiaphas bellowed, causing all the voices to go quiet.

The large man stood and stepped down from his chair. With dramatic power he took the floor, men quickly moving out of his way. He walked up and down the center of the room, tapping his staff on the stone floor. The high council eagerly awaited what Caiaphas had to say. "You do not realize that it would be a good thing for us if one man should die for the sake of the people—instead of the whole nation being destroyed."

Nigel's whiskers shook with anger—and glee. "Caiaphas doesn't realize what he just said. Little does he know that his warped view of sacrificing Jesus for the sake of Israel is exactly what the Maker intends. But not just for Israel. For the entire world."

Zeeb, Nahshon, Jarib, and Saar looked at one another, then back to Caiaphas. Zeeb finally stood and cleared his throat. "Are we to understand you to say that we should seek the death of Jesus of Nazareth?"

Caiaphas looked at this manipulative member of the Sanhedrin and smiled, knowing he and his scheming colleagues wanted nothing more than an approved mandate to accomplish what they had sought for so long. "Yes. And the sooner the better. For the sake of Israel."

With that Caiaphas left the chamber, and the high council broke up into small groups to further discuss this mandate. The spies were paid and dismissed. Zeeb and the others quickly filed out of the room to plot how they could best arrange the arrest of Jesus.

Nicodemus and Joseph of Arimathea looked at one another in alarm. They knew this was now beyond their control. They had warned Jesus to stay away from Jerusalem, but he had told them in so many words that he would return. He must be lifted up to draw all men to himself.

Nigel placed his head in his paws and shook his head. "Even though I know this is supposed to happen, I can't stand to watch it unfold."

"Watch what unfold?" the sweet pigeon asked.

Nigel climbed up on the pigeon, preparing to take off. "Another slaughter of the innocent."

419

Max smiled as he saw Nigel coming in for a landing where they were camped out for the night, a few miles north of Bethany. It had been a long time since Nigel had traveled by pigeon. Back when Jesus was born he had traveled all the way to Babylon via pigeon to escort the Wise Men to Bethlehem.

"Looks like ye still got yer wings, Mousie," Max greeted him.

"Indeed," Nigel said, gently sliding off the back of his carrier pigeon. "Thank you, my dear. You've been most helpful."

"Anytime, Nigel," the pigeon said before she flapped her wings and took off again.

"So, what did you learn?" Liz asked.

"The high council met to discuss Jesus' latest miracle of raising Lazarus. Caiaphas himself has given the order for Jesus to be killed, for the sake of Israel," Nigel reported. "The leading priests and Pharisees have publicly ordered that anyone seeing Jesus must report it immediately so they can arrest him."

"Oh, no!" Kate exclaimed, putting a paw to her face.

"Those no-good, wicked . . ." Max stammered as his anger raised the fur all along his back.

"Steady, Max," Liz said with a paw to Max's shoulder. "They are simply being used by the Maker to accomplish his divine purposes for Messiah."

"Jesus knows all about their plot," Gillamon assured. "That is why he has stopped his public ministry among the people and left the area around Jerusalem. Word of Jesus' miracle-working power is spreading like wildfire throughout the streets there. We're headed to the village of Ephraim for a few days before we head back for Passover."

Nigel's eyes widened. "Gillamon, are you telling us that things will transpire during Passover?"

"Everything will unfold with undeniable meaning and timing," Gillamon replied.

"The Passover Lamb," Liz said softly, her eyes welling up. She turned her gaze to the others and then to Gillamon. "Jesus will be the Lamb who takes away the sins of the world."

420

The group was very quiet and somber as the next few days passed. Jesus continued to teach wherever they went, and the women followers rejoined them from Capernaum. They wanted to join Jesus and the others as they made their way to Jerusalem for the Passover. The disciples were filled with awe, and the people following behind were overwhelmed with uncertainty. They knew things were heating up in clashes between Jesus and the Sanhedrin, but no one quite grasped what it all meant.

Jesus was walking ahead of them, alone. He was deep in thought. None of his followers knew how to approach him or even what to say.

Max studied Jesus and was filled with such deep respect he could hardly control his emotions. "There be two types of courage. One be the kind ye have when ye jest simply r-r-respond ta things. But there be a higher kind," Max went on. "When ye see a man who sees wha's comin' ahead, gr-r-rim though it may be, an' he has time ta turn back—an' easily could—but doesn't, aye, this be a higher courage then. Jesus be a hero unlike any I've ever known. The most courageous One there ever were."

"Perfectly said, Max," Nigel agreed. "Jesus has set his face toward Jerusalem, even though he knows what awaits him there. He's a hero indeed."

Max trotted up and walked with Jesus the rest of the afternoon, keeping him company.

Later that evening they stopped to rest under the shelter of some trees. They were about fifteen miles from Jerusalem, and would pass through Jericho on the way. When the people got settled, Jesus pulled the twelve disciples aside. They needed to hear what he had to say. And he needed to say it out loud. When the twelve were gathered around the fire, Gillamon and the animals settled under a tree nearby.

"Listen," Jesus said, "we're going up to Jerusalem, where the Son of Man will be betrayed to the leading priests and the teachers of religious law. They will sentence him to die and hand him over to the Romans. They will mock him, spit on him, flog him with a whip, and kill him, but after three days he will rise again."

Upon hearing this, Kate buried her face in Max's fur. Liz shook her head as her eyes filled with tears. Al surrounded her with his paws.

The disciples looked to the ground, none of them uttering a word.

"This is the third time Jesus has told them what is to come," Nigel noted. "But this time, with more horrific details."

421

Liz sniffed and wiped her eyes. "The disciples know that Jesus is Messiah, and they know he is going to die. But they do not know what to make of putting these facts together, no?"

"Yet they continue to follow him," Clarie said. "They love him so much they are willing to accept what is to come without understanding."

Max scanned the faces of the disciples. "I still wonder which one of them be the betr-r-rayer."

It was all Peter could do to bite his tongue and not denounce Jesus' words. He couldn't sit still, so got up to get a bite to eat. Some of the others followed him. But James and John went over to sit by Jesus.

"Master, we want you to grant us a special request," James said, looking at John and then at Jesus.

"What do you want me to do for you?" answered Jesus.

John spoke up, "Give us permission to sit one on each side of you in the glory of your kingdom!"

Jesus paused a moment before replying. Max's fur went straight up.

"I CANNOT BELIEVE THEY JEST ASKED JESUS THAT!" Max growled. "He jest told them wha' were goin' ta happen ta him with his *death!* An' all these two lads can think aboot be their own *ambition!*"

"Steady, Max," Liz said. "*Oui,* it is horrible, but watch how Jesus handles this."

"You don't know what you are asking," Jesus finally replied. "Can you drink the cup I have to drink? Can you go through the baptism I have to bear?"

"Yes," John answered, nodding eagerly.

"We can," James quickly added.

"You will indeed drink the cup I am drinking, and you will undergo the baptism which I have to bear!" Jesus replied. "But as for sitting on either side of me, that is not for me to give—such places belong to those for whom they are intended."

Nigel shook his head. "How little they understand about Messiah! They still think Jesus will have an earthly kingdom with right-hand men by his side."

"Aye, maybe one of these be the betr-r-rayer!" Max scowled.

"But consider this," Liz said. "These Sons of Thunder are ambitious enough to believe Jesus will be triumphant. They are in his inner circle, and stand ready to be at Jesus' side."

"At least their hearts be in the right place," Kate agreed.

"What did Jesus mean aboot the cup and the baptism?" Al asked, scratching his head. "I thought he were already baptized."

"The term 'cup' has long been used as a metaphor for the life and experience that the Maker hands to men," Liz explained. "David and Isaiah both used this term, no?"

"Right you are, my dear," Nigel interjected. "And when Jesus speaks of baptism, he is asking these two if they can face being submerged in the hatred, pain, and death Jesus will endure."

"And notice how Jesus doesn't even try to decide things that are for the Maker alone to decide," Clarie offered. "Here he is the King of all, yet he always obediently defers to his heavenly Father."

By this time Peter and the others had rejoined Jesus, James, and John by the fire, catching the end of their conversation.

"Who are you to ask such a thing of the Master!" Peter demanded to know. "What makes you think you deserve to be at Jesus' right and left side?"

"Oh dear, this could definitely cause a divide among the disciples," Nigel lamented.

Jesus held his hands up to silence the disciples, who were grumbling among themselves. "You know that the rulers in this world lord it over their people, and officials flaunt their authority over those under them."

Jesus eyed each of the disciples to make sure they understood him. They slowly murmured and nodded in agreement.

"But among you it will be different. Whoever wants to be a leader among you must be your servant, and whoever wants to be first among you must be the slave of everyone else," Jesus explained. "For even the Son of Man came not to be served but to serve others and to give his life as a ransom for many."

"That shut 'em up," Max said.

Liz nodded. *"Oui,* Jesus is making the standards of greatness crystal clear to these men. Service is the standard, not the ruling over others."

"Brilliant," Nigel said, shaking his head at Jesus' radical teaching. "Greatness consists not of reducing others to one's service, but in reducing oneself to *their* service."

Gillamon leaned back. "Jesus has always given himself as the example. He doesn't ask any of his followers to do what he hasn't done himself."

"Aye, an' he'll give himself ta pay for others ta have life," Kate said. "So these laddies really don't yet understand wha' they were askin' Jesus with all their ambition talk."

"Seems to me they should know—without a cross," shared Al, "there can't be a crown."

No one could add anything to Al's profundity. A chorus of quiet "Amens" drifted up into the night sky.

423

52

A Wee Little Man

"Bartimaeus? Blind Bartimaeus? He can see?!" the man exclaimed, handing the woman her purchase of fresh balsam.

The woman nodded as she handed the merchant the coins. "I saw it for myself. When that blind beggar heard that Jesus of Nazareth was coming down the road he called out to him, begging him for healing."

"And Jesus healed him? Just like that?" the man asked, astonished. "I've heard about how he dines with tax collectors and sinners, and heard rumors about his healing powers, but never gave him much thought, seeing as how he's never come here."

"Well, he's on his way into town, along with a big group—his disciples and other followers," the woman told him. "They're on their way to Jerusalem for Passover."

Zacchaeus stood in the shadows of the market, listening to this conversation. He frequently listened to the merchants around Jericho as they conducted business. As chief tax collector, he had risen to the top of his profession and become extremely wealthy by paying careful attention to the money exchanging hands in Jericho, the greatest tax center in all Palestine. He quickly learned if anyone tried to cheat on their taxes, and he showed no mercy to those who couldn't pay, throwing them out of their homes or shutting down their livelihoods. Zacchaeus had more money than anyone, and lived in the finest home in Jericho. And . . . he was miserable.

Like Matthew, he had made the choice to betray his countrymen by working for the Roman government. He collected the taxes for Rome and in turn pocketed tremendous amounts of money for himself. He long ago was kicked out of the synagogue and was a despised outcast of the Jewish community, hated by everyone. Were it not for the fact he was so short, he would have even been a physical bully as well. But he had money enough to hire thugs to rough up anyone who crossed him along the way.

Zacchaeus fiddled with the coin he had recently lifted with a little sleight of hand from a Roman centurion passing through Jericho on business for Herod Antipas. It was a denarius with the image of Caesar Augustus and his star that supposedly announced his deity. Zacchaeus rubbed his finger along the edge of the Star Coin where an indentation had marred it. The coin was still of value but it was defective.

As he studied the coin he saw how Augustus was remembered with the tribute by Tiberius, who had minted this coin. *How will I be remembered?* Zacchaeus thought to himself. He frowned at the answers that readily came to mind. No one would mourn when he was gone. In fact, they would rejoice. Thank goodness his parents hadn't lived long enough to see the kind of man he had become. At birth they had given him a name that meant "Righteous One." He laughed sadly. *I haven't lived up to my name now, have I? I'm a thief and a cheat. I'm defective like this coin. But I don't have any value. The only thing valuable about me is the money I possess.*

His heart was empty. His life felt meaningless. He had it all in terms of earthly possessions, yet he had nothing of real worth. He had heard of this Jesus of Nazareth and his radical teachings. People passing through Jericho passed on the latest news from the region, including the movement surrounding this Galilean. Jesus dined with tax collectors and sinners, drawing criticism from the Pharisees. He had even been called a blasphemer for healing on the Sabbath and forgiving sins. None of what this radical rabbi did made much sense to Zacchaeus. *Why would he purposely associate himself with people like me? If he was a man of God why did he defy the religious rulers? And how is it possible that he healed with such amazing power?* Blind Bartimaeus could now see. *Who is this Jesus of Nazareth?* Zacchaeus wondered.

Just then he heard voices at the end of the street. People were shouting as a crowd proceeded down the main road. "Jesus of Nazareth is here! Make way!"

Zacchaeus felt a pull on his heart to see Jesus for himself. He tried to get a glimpse of the approaching rabbi, but the crowds towered over him, blocking his view. He stood on tiptoe, he even tried to jump up to catch a glimpse, but the people only nudged him farther out of the way. He looked around and up at the trees lining the street. He had an idea.

"Ah, don't you love the aromas here?" Liz breathed in deeply, closing her eyes as she and Al rode in Clarie's saddlebags in the back of the caravan. "The balsam groves of Jericho perfume the air for miles. I've heard the roses of Jericho are exquisite as well."

Al lifted his nose, smelling the air. "Don't smell as nice as fish."

"Don't worry, Al, there's plenty of fish here in Jericho at the market," Gillamon said. "I'll make sure you get plenty before we part company."

"Part company?! Wha' do ye mean, Gillamon?" Max immediately wanted to know.

"Clarie and I won't be travelling on to Jerusalem with you and Jesus. From here on out, you will be on your own," Gillamon explained.

"But why in the world are you departing now, as Jesus is nearing the end of his . . ." Nigel stopped himself.

"You will understand when you reach Jerusalem tomorrow," Clarie said. "There is such a large crowd following Jesus now that we will simply slip away unnoticed. You will need to travel on foot from here on out. It's not far now."

Liz wrinkled her brow, curious as to this sudden change of plans. "Do we need to keep ourselves hidden from the disciples?"

"No, travel on with them for now," Gillamon instructed. "When you get to Jerusalem you can go off on your own so you are free to observe the events at will."

"When will we see ye again?" Kate asked.

"Soon, dear Kate," Clarie reassured her. "When the time is right."

Al's lip trembled. "I hate good-byes."

"It's not for long, Al," Gillamon said, giving the big orange cat a pat on the head.

"I say, what in the world is that chap doing up in a tree?" Nigel asked, pointing to the sycamore tree up ahead.

"Where?" Max asked, craning his neck to see. He grinned. "He's a wee little lad, ain't he?"

"It appears he is trying to see Jesus," guessed Liz. "His gaze is following in Jesus' direction."

Jesus was up ahead with his disciples, who surrounded him as he made his way along the crowded street. As they came to the sycamore tree Jesus stopped and smiled. He looked up and saw Zacchaeus sitting in the tree.

"Zacchaeus, come down immediately," Jesus called out as he looked up at the little man through the tree branches. "I must stay at your house today."

Zacchaeus was startled to hear Jesus call him by name. *How does he know my name?* He pointed to himself and Jesus laughed. "Yes, Zacchaeus, you! Come on down."

The little man quickly climbed down the branches and made a final jump, landing in the dirt with a thud. He smiled at Jesus and then noticed all the people staring at him. Not only were they shocked that the rabbi would bother to talk to the most despicable man in town, it certainly wasn't a very dignified place for a man of his position to be. Zacchaeus quickly dismissed the stares and greeted Jesus. *Why does he want to be with me?* He didn't bother to wait for himself to answer. For the first time in years, someone had called him by name and smiled at him, wanting to actually spend time with him.

"Certainly, Master," Zacchaeus said, bowing in respect and with a giddiness in his voice. "This way."

Jesus placed his hand on the little man's shoulder. "After you." He then turned to Matthew. "I'd like you to meet my friend, Matthew."

Matthew greeted Zacchaeus warmly as they started walking down the road. The other disciples looked at one another and shrugged their shoulders, falling in line to go with the Master to the home of this chief tax collector.

"I think he's a cute little man," Kate said with a perky grin.

"Well, 'cute' would hardly be the way these people would describe Zacchaeus," Gillamon disagreed as they walked along. "Do you hear what the people are saying?"

427

"Aye, they be murmurin' aboot Jesus, sayin', 'He has gone ta be the guest of a sinner,'" Max answered.

"Let 'em murmur," Kate said. "I think the wee little man is goin' ta be different after this dinner with Jesus."

"This be like a *déjà vu* scene," Al said as he happily chewed on some dried fish.

"*Oui,* like at Matthew's house," Liz said with a smile. "Jesus has turned this chief of sinners around over dinner."

People were gathered outside the house, listening to Jesus through the open door as he taught Zacchaeus.

Suddenly Zacchaeus stood up. His heart was full of emotion from Jesus' teachings. He longed to be reunited with Jehovah and his fellow Jews. He wanted to immediately turn from his corrupt life and become the "righteous one" his parents had named him to be.

"Look, Lord! Here and now I give half my possessions to the poor," Zacchaeus exclaimed, "and if I have cheated anybody out of anything, I will pay back four times the amount."

Murmurs of astonishment and approval rippled through the crowd. They couldn't believe what they were hearing. Zacchaeus had applied the maximum penalty for retribution, which was meted out for the crime of robbery. Four times the amount would never be voluntarily given by someone who had as much to repay as did Zacchaeus.

Jesus smiled and nodded in approval. "Today salvation has come to this house, because this man, too, is a son of Abraham. For the Son of Man came to seek and to save the lost."

"*C'est magnifique!* Another lost son of Israel is found, no?" Liz joyfully exclaimed. "How Jesus loves the prodigals in this world."

"Might I point out that the word Jesus used for 'lost' actually means 'in the wrong place'?" Nigel commented, straightening his spectacles. "Splendid analogy for the wee chap!"

"Aye, like Matthew, he were in the wrong place, but not anymore," Kate added happily.

"I have a story for you," Jesus said, directing his attention to the crowd at large gathered around Zacchaeus's door. The people eagerly leaned in to hear what Jesus had to say.

"A nobleman was called away to a distant empire to be crowned king and then return. Before he left, he called together ten of his servants and divided among them ten pounds of silver, saying, 'Invest this for me while I am gone.' But his people hated him and sent a delegation after him to say, 'We do not want him to be our king.'

"After he was crowned king, he returned and called in the servants to whom he had given the money. He wanted to find out what their profits were. The first servant reported, 'Master, I invested your money and made ten times the original amount!'

"'Well done!' the king exclaimed. 'You are a good servant. You have been faithful with the little I entrusted to you, so you will be governor of ten cities as your reward.'

"The next servant reported, 'Master, I invested your money and made five times the original amount.'

"'Well done!' the king told him. 'You will be governor over five cities.'

"But the third servant brought back only the original amount of money and said, 'Master, I hid your money and kept it safe. I was afraid because you are a hard man to deal with, taking what isn't yours and harvesting crops you didn't plant.'

"'You wicked servant!' the king roared. 'Your own words condemn you. If you knew that I'm a hard man who takes what isn't mine and harvests crops I didn't plant, why didn't you deposit my money in the bank? At least I could have gotten some interest on it.'

"Then, turning to the others standing nearby, the king ordered, 'Take the money from this servant, and give it to the one who has ten pounds.'

"'But, master,' they said, 'he already has ten pounds!'

"'Yes,' the king replied, 'and to those who use well what they are given, even more will be given. But from those who do nothing, even what little they have will be taken away. And as for these enemies of mine who didn't want me to be their king—bring them in and execute them right here in front of me.'"

Al put his paws up to his mouth. "This story has a scary endin'."

"Only for the enemies of the king, lad," Max said.

"I believe Jesus has just told a story not about money, but about his Kingdom," Liz suggested. "He knows his disciples and followers still believe he is setting up an earthly kingdom. This story is about them. He is going to leave them here to do his work for a time, entrusting them with the good news to multiply his Kingdom here in the world."

"Precisely, my pet!" Nigel echoed. "But the king's own people who didn't want him to be king will be treated harshly when Jesus returns in his glory."

"Aye, but the servants who invest an' multiply wha' he trusts them with will get a r-r-reward when he returns," Max added.

"The good servants will get more trust an' responsibility," Kate pointed out.

"Well done," Gillamon praised them. "You have become quite expert at interpreting Jesus' parables."

"But I'm afraid the disciples don't understand this one well," Nigel replied with a frown. "They look terribly confused."

"They will understand things far more on the other side of the cross," Gillamon said. "But until then, their confusion will only grow."

"I'm dr-r-readin' this week," Max frowned, hanging his head.

430

Gillamon put his hand under Max's chin and lifted his head to gaze into his eyes. "As hard as this week will be, remember what Jesus told you. His time is finally approaching, so you must let it come," he gently encouraged. "I know you'll want to fight against it with every courageous bone in your body, my friend. But remember what I've always told you."

"Aye—know that I be loved an' I be able," Max replied.

"That's right," Gillamon said, looking around at the Order of the Seven. "Know that you all are loved and able for the days ahead."

He stood and took Clarie by the reins. "It's time for us to go."

"Keep each other strong," Clarie said. "We'll see you soon."

Max put his front paws on Gillamon's legs. "I'll miss ye, Gillamon."

Gillamon gave Max one last petting. "I'll miss you, too. But I'm never far away." Max jumped back down and nodded as Gillamon reached out to touch each animal.

"Adieu, mes amis," Liz said. *"Bon voyage."*

Gillamon looked in Jesus' direction and their eyes locked. Jesus gave a slight nod of understanding and with that Gillamon and Clarie walked off into the night.

"Here!" Zacchaeus insisted, handing a bag of coins to Jesus as he also stood to depart. "Please take this money and use it as you will, and for whatever you need."

"Thank you, my friend," Jesus told Zacchaeus as he took the bag and handed it off to Judas, the treasurer for the disciples.

Judas took the bag and raised his eyebrows when he felt the weight of the coins. "We will make good use of this!"

"Ther-r-re's somethin' not quite r-r-right aboot him," Max growled, watching Judas.

Nigel tapped his finger on his mouth. "Hmmm . . . I've thought the same, old boy. He strikes a note of discord in my mind. Always seems a bit too preoccupied with money."

Zacchaeus suddenly felt the marred coin in his tunic. He didn't want to hold onto it any longer. "Oh, and take this, too, please." He stumbled and fell as he raced forward, the coin flying toward the animals. It rolled around and landed right before Liz. She recognized it immediately. *Armandus's Star Coin! How did this get here?*

Judas ran over and picked it up. "Got it." But instead of putting it in their coin bag, he hid it in the folds of his tunic.

Liz frowned at Judas. "I wonder who the *real* wee little man is here tonight."

431

53

REJOICE JERUSALEM: THY KING COMETH UNTO THEE

Armandus stationed his men at key points along the route to Jerusalem, fully aware of the dangers posed by the Zealots who were out to overthrow Roman rule. Herod Antipas rode along in his draped litter carried by multiple servants, growing more annoyed with every mile. He was uncomfortable with the continual jostling, even though he reclined on luxurious purple and white satin pillows. Herod insisted that his standard bearers and musicians loudly announce his arrival into Jerusalem for Passover, despite the warnings of his advisors after the recent attacks on his delegates. Not that he would observe Passover himself, but he wanted his subjects to know he was in the city for this event, attempting to garner their approval for political purposes.

"I count fifteen men on horseback and at least thirty foot soldiers," the scout reported. "There are five carts carrying supplies, and Herod's litter is well guarded. Our men are almost in position."

Barabbas and five of his men were well hidden behind an outcropping of rocks. As they saw Herod's entourage approaching, Barabbas held his hand up to ready his cohorts for the attack. He studied the line of guards as they neared the gates of Jerusalem. There were literally thousands of people descending upon the city, so the Zealots could easily blend in with the crowd as they approached Herod. Some of their men were hidden in a cart being pulled by oxen, ready to jump out for the attack.

"This is extremely risky," Barabbas said, looking into the faces of his men. "But the time for action is now. We need to strike while the masses are here. On my mark . . ." He hesitated a moment longer, gripping his dagger in his sweaty palm. The cart was almost in position near Herod's litter. "NOW!"

Barabbas and his men ran out into the open as the other men jumped out of the cart, using daggers to attack the line of Herod's guards. Armandus and his men immediately engaged the Zealots as a riot broke out. Herod heard the clashing of swords and men yelling and broke into a screaming panic.

"DEATH TO HEROD! THE KINGDOM OF HEAVEN IS AT HAND!" the Zealots cried as they attempted to reach Herod's litter.

One of the litter carriers was stabbed, causing the litter to falter, but two soldiers grabbed the attacker while another soldier kept Herod's litter upright.

433

Barabbas stabbed one of the soldiers, killing him instantly before he was surrounded by five Romans who wrestled him to the ground. Three of Barabbas's men escaped unnoticed into the crowd. Armandus's men quickly surrounded the remaining Zealots, killing four of them and capturing another two. "Take these rebels to the prison and the rest of you double up around King Herod!" Armandus ordered.

Herod's chief advisor, Felius, poked his head inside the litter. "My Lord, are you all right?" he asked in alarm.

Herod's face was full of fear and he was ashen from the assassination attempt. "No, I'm NOT all right! I might have been killed!"

"Your men captured the rebels and all is now secure. We're entering the gates now. You will be in your palace momentarily."

Armandus studied the crowd of people who had just witnessed this attack to gauge their reaction. They didn't cheer on the Zealots, but were still full of fear over Herod's potential reaction. They hurried along, staying clear of Herod's men. *Good,* Armandus thought. *This riot was quickly squelched. The people at large do not wish to join in.* He was relieved, for there were hundreds of thousands of Jews entering Jerusalem. A small riot could spread like wildfire.

"It's those followers of Jesus of Nazareth who have stirred things up!" Herod ranted once they were inside the palace. "They've been preaching all over Palestine about the Kingdom of heaven!"

"My Lord, from what we've been able to discern the followers of Jesus are not Zealots," Felius replied. "They do not preach violence against Rome, but have a message of peace. This Kingdom of heaven about which they speak is simply some lofty ideal. It's more a concept than an actual dominion."

"Tell that to the Zealots! They take this Kingdom of heaven talk to mean an overthrow!" Herod screamed, wild-eyed and still panicked.

"It is our belief that the Zealots are using the teachings of the Galilean for their own purposes. Jesus of Nazareth is not the real threat here," Armandus explained.

"MY kingdom is very real and it is here to stay!" Herod screamed, picking up and throwing a pitcher of water that a servant had brought in for him. The pitcher exploded on the wall, and water splashed everywhere. "I will execute these Zealots and any of these fanatical followers of Jesus who speak against ME!"

"Understood, my Lord. The Zealots are locked away, awaiting execution," Armandus reported. "Rest assured I will have our guards post an extra watch to help prevent any further insurrections while you are in Jerusalem."

Herod collapsed on the couch of pillows, resting his arm over his eyes. His rage suddenly turned into a pitiful whimper.

"Why do these people treat me, their king, this way? I should have been welcomed into Jerusalem after all I've done for them." Felius and Armandus shared an uncomfortable glance. For all the loud rants of Herod, at his core he was a fearful weakling who had no concept of how despised he really was. The people hated him as much as they had hated his father before him. But Herod's insanity kept him in a state of delusion.

"Rest now, my lord," Felius encouraged. "You are weary from the long journey and from your traumatic afternoon."

Herod rolled over and waved them off, signaling he wanted to be alone. Felius quickly ushered all the servants out of the room, closing the doors behind him as he and Armandus exited the royal chambers.

"Keep an eye on any disturbances you see," Felius instructed. "With a crowd this large during Passover, there is no telling what may happen in the streets of Jerusalem. There are certain to be more Zealots about."

Armandus struck his balled fist to his chest in salute and nodded. He turned away and pulled the plumed helmet from under his arm, putting it on and tightening his chin strap. As he walked out into the halls leading to the Praetorium, he considered the mounting tensions between the Zealots, Rome, and other factions that made Palestine a hotbed of hostility.

He knew that Jesus was being used by the Zealots to further their agenda of overthrowing Rome's rule in Palestine. They twisted his teachings to accommodate their desires for Israel to be ruled by their own true King of the Jews, not one of the puppet Herodian kings. Armandus had questioned what Jesus meant by 'the Kingdom of heaven.' He knew Jesus taught love and forgiveness, not war and hatred. But strangely enough, he also knew that the Sanhedrin despised Jesus of Nazareth as much as the Zealots despised Herod. If the Zealots were twisting Jesus' teachings for their own agenda, he wondered if the Sanhedrin would do the same.

435

When Jesus, his disciples, and his other followers were a short distance from the villages of Bethphage and Bethany at the Mount of Olives, he had everyone briefly stop and rest. He called over two of his disciples, Philip and Nathaniel, to give them an assignment.

"Go to the village ahead of you, and as you enter it, you will find a colt tied there, which no one has ever ridden," Jesus explained. "Untie it and bring it here. If anyone asks you, 'Why are you untying it?' say, 'The Lord needs it.'"

"As you wish, Master," Nathaniel said, and together he and Philip immediately went off to do as Jesus had requested.

Peter watched as the two disciples walked ahead. "Teacher, where are they going?"

"They are getting my transport. Today I will enter Jerusalem not as a worshipper," Jesus replied, "but as a King."

The old lady sat by a pile of palm fronds, weaving them into baskets, when she saw two men walking up the street. As they approached she saw them smile broadly when one of the men hit the other man in the chest with the back of his hand, getting his attention. They were pointing at her young donkey. She watched as the two men walked right up to the colt, and started untying it.

"Why are you untying the colt?" she asked them, slowly getting to her feet.

Philip and Nathaniel looked at one another. "The Lord needs it," Nathaniel explained.

The old lady reached down for a palm frond and walked over to the men. She smiled and handed it to Philip as she petted the donkey softly. The donkey looked up at her with its young, soulful eyes and she leaned over and rested her head on its muzzle, softly saying, "Hosanna!" She straightened up, nodded, and turned to go sit back down.

The two men gave her a curious look, shrugged their shoulders, and took the donkey by the reins to head back to Jesus. As they walked along, Philip twirled the palm branch in his hand. "How do you think the Master knew that this donkey would be there?"

"If he knew I was sitting under a fig tree those three years ago, he would know this donkey would be here," Nathaniel replied, remembering that first encounter with Jesus. "He knows everything before it happens, it seems."

"He even knew the donkey's owner would let us just take him," Philip said, looking back to glance at the old lady. But all he saw were her palm fronds and baskets. She was gone.

Jesus sat with the animals in the shade while they waited for the men to return. "This is it," he said.

"Are you ready?" Liz asked, softly putting her paw on Jesus' arm.

Jesus smiled and gently petted her on the head. "I am, Liz. I'm grateful this day has finally come."

"We're with ye all the way, Jesus," Max said.

"Thank you, Max. I'll especially need your support for the week ahead," Jesus said.

"Jesus, may I inquire as to why Gillamon and Clarie had to depart?" Nigel asked.

"They needed to make preparations for today," Jesus explained. "I'm an outlaw now, after the raising of Lazarus. The Sanhedrin have already ordered my arrest."

"So wha' are ye goin' ta do?" Kate asked with concern. "Enter Jerusalem in secret then?"

Jesus stood up and gazed in the direction of the magnificent city. "I'm going to boldly enter the main gate, loudly announced by the people." He saw the two disciples walking up the road with the donkey. "Here come our friends now."

"Where'd they get the donkey?" Al asked.

"You'll see," Jesus told the kitty and smiled, going to greet the men.

The animals watched as the men brought the donkey over to Jesus. As they threw their cloaks on the colt and helped Jesus up on its back, the donkey looked over at them with smiling, twinkling eyes.

437

"Don't tell me," Max said as he broke out in a grin. "I'd know those eyes anywhere."

"I say, is that who I think it is?" Nigel asked.

"Clarie?" Kate asked.

"But it is Gillamon!" Liz exclaimed. "Of course! Zechariah's prophecy! *Rejoice greatly, Daughter Zion! Shout, Daughter Jerusalem! See, your king comes to you, righteous and victorious, lowly and riding on a donkey, on a colt, the foal of a donkey.*"

"Splendid! And of course it must be a donkey never before ridden, as is only fitting for a king," Nigel said. "When a ruler comes riding a donkey, it signifies peace."

"*Oui,* as opposed to a ruler riding a horse, which is a sign of war," Liz added. "Jesus is the Prince of Peace."

They saw the shadow of a bird circling overhead. A pigeon, it landed next to Nigel.

"Clarie?" Kate asked.

"I'm Naomi," the pigeon replied. "Nigel, do you care for a ride?"

"Splendid to see you again! I would be overjoyed, my dear," Nigel said, bowing humbly with his paw draped across his chest. "Cheerio!"

he exclaimed as they took off to soar above the incredible scene below.

A surge of excitement rippled through the disciples and other followers as they began to cheer and accompany Jesus down the road. It didn't take long for the crowds to recognize Jesus, and they, too, started shouting and greeting him. As he went along, people spread their cloaks on the road. Others cut branches from the trees and spread them on the road. The crowds who went ahead of him and those who followed shouted,

"Hosanna to the Son of David!"

"Blessed is the king who comes in the name of the Lord!"

"Peace in heaven and glory in the highest!"

"Blessed is the king of Israel!"

"Aye, Jesus be comin' inta Jerusalem, boldly claimin' it as a King an' defyin' those Phar-r-risees!" Max cheered.

"Nothing could be so bold or daring, *ooh-la-la,* for an outlaw to defiantly enter the city! And the people are shouting 'Hosanna!' which means 'Save us now'," Liz told her friends in amazement.

"Sure, and Rabbi Isaac would say Jesus has a lot o' *chutzpah* to do that," Al added.

The disciples were hugging each other and celebrating that Jesus was so wildly received by the people, but none more so than Judas. He couldn't wait to meet his Zealot connections in the city after this triumphal entry. He could almost taste the coming victory for a newly established kingdom. Things were progressing perfectly.

A group of Pharisees walked along in the crowd and were appalled by what was happening. They shouted over the din of cheering, "Teacher, rebuke your disciples!"

"I tell you," Jesus replied as he rode along, "if they keep quiet, the stones will cry out." He shook his head at the blind Pharisees, who stood back and folded their arms in protest as the procession continued in full force.

Tears quickened in Jesus' eyes as he approached Jerusalem. He quietly spoke to the city. "If you, even you, had only known on this day what would bring you peace—but now it is hidden from your eyes. The days will come upon you when your enemies will build an embankment against you and encircle you and hem you in on every side. They will dash you to the ground, you and the children within your walls. They

438

will not leave one stone on another, because you did not recognize the time of God's coming to you."

Jarib, Zeeb, Saar, and Nahshon stood up on the wall overlooking the city and watched what was happening. They had heard the joyous shouts of the crowd surrounding Jesus when he called Lazarus from the tomb and raised him from the dead, and they were still spreading the word. Therefore many people, because they had heard he had performed this sign, went out to meet him.

"See, we are getting nowhere with this Jesus," Saar shouted in frustration, holding his hand out. "Look how the whole world has gone after him!"

"We can't arrest him like this," Jarib said. "Not when the people are surrounding him this way."

"He's become more popular than ever!" Nahshon lamented.

Zeeb stood silently, pursing his lips and squinting as he thought this through. His eyes studied the twelve disciples, who they knew were always by the side of this outlaw. His eyebrows went up as he saw one of the disciples walk over to talk with a group of known insurgents when they entered the city. "Perhaps we need someone on the inside to help us."

439

"Utterly thrilling to see Jesus' triumphal entry into Jerusalem from up here!" Nigel shouted, full of exhilaration with the sights below. He could see Jesus heading toward the Temple court area, followed by his disciples, all except for one. "Now where is *he* going?"

"Who? Jesus?" Naomi asked.

"No, Judas." Nigel frowned. "Let's find out. Please follow that man."

Before entering the Temple courts, Jesus stopped and slid to the ground. Putting his head near the donkey's ears, he whispered, "Thank you, my friend." The donkey nodded and closed its eyes tight.

At that moment, Nathaniel and Philip looked over to see the old lady standing there by the wall, lifting her palm frond in the air. "Hosanna to the king!" she called.

Giving each other an amazed look, they shrugged their shoulders and took the donkey over to her. "Thank you," they told her.

The old lady took the donkey and wrapped her hands around his muzzle and smiled. "Anything for the Lord."

The men nodded and turned to rejoin Jesus and the others as they entered the Temple courts. Thousands of people were milling about, and the familiar Passover sights, sounds, and smells filled the air.

Jesus looked up at the magnificent Temple and closed his eyes as he breathed a prayer. "Father, here I am, offering myself. Give me the strength and wisdom for the days ahead."

"Rabbi! Please, my little boy needs you," a man cried out, running to Jesus with a toddler in his arms. The little boy still clung to a palm branch and waved it around. "Please, I know you can heal him."

Jesus opened his eyes and smiled at the man with the lame boy whose legs were incapable of walking, running, or playing. He placed his hands on the toddler's legs. Soon the little boy began squirming to get down out of his father's arms. The man looked at Jesus and tears filled his eyes as he gently placed his son on the ground. Immediately the little boy began jumping and running around.

440

Cheers erupted from the crowd and a swarm of people descended on Jesus. He began healing the blind and the lame and the sick. "Hosanna to the Son of David," the children shouted, surrounding Jesus with smiles, hugs, and laughter.

A group of chief priests and scribes, the teachers of the Law, saw the wonderful things Jesus did and the children shouting in the Temple courts. They approached him indignantly.

"Do you hear what these children are saying?" they asked him.

"Yes," replied Jesus, smiling at the children, "have you never read, 'From the lips of children and infants you, Lord, have called forth your praise'?"

"No one's layin' a finger on Jesus," a surprised Max pointed out as the disgruntled priests stormed off.

"So much for them arrestin' him on sight then," Kate said happily.

"The Pharisees are afraid of the people," Liz observed, watching the masses, who had been captivated by Jesus, slowly start to depart. "They won't make a move when he's here in the Temple."

Evening was settling in. Jesus and his disciples got up to leave the courts to make their way to Bethany, at the Mount of Olives, where they would be staying during Passover.

Liz noticed Judas coming from another direction to join the disciples as they left the Temple area. She wrinkled her brow, suddenly realizing he had not been in the Temple area all afternoon.

"Mousie always says rats come out at night," Al said, looking at the darkening sky.

Liz frowned as she watched Judas. "They most certainly do, *mon cher*. They most certainly do."

THE UPPER HAND IN THE TEMPLE

I t was after midnight when Nigel rejoined Max, Liz, and the others at the Mount of Olives, where Jesus was encamped.

"Wake up!" Nigel whispered in Max's ear before scurrying over to Liz. "Do awaken, my dear. It is most urgent!"

Slowly Max and Liz roused and saw Nigel pacing back and forth, wringing his hands.

"Wha's goin' on, Mousie?" Max wanted to know.

"I've had the most distressing evening. And I believe I know who Jesus' betrayer will be," Nigel explained.

"Did you follow Judas?" Liz asked.

"Yes, how did you know?" Nigel asked as he adjusted his spectacles.

"I saw him return as Jesus and the disciples left the Temple, and it dawned on me that he had been missing all afternoon," Liz relayed. "Where did he go?"

"He went to a group of Zealots who are out to overthrow the Roman government by force," Nigel began. "Evidently there was an attempt led by a man named Barabbas earlier in the day. A group of Zealots actually attacked Herod as he entered the city. Most were killed or captured, but three escaped. Judas believes in their cause and gave them money to buy more weapons! He actually believes Jesus is going to usher in his new kingdom here as an earthly ruler, and has been giving money to the Zealots to prepare them to assist in the overthrow!"

"So Judas has been stealing money from the treasury of Jesus and the disciples," Liz said, shaking her head. "I suspected as much when I saw him take Armandus's coin that Zacchaeus gave to Jesus. I still don't know how Zacchaeus even came by it."

"Is Judas completely daft?!" Max growled. "Don't he know Jesus ain't aboot ta set up anythin' here on Earth right now?"

"I'm afraid not," Nigel lamented. "But there's more. The Star Coin went to the Zealots and I followed them. Through a series of transactions, it has landed in the hands of some Herodians who would love nothing more than to get Jesus out of the picture. Word is that Herod blames the attack today on Jesus' teaching that 'the Kingdom of heaven is at hand.'"

"Wha' a bloomin' mess!" Max said.

"*Oui,* but back to Judas," Liz said. "He has been stealing from Jesus and living a double life this entire time. If he plans to use Jesus' popularity as a platform to launch another agenda, he is dangerous."

"Ah, right you are. Once he sees that Jesus will not do as he desires . . ." Nigel began.

"That r-r-rat'll betr-r-ray Jesus in a heartbeat," Max finished grimly. "I jest don't understand how Jesus could've picked such a bad lad."

"Jesus knows all things, so he must have known about Judas even before he chose him," Liz said.

"That can only mean one thing," Nigel, with furrowed brow, told Max and Liz. "Jesus *needs* Judas . . . as an instrument of betrayal."

"This isn't good," Liz said. "I fear Jesus will be none too pleased." She, Max, Kate, Al, and Nigel were sitting in an alcove in the Temple, where the money changers and sellers had returned to fill the courts. Early this morning Jesus and the disciples had come to spend the day there.

As before, Jesus quickly grew angry and drove out all who were buying and selling there. He began to overturn the tables of the moneychangers and the benches of those selling doves. "It is written," he said to them, "'My house will be called a house of prayer,' but you are making it 'a den of robbers!'"

The merchants immediately left the area, but the people remained

443

behind. As before, the people surrounded Jesus with so much praising that the Temple guards didn't dare lay a hand on him, despite the charge of the Pharisees to arrest him. And also as before, the Roman guards looked on from the Antonia Fortress.

"Sir, should we send some soldiers down there?" one of the Roman guards asked.

Armandus marveled that Jesus had cleansed the Temple a second time, yet the Jewish leaders did nothing about it. He was relieved. "No, things have already settled, and the Temple guards didn't take action. But keep an eye out."

"Sure, all the people be lovin' Jesus' teachin'," Al said.

"Aye, but here come the chief priests an' the elders," Kate noticed. "An' they don't look too happy."

"Do they ever look happy?" Al asked.

444 Jesus looked up from where he sat as the group of disgruntled Jewish leaders approached. He didn't bother to stand.

"By what authority are you doing all these things?" one of the priests asked. "Who gave you the right?"

"I'll tell you by what authority I do these things if you answer one question," Jesus replied calmly. "Did John's authority to baptize come from heaven, or was it merely human?"

"*Ooh-la-la!* Jesus has turned the tables on them again, no?" Liz cheered. "Look at them trying to find an answer."

The chief priests huddled together to discuss how they would answer Jesus' question.

"Right!" Nigel agreed. "If they say John's baptism was from heaven, Jesus will ask them why they didn't believe John. But if they say it was merely human, they'll be mobbed because the people believe John was a prophet. Another stroke of genius!"

The Jewish leaders looked at one another uncomfortably. One of them finally replied, "We don't know."

"Then I won't tell you by what authority I do these things," Jesus responded.

"That be the lamest of the lamest answers the laddies could've given! Ha!" Max chuckled. "Way ta go, Jesus!"

"But what do you think about this?" Jesus followed up. "A man with two sons told the older boy, 'Son, go out and work in the vineyard today.' The son answered, 'No, I won't go,' but later he changed his mind and went anyway. Then the father told the other son, 'You go,' and he said, 'Yes, sir, I will.' But he didn't go. Which of the two obeyed his father?"

The chief priests replied in unison, "The first."

Jesus nodded. "I tell you the truth, corrupt tax collectors and prostitutes will get into the Kingdom of God before you do. For John the Baptist came and showed you the right way to live, but you didn't believe him, while tax collectors and prostitutes did. And even when you saw this happening, you refused to believe him and repent of your sins."

"He's not lettin' up for a second!" Kate said as Jesus began another parable.

"Now listen to another story. A certain landowner planted a vineyard, built a wall around it, dug a pit for pressing out the grape juice, and built a lookout tower. Then he leased the vineyard to tenant farmers and moved to another country. At the time of the grape harvest, he sent his servants to collect his share of the crop. But the farmers grabbed his servants, beat one, killed one, and stoned another. So the landowner sent a larger group of his servants to collect for him, but the results were the same.

"Finally, the owner sent his son, thinking, 'Surely they will respect my son.'

"But when the tenant farmers saw his son coming, they said to one another, 'Here comes the heir to this estate. Come on, let's kill him and get the estate for ourselves!' So they grabbed him, dragged him out of the vineyard, and murdered him.

"When the owner of the vineyard returns," Jesus asked, "what do you think he will do to those farmers?"

The religious leaders replied, "He will put the wicked men to a horrible death and lease the vineyard to others who will give him his share of the crop after each harvest."

Then Jesus asked them, "Didn't you ever read this in the Scriptures? 'The stone that the builders rejected has now become the cornerstone. This is the Lord's doing, and it is wonderful to see.'

"I tell you, the Kingdom of God will be taken away from you and

445

given to a nation that will produce the proper fruit. Anyone who stumbles over that stone will be broken to pieces, and it will crush anyone it falls on."

"They know Jesus is talking about them, no? They are the wicked farmers," Liz relayed. "Jesus used this verse from Psalm 118 to apply to himself. It was originally written to mean Israel as the stone, but now he is saying it is he! He is the foundation stone on which everything is built and the cornerstone that holds everything together."

Nigel raised a finger in the air. "And, for one to stumble or refuse his way means one will be crushed out of life."

"Like Nebuchadnezzar's statue dream!" Liz exclaimed. "Remember Daniel said the 'stone not carved by human hands' that would fall upon the feet and crush the enemies of God. Jesus is that stone."

"Brilliant!" Nigel cheered with a fist of victory raised high. "Jesus grows bolder by the hour in setting things right with his teaching!"

"Well, there the laddies go, losin' another round of questions with Jesus," Max observed as the chief priests quickly left the area. "Aye, but they'll be back, ye can be sure of that."

446

After the chief priests reported to the others how their question about John failed to entrap Jesus, they went back to the drawing board to find another way. They wanted to arrest Jesus on the spot, but they were afraid of the people who believed Jesus was a prophet and not to be touched. They would have to catch Jesus in an undeniable affront to God. Or Rome.

"This has to work," Saar said, grinning broadly. "There is no way around this question. He'll be trapped either way he answers!"

"Yes, but the question shouldn't come from us. It needs to come from those who are in a better position to uphold allegiance to Rome," Zeeb said, walking to the window.

Jarib slapped his hand on the table. "The Herodians! They are the perfect ones. They are loyal to Herod, but still hope for deliverance from Rome under his rule. There's enough of both sides of the coin there for them to ask the question."

"But the Sanhedrin and the Herodians are enemies!" Nahshon

pointed out. "What incentive could they have to partner with us on trapping Jesus?"

Zeeb smiled. "Didn't you hear? Herod blames all this Zealot attack business on the teachings of Jesus of Nazareth. The Herodians want to see Jesus out of the picture as much as we do."

"Oh look, another group coming to give it a fair go with Jesus," Nigel said. "Hmmm, this is most peculiar."

"What's peculiar, Mousie?" Al asked.

"This time, some of the Pharisees have brought along some Herodians. These types never mix," Nigel replied. He studied the men more closely. "By Jove, that's one of the men I saw last night. He has the Star Coin!"

"Teacher," the Herodian said with a sickly sweet smile, "we know how honest you are. You teach the way of God truthfully. You are impartial and don't play favorites. Now tell us what you think about this: Is it right to pay taxes to Caesar or not?"

Jesus smiled sarcastically. He knew their evil motives. "You hypocrites!" he said. "Why are you trying to trap me? Here, show me the coin used for the tax." He held out his hand.

One of the men pulled out a denarius and handed it to Jesus. Jesus held it and studied it for a moment, grinning. The disciples were standing nearby. "Why is he grinning?" Andrew asked. The others shrugged their shoulders.

"Whose picture and title are stamped on it?" Jesus asked, holding up the coin.

"Caesar's," they replied in unison.

"Well, then," he said, "give to Caesar what belongs to Caesar, and give to God what belongs to God."

The men immediately looked at one another, at a total loss for words, and turned and walked away, leaving Jesus holding the coin. Jesus smiled as they left, and he rubbed his finger along the marred edge of the coin. Andrew came over to Jesus. "Master, why are you smiling?"

Jesus held the coin up to show it to Andrew. "You see that star, just above the image of Caesar Augustus?"

Andrew squinted as he studied the coin. "Yes, I see it."

"That's *my* star," Jesus grinned and said. "This coin has *my* image on it." He winked at Andrew and gripped the coin, sharing a serendipitous laugh with the disciple.

"Bra-vo! Magnificent! That takes the biscuit!" Nigel cheered. "The coin is now in Jesus' possession!"

"And he has once again defeated the religious leaders with one of their 'unanswerable' questions," Liz echoed. "This one was especially clever, no?"

"How so, Liz?" Kate asked.

"Well, if Jesus had said it wasn't right to pay taxes to Caesar, they could have arrested him on the spot for being a traitor to Rome. And if he said it was right to pay taxes to Caesar, this would have discredited him in the eyes of the Jewish people who see only God as their King," Liz explained.

"I guess Jesus showed ye have to be a good citizen o' both God and country then," Al said.

Liz beamed and kissed Al on the cheek. "Well said, *mon cher!*"

448

The afternoon saw several more attempts by the Sanhedrin to corner Jesus. The Sadducees came, asking a question about marriage after the resurrection—which they didn't even believe in themselves—and the Pharisees attempted one more round of questions about the greatest commandment. Jesus fired back with answer after answer that left them defeated and looking even more foolish in front of the people. He lambasted them with a series of "woes," for their hypocritical, sinful behavior that had gone unchecked for far too long. And he posed one final question to the Sanhedrin about Messiah that finally shut them up, for they couldn't answer it. Jesus had decisively gained the upper hand in the showdown with the religious authorities.

"Beware of these teachers of religious law!" Jesus warned the people. "For they like to parade around in flowing robes and receive respectful greetings as they walk in the marketplaces. And how they love the seats of honor in the synagogues and the head table at banquets. Yet they shamelessly cheat widows out of their property and then pretend to be pious by making long prayers in public. Because of this, they will be more severely punished."

Jesus was tired. He sat down near the collection box in the Temple and watched as the crowds dropped in their money. Many rich people put in large amounts. Then a poor widow came and dropped in two small coins. His eyes filled with tears as he ran his finger along the edge of the Star Coin he still held on to. He knew she had truly given a gift to God, for she had given until it hurt. She had given all she had, entrusting herself to the care of God to provide for her needs.

Jesus called over his disciples. He pointed to the widow. "I tell you the truth, this poor widow has given more than all the others who are making contributions. For they gave a tiny part of their surplus, but she, poor as she is, has given everything she had to live on."

Judas folded his arms over his chest. "What can her pitiful contribution possibly matter?" he murmured under his breath, walking away.

Nigel was about to explode with that remark. He grabbed the fur on his head and held it. "Why that corrupt, arrogant, lying, no-good . . ." he spouted, his voice trailing off.

"Steady, Mousie," Kate said, putting her paw on Nigel's back. "Consider the source, aye? Wha' else would ye expect?"

Jesus sent the disciples on to Bethany, saying he would follow along. Once they had walked off, Jesus motioned for Nigel to come over.

"Jesus wants ye then," Kate encouraged. "Go on then, but be careful."

Nigel looked both ways and scurried over to Jesus, careful to stay out of the footpath of people but hidden within their robes that grazed over him.

"Yes, Jesus? You asked for me?" Nigel asked.

Jesus smiled. "Yes, my small friend." He held up the coin. "You and I both know where this coin has been. But it's time it finds a new home for a while before it reemerges in history."

Nigel clasped his paws together, intrigued. "Indeed! Where is it going?"

Jesus nodded to the widow who slowly made her way out of the Temple area. A basket was draped over her arm. "Take it to her, Nigel."

"Utterly splendid! Oh, won't she be simply delighted to find such treasure in her basket when she returns home?" Nigel cheered. He bowed with one foot forward and his tiny paw draped humbly over his chest. "It will be my honor, my Lord."

449

Jesus smiled and tears once again quickened in his eyes. "She will be dumbfounded to say the least, receiving more than she gave to the Lord today. If only everyone understood what she knows to be true. You can't outgive God."

"No, indeed! And might I add, one sleight of hand deserves another!" Nigel said, with a knowing grin. He put out his paw to take the coin from Jesus, then put it carefully into his mouth.

Jesus watched Nigel carefully navigate the throngs of people to make his way to the widow. Her wrinkled face was solemn as she walked away. Jesus' heart went out to her, for he knew she had nothing in her pantry at home. Nigel carefully scurried up her robe and sneaked into her basket. He dropped the coin and reappeared, giving a salute to Jesus before he scurried away again.

Jesus breathed in deeply and smiled. *Blessings, my daughter whom I love beyond measure. Don't be afraid. I will supply all your needs.*

WHERE YOUR TREASURE IS

The animals sat discussing all that had transpired in the Temple since Jesus' arrival a couple of days earlier. Things were heating up quickly. Earlier today Jesus had clearly told his disciples, "As you know, Passover begins in two days, and the Son of Man will be handed over to be crucified."

At that same time the leading priests and elders were meeting at the residence of Caiaphas, the high priest, plotting how to capture Jesus secretly and kill him. Nigel was listening in on their conversation:

"But not during the Passover celebration," they agreed, "or the people may riot."

"It is no longer a matter of 'if,' but of 'how.' Caiaphas and the Sanhedrin wish for the crowds to leave Jerusalem before they make a move to kill Jesus," Nigel reported later. "Yet Jesus says it will happen at Passover."

"He's setting the time for his own death, no?" Liz pondered. "Look at how Jesus is controlling the events. He has predicted exactly how and when he will be betrayed, mocked, tortured, and crucified. The Sanhedrin ultimately has no power over the divine plan that is unfolding. They will be used to bring things about at the perfect time."

"Aye, but it's goin' ta *feel* like they be in charge when it happens," Max lamented. "It's goin' ta be hard ta sit back an' watch it come."

451

"Jest remember that this is why Jesus came, me love," Kate comforted him. "An' he does it willin'ly."

"*Oui,* even though Jesus has done wonderful things these past three years in teaching and healing, they ultimately do not matter if his sacrifice isn't accomplished," Liz said gravely. "And by speaking the truth so boldly, he is quickly bringing it to pass."

"Few weapons against evil can rival the sword of truth," Nigel added. "And few are brave enough to wield it, for doing so carries a great cost."

Liz nodded somberly. "*Oui, mon ami.* And Evil's counterstrike comes with startling ferocity."

"So things will happen ta set the betr-r-rayal in motion soon," Max said sadly. "Wha's the update on Judas?"

"I haven't seen anything yet per se," Nigel answered. "But he does seem to be a bit touchy, and was actually angry over Jesus' latest announcement of his impending death."

"Aye, but not for Jesus' sake," Kate frowned, "but for his."

"If Judas seeks a takeover by Jesus as an earthly ruler, of course he must be disillusioned by now," Liz suggested. "Jesus has captured the people's hearts and won every argument against the existing religious rulers of Israel. Judas knows Jesus has supernatural powers to enable him to seize control, and the Zealots are waiting in the wings to be soldiers to usher in a victory."

"Brilliant observations, my dear," agreed Nigel. "So Judas must wonder *why* Jesus is so determined to die when he could have it all."

"Jesus ain't the kind o' Messiah the lad wants him to be," Al suggested.

"Big Al, ye're r-r-right!" Max affirmed. "We can't make Jesus out ta be who we want him ta be. We can't change him. He has ta change us."

Kate nodded. "Aye, ye can't use Jesus for yer own reasons. Ye have ta be used by him for his."

"Judas is as blind as the Sanhedrin," Liz said. "They believe they know better than God what this world needs Messiah to be."

"Dreadful mistake," Nigel said, shaking his head and clasping his paws behind his back. "Well, I shall watch Judas's every move from here on out."

"Look lively, Mousie," Max frowned. "Things could happen this ver-r-ry night."

Jesus and Lazarus were in a deep discussion while reclining at the table. Martha was busy serving all of them a grand feast in honor of Jesus and his disciples. The men ate their fill, enjoying the graciousness of this home and the bountiful food spread before them.

"Sources tell me the members of the Sanhedrin now seek to kill *me*, Jesus," Lazarus whispered.

Jesus nodded. "The Sanhedrin seek to destroy the evidence of your miracle by eliminating your life as a daily reminder to the people. Do not fear, Lazarus. They will soon have no reason to come after you."

Lazarus gripped Jesus' arm. "Master, I can't bear the thought that they will kill you. Isn't there another way?"

Jesus looked resolute and answered, "No. But nothing happens that has not been ordained from above. Stay strong."

Suddenly Lazarus's other sister, Mary, came and sat down next to them. Her face was full of emotion and her heart was heavy. Jesus smiled warmly at her with understanding. Mary took out a jar of expensive perfume and reverently poured it on Jesus' feet. She then unpinned her hair and wiped his feet. The house was immediately filled with the fragrance of the perfume. A hush fell over the disciples as they watched this scene, similar to the one involving the woman whom Jesus forgave as she wept and dried his feet with her hair.

453

Judas sat at the end of the table, seething with what was happening. *That perfume is worth a year's wages! What a waste!* His frustration had been mounting all day and he suddenly sat up and burst out, "Why wasn't this perfume sold and the money given to the poor?"

"Leave her alone," Jesus replied with a frown at Judas, fully aware of Judas's deceitful façade of caring about the poor. He knew Judas wanted the money for himself. "Why are you bothering this woman? She has done a beautiful thing to me. The poor you will always have with you, but you will not always have me. When she poured this perfume on my body, she did it to prepare me for burial. Truly I tell you, wherever this gospel is preached throughout the world, what she has done will also be told, in memory of her."

Judas sat back, resenting Jesus' rebuke. His disillusionment had quickly turned to anger, and now, with this, to hatred.

By morning, his hatred had turned to murder.

Nigel sat watching Judas, who was up before anyone. His eyes were darting back and forth and he was fidgeting with the corner of his cloak. He was obviously thinking about things, wrinkling his brow, shaking his head, and looking up at the ceiling. Suddenly he grew still and a wicked look covered his face. For just a few seconds his eyes flashed a menacing red. Nigel's fur stood on end. He had felt the presence of Satan before, and as he looked at Judas, it was unmistakable that Satan was fully present—he had entered Judas himself.

Judas got up and rushed outside, pulling on his cloak as he made haste on foot. He was heading straight for Jerusalem. Nigel didn't have time to alert any of the other animals so he followed Judas alone. He knew right where Judas was going.

Zeeb, Jarib, Nahshon, and Saar sat with their heads together, discussing the situation. Caiaphas and the chief priests and scribes had decided Jesus' fate, but no one could decide exactly how to take hold of Jesus.

"The people would cause an uprising the likes of which we've never seen! Then the wrath of Rome would fall upon us hard and fast," Saar snapped. "But there has to be a way to reach him." "As I mentioned to you before, we need a way inside Jesus' inner circle," Zeeb reminded them. "What better way to get to him?"

The others murmured agreement but no one had a solution. Then came a knock at the door.

"Come," Jarib called.

Two Temple guards opened the door, followed by several chief priests. And there behind them stood Judas. Zeeb's eyebrows went up in delight as he recognized this disciple of Jesus whom he had seen talking with some of the Zealots. "What was I saying?" he whispered as he stood and walked over to greet Judas.

"I am Zeeb," he said with a syrupy tone, his arms outstretched in greeting. "You are one of the followers of Jesus of Nazareth, correct? How can we be of service to you?"

Judas looked around at the men with a cold and calculating stare. There was an eerie understanding between them before he spoke a word. "What are you willing to give me if I deliver him over to you?"

Zeeb slowly turned and looked at the others, whose faces brightened immediately with surprise and delight. A surge of excitement ran through Zeeb, but he kept a calm demeanor.

"Please, have a seat, Judas," Zeeb said, ushering him over to the table to join him and the other priests. "Can we offer you something?" He clapped his hands and servants brought in a pitcher of water and a bowl of fruit. He then whispered in the ear of the Temple guard, who quickly ran out of the room.

Judas sat down and made himself comfortable. He liked being treated this way by these powerful men. It made *him* feel powerful, authoritative, and in control. He reached for a piece of fruit and took a bite. A rush of evil excitement coursed through him and he smiled at the men.

Zeeb sat down next to Judas. "It is very honorable of you to offer to do this, Judas. I think you agree with us that protecting Israel both from false Messiahs and the wrath of Rome is of the utmost importance."

Judas nodded slowly and swallowed the fruit. "Indeed. Jesus is not who I thought he was."

455

The Temple guard came back into the room and brought a box over to set on the table. Zeeb smiled and opened it. "We are prepared to offer you thirty silver coins for arranging the arrest of Jesus of Nazareth," he said as he reached in to take out a handful.

Judas smiled and held out his hand. As Zeeb counted out the amount, the sound of each coin echoed in the room. Nigel sat up high on the window ledge and jumped with each clink. His heart sank to see the price placed on Jesus' head set at the same amount as for a common slave. Mary had given the costly sum of a year's wages to lovingly anoint Jesus. Judas was accepting only a fourth of that amount to betray Jesus.

Where your treasure is, there is your heart also. Nigel remembered Jesus' words, and was sickened as he watched where Judas's heart was.

Judas put the coins into his personal money bag and clutched it with a wicked grin. He stood and Zeeb gave him instructions. "Look for the opportune time. We'll be waiting."

With that Judas left the room. The betrayal was set in motion. Nigel put his head in his paws and shook it in disbelief that this was actually happening. Gillamon had said Satan would return at 'the opportune time.' He shuddered as he realized that time had finally come.

Nigel watched as the men congratulated themselves for having arranged to 'protect Israel from the wrath of Rome.' The little mouse shook his head.

Sadly, now you will incur God's wrath instead.

LAST WORDS,
LAST SUPPER

I t's the festival of unleavened bread today," John said as Jesus and some of the other disciples sat together at the break of day.

Jesus nodded. "John, you and Peter go make preparations for us to eat the Passover."

"Where do you want us to prepare for it?" Peter asked.

"As you enter the city, a man carrying a jar of water will meet you," Jesus instructed. "Follow him to the house that he enters, and say to the owner of the house, 'The Teacher asks: Where is the guest room, where I may eat the Passover with my disciples?' He will show you a large room upstairs, all furnished. Make preparations there."

Peter and John got up. "As you wish, Master," Peter said as they walked over to Judas. "We need money to pay for the supplies for the meal."

Judas reached for the money bag tied to his waist and realized it was his personal stash—the one with the blood money. He moved his hands to the other side of his belt and pulled from the group's treasury. He counted out a few coins and put them in Peter's hand. "There, that should be sufficient."

"Good. Thank you, Judas," John said. "We'll see you there tonight."

Judas nodded and smiled. "Yes, for the Passover meal. See you tonight." As Peter and John walked off, Judas secured his money bag and looked up to see Jesus silently staring at him. Judas felt the weight of Jesus' gaze and turned to go find some breakfast.

When they were alone, the animals surrounded Jesus.

"How can you know what he is up to and remain silent?" Nigel asked, burdened by what he had seen.

"Aye, ye could kill him r-r-right now, on the spot!" Max growled, struggling to deal with what was happening.

Jesus' gaze followed Judas. "I will treat my betrayer with love until the end, giving him the opportunity to turn back from his course. But ultimately he alone is responsible for his sin."

"Jesus, please help us," Liz said. "I speak for all of us when I say we feel at a loss to know what to do."

Jesus turned and looked lovingly at the animals. "Go follow Peter and John, but stay out of sight. Once they leave the place arranged for the Passover meal, go to the upper room," Jesus instructed. "Stay there behind the water pots while Peter and John return to prepare the meal. The rest of us will arrive at sundown, and you will be able to witness everything unfolding from there." He paused and breathed in deeply. "Please pray. Pray for me. Pray for my disciples. Pray for my mother. I won't get to speak with you any longer, but I will know you are there, hidden, and supporting me. And when I am gone, please go to my disciples and my mother and comfort them. That is the greatest thing you can do for me."

Liz's eyes welled up with tears as she went to fall into Jesus' lap. "We will, Jesus. We will do everything you ask. *Je t'aime.*"

Jesus reached down and picked Liz up, holding her tightly in his arms, and gave her a kiss. "Thank you, Liz. I love you, too, little one. *Adieu.*"

Al sat by, his lip quivering with grief. Jesus set Liz down and reached over to place his hand on Al's back. "Be brave, Albert. I'm grateful you are here. You make everyone feel better. Never stop being you."

Tears filled Al's eyes. "I'll try." He lifted a paw to wipe his eyes, then went and hugged his wife, Liz, who wept softly.

Kate and Max next came up to Jesus and he enveloped them both with a big hug. "You two protect the others. Never have there been two dogs I could rely on more. Thank you for being my devoted, fearless friends."

"Oh, Jesus, how I wish things could be different," Kate cried. "But I understand. We'll be there all the way."

Max could barely stand to look Jesus in the eye. He shook his head and then buried his face in Jesus' robe, sobbing. "If I could take yer place, I would."

Jesus lovingly petted Max and whispered in his ear, "I know, Max. You are brave, and your heart is true. I am proud and grateful you are mine."

Finally, Nigel stood by to tell Jesus farewell. "I'm afraid there are no words . . ." he started before taking off his spectacles and wiping away his tears.

Jesus picked Nigel up in his palm and brought him up to his face. "Sometimes words aren't needed, so let what you are feeling settle quietly into your heart. Someday you will have the words, and, to go with those words, a melody that will bless the world."

Nigel wrinkled his brow as he didn't quite understand Jesus' statement. But he bowed humbly. "I am your most humble servant, my liege."

459

Jesus placed Nigel gently on the ground with the others. He smiled with sadness but also with confidence. "Thank you all for who you are and what you mean to me. Go now. I will see you on the other side of the cross."

Max, Kate, Liz, Al, and Nigel somberly nodded and walked off to catch up with Peter and John. Their hearts were heavy and breaking, and no one spoke a word.

"Jesus thinks of everything," John smiled and said as he and Peter saw the man with the water jar walking down the road.

"Yes, and sometimes what he thinks doesn't make sense," Peter said. "Men never carry water jars. That's a woman's task! Still, the Master has his reasons."

They followed the man with the water jar until he entered a house two stories high with an outside staircase leading to an upper room. John and Peter stepped inside and there sat an old man. "Excuse me," John said, "the Teacher asks: Where is the guest room, where I may eat the Passover with my disciples?"

The old man smiled. "Follow me."

He led Peter and John up the stairs and into a room furnished with a large U-shaped table, prepared with pillows surrounding it. The table was set with empty serving bowls and cups. The man with the water jar entered the room and placed it on the table.

"I've taken the liberty to make sure the house is fully prepared. There is no leaven anywhere, so all is clean and ready for you," the man informed them. "Since this is a private meal, there will be no servants to wash the feet of the guests, but here is the basin of water and a towel. The fire and roasting pit are outside."

Peter and John put their hands on their hips and looked around the room. "This is perfect. Thank you."

With that the men walked back outside. The old man bid them farewell and walked off down the street. Peter and John took off in the other direction to the market to purchase the unleavened bread, wine, bitter herbs, salt, fruits, and nuts, and of course to the Temple for the Passover lamb. The man with the water jar walked over to a patch of bushes. He pulled back the leaves and spied the animals, startling them.

460

"They're gone, so you can go up now," the man said. He had beautiful blue eyes.

"Gillamon?" Kate asked.

"Clarie, actually," the man replied. "Gillamon had to go elsewhere."

"Oh, *mon amie,* I am so happy to see you," Liz said. "Will you be able to stay with us?"

"No, I have other tasks, but you will be safe here, and well hidden," Clarie told them. "As I'm sure Jesus explained, things will all begin tonight. Be strong and I will see you soon."

Clarie let the leafy branches go back in place. When the animals came out to go up the stairs, she was gone.

Liz and Nigel quietly informed the others about the things Peter and John were preparing for the meal. "To review, the Passover feast commemorates the events of Israel's delivery from slavery in Egypt," Nigel explained. The angel of death visited Egypt, but passed over the homes of the Hebrews, who were kept safe by putting the blood of a lamb without blemish on the doorframe. So a lamb is sacrificed and prepared every year to remember that event." Al wore a sad look. "I hate that part. I hope Clarie didn't have to do that task today!"

"I am certain she did not, *mon cher,*" Liz assured him. "Now, because the people had to leave so quickly, they had to make bread without leaven. In addition to the unleavened bread and the lamb, there are four items necessary for the Feast, no? One is a bowl of salt water, to remind them of the tears they had shed while in Egypt and the salt waters of the Red Sea that the Maker parted."

"Splendid remembrance idea," Nigel added. "A second item is a collection of bitter herbs, composed of horseradish, chicory, endive, lettuce, horehound, and the like, to remind them of the bitterness of slavery."

"*Oui,* and third is a paste called Charoshet, which is a mixture of apples, dates, pomegranates, and nuts," Liz added.

"That sounds tasty. Wha's that for?" Kate asked.

"It reminds them of the clay with which they were forced to make bricks in Egypt," Liz explained. "They place sticks of cinnamon in the paste to remind them of the straw used to make the bricks."

461

"Finally there are four cups of wine," Nigel said, straightening his spectacles. "Each cup represents a promise of the Exodus from the Maker: 'I will bring you out from under the burdens of the Egyptians; I will rid you of their bondage; I will redeem you with an outstretched arm; and I will take you as my people and will be your God.'"

"So Jesus an' the disciples will observe these things on the night of Jesus' betrayal," Max said. "I think he's got some meanin' in all of this. I'm beginnin' ta connect his timin' then."

"Brilliant deduction, old boy," Nigel said. "Right. The whole Passover feast is about deliverance, and the Lamb is the symbol of safety and salvation from death."

"*Oui,* and the covenant promises of God will be woven into what Jesus will do," Liz added softly. "Deliverance from the bondage of sin . . ."

"And redemption with outstretched arms..." Nigel paused as Jesus and the other disciples arrived, swallowed hard, then continued, ". . . with the blood of the Lamb."

"I can't believe he let Judas sit next ta him!" Max whispered hoarsely.

The animals looked at the men reclining at the table, enjoying the meal. John was seated at Jesus' right and Judas, in the position of honor, on his left.

"Indeed, but he told us he would show love to his betrayer up until the end," Nigel answered. "Oh my, but this is shocking. Look at what Jesus is doing now."

Jesus got up from the table, took off his robe, wrapped a towel around his waist, and poured water into the basin used for washing guests' feet. Then he began to wash the disciples' feet, drying them with the towel he had around him. The disciples looked at one another uncomfortably. This was unheard of, for a rabbi to perform such a lowly task!

Jesus came to Peter. "Lord, are you going to wash my feet?"

Jesus replied, "You don't understand now what I am doing, but someday you will."

"No," Peter protested, "you will never ever wash my feet!"

Jesus replied, "Unless I wash you, you won't belong to me."

Peter exclaimed, "Then wash my hands and head as well, Lord, not just my feet!"

"A person who has bathed all over does not need to wash, except for the feet, to be entirely clean. And you disciples are clean, but not all of you," Jesus said.

"Judas," Liz whispered. "He's referring to Judas. But even now, Jesus still washes his feet. Incredible!"

After washing their feet, Jesus put on his robe again and sat down. "Do you understand what I was doing? You call me 'Teacher' and 'Lord,' and you are right, because that's what I am. And since I, your Lord and Teacher, have washed your feet, you ought to wash each other's feet. I have given you an example to follow. Do as I have done to you. I tell you the truth, slaves are not greater than their master. Nor is the messenger more important than the one who sends the message. Now that you know these things, God will bless you for doing them."

The disciples quietly nodded and began discussing what Jesus had done, stunned by his behavior. But soon they began eating. Then Jesus made a stunning announcement: "I tell you the truth, one of you eating with me here will betray me."

The men were greatly distressed, and looked at one another and

462

down the row of faces to their right and their left, murmuring, "Am I the one?"

"It is one of you twelve who is eating from this bowl with me," Jesus said. "For the Son of Man must die, as the Scriptures declared long ago. But how terrible it will be for the one who betrays him. It would be far better for that man if he had never been born!"

"Even now, Jesus is warning Judas of what is to come," Nigel predicted. "Judas can still turn back now if he chooses."

Peter caught John's eye and mouthed, "Who's he talking about?"

John nodded and leaned over to Jesus and asked, "Lord, who is it?"

Jesus responded quietly, "It is the one to whom I give the bread I dip in the bowl." He reached over, pulled off a piece of bread, dipped it, and gave it to Judas. Judas smiled and took the bread and ate it. Jesus leaned in and said, "Hurry and do what you're going to do."

Judas locked eyes with Jesus and gave a cold, unfeeling stare. He then looked around the table and saw that the disciples had resumed eating, talking quietly among themselves. He casually got up and made his way out the door into the night.

"Those laddies don't even know wha' Jesus meant," Kate noted. "They probably think Jesus were tellin' him ta go an' pay for the food or ta give some money ta the poor."

"Judas didn't turn away from his course," Nigel said, shaking his head. "He's heading into the darkness."

Al frowned. "Aye, it's always night when ye turn yer back on Jesus."

"What do you mean, *cher* Albert?" Liz asked.

"That's when ye get lost in the dark," Al explained.

As soon as Judas left the room, Jesus spoke up. "I am with you for only a short time longer. You are going to look high and low for me. But just as I told the Jews, I'm telling you: 'Where I go, you are not able to come.' Let me give you a new command: Love one another. In the same way I loved you, you love one another. This is how everyone will recognize that you are my disciples—when they see the love you have for each other."

Jesus swallowed hard and expressed deep pain in his eyes. "Tonight all of you will desert me. For the Scriptures say, 'God will strike the Shepherd, and the sheep of the flock will be scattered.' But after I have been raised from the dead, I will go ahead of you to Galilee and meet you there."

463

Peter sat up. "Even if everyone else deserts you, I will never desert you."

"Simon, Simon, Satan has asked to sift each of you like wheat. But I have pleaded in prayer for you, Simon, that your faith should not fail. So when you have repented and turned to me again, strengthen your brothers."

Peter shook his head and said, "Lord, I am ready to go to prison with you, and even to die with you!"

Jesus looked at his boisterous disciple in love mixed with sadness. "Peter, let me tell you something. Before the cock crows tomorrow morning, you will deny three times that you even know me."

"This is worse than I thought!" Nigel lamented, watching Peter shrink back onto his pillow. "They'll all desert him in his hour of need!"

"An' Peter? His number one disciple will deny him thr-r-ree times?" Max wondered in astonishment. "Jesus called him Simon again, 'cause he'll act like his old self."

464

"But Peter's heart be in the right place," Kate suggested. "He's not like Judas, who's goin' ta betray Jesus on purpose."

"*Oui,* Kate, Peter and the others love Jesus but will have a moment of fear and weakness," Liz said. "But look how Jesus has already told Peter he will return to him, and to help the others. Such amazing love, no?"

"Indeed. He doesn't condemn them, sad as he is," Nigel added. "He even offers Peter hope. Jesus said he'll meet them in Galilee after his resurrection, but I don't think they even heard those words."

Jesus took some bread and blessed it. Then he broke it in pieces and gave it to the disciples, saying, "Take it, for this is my body." The men slowly ate the bread, trying to understand what Jesus was doing.

Then Jesus took a cup and gave thanks, then handed it to them. "Drink from it, all of you. For this is my blood that establishes the covenant; it is shed for many for the forgiveness of sins. But I tell you, from this moment I will not drink of this fruit of the vine until that day when I drink it in a new way in my Father's Kingdom with you."

Jesus looked around the room. All hearts were heavy, including his. "Don't let your hearts be troubled. Trust in God, and trust also in me. There is more than enough room in my Father's home. If this were not so, would I have told you that I am going to prepare a place for you? When everything is ready, I will come and get you, so that you will always be with me where I am. And you know the way to where I am going."

"No, we don't know, Lord," Thomas said. "We have no idea where you are going, so how can we know the way?"

Jesus told him, "I am the way, the truth, and the life. No one can come to the Father except through me."

Jesus continued talking about many wonderful promises.

"He's made a new covenant," Nigel told the group. The promises of the old covenant between the Maker and men were based on the Law, which man has been unable to keep. They've broken the relationship with the Maker over and over."

"*Oui,* so Jesus is making a new agreement," Liz added. "It is not dependent on man keeping the Law, but on Jesus' blood alone."

"So the new covenant be based on love now, not law," Kate said.

"If you love me, show it by doing what I've told you," Jesus continued. "I will talk to the Father, and he'll provide you another Friend so that you will always have someone with you. This Friend is the Spirit of Truth. The godless world can't take him in because it doesn't have eyes to see him, doesn't know what to look for. But you know him already because he has been staying with you, and will even be in you!" Jesus looked at each of his disciples and saw the despair creeping into their eyes.

465

"I will not leave you orphaned," Jesus smiled and said. "I'm coming back. In just a little while the world will no longer see me, but you're going to see me because I am alive and you're about to come alive. At that moment you will know absolutely that I'm in my Father, and you're in me, and I'm in you. The person who knows my commandments and keeps them, that's who loves me. And the person who loves me will be loved by my Father, and I will love him and make myself plain to him.

"I am leaving you with a gift—peace of mind and heart. And the peace I give is a gift the world cannot give. So don't be troubled or afraid. Remember what I told you: I am going away, but I will come back to you again. If you really loved me, you would be happy that I am going to the Father, who is greater than I am. I have told you these things before they happen so that when they do happen, you will believe."

Jesus stood up from the table. "I don't have much more time to talk to you, because the ruler of this world approaches. He has no power over me, but I will do what the Father requires of me, so that the world will know that I love the Father. Come, let's be going."

One by one the disciples got up and followed Jesus out the door. The animals waited until the coast was clear before they also left.

"Jesus is certain of his death but he is also just as certain of something that gives us all hope, no?" Liz said.

"What then? I could use some hope aboot now," Al asked.

"Jesus is also just as sure of his glory and resurrection!" Liz said.

"Aye, he'll be the King of Kings in heaven then!" Kate said.

"That's the part I wish we could get ta first," Max said sadly.

Nigel slowly nodded in agreement, but then answered, "But before the coronation, first must come the cross."

THE GARDEN

The incessant knocking on the door annoyed Zeeb and the others. Here he was, in the middle of delivering an eloquent account of Israel's deliverance from Egypt around their Passover meal, and someone dared to interrupt them.

A servant opened the door and immediately Judas stepped in the room. "Pardon the interruption, but the opportune time has come."

Zeeb slowly placed his cup of wine on the table and his look of irritation melted into one of ecstatic delight. He motioned for the others who immediately got up and left the room with him and Judas. He sent messengers immediately to notify Caiaphas and a small contingent of chief priests and other Sadducees and Pharisees. They soon were clustered together as Judas explained the plan.

"Jesus has been staying outside the city walls over on the Mount of Olives every night. A wealthy friend has given Jesus and his disciples permission to use his private garden of olive trees called Gethsemane," related Judas. "After the meal I know they'll head there. Since the masses of people are all occupied tonight with their celebrations, there won't be throngs of people surrounding Jesus. It's the perfect time to arrest him."

"We can take our Temple guards with us," Saar said.

"That's not good enough," Caiaphas said with a booming voice. "We know that this man possesses supernatural powers."

"What do you suggest, Caiaphas?" Zeeb asked.

"I think a cohort of Roman soldiers is sufficient to handle any resistance from the Galilean," Caiaphas replied, motioning to his servants. "I'll set things in place now."

Judas's eyes grew wide at the thought of up to six hundred soldiers armed for battle surrounding Jesus and his small band of men.

As Caiaphas stood to leave, he smiled at Judas. "Well done, son of Israel. Your services have saved us from a destructive adversary." Then he turned back to Zeeb and the others. "Bring Jesus to my father-in-law's house."

Judas bowed respectfully as the high priest left the room. "Excellent work, Judas. I knew we could count on you," Zeeb said as they made their way out to the courtyard. "Since it is dark, our guards need to make sure they arrest the right man. How do you propose we identify Jesus?"

"With a kiss," Judas said. "I'll greet him as I always do."

A wicked grin crept upon the faces of the men. "A brilliant suggestion, Judas. Jesus would never suspect your real intentions then," Nahshon said, slapping Judas on the back.

468

Together the men went outside and awaited the arrival of the soldiers to escort them to the garden. Judas's resolve only grew as he felt intoxicated by the power he now wielded. His mind raced with what could be next in his future. After he performed this service for the Sanhedrin, there were bound to be even greater things in store.

Jesus and the disciples walked through the moonlit landscape of the Kidron Valley on their way to the Mount of Olives. He still had much to tell these men, so he kept teaching as they walked along. They passed some grapevine trellises and Jesus pointed to them. "I am the real vine and my Father is the farmer. He cuts off every branch of me that doesn't bear grapes. And every branch that is grape-bearing he prunes back so it will bear even more. You are already pruned back by the message I have spoken. Live in me. Make your home in me just as I do in you. In the same way that a branch can't bear grapes by itself but only by being joined to the vine, you can't bear fruit unless you are joined with me.

"I am the vine, you are the branches. When you're joined with me and I with you, the relation intimate and organic, the harvest is sure to be abundant. Separated, you can't produce a thing. Anyone who separates from me is deadwood, gathered up and thrown on the bonfire. But if you make yourselves at home with me and my words are at home in you, you can be sure that whatever you ask will be listened to and acted upon. This is how my Father shows who he is—when you produce grapes, when you mature as my disciples."

"Even now, Jesus is giving the disciples words of wisdom that will stick with them forever," Nigel marveled as he rode along on Kate's back.

The animals were free to travel within earshot of Jesus and the men under cover of darkness.

"*Oui,* and how fitting. They will remember this illustration every time they see a vine, eat a grape, or sip the wine as Jesus asked them to remember him," Liz noted.

"I've loved you the way my Father has loved me," Jesus continued. "Make yourselves at home in my love. If you keep my commands, you'll remain intimately at home in my love. That's what I've done—kept my Father's commands and made myself at home in his love.

469

"I've told you these things for a purpose: that my joy might be your joy, and your joy wholly mature. This is my command: Love one another the way I loved you. This is the very best way to love. Put your life on the line for your friends. You are my friends when you do the things I command you. I'm no longer calling you servants because servants don't understand what their master is thinking and planning. No, I've named you friends because I've let you in on everything I've heard from the Father.

"You didn't choose me, remember; I chose you, and put you in the world to bear fruit, fruit that won't spoil. As fruit bearers, whatever you ask the Father in relation to me, he gives you. But remember the root command: Love one another.

"Jesus is love, jest like his Father," Kate said.

"If you find the godless world is hating you, remember it got its start hating me. If you lived on the world's terms, the world would love you as one of its own. But since I picked you to live on God's terms and no longer on the world's terms, the world is going to hate you.

"When that happens, remember this: Servants don't get better treatment than their masters. If they beat on me, they will certainly beat on you. If they did what I told them, they will do what you tell them. They are going to do all these things to you because of the way they treated me, because they don't know the One who sent me. If I hadn't come and told them all this in plain language, it wouldn't be so bad. As it is, they have no excuse. Hate me, hate my Father—it's all the same. If I hadn't done what I have done among them, works no one has ever done, they wouldn't be to blame. But they saw the God-signs and hated anyway, both me and my Father. Interesting—they have verified the truth of their own Scriptures where it is written, 'They hated me for no good reason.'

"I've told you these things to prepare you for rough times ahead. They are going to throw you out of the synagogues. There will even come a time when anyone who kills you will think he's doing God a favor. They will do these things because they never really understood the Father. I've told you these things so that when the time comes and they start in on you, you'll be well warned and ready for them."

Max wrinkled his brow. "These laddies have been given fair warnin' of wha' followin' Jesus will br-r-ring 'em. I sure hope they can handle it then."

"In time, I'm sure they will," stated Nigel. "But they have quite a bit of tuning and practicing before they can stand up to the rigors of being Jesus' ambassadors."

As they approached the garden, Jesus opened the gate and they were greeted by the shadows of gnarled trunks of massive olive trees, lined in row after row. Jesus had the men sit down. "I need to lift us all up in prayer." The disciples closed their eyes and lowered their heads as Jesus raised his arms and eyes to the heavens.

"Father, it's time."

Immediately, tears quickened in Liz's eyes. A lump tightened Max's throat.

"Display the bright splendor of your Son so the Son in turn may show your bright splendor. You put him in charge of everything human so he might give real and eternal life to all in his charge. And this is the real and eternal life: That they know you, the one and only true God, and Jesus Christ, whom you sent.

"I glorified you on earth by completing down to the last detail what you assigned me to do. And now, Father, glorify me with your very own splendor, the very splendor I had in your presence before there was a world.

"I spelled out your character in detail to the men and women you gave me. They were yours in the first place; then you gave them to me, and they have now done what you said. They know now, beyond the shadow of a doubt, that everything you gave me is firsthand from you, for the message you gave me, I gave them; and they took it, and were convinced that I came from you. They believed that you sent me. I pray for them.

"I'm not praying for the God-rejecting world but for those you gave me, for they are yours by right. Everything mine is yours, and yours mine, and my life is on display in them. For I'm no longer going to be visible in the world; they'll continue in the world while I return to you.

"Holy Father, guard them as they pursue this life that you conferred as a gift through me, so they can be one heart and mind as we are one heart and mind. As long as I was with them, I guarded them in the pursuit of the life you gave through me; I even posted a night watch. And not one of them got away, except for the rebel bent on destruction.

471

"Now I'm returning to you. I'm saying these things in the world's hearing so my people can experience my joy completed in them. I gave them your word; the godless world hated them because of it, because they didn't join the world's ways, just as I didn't join the world's ways. I'm not asking that you take them out of the world but that you guard them from the Evil One.   They are no more defined by the world than I am defined by the world. Make them holy—consecrated—with the truth; your word is consecrating truth. In the same way that you gave me a mission in the world, I give them a mission in the world. I'm consecrating myself for their sakes so they'll be truth-consecrated in their mission.

"I'm praying not only for them but also for those who will believe in me because of them and their witness about me. The goal is for all of them to become one heart and mind— just as you, Father, are in me and I in you, so they might be one heart and mind with us. Then the world might believe that you, in fact, sent me. The same glory you gave me, I gave them, so they'll be as unified and together as we are—I in them and you in me. Then they'll be mature in this oneness, and give evidence to the godless world that you've sent me, and loved them in the same way you've loved me.

"Father, I want with me those you gave me, right where I am, so they can see my glory, the splendor you gave me, having loved me long before there ever was a world. Righteous Father, the world has never known you, but I have known you, and these disciples know that you sent me on this mission. I have made your very being known to them—who you are and what you do—and continue to make it known, so that your love for me might be in them exactly as I am in them."

When Jesus stopped, he lowered his head and his hands. The disciples looked up and saw that his face was full of burden and pain. "Peter, James, and John, please come with me. The rest of you sit here while I go and pray."

"That was the most magnificent prayer I have ever heard," Liz said, wiping her eyes. "Jesus prayed not only for himself and for these disciples, but he looked down through time and prayed for every believer to come."

"Extraordinary," Nigel said softly. "And he is not finished praying."

The animals quietly moved around the tree trunks, following Jesus and the three disciples farther up the garden path.

Jesus began to look unstable on his feet and stopped on the path. He turned to Peter, James, and John, and his breathing was labored. "My soul is crushed with grief . . . to the point of death. Stay here and keep watch with me."

The disciples did as he asked and sat down against some tree trunks. Their faces also showed concern, but they remained quiet as they watched Jesus walk on a little farther. They leaned their heads on the tree trunks and closed their eyes.

Jesus staggered and fell to the ground. Max wanted to run to his side, but Kate kept him still.

His voice cracked and his lower lip quivered as he prayed with a face upturned to the heavens. "Abba, Father," he cried out, "everything is possible for you. Please take this cup of suffering away from me. Yet I want your will to be done, not mine."

The heaviness around Jesus and in the garden was felt by all of them. Jesus sobbed and shook as he dropped his head and gripped the ground with his fingers. The olive trees even seemed to bend toward him.

"Jesus be strugglin' so," Kate wept. "Like a wee lad, he called the Maker 'Daddy.'"

Liz swallowed hard, and her voice broke. "His human side is

wrestling with what is coming. He knows everything that is going to happen, and is honestly asking the Maker if there is any other way to save humanity."

"What do he mean by the cup?" Al asked, his eyes full of tears.

"The cup represents the cross," Nigel said, clearing his throat. "And it is filled with the sins of the world. Every man, woman, and child—past, present, and future—every thought, deed, action will be heaped upon Jesus all at once."

"Aye, so it's not jest the physical part of this ordeal that will be so hard," realized Max. "It's the horror of becomin' sin itself that's grippin' Jesus' spirit."

"The blameless lamb of God will in one moment become every evil deed in history," Nigel said. "It's unthinkable."

"So I believe Jesus is trying to understand why this is the only way," Liz said softly. "He knows he would not be any less holy or righteous if he allowed the sin-sick human race to suffer the consequences of their rebellion against the Maker."

473

"But love," Kate whimpered. "His love for them makes him willin' ta obey the Maker's plan."

After a while, Jesus slowly got up and returned to find the disciples asleep. "Simon, are you asleep?"

Peter slowly opened his eyes and nudged James and John, who also woke up.

"Couldn't you watch with me even one hour? Keep watch and pray, so that you will not give in to temptation. For the spirit is willing, but the body is weak." Jesus took in a deep breath and left to continue praying.

The disciples kept their eyes open for a moment, but they were physically overwhelmed with the despair of what Jesus had told them. Sleep was a welcome escape.

Jesus felt weak and again stumbled to the ground. He lay on his side and raised his hand to heaven. "My Father, if this cannot pass unless I drink it," he swallowed hard, "your will be done."

Liz looked around the garden of Gethsemane. How she adored gardens! They were always her favorite hobby. But a sudden realization washed over her. Gethsemane means 'olive press.' Jesus was being pressed for a decision. "It was in a garden that Adam and Eve first made the decision to break away from the Maker. Now in *this* garden, a decision must be made by Jesus to restore what was broken."

"The Maker restores every detail," Max said, astounded.

Nigel studied Jesus, who was struggling physically, emotionally, mentally, and spiritually because of Adam's first wrong decision in the Garden of Eden. Isaiah's words came to mind: *"A man of sorrows, and acquainted with grief."*

Again after a time of anguished prayer, Jesus got up and returned to his disciples, who were again sleeping. They couldn't keep their eyes open. And they didn't know what to say. Jesus walked back a third time and knelt on the ground in agony.

"Abba, please!" Jesus cried. He put his hands up to his face, and when he pulled them away, they were streaked with blood. He was in such agony of spirit that his sweat fell to the ground as great drops of blood. He threw his head back and raised his hands in the air. "Please!"

Suddenly a beam of light appeared next to Jesus.

474

"It's an angel!" Liz exclaimed through tear-streaked eyes.

A faint glimmer of relief coursed through the animals as they watched the angel quietly wipe Jesus' brow. The angel tenderly cared for him, whispering in his ear, and strengthening him. After a while, Jesus ceased the physical struggle and closed his eyes, sitting quietly as the angel slipped away.

"Jesus has learned to do what every spirit must do," Nigel told the others. "He's accepted what he doesn't understand. The will of his Father summons him to obey despite what he feels."

"And because he were on his knees first, he'll now be able to stand to face wha's comin'," Al said, watching as Jesus calmly stood to walk back to the disciples.

Jesus stood above Peter, James, and John, who for the third time were sleeping. "Go ahead and sleep," he told them. "Have your rest. But no—the time has come. The Son of Man is betrayed into the hands of sinners," he said as he saw a long row of torches coming up the path toward the garden. "Up, let's be going. Look, my betrayer is here!"

Peter, James, and John roused quickly at Jesus' warning. "Master?" Peter asked, rubbing his eyes. He looked at the other two as Jesus began walking toward the other eight disciples.

Jesus stopped and stared into the dark shadows at the entrance to the garden. Suddenly Judas emerged alone and rushed up to Jesus. His eyes were wild and unnatural looking.

"Greetings, Rabbi!" Judas exclaimed as he gave Jesus the signal kiss.

Jesus' eyes remained open. "Judas, you would betray the Son of Man with a kiss?"

Judas pulled back and gave Jesus a silent, questioning stare.

"My friend, go ahead and do what you have come for," Jesus said as he stepped around Judas and called into the darkness. "Who is it you want?"

"Jesus of Nazareth," a voice shouted back from the shadows.

"I AM he," Jesus said with bold assurance.

At the sound of Jesus' authoritative voice, the mob of men fell to the ground. They were carrying torches, lanterns, and weapons that crashed together as they were overcome with fear.

"That wasn't just Jesus' voice they heard," Liz said. "They heard the voice of I AM!"

After a moment the glimmer of torches grew into a steady stream of soldiers entering the garden. The disciples instinctively surrounded Jesus. Peter quietly pulled a short sword from his belt and hid it under his robe. The eerie torch lights flooded the clearing, glinting off the hundreds of swords and spears carried by the Roman soldiers and Temple guards.

Jesus' face showed no fear as he scanned the mob of faces, looking for the commander in charge.

Again he asked them, "Who is it you want?"

"Jesus of Nazareth," the head commander of the Temple guard said authoritatively as he strode toward Jesus.

"I told you I am he. If you are looking for me, then let these men go," Jesus said, motioning to his disciples.

The commander nodded and motioned for three men holding chains to take Jesus. As they walked toward Jesus with clanking irons, Peter suddenly raised his sword high and lunged forward. Peter tried to strike at the head of one of the three servants, but his sword bounced off the man's helmet, slicing off his ear. The man dropped the chains and screamed in pain, grabbing where his ear had been and blood now gushed forth.

Immediately men began yelling and the circle of flames tightened

475

around Jesus and his disciples. "NO more of this!" Jesus shouted as he quickly reached down and picked up the man's ear. He placed his hand against the man's head and instantly the bleeding stopped. The servant immediately felt the warmth of Jesus' touch radiate through him as the severed ear was completely healed. A hush of silence fell over the mob at this healing miracle of grace from Jesus to a man who had come to arrest him.

Jesus looked at Peter, who still held his bloodied sword, but whose face was full of panic. "Put away your sword," Jesus told him. "Those who use the sword will die by the sword. Don't you realize that I could ask my Father for thousands of angels to protect us, and he would send them instantly? But if I did, how would the Scriptures be fulfilled that describe what must happen now?"

Peter slowly lowered his sword and stepped back, scowling and feeling helpless. Jesus held out his arms and allowed the men with the chains to clamp them tightly on his hands and feet. The heavy chains were draped across his chest.

476

Jesus looked around the crowd of chief priests and Pharisees. Zeeb, Saar, Jarib, and Nahshon stood by, chins raised in the air. "Am I some dangerous revolutionary, that you come with swords and clubs to arrest me? Why didn't you arrest me in the Temple? I was there teaching every day. But this is all happening to fulfill the words of the prophets as recorded in the Scriptures."

The commander grabbed Jesus by the arm, understanding full well that Jesus was mocking the cowardice of these religious leaders for coming at night, and so heavily armed. "Let's go."

The guards roughly pushed Jesus out of the garden as the entire mob murmured and jeered at him. They began walking down the hillside, and Jesus struggled with quick steps against the chains that bound his feet.

Immediately the disciples held their heads in despair before fleeing in every direction.

The animals sat holding each other, weeping as they watched Jesus' arrest and the disciples' desertion. It felt surreal to watch everything unfold just as Jesus had predicted it would happen.

"'Strike the shepherd, and the sheep will be scattered,'" Nigel quoted from Zechariah. "The disciples all fled, just as Jesus told them at supper they would."

"Jesus were in contr-r-rol of ever-r-rythin' that jest happened," Max said. "From displayin' his author-r-rity by statin' who he were an' dir-r-rectin' who would be arr-r-rested, ta healin' the lad's ear an' willin'ly bein' led away."

"*Oui,* after Jesus won the victory over the decision of obedience in the garden, his power and authority blazed forth," Liz echoed.

"Even with that violent kiss," Kate said, wiping her eyes.

They watched the blaze of torches marching back up the Kidron Valley into the gates of Jerusalem.

"Aye, but now the Shepherd be the Lamb," Al lamented.

477

DENIED

Peter wrapped his cloak tightly around his shoulders as he stood in a darkened doorway near the entrance to the city. The chilly night air only added to his misery, his breath rising as a cloud of mist. His heart pounded when he heard the voice of the Roman cohort commander ordering his six hundred soldiers to peel off from the processional mob returning from the garden and head back to the Praetorium. The contingent of Temple guards, servants, and Pharisees continued on toward the palace of the high priest.

Peter gasped and stepped back into the shadows as the mob passed by. He scanned the crowd and clenched his fists as Judas walked past, talking with his conspirators about their quick success in apprehending Jesus. He wanted to wrap his hands around the neck of that lying traitor. But then he heard the clanking of irons and a lump grew in his throat as Jesus shuffled along, being pushed now and then by the gruff guard. Peter was terrified of being found anywhere near this group, but his heart told him he had to be near his Lord.

After the mob passed by, he suddenly saw John walking at a distance, following them. Peter jumped out of the shadows and grabbed the other disciple by the arm, giving him a terrible fright. "John! You're following them, too?"

"I have to. I have to do something. Be there. Something," John replied. "They're taking him to Annas in the high priest's palace compound. My father's family knows his servants well, having supplied the palace with salt fish for years. I'm hoping I can get in to see what's happening."

"Can you get me in, too?" Peter pleaded. "I . . . I have to be there where he is."

"Come, let's follow on and I'll see what I can do," John said.

The two disciples kept their distance behind the mob as they walked the darkened streets of Jerusalem, gaining some relief that they at least had each other at this horrific moment. Behind them walked the animals.

"Who be Annas anyway?" Max asked. "I thought Caiaphas were the high priest."

"Annas is the father-in-law of Caiaphas, and was high priest for almost ten years. Four of his sons also held the position, so the family has been entrenched in this seat of power for years," Nigel explained. "And if the truth be known, they are the corrupt ones behind the robbers Jesus cleared from the Temple. All those money-changing and sacrifice-selling vendors are housed in what is called 'Annas's Bazaar.'"

479

"*Oui,* and this family has grown extremely rich from their money practices at the Temple," Liz spat. "Before Israel came under Roman rule, the high priest held the office for life, but when Roman governors were established here, the office became a matter of bribery, being filled by the highest bidder willing to submit to Rome. *C'est* despicable!"

"So when Jesus cleared the Temple, I'm afraid he made a direct attack on the house of Annas and the man's vested interests there," Nigel continued. "He is notorious to the Jews and although Caiaphas has the current title, Annas remains the shadowy power behind the throne in Jerusalem."

"Mousie, ye say rats come out at night, and this Annas sounds aboot like the leader o' the pack," Al commented.

Kate bristled. "So what will Annas do with Jesus? It's the middle of the night!"

"It will be some sort of an interrogation, no?" Liz said. "Let's get there and we'll know for sure."

"That's Peter an' John up ahead!" Max exclaimed. "Looks like they be tryin' ta get inside then."

Massive, imposing walls surrounded the palace compound, and torches placed along the wall gave it an intimidating appearance. Large iron gates creaked open for the mob who marched through the front entrance leading to an inner courtyard. Beyond the large courtyard was a series of passages leading to various buildings in the complex. As the mob took Jesus on to the house of Annas, John told Peter to wait while he went on ahead. Once inside, he talked with a servant he knew and asked for Peter to also be admitted. The servant motioned to the young woman who was tending the gate. She opened the gate and Peter slipped inside.

"Stay here while I go see what's happening," John instructed before he quickly walked off.

Peter nodded and pulled his cloak higher up over his head, trying to cover his face.

The animals came near the gate to assess the situation.

"We simply must get inside," Nigel insisted.

Liz nodded as she surveyed the walls and the gate. "*Oui,* I agree. I am small enough to fit through the bars of the front gate, so we can go together. Max, please remain here with Kate and Albert while we go in."

"Aye, Lass, we'll keep an eye out for things here," Max said.

"Be careful," Kate called after Liz and Nigel as they quietly went up to the gate and slipped in unnoticed.

Liz and Nigel saw Peter standing there with the young woman who tended the gate.

"Are you one of this man's disciples, too?" she asked him.

"No, I am not," retorted Peter, looking around the courtyard. He saw some servants and officers around a charcoal fire, warming themselves. Peter walked over and stood there with them, keeping himself warm, and trying to blend in with the group.

"Oh dear, that's one denial," Nigel frowned and said as they hurried to find Jesus.

The guards ushered Jesus into a large room where a select number of the religious elite were gathered. John quietly made his way inside, but remained in the back of the room. At the front of the room was a large empty chair. The guards roughly shoved Jesus to where he stood in front of and facing the chair while they took positions behind him and to either side. Liz and Nigel carefully entered the room and hid behind a large piece of pottery.

"I don't like this, Nigel," Liz said. "Members of the Sanhedrin are gathered here, at night and during a festival. If they intend to have a trial, they are already violating their own rules of procedure!"

"Indeed, this is clearly illegal by Jewish law," agreed Nigel. "All trials are only to be held in the Hall of Judgment in the Temple area, and in full view of the public!"

Tension filled the room as all who were gathered there waited in silence for Annas to arrive. A door slammed open and in walked the old patriarch of the family, dressed in his fine robes of authority. He wore a scowl on his face as he made his way to the chair and sat down, taking care to arrange his robes. He looked up and met the confident gaze of Jesus.

"Twice you entered the Temple area, overturned the tables, and drove out the merchants," Annas began with a condescending tone. "Not only did you disrupt the sacred atmosphere of the Temple, you disrupted the order of how things are done in providing sacrifices. You proceeded to teach questionable things in the Temple and from what I've heard, in the synagogues all over Judea and Galilee. Tell me, what exactly are you trying to teach the people of Israel? And what about this band of followers of yours? Who are they?"

481

"How dare he accuse Jesus of disrupting the 'sacred atmosphere'!" fumed Nigel. "Jesus disrupted the *unsacred* atmosphere!"

"Steady, *mon ami*," Liz whispered.

"I have always spoken quite openly to the world," Jesus calmly replied. "I have always taught in the synagogue or in the Temple where all the Jews meet together, and I have said nothing in secret. Why do you question me? Why not question those who have heard me about what I said to them? Obviously they are the ones who know what I actually said."

One of the officers gritted his teeth, strode up, and slapped Jesus with his open hand. "Is that the way for you to answer the high priest?"

Jesus flinched but stood steadfastly. He slowly turned his gaze to the man who hit him. "If I have said anything wrong, you must give evidence about it, but if what I said was true, why do you strike me?"

"Jesus is calling them out on their own procedures himself," Liz noted. "He knows he is being denied due process of Jewish law. Every trial is supposed to begin by presenting the evidence of innocence before evidence of guilt is presented. And that evidence must come from independent witnesses, not the accused or the accuser! Jesus is saying that if he has said anything illegal, witnesses should be called. He has simply stated the law, so why hit him?"

"Yes, and he knows the accused cannot be compelled to testify against himself. I fear they have already come to a verdict and a sentence," Nigel said. "Now they're fishing for a charge to make it all appear legitimate."

Annas stood and waved his hand. "Send him to Caiaphas." He glowered at Jesus, then turned and walked out of the great hall.

The guards gripped Jesus by each arm and shoved him out of the room back to the courtyard and on to the house of Caiaphas. As Liz and Nigel stayed clear of the group of men making their way across the palace compound, they passed by Peter, who was now sitting near the fire, warming his hands.

A man leaned forward and studied Peter's face, which was lit up by the glowing fire. "You also were with Jesus the Nazarene! You must be with him."

482

"Man, I am not!" Peter snapped, pulling his cloak around himself.

Liz's heart fell. "That makes two denials. Jesus said Peter will deny him three times before the cock crows."

Nigel looked around while they scurried across the courtyard. "I don't see signs of any such birds here. And isn't there a Jewish law that such livestock cannot be raised in the Holy city? Hmmmm . . ."

Liz and Nigel scurried inside the great hall of Caiaphas. They saw a side passage with steps leading up to a balcony overlooking the great hall. Together they hurried up the steps and found a spot where they could see everything, waiting for things to begin.

The crowd here was much larger, with almost the entire Sanhedrin gathered. Jesus stood at the front of the room, where Caiaphas sat in his full high priestly garb of rich blue robes and breastplate inlaid with twelve different precious stones, representing the twelve tribes of Israel. His ornate headdress completed the full garb of the high priest of Israel, who looked ready to perform his duties in the Temple.

The chief priests and council members immediately began calling witnesses who eagerly got up to testify against Jesus. They were looking for evidence that would be enough to sentence him to death.

"They have nothing on Jesus," Nigel noted. "Plenty of witnesses are willing to bring in false charges, but nothing is adding up. In fact, these false witnesses are canceling each other out!"

Finally a few of the witnesses stood up and lied: "We heard him say, 'I am going to tear down this Temple, built by hard labor, and in three days build another without lifting a hand.'"

"What do you have to say to the accusation?" Caiaphas asked Jesus. Jesus was silent.

"They are twisting Jesus' words with this half-truth!" Liz said. "Jesus told them, 'Destroy this temple, and in three days I will raise it up.' He was talking about his *body.*"

"This ludicrous charge still isn't enough to convince the Romans that killing Jesus will serve their interests. They need more," Nigel stated, folding his arms over his chest.

Caiaphas rose from his chair and walked over to stand in front of Jesus. He lifted his finger and pointed it in Jesus' face. With a clenched jaw he asked, "Are you Messiah, the Son of the Blessed?"

It felt as if all of heaven and earth held their breath as they waited for Jesus' reply. If he said 'no' he could walk away free. If he said 'yes' he was signing his own death sentence. But Jesus wasn't here to defend himself. He was here to fulfill the plan of God. And his answer would be the catalyst to set the full plan in motion.

483

Jesus looked Caiaphas confidently in the eye. "Yes, I am, and you'll see it yourself: the Son of Man seated at the right hand of the Mighty One, arriving on the clouds of heaven."

Caiaphas's eyes widened and he cried out as if he were in pain, ripping his clothes. "Did you hear that? After that do we need witnesses? You heard the blasphemy. Are you going to stand for it?"

The din of voices cried out in condemnation: "Death! Death! Death!"

Some of them ran up and started spitting at Jesus. The rough guards grabbed him while one of the officers blindfolded him. They started taking turns hitting Jesus in the face with balled fists. "Who hit you? Prophesy!" they screamed and mocked.

"Oh, Nigel, I can't bear this!" Liz cried, turning to run down the stairs.

Nigel followed Liz outside as the gang of guards and officers continued to punch and slap Jesus without mercy. The two ran over to the side of the courtyard where Peter remained while the mob pushed Jesus outside.

"Listen to his accent," a man said, pointing at Peter. "This man was certainly with Jesus, since he's also a Galilean."

But Peter stood up and shouted, "Man, I don't know what you're talking about! May I be struck down if I'm lying!"

Immediately, while he was still speaking, the trumpet call sounded, announcing the 3:00 a.m. changing of the Roman guard at the Antonia Fortress.

"Cock-crow!" Liz exclaimed. "The Latin word for trumpet call is *gallicinium,* meaning "cock-crow"! That's what Jesus meant!"

At that moment, Peter looked up as Jesus was pushed right by him and they locked eyes. Jesus' words rushed into Peter's anxious mind: *Before the cock crows today, you will deny me three times.* Not only was he overwhelmed by Jesus hearing his third denial, Peter gaped in horror at Jesus' face, now bloodied with swollen eyes from where he had been punched repeatedly.

484

Peter's mouth fell open in silent despair and he ran away from the fire and out the front gate. Max watched him run a short distance away and collapse on the ground, weeping bitterly.

Liz and Nigel ran over to rejoin the other animals. Liz fell into Al's arms, weeping as well.

"Wha' happened in there?!" Max asked.

"It was horrific," Nigel said. "Because things happened so fast with Judas coming to them, they arrested Jesus before they had a plan. Jesus was put through two illegal mock trials, beaten, denied due process of law . . ."

"And denied by Peter," Liz said. "Just as Jesus predicted, but to make it worse, Jesus heard Peter and looked right at him at that moment."

Tears welled up in Kate's eyes. "This be devastatin'! They beat Jesus? Where do they have him now?"

"They will hold Jesus until daybreak. Caiaphas has ordered the Sanhedrin to reconvene at their official place of judgment in the hall at the east end of the Royal Portico of the Temple," Nigel explained. "But it will all be for show. They've already found Jesus guilty and have come up with a charge strong enough to present before Rome for death—treason."

"Sounds like Jesus has 'em right where he wants 'em," Al said, amazing the others with his insight, for that was exactly the case.

Max lowered his head and shook it. He then looked over in Peter's direction. "I know how the lad feels. He feels like a failure. Wha' he did were bad, but ye got ta admit Peter's been brave all night. He drew his sword an' were willin' ta take on the mob ta protect Jesus. Then he followed him here where it be dangerous for *him* ta be arrested, too."

"I must say you are right," agreed Nigel. "Each time Peter was asked if he was with Jesus, even though he wrongly denied him, he didn't run away from the danger. He stayed put."

"Jesus knew that the r-r-real Peter were the one who called him Messiah an' said he'd die for him, an' who followed him here in the face of danger," Max said. "Jesus knew it weren't the r-r-real Peter who would deny him an' r-r-run away in a moment of weakness. He knew down deep the r-r-real Peter were br-r-rave."

"So Peter failed because he were brave and not a coward then," Al posed. "Sure, there's no denyin' that."

"I can't help Jesus, but I can help Peter. Jesus asked us ta comfort his disciples," Max said. "He needs someone who understands when ye fail at bein' brave, even if he doesn't know the r-r-real me."

"Go, me love," Kate said, nudging Max with her head.

"*Oui,* we will be in the Temple area," Liz told him. "And Maximillian, Jesus would be very proud of you."

Max nodded silently and trotted off to find Peter. He found him leaning against a darkened wall, physically writhing and sick to his stomach from grief. Max slowly walked up to Peter and just stood there. Peter jumped when he saw the shadow of a figure next to him, but then recognized the little dog.

"Tovah? How did you get here?" Peter said, reaching with trembling hands for Max. He pulled Max to him and clung to the little dog as if he were the last friend he had in the world. "How can I ever face Jesus again after what I've done?" he sobbed, rocking Max back and forth. "I'm so ashamed. I've failed my Master."

Give it time, lad, Max thought as he simply let Peter hold on to him. *Ye'll get past this. Jesus said so. Ye'll come r-r-roarin' back as a br-r-rave leader. But for now, let the tears come then.*

485

"We dare not make a martyr out of him," Saar warned as he walked with Zeeb and the others to where the Sanhedrin were gathering for Jesus' public trial. "The influence of martyrs only grows after their death."

"Yes, Jesus is too popular with the people to assassinate him," Jarib echoed. "But if the masses see him as just another false Messiah, they'll be glad he's dead."

"Which is why our plan to discredit him as a blaspheming revolutionary who would seek to take over Rome's authority is brilliant," Zeeb said. "He'll be publicly executed by Rome, not by us."

"We couldn't have come up with a better plan to get rid of Jesus," Nahshon enthused. "And he walked right into it, as if he were willingly going along with his own condemnation!"

Their footsteps echoed off the walls of the Hall of Judgment, which had been designed to resemble the ancient threshing floor where farmers would separate the wheat from the chaff. This was the forum where all matters of justice were presented to the public. Liz, Al, Kate, and Nigel were tucked away behind one of the many columns that ran along the long hall that opened to the outer courtyard. The area was packed with people who were in the Temple area for the Passover.

Liz gasped when she saw Jesus being brought out to stand before the Sanhedrin. His face was now black and blue from the beating he was given in the night. One eye was swollen shut and his lip was cut and bloodied. He still wore the heavy iron shackles that bound him hand and foot. Al placed his paw on Liz's shoulder as silently they watched the third trial begin.

Caiaphas and all seventy members of the Sanhedrin were gathered together. In order to maintain the appearance of propriety, they began the trial in daylight, in public view, but they continued to blatantly violate the rules of procedure. But the pursuit of truth and justice wasn't their objective in the first place. Jesus was already condemned. This trial was just for show.

Zeeb walked forward and stood in front of Jesus. "Are you Messiah?"

Jesus took a deep breath. "If I said yes, you wouldn't believe me. If I asked what you meant by your question, you wouldn't answer me. So here's what I have to say: From here on the Son of Man takes his place at God's right hand, the place of power."

They all said, "So you admit your claim to be the Son of God?"

"You're the ones who keep saying it," Jesus replied.

Zeeb stretched out his hands. "Why do we need any more evidence? We've all heard him as good as say it himself."

Caiaphas nodded at Zeeb, who motioned for the Temple guards to usher Jesus away. The council disbanded and broke into small groups who murmured among themselves.

"Look, there are Nicodemus and Joseph of Arimathea," Nigel said. "They are obviously in utter dismay."

"They aren't the only ones," Liz said. "Look who else is here."

Judas watched the guards taking Jesus away, and his face was full of remorse after hearing that Jesus was condemned to death. Jesus was going in one direction and Zeeb and the other elders were going in another. Judas hesitated only a moment before he ran after Zeeb and the others who were walking into the Temple area where only priests could enter. Just as Zeeb entered the forbidden area, Judas called after him. Zeeb turned and came and stood with his hands clasped together. "Yes, Judas?" he asked with an irritated tone.

Judas shook his head sadly. "I have sinned, for I have betrayed an innocent man."

"What do we care?" Saar snapped as he and the others came up behind Zeeb. "That's your problem."

Judas's jaw dropped in shock at their response. Why were they treating him this way? He wrinkled his brow as he dug for his money bag that held the silver coins. He gripped it tightly and threw it into the sanctuary where it landed with a thud. Judas then turned and ran away from the Temple courts.

Nahshon walked over and picked up the coins. "It wouldn't be right to put this in the Temple treasury, since it was blood money."

The men thought a moment and discussed a few ideas. Nigel listened in as he had scurried over to hear what was discussed. When they disbanded he ran back to Liz and the others to report.

"Judas returned the thirty pieces of silver," Nigel began, winded from running about. "He actually has realized what he's done and feels remorse for betraying Jesus. Those hypocrites debated about what to do with the money since it 'wouldn't be right' to put it in the Temple treasury. They're going to buy the potter's field, and make it into a cemetery for foreigners."

487

Liz shook her head as they watched Judas run off. "Do you realize we've just seen another prophecy fulfilled? Jeremiah wrote, 'They took the thirty pieces of silver—the price at which he was valued by the people of Israel, and purchased the potter's field, as the Lord directed.'"

"All his years with Jesus taught Judas nothin'," Kate lamented. "If he had run after Jesus an' begged forgiveness, he would've been given grace. That goes ta show ye that jest bein' around godliness don't make ye godly."

"*Oui,* and it is not enough to simply be sorry," Liz added. "Failure to confess sin and receive forgiveness only leads to more pain. Judas slowly started deceiving little by little until it led to full betrayal."

"Indeed, and Satan can use anyone bearing unresolved sin to work against the Maker," Nigel echoed. "But when the evil one has done all the damage he can, he'll do away with the one he used."

"Only now Judas sees the ugly truth of wha' he's done, an' it's too late," Kate said. "He were used as a tool an' now will be tossed aside."

488

"Sounds to me like Judas sold *himself* for thirty pieces o' silver," Al noted.

The animals would later learn that Judas ran out of the gates of the city, located a lone tree overlooking a cliff and hanged himself there. Because he didn't run to Jesus, he not only was denied forgiveness, but denied life itself.

LIKE A LAMB,
HE OPENED NOT
HIS MOUTH

hat is it?!" Pilate snapped as his servant woke him. His head was aching from a night of restless sleep.

"Sir, I am sorry to wake you. I know the hour is early but there are some elders from the Sanhedrin here to see you," the servant explained. "They have a man in custody whom they need to present to you."

Pilate sat up in bed and rubbed his face. "These people!" he growled. "They are forever pushing me to the edge with their demands." He pulled back his covers and stomped over to the basin of water, splashing his face and drying it with a towel. He mumbled curses into the towel.

The servant stood by, holding Pilate's tunic and Roman body armor. Pilate threw the towel on the floor and went over to get dressed. "Very well, show them into my hall," Pilate instructed.

The servant hesitated. "Um, sir, I'm afraid you'll have to go out to them. They claim they will be defiled if they enter your headquarters."

Pilate glared at the servant. Then he gave a sarcastic laugh and shook his head. "Of course, entering a Gentile's home defiles them. Ever true to their rules," he nodded. "Tell them I'll be right there." As the servant bowed and left the room, Pilate buckled his breastplate and muttered, "I hate coming to Jerusalem."

Pilate's primary headquarters were in balmy Caesarea on the Mediterranean Sea, but he always came to Jerusalem for the major festivals, when the population grew to ten times its normal size. Part of Rome's success in worldwide domination was in part due to demanding law and order from their provinces. As acting prefect, or governor, Pilate was beholden not to the Roman Senate but to the Roman Emperor Tiberius himself to keep the province under control. Jerusalem was always a volatile place, but during these huge festivals it was a powder keg waiting to explode. Pilate knew his position with the Emperor was tenuous at best since his appointment here five years ago. He often wished he had heeded the advice of his predecessors in dealing with these difficult and complex conquered people of Israel. Before his arrival in Judea he had considered the former prefects pushovers and he wasn't about to fall into the same trap of bowing to the whim of these obstinate people.

490

When Pilate first arrived in Caesarea, he sent an army to spend the winter in Jerusalem, sending a clear message that the new governor was in command of the region. His army arrived, carrying shields bearing the image of Caesar, which they displayed in all the public squares, as was consistently done all over the Empire. He even had the shields mounted in Herod's Palace, which didn't set well with the tetrarch of Galilee. Herod Antipas understood the religious sensitivities of the Jewish people, who vehemently opposed any hints of idolatry. Rome viewed Caesar as a deity, so for his image to be plastered all over Jerusalem was an affront to the Jews. They even had money changers to change the coins with Caesar's image over to their own currency before it would be acceptable to be placed in the Temple treasury. It had taken the Babylonian captivity to finally cure the people of Israel from chasing after false gods as they once did. But now their resolve to oppose false gods was as fierce as their previous worship of them.

Herod Antipas and Pilate's predecessors had taken great care to remove the "graven images" carried on Roman flags that the Jewish people held as a violation of their religious laws. But Pilate ignored such actions. Rome was in charge, after all, and Rome worshipped many gods. Israel would just have to submit.

But Pilate soon found out these Jews were serious to the point of death about upholding their laws concerning their God. A mob of Jewish leaders traveled to Pilate's headquarters in Caesarea and staged a protest, which put Pilate in a difficult situation. If he removed the images he not only would appear weak, it would be an affront to Caesar. Yet he was charged with keeping the peace with the province.

After five days of protest the Jewish leaders simply would not go home, so Pilate ordered them to meet him in the amphitheater. He went and sat in his viewing seat and ordered his soldiers to surround the Jews gathered there, but to conceal their weapons. Pilate threatened the Jews that if they did not cease their protest and return home, he would order his soldiers to kill them on the spot. With that the Jewish leaders threw themselves to the ground and bared their necks, claiming they would willingly die before transgressing their sacred laws of not allowing any graven image to remain in their midst. Pilate was moved by their resolve and reasoned that he could not very well arrest or slaughter an entire nation. He ordered the images removed from Jerusalem and returned to Caesarea.

491

Meanwhile Herod Antipas wrote to Tiberius himself about the issue of the shields mounted all over his palace and the revolt of the Jewish people. Pilate had greater authority than Herod, so Pilate hated Herod for going over his head directly to the Emperor. Tiberius soon warned Pilate in a letter that he had best respect the religious requests of the Jews or face removal from office. Pilate also hated the Jewish people who repeatedly butted heads with him on issue after issue, and never hesitated to threaten him with reports to Rome. So while he was the Roman governor of the province, Pilate felt he was governed by the laws of this mysterious God of Israel. Pilate enjoyed his prestigious post in Caesarea, so he traveled to Jerusalem on occasion. He didn't want to do anything to endanger his career.

Pilate walked out into the courtyard and saw a contingent of the Sanhedrin standing in a semi-circle around a prisoner. He immediately noticed the dried blood and the swollen condition of the man's face, and the chains draped over his chest that bound his hands and feet. A boisterous crowd was growing behind the Jewish leaders, which Pilate knew was full of Zealots and other revolutionaries who congregated here in Jerusalem during Passover. He immediately saw the volatile situation unfolding before him. The man in custody was this commonly named Jesus whom he had heard was some religious fanatical teacher who had offended the Sanhedrin.

He got right down to business, sitting in the judgment seat before them. Pointing to Jesus, Pilate asked, "What is your charge against this man?"

"We have found this man subverting our nation," Saar offered.

"He opposes payment of taxes to Caesar and claims to be Messiah—a king," Jarib added.

"We wouldn't have handed him over to you if he weren't a criminal!" Nahshon insisted.

"Then take him away and judge him by your own law," Pilate told them with a wave of his hand, knowing this was yet another issue regarding violation of their religious laws.

"Only the Romans are permitted to execute a prisoner," Zeeb reminded Pilate.

492

Execute? This was serious. These leaders wanted this man dead. Pilate studied Jesus, who stood quietly before him, his gaze fixed on the ground.

Then Pilate motioned for Jesus' attention. "Don't you hear how much they are testifying against you?"

Jesus looked up but didn't answer Pilate on even one charge. Pilate locked eyes with Jesus while the chief priests and elders continued their accusations. But while Pilate looked at Jesus, the sounds of their voices were drowned out as he thought to himself, *Amazing! Never before have I seen a prisoner not give a single protest. Perhaps he knows what I know. These charges are political lies born from jealousy. If there were any merit to their accusations he would answer.*

Pilate stood and walked away, leaving the elders standing in the courtyard. As he entered the Praetorium, he ordered for Jesus to be brought to him inside. He wanted to discuss this with the man in private.

Jesus entered the hallway, still bound and barefoot. The clanking irons echoed off the marble floor as he shuffled along. Pilate wrinkled his brow as he saw this man laboriously walk and then stop to stand before him, docile as a lamb. There was no protest from this Jew about entering a Gentile dwelling. That alone spoke volumes to Pilate. He was of a different mindset altogether than the others.

"The Jewish leaders accuse you of being a revolutionary," Pilate began, giving a sarcastic laugh as he studied Jesus. "You hardly strike me as the type. And you also don't give the appearance of one who incites the people not to pay taxes. But what is this about your claim to be Messiah? Are you the King of the Jews?" he asked him.

Jesus finally spoke. "Is this your own question, or did others tell you about me?"

"Am I a Jew?" Pilate retorted with a tone of contempt. "Your own people and their leading priests brought you to me for trial. Why? What have you done?"

"My Kingdom is not an earthly kingdom. If it were, my followers would fight to keep me from being handed over to the Jewish leaders," Jesus replied confidently. "But my Kingdom is not of this world."

Pilate looked Jesus up and down as he circled him. Despite his pitiful appearance, Pilate was impressed with his majestic demeanor. "So you *are* a king?"

Jesus responded, "You say I am a king. Actually, I was born and came into the world to testify to the truth. All who love the truth recognize that what I say is true."

493

"What is truth?" Pilate asked wearily, leaning over in Jesus' ear. But he didn't wait on an answer. He left Jesus standing there as he turned and walked back outside.

Nigel looked on from a ledge high up in the hall as a Roman guard took Jesus by the arm to return him to the courtyard. *You've just been talking with Truth itself.*

Pilate put his hands on his hips and stood in front of the people outside in the courtyard. "He is not guilty of any crime."

But together the men began to protest in unison, lifting their fists as they animated their speech: "He stirs up the people, teaching throughout all Judea, from Galilee where he started even to here."

Pilate's eyebrows and spirits rose when he heard where Jesus was from. "So, he's a Galilean?"

"Yes, from Nazareth," Zeeb answered.

There may be a way out of this dilemma for me, Pilate thought to himself hopefully. *Jesus legally is under Herod's jurisdiction. And Herod is here in Jerusalem for Passover. So, let my nemesis handle this! He is the one who cares so much about these people and their religious laws.*

Pilate clapped his hands for two of his guards. "Take this Jesus of Nazareth to Herod Antipas. As Tetrarch of Galilee, this is his problem."

"Yes, Sir," the guards responded, saluting him. They grabbed Jesus by the arms and led him out of the courtyard to head to the palace, where Herod was staying for the Passover.

As the group of elders followed the soldiers escorting Jesus, Nigel scurried out to rejoin Liz and the others, who were hiding in the courtyard.

"Pilate knows Jesus is innocent, that much is certain," Nigel reported. "But he's faced with yet another challenge by the Jewish religious leaders, who are pressing him to abide by their wishes. Pilate has passed Jesus off to Herod, who is in town for the Passover."

"Oui. Herod's presence here in Jerusalem has provided the perfect out for Pilate. But Herod has wanted to see Jesus in person for a long time, and I fear what he'll do," Liz worried. "Nigel, we need to see what happens next. Can you follow them to Herod's palace?"

494

"Aye, we'll stay here an' keep a lookout for Max," Kate added.

"Excellent idea, my dears," Nigel said, spotting his pigeon friend Naomi. "I'll return with a report as soon as I can."

"Be careful, *mon ami,*" Liz warned as Nigel scurried across the crowded streets. She watched Nigel climb on top of the bird and take off above the city. He saluted as they flew by. "How did we ever get by without Nigel and his pigeons?" Liz wondered aloud.

Herod's eyes lit up and he clapped his hands in delight when he heard Jesus of Nazareth had been brought to him. He swallowed a bite of his breakfast and wiped his mouth, brushing the crumbs from his silky tunic. "Bring him in!"

Armandus stood in Herod's chamber and a wave of shock flew over him as Jesus was ushered into the room. *What is happening?!* he wondered when he saw Jesus' severely beaten appearance. Armandus's heart sank to see him like this. But the Roman soldier showed no outward signs of dismay. He stood quietly at attention.

"Felius, from the looks of him, I think you were right about this Jesus of Nazareth. He's no Zealot," Herod said, almost giddy with laughter and relief. He was surrounded by his entourage of servants, who smiled and laughed with him. "But you are a supposed miracle worker. So? Let's see something!"

Jesus stood there, silent.

Herod's smile faded. "Aren't you going to show me your great powers I've heard so much about? I hear you make the blind see and even raise the dead." The crowd murmured to each other. "Come now, show us something spectacular!"

Jesus remained quiet, his gaze fixed on the floor. He said not a word.

"Herod, if I may, this man is indeed a threat to Rome," accused Zeeb.

"He claims to be the King of the Jews," Jarib offered.

Herod raised his eyebrows. "Well, well, well, is that so?" He stood to walk around Jesus and began to speak with a voice dripping with sarcasm. "He certainly *looks* dangerous, doesn't he?"

This drew laughs from the crowd. Herod pointed to his own crown. "But if you check your records, I am more the king of the Jews, one of them appointed by my father. Ah, the rumor of the 'rightful' King of the Jews, could that be it? My father once had a similar threat but he took care of it by killing all the newborn male babies who could grow up to threaten his rule."

495

Armandus shut his eyes tightly and thought of his father, who had been ordered to oversee that travesty.

"So, did you escape my father's sword?" Herod mocked Jesus.

"YOU BETTER BELIEVE HE DID!" Nigel shouted with a fist held high. He then quickly covered his mouth lest he be heard squeaking in his hiding place.

"Tell us your plans for your *glorious* Kingdom," Herod insisted. "Do you plan to establish your throne here and then march on to Rome and overthrow Caesar himself?"

More laughs rose from Herod's crowd. But the chief priests and elders raised their voices again, shrilly accusing Jesus of the charges.

Jesus didn't bother to look up or to utter a word.

Herod's face twisted with anger at Jesus' silent affront to him. He reached over and lifted up a piece of Jesus' matted hair and sneered at him in disgust. But then his face grew a wicked grin. "Oh, forgive me for touching you, Your Majesty!" Herod mockingly bowed. "And look, that's no way for a king to dress. Bring him one of my robes! Hurry!" He clapped his hands and a servant quickly brought in an elegant purple robe.

"Let my soldiers help you look like a proper king," Herod said, standing back with his arms folded across his chest, nodding over in Armandus's direction.

Velius and Ulixes nudged one another and walked over to snatch the robe from the servant. Armandus clenched his fists and took one step forward, then caught himself. He didn't want to be a part of this cruel mockery, but was powerless to stop it. He stayed put and watched as his two subordinates laughed and jeered as they roughly wrapped the robe around Jesus' shoulders. Laughter erupted from Herod's crowd as they all joined in the taunting and jeering of this oh-so-powerful king.

Jesus silently endured the ridicule, which only irritated Herod further. "I tire of this," he said after a few moments. He motioned for Armandus to come over to him, and the Roman centurion did so immediately, then snapped to attention.

496

"Armandus, you and your men accompany this 'king of the Jews' and report to Pilate that I find nothing but humor about this man and the charges against him. He is innocent," ruled Herod. "Go and do whatever Pilate instructs with him. I'm impressed that he asked for my opinion in the matter, so I will assist him with the handling of this problem by sending you and your men to be at his disposal."

"Sir, yes, Sir!" Armandus said with a balled fist to his chest, saluting Herod. "Bring him," Armandus ordered Ulixes and Velius, who grabbed Jesus.

Jesus and Armandus briefly locked eyes but Armandus quickly looked away, leading the men out of the room. Following on their heels were the protesting chief priests and elders, who weren't going to let up for a moment until Jesus was dead.

"Oh dear," Nigel whispered, putting a paw to his mouth. "Armandus is now drawn into this ugliness."

Liz, Kate, Al, and now Max surrounded Nigel as he landed with a report of all that transpired at the trial in front of Herod.

"Not guilty," Nigel said. "Jesus stood there not uttering a word, and Herod found him not guilty."

"This makes two judges, impartial representatives of Rome, who have found Jesus not guilty, no?" Liz said. "And this is one of the requirements of the Jewish law that two independent witnesses testify to the innocence of the accused."

"I fear it will make no difference," Nigel lamented, shaking his head. "The Sanhedrin know they have Pilate's back up against the wall, and will stop at nothing until they get their way."

"But wha' can they do now that Jesus has been found innocent by two R-r-romans?" Max growled.

Liz wrinkled her brow as she thought this through. She snapped her head up as a thought occurred to her. "Pilate has another way out of this! It is a tradition that the Roman governor releases one prisoner each year in honor of the Jewish Passover festival. He could simply release Jesus!"

"Aye, maybe that's how he'll be able ta get out of this," Kate agreed hopefully.

"But Jesus said he were goin' to the cross," Al reminded everyone. "So ain't that what we should expect then?"

497

The group solemnly nodded as they realized Al was right. Jesus said he would be turned over to the Gentiles and be crucified. And Pilate was the sole Gentile in Jerusalem who would determine the course of events. However it played out, the end result was inevitable.

"I'm afraid there's more," Nigel lamented. "After mocking Jesus and dressing him up in a kingly robe, Herod ordered Armandus and his soldiers to take Jesus back to Pilate. It's a peace offering from Herod to Pilate, if you will, and Herod ordered Armandus to do whatever Pilate instructs."

"*Our* Armandus?" Liz said, wide-eyed. "Oh, this can't be happening! He must be sick with these orders."

"Indeed, he is. I could see it written all over his face," Nigel replied with a frown. "But he is a faithful soldier and will do as he is ordered. Utterly dreadful situation for him."

"Lucifer's warning!" Liz put a paw to her face in horror. She looked Nigel in the eye. "That night when Marcus let Jesus' family escape the slaughter of the innocents, he said the sword of Antonius would find Messiah yet!"

"An' now Marcus's lad has been put dir-r-rectly in charge of guar-r-rdin' Jesus as he goes back ta Pilate," growled Max. "That wicked devil be br-r-ringin' it ta pass!"

"If things proceed as Jesus predicted, and we know they will, Jesus will go to the cross one way or another," Nigel told his friends with a voice full of encroaching horror. "And Armandus will be the one responsible to carry it out."

60

And with His Stripes
We Are Healed

Pilate sat drumming his fingers on his desk in the Praetorium, waiting on Herod's answer. He was formulating a response plan depending on how Herod determined the fate of Jesus of Nazareth. If Herod found him guilty, he still would be faced with the predicament of executing him, which he didn't want to do. Or, if Herod found him not guilty, he would be faced with the hounding by the Sanhedrin, who would appeal their case.

"Sir, Herod has sent his answer with one of his centurions," Pilate's servant announced. "He is waiting outside."

"Send him in immediately," Pilate ordered.

Armandus came striding into Pilate's headquarters and extended a formal salute. "Sir, I am Armandus Antonius, centurion assigned to Herod Antipas. He has sent me to tell you he finds Jesus of Nazareth not guilty of the charges against him."

Pilate closed his eyes in relief and nodded. "So, he actually agrees with me. Where is Jesus now?"

"Sir, Jesus is with two of my men outside. Herod ordered that I report to you and offer our services in order to assist you with this matter, since we are soldiers in the jurisdiction of Galilee," Armandus answered.

Pilate raised his eyebrows upon hearing Herod's offer of assistance, pleased that Herod was finally acting like an ally and not an adversary.

Knowing that Herod held favor with Tiberius, Pilate's spirits were encouraged that perhaps that favor would be extended to him as he partnered with Herod on this issue.

"Very well. I have been considering options for what to do with Jesus depending on Herod's response," Pilate said. "I take it the Sanhedrin were none too pleased by Herod's verdict."

"No, Sir, they are extremely upset and are demanding an audience with you to make an appeal of their case," Armandus reported.

"What a surprise," Pilate replied with a sneer. "Rome has a custom of releasing a prisoner each year in honor of the Jewish Passover festival. I will offer to release a prisoner to the people—either Jesus of Nazareth or the worst one in our custody. Because Jesus is so popular with the people at large, surely they will choose Jesus. Tell me who we have awaiting execution."

"Three Zealots arrested for an insurrection against Herod earlier in the week," Armandus replied. "I arrested them myself, Sir."

"Who is the worst of the three of them?" Pilate asked.

"Barabbas is the ringleader of the group, and is a notorious murderer and thug, accused of theft as well," Armandus explained. "The other two are common thieves hired by Barabbas."

Pilate smiled. "Perfect. I will let them choose Jesus or Barabbas. I'm certain the people will choose the peaceful 'king of the Jews' over the murdering Zealot."

In addition to hating the thought of Barabbas out of prison and free to attack again, Armandus was flooded with relief that Jesus could be released. It would be worth it for Barabbas to be a substitute for Jesus. "Indeed you are right, Sir! This is an excellent plan," Armandus enthusiastically told Pilate.

"Good. Go call the leading priests and other religious leaders, along with the people, and I will announce my verdict," Pilate ordered.

"Yes, Sir!" Armandus saluted again and turned to do as commanded.

Pilate smiled and clapped his hands with a feeling of triumph over the Jewish leaders. This day was turning out better than it began. Not only did it appear he and Herod had a new alliance and friendship that could lead to greater favor from Emperor Tiberius, the people of Israel would choose to release Jesus, thereby getting Pilate off the hook with the Sanhedrin.

Jesus stood there in the purple robe Herod had placed on him. Ulixes and Velius stood on either side of him. When Pilate saw him he had to laugh at Herod's sense of humor. He walked by Jesus and said to Ulixes, "Herod wanted him to look the part?"

"Yes, Sir," Ulixes replied with a grin.

Armandus walked up to Pilate. "Sir, the chief priests, elders, and people are assembled as you requested."

Pilate looked out to the courtyard where thousands of people had assembled. The Sanhedrin were huddled together off to the side. *Good, the people outnumber the Sanhedrin by thousands,* Pilate thought to himself after seeing the crowd. Hundreds of Roman soldiers were posted at strategic points outside the Antonia Fortress, donned in their red cloaks and silver helmets, spears held at attention. Pilate walked over to the judge's seat and sat down.

"You brought this man to me, accusing him of leading a revolt. I have examined him thoroughly on this point in your presence and find him innocent. Herod came to the same conclusion and sent him back to us. Nothing this man has done calls for the death penalty," Pilate began, watching the predictable reaction of the Sanhedrin who began to raise their voices in protest. Pilate held up his hand. "You have a custom that I release one prisoner to you at the Passover. Which one do you want me to release to you—Barabbas, or Jesus who is called Messiah?"

501

At that moment, Pilate's servant came running over to him and handed him a note. "Sir, your wife sent this and said it was imperative we deliver it to you immediately."

While Pilate was preoccupied with the note, the chief priests and elders quickly moved into action. "Hurry, tell the people to shout for Barabbas's release and Jesus' death!" The men spread out like a swarm of flies, running through the crowd with the command, implying that this was not a suggestion.

Leave that innocent man alone. I suffered through a terrible nightmare about him last night, Pilate read. He wrinkled his brow and a feeling of uneasiness came over him. *How did she even know I was dealing with Jesus this morning? My wife has always been superstitious, but how can this be explained? She knows he is innocent as well.* He paused a moment but realized he needed to return to the matter at hand. At least he was trying to free him at this very moment.

Pilate looked up and cleared his throat. "Which of these two do you want me to release to you?"

The crowd shouted back, "Barabbas!"

Pilate felt like he had been hit in the gut with this shocking response from the crowd. This wasn't supposed to happen! "Then what should I do with Jesus who is called Messiah?"

They shouted back, "Crucify him!"

"Why?" Pilate demanded, now growing angry at the people. "What crime has he committed?"

But the mob roared even louder, "Crucify him!"

Pilate saw he wasn't getting anywhere and that a riot was developing. So he sent for a bowl of water. He would use one of their own Jewish customs against them. *They want blood! But I cannot crucify Jesus. Perhaps if I have him flogged, that will be sufficient to satisfy their thirst for blood. Once they see he has paid for their trumped-up charges, surely that will be sufficient.*

502

Pilate stood and washed his hands before the crowd, announcing, "I am innocent of this man's blood. The responsibility is yours!"

And all the people yelled back, "We will take responsibility for his death—we and our children!"

Pilate squinted in disgust as he scanned the crowd, taken aback by their sheer hatred for Jesus of Nazareth. He thought Jesus was loved by the people! He had heard about the moving reception they had given Jesus when he entered Jerusalem. *How could the people turn on him so quickly? And they're so thirsty for his blood that they would put the blame on their own children? I will never understand these people.*

He walked over to where Armandus and his men stood with Jesus, and placed his hands on his hips. Pilate furrowed his brow and tightened his lips. "Take him and have him flogged. Then bring him back here." Pilate turned and walked back into the Praetorium.

Armandus immediately felt sick to his stomach but held himself together. "Yes, Sir."

"Come on, Your Majesty," Velius whispered sadistically in Jesus' ear, laughing.

"Someone needs a coronation," Ulixes echoed wickedly.

"No! No! Not this!" Liz sobbed and cried as they watched the soldiers leading Jesus out of the courtyard over to the Antonia Fortress, where an entire cohort of six hundred soldiers were gathered.

"They're goin' ta torture him!" Kate wept, as she and Liz clung to each other. Al enveloped both of them with his arms.

"Jesus said they would," Max growled, feeling helpless. They all felt helpless. They *were* helpless. Max stood, as if ready to run, but knew he must stay put. "Mousie, wha's goin' ta happen ta Jesus?"

"Roman scourging is merciless," Nigel whispered to Max softly, out of earshot of the girls, sickened by what was happening to Jesus. "They chain the victim's wrists to either side of a wooden pillar with his back exposed. They use a trained expert called a *lictor*, who knows how to inflict the worst damage imaginable. He uses a leather whip called a *flagrum*, which has tails tied and knotted with bits of metal and bone. Victims suffer lacerations on the skin and deep cuts and bruises in the muscles underneath. Depending on the ferocity of the lictor, victims can have punctured lungs or broken ribs."

503

Max frowned and shook his head. "How long do it last?"

Nigel shut his eyes tight at the horror of the situation. "Most victims go into shock in as little as five minutes, so the lictor will deliver three or four blows and then back off, allowing the victim to somewhat recover. But time is given for the victim to be taunted by the soldiers. The Jews limit scourging to thirty-nine lashes, and only to the back and shoulders, but the Roman lictors are given no restrictions," he related as he paused to take a deep breath. "Back, legs, shoulders, face, chest— nothing is off limits and the flogging can continue until the soldiers are sufficiently entertained."

"Entertained?" Max asked in disbelief. "Ye mean ta tell me those soldiers actually *enjoy* doin' this?"

Nigel frowned. "Not all of them, certainly, like Armandus, who doesn't want to see this happen to Jesus. But the reality is that many of these soldiers have been hardened by Rome's conquests."

Max walked over to Liz, Kate, and Al. "Jesus asked us ta pr-r-ray," he reminded them. "There's nothin' else we can do." With that they all bowed their heads and prayed for Jesus.

Armandus stood in the back of the company of soldiers, not wanting to have anything to do with the gruesome affair taking place. Jesus' clothes were removed and he was roughly tied to the low whipping post. Soon the lictor came out with a leather mask over his face that gave him a fierce appearance. He picked up the flagrum and snapped it on the ground as the company of soldiers cheered his approach, clapping their hands. He raised his hand back and struck Jesus across the back with the whip.

The horses in the corral nearby all jumped and snorted the moment the whip found its mark. Jesus gripped the iron rings of the whipping post and cried out in agony. The lictor pulled back and struck again and again, each time hitting other areas of Jesus' body and inflicting more damage. Jesus began to faint, so the lictor stopped. The Roman soldiers took this as their cue to taunt and ridicule Jesus. Armandus couldn't stand to watch this. He quietly stepped away, unnoticed by the others. The scourging went on and on until Jesus was completely covered in blood.

504

"I have an idea!" Ulixes whispered in Velius's ear as he spied the overgrowth of thorns growing at the far end of the complex. "Come on!"

Together the two soldiers went over to the thornbush. Ulixes took out his dagger and cut off several pieces, handing them to Velius. "What are you doing?"

"The king needs a crown," Ulixes replied with a wicked grin. "But be careful, these thorns are at least three inches long and as sharp as your sword,"

Velius laughed. "I get it," he said as he carefully started weaving the thorns into a circle. "Ouch!" he yelled when he pricked his thumb, dropping the crown of thorns, and putting his thumb in his mouth. "That hurt!"

Ulixes picked up the crown and wove in the last piece of the thorny vine. "There, that looks perfect!"

Together the two soldiers ran back over to join the others. Ulixes held up the crown of thorns. "Look what we have—a crown fitting for the king of the Jews!"

The company of soldiers began laughing and clapping at Ulixes's sick joke. He walked over and placed the crown of thorns on Jesus' head. "Here's your crown, Your Majesty," the wicked soldier said with gritted teeth. At that moment his eyes flashed red and he pushed the thorny crown down on Jesus' head. Jesus closed his eyes and groaned in pain as he felt blood begin to trickle down into his face.

Ulixes stepped back and mockingly bowed and raised his arms up and down. "Hail, Your Majesty!" The other soldiers immediately joined in the mockery.

"Here, let me release your king before he dies," the lictor joked as he went over to take Jesus' arms out of the shackles. "He's had enough of this."

As the lictor released him, Jesus immediately fell to the hard ground, struggling to breathe. His body was covered with gashes and bloody stripes, and he lay in a pool of blood.

"Get him up," one of the soldiers shouted, grabbing the purple robe where they had tossed it. "He needs his robe!"

"And a scepter!" another soldier yelled as he ran to get a stick.

Together the soldiers picked Jesus up and made him stand in place while they put the purple robe on him and thrust the stick into Jesus' bloody hand.

505

They bowed low before him and jeered him with the words, "Hail, Your Majesty, king of the Jews!" Then they spat on him, and took turns hitting him with their fists. They had turned into a bloodthirsty, crazed mob, coming at Jesus from all directions. Ulixes took the stick and hit him on the head with it, laughing maniacally.

"ENOUGH!" Armandus yelled as he returned to see the horror of what they were doing to Jesus. He strode over and pulled the soldiers off him. He took the stick from Ulixes, who glared at him with an evil, unnatural look in his eye. "That's enough! This prisoner will be returned to Pilate now!"

Armandus threw the stick on the ground and put his arm under Jesus' elbow to steady him while he commanded the men to get away from them. Jesus was trembling from shock and blood loss, and was barely able to stand. "I've got you," he barely whispered so no one could hear him but Jesus. Then in a louder voice, "We're taking you back to Pilate."

Armandus took Jesus to the end of the darkened corridor just outside the courtyard and ordered Ulixes and Velius to report to Pilate that the prisoner had been flogged and was ready to be presented. He wasn't about to leave Jesus alone with these two blood-crazed soldiers. As the soldiers marched off to Pilate, Armandus supported Jesus, allowing the bloodied man to place his full weight on him. It was the first opportunity he had alone with Jesus. "Master, I'm sorry. I don't understand why this is happening, but I can't stop any of it."

Jesus struggled to speak, still reeling from the trauma and shock of the scourging. "Do not blame yourself, Armandus. This is not your doing. The Son of Man must be lifted up for the salvation of the world."

Armandus wrinkled his brow. He didn't understand any of this. He saw the soldiers return and moved away from Jesus, propping him back up on his own two feet. "Pilate said to bring him out now, Sir," Velius reported.

Pilate went outside again and said to the people, "I am going to bring him out to you now, but understand clearly that I find him not guilty."

Then Jesus slowly came out wearing the crown of thorns and the purple robe. The crowd, and even Pilate, gasped when they saw him. Pilate pointed at Jesus and announced, "Behold, your king!"

The animals also gasped as they gazed on the unrecognizable form of their friend, their master, their Messiah. Liz and Kate hid their eyes, unable to handle the shock. Al began to cry. Max could barely swallow the lump in his throat.

"This is far worse even than I described to you earlier. Unspeakable," Nigel said, putting his paw to his head, shaking it in disbelief. Suddenly the words of Isaiah came crashing into his mind: *But he was wounded for our transgressions, he was bruised for our iniquities: the chastisement of our peace was upon him; and with his stripes we are healed.*

The leading priests and Temple guards began shouting, "Crucify him! Crucify him!"

"Take him yourselves and crucify him," Pilate said, walking away with a wave of his hand. "I find him not guilty."

Zeeb stepped forward and called after him. "By our law he ought to die because he called himself the Son of God."

When Pilate heard this, he stopped in his tracks, more frightened than ever. Not only had the letter from his wife made him feel uneasy, but to hear that Jesus said he was the Son of God made Pilate break out in a sweat. As a Roman, Pilate was naturally superstitious and believed in all gods, which were accepted into the Roman culture. But this God of Israel was something different. If Jesus truly were the Son of *this* God, Pilate could be in mortal danger. He motioned to Armandus to bring Jesus with him back into the headquarters again. He walked ahead and Armandus took Jesus by the arm and escorted him in.

Pilate exhaled, pulled his fingers through his silver, cropped hair and paced around the room. Armandus soon ushered Jesus in to stand before him and stepped back. Pilate got right in Jesus' face.

"Where are you from?" he asked with a hushed but strong voice.

Armandus knew Pilate wasn't talking about Galilee or anywhere here on Earth. But Jesus gave no answer.

"Why don't you talk to me?" Pilate demanded as he raised his voice, more out of panic than anger. "Don't you realize I have the power to release you or crucify you?"

Jesus slowly lifted his gaze and looked directly at Pilate. "You would have no power over me at all unless it were given to you from above. So the one who handed me over to you has the greater sin."

507

Pilate and Armandus shared a startled look. Pilate stepped back and shook his head before turning and stomping back out to the Jewish leaders.

"You *must* release this man," Pilate again insisted. "He's been flogged within an inch of his life as it is. Surely this should satisfy you."

"If you release this man, you are no friend of Caesar," Caiaphas spoke up in a commanding voice. "Anyone who declares himself a king is a rebel against Caesar."

Pilate stood back and silently stared at them in disbelief. Here these people were, contradicting their core beliefs. They were willing to abandon it all if it meant being able to eliminate Jesus.

As he sat down on the judgment seat, Pilate motioned for Armandus to bring Jesus out to them again. He would make one final plea before the people. As Jesus stood before the crowd, Pilate said to them, "Look, here is your king!"

"Away with him!" they yelled. "Away with him! Crucify him!"

"What? Crucify your king?" Pilate asked.

"We have no king but Caesar," the leading priests shouted back.

That was all Pilate needed to hear. It was over. The Jews had chosen Caesar over the king of the Jews, and wouldn't hesitate to tell Tiberius that Pilate actually argued against their decision. He put his head in his hand and with a defeated voice ordered, "Release Barabbas." He took a deep breath and stood. "Crucify Jesus of Nazareth."

"Pilate tried desperately all day to put the decision about Jesus off on someone else," Liz said with a broken voice as they watched Pilate leave and saw Jesus carried away.

"But there be no escape from a personal decision aboot Jesus," Al added.

"Indeed, everyone must decide what to do with Jesus," Nigel agreed. "Accept him or reject him."

Kate shook her head sadly. "Pilate finally made his decision, rejectin' Jesus after all. He chose saving himself an' his position with Rome over doin' the right thing."

"An' nobody will ever forget him for it," Max said, "least of all, the Maker."

508

Barabbas sat with his back leaning on the dank dungeon wall of the Antonia Fortress and closed his eyes to fight back the wave of terror that now engulfed him. All morning he had heard his name chanted by crowds in a roar of celebration from the courtyard above. He could occasionally make out the voice of Pilate speaking to the crowd, assumedly claiming victory over this enemy of Rome who had been captured. Now he and his fellow insurrectionists would be made an example of so the people would see what happens to anyone who defies Rome.

He could barely make out his name until the crowd started chanting over and over, *"Give us Barabbas!"* The blood drained from his face as the words then changed to the muffled sounds of, *"Crucify him! Crucify him!"* A horrific death awaited him and the two thieves who had been arrested with him.

"They're coming for us!" one of the thieves cried out in panic as they heard the distinct sound of the Roman soldiers' feet echoing down the stone corridor.

"This is your fault!" spat the other thief. "Your failed riot has killed us!"

The three men listened as the footsteps stopped and the jangling of keys sounded outside their cell door. Their hearts began pounding wildly as the door suddenly slammed open and three Roman soldiers rushed in.

Two legionnaires grabbed the thieves and dragged them out into the corridor, the prisoners screaming as they were carried away to be prepared for crucifixion. Barabbas recognized the centurion as the same one who had arrested him the day of the failed attempt to assassinate Herod Antipas. But he was covered in blood. Barabbas swallowed hard. This blood belonged to another man. Fear soon mixed with rage as the centurion shoved him out of the cell but in the opposite direction of the other prisoners.

Barabbas decided he would verbally unleash his rage on this Roman. Nothing mattered anymore anyway. "You Roman thugs will someday feel the wrath of God when he raises up his people against you in great numbers!"

"Shut up!" Armandus yelled, giving Barabbas a hard shove.

"Were you given the reward of crucifying me yourself since you saved Herod from my blade?" Barabbas continued.

As they neared the barred exit door ahead, Barabbas had to squint against the bright sunlight that poured in. His eyes began to water after having been plunged into darkness for days. He needed to allow his eyes to adjust, so he closed them for a moment as the centurion stopped him in the corridor. He heard the soldier's keys jangle to unlock the door, pushing it open. The soldier then removed the shackles from his wrists and shoved Barabbas out the door.

"Get out!" Armandus ordered. He then slammed the barred door behind him, locking it from the inside.

"I don't understand," Barabbas said in shock, holding his hands up to shield his eyes from the bright sunlight.

"You're free, Barabbas. Someone is taking your place," Armandus scowled. "And unlike you, *this* man is innocent."

"Who? Who is taking my place?" Barabbas had to know, his heart beating wildly inside of him.

"Jesus of Nazareth," Armandus replied. His voice trailed away.

Barabbas lowered his hands and saw they were covered with the blood that had been on the Roman. He wiped his hands on his grimy clothes. *Who's blood?* he wondered. The realization that he was not going to die washed over him as he looked at the stripes of blood now on his tunic. *Thankfully it's not mine.*

THE KING OF THE JEWS

H ere you go, Your Majesty," Ulixes mocked as he roughly tied the wooden sign around Jesus' neck. "This should make it official. Pilate even ordered it written in three languages so everyone will know that you are indeed the King of the Jews!"

"He's got his crown and his title," Velius jeered. "Now he needs to get up on his throne so people can bow before him!"

Jesus could barely stand, but quietly endured the continued taunting as the soldiers prepared him and the two thieves for crucifixion. Each was made to wear a *titulus,* or sign around his neck, indicating the crime he had committed. The criminals would be marched through the streets by the longest route possible, so everyone along the way could read about their crimes. The signs would then be attached to their crosses to warn others what surely awaited them if they committed the same crime.

"Mon Dieu!" Liz exclaimed as she and the other animals moved to where Jesus was being held. The death march was ready to begin. "The crown of thorns! This was foreshadowed in the Garden when man fell, and later when Abraham was about to sacrifice Isaac."

"How so, Liz?" Kate asked tearfully.

Nigel's eyes widened with Liz' revelation. "Indeed you are right, my dear. Thorns represent the fall of man when God told Adam the ground would be cursed with thorns and thistles because of his sin. And when Abraham was about to sacrifice Isaac, a substitute ram was caught in the thicket of thorns by its head!"

"Aye, Jesus were foreshadowed all along," Max observed. "His blood be on ever-r-ry page of the Scr-r-riptures."

"*Oui*, and the wooden sign around Jesus' neck also is full of meaning," Liz added, trying to find confirmation of the plans of God in the horror of this moment. "Pilate ordered Jesus' sign to be written in Greek, Latin, and Hebrew. These nations are responsible for giving the world three vital things for people to live together. Greece gave the world beauty of form and thought, Rome gave the world law and good government, and Israel gave the world worship of the one true God."

"Jesus be all o' these things, and more," Al sniffed and said. "So in their own language, Jesus be called the King o' the Jews?"

The Jewish leaders were arguing with Pilate about the sign around Jesus' neck. Pilate had had enough. He threw up both hands in front of them and forcefully gestured, "What I have written, I have written!" He then stomped off and left the soldiers to their work. He was ready to end all involvement with this miscarriage of justice. The Jewish leaders looked at one another and folded their arms in disapproval. But they had pushed Pilate as far as they could.

511

Armandus was in charge of four soldiers who were preparing the three men to be led to the crucifixion site. Two of the legionnaires were Armandus's men, Ulixes and Velius, and they were assigned to Jesus. The other two were from Pilate's regiment from Caesarea, and were assigned to the two thieves. They readied the two thieves with their signs and placed the crossbeams over their shoulders. Ulixes and Velius lifted Jesus' crossbeam and harshly placed it across the nape of his neck, trying to balance it along his torn shoulders.

Max growled. "Wha' be they doin' ta him now?"

Nigel frowned and cleared his throat. "It is customary for each criminal to bear his own cross as a testimony of his guilt, so they are placing the *patibulum*, or crossbeam, on each man's shoulders. Each will have to carry it to the place of crucifixion where the *stipes*, or vertical beam, awaits them. The crossbeam's terribly heavy, weighing seventy pounds or more."

Al's lip trembled as he inquired hesitantly, "What exactly happens then?"

Liz gasped and tears quickened in her eyes, but she knew they should be prepared for what was to come. Nigel continued, "Crucifixion was invented by the Persians, who desired their victims to be 'lifted up' off the ground, so as not to defile the earth belonging to their god Ormuzd. The Carthaginians picked it up from the Persians, and then the Romans picked up the practice." Liz shook her head. "But because it is the most cruel and horrific means of death ever invented, it is illegal to inflict it on a Roman citizen. It is meant only for rebels, runaway slaves, and the lowliest of criminals."

"And to think that Rome is known for its justice," Nigel said, shaking his head. "Jesus was found not guilty by Pilate and Herod in their Roman courts. On his desk every Roman official has a figure of Janus, the two-faced god, to remind him to look forward and backward, at both sides of the question. In Roman courts, the innocent and the guilty always get justice—not mercy, but at least justice. But this . . . this is a mockery of justice to send an innocent man to such a horrific death."

"So the Jews and the Gentiles both looked the other way on the very things they be known for: God and the Law. That's aboot as two-faced as it gets," Al noted. "Both groups be guilty o' doin' this to Jesus."

"*Oui,* Albert, they are the ones who at this point in time are about to kill Messiah," Liz affirmed. "But the reality is that every single man, woman, and child across time since Adam is responsible, for Jesus is willingly doing this to die for the sins of every single soul."

"'The wicked band together against the righteous and condemn the innocent to death,'" Nigel recited, quoting yet another prophecy of Messiah from Psalm 94. "In the Maker's court, one day every person will have to give an account of what they did here on Earth. Judas, Pilate, Herod, and Caiaphas will be judged for what they did to Jesus, but so will every other soul because of their sin. Sadly, all are guilty of the charges and owe a debt that, without Jesus, must be paid by a dreadful eternity apart from the Maker."

Al gulped. "Ye mean . . . in hell?"

"*Oui.* The Maker loves the world but his justice demands that sin be paid for. But for those who believe in Jesus, he'll take their place in the Maker's court. Jesus will look at them, smile, and say, 'Not guilty. I've paid their debt in full,'" Liz added, the full understanding of Jesus' mission becoming clearer with each passing moment. "This is how every soul can gain eternal life with the Maker in heaven!"

"For God so loved the world, he gave his only son so whoever believes in him won't perish but'll have eternal life," Al recounted. "Is this what Jesus meant then?"

"Aye, Big Al. That's exactly wha' Jesus meant. No one be killin' Jesus—even though it looks that way," Max observed. "He's giving up his life willingly. He's the one who planned this ta happen ta save the world then."

"No one has ta be separated from the Maker when they die. He's givin' them a way out—a way ta be with God in heaven forever!" Kate said joyfully. The hope of the moment was overshadowed by what would have to happen to make this possible. "So wha' will happen ta our Jesus now?"

"Right. I'll try to explain this the best way I can, but I'm afraid there is simply no way to put it mildly," Nigel began. "Once they arrive at the place of The Skull, where the Crucifixion will be held, they will remove the condemned men's clothes to humiliate them. They will take the crossbeam and attach it to the vertical beam to form a 'T,' and make each man lie on his cross. While two soldiers hold him down," Nigel said, a lump in his throat, "two others will drive five-inch long nails through his palms close to the wrist. They do this in order to cause intense pain at the median nerve of the arm and forearm, and to support the weight of the victim while on the cross. Next they will place his feet flat on the *stipes*, bending his knees, and drive a nail through each foot. As the soldiers then tilt the cross up and guide it into a hole, the jarring motion and the hammering of support wedges in the hole to stabilize the cross cause shocking, horrific pain."

Max shook his head, trying to grasp that this would be happening to Jesus. "How long will they have ta hang there?"

"I pray mercifully not long," Nigel replied. "Sometimes victims stay on their crosses for days on end."

"Days?! How can that be?" Al asked in anguish.

"The cause of death is not the nails. Some victims are simply tied with ropes to the cross without nails, which might sound more merciful but their suffering is prolonged," Nigel explained. "Death from crucifixion usually comes from exposure to the elements of heat and cold, dehydration, or lack of water, starvation, or suffocation. You see, victims have to continually move to momentarily relieve the pain in their wrists, arms, shoulders, chest, and legs. After a while they become so tired they can't lift themselves up to catch their breath or even have the lung power to exhale. For nailed victims, they experience blood loss, shock, and even heart failure. But victims have been known to last for days on the cross, depending on how badly they were scourged prior to crucifixion. It's simply incomprehensible that man could have invented something so 'excruciating'—and this is where that word comes from."

"Because Jesus suffered such a brutal scourging, he will not be physically able to last as long as others might," Liz added in a broken voice. "We also have the hope that the Sabbath and the Passover begin at sundown today, and by Jewish law, victims must not be left on the cross."

"So it will be a matter of hours, not days then," Max surmised. "These will be the longest hours the world has ever seen."

Armandus stood clenching his jaw as the four legionnaires formed a square around Jesus and the two thieves. They would walk them along the crowded, narrow streets of Jerusalem, out the gates of the city to Golgotha. For some reason Armandus suddenly remembered the Via Sacra in Rome—the Sacred Way—and how it represented triumph as the men meandered through the streets of Rome before the crowds. *This walk will be the opposite for Jesus. This road is the Via Dolorosa—the way of suffering and sorrow*, he thought to himself, gripped with anguish. *There will never be anything sacred about this way.*

"We're ready, Sir," Velius said as the soldiers got into position around the prisoners.

"Very well," Armandus said as he began walking forward. He suddenly heard a groan and the sound of a man hitting the stone pavement. He turned and saw it was Jesus lying there, clearly unable to carry the weight of the crossbeam. His back and muscles were too damaged to support the beam, and his strength was drained from the loss of so much blood.

"Get up!" Ulixes said, kicking Jesus. "That's no way for a king to act!"

Armandus walked back and shoved the cruel soldier in the chest, snapping, "You fool, the man was scourged so brutally that he can't carry this much weight!" He looked around and saw a man standing at the edge of the street where Jesus was. He placed the end of his spear on the man's shoulder. "You—carry this man's cross."

The man's face filled with fear and his two sons gripped him by the shoulders. He turned to them, handing them his knapsack and whispered, "Alexander and Rufus, follow along so I won't lose you. I must do as the centurion commands." The young men nodded as their father stepped forward. "Sir, I am Simon, from Cyrene. I will do as you say."

Armandus nodded and barked at his men. "Take the cross off Jesus and put it on this man." After the soldiers untied the crossbeam from Jesus' shoulders, Armandus slowly helped Jesus to his feet, whispering to him, "I've got you."

Jesus shut his eyes and nodded. A large crowd trailed behind, including many grief-stricken women who began wailing.

As the soldiers seized Simon to put the cross on him, Jesus turned to the women. He raised his gaze and said, "Daughters of Jerusalem, don't weep for me, but weep for yourselves and for your children. For the days are coming when they will say, 'Fortunate indeed are the women who are childless, the wombs that have not borne a child and the breasts that have never nursed.' People will beg the mountains, 'Fall on us,' and plead with the hills, 'Bury us.' For if these things are done when the tree is green, what will happen when it is dry?"

Armandus looked at Jesus in awe. *Even now, he's preaching to the people, more concerned about them and their futures than his own.*

"He's prophesying," Liz noted. "Jesus is the green tree, and he is saying if such horrible things happen while he is here, how terrible it will be when he is not here and God's wrath falls upon them for rejecting Messiah."

Suddenly a murmuring developed as Mary was escorted by several women to the front of the crowd. Her face was full of anguish, and tears streamed down her cheeks as she looked on her firstborn son. She reached out a cloth to wipe his face, looking first to Armandus for approval. Armandus swallowed hard, thinking how it would be if this were his mother and he were in Jesus' place. He nodded respectfully and stepped back to watch a tender scene.

No words were spoken, but the loving touch of a mother to her son left the crowd speechless. Mary gently dabbed the cloth on Jesus' face, struggling to wipe his eyes without causing him further pain, since they were so badly swollen and bruised. Tears fell down her face as she looked at the crown of thorns, shaking her head.

Anger welled up inside of Armandus. He reached over and removed the crown of thorns, tossing it in the street. Mary gently dabbed at the blood on Jesus' brow, choking on her tears.

515

"The man is ready, Sir," Velius said when Simon was prepared with the crossbeam tied to his shoulders.

Armandus took Mary by the arm and she suddenly whispered in Jesus' ear. "Your Father's hands, Jesus, you are in your Father's hands." She fell back into the arms of the other weeping women as Jesus was pushed away from her touch.

Armandus resumed his position at the front of the procession, and tried to shake off the emotion of that moment. They walked on to Golgotha, known as the place of The Skull for its craggy cliffside appearance resembling a skull.

The animals followed along, weeping as much for Mary as for Jesus.

Once they reached Golgotha, things happened quickly. The soldiers offered the victims wine drugged with myrrh. The two thieves eagerly drank the elixir, taking any chance they could to alleviate their pain. But Jesus quietly refused it. He was going to face the salvation of mankind with his senses fully intact. Armandus looked at Jesus in continuing awe as he removed the sign from around Jesus' neck. It was covered with blood, staining the wood with a reddish-brown hue. He handed it to Ulixes, who would affix it to the top of Jesus' cross.

As they removed the crossbeam from Simon's shoulders, he bent forward, resting his hands on his knees and catching his breath. Even for a strong, healthy man the burden of carrying the cross was intense. He heard the clank of the Roman hammer nailing the crossbeam to the stipes and raised his gaze. Simon locked eyes with Jesus, experiencing a sense of sadness and an indescribable feeling that he had just participated in something significant. In Jesus' eyes he saw gratitude mixed with love for him. Simon lingered a moment longer, until the two brusque legionnaires grabbed Jesus. He turned and walked back to find his sons. He didn't want to be alone as the events unfolded.

Ulixes and Velius pulled off Jesus' clothes and threw them on the ground, leaving him dressed only in a loincloth. His robe was soaked with blood. The soldiers roughly handled him and forced him to lie back on the prepared cross. Armandus watched as Pilate's two soldiers lay across Jesus' body, bracing for him to resist the process. Amazingly, Jesus stretched his arms wide, shutting his eyes as he submitted to his inevitable fate.

516

Velius and Ulixes each took one of Jesus' wrists and stretched his arms so tightly on the crossbeam that Jesus' shoulders pulled out of joint. They took the huge nails and as they raised their hammers high in the air, Armandus shut his eyes tightly with the first clank of the hammer onto iron. Jesus groaned as the nails entered his wrists, tears of agony streaming down his face. Ulixes's eyes flashed red with delight and a wicked smile grew on his face.

Armandus had to turn his back and act as if he was disinterested in order to make it through this nightmare. He walked over to the two thieves who knelt on the ground, arms bound to their crossbeams, and waiting their turn for the same fate. He listened as the other nails were driven into Jesus' feet, followed by the groans of this innocent, loving man who didn't fight his executioners.

"One, two, heave," he heard Velius instruct as they lifted Jesus' cross high in the air. He heard the sickening thud of the cross landing in the hole, and Jesus crying out in pain. But what Armandus heard next made him turn around and face Jesus in disbelief.

517

"Father, forgive them, for they don't know what they are doing," Jesus said softly.

How can he possibly say this? Armandus wondered. *And to whom is he speaking?*

As the soldiers left Jesus to move on to repeat the horrific procedure with the two thieves—one on his right and one on his left—Armandus gazed at Jesus hanging there and read the wooden sign above his head, written in three languages: JESUS OF NAZARETH: KING OF THE JEWS.

Why would the Jews kill their king? Armandus wondered. *What possible threat did he pose to them?* Suddenly he made a startling connection of events in his mind. *Herod the Great also wanted to kill the King of the Jews. Why? Who is he?!*

It was nine o'clock in the morning. Armandus's mind was swirling with questions and he already felt a sickening heat enveloping him, unnatural for springtime. He shuddered and wiped his brow with the back of his arm, hoping this day would pass quickly. Nothing about this day felt natural. He gazed at Jesus suffering on the cross. *Who really is this Jesus of Nazareth?*

62

WHO IS THIS KING?

It didn't matter that this was a foregone conclusion. It didn't matter that they knew hundreds of years ago from prophecy that Messiah would die via crucifixion. Now that they knew Jesus personally, nothing that they *knew* mattered. All that mattered at this moment was how they *felt*. They had benefited from life with Jesus since the moment of his birth. They watched him grow as a young, happy, caring boy. They saw him begin his ministry and affect countless lives with his healing touch and his words of grace and guidance. Jesus was a beacon of light and love in a dark world, bringing hope to the hopeless and love to the unlovable. He was Emmanuel, God with Us. He was the Way, the Truth, and the Life. But now they saw him dying before their eyes. And they were heartbroken.

Liz and Kate hugged each other as they sobbed. Max, Al, and Nigel stood by as silent sentinels, resigned to the fact that what was happening was Master-planned and well beyond their control. They slowly watched the crowd gather around Jesus' cross: his mother Mary, Mary Magdalene, Salome, and Mary, the wife of Clopas. The love these women had for Jesus kept them clinging to him even at the cross. They were unashamed to stand below the cross of this man rejected by the world. Suddenly and surprisingly, John appeared. One lone disciple had finally shown up.

As John looked at Jesus, crucified between two thieves, a wave of understanding and shame washed over him. He and his brother James had brazenly asked to be placed at the right and the left side of Jesus, but Jesus had told them they didn't truly know what they were asking. "Of course we can handle it!" the Sons of Thunder had arrogantly answered him. John closed his eyes and shook his head with regret. *How could I have been so foolish?*

Surrounding these few who stood at the foot of the cross out of love for Jesus were those who stood at the cross out of hatred and avarice. The laughter of the soldiers was like a dull knife stabbed in the back. It was out of place, unexpected, and irreverent. They gambled for Jesus' clothes by throwing dice. They divided Jesus' clothes among the four of them. They also took his bloody robe, but it was seamless, woven in one piece from top to bottom.

"Rather than tear it apart, let's throw dice for it," Ulixes suggested with a callous grin.

"Dogs surround me, a pack of villains encircles me; they pierce my hands and my feet . . . They divided my garments among themselves and threw dice for my clothing," Nigel softly recited, remembering the prophecies from Psalm 22. "Astounding. David wrote these prophetic words before crucifixion had even been invented."

The crowd watched and the Jewish leaders scoffed. "He saved others," Zeeb started to taunt, "let him save himself if he is really God's Messiah, the Chosen One."

The soldiers mocked him, too, by offering him a drink of sour wine. They called out to him, "If you are the King of the Jews, save yourself!"

The people passing by shouted abuse, shaking their heads in mockery, following the cue of their leaders. "Look at you now!" they yelled at Jesus. "You said you were going to destroy the Temple and rebuild it in three days. Well then, if you are the Son of God, save yourself and come down from the cross!"

Over the course of the next three hours, the leading priests, the teachers of religious law, and the elders took turns mocking Jesus. "He saved others," they scoffed, "but he can't save himself! So he is the King of Israel, is he? Let him come down from the cross right now, and we will believe in him! He trusted God, so let God rescue him now if he wants him! For he said, 'I am the Son of God.'"

"But I am a worm and not a man, scorned by everyone, despised by the people. All who see me mock me; they hurl insults, shaking their

519

heads. 'He trusts in the Lord,' they say, 'let the Lord rescue him. Let him deliver him, since he delights in him,'" Liz echoed from Psalm 22. She had dreaded seeing this psalm fulfilled before their eyes.

"The fact that Jesus isn't comin' down *pr-r-roves* he's Messiah," Max said in a broken voice. "If he did leave the cr-r-ross, he couldn't save the world."

"Aye, Jesus is showin' that there be no limit ta the love of the Maker," Kate added, wiping her eyes. "There be nothin' his love wouldn't do for the people he created, even dyin' for 'em."

Even the criminals who were crucified with Jesus ridiculed him. One of them scoffed, "So you're Messiah, are you? Prove it by saving yourself—and us, too, while you're at it!"

Something suddenly changed in the other criminal. "Don't you fear God even when you have been sentenced to die? We deserve to die for our crimes, but this man hasn't done anything wrong." He winced as sudden pain shot through his arms. "Jesus . . . re- . . . remember me when you come into your Kingdom."

520

Jesus gasped for breath and slowly turned his gaze toward the criminal. "I assure you . . . today you will be with me in paradise."

Jesus writhed in pain and rose up on his feet to seek temporary relief from the agony in his wrists. The pain then attacked his feet and he lowered himself back down, shaking with searing pain beyond comprehension. His gaze drifted to the crowd below. He saw his mother standing there beside John. The long-ago-prophesied sword was piercing her heart as men pierced her son.

Jesus licked his dry, cracked lips and struggled to form his words. "Dear w-w-woman . . . here is your son." He looked at John. "Here . . . is your mother."

John wrapped his arm around Mary, understanding Jesus' directive that he was to now look after the mother of Messiah.

He's prayed for his murderers, promised Paradise, and now provided for his mother, Armandus thought to himself. *Who does that while struggling to hang on to life? Who is he?*

"Wha's that comin'?" Max asked, his head up at attention.

"Where, old boy?" Nigel asked, looking in the direction where Max stared.

"That dark thing," Max answered.

The animals watched a strange phenomenon creeping along the horizon. It looked like a black curtain being pulled across the sky. It soon blocked out the noonday sun high overhead.

"Could it be an eclipse?" Nigel wondered.

"*Non, c'est impossible,*" Liz answered. "The moon is in its full phase. This has to be supernatural."

Armandus looked at the ominous sky that brought with it a chill in the air. The sky was dark but these were not clouds. His eyes roamed the heavens but it looked as if they were completely cut off from the earth.

The shroud of darkness lasted three hours. During that time, the animals watched as Jesus uttered not a word, but wore a look of unimaginable grief. His eyes gazed into the distance, widened with shock and disbelief. His mouth would occasionally open as if viewing a horrible scene, and he would shake his head sadly. He sobbed and sobbed and sobbed, which robbed him of precious breath.

"I think he's seeing every sin of man played out across all time," shared Nigel with a heavy heart.

521

"*Oui,* this is why the darkness covered the earth. Heaven could not watch as Jesus took on the sin of the world," Liz wept. "As he became sin itself."

Nigel nodded. "Jesus now understands humanity as he never has before. He has never known what sin feels like, or what being separated from the Maker feels like."

"Nobody can really understand what ye go through unless they've been through it themselves," Al remarked. "Because Jesus felt every single sin o' every single person, he truly be the only one who can now understand 'em. He's been there. Sure, and he's done that."

"Aye, an' he's *paid* for it on top of it all. For the first thr-r-ree hours, Jesus were sufferin' *at the hands of* man," Max said. "For the last thr-r-ree hours, he were sufferin' *for* man."

Suddenly the dark skies began to swirl into storm clouds. A single drop of water fell from the sky and landed on Jesus' face.

"I think the Maker be cryin'," Al said with a trembling lip as he, too, began to cry.

Jesus' eyes widened and he frantically searched the heavens. With a loud voice, he screamed, *"Eli, Eli, lema sabachthani?"*

Liz shook her head, weeping. "He's quoting the first verse of Psalm 22: 'My God, my God, why have you forsaken me?'"

A rumble of thunder raced across the sky, and a rush of wind began to blow.

Some of the bystanders looked at one another trying to understand what Jesus was saying. They misunderstood and thought he was calling for the prophet Elijah. But others responded, "Wait! Let's see whether Elijah comes to save him."

Jesus lowered his gaze and shut his eyes. He licked his lips and with a broken voice, said, "I am thirsty."

Armandus grabbed a hyssop branch and a sponge and plunged it into a jar of sour wine that was sitting there for the soldiers to drink. He reached and held it up to Jesus' lips, striving to ease his new friend's suffering.

After Jesus tasted it, he looked at Armandus with those piercing green eyes. In that moment, Armandus knew. He finally knew who Jesus was.

522

A series of flashbacks played across his mind. "I like his eyes!" the toddler Armandus had told his mother about the baby friend who visited his family's home in Jerusalem. That baby was Jesus! And that day as a teenager when he bought the oil lamp in Jerusalem—the young Jewish boy with the worn clothes and the captivating green eyes who smiled at him in the street, causing him to have a distant feeling of familiarity. It was Jesus! That day Jesus healed his servant in Capernaum, there was something in those eyes that haunted Armandus, something familiar. Now he knew who Jesus was all along. He was the child his father and mother knew—this is the one child his father had allowed to escape the night of the slaughter of the innocents. Jesus was the child his father had saved!

Jesus pulled himself up one last time. With a loud voice he exclaimed, *"Tetelesai!"*

Nigel let out a mournful groan as he interpreted Jesus' word: "Paid in full!"

"Father, into your hands I commit my spirit," Jesus softly said. His chin dropped to his chest, and he was gone.

Mary threw her head back and let loose a sorrowful cry. Her son's last words were the ones she had taught him as a child to pray before he went to sleep every night. Now he uttered them as he went to be with his Father.

Immediately an earthquake shook the ground and everyone cried out in fear, dropping to their knees. A giant crack ran under Armandus's feet and he knelt down and clutched the earth with both hands. His emotions raged as violently as the stormy sky that was suddenly illuminated with widespread lightning and deafening thunder. The heavens broke open with a deluge of stinging rain. As the crowds screamed and began running away, Armandus slowly got to his feet.

The centurion gazed on this Jesus who had been in his life all along, and who did things no mere human could ever do. The rain began washing the blood from Jesus' body, and it pooled on the muddy ground below. Yes, Armandus now knew exactly who Jesus was.

"Surely he was the Son of God!"

WORTHY IS THE LAMB

"What is that sound?" one of the priests shouted. He stopped in the middle of preparing the sacrificial lamb for Passover at the designated three o'clock hour to listen.

"It sounds like something tearing," another priest nervously answered. "The sound is coming from the Most Holy Place!"

The priests ran toward the Holy of Holies, the most sacred place in all Israel. It was here the presence of God resided, and where the Ark of the Covenant holding the Ten Commandments once was kept. After the Babylonian invasion and destruction of Jerusalem the Ark was never seen again, but the sacred Foundation Stone, or the rock where Abraham offered up Isaac, remained. Only the high priest could enter the Holy of Holies, and only on one day each year—the Day of Atonement, or Yom Kippur—the day all sin was obliterated.

Hanging in front of the Most Holy Place was a curtain of blue, purple, and scarlet yarn and finely twisted linen, with woven cherubim throughout. It was hung with gold hooks on four posts of acacia wood overlaid with gold and standing on four silver bases. The curtain separated the Holy Place, where priests could gather, from the Most Holy Place, where God was. A series of separation points in the Temple separated the Jews from the priests, and the Gentiles from the Jews. If you were a common person, Jew or Gentile, personal access to the presence of the one true God was denied. But all that was in the process of changing.

A group of priests ran to the Most Holy Place from all over the Temple but fell back in fear as they saw the unthinkable occurring before their eyes. The sixty-foot-long curtain was being torn from the top to the bottom, by unseen hands. The sound of the thick fabric tearing drove fear into the hearts of these priests, for they knew they would be exposed to the presence of God. The ground shook from a violent earthquake under their feet and they scattered in all directions, spreading the word of the veil of the Temple being torn in two. They would later learn that this happened at the precise moment Jesus of Nazareth died on the cross.

"Sir, orders from Pilate," a legionnaire said, handing Armandus a small scroll.

Armandus snatched it from the soldier and unrolled it, reading Pilate's instructions as the rain pelted the paper. He nodded and excused the messenger. Pointing at Pilate's men in charge of the two thieves, he said, "Listen up, men. On request of the Jewish leaders, Pilate has ordered that the legs of these men be broken to hasten their death in accordance with their law. These bodies need to be removed before sundown. Make it so." He looked at Jesus' lifeless form, and at the two thieves who struggled to hang on to life. It would ultimately be merciful, as death would come more quickly to them. But for Jesus, it was unnecessary.

As Pilate's men immediately took to the task, Ulixes spoke in a low tone to Velius. "How do we know the king is *really* dead?"

Velius grinned at Ulixes as the callous legionnaire grabbed Armandus's spear that was leaning against a post. Ulixes hurriedly went up to Jesus, his eyes flashed red, and he shouted almost in victory, "HA!" as he thrust the spear into Jesus' side. Immediately water mixed with blood flowed out. He tossed Armandus's spear on the ground and looked up at Jesus with eerie satisfaction.

Armandus stomped over and grabbed Ulixes's shoulder armor, spinning him around. "That's a sure sign of death! Now go ready the ropes!"

"Yes, Sir! The king is truly dead, Sir!" Ulixes said with a laugh as he and Velius got the hammers and ropes, and lifted two ladders up behind Jesus' cross.

Armandus clenched his jaw as he watched Mary fall to her knees with arms raised, eyes pleading as she cried, "Please, with care, with care!" He instinctively took a step toward her to offer aid, but others rushed to her side, supporting her there on the filthy ground. Armandus remained where he was, but anger consumed him as he turned his gaze upward to see the work of his soldiers.

Ulixes and Velius stood on ladders leaning against the gnarled cross as they carried out with callous precision the task they had performed countless times before. One legionnaire hammered the iron spikes back through blood-drenched wood while the other slipped a rope under the dead body to catch it as it fell forward, slowly lowering it to the ground. The soldiers carried on, laughing about their winnings from casting lots for this dead man's cloak.

"Maybe they'll treat me like a king when I stroll through the city tonight wearing that robe!"

"Hail, great Ulixes!" Velius replied with a sarcastic bow as they reached the ground.

The cold-hearted soldiers ignored the group of Jews gathered around Jesus' body, weeping and clinging to one another. His mother refused to be comforted. She held tightly to her son, her head thrown back as she wailed in sorrow, rocking his lifeless form back and forth.

Ulixes picked up the spear belonging to Armandus and together the soldiers walked over and stood face-to-face with their commander. Ulixes wore a look of inappropriate humor and silent indignation as he handed the bloody spear to the centurion.

"Our work is finished here, Sir. Are we relieved?" Velius asked.

Armandus grabbed his spear so tightly his knuckles turned white as his eyes bored into the face of Ulixes. How he wanted to thrust the cold blade into this one who had tortured and mocked Jesus. Yes, these were typical brutal Roman soldiers who carried out their assignments with undeniable precision and impeccable obedience. But this one—Ulixes—there was something evil about him. He had pushed the limits of Roman brutality today, enjoying every minute of it in a way that could be described as nothing short of inhuman. All Armandus could muster was a nod of agreement as he struggled to maintain self-control. He couldn't allow himself to stoop to the level of mindless brutality of this soldier, despite the rage he felt inside.

With that the soldiers picked up their personal effects from their crucifixion post and prepared to depart. Suddenly, something caught Ulixes's eye. He grinned wickedly and walked over to the cross. He looked back at Velius. "We forgot something."

Ulixes climbed back up the ladder with an iron bar and pried loose the wooden sign that had been nailed in place above the head of the dead man. He jumped from the ladder and landed on the ground with a thud, splashing mud onto the mourning family. He smiled as he read the sign and carried it over to Armandus.

"The criminal's sign, Sir," he said with false sincerity. "An untimely death but a fitting end to his reign. We have protected our Emperor from the threat of this one today. Hail, Caesar!" The depraved soldier saluted his commander and waited for a reply as rain splashed off his outstretched arm.

It was all Armandus could do to return the salute of the wicked soldier, but to not do so would signify treason against their sovereign Roman Emperor. He quickly saluted and the wicked grin grew on the face of his subordinate soldier. Armandus leaned in and got eye-to-eye with Ulixes, allowing the tip of his spear to rest on the man's chest. "Never usurp my authority again, or it will be you facing an untimely death."

Ulixes gritted his teeth. "Yes . . . Sir." The soldier tossed the wooden sign into the mud.

"Get out of my sight," Armandus scowled as Ulixes turned away.

Velius picked up the dead man's robe and draped it around Ulixes's shoulders. Ulixes and Velius left the scene and walked back down the steep hill. Their laughter and mocking resumed once they were out of earshot of Armandus. Other soldiers joined in the fun of hailing the "royal Ulixes" in his new robe as he gallantly walked back into Jerusalem.

Armandus returned his attention to the grieving mother. Suddenly two well-dressed men approached her, with servants in tow. They knelt down to place their arms around the mother. Pharisees?

What should they care? Armandus questioned himself. *They are the ones who condemned this man. How dare they pay respects to his mother!*

But as Armandus watched, he noticed that these men cared not that their expensive, prestigious robes were quickly drenched with the blood and mud that ran over the ground in a torrent. Their grief was genuine.

One of the men suddenly looked up at Armandus with pain in his eyes. The centurion and the Pharisee shared a moment of strange bewilderment. The man stood and walked over to Armandus.

"I am Joseph of Arimathea," he explained with a hand over his heart. "Pilate has given Nicodemus and me permission to remove the body."

Armandus felt something he couldn't quite identify. Relief? Gratitude? Finally, here was a show of respect for this dead man that Armandus was unable to give him. Shame. He felt shame.

"Of course," Armandus uttered after clearing his throat and dropping his gaze to the ground.

Joseph stood there, waiting, not daring to touch the Roman. Armandus lifted his head and gazed deeply into the eyes of this Jew. The man did not speak immediately, but peered into the soldier's soul, somehow understanding the depth of regret buried there.

"Know this," Joseph finally said. "You are not responsible for this man's death."

Confusion swept over Armandus. His mind silently screamed, and all he wanted was to escape this scene. He clenched his jaw, brusquely straightened up, and nodded to the strange man. "Be swift with the body."

The Roman centurion looked once more upon the grieving mother. As the servants gently took her son from her arms, she locked eyes with Armandus and in them he saw the pain only a mother having lost a child could express. Her eyes. Jesus had her eyes. And in that powerful moment before his death, those eyes had looked directly at Armandus with such compassion the soldier finally realized who he was.

Armandus shook his head and turned away. He could not accept what was happening. He was responsible! How could this Jew say such an outrageous thing? It was his sole responsibility to carry out this despicable deed. *Enough!* his mind silently screamed as he quickly walked away from the horror of this dark day in Jerusalem.

From a distance, the animal friends stood in silent grief as they watched the humans carry Jesus away from the three empty crosses. The rain continued to lash the earth, as if nature itself were furious with what had happened here. Already nervous from the earlier earthquake and now this torrential downpour, the humans quickly departed the place of The Skull and made their way home. The small creatures walked to the scene, barely able to speak as they gathered around the muddy pool of blood at the foot of the cross.

"No amount of prophecy could have prepared me," Liz said softly, her voice breaking with each word, "for the reality of this day."

"Aye," Max echoed as he put a paw gently on Kate's back. He softly nuzzled his mate, who shook with silent sobs.

"Indeed," Nigel added, wiping his eyes unashamedly.

Al's lip quivered as he sobbed uncontrollably. "I jest don't understand. Why? Why him? Why?"

Nigel walked over to the sign lying in the mud, rain splattering off the wood and covering his white fur with remnants of blood. "Because of this."

The animals gathered around Nigel and the sign. Liz closed her eyes and nodded in understanding. Max's brow wrinkled with anger. Kate shook her head in grief. Al cocked his head to one side. "Mousie, what does INRI mean?"

Nigel adjusted his spectacles and cleared his throat.

529

"INRI represents the Latin inscription IESVS • NAZARENVS • REX • IVDÆORVM," Nigel responded, placing his paws respectfully on the crude wood. He looked up at Al and the others and took a deep breath before continuing. The mouse could hardly bear to speak another word. He slowly looked into the grieving faces of these who had walked with Messiah from the joyous moment of his birth and now stood here in the sorrowful moment of his death.

Suddenly Liz stepped forward and placed her dainty paw on the sign, her tears falling onto the wood. *"Mon Cher Dieu!"* she exclaimed, looking up at the cross. She turned her gaze to Nigel. "This is more than just a wooden sign. It is an answer."

"I'm afraid I don't follow you, dear girl," Nigel replied as he examined the sign.

"It is the clear answer to the question the Magi asked when they first arrived in Jerusalem," Liz explained with great emotion in her voice.

"Aye, the question aboot Messiah that led ta that dark day in Bethlehem," Max added with a frown, remembering King Herod's response.

Kate smiled sadly as she thought about the happy days before that horrible night. She recited the Magi's question: "Where is he, the newborn King of the Jews?"

The friends stood there for a moment as they remembered the events that followed that night so long ago.

"So ye're sayin' the Wise lads asked the question way back then and the Roman lads answered it today by writin' on this sign?" Al finally asked, not realizing the profound meaning of his question.

Nigel tightly closed his eyes and nodded his head in agreement. He opened his eyes, cleared his throat, and reverently translated the Latin inscription on the sign:

"Here is Jesus of Nazareth, the King of the Jews."

"Twenty-eight," Liz said. "I count twenty-eight prophecies that were fulfilled while Jesus was on the cross, with these two after his death: "Not one of his bones will be broken" and "They will look on the one they pierced.""

"The sword of Antonius will find Messiah yet," Nigel recited, recalling Lucifer's words. "This is what Lucifer meant, that Armandus would oversee the execution of the one child his father let go. Armandus's own spear found Messiah, piercing his side."

"Aye, but little did Lucifer know that his evil threat would actually fulfill the prophecies Liz jest told us aboot," Kate said in anger. "That devil were actually employed by the Maker ta make the prophecies aboot Jesus come true!"

"I love ta watch the Maker turn everythin' the devil does back on his slimy head," Max huffed.

"Jesus were already dead so they didn't break his legs," Al said sadly. "So how do ye think Jesus died?"

"From what I can surmise, with the water and blood that came from Jesus' side," Nigel said gently, "it appears his heart ruptured."

Tears fell down Liz's cheeks. "Jesus literally died of a broken heart as he paid for the sins of the world."

"As the Maker took a rib from Adam's side to make his bride, Eve, while he slept, could it be that He took from Jesus' side his heart to make Jesus' bride?" Clarie said, suddenly appearing as a lamb standing beside them. Her loving eyes and gentle voice brought welcome relief.

"Oh, Clarie!" Kate exclaimed, giving the lamb a warm embrace. "I think the Maker knew we needed ta see ye."

"*Oui, mon amie,* how glad we are to see you," Liz echoed, kissing the lamb on both cheeks. "What do you mean? Jesus' bride?"

"All those who will follow Jesus after his resurrection will become known as 'the church,' which he will lovingly refer to as his 'bride,'" Clarie explained. "He already loves her enough to have died for her, giving his heart freely for her. Someday he'll come back for her and bring her to heaven for all eternity."

The animals were stunned by the wonder and beauty of this revelation. It was mysterious and hard to understand.

Clarie saw they were trying to comprehend the meaning of this. "You will understand with time," she smiled.

"Wha' will happen ta Jesus' body now?" Kate asked quietly.

"Well, they don't have much time, but Joseph and Nicodemus will carefully clean Jesus' body, anoint it with oil, and then wrap it in a single linen cloth," Clarie explained. "Usually they use a large amount of myrrh and spices and wrap the body from head to toe in strips of linen soaked in a mixture of spiced resin, but there won't be time to prepare Jesus' body completely before they have to roll the stone in front of the tomb."

531

"Why won't they have time then?" Al asked.

"Sunset is fast approaching, and with it, the Sabbath. They must obey the Jewish law that the body of someone executed must be buried on the same day he dies," Liz jumped in to explain. "So Joseph and Nicodemus are hurriedly trying to keep two of the Maker's commandments before the sun goes down."

"That's exactly right, Liz," Clarie affirmed. She looked over at Nigel, who was looking at Jesus' sign, touching it softly.

"Wor-thy is the Lamb, that was slain," Nigel sang softly. He looked up with grieving eyes, not understanding how or why he would or could sing at a time like this. "Where did that come from?"

Clarie walked over and softly kissed the little mouse on his head. "It came from your heart, dear Nigel." She looked over at Max. "Max, would you please pick up Jesus' sign and carry it with us?" "Aye, Lass, but why do we need it?" Max asked.

Clarie started walking in the direction the men had taken Jesus' body. "You'll know why soon."

Max reverently picked up the sign lying in the mud and covered with blood. He closed his eyes and fought back the tears as he fell in line behind Clarie and the others. As the animals walked on to the Garden tomb where Joseph and Nicodemus were hurriedly preparing Jesus' body, the rain suddenly stopped and the sky began to clear. The sun appeared just long enough to give their eyes and hearts a welcome relief of hope with the light after the darkness of this horrific day.

As they reached the tomb carved into the hillside, they saw the men roll the massive stone in front of the entrance. Joseph, Nicodemus, and their servants walked away and the animals saw two of the women who had been hiding in the Garden also scurry home. The women had followed to see where Jesus would be laid. But now the sun was setting and the Sabbath had begun. Everyone needed to get home.

The animals gathered around the tomb, knowing Jesus' body was on the other side of that huge, cold, round stone. All was quiet. Not even the birds were singing. All nature itself was grieving.

Liz walked up and placed her dainty paw on the stone, weeping. "We can no longer get to our Jesus."

"Aye, the separation be too great," Kate added, joining Liz and placing her paw on the stone.

Max, Al, and Nigel joined them next to the stone, just wanting to be close to Jesus, even though they knew they couldn't get to him. The five friends held a silent vigil of grief.

Clarie stood behind them, so proud of how they had walked with Jesus every step of the way, never faltering in their mission. Perhaps their greatest challenge was when they were called to simply stand by and allow the events of Jesus' death to unfold. Oh, if they only could see all that was coming! Clarie would have to wait right along with them, but she still could offer them some hope to lift their spirits.

"Liz, you are almost always right, but in this case, you couldn't be more wrong," Clarie said.

Liz turned to her lamb friend and wrinkled her brow. "I am sorry, but I do not understand, *mon amie.*"

"Jesus has provided a way of access to himself and to his Father that has never until now been available to all creation since the Fall in the Garden," Clarie explained. "Today at the moment of Jesus' death, the veil in the Temple was rent in two, from top to bottom. There is no longer any barrier to get to the Maker, all because of what Jesus did."

"You mean the veil to the Most Holy Place? It was torn? But how?" Liz said excitedly. "It is made of knitted wool. It is simply not possible to

532

tear it! The weight and strength of it cannot be torn by human hands!"

Clarie pursed her lips and gave Liz a look of *Come now, you should know better than to say something is impossible.* "Exactly."

Liz smiled sheepishly and nodded. "*Oui*, but with the Maker, nothing is impossible!"

Max gently placed Jesus' sign on the ground. "Aye, so ye're tellin' us that the dividin' cur-r-rtain that kept the people away fr-r-rom the Maker were r-r-ripped apart by the hand of the Maker himself?"

"He must want everyone to be able to get to him now," Al said, drawing appreciative looks of understanding from the others.

"Jesus said he were the Way ta the Father!" Kate enthused. "He's paid the price for all ta reach him."

"Utterly sublime!" Nigel added. "Just as Jesus' body was torn for men, now the Maker has torn the dividing veil. No longer must anyone go through priests, good deeds, or sacrifice to reach him. Through Jesus' sacrifice, direct access to the Maker is forevermore granted. He was the final sacrifice the Maker will ever require. Worthy is the Lamb indeed."

533

Clarie beamed at seeing the understanding of the animals. Suddenly they heard the voices of soldiers approaching. "Hurry, hide!"

Max picked up the sign and ran behind the bushes with the others. They saw the glow of the torches first, and then the familiar brusque voices of soldiers approaching the tomb.

"Those Jewish leaders are the most paranoid bunch I've ever seen," Velius joked. "I can't believe they actually asked Pilate to post us here to guard a dead body!"

"Yeah, as if he's going to get up and escape!" Ulixes laughed. "I thrust the spear into him myself. Jesus was *dead* when we took him off the cross."

"It's not that they think this Jesus is going to rise from the dead, even though he claimed it. They're afraid his disciples will come and try to steal the body and *say* that Jesus rose from the dead," one of the Temple guards explained to them. "The Jewish leaders knew you two men were on the crucifixion detail and might I add, it didn't escape them that you *enjoyed* it. They know they can trust your opinion that Jesus is in fact dead."

"Yeah, well, it's only a couple of days. The pay is good, and it's from the Temple treasury at that," Velius said as he pulled out the cord to tie across the stone that had been rolled in front of the tomb.

"Our commander was glad to get rid of us for a while, too," Ulixes said as he helped to secure the cord. He took out a glob of wax and mashed it on top of the cord. He brought his torch close enough to slightly melt the wax while he pressed the Imperial Seal of Rome into the glob, leaving an impression in the wax. He then stood back and grinned at the tomb.

"Jesus' fate is sealed," Ulixes said with a wicked laugh. "The king is dead."

ENCORE: LONG LIVE THE KING!

Kings will stand speechless in his presence.
—ISAIAH 52:14

64

I KNOW THAT MY REDEEMER LIVETH

Here we are again, in another garden, no?" Liz posed. "The most important encounters between man and the Maker have taken place in gardens. I wonder if this is why I am so drawn to them."

Liz and the animals had remained near the Garden tomb, not wanting to leave. They stayed hidden from the soldiers guarding the tomb, and comforted each other as best they could. Faint pink ribbons of light began to streak across the dark sky.

"Aye, Lass. Methinks we're goin' ta see the best gar-r-rden meetin' yet," Max said cheerfully. "R-r-remember, all of ye, Jesus said he would r-r-rise on the third day!"

"I wish it would hurry up and get here," Al said with his head resting on his front paws. "I can't stand to be so sad for so long."

Clarie breathed in deeply as a gentle breeze blew through the garden. She smiled and gazed at the tiny rays of light appearing in the sky. She looked around at the animals. "Al, you won't have to wait any longer. It's time."

Kate's sad eyes widened. "How can it be the third day already?"

"The Jews count any part of a day as a 'day' so Friday, Saturday, and now today, Sunday, make three," Liz explained excitedly. *"C'est magnifique! Le troisième jour est arrivé!"*

"Aye, and the third day be here, too!" Al cheered.

"Splendid! Oh, how I've longed for this day!" Nigel exclaimed with a fist of victory raised in the air.

Clarie walked over to Nigel and leaned her head in close to his. "Nigel, since seals are your specialty, would you do the honors?"

Nigel's eyes widened and he placed a paw on his chest. "I say, you want *me* to break the seal on Jesus' tomb?"

"No one deserves it more, Mousie," Max announced, giving Nigel a nudge.

"*Oui*, what a wonderful honor, *mon ami!*" Liz encouraged.

"Jesus wouldn't have it any other way!" Kate added.

Al braced himself for impact and shut his eyes tightly. Max looked at him and frowned. "Wha's wr-r-rong with ye, lad?"

"Goin' into the IAMISPHERE be one thing," Al gulped. "Wakin' I AM be a whole 'nother thing."

Clarie laughed softly. "Actually, Al is not far off. Once the seal is broken, we all need to brace ourselves."

Nigel smoothed his fur and whiskers, making sure he looked his best. He straightened his spectacles and bowed humbly with one foot forward and a paw draped across his chest. "It will be my highest honor." With that he scurried over to the tomb, careful to avoid being seen by the soldiers.

The animals watched as Nigel jumped from rock to rock and up to the cord that was tied around the stone. They held their collective breath as the little mouse carefully walked across the cord to reach the seal, slipping once. He looked over at the group, who all gave him encouraging nods and smiles.

Nigel closed his eyes. He let go a deep breath and sang-whispered, "I know that my Redeemer liveth." He wrinkled his brow, curious as to why he once again was singing, but began to nibble on the Roman seal. As soon as he broke through the wax, the earth began to rumble and the cord split. Nigel grabbed one end of the cord and swung to the ground. As soon as his paws hit the dirt, a violent earthquake erupted and light filled the Garden. Rocks tumbled all about the soldiers, who covered their heads with their hands.

The animals looked up to see an angel descending from heaven. He landed right in front of the stone. His appearance was like lightning!

538

His robe was as white as snow. He stretched out his strong arms over the stone and easily rolled it aside. The angel then jumped up and sat on top of the stone. He looked over at Nigel and smiled at him with a wink.

The guards screamed in fear from what they had seen and then proceeded to faint.

"Those bully lads scr-r-ream like lassies," Max chuckled as he trotted over to the tomb, followed by the others.

Nigel looked up at the angel and then in the tomb. "May I?"

"Of course! Come and see!" the angel said excitedly, his hand extended in welcome toward the open tomb. "All of you, come and see that he is risen!"

Nigel was the first to peek inside the tomb, and he was soon joined by the others, who stood with him gazing in. There on the slab where Jesus' body had been laid they saw nothing but his bodiless grave clothes lying there, undisturbed. His head covering was still in its original shape, but was flat. The long linen shroud also was still in the shape of his body, but also was flat.

539

"He's r-r-risen jest like he said!" Max exclaimed, pushing on in and running to the slab.

"*Oui,* his shroud is here but it is still lying in place as if he simply passed through it!" Liz exulted, tears of joy now filling her eyes. "He is risen!"

"Brilliant! And unlike Lazarus, who had to be unbound from his grave clothes, Jesus has sent the clear message that nothing can bind him," Nigel added. "Not a stone, not grave clothes, not death itself!"

"Praise the Maker, our Jesus be alive!" Kate said, hugging Al.

"Aye! He ain't called I WERE, but I AM," Al cheered. "But where be Jesus now?"

"You'll see him soon," Clarie said. "It's going to get very busy here in the Garden."

Suddenly another angel appeared in dazzling clothes, sitting on the slab in Jesus' tomb. "Greetings!"

The animals bowed respectfully before the powerful angel. "That's our cue. Time to go," Clarie said. The group went back outside and resumed their hiding position. "You're going to love this."

"How will we roll away the stone?" they heard a woman's voice say from around the corner.

Soon the animals saw Mary Magdalene, Salome, Joanna, and other women they had seen at the foot of Jesus' cross, except for his mother, Mary. Their faces wore expressions of intense grief, and in their hands they carried jars full of spices.

"They've come to complete the process of anointing Jesus' body," Clarie whispered.

"They be in for a gr-r-rand sur-r-rpr-r-rise then," Max answered in a hoarse whisper.

As the women walked up to the tomb, they saw the soldiers lying there unconscious and the stone rolled away. Mary Magdalene stopped in her tracks and put her arm out in front of the women in alarm. "What has happened?"

Together the women slowly, carefully inched their way toward the tomb. They held on to each other and gradually came to the entrance. The women peered inside and saw Jesus' grave clothes lying there.

"He's gone!" Mary Magdalene said as she immediately took off running.

540

The other women were too much in shock to react when suddenly they saw the two angels radiating light inside the empty tomb. Their presence was blinding and struck fear into the women's hearts. The women immediately bowed with their faces to the ground.

One of the angels asked, "Why are you looking among the dead for someone who is alive? He isn't here! He is risen from the dead!"

"Remember what he told you back in Galilee, that the Son of Man must be betrayed into the hands of sinful men and be crucified, and that he would rise again on the third day," the other angel echoed with a brilliant smile. "But go, tell his disciples and Peter, 'He is going ahead of you into Galilee. There you will see him, just as he told you.'"

The women suddenly remembered Jesus' words, but were so full of fear and confusion that they quickly left the tomb. They glanced over and saw the soldiers beginning to rouse, and their hearts began pounding in their chests. "Hurry, we have to get away from here," Salome urged. "And we must tell no one!"

As the women ran off, Ulixes, Velius, and the Temple guard sat up, trembling from head to toe. They looked at one another in fear. "We must report this to the Jewish leaders," the Temple guard said in a broken voice. Together they picked up their spears and ran away.

"Cowards!" Max called after them.

As the women rounded the bend, there in front of them stood Jesus. He wore a pure white robe and his face radiated robust health and power.

"Good morning!" Jesus smiled and said.

The women gasped in awe and joy, fell at his feet, and worshiped him, crying, "Master! You're alive! We don't understand!"

Jesus gently placed his hand on their heads. "Do not be afraid. Go and tell my brothers to leave for Galilee, and they will see me there."

Then suddenly, Jesus was gone.

The women laughed with joy and hugged one another tightly. "We've got to tell the eleven! If we spread out, we can find them." The women got to their feet, tingling from head to toe with the miracle of seeing their risen Lord. Their fear vanished and they ran as fast as they could to find the disciples.

Peter and John jumped when they heard the knock on the door. Fear coursed through them afresh as they wondered if the Jewish authorities had found them. John looked to the room where Jesus' mother, Mary, slept, exhausted from the grief of losing her son. *What will she do if we are taken?* John worried to himself. They paused a moment and waited. The knocking resumed and this time they heard a hushed voice. "It's me, Mary Magdalene."

Peter let go a heavy sigh of relief and shut his eyes tightly. John got up and cracked open the door to make sure she was alone. When he saw it was she, he opened the door and quickly ushered her inside. She put her hand to her mouth as tears filled her eyes.

"Something has happened," she began. "We went to the tomb to anoint Jesus' body with spices, but when we got there . . ." She stopped and shook her head sadly.

"Yes? What, Mary?" Peter asked insistently. "What happened?"

"The guards were lying there unconscious, the stone was rolled away, and Jesus . . . he was gone," Mary finally spilled out. "Someone has taken him!"

Peter and John looked at one another in alarm, and mindlessly left Mary sitting there as they ran out the door. They were heading for the tomb to see for themselves.

After the men left, Mary Magdalene stood up and walked out, slowly closing the door behind her. She didn't know what else to do, so she decided to go back to the tomb. She had to find out where Jesus was.

Jesus' mother, Mary, emerged from the other room, her hand on her chest. She smiled and closed her eyes, tears of joy streaming down her face. Overhearing Mary's report, she tapped her hand on her heart. "My Jesus, you are alive!"

"It's John!" Liz exclaimed as the disciple reached the tomb, stopping outside and falling to his knees as he peered inside the empty tomb. The animals had moved closer to the tomb where they could hear and see everything, but they still remained hidden behind a shrub.

"Aye, an' Peter," Max added as Peter ran and put his hand up on the stone, out of breath from running. He looked inside and stepped around John, boldly entering the empty tomb.

The angels veiled themselves so Peter and John couldn't see them.

Peter walked over and looked at the undisturbed grave clothes. He furrowed his brow and ran his fingers through his hair, struggling to understand what had happened.

John slowly joined Peter in the tomb, and as he stood there, Jesus' words suddenly rushed back into his mind. *"Listen, we're going up to Jerusalem, where the Son of Man will be betrayed to the leading priests and the teachers of religious law. They will sentence him to die and hand him over to the Romans. They will mock him, spit on him, flog him with a whip, and kill him, but after three days he will rise again."*

Everything suddenly fell into place. John grabbed Peter by the arm and exclaimed, "He's alive!"

Peter looked at John with confusion. He still didn't understand and was blinded with grief. The animals saw Peter and John exit the tomb and hurriedly walk away.

"John gets it, but Peter still doesn't see," Nigel said.

"Oui, Peter is not only blind with the grief of Jesus' death, but with the grief of having betrayed his Lord," Liz agreed. "This heavy burden has Peter's heart so captive with pain that even at this moment of victorious evidence, he just can't see it."

After a moment they saw a glow of light once more coming from the tomb. And they heard the soft weeping of Mary Magdalene. She walked back to the tomb, stooped, and looked in. She saw the two white-robed angels, one sitting at the head and the other at the foot of the place where the body of Jesus had been lying.

"Dear woman, why are you crying?" the angels asked her.

"Because they have taken away my Lord," she replied, "and I don't know where they have put him."

Mary turned to leave and saw someone standing there. It was Jesus, but she didn't recognize him. The animals gasped with joy at seeing Jesus for the first time.

"Dear woman, why are you crying?" Jesus asked her. "Who are you looking for?"

"The lass be blind with tears," Kate observed, her chin quivering at seeing Mary's pain. "An' deaf with grief. She doesn't even recognize his voice."

Mary placed her hands on her eyes, shaking her head before answering this man she thought was the gardener. "Sir, if you have taken him away, tell me where you have put him, and I will go and get him."

"Mary," Jesus said softly, smiling with his arms spread out.

Mary's head immediately snapped to attention as she recognized Jesus' voice. *"Rabboni!"* she exclaimed as she fell at his feet, holding on to him, weeping now with joy and relief.

Jesus gently reached down and touched her. "Do not hold on to me, because I have not yet gone back up to the Father. But go to my brothers and tell them I am returning to him who is my Father and their Father, my God and their God."

He helped her to her feet and their eyes locked. Jesus was filled with compassion for her and knew she was trying to grasp what was happening. "Go, now."

Mary smiled and without another word ran off to tell the others, this time, that Jesus was not in the tomb because he was alive. In a flash, Jesus was gone.

"We didn't get to see him!" Al said sadly, stepping out from the bush and running into the tomb to see if he was in there. "The angels be gone, too!"

The others followed Al into the tomb. They were full of joy but also shared Al's sadness that they didn't get to talk to Jesus. Clarie smiled and nodded as she looked at her friends. It was time.

"Now that you've seen that Jesus is risen, it's time for you to remember," Clarie said.

"Remember what, *mon amie?*" Liz asked.

Clarie smiled. "Not what, but *when.* Max, will you go get Jesus' sign?"

Max looked at her with a furrowed brow. "Aye, wha'ever ye say, Lass."

As Max ran outside, Clarie lowered her head to Nigel. "Nigel, would you please take the reed from behind my ear that you took from the Jordan River the day Jesus was baptized?"

"Certainly, my dear," Nigel said, gently pulling the reed and holding it fondly in his hands.

Max came back inside the tomb and placed the sign gently on the stone floor. "Here ye go, Lass."

"Thank you, Max," Clarie said. She looked around at the curious animals who wondered what she was doing. She pointed to the sign. "This is no ordinary sign." She nodded to Nigel, "And that is no ordinary reed. You were sent here in time to retrieve them for a grand mission. There's a reason you've been singing when you didn't understand why, Nigel."

Nigel wrinkled his brow and rubbed his chin, trying to remember. "I'm afraid I'm at a loss, my dear."

Suddenly they heard Gillamon's voice echo off the walls of the empty tomb: "Deep in your subconscious will be these things to watch. They will give you a fresh passion that you will need when you return to the year 1741. As you go back in time to Jesus, watch him, the *Maestro, again. Watch as he carefully chooses his twelve instruments, tuning them to perfection in order to bring a full symphony of purpose into being. Once more feel the crescendo of his life symphony to its climactic end of the Passion. Feel the thrill of Messiah's mighty encore, which has left believing audiences applauding ever since that day. You see, in order to truly make beautiful music, one must know the Subject well, and feel it deep in the soul.*"

"And the *Subject* is Messiah!" Nigel replayed his response, now fully remembering, a jolt of excitement running through him.

"*Bien sûr!*" Liz exclaimed. "Handel! Jennens! The libretto for *Messiah!*

544

We've been sent back to revisit our time with Jesus in order for Nigel to freshly experience the Savior's life. Nigel, you are to inspire Handel's music with your violin."

"Aye, we were also sent ta get things Mousie needs for his new violin!" Max exclaimed.

Nigel held up the reed in his hand. "My bow." He walked over and tenderly touched Jesus' blood-stained sign. "The wood for my violin."

"Ye still need the hair from a grey stallion's tail then," Kate added.

"Achilles!" Liz exclaimed. "We must find Achilles!"

Clarie smiled and nodded. "Exactly, Liz. He's with Armandus at a place you should well remember."

"The home of Antonius?" Liz asked hopefully.

"Indeed," Clarie affirmed. "In the garden. Where another encounter with Jesus is soon to take place. Shall we?"

"Aye, there be no time like the present!" Al exclaimed, trotting away from the empty tomb. He knew exactly where they needed to go.

545

65

TELL YOUR FATHER

"Shhhh, hurry!" Clarie urged as the animals made their way into the garden courtyard. "Find a hiding spot. He's coming!"

The animals each found a place to hide. Al lifted his head, startled by what he saw. "What's wrong with him?"

Liz gasped and put a paw to her mouth. "Oh, no! Achilles has been wounded!"

The magnificent grey stallion lay on his side, breathing heavily. His body shuddered and he struggled to lift up his front leg. Achilles was in pain.

Armandus walked into the courtyard with a poultice and knelt down by his beloved horse. "Here you go, my friend. Let's see if this brings you any comfort."

"His leg," Liz observed sadly. "It is swollen from an injury. *C'est tragique!* Armandus may have to put Achilles down."

Armandus winced as Achilles grunted from the pain. He sat down next to his horse in the courtyard of his parents' grand home in Jerusalem. He looked around at what was once a happy place for him. When his parents moved back to Rome, they agreed to allow Armandus to keep the property for his use, knowing he would be stationed in this region for an indefinite period of time. It was eerily quiet as he looked around the neglected garden that had been his mother's pride and joy. It was her place of solace. There in the middle of the garden was the carved statue of Libertas, bearing the resemblance of his mother's face, with a carved cat figure at the base. Armandus laughed sadly. "If the Jewish leaders knew that this idol was within the walls of Jerusalem, they would be banging down the doors, demanding its removal," he said to Achilles. "But I won't let them in. I won't let anyone in. No one is going to take you from me."

When Pilate had released Armandus back to Herod Antipas, he sent word that Armandus had performed extraordinarily well in "that Jesus matter." As a reward, Herod gave Armandus two days' leave. When Armandus gratefully returned to the Antonia Fortress he was horrified to see that Achilles had suffered this leg injury when the earthquake hit on Friday. All the horses rose up in alarm that day, and Achilles's leg fell into a crack, leaving him wounded. Armandus immediately brought the lame horse here, where he could privately care for him. But it appeared there was nothing he could do.

Tears filled Armandus's eyes as he pulled back the poultice. It was hopeless. His horse was wounded beyond hope. He shook his head. Too much grief. Too much death. Too much loss. "I don't think I can take losing you, too."

547

Suddenly he heard someone banging at his door and he immediately wiped his eyes and got to his feet, running to the door. As he opened the window latch, there stood his two legionnaires, Velius and Ulixes. Their eyes were wild with fear.

"Sir!" Velius exclaimed as Armandus opened the door. "We've just come from guard duty and have some disturbing news to report."

"What has happened?" Armandus said with his hands on his hips.

"Pilate appointed us to guard the tomb of that Jesus of Nazareth, along with one of their Temple guards," Ulixes explained. "This morning at the tomb . . ." He stopped and looked at Velius.

"Well, get on with it!" Armandus shouted.

"Sir, an earthquake happened, and we saw a man who looked as bright as lightning suddenly appear," Velius continued.

"He rolled away the stone in front of the tomb, and sat on it," Ulixes jumped in. "Sir, the body just vanished. Jesus is gone."

"Did someone take the body?" Armandus asked, wide-eyed at this incredible report.

The two soldiers looked at one another. "No, his grave clothes were there neatly in place, like he just disappeared out of them," Velius explained. "And that bright man that rolled away the stone—he wasn't human. He looked like a god. And he had the strength of a god."

"But the Jewish leaders want us to tell everyone that someone took the body," Ulixes added. "The Temple guard had us report to them first. They gave us a huge sum of money and told us to report that we had fallen asleep and that Jesus' disciples came and stole the body."

"They vowed to protect us should this word get back to Pilate," Velius further explained.

"But that story doesn't even make sense," Armandus frowned and said. "If you were asleep, how would you know that Jesus' disciples had stolen the body? And for a Roman soldier to fall asleep is punishable by death!"

"Sir, we know," Ulixes pleaded. "We know what happened, but we took the money and agreed to spread the story as the Jewish leaders instructed us. We didn't know what else to do."

"Go back to the Antonia Fortress and wait for me there," Armandus instructed. "And speak of this to no one."

"Yes, Sir!" the two soldiers exclaimed, respectfully saluting their commanding officer before turning to leave.

Armandus shut the door and rubbed his face with his hands. His mind was reeling with this news. Jesus had claimed that he would rise from the dead. Could it be true? The centurion shook his head. Rising from the dead was impossible. There must be some other explanation. As he walked back to where Achilles lay, he stopped and stared at the statue of Libertas. She represented liberty, freedom. Armandus looked at her longingly, wishing he could be free. He felt imprisoned to guilt, pain, sorrow, and impossible burdens placed before him. If only this goddess were real. But now, after Jesus, Armandus doubted all of Rome's gods and theology. He had come to feel there was only one true God. But he had killed God's Son. Surely the pit of Hades was all that awaited him now.

Achilles snorted in pain, and Armandus ran over to him. The horse was sweating and clearly in agony. It was time to get back to his men and his duty, but Achilles couldn't return with him. He knew what he must do. Armandus pulled his sword from its sheath as his eyes filled with tears at the horrible task before him. He fell over his horse to embrace him one last time, weeping and softly whispering, "I'm sorry, my friend. I'm so sorry."

548

"Why are you crying?" a voice from behind him asked.

Armandus quickly turned around with his sword raised, startled at the presence of someone who had invaded his home. There stood Jesus. Armandus's eyes filled with fear, and his throat tightened so much he couldn't say a word.

Jesus simply smiled. "Put away your sword." He proceeded to kneel down next to Achilles and placed his hand on the horse's leg.

Armandus watched in disbelief as he saw Jesus' pierced hands now tenderly touching Achilles. *How is this possible?!* he wanted to know.

Suddenly Achilles whinnied and rose up to stand tall on his feet, strong and completely healed. He stomped his foot and vigorously nodded his head, as if to say, "Thank you!"

Armandus dropped to his knees and bowed low before Jesus, swimming in a sea of emotions. "Thank you, my Lord! Thank you for healing Achilles! Oh, please forgive me! Forgive me for all I've done."

"I already have, remember?" Jesus put his hands on Armandus's shoulders. Armandus turned his gaze to look upon this man who was indeed the resurrected Son of God. Jesus gripped him by the hand and helped him to his feet. Armandus immediately embraced Jesus, overcome with gratitude. For the first time, he was experiencing the grace and forgiveness of the one true God, and it was unlike anything he had ever known. "I've got you," Jesus smiled and said.

549

Armandus wept for joy and leaned back. "Yes, you do, my King. Please, tell me how I can be one of your disciples."

"When you return to Capernaum, find Peter," Jesus replied. "He'll show you how."

"I will, but where are you going? You're alive now! Won't you stay here and establish your kingdom?" Armandus asked. "No one can doubt that you are the Son of God any longer! You have the power to come back from the dead."

"My kingdom is not an earthly kingdom, but will be composed of men just like you," Jesus said. "I will be here for a short while after I meet with my disciples and others, including some now on the road to Emmaus. Then I will return to my Father in heaven."

"I don't understand," Armandus said.

"You will, with time," Jesus replied. He looked around the courtyard and smiled. "Our parents were friends. You and I met here as children."

"Yes, I know," Armandus replied sadly. "The day you died, I finally understood who you were."

"Armandus, tell your father. Tell him about me and all that has happened," Jesus urged. "He has grieved these many years over what he did to the children of Bethlehem that horrible night so long ago. Tell him the child he saved has now saved the world."

Armandus looked down and nodded. "I will, my Lord. I will tell him."

When he looked up, Jesus was gone. Armandus looked around the courtyard and raised his hands toward the heavens. "Thank you, my King!" He ran over and embraced Achilles. "Oh, Achilles, you are well! I don't have to lose you. I will ride you out of here!" Jesus had given Armandus everything: forgiveness, healing, hope, a future, and a message. Armandus would not let Jesus down.

"Stay here, Achilles. Let me get my things and together we'll ride to the Fortress," Armandus exulted.

As soon as Armandus was gone, Nigel quickly jumped down to land on the horse's back and ran along his head to stand on his nose. "Good day, Achilles. I have long admired what a fine stallion you are. My name is Nigel P. Monaco, and I am on mission for the Maker. Might I ask to remove one of the hairs from your tail? It's terribly important."

"*Buon giorno*, Nigel," Achilles answered in a thick Italian accent, trying to look at the mouse without crossing his eyes. "It would be my honor to serve the Maker, especially after all he has done for me, eh? Take as many as you need."

"Simply *splendid* of you, old boy!" Nigel cheered. "But one is sufficient. My friend will assist with this endeavor." Nigel pointed to Al, who jumped up on a rock wall next to where Achilles stood.

Al waved and gave a goofy grin. He reached up and grabbed one of Achilles's tail hairs and yanked hard. At that moment, Achilles's natural reflex made him kick his hind leg, sending Al flying across the courtyard. Al landed right on the Libertas statue and slid down to where he was face-to-face with the carved image of Liz, who had posed for the base. "Why hello, me love," Al said before his eyes rolled back in his head and he passed out.

Achilles and Nigel gritted their teeth as they watched Al sail across the courtyard. "*Mi dispiace!* I hope *il gatto* is all right."

"He'll be fine, I assure you," Nigel said. They heard Armandus's footsteps coming down the tiled corridor. "I must be going. Thank you again!"

"Prego, Nigel," Achilles replied with a grin.

Armandus lifted the saddle up onto Achilles. "I never thought I'd ever be able to put this on you again." He secured the saddle and walked Achilles out of the courtyard, smiling and shaking his head in wonder and awe. Armandus climbed up in the saddle once they were outside. "Long live the King! *Magna est veritas et praevalebit!*" Armandus exclaimed as he squeezed Achilles with his heels and the horse galloped off.

Immediately Liz and the others ran over to check on Al. "Speak to me, *cher* Albert."

Al's eyes fluttered open and he rubbed his head with his paw, now sitting up. "I jest had the craziest dream. I were flyin' like Mousie on a pigeon. But then, Liz, ye turned ta stone and I fell like a rock." He held up the hair from Achilles's tail and asked, "Where'd I get this?"

Liz breathed a sigh of relief and hugged Al as Nigel reached over to get the hair. "I'll take that off your hands, old boy."

"Wha' did the lad say when he were r-r-ridin' off then?" Max asked.

"Great is the truth and it will prevail," Nigel translated.

"Oh, this were wonderful ta see! Jesus healed Achilles an' gave hope ta Armandus," Kate noted happily.

"Aye, an' that lad will give hope ta his father," Max added. "There's nothin' as powerful as gr-r-race ta give ta those who feel they be unforgivable."

"Well, your mission here is accomplished," Clarie said. "You've got everything you need for Nigel's violin."

"Oui, and I cannot begin to imagine the music that will come from those items!" Liz cheered.

"Aye, the r-r-reed from the Jor-r-rdan, the wood from Jesus' sign, an' hair from the R-r-roman's horse," Max affirmed.

"Not hair from just any horse, mind you," Nigel said with a jolly twinkle in his eye. "But the hair of the horse healed by the power of resurrected Messiah!"

"Oh, Nigel, I be so excited for ye!" Kate said, hugging the little mouse. "I can't wait ta hear wha' comes from yer fiddle."

"Me as well, dear Kate," Nigel replied, studying the sign. "I say, though, when we bring these items back to Shandelli to make my violin, I don't see how we can reveal the entire sign. Plus he doesn't need this much wood."

"But of course, you are right, *mon ami,*" Liz agreed. "Perhaps you should take just a portion of the sign."

They studied the sign for a moment. "Right," Nigel concurred. "The acronym INRI represents the Latin inscription IESVS • NAZARENVS • REX • IVDÆORVM (Iesus Nazarenus, Rex Iudaeorum). Since the REX means "KING," I'm terribly drawn to using the 'R.'"

"I think that is perfect, *mon ami,*" Liz said with her dainty paw on his back. "And did you notice how beautiful the color of the wood is where Jesus' blood has stained it there?"

"Stand back then," Max said as he picked up a sharp rock. He lifted the rock high and plunged it into the sign, breaking it apart at the 'R'. It was a clean break. He made another plunge, separating the 'R' from the 'I.'

552

"Good show, old boy!" Nigel exulted, picking up the segment of wood. "It's perfect!"

"Very well, it's time for you to return to 1741," Clarie instructed the group. She pointed to the remains of Jesus' sign. Suddenly the dried blood on the sign began to liquefy and formed a circle. Soon it rippled into the Seven Seal. It was time to break the seal and enter the IAMISPHERE.

Kate's smile faded. "That means we have ta tell ye good-bye." The Westie went over and embraced her lamb friend.

"Good-bye, sweet friend," Clarie said tearfully. "I'm so proud of you all."

Liz also embraced Clarie. *"Merci beaucoup,* Clarie, for everything. We hope to see you soon."

"Don't worry," Clarie replied playfully. "I'll see you again soon. You never know where I might turn up." She winked and gestured to the sign. "Nigel, if you please."

"Certainly, my dear. Farewell," Nigel bowed and said, kissing her extended front foot. "Is everyone ready?" He looked around the courtyard one last time and said, "Hallelujah!" before nibbling the seal.

In a flash the sign exploded and they disappeared into the IAMISPHERE.

TIME FOR MUSIC

The rush of wind and swirling panels in the IAMISHPERE only added to the exuberance of the group. The grief of losing Jesus all over again was overshadowed by the victory of his resurrection. The animals were swept up in the triumph of Messiah.

"Welcome back, my friends," Gillamon's voice echoed as he slowly came into view before them. "By your expressions I believe you had a successful mission. Did your time with Jesus stir your hearts as planned?"

"Indeed! Utterly brilliant idea for us to go back to Jesus, Gillamon!" Nigel enthused. "I truly feel I now have the passion necessary to assist Handel in composing *Messiah*."

"*Oui,* and we have the required items for Nigel's new violin," Liz added. "His *divine* violin, no?"

Nigel held up the piece of wood and Gillamon's eyes filled with emotion at seeing the 'R'. "This is the only remaining piece of wood from Jesus' sign, but from it will come music like nothing else in history. Well done," the wise old mountain goat told the group.

"So, Gillamon, wha' be our next steps in the mission?" Max asked.

"You will re-enter time at the precise moment you left in 1741. In fact, Shandelli will be in the kitchen getting Nigel that piece of cheese, so you will have a moment or two to get situated in Handel's composing room," Gillamon explained.

Al's ears perked up. "I been so busy with Jesus' resurrection and all that I forgot to eat! Hooray, there be cheese back in 1741!"

"Nigel, you will of course work with Shandelli to build your new violin, but you only have one month before it is time for the music of *Messiah* to be born," Gillamon instructed. "You will need to provide the new items with vague explanation to our stickbug friend. Little will he realize he is handling wood touched by Jesus."

"I will do my best to withhold the details, although I shall be bursting to share the glory of these items with Shandelli," Nigel said with a jolly voice. "But I understand the importance of secrecy."

"Liz, you and Al are to make a trip to Ireland immediately upon returning," Gillamon explained.

Al's eyes lit up. "Me homeland! We get to visit me old green sod?"

Gillamon chuckled. "Yes, Al, your country will have the privilege of inviting Handel to perform *Messiah* for the first time in Dublin."

"I bet London will be green with envy aboot that!" Al said, proud of his Irish roots.

"What exactly are we to do there, Gillamon?" Liz asked.

554

"You must get Lord William Cavendish to write a letter inviting Handel to perform a series of benefit concerts next spring in Dublin," Gillamon answered. It will be this letter that finally inspires Handel to get working on *Messiah.*"

"*C'est magnifique!* This is perfect for *Monsieur* Handel to have an entirely new audience to debut *Messiah*, away from the negative atmosphere of London," Liz observed. "But, Gillamon, travel to Dublin will take some time, as will the return letter. If Handel is supposed to begin writing *Messiah* in a month, I do not see how we have the time to get there and back."

Gillamon grinned. "Look around you, Liz. You are in the IAMISPHERE. Before now, you have used it to travel across *time*. How else might you use it?"

Liz thought a moment before her eyes brightened with realization. "We can travel across *distance* as well in the IAMISPHERE, no?"

"Exactly. You have all the time in the world," Gillamon assured her. "You can get to Dublin and return on the day of your choosing. You can go there and be back before dinner, if you wish. Just as you seemingly have been gone for twenty-four years to be with Jesus, it's really only been a moment in time. Shandelli has only just now gone to the kitchen for Nigel's cheese."

Al struggled to wrap his mind around the concept of traveling through time in the IAMISPHERE. "So the cheese won't have aged twenty-four years while we were gone? That's good because it would be a wee bit dry."

"Ye two can have a second honeymoon!" Kate encouraged.

"Aye, go enjoy yerselves an' we'll handle Handel," Max added. "So wha' do Kate an' meself need ta do then, Gillamon?"

"You will need to fiercely guard Handel's house from the beastie who destroyed Nigel's first violin," Gillamon said with seriousness. "Thankfully the enemy has just left Handel's house, so he will think his mission is accomplished. It will take a while before he discovers the replacement. Maintain your post at the Butcher of Brook Street, but keep your eye out here."

"Wha' aboot David Henry? Should we check up on him then?" Kate asked.

"Indeed, Kate," Gillamon replied. "He needs to know what Handel is working on, and about his trip to Dublin when the time comes. We want him eager to hear *Messiah* when Handel first performs it here in London."

555

The IAMISPHERE spun rapidly until a single large pane appeared. It was Handel's composing room, July 1741. Nigel's broken violin still sat on the floor, and Jennen's letter with Al's inkblot pawprints remained on the desk. Al gulped in fear, remembering the mess he had made.

"Liz, maybe we need to stay in Ireland for a long time then," Al suggested, worried that he would be banished from Mrs. Rice's kitchen.

"Liz, when you are ready to depart for Dublin, the seal will be on the desk." Gillamon placed his hoof in the pane. "Go, my friends, and know that you are loved and able. Time for music."

Suddenly the animals were assembled in Handel's composing room, right where they had been when their journey in time to be with Jesus began.

"Nigel, quickly, hide the new violin items before Shandelli returns," Liz urged. "He does not need to know we already have them."

"Right!" Nigel said, scurrying up the bookcase to hide them behind some books. He touched them tenderly and breathed a soft prayer, "Please, Maker, do not let anything happen to these priceless items."

Just as Nigel returned to the floor, Shandelli came walking into the room, still wearing a somber face. In his twiggy hands he held a piece of cheese. *"Signor* Monaco, here is your cheese. Please do not be sad, we will think of something, *amico."*

Nigel happily took the cheese. "Why thank you, old boy! I say, this is a splendid choice of cheese." He nibbled a bite and smiled. "Delicious! It was terribly good of you to get it for me."

Shandelli wore a look of confusion as to the quick change in Nigel's demeanor. Liz got Nigel's attention from up on the desk and motioned for him to act sad about his violin. She rubbed her eyes like she was crying. Nigel realized his behavioral error and immediately tried to correct it.

Nigel then raised the back of his paw, setting it upon his brow in dramatic flair. "Oh, but the finest cheese cannot erase my sadness over the loss of my violin!"

"He be layin' it on a wee bit thick," Al whispered to Liz, who rolled her eyes at Nigel's overly dramatic performance.

"Naturalmente, you should feel sad, but we will start again!" Shandelli exclaimed determinedly. He clapped two of his hands together. "Max and Kate, *per favore,* can you go retrieve items again for Nigel's new violin?"

"Aye, we'll be glad ta, lad," Max replied with a wide grin. "We'll get everythin' first thing tomorrow."

Nigel peeked out from under his paw and winked at Max. "Oh, I am most grateful to you all, my friends. And I believe that this new violin will be even better."

"Certamente! Of course it will be even better! Now that I've made one mouse-sized violin, I can only improve on the design, eh?" Shandelli gestured with his twiggy fingers. *"Detto fatto!"*

"Bon! Merci, Signor Shandelli," Liz said, jumping off the desk. "Now since it has been quite a long day for all of us, why don't we retire?"

"Aye," Max yawned. "I could do with a wee bit of shuteye then. Kate an' me will be on our way back ta the butcher." He walked over to Nigel. "Sleep well, Mousie. Ye've had a busy day."

"My most heartfelt thanks," Nigel said, bowing with his paw draped across his chest. "I plan to sleep well. You do the same. It's been a busy day for all of us." He and Max shared a grin. They had been up since Resurrection morning. A busy day indeed.

"Buona notte," Shandelli said, following Max and Kate out of the room.

Liz stretched out long across Handel's desk, yawning. *"Cher* Albert, we will leave in the morning, no?"

Al jumped off the desk. "Sure thing, Lass. For now, I'm goin' to fill up on some 1741 food!"

"Buon giorno, Signor Monaco," Shandelli greeted Nigel in the shed.

"I hope I'm not intruding too early in your day," Nigel said, carrying a bundle wrapped in a piece of cloth. "I have the replacement items for my violin."

Shandelli's eyes widened on the side of his face, causing Nigel to chuckle softly at the animated stickbug.

"Fantastico!" the stickbug cheered, holding out his twiggy arms in greeting. "But how did Max and Kate get the items so quickly?"

Nigel wrinkled his nose to think of the right explanation. "Oh, it only took a moment in time. I think you'll be pleased with what they found." Nigel laid the bundle on the table and slowly unwrapped the items.

557

Shandelli reached down and lifted the wood from Jesus' sign, studying it closely. "Ah, this wood has an unusually beautiful red hue."

"You said beautiful music always begins with a carpenter. I assure you, the finest carpenter who ever lived is the one who made this wood so beautiful," Nigel said, trying not to be emotional.

"What is this 'R' on the wood?" Shandelli asked, his big buggy eyes holding the wood up close.

"No doubt the carpenter's signature," Nigel said, clearing his throat. "And look at this fine horse hair and new bow stick."

"Si, si, very nice, very nice," Shandelli said, touching the other items. *"Signor* Monaco, I promise you, your new violin will make the finest music in all the world!" He proceeded to pull out the diagram for making the violin.

Nigel folded his arms across his chest, grinning broadly as he watched Shandelli prepare the tiny tools to begin construction of the new violin. "Of that I have no doubt, old boy."

"Are you ready, *mon cher?"* Liz asked Al as they sat on Handel's desk.

"I'm as ready as I'll ever be to go into that scary place," Al said, squeezing his eyes shut.

"Since we will have to break the seal ourselves when we wish to return from Ireland, I thought it best to break it myself here," Liz said, studying the fresh Seven Seal. She lifted up her paw and 'sprung' her pointer claw. "Here we go," she said as she dug her claw into the seal. *"Bon voyage!"*

Immediately they were inside the IAMISPHERE with the green scenery of Ireland swirling around them. "Oh, Albert, I did it! Look!" Liz announced excitedly.

Al slowly opened his eyes and started purring at the sight of the beautiful scenery of his beloved homeland. "Aye! There she be!"

"Well done, Liz," came Clarie's voice. "I told you I would see you soon."

"Clarie! But this is a wonderful surprise!" Liz greeted the lamb, kissing her on each cheek. "We just said farewell to you yesterday."

"Gillamon decided I could be of assistance to you on the Ireland mission," shared Clarie.

"Ireland be a perfect place for a lamb," Al said happily.

"Except I will be a homeless girl for this mission," Clarie replied. "And you will be my pets."

"Magnifique! But you will make a pretty girl! How will this work?" Liz asked.

"Lord Cavendish will need to 'find' me on the street, and help me to the orphanage," Clarie explained. "I will ask him to please take care of you for one night, and then he can let you go."

"Oui, this will be enough time for me to write the suggestion letter," Liz replied.

"What letter is that?" Clarie asked.

"The one suggesting the benefit concert by inviting *Monsieur* Handel to Dublin," Liz replied with a coy grin. "Anonymous letters are my specialty, no?"

"There be Dublin!" Al pointed happily. He trotted fearlessly over to the pane and put his paw right into the lush green hillside and immediately they were standing on Irish soil.

"Al, Gillamon would be proud of you," Clarie cheered. "I've never seen you so brave in the IAMISPHERE."

"I jest kept me eyes on the green," Al said, rolling around happily on his back in the green grass, his fluffy belly fur blowing in the gentle breeze. "Sure, and it's great to be back."

558

"*Bon,* which way to meet Cavendish?" Liz inquired.

"Follow me," Clarie said. As she walked through the green grass, she slowly morphed from a lamb into a seven-year-old little blonde-headed girl wearing tattered old clothes and no shoes. She turned around and smiled, a smudge of dirt on her face. "How do I look?"

"You are *très jolie, mon amie!*" Liz replied in wonder to see yet another transformation of their lamb friend.

Al's jaw hung open. "I knew the green grass o' Ireland were magical but this takes the biscuit, as Mousie would say."

Clarie giggled. "Good. Okay, stay right underfoot. Let's go find Cavendish."

Together the threesome entered the city limits of Dublin and soon heard the familiar sounds of the hustle and bustle of an eighteenth-century city street. Horses clip-clopped along the cobblestone streets, merchants called out their wares and bartered with customers, a baby cried from within an open window, and children played happily in a courtyard. Soon they came to Fishamble Street.

559

"Fish-amble Street? Be there fish here?" Al asked hopefully.

"I'm sure there is fish at one of the pubs on this street, Al. But Lord Cavendish passes by here every afternoon to inspect the progress of the new Music Hall construction," Clarie said, looking for the man. "That's the orphanage right over there, behind those walls."

Liz stared at the stone walls and realized so many children were left alone in the world without parents. It made her sad to think of any child out here alone on the streets. "Of course! The orphanage! That can be the place to benefit from Handel's performance of *Messiah!*"

Suddenly Clarie jumped. "There he is! Okay, get ready, we're on."

Lord Cavendish was rather plainly dressed for a man in the Irish upper class, and he walked speedily along his way. Clarie cleared her throat and began singing a sweet Irish tune. Her voice was so beautiful it startled Lord Cavendish. He stopped and listened as she sang, mesmerized by her striking blue eyes.

Dreaming in the night, I saw a land where no-one had to fight,
Waking in your dawn, I saw you crying in the morning light,
Sleeping where the falcons fly, they twist and turn all in your
air blue sky,

When living on your Western shore, saw summer sunsets, asked for more,
  I stood by your Atlantic sea, and I sang a song for Ireland.

When Clarie finished she gave Lord Cavendish an endearing smile and curtsey. He smiled back and tilted his head as he looked at her. "You have a voice from heaven, child."

If you only knew, Monsieur, Liz thought to herself.

"Thank ye, Sir," Clarie replied humbly. "Might ye be able to spare a coin so I can feed me kitties?"

Lord Cavendish frowned and looked around. "Where is your home?"

Clarie played her part well, lowering her head. "I don't have a home. Me mum were taken to Debtor's Prison and we lost our home."

Lord Cavendish dropped to his knee and looked her in the eye. "And you're living out here all alone? No, this won't do. Come, I'm taking you to the orphanage."

"Thank ye for yer kindness, Sir," Clarie said, tears welling up in her big blue eyes. "But what about me kitties? I can't jest leave them alone. They're all I have."

"But we must get *you* cared for, little one," he replied.

Clarie looked down at Liz and Al, giving them a wink. "I'll go with ye if ye promise me to care for them at least for tonight. Please give them some food. Will ye promise me?"

Liz batted her eyes, purred, and rubbed along the man's knee. Al smiled his goofy grin. Lord Cavendish would not have any one else know this, but he had a soft heart for children and animals. This poor little girl had lost everything. What would it hurt to keep a promise to care for her pets for one night?

"Very well, I promise," Lord Cavendish replied. "But only if they keep up with me while we get you settled."

"Do not worry about that, Monsieur," Liz meowed.

Lord Cavendish smiled, took Clarie by the hand, and together they walked to the orphanage. When they got to the gate, Clarie knelt down and hugged Liz and Al. "I'll miss ye but this nice man has promised to feed ye tonight. Don't be afraid. The Maker will take care of ye after that." She added a few tears for full effect and turned her sad gaze to the man. "Okay, Sir, I'm ready."

560

The kind man's heart broke at the tenderness of this small child lost in a cold world. But her thoughts were about her animals. He would keep his promise to her. He took Clarie by the hand and walked her inside. A kind woman greeted Lord Cavendish and ushered Clarie inside. He promised he would check in on her soon.

As Lord Cavendish exited the gate, Liz and Al were ready to follow him home. He looked behind as he walked along the street, these two cats staying right at his heels. He laughed to himself, *It's as if they know where we're going.*

Liz and Al exchanged a smile. Soon they were at the Cavendish home where Mrs. Cavendish was more than happy to welcome the cats, making a fuss over them. Al was once again in heaven as she gave them warm milk and scraps from dinner, and even a cozy blanket to sleep on. After the Cavendish family had retired, Al promptly fell asleep, and Liz went to work.

Liz carefully explored the house until she found the study. *"Voila!"* she exclaimed as she found fresh paper and ink sitting there on the desk. "This is all too easy." She sat down and thought a while to come up with the perfect words to move Cavendish to contact Handel. She gripped the pen, and began to write.

561

Dear Sir:

I am writing to ask you to please help the lost children of Dublin. I have recently traveled to your fair city from London and learned of the sad situation of the children here. Some lose their parents in death. Many parents fall upon hard times, unable to pay their debts, and are sent to the Debtor's Prison, leaving their children alone. Gratefully the orphanage is a place of refuge for these children, but is sadly in need of money to care for them. Have you met one of these children alone in the street? It is heartbreaking, to say the least. Families can be reunited for only a small amount of money to pay for debts owed.

I am well connected with the musical world in London, and I understand you share a love for the arts. As you are in process of constructing a new music concert hall on Fishamble Street, might I suggest a benefit concert that would not only fill your hall, but benefit children and their destitute parents in the process? George Frideric Handel is one of the top composers in London and I happen to know he is a good Christian man with a tender heart for charitable causes. I have no doubt he would come to Dublin if you invited him. Proceeds from the concert could go toward the orphanage, the prison, and even the hospital, caring for many lost lambs as our Lord Jesus Christ charged us to do in His name. Thank you for considering my suggestion and may God bless your charity.

Your Humble Servant,

LB

Liz was careful to smudge her signature to make it unreadable. She smiled as she read the letter back to herself. She especially liked the 'lost lamb' part. *Brilliant, Clarie!* she thought to herself. *If this doesn't get him to invite Handel, I don't know what will.* She folded the letter, affixed a seal and left it sitting on the desk of Lord Cavendish. If he wanted her and Al gone in the morning, he had best get busy writing his own letter to George F. Handel. Liz wasn't going anywhere until he did.

DINNER FOR THREE

L ord Cavendish rose early, his mind troubled about the little girl he found in the street the day before. He walked downstairs to his study to attend to his correspondence when he saw a strange letter sitting on his desk. Liz sat in the corner, watching him, her tail slowly curling up and down.

As he started reading he put his hand to his mouth in amazement. *Who wrote this letter?* he thought as he squinted at the smudged signature. He shook his head, unable to read it. *How is it possible that my exact experience with the little girl was expressed in this letter?* He stared out the window and tapped the letter in his hand, thinking.

"Well, whoever you are, you have just given me a brilliant idea!" Lord Cavendish said out loud to himself. He busily took out a sheet of paper, dipped his pen in the ink, and began to write. "To George F. Handel, . . ." he mumbled as he quickly wrote out the letter.

"Je vous en prie, Monsieur," Liz smiled and said from the corner. "Mission accomplished," she announced as she sauntered out of the room, her tail raised in the air. She walked over to where Al slept and smiled. Drool ran down his chin and he wore a goofy grin. *"Bonjour,* Albert. Time to go," Liz told her mate.

"Not 'til I've rolled this fishy cheese down the street," Al mumbled in his sleep.

Liz giggled, shaking her head. "I suppose we have time for you to finish your dream, no?"

LONDON, AUGUST 21, 1741

The rain pellets bounced off the windows as Peter gazed out onto Brook Street. He sighed deeply. Things were growing as dreary as the weather around Handel's House. Peter wondered how long Handel would remain in this house. If things didn't start picking up for Handel's work, they all could be moving out soon. Handel stubbornly clung to his beloved opera, while so many opportunities awaited him with writing English oratorio. If only he would cut opera loose and allow the changing musical winds to fill his composing sails, then things could turn around. He could win over a new audience and start again. But no one could make the independent Handel do anything he didn't want to do. Handel had to choose to get going again, and the world would just have to wait on his next move.

564

Peter heard a knock at the front door. He walked over and opened it to find a courier standing there in the rain.

"Evenin', Sir. Letter for Mr. Handel," the courier said, tipping his hat.

"Thank you, and good-evening to you as well," Peter replied, taking the letter. The courier quickly left to make his way down the rain-soaked street. Peter shut the door and studied the letter.

"Ireland. Hmmmm," Peter mumbled to himself as he climbed the stairs to deliver the letter. He met Handel coming down the stairway.

"Who vas dat, Pater?" Handel asked, putting on his tricorne hat.

"A courier, Sir," Peter said, extending the letter. "From a Lord Cavendish in Ireland. Do you know this gentleman?"

"No, but he I tink he must know me." Handel took the letter and gave it a passing glance before sticking it in his coat pocket. "I am going out. Tell Mrs. Rice I von't be eating in tonight."

"Very well, Sir," Peter said, walking Handel back to the door. "Have a good evening."

"Ya," Handel said as he left the house and took off down Brook Street.

Liz was sitting there beaming up at Peter when he closed the door again behind Handel. He looked at her, smiled, and reached down to scratch her under the chin. "Let's hope that letter contains good news for Mr. Handel, little cat."

"*I can assure you, it does, Monsieur!*" Liz meowed happily. She was ecstatic to see that the letter had finally arrived. She ran off to find Nigel. Things would start happening soon. He needed to be ready.

Handel's foot splashed in a deep puddle, sending water up his leg. He scowled and grumbled in German, Italian, and French as he pulled his cloak tightly around himself.

A crash of thunder boomed in the distance and the rain poured even harder. The wind suddenly picked up and was so fierce Handel had to lean into it just to stay upright.

Maybe I should go home, he thought to himself, doubting his reasons and ability to be eating out. He looked up and noticed he was almost at the tavern. *I vill go eat anyway. Maybe dis tempest vill be over by the time I leave.*

Suddenly a flash of lightning lit up the sky. "Everyting becomes easy to see vit de light. I vish you vould strike me vit inspiration," he begged as he looked up at the raging sky.

565

Handel felt instant relief as he saw the tavern sign swinging in the wind, its iron chains creaking wildly. He stepped inside and was greeted by a servant who took his rain-laden cloak.

"Quite a storm out tonight, Sir," the servant said.

"Ya, I vish I had an ark," Handel quipped as the servant led him to a table. Handel grunted as he sat down and stomped his soggy feet on the floor. "Someting hot to drink."

"Yes, Sir, right away, Sir," the servant replied.

Handel looked around the darkened room, lit by tin lanterns with tall candles and glass globes. On his table was a single candle. He put his hands over the flame and rubbed them together, trying to warm them. Even though it was August, a blustery, rainy night in London could chill a person to the bone.

The servant came back with a hot mug and placed it before Handel. "Here we are, Sir. Now, what will ye have for supper?"

"Please bring me," Handel said as he studied the menu, "a ham, tree helpings of potatoes, tree helpings of roasted vegetables, and an apple pie. Ya, dat should be enough."

The servant's eyes grew wide and he nodded as he took the menu from Handel. "Very well, Sir." *He must be having guests,* the waiter thought as he headed to the kitchen.

Handel picked up his mug and sipped it, closing his eyes in delight. "Ah, now dis is vorth valking tru de Great Flood to sip." He sat a long while, warming up and getting dry. *I vonder if Noah got tired of vat he had to do. All dat time building dat ark, taking care of dose animals, dealing vit de rain, vit no place to land. I feel like I've got no place to land. My opera is gone. My public doesn't appreciate me anymore. Vat is to become of me, I vonder?*

After several more moments had passed, Handel noticed the servant delivering food to the other tables. He began to grow irritated.

"You," Handel gestured to the servant, who came running to the table. "Vy do you keep me so long vaiting?"

The servant held out his hands as if to point out the obvious. "We are waiting until the company arrives."

A big frown appeared on Handel's face. "Den bring up de dinner *pretissimo,*" he demanded, slamming his fist on the table. "I AM de company!"

The servant's face flushed with embarrassment as he rushed off to get Handel's "dinner for three."

"Bah!" Handel barked, sticking his hand in his pocket. He felt the small number of coins he had to pay for his meal, but then his hand clasped the letter.

"Ah, de letter from Ireland. Vat could dis be about?" he said as he broke the seal and pulled out the letter from Lord Cavendish. His lips mumbled as his eyes eagerly scanned the page. "He vants me to give a concert in Ireland? For de children, ya?" He scratched his chin in thought. *A new public, a good cause. Dis could be someting to help me. But vat to write?*

The servant was followed by an assistant who helped carry the two trays of food over. Together they quickly set the food before Handel while Handel held up his cup. "Ah, tank you. And more to drink, ya?"

Handel's mind was racing as he eagerly began eating his dinner. Already his spirits were lifting as he thought about the possibility of getting out of London to perform in Ireland.

The servant returned with Handel's drink and was shocked to see so much of the food already gone. *Looks to me as if two guests showed up.*

Handel was suddenly galvanized and ready to rush home to see what he could compose for the benefit concert in Dublin. He took a swig and reached into his pocket for the coins to pay for his large dinner.

Suddenly his finger ran along the marred edge of his favorite coin. The Star Coin. He pulled it out and studied it as he had done countless times since he acquired it in Rome so many years earlier. A feeling of certainty came over him and at last in that moment he knew without a shadow of a doubt. This was not Caesar's star. It was *Messiah's* star. This Roman coin had Messiah's image stamped upon it.

A cascade of inspiration washed over Handel. "Messiah! Jennens's libretto! *Dat's* vat I vill write!"

Handel hurriedly put his coins on the table to pay for dinner but gripped the Star Coin tightly. *For unto us a child is born,* he thought with a grin.

567

"Are you ready, *Signor* Monaco?" Shandelli asked him.

Nigel stood in the garden shed, surrounded by Max, Kate, Liz, and Al. His eyes were closed, but pointed in the direction of Shandelli, who wanted to surprise him. The rain pounded on the roof, and the wind blew wildly outside, adding to the drama of this moment.

"Bravo! Hold out your paws," Shandelli instructed.

Nigel's heart was beating rapidly as he held out his paws. He was smiling broadly with his eyes still closed. The others exchanged glances of excitement for their mouse friend.

Shandelli gently placed the cloth-covered violin in his paws. *"Signor* Monaco, your new violin."

Nigel's eyes fluttered open and he looked at Shandelli, who clasped his hands in delight. "Thank you, my good friend."

"Prego, Nigel, *Prego,"* Shandelli responded warmly.

"Go ahead, Mousie. Open it then!" Max urged him.

Nigel took a deep breath and carefully removed the cloth from the violin and looked upon it in awe. It was even more beautiful than his first violin. His mouth gaped open as he slowly took it in hand. The round portion of the 'R' comprised the body of the instrument, its carving still visible around the edges. It truly was a violin fit for a king.

"And your new bow," Shandelli said, handing him the new bow he had been hiding behind his back. "I must say I have never felt a stronger horse hair, nor a more solid reed for a bow."

"*C'est très belle!*" Liz exclaimed joyfully. "*Signor* Shandelli, you have outdone yourself!"

"*Grazie,*" Shandelli said humbly with a bow. "I cannot wait to hear *Signor* Monaco play it."

"Oh, do play us a few notes, Nigel," Kate pleaded happily.

Nigel held the violin and bow to his chest. "I feel like I must wait to play it until I play it first for *Messiah.*"

"How do ye know it will play okay?" Al asked, then looked at Shandelli with an embarrassed grin. "No offense then."

"I know it will play because of the master violin maker who made it, and because of the *Maestro* who ordained it," Nigel replied as he continued to study the beautiful wood stained by Jesus' blood.

"Well, as the fiddlers always say in Ireland, 'the older the fiddle, the sweeter the tune,'" Al recounted. "And that fiddle right there may be new but with seventeen-hundred-year-old wood it should make a grand tune!" This immediately drew looks of alarm from the animals.

Max bonked Al and whispered, "Shhhh, kitty! The big-eyed beastie don't know where we got the wood then!"

"Ah, what I mean is that since Mousie will play tunes aboot what *happened* 1,700 years ago, it should make pretty music!" Al quickly corrected with a weak grin.

"So as I was saying, I will wait to play for Mr. Handel. I hope that is agreeable to you," Nigel offered to Shandelli.

"But of course! I think you will play even more powerfully when the story of Messiah begins, eh?" Shandelli replied.

"Well, we won't have to wait long because I believe tonight will be the night, when Handel returns," Liz posed. "He has the letter from Lord Cavendish, so it is only a matter of time."

"Indeed you are right, my dear," Nigel agreed. "I feel we best get inside and be ready."

"Do ye hear that?" Max asked.

"No, *mon ami,* what is it?" Liz asked.

"The storm be over," Max said, opening the door. He grinned and looked back. "The r-r-rain stopped."

"Thank the Maker. Now we can get back to the house without getting my violin wet. Catgut does not respond well to moisture," Nigel explained.

Al instinctively grabbed his belly, forgetting about the term not referring to cats. "Well, *this* cat do. I'm goin' to get some milk."

While Al trotted back to the house, Max and Kate gave Nigel parting hugs. "Okay, Mousie, this be it. We'll be prayin' ye through," Kate said affectionately. "Ye'll play pretty, I know it."

"Aye, an' we'll be guardin' the house from any beasties that tr-r-ry ta come near ye," Max reassured. "Go in there an' play for Jesus as if he were in the r-r-room."

"Indeed I shall. Thank you both," Nigel replied. "I only pray that I shall play well enough to earn the applause from our Jesus, to know that he is pleased."

"I'm sure you will, *mon ami,*" Liz encouraged. They heard the front door slam. Handel was home. "Come, it is time."

569

Nigel's Nightly
Serenades

"Vere is it? Vere is it? Vere is it?" Handel murmured as he looked around his composing room for Jennens's libretto of *Messiah*. Suddenly his eyes landed on it and he clapped his hands once. "Ah! Dere you are!"

He walked over to plop down on the settee where Al was already lying, sound asleep. Handel reached over and stroked Al while he read through the libretto. "'Part de First, De Prophecies of Isaiah,' ya, gut, gut." He read on and nodded, liking what he saw. "'Part de Second, De Passion of de Christ.' Dis is vonderful, ya. Hallelujah, ya, ya."

Nigel, Liz, and Shandelli hid in the corner, reveling in seeing their appointed mission begin its climactic realization. Nigel's heart was beating so fast in anticipation of playing for Handel that he kept taking deep breaths, holding his violin and bow at the ready. Liz placed her dainty paw on Nigel's back, trying to calm his nerves.

Handel yawned with a growl that startled Al. Al popped his head up and blinked, having come out of a deep sleep. He had to remember where he was. Once he did, he quickly put his head down and fell back asleep.

"I tink you have de right idea, cat," Handel yawned. "But I vish to finish reading dis. 'Part de Tird, Christ as Savior and Victor,' very gut, very gut." He yawned again and shook his head. He rubbed his eyes and said, "I vill begin tomorrow, ya. For now I must sleep. Good night, cat." He gave Al a parting petting and closed the libretto, carrying it upstairs to his bedroom.

Nigel looked at Liz and Shandelli, swallowing hard. "I believe that is my cue."

"Go, *Signo*r Monaco. Play for the *Maestro*," Shandelli encouraged.

"*Oui*, this is your big moment, *mon ami*," Liz added warmly. "You will be wonderful!"

"I thank you, my friends. Liz, may I ask you to please assist by reading to me from the libretto? I feel I shall play best if I hear the words read aloud first," Nigel explained.

"*Bien sûr!* It will be my honor!" Liz enthused.

"Splendid. Shall we, my dear?" Nigel asked, his paw out.

Liz smiled and together she, Nigel, and Shandelli followed Handel upstairs. The oil lamp on his nightstand gave the room a cozy glow. His bed was canopied with luxurious crimson harrateen and silk braid fabric with matching bolster, pillows, linen sheets, blankets, and quilt. The same red fabric hung in the windows. Handel walked over to draw the curtains for the night, setting the libretto next to the oil lamp.

571

"Perfect!" Liz whispered.

Handel undressed, put on his nightshirt, and took the Star Coin out of his pocket. He kissed it and set it down next to the libretto on the nightstand. With a grunt he climbed into bed, pulling his covers up to his chest as he positioned himself in his typical upright sleeping position. Slowly his eyes closed, and he drifted off to sleep.

Nigel, Shandelli, and Liz jumped onto the nightstand. Liz opened the libretto and she and Nigel locked eyes, smiling. They had come so far together, from Liz assisting Jennens with these words, going back in time with Jesus, and bringing forth Nigel's divine little violin. It was a magical moment.

"Part the First," Liz softly whispered. "Sinfony (Overture). E minor. Grave—Allegro moderato."

Nigel nodded and smiled. He jumped over to Handel's bed and slowly walked up onto his pillow, right by his ear. He raised the violin to his chin, lifted his bow, closed his eyes, and took a deep breath.

As Nigel drew his bow across the strings, a holy sound filled the room. Liz and Shandelli gasped at the sheer beauty of the notes resonating from Nigel's violin. Nigel swayed back and forth, swept up in the divinely inspired music that poured out of his heart and mind into his bow.

"Never before have I heard any violin produce a sound so magnificent, not even Stradivari's Messiah violin," Shandelli whispered in awe. "The sound of this second violin is better than the first."

Tears filled Liz's eyes. Shandelli was unaware of the origin of the items for Nigel's violin: Jesus' blood-stained sign from the cross, the Jordan River reed, and Achilles's hair infused with the touch of the resurrected Messiah. "Just like Jesus was the second Adam. When man fell, a new man came to pick him back up. Messiah makes all things new and better than before."

The animals were suddenly startled as Handel began to also sway along with Nigel, clearly hearing the music. But he didn't wake. They all exhaled with relief.

When Nigel had completed playing the Overture, he looked over and nodded to Liz. She smiled and read the next movement. "Recitative, accompanied in E major. *Comfort ye, comfort ye my people, saith your God: speak comfortably to Jerusalem, and cry unto her, that her warfare is accomplished, that her iniquity is pardoned. The voice of him that crieth in the wilderness, prepare ye the way of the Lord, make straight in the desert, a highway for our God.*"

Liz's heart was full to bursting as she heard Nigel play the music that would make Isaiah's words spring forth into indescribable sound. Nigel and Handel swayed in unison. Shandelli closed his eyes and lifted his twiggy arms as if seeing the notes appear on the page himself.

Soon Nigel stopped and, once again, Liz read the next segment. "Song, E major. *Ev'ry valley shall be exalted, and ev'ry mountain and hill made low, the crooked straight, and the rough places plain.*"

Nigel's rhythm picked up with this next song, and his entire body grew animated. Handel also responded in kind, smiling in his sleep with the lively tune.

After a few moments of playing, Nigel stopped and whispered, "One more segment, if you will, my dear."

Liz nodded. "Chorus, A major. *And the glory of the Lord shall be revealed, and all flesh shall see it together; for the mouth of the Lord hath spoken it.*"

As Nigel played, Liz and Shandelli swayed back and forth, closing their eyes in sheer wonder and awe of this song that for now only gave the melody with a single instrument. They imagined the full orchestra and compliment of voices that would one day make this powerful chorus resound in countless concert halls around the world.

Finally, Nigel slowly lowered his bow and breathed a silent prayer, "Thank you, Maker. Thank you, Jesus, my Messiah."

Liz embraced Nigel as together they jumped down onto the floor. "You did it, *mon ami!* You played beautifully!"

Shandelli put his twiggy hands on top of his chest. "Never before have I heard such beautiful music. *Bravo, Signor* Monaco!"

Nigel bowed humbly and took a deep breath. "Thank you both. But it was as if I weren't even playing that music. When I pulled my bow across the strings, the music just took over and played itself, truly!"

"The *Maestro* was playing through you, Nigel," Liz affirmed the little mouse. "That is why. When he asked you to do all you could, he did the rest, bringing out the notes."

573

Nigel straightened his spectacles. "Indeed. Now to see if those notes appear on Handel's pages tomorrow."

The three friends watched a moment as Handel slept. Little did they know that Nigel's notes filled the composer's dreams with page after page of music.

As morning dawned, Handel woke with a start, rubbed his eyes, and jumped out of bed. He saw the open libretto sitting on his nightstand and wrinkled his brow, not remembering if he had left it that way the night before or not. No matter. He put on his red dressing robe and cap, picked up the libretto, and hurried down the stairs to his composing room.

Liz was curled up next to Al on the settee when she was awakened by Handel's heavy footsteps on the stairs. She looked up to the Rembrandt painting hanging on the wall above Handel's clavichord. Nigel and Shandelli were sleeping high above on the wide frame of the painting. "Wake up! He is coming!"

Nigel and Shandelli roused quickly and nodded. Handel came bounding into the room and rustled around for some fresh lined music paper. He pushed other musical pieces aside and made room to begin writing. He picked up his feather quill pen, dipped it in the ink, and wrote the necessary musical marks on the score.

Peter came into the room and smiled. "Good morning, Sir. I see you are busy at work already. Wonderful! May I bring you some breakfast?"

"Ya, good morning, Pater," Handel replied, not bothering to look up but continuing to write. "I am not hungry. I have important vork to do."

Al sat up. *"I'm hungry, lad! I'll eat for the two o' us,"* Al meowed to Peter.

"I'm happy to hear it, Sir," Peter replied with delightful surprise at Handel's lack of appetite for food but his raging hunger to once again compose. "I shall check in on you later."

Handel grunted something but kept writing. Peter motioned for Al to follow, closing the door behind them.

Nigel peered over the picture frame, eagerly waiting to see Handel's notes appear on the page. As Handel furiously wrote a torrent of notes, Nigel's eyes filled with tears. It had worked. Handel was writing out the very notes of the melody Nigel had played in his ear during the night, adding all the other parts to build upon that base.

The Maker had asked this tiny mouse to do what he had never before done—to play a violin. A mouse-sized violin made by a Stradavari-trained stickbug from Italy with items made by the touch of Messiah himself. It was all so impossible, yet it was happening before their eyes.

Nigel glanced over at Liz and gave her an affirmative nod. Liz smiled and jumped up on Handel's desk. She wanted to see the music for herself.

"Do you vish to help me write *Messiah,* cat?" Handel chuckled.

"Do you mean besides providing the words I assisted Isaiah in writing, and Jennens in gathering for the libretto?" Liz meowed playfully. *"No, but my mouse colleague will help you from here on out with the music, as he did last night."*

"I am glad you approve of my vork den," Handel said, putting his hands on the clavichord to play the notes he had just written. She glanced up and smiled at Nigel, who wiped his eyes with emotion at hearing his music played back with the embellishment of Handel's skillful composition.

Liz remained on Handel's desk while Nigel and Shandelli watched the composer gush page after page of music for the rest of the day.

A soft knock came at the door. "Mr. Handel, may I ask what you are working on? And might you be ready to eat something?" Peter asked. He walked in with a plate of food, setting it down for Handel.

Handel put down his pen and stretched his arms back. "Ya, Pater, tank you. I am vorking on *Messiah* dat Jennens sent to me, vit dese two cats," Handel said, playfully scratching Liz under the chin. "I vill go to Dublin and perform *Messiah* for a charity concert." He mindlessly handed Peter the letter as he picked up a roll, taking a bite and washing it down with some hot chocolate.

Peter scanned the letter and looked up, beaming. "This is wonderful news, Sir!"

"Ya, now I need to vork, and I don't vant to be interrupted. You can leave my food by de door and I vill get it ven I vant it, ya?" Handel instructed him.

"Yes, Sir," Peter replied, "and I will deal with any contacts or visitors so you will not be disturbed,".

575

"Gut, gut, Pater, tank you," Handel replied with an animated nod. "I don't know if dis *Messiah* vill be of much good to my listeners but I shall do my best vit it."

"I'm sure it will be splendid, Sir!" Peter encouraged.

"Ya, okay, go away now. I have vork to do," Handel ordered, handing Peter his cup.

Peter chuckled. "Yes, Sir." He left the room and softly closed the door behind him.

Handel worked well into the evening before finally laying down his quill. He stood and stretched his back. He then picked up the last page he had written and looked it over one last time. "Ya, it's good. Vat do you tink, cat?"

"*C'est magnifique!*" Liz meowed in reply.

Handel extended one leg forward and bowed. "I am glad you approve. I vonder if Jennens knew someting I don't about you, cat. But I am glad you came, ya, you and dat big, eating cat." His stomach growled. "I vill eat now, too."

When Handel left the room, Nigel and Shandelli jumped down and joined Liz on the desk. Nigel placed his paw on the first pages of *Messiah,* beaming with joy. "I can hardly believe it, but here it is before my eyes," the little mouse marveled.

"*Oui, Messiah* is born!" Liz cheered. "Are you ready to repeat the routine again tonight?"

"Yes, my dear, I am ready," Nigel replied with humbly. "I suppose we shall have a tiring few weeks ahead."

"From studying the libretto, I estimate it will take three weeks, if Handel works at this same pace each day," Liz surmised. "I believe you set the perfect tempo last night, *mon ami.*"

"*Bravo!*" Shandelli applauded. "I am honored to watch this masterpiece unfold, and look forward to each note!"

"Most kind, *Signor* Shandelli," Nigel said. "It would not have been possible without your help. I am terribly glad you are here. Now I propose we eat and get ready for tonight's serenade."

576

Once again, everyone resumed their positions in Handel's bedroom and Nigel began playing after Liz read to him the first segment of the nightly serenade. When she came to the second part her mind flashed with memories of Jesus clearing the Temple in Jerusalem:

> "The Lord whom ye seek will suddenly come to his Temple, ev'n the messenger of the covenant, whom ye delight in: Behold he shall come, saith the Lord of hosts . . . But who may abide the day of his coming? And who shall stand when he appeareth? For he is like a refiner's fire . . . And he shall purify the sons of Levi, that they may offer unto the Lord an offering in righteousness."

As Nigel played each part, Liz could see the words describing the scenes of their time with Jesus. No wonder Gillamon had sent them back to relive those years with the Savior. While they were with the Savior, these passages of Scripture were acted out before their eyes. Now they were being acted out in music for their ears.

Handel continued to sway in his sleep. Nigel paused and nodded. Liz smiled as she read the next segment. They were moving into the story of Jesus' birth.

"Recitative, A. 'Behold, a virgin shall conceive and bear a son, and shall call his name Emmanuel, God with us.' This will be Kate's favorite part," Liz whispered, thinking of all the events surrounding the Christmas story.

"Chorus, G Major. 'For unto us a child is born, unto us a son is given; and the government shall be upon his shoulder, and his name shall be called Wonderful, Counselor, The Mighty God, The Everlasting Father, The Prince of Peace.'"

Nigel almost danced as he played the happy pronouncement of Jesus' names. He steadily built the song up to a crescendo, giving musical exclamation points to each name. Liz smiled as they worked on through the segments telling the glorious story of Jesus' birth: the shepherds, the angels, the Magi.

Finally Nigel came to a stopping point, spent from playing. Together they called it a night.

Nigel's nightly serenades continued with the same routine, followed by Handel writing out the following day what Nigel had played in his ear the night before. Part One was completed in six days, and it was time to begin the section on the Passion with passages from Isaiah 53 and Psalm 22.

Liz read the libretto with tears and a broken voice. Nigel wept as he played, with the emotion of the fresh meaning of the words having just been supplied by their time with Jesus.

"Chorus, G minor. 'Behold the Lamb of God, that taketh away the Sin of the world . . .'

"Song, E flat major. 'He was despised and rejected of men, a man of sorrows, and acquainted with grief. He gave his back to the smiters, and his cheeks to them that plucked off the hair: He hid not his face from shame and spitting.'"

Liz cleared her throat with emotion. "Chorus, F Minor. 'Surely he hath borne our griefs and carried our sorrows: He was wounded for our transgressions, he was bruised for our iniquities; the chastisement of our peace was upon him . . . And with his stripes we are healed.'"

Liz sat on Handel's desk for nine days, watching the emotion fill his eyes as he composed the music for these passages of Jesus' scourging and crucifixion. The feelings she had were indescribable. Many, many years earlier she had sat on Isaiah's desk as he wrote these words. She watched the prophet as he leaned over onto his knees, sobbing. That was the night she spoke to Isaiah, and they both pondered what his prophecies of the suffering Messiah could mean. She had seen the Messiah suffer with her own eyes, fulfilling each and every word Isaiah had written. Now, she sat on Handel's desk as he put to music these same words. *I am blessed to have experienced it from beginning to end,* she thought. "Merci, Maker. Merci, Messiah," Liz breathed a silent prayer.

"He hasn't come out in days," Peter told Mrs. Rice. "I've heard him weeping as he writes. But I don't want to disturb his work."

"Well, you had best check on him tomorrow morning before he gets started for the day," Mrs. Rice urged with a frown. She tossed Al a piece of cheese. "We don't want our Mr. Handel to drop dead from lack of food."

Al's eyes widened at the thought. He took the cheese in his mouth and carried it upstairs to where Nigel and Liz sat, discussing the night ahead. Shandelli and Handel were both exhausted and had already gone to their respective beds. Scattered around Handel's bedroom were scored pages of music, blank pages, and the libretto. Although he worked primarily at his desk, Handel wrote wherever and whenever the inspiration struck.

"Here ye go, Mousie," Al said, giving him the cheese. "Ye composers need to keep up yer strength then."

"Why thank you, old boy," Nigel said, taking a bite out of the cheese. "It's terribly kind of you."

"*Bon,* Albert," Liz said. Then looking over the libretto, she went on, "Well, tonight is the night we have both anticipated for a long time. It is time for *The Hallelujah Chorus.*"

"Indeed, and I am most anxious to see what comes," Nigel said, adjusting his spectacles. "We both agree this could be the most important piece of the entire *Messiah.*"

"*Oui,* for it shows Jesus in his glory as King of Kings, and Lord of Lords," Liz replied.

"And he shall reign for ever and e-ver," Al added, punctuating each word.

Nigel and Liz looked at him in amazement. "Brilliant! I like the way you phrased that, old boy!"

"That's how I'd sing it," Al replied.

Suddenly the soft glow from the oil lamp grew brighter and Clarie appeared before them as a lamb. She looked at Handel fast asleep and then smiled at her friends. "Hello, dear friends! This is a special night."

"*Bonsoir,* Clarie." Liz greeted her with a kiss on each cheek.

"I thought ye were in the orphanage," puzzled Al with a wrinkled brow.

"I can break out every now and then," Clarie said with a wink. "I'll be back by morning."

Turning to the little mouse, Clarie continued, "Nigel, Jesus sent me to tell you that as you play tonight, remember Resurrection morning, when all the pain and sadness were gone, and the victory had been won. Remember what it felt like when he was restored to you. He said to give you this message: 'Nigel, I know you can play in such a way that the world will know how heaven opened up in all its glory and welcomed me—how my Father welcomed me back. That is how it is in heaven, and all the world will see it one day when I return in victory as King of Kings.'"

579

Nigel bowed and lowered his head. "Thank you for this message, my dear. I will play my best for the King." He looked up at Liz. "Let us begin."

Liz resumed her position at the libretto and Nigel with his violin in hand by Handel's ear.

"Chorus, D major," Liz said with a broad smile. "'Hallelujah! For the Lord God omnipotent reigneth. The kingdom of this world is become the Kingdom of our Lord and of his Christ; and he shall reign for ever and ever, King of Kings, and Lord of Lords.'"

Although Nigel had been playing with exquisite perfection these past two weeks, as he began to play the notes for *The Hallelujah Chorus,* he entered an entirely new realm. Handel was physically moved in a greater way, too, as his head moved back and forth with the music. When Nigel put down his violin, he released a heavy sigh of exhaustion and bowed. Morning would soon reveal the glory of the King.

Handel woke before sunrise. Liz and Al were sleeping on the floor and Nigel was curled up under Handel's bed, out of sight. When Handel's feet hit the floor, the animals jumped. He was racing around the room, mumbling to himself. He pulled back the curtains, grabbed some of the unused pieces of lined paper, turned up his oil lamp, and began to write. He was filled with a sense of urgency to capture the notes flowing through his mind, and couldn't spend even a moment to walk downstairs.

Al remained asleep while Nigel joined Liz on the floor, quietly watching Handel. He was furiously writing out notes, humming bars of *The Hallelujah Chorus*, and using forceful hand motions to sing out the words: "HAL-le-lu-jah! HAL-le-lu-jah!"

Slowly as the sun began to rise, Handel began singing, "KING OF KINGS!" At that moment, his eyes widened with an expression of awe as he gazed out the window. Suddenly he dropped to his knees on the floor and exclaimed with his arms raised, "My King and my God!"

"What is happening?" Nigel asked in alarm.

"This is what he is seeing," Clarie said, appearing again with them, but keeping her presence veiled from Handel.

Liz and Nigel looked on at the incredible scene before their eyes, as they were allowed to see what Handel saw. They saw all of heaven opened up before them. God was seated on his throne, and Jesus was at his right hand. Angels encircled the throne, singing praises. Liz's heart caught in her throat to see Jesus, and then Isaiah and John standing nearby. In a flash the vision was gone.

Handel put his hand on his chest and was breathing rapidly after the heavenly vision. He was tingling from head to toe. "Hallelujah," he whispered reverently as he got back up to sit in his chair. He picked up his quill and finished writing out the score. When he was finished, he put down his quill, sat back in his chair, and shook his head in amazement.

Peter quietly knocked at the door. "Sir, may I come in?"

"Ya, Pater, come," Handel answered. "Vat day is today?"

Peter carried a tray of hot chocolate in and set it on Handel's desk. "It's the sixth of September." When he saw Handel's face, he was taken aback. "Sir, you look different. Are you all right?"

Handel smiled and in a very uncharacteristically subdued voice said,

580

"I just wrote a chorus. *De Hallelujah Chorus.* About de reign of Messiah as King of Kings forever."

"It must have really moved you, if I might say so, Sir," Peter observed, still studying his employer's face. "You look radiant."

Handel looked Peter in the eye and swallowed hard. "I tink I did see all Heaven before me, and de great God himself." He returned his gaze out the window, longing to see the beautiful vision again.

Peter realized what a sacred experience Handel was having. "Well, then I expect your music will help the rest of us see heaven when we hear it."

Handel didn't respond, but shut his eyes tightly. Peter didn't say another word, but quietly left the room.

After a moment, Handel picked up the libretto to see what was next to write.

"I know that my Redeemer liveth," he recited. He stared back out the window and smiled. "Ya, dis I know for sure."

581

WHEN IRISH EYES ARE SMILING

Three weeks and three days to write a three-part oratorio that takes three hours to perform," Liz announced to the group with pride.

"Sure be a lot o' threes with Messiah," Al observed, counting on his fingers.

"Handel has finished *Messiah* and we could not be more proud of you, Nigel, for serenading him through," Liz went on. Max, Kate, Al, Liz, and Shandelli were gathered in the garden to celebrate, and erupted in cheers over Nigel's accomplishment.

"Thank you, my dear Liz," Nigel said, bowing his head humbly. "I couldn't have done it without all of you."

"Aye, 'tis always a team effort when ye're workin' for the Maker, but ye should be pr-r-roud of wha' ye done, Mousie," Max offered with a wide grin.

"So wha' happens now?" Kate asked.

"It seems our Mr. Handel has been so rejuvenated to write oratorio that after a few days of rest he has begun working on his next work, *Samson,*" Liz explained. "But I heard him talking to Peter about making arrangements to depart for Dublin at the first of November. He is shipping over his own organ, and will give several concerts over the winter season, waiting to debut *Messiah* in the spring."

"Sure, it's a good thing he likes writin' his ora-oreos now," Al said, relishing some newly arrived biscotti from Handel's latest food shipment from Italy. "He's been orderin' more treats again."

"Al, with your love of cookies, I look forward to watching you discover what the humans invent one day," Gillamon chuckled warmly, suddenly appearing in the garden.

"Gillamon! It's gr-r-rand ta see ye!" Max cried as he ran over to his old friend.

"I am happy to see you all, and so very proud of how well you've done with this mission," Gillamon replied. He turned to Shandelli, whom he had not yet met in person. *"Signor* Shandelli, I am Gillamon. I wanted to personally come to thank you for your assistance with Nigel's violin."

Shandelli's big eyes blinked in surprise to see a mountain goat standing in the garden. He bowed respectfully. *"Prego, Signor* Gillamon. It was my honor. I have heard much about you from these friends who admire you."

Gillamon nodded majestically. He looked around at the others. "You are almost finished. There remain only a few more tasks ahead."

583

"Jest give the word, an' consider it done," Max said eagerly.

"Oui, what remains for us?" Liz asked.

"As you've already explained, Liz, Handel will indeed be leaving for Ireland soon, and the first performance of *Messiah* will be in the spring," Gillamon explained. "Nigel, Shandelli, Liz, and Al will travel to Ireland for the grand debut. You are to assist where you can to make sure the concert is well attended. We want to give Handel a strong start."

"Utterly splendid!" Nigel cheered. "Oh, I can't wait to see and hear the music come to life!"

"Ye deserve it, Mousie," Kate smiled and said. "Wha' will Max an' me need ta do then?"

"Kate and Max, you are to make sure David Henry knows about *Messiah's* premiere in Dublin," Gillamon explained. "And it is crucial that David attends the London premiere when Handel returns. Handel will need his support, but more importantly, what he writes in a letter will carry great weight with another who reads his words."

"How will we know aboot things there if we're here keepin' an eye on Br-r-rook Str-r-reet?" Max asked.

"Liz, why don't ye write an anonymous note in the Dublin newspaper like David Henry do here in London?" Kate suggested. "Jest give us yer code name an' send the paper ta the Butcher shop."

"Aye, then we'll jest dr-r-rop the paper at David Henry's place so he can r-r-read aboot things," Max added.

"How aboot 'Irish Eyes' as our code name since we'll be doin' the spyin' an' reportin' in Ireland," Al suggested. He took another bite and mumbled, spreading biscotti crumbs everywhere. "And I be Irish, ye know."

"Brilliant suggestions, all of you!" Nigel enthused with a jolly smile. "I say, we could get rather good at this espionage business. It is rather thrilling, isn't it?"

"*Bon.* This sounds like a perfect plan," Liz agreed.

"Indeed it does," Gillamon approved. "After the London premiere of *Messiah,* your mission with Handel will be complete."

"Where will we be headed then, Gillamon?" Max asked.

"That will depend on David Henry's letter," Gillamon said with a wink. "For now, focus on the tasks at hand."

Nigel rubbed his paws together. "Right! Next stop, Ireland!"

584

"They love him here!" Liz rejoiced with Clarie on the orphanage playground. "He wrote to Jennens that 'I cannot sufficiently express the kind treatment I receive here.' He has sold out all his winter concerts and will be advertising for *Messiah's* premiere soon."

"Aye, he's a happy Handel," Al added with a goofy grin. "I've never seen him laugh this much. Sure, that's because Ireland be such a happy place."

"I'm glad to hear it! After feeling so rejected by the London elite, I know it has boosted Handel's spirits to receive such encouragement," Clarie said happily. "Lord Cavendish is pleased with Handel's reception, too. He's been here and has requested that I be able to attend the concert along with a few of the other orphans."

"*C'est bon!* So you will be there to hear *Messiah,*" Liz exclaimed.

"I would have been there one way or another, of course," Clarie said with a wink, giving Al a plate of food.

"So how long will we stay here at the orphanage with ye then?" Al asked. "I like the food."

"You will soon return to London, and my 'mum' will conveniently be released from debtor's prison with the money raised by the concert," Clarie said. "That will be the story that is told when it is time for me to depart."

"Gillamon said we need to assist with the concert to help Handel. We need to pack as many people into that concert hall as possible," Liz said, studying some ladies walking along the street in their wide hooped dresses, escorted by gentlemen carrying swords at their belts. "It only holds 600 people, but I believe there is a way to add more."

"How, Liz?" Clarie asked.

Liz turned her head back and gave Clarie a coy grin. "By a simple change of attire, perhaps?"

Nigel wiped away the tears of joy. "Handel's rehearsal of *Messiah* was exquisite! Oh, just to hear it even *practiced* surpassed my grandest hopes. Handel has selected four perfect soloists!"

"*Sì, sì, Signor* Monaco!" Shandelli added. "And the twenty-six boys from the Cathedral choirs are *magnifico!*"

"All Dublin is talking about it, no?" Liz said, pleased, tapping the newspaper. "*Voila!*"

585

Nigel walked over to stand on *The Dublin News Letter* where Liz pointed. He adjusted his spectacles and read the notice:

"*Yesterday morning, at the Musick Hall there was a public rehearsal of* Messiah, *Mr. Handel's new sacred Oratorio, which in the opinion of the best judges, far surpasses anything of that nature, which has been performed in this or any other Kingdom . . .*"

Nigel looked up and gave a jolly chuckle. "What a splendid review! My dear, however did you get this submitted to the newspaper?"

"Oh, I have my ways," Liz said with a knowing grin. "But there is more, *mon ami.*" Liz tapped on the other newspaper sitting there, *The Dublin Journal.*

Nigel smiled and read the other review: "*Yesterday, Mr. Handel's new Grand Sacred Oratorio, called,* Messiah, *was rehearsed to a most grand, polite, and crowded audience, and was performed so well, that it gave universal satisfaction to all present; and was allowed by the greatest judges to be the finest composition of musick that ever was heard, and the sacred words as properly adapted for the occasion.* My dear, you have simply outdone yourself!"

"Aye, she's even suggested that lassies become hoopless," Al added.

Nigel gave Al a confused look. "I don't quite follow you, old boy. Do you mean to say, 'hopeless'? Whatever for?"

"No! *Hoopless.*" Al encircled his paws around his robust belly and hips. "Ye, know, hoops that the lassies like to wear to make their dresses poofy."

"*Oui, mon ami,* I considered the amount of space that such hoops take. By my calculations the music hall can fit at least one hundred more guests if the ladies attend without them," Liz explained. She pointed to the additional notice in the paper.

> *Many Ladies and Gentlemen who are well-wishers to this noble and grand charity for which this oratorio was composed, request it as a favor, that the Ladies who honor this performance with their presence would be pleased to come without hoops (hoop-framed skirts), as it will greatly increase the charity, making room for more company.*

586

"See? The lassies will be hoopless," Al said.

Nigel gave a robust chuckle. "Brilliant, my dear! Simply brilliant!"

"*Merci.* I have arranged an additional notice on the day of the concert to request that the gentlemen come without their swords to increase space for the audience as well," Liz continued.

"*Bravo!* That should make it easy for a large crowd to attend," Shandelli cheered.

"Precisely *seven* hundred," Liz said with a smile. "It seemed like a perfect number to give *Monsieur* Handel the start he needs, no?"

"And lookie here," Al said with a goofy grin, pointing to another notice in the paper. "This were me idea for Max and Kate to read."

Nigel and Shandelli leaned in to read the notice. "Irish Eyes Are Smiling."

Nigel, Shandelli, Liz, and Al sat way up high by the windows in the Musick Hall, clinging to one another in anticipation of this event that had been their multi-year, multi-era mission. Today was Tuesday, April 13, 1742, but thousands of years of preparation had led up to this day. Clarie sat in the audience with Lord Cavendish and the other children. She looked up and smiled at the animals.

"Look at all the hoopless lassies," Al remarked. "Sure, and they all look skinnier to me."

"I hate to say it, but I'm dreadfully nervous," Nigel said, smoothing his twitching whiskers. "It's been seven months since Handel completed *Messiah,* and now the moment has arrived to see what the world thinks of our work."

Liz placed her dainty paw on Nigel's back. "Exactly, *mon ami. Seven* months. Perfection. I'm sure your nerves will ease when the music begins and you see the world embrace *Messiah."*

"Let us hope *Signor* Handel is not nervous, eh?" Shandelli said.

Handel stood in the corridor and breathed in deeply through his nose, letting his breath go as he listened to the sounds coming from the Musick Hall. The orchestra was warming up and a strange beauty of discordant sounds filled the air. Violinists played through their various parts from the score for a few last moments of practice. The trumpeter's horn ran up and down the scale and the cellists carefully tuned their beautiful instruments.

587

Above the sound of the instruments preparing for the concert was the hum of the crowd now packed into the hall. Handel had smiled when he read the requests in the newspaper for the ladies to not wear hoops and the gentlemen to leave their swords at home. "Dat is brilliant, ya!" he said with a solid pound on his harpsichord. "Whoever tought of dis should get into de concert free."

Suddenly he heard the roar of applause as the choir and four soloists entered the hall to take their places for the concert. The time had finally come for *Messiah's* debut. A hush fell over the crowd and that was his cue.

"May my vork be pleasing to your ear," Handel whispered prayerfully as he walked out to take his place at the harpsichord.

The crowd erupted into even louder applause until Handel took his seat and got settled. When he lifted his hands the audience immediately fell silent. The musicians held their hands in position on their instruments and locked their eyes on Handel.

With one swift, downward motion of Handel's hand, the first notes of *Messiah* filled the hall.

THE KING
OF KING'S MUSICK

Max and Kate sat behind some crates in the butcher shop, waiting for the butcher to stop talking with the courier. *Get on with it, lads!* Max impatiently thought to himself.

"So I hear Mr. Handel is quite the hit in Dublin," the courier said, handing the butcher a stack of newspapers.

"Really now, is that so?" the butcher said. "Well, he's been gone from Brook Street so long my business has suffered. He's always been my best customer. I hope he comes home soon!"

The two men enjoyed a laugh before parting ways. The butcher set the stack of papers aside and went to prepare the day's meat.

"Did ye hear that?" Kate asked happily. "Handel be a hit! Let's look for wha' Liz put in the papers."

"Aye, 'tis gr-r-rand news! Ye take this one, an' I'll look at this one," suggested Max, dividing up the papers.

Together Max and Kate looked through the papers spread out on the floor, carefully lifting each page with their teeth.

"Look, me love, here's one from April 9," Kate said. *"Yesterday morning, at the Musick Hall there was a public rehearsal of the Messiah, Mr. Handel's new sacred Oratorio, which in the opinion of the best judges, far surpasses anything of that nature, which has been performed in this or any other Kingdom . . ."*

"Aye, there be somethin' in *this* paper, too, givin' Handel a gr-r-rand r-r-review then," Max reported. He wrinkled his brow. "An' somethin' aboot hoops?"

His eyes kept scanning the paper, looking for the code from Liz. Finally a big grin appeared on Max's face. He tapped the paper. "Look here, Lass."

Kate leaned over to Max's paper. "Irish Eyes Are Smilin'?" she read, looking up at Max.

"Aye, an' ye know wha' they say aboot the Ir-r-rish," Max said with a mischievous grin. "When Ir-r-rish eyes be smilin' they be up ta somethin'!"

Kate playfully nudged Max. "Well, they obviously be up ta somethin' *good* then. Looks like they accomplished their mission ta help Handel. Look at this *Dublin Journal* paper from April 17!"

Max's eyes grew wide with excitement. "Aye! Hurry, Lass, let's get these papers together. He's got ta read this!"

Max and Kate carefully refolded the papers and carried them out of the butcher shop. Today they would be paper dogs, delivering good news to David Henry.

589

"Well, I heard even Jennens himself is upset that Handel performed his new oratorio in Dublin of all places," a man said as the trio of businessmen stood on the corner with their newspapers, gossiping. "How Handel would prefer those lowly Irish rabble to a refined British audience is beyond me."

"I have it on good word that Jennens even said he was disappointed in what Handel did with his *Messiah* libretto. He said Handel composed it in too great a haste and should have taken at least a year to work on it to make it the best of all compositions," the second man shared. "He actually said he would 'put no more sacred words into Handel's hands to be thus abused!'"

"Oh, it's far worse than that!" the third man jumped in. "That chap Holdsworth told Jennens he was sorry to hear that Handel is such a *Jew*. He actually wrote, 'His negligence, to say no worse, has been a great disappointment to others as well as yourself, for I hear there was great expectation of his composition.'"

"Indeed, and Jennens told Holdsworth he did Handel too much honor to call him a Jew! He said, 'A Jew would have paid more respect to the prophets. The name of *Heathen* will suit him better.' Jennens went so far as to call Handel too lazy and obstinate to work on the weak parts Jennens has suggested to make it fit for a public performance."

"Shocking to hear all of this!" the first man replied, shaking his head. "While Handel is preparing the London debut, I've heard tell that there's such a clamor around town from the religious elite against him performing it at all. They claim Handel dares to present such a sacred piece about Jesus Christ as an 'entertainment' in a theatre, when such words only belong in a church!"

Max was about to attack the trio of businessmen upon hearing their malicious conversation about Handel. Kate had to hold him back as they hid behind the bushes listening in.

"I cannot believe wha' I be hear-r-rin'!" Max growled. "The ar-r-r-r-rogance of these supposedly upper class men of London makes me sick! They called the Ir-r-rish 'lowly r-r-rabble?' THEY be the r-r-rabble if ye ask me! An' JENNENS! How DAR-R-RE he talk aboot Handel that way!"

"Steady, Max," Kate said with a stern look on her face. "We shouldn't be surprised. Nothin's changed much in seventeen hundred years when it comes ta Messiah."

Max wrinkled his brow. "Wha' be ye sayin', Kate?"

"Well, Messiah gave his first appearance ta the lowly shepherds, not the elite in Israel, didn't he? Jest like the Maker arranged for Handel's *Messiah* ta first be given ta those considered on a lower rung on the social ladder than these British elite," Kate explained.

"Aye, I see that," Max agreed.

"An' Messiah were also rejected by the folks in his hometown of Nazareth, weren't he? Jest as it appears Handel's hometown of London be rejectin' *Messiah* now," Kate continued. "Then Messiah were constantly accused by the Pharisees aboot breakin' their rules like healin' in the Temple on the Sabbath."

"Aye, an' now the modern day Phar-r-risees be more concerned aboot where *Messiah* should be performed based on wha's acceptable ta their rules," Max added. "Instead of bein' glad such gr-r-rand music an' words aboot Jesus be shared with more people in a theatre, they be more worried aboot it not bein' sung in a church!"

"Messiah had his Judas. One of the ones closest ta Jesus betrayed him," Kate further observed. "An' the one closest ta Handel's *Messiah* has said hurtful words against it then. Not that I'd call Jennens a Judas. I know he said those things bein' upset, an' we've all been guilty of that. Even Judas later regretted wha' he'd said."

"Kate, Lass, ye be quite the wise one," Max said. "Ye paint a picture that shows how Jesus went through the same things humans have ta go through even today. Anyone who tries ta share aboot Messiah will face opposition from the world then."

"Aye, that's wha' happened ta all the disciples," Kate reminded him sadly. "All but John were killed for followin' Jesus, but because of wha' they did, the world knows aboot Jesus today."

"An' not a one of them r-r-regr-r-retted it then. They knew it were all worth it ta be bold for Jesus," Max said. He nodded and took a deep breath. "All right, Lass. Handel will jest have ta deal with it, too. I hope he feels like it all be worth it."

591

"He only has ta please an audience of One," reminded Kate. "An' I think he will, even here in London."

Max grinned and leaned over to kiss Kate on the cheek. "That's wha' I love aboot ye. Ye know how ta speak the truth in love."

Kate smiled. "Let's hope David Henry does the same."

"Aye, let's get the truth aboot Handel's *Messiah* in his hands r-r-right now," Max replied, picking up the papers to continue on their mission.

As Kate walked ahead, Max grinned and couldn't resist giving the trio of businessmen a parting gift, right on their shoes.

LONDON, MARCH 23, 1743

"I think you *should* take your violin, *Signor* Monaco," Shandelli passionately encouraged Nigel with his twiggy hands in the mouse's face. "*Certamente,* it is appropriate to have it at the *concerto.*"

"Very well, I shall," Nigel replied, grooming his whiskers and making sure his spectacles were squeaky clean.

"You look very handsome, *mon ami,*" Liz encouraged her mouse friend. "Why are you so nervous for this performance after such a splendid debut in Dublin?"

"Thank you, my dear," replied Nigel, bowing. "For one, King George II will be in attendance, so *Messiah* will be performed for royalty! And then there's been all this nasty business in the paper about Handel's scandalous choice of the theatre at Covent Gardens and not a church for the performance."

"Pffft!" Liz spat with a paw in the air, dismissing the thought. "We will not allow these modern-day Pharisees to interfere with this big moment, so I want for you to put it out of your head this instant."

Nigel nodded. "Right you are, Liz. I will."

"*Bravo.* Shall we be going?" Shandelli cheered. "Max, Kate, and Al are waiting for us at the butcher shop."

"*Oui,* the concert begins in a few short hours. We need to sneak inside and take our hidden positions," Liz agreed. "This time, we're all going to hear *Messiah!*"

592

David Henry sat in the grand theatre hall, gazing up at the elegant architecture and décor of this beautiful place. *How could anyone think that there exists any place that is inappropriate to sing about Messiah?* he thought to himself. *I grow so weary of those who try to prevent the good with such small-minded thinking.*

His thoughts were interrupted as he had to make way for a beautiful lady and gentleman to pass along his row to the two open seats next to him. David stood and respectfully made room. "Good evening."

"Thank you," the passing man said. Once they were seated, he leaned over to David, who held a dated copy of a newspaper in his hand. "I see you read the *Dublin Journal?*"

"Well, yes, I received a few copies of it recently. I was very interested to read of Mr. Handel's success with *Messiah's* debut there," David replied. He opened it to the article that raved about the performance, pointing to it.

"The best judges allowed it to be the most finished piece of Musick. Words are wanting to express the exquisite delight it afforded to the admiring crowded audience. The

Sublime, the Grand, and the Tender, adapted to the most elevated, majestic, and moving words, conspired to transform and charm the ravished Heart and Ear."

The man smiled, and the smile lines around his eyes made his warm blue eyes twinkle with appreciation. "Yes, I read that article as well. But this lovely lady actually attended the concert herself. My dear, do you wish to share with . . . I'm sorry, I didn't get your name?"

"Henry. David Henry. I am humbled to make your acquaintance, Mr. . . .?"

"Gillamon. And this is Lady Clarie," the man said, gesturing to the lovely lady sitting on his left.

The beautiful lady leaned forward and smiled with her striking blue eyes. "Pleased to meet you, Mr. Henry."

"The honor is all mine, Lady Clarie. So you were actually at the concert?" David asked excitedly.

"Oh yes, and it was beyond anything the world has ever heard, or will ever hear," reported Clarie. "This music is in a category all its own. Mr. Handel has created a masterpiece."

"I've been eager to hear *Messiah* after reading this review," David replied. "But unfortunately, London seems to be giving Handel a lukewarm reception with all the criticism."

"A prophet is never welcome in his own hometown, is he?" Gillamon said with a resolute yet positive expression. "And the light shineth in darkness; and the darkness comprehended it not."

David thought a moment. "That Scripture is from John? Indeed, it is quite fitting."

A murmur rippled through the crowd as the orchestra began to play music announcing the entrance of the king. Immediately the crowd stood as King George II entered the theatre. As he passed, people in the rows bowed and curtsied out of respect for royalty. He took his seat in the special box seat designated for the monarch.

"There's the king!" Nigel exclaimed. The animals were hidden across the theatre, high up in an alcove.

"And there is David Henry," shared Liz, after scanning the crowd and finding him at last. "Well done, Max and Kate. He is here!"

As Max followed where Liz was pointing, he saw the man and

593

woman next to David Henry. Suddenly the man turned up his gaze and locked eyes with Max, smiling and giving him an affirming nod.

"An' there be Gillamon!" Max said. "Sittin' r-r-right next ta him!"

Kate's eyes widened and her perky grin showed her perfect little white teeth. "An' Clarie be with him!"

"Where?" Shandelli protested. "I don't see a mountain goat in here!"

Liz had to think quickly about explaining Gillamon's appearance as a gentleman. "Ah, *Signor* Shandelli, we'll have to explain this all later, no? Oh, but shhhh . . . Here comes *Monsieur* Handel!"

Immediately Liz began applauding with the rest of the audience, trying to divert Shandelli away from trying to find Gillamon. Shandelli's attention turned to the events taking place on stage, and he quickly forgot about looking for a mountain goat in the theatre.

Handel bowed low with one foot forward in the direction of King George, who returned the gesture with a royal nod.

Nigel took a deep breath and gripped his violin.

594

Liz looked over at her mouse friend and tears welled up in her eyes. "Play, *mon ami.* Play your violin. You know it well, so play as Handel conducts *Messiah.*"

Nigel smiled, bowed, and held his violin up to his chin, waiting for Handel to begin. Handel raised his arms, then with one swift, downward motion from him, the orchestra began to play. Nigel closed his eyes and joined the other violinists in playing the majesty of notes that filled the concert hall with divine music.

Liz leaned over and whispered to Max and Kate, "We're nearing the finish of the second part. Here comes *The Hallelujah Chorus!*"

After only a few measures of *The Hallelujah Chorus,* an incredible thing happened. King George II stood. Then the rest of the audience stood, following his example.

"Looks like he knows *the* King," Al said to Nigel, who continued to play on.

"Wha's happenin'?" Max whispered to Liz.

"It appears the king recognizes a Sovereign Ruler even greater than himself as he hears these words," relayed Liz, choked up with emotion. "King of Kings, Lord of Lords."

The power of *The Hallelujah Chorus* filled the hall. Every member of the audience was swept up by the majesty of the performance. David Henry was in awe of seeing the king of England stand. This was unheard of, and he marveled at the power of Handel's *Messiah*. Or rather, the power of Messiah himself.

When the choir finished the last 'Hallelujah' the king began applauding, followed by the rest of the audience. Handel turned around to face the king and bowed. In that moment, the Lord spoke gently to Handel's heart: "NOW DO YOU SEE? I HAD AN EARTHLY KING PASS YOU OVER FOR MASTER OF THE KING'S MUSICK BECAUSE I NEEDED YOU TO BE THE MASTER OF THE KING OF KING'S MUSICK. I AM THE KING OF KINGS."

Handel shut his eyes and placed his hand over his heart. "Thank you, my King and my God!" he prayed silently. He raised his gaze and wore a radiant smile. Handel instantly knew he had pleased the only One he truly cared about. Nothing anyone said from here on out mattered. The King of Kings was pleased, and that was reward enough.

While the people continued to wildly applaud, the animals suddenly heard an unusually loud applause coming from the balcony. Liz looked over to seek out the source of the applause and her heart caught in her throat. She turned to Nigel and placed her paw on his small frame, pointing to the source. All the animals turned to see where she pointed, and were filled with awe.

The sound of applause came from a pair of nail-scarred hands.

Tears quickened in Nigel's eyes. He put his hand over his heart and bowed humbly. When he raised his gaze, Jesus smiled and responded with a supremely royal nod. Then, suddenly, he was gone.

Nigel's audience of One was pleased. The *Maestro* himself applauded his work, and in the end, that's all that mattered.

Epilogue: The Letter

avid Henry lit the candle on his desk and reached for his Bible. As he flipped through the Old Testament, then the New, he smiled to see the passages he had heard sung tonight in Handel's *Messiah*. Isaiah. Haggai. Zechariah. Malachi. Matthew. Luke. *Ah, and here we are, John.* He found John 1 and began to read:

In the beginning was the Word, and the Word was with God, and the Word was God. The same was in the beginning with God. All things were made by him; and without him was not any thing made that was made. In him was life; and the life was the light of men.

And the light shineth in darkness; and the darkness comprehended it not.

There was a man sent from God, whose name was John. The same came for a witness, to bear witness of the Light, that all men through him might believe. He was not that Light, but was sent to bear witness of that Light. That was the true Light, which lighteth every man that cometh into the world. He was in the world, and the world was made by him, and the world knew him not.

He came unto his own, and his own received him not.

But as many as received him, to them gave he power to become the sons of God, even to them that believe on his name: Which were born, not of blood, nor of the will of the flesh, nor of the will of man, but of God.

And the Word was made flesh, and dwelt among us, (and we beheld his glory, the glory as of the only begotten of the Father,) full of grace and truth.

David paused a moment and thought about what that meant. The Light—Jesus—came into the world, and the world didn't understand him. It took a while for the world to begin to understand him. And the world began to understand the Light from the voices of those who told his story. And that was all he asked his followers to do. Simply tell his story.

He read another passage further down. "I am the voice of one crying in the wilderness, Make straight the way of the Lord."

John the Baptist was that voice. And that voice was silenced by evil men who didn't want to hear what he had to say. But even when John was killed, others rose up to keep speaking about the Light, and all the Light represents. The twelve Disciples started a movement that turned the world upside down. They spoke boldly and unashamedly about Messiah. And the world persecuted them for it. But other voices rose up, and have been rising up for more than seventeen hundred years to speak boldly about the Light of the world: Messiah.

Messiah. Handel's is yet another voice that has risen to speak about Messiah through music. And the world has sought to silence that voice.

David smiled as he thought to himself, *What the world doesn't understand is that the VOICE will never be silenced. Truth cannot be held back. It always will be victorious, if spoken boldly. God has given me a platform and a voice to speak the truth, and I intend to use it whenever I can, just like Jesus' cousin, John.*

John. Suddenly he thought about *his* cousin. *I must tell John about this!* He took out a fresh piece of paper, and dipped his quill in the ink.

598

From   David Henry,
        LONDON, England
        23 Mar 1743

To   John Henry,
        Hanover CO, VIRGINIA

Greetings, Cousin:

I trust this letter finds you and yours well and prospering. I have just returned from a most miraculous evening. The great composer George F. Handel gave a sublime London debut of his new Sacred Oratorio, called *Messiah.*

I must say I was moved greatly by the words comprised of prophetic texts from Isaiah and others, and the gospel accounts of our Lord. It truly is the most remarkable music I have ever heard, and I pray that one day you will be able to hear it performed in the colony of Virginia.

His Majesty King George II was in attendance and surprised the audience when he stood during an especially powerful part called *The Hallelujah Chorus*. I have obtained a copy of the libretto which was printed for the audience and will enclose it herewith. I can only surmise that even the great King of England recognized the King who is Sovereign even over his own rule. I pray our king never forgets this truth. As Isaiah's words about Messiah were powerfully relayed in song: the Government shall be upon HIS shoulder.

Despite the glory of the evening, I must tell you that Mr. Handel has experienced a backlash of persecution for this work, and who knows if it will ever become an oratorio that is played beyond a small number of performances this season. Handel went against London's religious elite who criticized his choice of venue for such a sacred work, namely Covent Garden Theatre. How preposterous to attack such a magnificent, godly work for something so completely meaningless!

A gentleman sat next to me in the performance, a Mr. Gillamon, and as we discussed Mr. Handel's situation, he reminded me of John 1:5. If Messiah himself was misunderstood and persecuted when he came into the world, why should his followers not also be misunderstood and persecuted? In fact, our Lord said that this would indeed happen. I have been pondering those followers across time that have given voice to the truth, and have come to realize something important.

If only one voice of faith will rise up and speak (or sing, or write, using whatever gift the Lord has given him,) the history of the world will be changed.

I have been inspired to contemplate what my one voice can do, and will do in this world for the good. I wish to

599

impart that same thought to you, my cousin. You are over in the New World. Perhaps your one voice will change the history of America. Or even that fine young son of yours, young Patrick. Perhaps his one voice will rise up and change history. Time will tell, as it always does.

I pray you to give my best to your family, and may our Lord bless your endeavors.

Your Humble Servant,

David Henry

David sealed the letter and locked it in a metal box of outgoing correspondence. When he blew out the candle and left the room, the rat's glowing red eyes narrowed from the open window. *Looks like I'll be sailing to the colonies,* the rat thought with a grimace, *along with that letter.*

A (Lengthy) Word
from the Author

Now there are also many other things that Jesus did.
Were every one of them to be written, I suppose that the world itself
could not contain the books that would be written.
— John 21:25

Preach it, John! My esteemed fellow author indeed knows what he's talking about. Trust me, I couldn't even fully write about all of the things Jesus did that *were* written down. I know how overwhelmed John and his three colleagues must have felt in trying to capture everything Jesus did. I have to admit it was a bit overwhelming as I began the process of tackling a book on the life of THE central figure in all of history: Jesus Christ.

Four Gospels. Eighty-nine chapters. All of Jesus' life and mission is captured in these books of Matthew, Mark, Luke and John. But of the eighty-nine chapters, only four of them cover Jesus' life before he was thirty years of age. So a three-year span of Jesus' ministry is covered in eighty-five chapters. And of these, twenty-seven deal with Jesus' last eight days of life. What do all of these statistics tell you?

Well, even though Jesus' three-year ministry was full of wonderful teaching and miracles, the main reason for Jesus' coming was the last week of Jesus' life. That's where the emphasis of his story needs to be. For if you focus on his good teaching and compassionate healing, but miss the Passion, you've missed it all.

So, I've done the same. I haven't covered every single scene in the fifty-eight chapters of Jesus' ministry. I've hit the highlights, major scenes and crucial things to know about the road leading to the cross. But I've omitted repetitive scenes, similar teachings and miracles. But when it comes to the Passion, every word is there. These are the most important scenes of the book, and I made sure I was as thorough there as humanly possible. My goal was not to regurgitate all four gospel accounts, but to present the major scenes of Jesus' ministry. Besides, you need to go read the original accounts yourself anyway. I challenge you to go find the segments of Jesus' teachings that I did not include, and think about what they looked like after getting a feeling for the other scenes I've written. Perhaps the unwritten scenes in my book will take on new life as you read them from the four Master writers.

As with all my books, and *especially* this one, I want to be crystal clear with my readers where I've taken liberties with the factual events that I've woven a fictional story around. Let's start with Jesus, then we'll move to Handel.

One of the greatest challenges of writing this book was working from a "Harmony of the Gospels." That means taking the events written from four different points of view that were not written in chronological order, and combining them into singular scenes and in order. Some events were only recorded by one or two gospel writers, and some were recorded by all four, but with seemingly contradictory details. There is no contradiction in the truth of what happened, just the perception of the authors. Just as if you were to have written this book, you would write it completely differently than I have, even though the subject matter is the same. Or if you and I were to witness a huge event and write down what we saw, the accounts would be different based on where we were standing, what we were able to see, what we perceived, etc. It's the same here with the gospels. So don't be alarmed as you read different accounts in the gospels. Each gospel writer wrote to different audiences and God knew exactly what perspective of Jesus would speak best to each group, so their pens were divinely inspired to record exactly what they wrote.

Matthew wrote to the Jews, and includes much about the Old Testament prophecies to point to the Messianic proof of Jesus. Mark wrote to a Roman audience, so provides an action oriented, less detailed account that would speak to the Roman mentality, giving them a non-Jewish identification with the message of the gospel. Luke provides a very Gentile intellectual approach to present Jesus with universal appeal to all cultures with exhausting detail. As a physician, Luke actually used the word that his account is an "autopsy" of the facts he had endlessly researched to give a full picture of the life of Jesus. John is best known as the "universal Gospel" as his account is the one that most people can easily understand. John wrote simply and emphasized faith in Christ as

Savior. That said, here is where I took liberties with their work:

Jesus learning he was Messiah: We don't know when or how Jesus understood he was Messiah. I used the fictional tool of Mary's journal to aid him, and nine seemed to be a reasonable age. He knew that he was Messiah at age twelve, but I feel certain that he knew earlier than that.

Rabbi Isaac: He is a fictional character, but Jesus would have had a Rabbi. I also took liberties with his speech, giving him some humorous, lively (and not yet created) Yiddish terms. Read *The Prophet, the Shepherd, and the Star* for more background on this lovable character.

Names of Jesus' sisters: we don't know their names, or how many he had, but we do know there was more than one.

Jesus left behind in Jerusalem: We don't know how Jesus got left behind when Mary and Joseph departed Jerusalem, but the scenario I've presented of miscommunication over traveling with the men or women seems the most plausible from all the commentaries I read.

Roman family of Antonius: This is a fictional family and the interplay with Jesus, Mary and Joseph is as well. However, there really was a Centurion in Capernaum and at the foot of the cross, and there would have been a Centurion overseeing the slaughter of the innocents as well.

Four Pharisees/Sadducee: Zeeb, Nahshon, Sarib and Jarib are fictional in name and in movements, but represent every encounter by the Sandhedrin recorded in the gospels.

Roman soldiers: Velius and Ulixes are fictional.

Matthew before he became a disciple: The interplay I've presented with Jesus and Matthew prior to Jesus stopping at his tax collecting booth is fictional, but plausible. Matthew indeed was a spiritual prodigal that came back with Jesus' graceful touch.

Assigning Disciples: Many times in scripture, Jesus instructed disciples to do something, but no names are given. In these cases I "assigned" specific disciples for the tasks, i.e. Philip and Nathaniel to get the donkey for Jesus to ride into Jerusalem.

Jesus' healings: Many of Jesus' actual healings from scripture are recorded, but I have added some fictional ones as well.

Time: I compressed the last five months of Jesus' ministry for the sake of keeping the flow of the story moving.

Jesus writing in the dirt: No one knows what Jesus wrote, although many have speculated. It seemed plausible that he would have pointed out the accusers' sins, making them drop the stones they had ready to hurl at the woman caught in adultery.

Judas' interaction with the Zealots: this is my fictional take on what Judas may well have been doing with the money that we know he did steal from the disciples' treasury. There has been much speculation on what was going on in his heart and mind, so I've written his character based on what I felt was the most plausible unfolding events with his betrayal.

Cock crow: I used the best interpretation of what Jesus meant from the commentaries I read, that it was not a physical rooster, but a specific time for the changing of the Roman guard known as the cock crow.

Mary on the Via Dolorosa: this is a fictional encounter with Mary wiping Jesus' brow as he fell on the way to the cross.

Lord's Prayer: I combined Matthew's longer version from the Sermon on the Mount with Luke's shorter version that was placed in a different setting with the disciples and Jesus.

The Star Coin: I had a lot of fun using this "prop" passing through the hands of Armandus, Zacchaeus, Judas, Jesus, the Widow and finally Handel. This was an actual coin minted by Rome as I described it, and I'm proud to own one that I will use for show and tell at my creative writing workshops.

I'm not ambitious, am I? Ha! So let's put another life story into this already massive book. Let's add George Frideric Handel to the mix! It was doubly overwhelming to tackle this other historical giant in this book, but I feel it worked beautifully. You can read Michael P. Monaco's account of how this happened in the book flap, but God struck me with the thread of writing the life of Christ within the story of Handel writing Messiah, sitting at Michael's concert in the Capitol Building in Williamsburg, VA. I had heard Michael relay the story of King George II choosing Greene over Handel countless times, but on this one particular night in October 2010, I heard it with my Author Hat on, and the plot soared into being from that moment.

God spoke to me on another pivotal night: Christmas Eve 2011. I was sitting at the Christmas Eve service at Church of the Apostles in Atlanta when he said, "You need to get to London and sit in Handel's composing room and write." I replied, "Seriously, God?" To which he replied, "SERIOUSLY."

I went home that night, emailed Handel House Museum in London and they graciously agreed for me to do just that. So on March 5, 2012, I sat in the very room where Handel wrote Messiah and wrote Chapter 67 (Dinner for Three) and Chapter 68 (Nigel's Nightly Serenades). I cannot begin to tell you how surreal that was, and I pray you can see that the inspiration I experienced was off the charts, especially in Chapter 68. Here are some other things you might like to know about the Handel part of this book:

Stradivarius "Messiah" Violin: This is an actual violin made by Stradivari but was not named "Messiah" until the 1800's.

Dinner for Three: this was a real anecdote about Handel who did indeed have a large appetite. All of the "funny stories" recounted about Handel are taken from his biographies. He was quite the colorful fellow.

Jennens' Letter: Jennen's letter to Holdsworth in Chapter 9 is his actual letter about the oratorio he had completed for Handel. The subject was indeed Messiah.

Newspaper Articles: all of the articles printed in the *Gentleman's Magazine*, the *London Daily Post*, *The Dublin News Letter* and the *Dublin Journal* (written either by David Henry or Liz) were actual accounts printed at the time. I took the liberty of assigning their "authors."

David Henry: He was the real first cousin of John Henry (father of Patrick Henry.) I was thrilled to see in my research that he indeed liked to write anonymously, so for the actual anonymous entries benefiting Handel, it worked beautifully to make them come from David's pen. Was he really at the London premiere of *Messiah?* I haven't been able to find proof of that, but as Editor of *Gentleman's Magazine*, it is entirely plausible that he could have been there. And his letter to cousin John

Henry? All fiction. But stay tuned to see what happens with that letter in *The Voice, the Revolution, and the Jewel (2014)*.

Handel's House: there was no garden out back, only a cobblestone street. I took liberties with having the shed for the animals to meet. Please visit www.handelhouse.org to take a photographic tour where you can see his bedroom just as I described it, as well as his composing room.

Butcher of Brook Street: this was a fictional store, but you will not believe what I saw when I visited Handel's House in London. Standing at Handel's front door, I turned my gaze down the street where I had envisioned the fictional butcher shop, and right in the spot where I had placed it was a massive Scottie Dog storefront sign! So, *of course,* Max and Kate must have been there in 1741.

Trio of London Businessmen: as with the Pharisees, these are fictional men but represent the true sentiments of real people at the time. Their "gossip session" on the corner in Chapter 70 consists of actual statements made in letters/papers at the time, condemning Handel about his new oratorio of *Messiah*.

King George II: Yes, he really did stand during the *Hallelujah Chorus*, and that is why we stand today when it is performed.

Messiah's Success: You may be surprised to learn that it took years for *Messiah* to really take off, due to the controversy surrounding the setting for performing the masterpiece. In 1749 Handel became actively involved with the Foundling Hospital in London which was an orphanage, offering to perform a benefit concert of *Messiah* to raise money to build a Chapel there. The concert was a sell-out as the setting and cause seemed to resolve any conflicts that the "good people of London" had about the work being performed outside a church. This benefit concert became an annual event continuing past Handel's death in 1759 all the way to 1777.

Handel willed a gift to the Founding Hospital in the third codicil to his will: "I give a fair copy of the Score and all the parts of my Oratorio called *The Messiah* to the Foundling Hospital." Handel died on April 14, 1759, and within two weeks, that score was copied and delivered per his request. And on March 2, 2012, I was privileged to hold that actual score in my hands with the gracious permission of Librarian Katharine Hogg and the Foundling Museum in London. I encourage you to visit www.foundlingmuseum.org.uk to learn more. To see pictures of me (and Nigel) with the 1759 score, please visit my Facebook page: Jenny L. Cote.

It's hard to imagine that such a beloved work as *Messiah* had such a difficult beginning, but it persevered to become the greatest musical masterpiece in history. As it should, given its *Subject* matter. But as Kate so wisely told Max, "Nothin's changed much in 1,700 years when it comes ta Messiah." And as Max replied, "Anyone who tries ta share aboot Messiah will face opposition from the world then." People have been opposing Messiah—Jesus—since the beginning, as well as those who write about, sing about or talk about him. Sadly the dark still doesn't welcome the light, for it does indeed make the rats scatter. "Rats. Utterly dreadful," as Nigel says.

Jesus asked his disciples, "Who do you say that I am?" He's still asking that question today. Have you answered it? Have you decided what to do about Messiah? There can only be two responses. I pray you know in your heart and have let Jesus know that HE is indeed your Savior and Lord. He loves you so, and would have done everything written in this book if you were the only one he needed to come and save. If you come to know Jesus as your Messiah after reading this book, it would thrill my heart to know about it. I love hearing from my readers on how my books move them, so please drop me a line at:

607

jenny@epicorderoftheseven.com

Handel and I have a lot in common. Jesus is my Messiah, and he is my audience of One that I care about pleasing with my work and my life. When Handel would finish composing a piece of music, he would sign his initials G F H along with the inscription S.D.G.: Soli Deo Gloria. It means "Glory to God Alone."

So with that I end this work as Handel did his:

S. D. G.
J L C
March 2012

BIBLIOGRAPHY

Barclay, William. *The Gospel of John*. Philadelphia: Westminster, 1975. Print.

Barclay, William. *The Gospel of Luke*. Philadelphia: Westminster, 1975. Print.

Barclay, William. *The Gospel of Mark*. Philadelphia: Westminster, 1975. Print.

Barclay, William. *The Gospel of Matthew*. Philadelphia: Westminster, 1975. Print.

Blomberg, Craig. *Matthew*. Nashville, TN: Broadman, 1992. Print. The New American Commentary.

Borchert, Gerald L. *John 1-11*. [Nashville]: Broadman & Holman, 1996. Print. The New American Commentary.

Borchert, Gerald L. *John 12-21*. Nashville: Broadman & Holman, 2002. Print. The New American Commentary.

Brooks, James A. *Mark*. Nashville, TN: Broadman, 1991. Print. The New American Commentary.

Bullinger, E. W. *Number in Scripture: Its Supernatural Design and Spiritual Significance*. Grand Rapids, MI: Kregel Classics, 2007. Print.

Burrows, Donald. *Handel: Messiah*. Cambridge: Cambridge UP, 1991. Print.

Cowman, Charles E., and James Reimann. *Streams in the Desert: 366 Daily Devotional Readings*. Grand Rapids, MI: Zondervan Pub. House, 1997. Print.

Cox, Steven L., Kendell H. Easley, A. T. Robertson, and John Albert Broadus. *Harmony of the Gospels*. Nashville, TN: Holman Bible Pub., 2007. Print.

Eldredge, John. *Beautiful Outlaw: Experiencing the Playful, Disruptive, Extravagant Personality of Jesus*. New York, NY: FaithWords, 2011. Print.

Fleming, Ed.D., James. *The Explorations in Antiquity Center*. LaGrange, GA: Biblical Resources, 2007. Print.

Gower, Ralph. *The New Manners & Customs of Bible times*. Chicago: Moody, 2005. Print.

Gutmann, Peter. "Classical Notes - Classical Classics - Handel's Water Music and Music for the Royal Fireworks, By Peter Gutmann." *Classical Notes, Peter Gutmann, CD Reviews, Articles, Expanded Goldmine Columns*. Web. 03 Feb. 2011. <http://www.classicalnotes.net/classics/watermusic.html>.

Halley, Henry Hampton. *Halley's Bible Handbook: An Abbreviated Bible Commentary*. Grand Rapids, MI: Zondervan Pub. House, 1965. Print.

"Handel House Museum - History of the House." *Handel House Museum -*. Web. 08 Feb. 2011. <http://www.handelhouse.org/the-house/history/>.

"Handel House Museum - Wikipedia, the Free Encyclopedia." *Wikipedia*. Web. 08 Feb. 2011. <http://en.wikipedia.org/wiki/Handel_House_Museum>.

Hogg, Katharine, and Donald Burrows. *Handel the Philanthropist*. London: Foundling Museum, 2009. Print.

Hogwood, Christopher. *Handel*. London: Thames & Hudson, 2007. Print.

Holy Bible: New International Version. Grand Rapids, MI: Zondervan, 2005. Print.

Holy Bible, Red-letter Edition: Holman Christian Standard Bible. Nashville: Holman Bible, 2004. Print.

Josephus, Flavius, Paul L. Maier, and Flavius Josephus. *Josephus, the Essential Works: A Condensation of Jewish Antiquities and The Jewish War*. Grand Rapids, MI: Kregel Publications, 1994. Print.

Knight, George W. *The Holy Land: An Illustrated Guide to Its History, Geography, Culture, and Holy Sites*. Uhrichsville, OH: Barbour, 2011. Print.

Lucado, Max. *Just Like Jesus*. Nashville, TN: Word Pub., 1998. Print.

Luckett, Richard. *Handel's Messiah: A Celebration*. New York: Harcourt Brace, 1995. Print.

MacArthur, John. *The Jesus You Can't Ignore: What You Must Learn from the Bold Confrontations of Christ*. Nashville, TN: Thomas Nelson, 2008. Print.

MacArthur, John. *The MacArthur Bible Commentary: Unleashing God's Truth, One Verse at a Time*. Nashville, TN: Thomas Nelson, 2005. Print.

MacArthur, John. *Twelve Ordinary Men: How the Master Shaped His Disciples for Greatness, and What He Wants to Do with You*. Nashville, TN: Nelson, 2002. Print.

The Macarthur Study Bible English Standard Version, Brown/crimson, Trutone. Crossway, 2011. Print.

McGee, J. Vernon. *Thru the Bible with J. Vernon McGee*. Vol. III. Nashville: T. Nelson, 1981. Print.

McGee, J. Vernon. *Thru the Bible with J. Vernon McGee*. Vol. IV. Nashville: T. Nelson, 1981. Print.

Moore, Beth. *Jesus: 90 Days with the One and Only*. Nashville, TN: B & H Group, 2007. Print.

Peterson, Eugene H. *The Message: The Bible in Contemporary Language*. Colorado Springs: NavPress, 2002. Print.

The Revell Bible Dictionary. Old Tappan, NJ: Fleming H. Revell, 1990. Print.

Riding, Jacqueline, Donald Burrows, and Anthony Hicks. *Handel House Museum Companion*. London: Handel House Trust, 2001. Print.

"River Thames." *Wikipedia, the Free Encyclopedia*. Web. 02 Feb. 2011.<http://en.wikipedia.org/wiki/River_Thames>.

Rodgers, Nigel, and Hazel Dodge. *Roman Empire*. New York: Metro, 2008. Print.

Sanctuary: A Devotional Bible for Women. Carol Stream, IL: Tyndale House, 2006. Print.

Stein, Robert H. *Luke*. Nashville, TN: Broadman, 1992. Print. The New American Commentary.

610

Swindoll, Charles R. *Jesus: The Greatest Life of All*. Nashville: Thomas Nelson, 2008. Print. Great Lives from God's Word.

Van Til, Marian. *George Frideric Handel: A Music Lover's Guide*. Youngstown, NY: WordPower, 2007. Print.

Zodhiates, Spiros, Spiros Zodhiates, Warren Baker, James Strong, and James Strong. *The Hebrew-Greek Key Word Study Bible: King James Version*. Chattanooga, TN: AMG, 1991. Print.

GLOSSARY OF WORDS AND PHRASES

Handel's Terms

Col pugno!	Musical term for 'with the fist, bang the piano with the fist.'
Den, Dat, Dis, De, Dey	When, That, This, The, They
Gut	Good
Pater	Peter
Pretissimo	Italian musical term for extremely fast
Vat de dyfil?	What the devil?
Ya	Yes

Liz's French Terms

Bien sûr!	Of course!
Bon	Good
Bonjour	Hello/Good day
Bon voyage	Good journey
C'est magnifique	It is magnificient/incredible
C'est tragique	It is tragic
C'est très belle	It is very beautiful
Cher/Chere	Dear
Comprenez-vous?	Do you understand?
Dieu est bon	God is good
Je vous en prie	You are welcome
Le troisième jour est arrivé!	The third day is here
Merci	Thank you
Mon ami/amie	My friend (masc./fem)
Mon Dieu	My God

Monsieur	Mister
N'est ce pas?	Isn't that so?
Non, c'est impossible	No, it is impossible
Oui	Yes
Quel dommage	What a pity
Petit déjeuner	Breakfast
S'il vous plaît	Please
Très bien	Very well, very good
Très jolie	Very pretty

Shandelli's and Achilles's Italian Terms

Amico	Friend
Applauso	Applause
Arrivederci	Goodbye
Bravo	Good/Well done
Buon giorno	Good day
Buon sera	Good evening
Buona notte	Good night
Certamente	Of course
Che cosa c'è?	What is the matter?
Ciao	Hello/hi
Ciò che Dio vuole, Io voglio	What God wills, I will
Concerto	Concert
Detto fatto	No sooner said than done
Fantastico	Fantastic
Glorificare Dio	Praise God
Grazie	Thank you
Il gatto	The cat
Magnifico	Magnificent
Mi dispiace	I am sorry
Migliore	Best
Mi scusi	Excuse me
Musicale	Musical
Naturalmente	Naturally, of course
Per favore	Please

Prego	Don't mention it/it's a pleasure
Sì	Yes
Signor/Signora	Mr./Mrs.
Viva il rè	Long live the King

Armandus's Latin Term

Magna est veritas et praevalebit	Great is the truth and it will prevail

Rabbi Isaac's Hebrew (and Yiddish) Terms

Ahava	Love
Al Tedag	Don't worry
Am Yisrael	The people of Israel
Az mah?	So what?
Azoi?	Really?
Be'tach	Sure!
Boker tov	Good morning
Chutzpah	Utter nerve, audacity
Ein brerah	No choice
Elokei	My G-d
Elokim yerachem	G-d will have mercy
HaRosh mistovev	My head is spinning
Kacha kacha	So-so
Kolboynik	Know-it-all
Laila tov	Goodnight
LeChayim!	To life!
Lo yitachem	It is not possible
Mah lechnah?	What's it to you?
Mazel tov!	Congratulations!
Meshuga	Crazy
Nu? So?	Well?
Oi!	Denotes disgust, pain, astonishment, or rapture
Oi Vai lz mir!	Woe is me!

615

Savlanut	Patience!
Shalom	Peace, hello, goodbye
Sheket!	Quiet!
Toda	Thank you
Yeled	Child

Nigel's British Terms:

Ace	Brilliant
Cheeky	Flippant / arrogant / smart aleck
Completely mental	Crazy
Cracking	The best
Crikey	Exclamation of surprise
Ergo	Latin for "therefore"
Fancy	To desire (something)
Jocularity	Joking around
Jolly	Very, or to emphasize the point
Smashing	Terrific
Takes the biscuit	Outdoes everything else and cannot be bettered

ABOUT THE AUTHOR

Award winning author Jenny L. Cote developed an early passion for God, history and young people, and beautifully blends these passions together in her two fantasy fiction series, *The Amazing Tales of Max and Liz*® and *Epic Order of the Seven*®. Likened to C.S. Lewis by book reviewers and bloggers, Jenny L. Cote opens up the world of creative writing for students of all ages and reading levels through fun, highly interactive workshops. Jenny has appeared to over 20,000 students at lower, middle, high school and universities in the US and abroad. Jenny is available to speak to schools, homeschool groups, churches, libraries, professional and community groups. To schedule a talk, reading and/or book signing, or interview please visit her website at www.epicorderoftheseven.com.

A native of Norfolk, Virginia, Jenny holds two marketing degrees from the University of Georgia and Georgia State University. Prior to writing her career focused on strategic planning and marketing, specifically in healthcare at Children's Healthcare of Atlanta. She now writes and speaks full time and lives in Roswell, Georgia, with her husband Casey and son Alex. Jenny is active in the Student Ministry at Dunwoody Baptist Church, and enjoys reading, research, museums, music, travel, meeting people, fitness and finding any excuse she can to get to the beach.

. . . AND HER BOOKS

The Amazing Tales of Max and Liz® is a two-book prequel series that begins the adventures of brave Scottie dog Max and brilliant French cat Liz through the stories of Noah's Ark and Joseph. Book One: *The Ark, the Reed, and the Fire Cloud* (winner of the 2009 Gold Award in the Reader's Favorite Awards for Children's Chapter Books) is currently in pre-production for a 3-D animated feature film. Book Two: *The Dreamer, the Schemer, and the Robe* (winner of the 2010 Reader's Favorite Gold Award for Children's Chapter Books) brings Max, Liz, and friends to work behind the scenes in the life of Joseph in the land of Egypt. *The Epic Order of the Seven®* series picks up where the Max and Liz series left off. Book One: *The Prophet, the Shepherd, and the Star*, (winner of the 2011 Reader's Favorite Gold Award for Christian Historical Fiction) gives Max, Liz, and the gang their most important mission yet: preparing for the birth of the promised Messiah. Their seven-hundred–year mission takes them to the lives of Isaiah, Daniel, and those in the Christmas story.

Please visit:

www.epicorderoftheseven.com

and the

Jenny L. Cote Facebook Page

ALSO FROM JENNY L. COTE

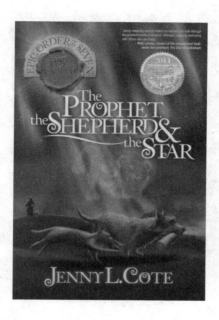

The Prophet, the Shepherd & the Star

ISBN-13: 978-0-89957790-6

Max, Liz and their Order of the Seven team of animal friends are given their most important mission to date—to help bring the promised Messiah into the world. Seven hundred years before the Nativity, they must protect the prophet Isaiah as he writes the crucial prophecies about the coming Messiah. They go with Daniel into Babylonian Captivity of the fiery furnace and the lions' den where a secret scroll is hidden away for the wise men to someday discover. Finally they must stop the many evil plots to prevent Jesus' birth, assist Mary and Joseph in their arduous journey to Bethlehem, and aid their escape from the evil King Herod.

Also from Jenny L. Cote

The Amazing Tales of Max and Liz® Series

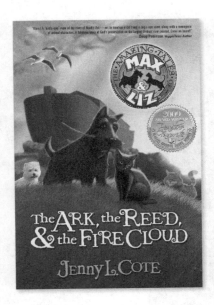

A magical adventure of animals traveling worldwide to Noah's ark. Max, a brave Scottish Terrier meets Liz, a brilliant French cat, on the way to the ark, along with a whimsical team of animal sojourners. Max and Liz become the brave leaders for the humorous and often perilous journey. Once aboard they help other animals through the flood and the long voyage, but also must foil a plot by a stowaway who is out to kill Noah and stop his mission of saving the animal kingdom as well as the human race.

Book One: *The Ark, the Reed, and the Fire Cloud*
ISBN-13: 978-089957198-0

A thrilling adventure to uncover the captivating story of Joseph in mysterious Egypt. They waited for centuries for their first mission as God's envoys in history, but Max and Liz finally get to work behind the scenes in the life of Joseph. All looks hopeless for the young teenager as his brothers sell him into slavery in Egypt. Max and Liz must combat the forces of evil that are out to thwart their plans, leading them into mysterious adventures with pyramids and mummies. If they fail in this mission, all of Egypt and surrounding nations will suffer from famine, and the Hebrew nation will never be born.

Book Two: *The Dreamer, the Schemer, and the Robe*
ISBN-13: 978-089957199-7

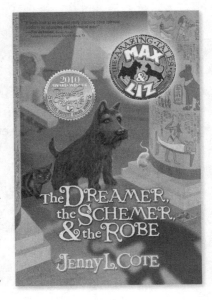